Convenie...

**These three Bravo men *had* to get married—
or did they?**

Cash Bravo
did it to give his unborn baby a father.

Nate Bravo
did it so his dear friend Megan
could keep her ranch.

And Zach Bravo...
well, he was madly in love, even though
his intended had eyes for another man.

**So the Bravo men's marriages
began in name only—but were they destined
to be love matches after all?**

"Christine 'is' romance. Nobody does it better."
—Georgia Bockoven, bestselling romance author

CHRISTINE RIMMER

BRAVO
FAMILY TIES

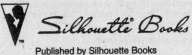
Silhouette® Books

Published by Silhouette Books

America's Publisher of Contemporary Romance

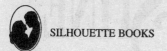 SILHOUETTE BOOKS

ISBN 0-373-18507-3

by Request

BRAVO FAMILY TIES

Copyright © 2002 by Harlequin Books S.A.

The publisher acknowledges the copyright holder of the individual works as follows:

THE NINE-MONTH MARRIAGE
Copyright © 1998 by Christine Rimmer

MARRIAGE BY NECESSITY
Copyright © 1998 by Christine Rimmer

PRACTICALLY MARRIED
Copyright © 1998 by Christine Rimmer

Visit Silhouette at www.eHarlequin.com

Printed in U.S.A.

CONTENTS

Dear Reader,

Here they are: the first three books in the Bravo family saga. These were the *only* Bravo books I originally intended to write.

So much for what I originally intended. Your response to these first three stories has been so enthusiastic, I've since written nine more Bravo tales. Watch for the newest ones, coming from Silhouette Special Edition in August, October and December of this year.

But back to when I started....

My idea was to write about three strong, sexy and *difficult* men: Cash, Nate and Zach Bravo. Their fathers were brothers. And each of them has inherited a third of their grandfather's ranch, the Rising Sun, in northeastern Wyoming. Cash and Nate are what you might call nonmarrying men. They have never *been* married and they never plan to *get* married. As for Zach, he took a chance on marriage once and it was a disaster.

What do these guys need?

The right women.

For Cash, that would be Abby Heller. Abby's fifteen years younger than he is, but make no mistake—she's all woman. Nothing will stop her from getting her man.

And for Nate? Megan Kane. When her father's will forces her to marry and have a baby or lose her home, who else would Megan go to for help but the only man she has ever loved?

And what about Zach? His woman would be sweet, widowed Tess DeMarley. The two of them start out with a purely practical arrangement. She needs a husband and a father for her child; he needs a good wife to run the ranch with him. Does the marriage *stay* practical? I think you know the answer to that one.

So please. Come with me now to Medicine Creek, Wyoming, and meet the original troublesome, hard-loving, tough and tender Bravo men.

Yours always,

Christine Rimmer

THE NINE-MONTH MARRIAGE

For Phylis Warady.
Thanks, Phyl, for the tea and the company,
the funny stories, the kind words and
the thoughtful advice—
not to mention watering my houseplants
and taking care of Jesse's lizard.
You are a treasure.

Chapter One

Abby Heller heard a buzzing sound. She rolled to her back and opened one eye. It was light in the room: definitely morning. Not that Abby cared. She'd been up until three.

The buzzer sounded again. Abby put it together; there was someone at the door.

"Go away," she whispered at the faint watermark on the ceiling. Then she pulled the covers over her head.

Again, the buzzer sounded, like some irritating electronic sheep: "Baaaaaaa!"

And then it happened: everything in Abby's stomach started to rise.

She stuck out a hand, groping for the saltines on the cluttered table by the bed. At the same time she sucked in air slowly, and then slowly let it out.

A pocket calculator and an empty Dr Pepper bottle

clattered to the carpet before her fingers closed on the waxed-paper wrapper. She pushed the covers off her face and dragged herself to a sitting position. Still breathing with great care, she fumbled with the roll of crackers.

"Baaaaaa!"

Her stomach roiled. She shot a look of absolute loathing at the scarred wooden door of her furnished studio apartment. And then, with grim determination, she stuck a cracker in her mouth. Slowly she chewed, taking long, careful breaths at the same time. She swallowed with caution, stuck in another cracker and chewed some more. The feeling that she would lose the contents of her stomach began to subside.

She got the second cracker down—and dared to hope it would be okay, that she wouldn't spend the next fifteen minutes hugging the bathroom fixtures after all.

"Baaaaaa!" the buzzer bleated again. And then a fist hit the door—three sharp raps.

She shot a glance at the clock by the bed. When she saw the time, she let out a sound so low and ominous it could only be called a snarl. Whoever had come pounding on her door at 7 a.m. was going to regret it.

Muttering an oath that would have made her mother furious, Abby tossed the crackers on the nightstand, threw back the covers and stalked across the room to the door. She looked through the peephole.

And saw Cash Bravo on the other side.

"Oh, God," she breathed in horror. Her stomach lurched. She pressed her hand to her mouth.

Miraculously, she didn't throw up.

His fist hit the door again. The buzzer buzzed, "Baaa—baaa—baaaa!" And Cash called out, "Abby! I know you're in there. Come on. Open up."

For a moment, she considered grabbing her car keys and heading for the service porch off of her minuscule kitchenette. She could be down the back stairs before he realized she'd gone. The big T-shirt she'd slept in might not be appropriate for day wear, but it was decent enough for a drive in the car.

But then she shook her head. Running would get her nowhere. If Cash Bravo wanted to find her, he would.

No. Better to face him down and get it over with.

"Abby! Now!"

The hard command in his voice told her more than she wanted to know. If she didn't do something, he would beat the door down.

"Just a minute!"

She flew to the bathroom door and snatched her robe from the nail there. She shoved her arms in it, then knotted the belt. Then, turning, she caught a glimpse of herself in the streaked mirror over the bureau next to her bed.

A miserable groan escaped her. She looked awful, her skin pasty, her hair all tangled and lank. Ugly dark splotches marred the skin under her eyes. Oh, she didn't want him to see her like this! Partly because of stupid pride. And partly because he might guess—

She did not allow her mind to complete the thought. He was not going to guess. No one would know until she was ready—especially not Cash. And if he started in about how bad she looked, she would tell him she was just tired, from working so late.

"Abby!" He buzzed for the umpteenth time—and then he did a little more pounding for good measure.

"Coming…" The room was a mess, her clothes and books and shoes scattered everywhere. She'd always been that way: someone with places to go and things to do and no time for keeping house. For once, though, she wished she had a moment to—

"Abby!"

"All right!"

She marched to the door, yanked it open—and utterly despised herself for the hard fist of longing that closed around her heart as her eyes met his.

He stared for a moment, then muttered accusingly, "You look like hell."

She decided the best way to handle that remark was not to dignify it with an answer. Besides, he didn't look so great himself. His bronze skin had a gray cast to it. She would bet he'd kept some bartender real busy last night.

"Are you going to let me in?" Without waiting for an answer, he moved toward her. She stepped back, clearing the doorway—and gaining a little distance from him. She didn't want to be too near him, to feel the warmth he radiated or to smell the scent of his skin.

His sky blue eyes surveyed her poor little room. She tried not to grit her teeth as she watched him. She knew his every expression. Right then, his jaw looked like granite and his mouth made a flat line; he was dismissing everything that he saw.

When he was through looking around, he turned to her. "What's going on?"

She backed up a few more steps—until she bumped into the end of the bed. "What do you mean?"

"You know damn well what I mean. Spring semester ended weeks ago. And you're here in Denver instead of home where you belong. Why?"

"Cash, look—"

"We've called. Both your mother and me. Left message after message. But you never call back."

"Cash—"

"Why?"

She stared at him, aching with the sudden foolish need to launch herself at him, to feel his strong arms go around her. And to tell him everything, all of it—including how scared she was, and how tired. But of course she couldn't do that, couldn't go running to Cash this time, as she'd done all of her life until now. Now Cash himself was the problem—or at least a major part of it.

She folded her arms over her stomach, hunched her shoulders and tried to speak calmly. "I just…I wanted a change." It came out sounding almost as pitiful and lost as she felt.

His eyes seemed to bore right down into the center of her. "You never wanted a change before."

"Well, now I do." Her robe had fallen open a little in front. She straightened it, avoiding those eyes.

She heard him sigh. He was turning away when she looked up, alligator boots striding across the worn gray carpet, moving toward the arch that framed her kitchenette.

In front of the arch stood a Formica-topped table, on which Abby had set up her computer. Cash dropped into one of the table's three chairs, leaned back and scrubbed both hands down his face. "It's all my fault, isn't it?"

"No. Of course not."

He lowered his hands. Their gazes locked. "Abby, you never were a very good liar. Just lay it out like it is, all right? You don't want to come home because of me, because of what happened."

He looked so utterly miserable. Longing squeezed her heart again, hard and painfully sweet—to go to him, to pull him close, to run her fingers through his silky dark-gold hair.

But she stayed where she was. And she spoke in careful, reasonable tones. "It's not your fault. Or at least, it's no more your fault than mine."

"But it *is* the reason you won't come home."

She dropped to the end of the bed. "Cash, I need some time. Please understand. I need to think things through."

He shoved a stack of accounting books aside, making room to rest an elbow on the table's edge. "I don't want this for you." He gestured broadly. "Living in a place like this. Working in some cheap bar."

She sat up straighter. "How do you know where I work?"

He just looked at her.

She thought of Nate. Nate Bravo was Cash's cousin, but they were more like brothers, really. Nate was a private investigator. "Nate?" she demanded, anger sparking. "You put Nate on me?"

He shook his head. "Uh-uh. I followed you myself. Last night. Then I went back to my hotel and got blasted. And then this morning, well…here I am."

It all seemed so pitiful. "Oh, Cash.…"

"You're just a kid. And I know you looked up to me. *Trusted* me…"

She hated the self-loathing in his voice. She wanted to yell at him, to demand that he stop blaming himself. But at least one of them had to remain reasonable. "Cash, I'm twenty-one years old. Not as ancient as you are, maybe. But old enough to take responsibility for my own actions. I don't blame you, honestly."

He leaned toward her, hope kindling in his eyes. "Then come home to Medicine Creek where you belong. Work for me through the summer, the way you always have. That *is* what we agreed.''

"Cash—"

"No. Listen. Remember." He spoke with such urgency, as if he really believed that she needed reminding of the things they had said, as if reminding her would make her abide by them. "You told me you'd go back to Boulder, finish out your semester. And then you were supposed to come home. We said that we were going to put what happened behind us. And we can do that. I know it. We can make things the way they used to be."

She gazed at his beloved face, thinking that maybe *he* could go back, but she couldn't. Not ever.

Until that night two months before, Cash had been her best friend. He had been like a big brother, yes— someone who looked out for her, someone who wanted to help make all her dreams come true. But there had been even more than that. They'd shared something so special. They had been true comrades, in spite of the difference in their ages.

But now, everything had changed. Now, if she let herself be near him, she'd end up just like every other woman he knew, looking at him with hungry eyes, mooning after him all day long. She didn't think she could bear that. She had better things to do with herself than moon after a man—even if that man was Cash.

"Come home," he said again.

She drew back her shoulders and spoke with finality. "No, Cash. I'm sorry, but I can't go home now."

He scowled at her. She didn't waver. And then his eyes narrowed. "Is there something you should tell me about?"

Though her pulse shot into overdrive and sweat

broke out under her arms, she neither blinked nor shuddered. "Like what?"

"Abby, we weren't..." His cheeks puffed as he blew out a breath. "Careful. And it *was* your first time."

She looked away, toward the door, praying he would just let it go.

Her prayer got her nowhere. He forged on.

"You weren't using anything—you couldn't have been. And me, well, I acted like a damn fool all the way around."

She continued looking toward the door.

"Just tell me. Are you pregnant?"

It was the moment. The moment to say it. But she simply could not deal with having him know. Not right then. Not yet....

So she turned her head, looked him right in the eye and told a whopper of a lie. "No."

His big body visibly relaxed. "Well. At least we don't have to face a disaster like that."

"Yes." Her voice sounded funny, pinched and tight. She coughed to loosen her throat. "At least not that."

There was a pencil on the table, next to the stack of accounting books. He grabbed it, began idly tapping it on the tabletop, his watchful eyes studying her at the same time. Then all at once, he tossed the pencil down and stood. "You're too skinny. Get dressed. We'll get some breakfast into you."

Breakfast was the last thing she wanted to deal with right then. "No, Cash. Really, I—"

"Don't argue. I plan to stick around this town for a few days. I want to make sure you're going to be all right."

She dragged herself to a standing position and, with

considerable effort, kept her voice reasonable. "Cash. I'll be fine. Believe me. But you have to let it go. You have to let *me* go."

The tension was back, in his shoulders and around his eyes. "Damn it, Abby. You're as good as family to me. We had plans."

"Plans change."

"What does that mean? Are you talking forever? Are you saying you'll never come home?"

She wanted to drop back to the bed, burrow beneath the rumpled covers—and never come out. "Look, Cash. I don't know. Just, please, let me be for now."

But he refused to hear her. "Put on some clothes. We'll go eat."

She regarded him, shaking her head, absolutely certain that she could not face a plate of eggs at any time in the near future.

Still, if it was the only way to get rid of him...

"Breakfast," she bargained. "That's all. You'll say whatever else you think you have to say to me. And then you'll go home."

"I said I'm staying awhile."

She gave him her hardest look. "And I said you're not. Breakfast. And then you go."

He glared at her, but couldn't keep it up for long. He hung his head. "You hate me." He looked absolutely desolate.

Though he was fifteen years her senior, right at that moment, she felt a thousand years older than he would ever be. "No. I do not hate you. I could never hate you. But I need to be away from you, and...everything I grew up with, for a while. Until I figure things out. Nothing's...the way it used to be. And I'm having some trouble dealing with that."

She watched the deep sadness that clouded his eyes, a sadness that matched her own. "Ty," he said with quiet regret.

She nodded. Abby's father, Ty Heller, had been top hand at the Bravo family's ranch for almost thirty years. Two months ago, he had rolled his ancient pickup down a ravine and broken his neck. Abby still had trouble believing that he was really gone.

Cash took a step toward her. "Abby…"

"Don't." She threw out a hand to ward him off.

He stopped, though his eyes pleaded with her. It had been the night of Ty's funeral when Cash had come to her, to offer comfort. To be comforted himself….

"Try to understand." Her voice was hardly more than a whisper. "I need some time here in Denver. On my own."

"Abby…"

"Let me go, Cash."

She saw the change in him as he accepted her will. He had a young man's face as a rule; a boyish look about him that women loved. But right then, he looked older than his thirty-six years.

"All right," he said flatly. "Breakfast. We'll talk a little more. Then, if you still want me to, I'll go."

At a coffee shop a few blocks from Abby's apartment, Cash ordered a western omelette and a stack of pancakes.

"I'll have a bran muffin," Abby said.

Cash took her menu from her. "You need eggs." He aimed one of his knock-'em-dead smiles at the waitress. "She'll have eggs. Scrambled. With sausage. Hash browns, sourdough toast and—"

"Cash."

"—a large milk."

"Just tea and the muffin," Abby said to the waitress.

The waitress looked at her patiently. "But, honey, he thinks you should have—"

"Tea and a muffin," she repeated through clenched teeth.

Cash said, "You'll want those eggs the minute you get them."

"For the last time. Tea. A muffin. That's all."

The waitress looked at Cash, a rueful, "what shall I do now, master?" sort of look. What was it about the man? All he had to do was smile at women, and they forgot that they had the right to vote now.

"It's my breakfast," Abby insisted.

"You need protein," Cash said.

She slapped her palm on the table. "Stop."

He widened those baby blues. "Stop what?"

"I can order my own food. You back off. I am not kidding."

For a suspended moment, they stared at each other, eye to eye and will to will. And then, elaborately, he shrugged. "You want to starve yourself I guess that's your business."

"You bet it's my business."

He turned a sheepish smile on the waitress. "Sorry, ma'am. I guess she just wants that muffin after all."

"Oh, it's no problem. Really. Is that all, then?"

"Yeah, I think that'll do it." He glanced at her name tag and then zapped her with another smile. "Betty."

Blushing prettily, Betty finished scribbling the order. Then she trotted away to do her master's bidding.

They got their food quickly, which was par for the course with Cash. He had a talent for making others want to please him. Women—and men, too—seemed to fall all over themselves seeing that his needs were met. And really, Abby thought, it didn't surprise her that people responded to him. He was generous and kind. And he gave others the feeling that he really *saw* them and cared about them.

He dug right in when Betty set his plate before him. Abby ignored her muffin and watched him, feeling fond in spite of herself, thinking how handsome and healthy and fine he was, even after a night spent drinking too much. A gorgeous man, all the way around.

He looked up from his plate to catch her watching him. She instantly dropped her gaze to her untouched muffin.

"You eat that," he commanded. She picked it up and began peeling off the paper muffin cup. She had popped a bite into her mouth and was chewing obediently, when he asked, "You will come home and see your mom before school starts again, won't you?"

She sipped tea, stalling, wishing he'd asked just about anything else but that. Abby loved her mother, but the two of them rarely saw eye to eye on anything. It had been Ty who understood her. And she didn't even want to think about what would happen when Edna Delacourt Heller learned about the baby.

So she *wouldn't* think about it. Not for a while yet, at least. And as far as the fall semester at C.U. went, well, she doubted she'd even be going. Right now, she needed to earn and save money. To that end, she was working two jobs. She served cocktails all night, which Cash had discovered. What he didn't know was that from nine to three, Monday through Friday, she waited tables at a coffee shop much like the one they sat in right now. She spent what spare time she had in search of bookkeeping work, which she prayed she would find before she got too big to be on her feet day and night.

Cash was watching her, waiting for an answer. "Well?"

She broke off another piece of muffin. "I'll try to get home for a visit as soon as I can."

He made a sound in his throat, an impatient sound. "Your mom needs to see you. You're all the family she's got now. And she's still grieving, with your dad gone."

"I said I'll try, Cash."

He dropped his fork, hard enough that it clattered against his plate. "Just say when you're coming. I'll make arrangements *not* to be around. How's that?"

"Stop." She aimed a look at him, a look as fierce and fiery as she could make it.

Carefully, he picked up his fork and finished his omelette.

Half an hour later, they arrived back at her apartment. She tried to tell him goodbye at the door, but he refused to take a hint. He pushed past her and gained the sanctuary of her room.

"One more thing," he announced, as he felt for the inside pocket of his western-cut suede jacket.

She knew what was coming. "Do not get out that checkbook."

He ignored her. He went over to the table, pulled out his platinum Cross pen and scribbled out a check. "Quit working at that bar." He ripped the check from the book and held it out to her. "This should hold you over until you can find something worth your while."

She remained at the door, her hands behind her back. "I can manage on my own."

"I'll just leave it right here."

"No."

Shaking his head, he put the check on the table. Then he slid the checkbook back to his pocket and put his pen away. "Well, I guess there's nothing more to—"

Before he could get the rest out, she marched over, picked up the check and tore it in half, then tore the halves in half. After that, she threw the pieces in the air. Together, they watched them drift to the carpet at their feet.

He looked down at the torn remnants of his generosity. "What the hell good is that supposed to do?"

"What part of *no* was unclear to you?"

He pushed back the sides of his jacket and braced his hands on his lean hips. "This is stupid. Pointless. I've always helped you before. I've paid for half of your education, and you were never too proud to let me."

"Things were different then. You were investing in me. The more I learned in college, the more use I was to you."

"And now you're not?" He loomed closer, his voice rising in volume with his frustration. "What are you telling me? Are you saying that you're never coming back to work for me because I blew it and took you to bed?"

"Quiet down."

"Then answer me."

"All right. I'm saying I don't know. I'm saying I need time. I've *been* saying that all morning. But you're a pigheaded man. And you just aren't hearing."

"You're never going to forgive me, are you?"

"It's not a matter for forgiveness."

"That's what you say."

"Because it's true."

He took a step closer, so he was looming above her. "Then if you don't have to forgive me, why won't you—"

She cut him off. "I mean it, Cash. I am not coming home. You just have to let me be for a while."

"Abby, you have to listen. You have to see—"

"No." She tried to back away.

"Don't—" He reached out and grabbed her, his big hands closing on her upper arms.

She froze, sucking in a shocked gasp.

"Abby…" The word was an agony. And also a caress.

For a moment, she forgot how to breathe. Images of that night in April flashed through her mind.

Sorrow; he had looked at her with such sorrow. Sorrow for Ty, who had been like a father to him, and sorrow for her, too. In Cash's eyes that night she had seen all the sadness of the world. At first. But then, as she watched, that sorrow had changed to something else altogether.

She had felt as if her heart were lifting, rising to meet the look in his eyes. She had surged up, to press her open lips against his neck—to taste him with her tongue. He had made a sound then, an urgent, hungry sound. And reached for her. His mouth had covered hers, hot and consuming, tasting slightly of whiskey and the cigarettes he kept swearing he was going to give up.

After that first burning kiss, he had pulled away, looked down at her. His warm breath came ragged against her face. "Abby?" A question. A plea.

"Cash," she had answered, and dragged his head back down so that his lips could meet hers once more.

Abby closed her eyes, shutting out the sight of him

now—and the memories of him then. Very gently, Cash released her.

"See?" she whispered, making herself look up at him again. "It can never be the same."

He stepped back, away from her. "You find a way to see your mom," he commanded harshly. "She hasn't been herself since your dad died. She needs you." And then he turned and went out the door.

Chapter Two

Cash flew his little Cessna four-seater out of Denver into Sheridan. From there, he got in his Cadillac and headed for home, which was Medicine Creek, a town with a population that hovered just below the thousand mark, not far from the eastern slopes of the Big Horn Mountains in northern Wyoming.

Medicine Creek looked like any number of small towns in the West. Its Main Street consisted primarily of flat-roofed buildings made of brick. The buildings housed bookstores and gift shops, a couple of diners and a couple of pricier restaurants. There was a new library, with floor-to-ceiling windows in front and a pretty good selection of books inside. There was the Oriental Hotel, which the Medicine Creek Historical Society had succeeded in having declared a historical building a few years before; both Teddy Roosevelt and the Sundance Kid had slept there—Sundance reputedly with his lady love, Emma Pace.

Cash lived in a big house of slate and brick on North Street. It was a nice, quiet street lined with cottonwood trees. He'd had the house built to his own specifications a decade earlier. As a rule, he enjoyed the large, airy rooms and vaulted ceilings. He was a man who liked lots of space. But that day, the damn big rooms seemed to echo. The house felt too empty.

He picked up the phone and called the ranch. Edna answered on the third ring.

"Rising Sun Ranch."

She sounded tired, he thought. He knew her so well. She'd treated him like her own when he'd come to live with his grandparents all those years ago; a ten-year-old boy who'd needed someone to mother him, though nothing would have made him admit it at the time.

"Edna?"

He knew she was smiling even before she said his name.

"Cash. I was hoping we'd hear from you today."

He also knew she was hoping he'd have something good to tell her about Abby.

So much for Edna's hopes.

"What's for dinner?" he asked.

"Oh, roast chicken. Oven-browned potatoes. Snap beans with bacon. Fresh-baked bread, gelatin mold salad...."

"I'll be there in an hour."

They sat down to eat around seven. There were just three of them: Edna, Cash and Zach, Cash's cousin. Zach Bravo had been running the Rising Sun since their grandfather, Ross Bravo, had died five years before.

The table seemed even bigger than usual, with only the three of them. But Edna liked to eat there. She'd assumed the role of hostess at Bravo family events almost a quarter of a century before, after Cash's grandmother, Matty, passed away. Then, five years ago, after Ross had been laid to rest beside Matty, Zach had invited the Hellers to move out of the foreman's cottage across the yard and into the main house. Edna had quickly agreed.

But even before the Hellers actually moved in, it had always seemed to Cash as if the house belonged as much to them as it did to the Bravos. Edna kept the rooms smelling of lemon wax; she hummed in the kitchen while she cooked for the family and the hands. Ty used to sit out on the wide front porch of an evening, his boots up on the porch rail—a man who felt himself at home. And whenever Cash came out from town, they all ate together, as a family: Zach, Cash, Ty, Edna—and Ross, before his death. Nate, too, whenever he showed up for a visit. And Abby...

It caused a tightness in Cash's chest to think of her. But he couldn't help himself, sitting here at this table, where she'd eaten pretty much all of her dinners for the first eighteen years of her life.

Abby had been born at the ranch, over in the foreman's cottage, during a spring blizzard when there'd been no way for Edna to make it to the hospital in Buffalo. Cash had been scared to death for Edna, since his own mother had died in childbirth. But Edna had lived. And produced the miracle of Abby. They hadn't let him in the cottage during the birth. But not long after, as soon as mother and child had been cleaned up, Ty had come out and found him skulking around the front door, scared to death of what might be happening inside.

"Get your butt on in here, boy," Ty had commanded. Inside, Ty had let him hold Abby, so tiny and red faced.

Right now, it seemed to him that he had sat at this table and watched her grow up. He could see her as if she really were there across from him, at about three years old—the age when Edna had declared her ready to eat with the big folks. She'd thrown a handful of boiled carrots across the table and been sent to her room in disgrace.

He recalled her at six—or was it seven?—wearing jeans and a T-shirt, her mouth set in a mutinous line— just before Edna sent her away again, because she had dirt under her nails and Edna wouldn't stand for that. And at eleven, all dressed up for some reason in a pretty blue dress. And at fifteen, when he'd noticed she was wearing eye makeup. Cash had frowned at her, wondering why she thought she needed to wear makeup. She had stuck out her tongue at him. And by then she'd been smart enough to wait until Edna couldn't see.

"So how's Abby doing down there in Denver?" Zach asked into the silence that had settled over the table. Zach was like that; sometimes they all wondered if he thought of anything but cows and bulls and the land he loved more than the average man could love a woman. But then he'd open his mouth and out would come exactly what everyone else was wondering about—but didn't have the nerve to mention.

Cash shot a glance at Edna. She seemed composed,

though she'd set down her fork and her smile looked pinched at the corners.

"Yes," Edna said, sounding too polite. "How *is* Abigail?"

Cash recalled dark circles under hazel eyes and a fleabag one-room apartment strewn with clothes and books. "She seemed...okay."

Edna waited, still smiling her pinched smile at him. Zach waited, too, watching Cash, wearing one of those completely unreadable *Zach*-like looks.

"What?" Cash said, as if he didn't know.

"'Okay' doesn't tell us a hell of a lot," Zach said dryly.

"All right." Cash had the urge to loosen his collar, a stupid urge, since his shirt was already open at the neck. "I'm getting to it."

They went on watching him.

"She's working a lot. She's real busy. She seemed...tired."

"Where is she working?" Edna asked.

"Mac's Mile High, I think it's called."

"Mac's Mile High *what?*"

He coughed. "Saloon. Mac's Mile High Saloon."

"A bar." Edna put her slender, work-chapped hand over her heart. *"Why* is she doing this? What has come over her?"

Her father's dead. And on the night of the day that they put him in the ground, I took her virginity out in the barn, Cash thought. That's why she's doing this. That's what's come over her.

"She should be here, at home," Edna said. "Working for you. The way she's always done since she was sixteen."

Cash said nothing; he just sat there, despising himself.

"That's what I really don't understand," Edna went on. "Of course, we all know that Abigail and I have our differences. And I can almost understand that she might want to take off on her own for a time, after…losing Ty. But that she'd do this to *you*, Cash. That she'd not show up to handle your office, when you were counting on her. After all you've done for her, it just doesn't—"

Cash couldn't take any more. "Edna. The office isn't a big deal."

"Oh, you say that, but still—"

"I mean it. It's nothing. I hardly use it anyway. It's just an address to put on my letterhead. And Renata is there. She can handle the phones and the mail."

"It's not the phones. Or the mail. And I know that *you* are the heart of Cash Ventures, Incorporated, that it's your charm and your willingness to take a chance, not to mention your good sense for a strong investment, that makes you a successful man. But I also know how you and Abby are. Always with your heads together, always making plans. And she *has* become quite useful to you, since she's learned so much about number cracking and all."

"Number crunching."

"Yes. Exactly. Did you tell her to call me?"

Had he? In so many words? He couldn't exactly remember.

"You didn't tell her to call me?"

The hurt in her eyes, hazel eyes like Abby's, broke his heart.

"Cash?"

"I...told her to get home to see you, as soon as possible."

"Did she say that she would?"

He couldn't bear to give her the truth. So he didn't. "Uh, yeah. She did. You know she did."

"Oh, I don't understand." Edna shook her head. "I just don't understand. She could at least return my calls."

Zach spoke softly. "She's twenty-one. A grown-up. Maybe we have to let her do things her own way now."

Edna pressed her lips together, collecting herself. And then she gave Zach a brave smile. "Yes. I know, I know." She turned her smile on Cash. "Thank you. For going. For checking to see that she's all right."

"Damn it, don't thank me!" The words exploded out of him, harsh and angry, full of all the frustration he was trying so hard to control.

Edna's smile wavered. "Cash?"

He sucked in a long gulp of air. "I'm sorry. I'm...a little on the edgy side, I guess."

Edna nodded sadly. "Yes, I know. I understand."

There was a long, heavy silence, which Zach ended by asking, "Was that apple pie I saw on the kitchen counter?"

Edna put on her brave smile again. "It certainly was." She pushed back her chair and stood. And then, for a moment, she wavered and leaned on the table.

Both Zach and Cash jumped to their feet.

"Edna?" Zach asked. "You all right?"

She pushed away from the table and smoothed her hair with a shaky hand. "Fine."

"You look pale," Cash said. "Maybe we should—"

"I said I'm fine. I simply stood up too fast, that's all."

"But—"

"No buts. Both of you sit down." She was already in motion, gathering up their empty plates. "I'll just go and see about fresh coffee and that pie."

Cash stayed after dinner to go over the accounts with Zach.

The ranch, which covered roughly a hundred square miles and was home to around twelve hundred head of cattle, belonged jointly to the three Bravo cousins: Cash, Zach and Nate. But in an era when beef prices never went high enough and one drought seemed to follow another, it was Zach who made the Rising Sun Cattle Company a going concern. For years now, both Cash and Nate had pretty much gone their own ways. Neither of them would have minded at all if Zach just took care of the place and let them show up when the urge struck—or gave them a call when he turned up shorthanded during calving season or at branding time.

But Zach took his stewardship seriously. So whenever Cash or Nate came out to the ranch, they always seemed to end up crowded around Zach's computer, staring at columns of numbers that proved Zach was doing one hell of a job.

By the time they finished that night, eleven o'clock had come and gone. Cash decided against driving back to town.

"You know your room is always ready for you," Edna told him fondly. Though it had long ago been done over into a guest room, Edna still called it *his* room. She always put him there whenever he stayed the night.

Unfortunately, he'd forgotten that he could see the barn from the window of that room. So instead of going to bed, he ended up standing in the dark, looking out at the silvery light of the full moon reflected off the barn walls.

And remembering what he had no right to remember...

Hearing again the sound of Abby's sobs, which had led him to her, in one of the vacant stalls. Smelling the humid, pungent odors of hay and animals. Feeling once more the sudden, shocking, incredible caress of Abby's mouth against his throat; her sweet, ragged breath across his skin. Seeing the absolute trust in her eyes when he looked down at her—and covered her mouth with his own....

With a low oath, Cash turned away from the window. He threw himself on the bed fully clothed, not even bothering to pull off his boots. He ached for a cigarette. Just one.

But he'd given them up again, this morning, after smoking a whole pack in the bar of his Denver hotel last night.

He closed his eyes. He started counting oil wells, which was his own private joke on himself. His daddy, Johnny Bravo, had made it big on an oil well that came in a gusher down in Carbon County. Cash had invested in an oil well or two himself in his time. So when he couldn't sleep, he didn't count sheep. He counted oil wells.

Somewhere around three or four thousand, he must have dropped off.

He dreamed of things he had no right to dream of. Later, he awoke and found himself staring at the ceiling, remembering those dreams, hard as some randy

kid. He lay there, hating himself some more, not only
for what he'd done but for the fact that remembering
what he'd done had the power to arouse him. On top
of hating himself, he tried to figure out what in the hell
he could do to make things right again.

He couldn't come up with a damn thing. And he
couldn't get back to sleep, either. He glanced at the
clock on the bedstand to his right. It was nearing
5 a.m. He'd slept longer than he'd thought. Soon Zach
would be up. A rancher to his bones, Zacharius Bravo.
He never took a vacation and rarely gave himself a day
off. Three hundred sixty-five days a year, he was up
before dawn, whether there was any reason to be up at
that godforsaken hour or not.

Edna would be up shortly, too, banging those pots
and pans, getting breakfast ready for Zach and the three
hands out in the trailers next to the foreman's cottage.
If Cash wanted to sleep in, she'd always fix him something special later on.

Well, this was one day when he wouldn't put Edna
out. He swung his boots to the floor and sat up with a
groan. He raked his hair back with his hands. As he
rubbed his gritty-feeling eyes, it occurred to him that
he should probably hit the shower. But he wanted coffee first.

Downstairs, he stood for a minute in the doorway to
the kitchen. Edna was there, at the table bent over some
papers. He waited for her to look up and see him.

And when she did, he had to stifle a gasp. Her face
had a bluish cast and the skin around her lips was dead
white.

"God. Edna…"

She smiled, a death's-head grin, and gamely held up

a pen. "I was trying to write to her. I thought maybe a letter would make her see—"

"Edna, what the hell is wrong with you?"

She waved the pen, as if his question meant nothing. "I just want her home. I want to see her. I need to see her. Sometimes I wake up in the morning and I wonder if there's anyone left for me. Without Ty. Without my little girl…"

"Edna, *what is wrong?*"

For a moment, she kept smiling that scary smile, and then she frowned. "I don't know. I've been up all night." She put a fist against her chest. "This crushing pain. Like someone dropped a boulder on me, right here. All night long."

He was already at the phone, dialing 911.

"I kept thinking it would go away," he heard Edna murmuring as he waited for someone to pick up the damn phone on the other end. "I didn't want to wake you or Zach. You boys need your sleep…."

Chapter Three

"We should call Abby," Zach said hours later.

Cash and his cousin sat in the small waiting room of the hospital in Buffalo. The doctor had just been out to explain to them that it looked as if Edna had had a heart attack—but they couldn't be sure yet. Half of her heart had stopped working, the doctor had said, but they were confused about her blood test results. A helicopter would take her to the big hospital in Billings right away, where they would learn more.

"Do you want me to do it?" Zach asked.

Cash blinked and tried to stop worrying about Edna. "What?"

Zach sighed. "Do you want me to call Abby?"

"What for?"

"Because she should know."

Cash stared at his cousin. Then he nodded. "You're right. And she should be here." He stood. "I'll go get her. Right now. Can you hold down the fort on this end?''

"Hell, Cash."

"What? You know she'll get to Billings one way or another. Might as well fly her myself."

"Yeah, but..."

Cash saw something in Zach's eyes he wasn't sure he liked. All at once, he wondered how much his cousin knew. "But what?"

"Maybe she'd like a little warning."

"Warning? What for? She doesn't need a warning. She needs to be with her mother."

Zach shook his head.

"What?" Cash demanded again. "You got something on your mind, you better say it."

Zach shrugged. "No, you're right. She'll want to be with Edna, pronto. So go get her."

One by one, Abby set three longnecks in front of three thirsty urban cowboys, then she scooped up the icy mugs from her tray and plunked them in the middle of the table. "Enjoy."

"Thank you, ma'am." The tallest of the three customers pushed back his white Stetson and tossed some bills on her tray.

"I'll be right back with your change."

"You keep that."

Abby murmured her thanks and turned for the bar. She got about two steps before she saw Cash standing over by the door, scanning the club and looking break-your-heart handsome.

Her mouth went dry and her pulse went crazy. Before she could move another inch, he saw her. She felt pinned to the spot by those eyes of his.

But she didn't stay pinned. She marched to the bar, set down her tray and muttered to Mac, the bartender and owner, "I need a break."

Mac, who saw everything, was looking at Cash. "Ten minutes. No more."

"No problem," she said, with more assurance than she felt.

She approached Cash. "This way." She led him through a side door to another room furnished much like the main bar, with small round tables and bentwood chairs. Mac called it the party room and rented it out to groups.

Abby flicked a wall switch. The overhead lights came on, harsh and much brighter than the dim lights in the main bar behind her. She closed the door and gestured at a chair. Cash dropped into it.

She looked at him in the brighter light—and felt the first stab of alarm. Until that moment, she'd imagined it was just going to be more of the same: he demanding she come home and she insisting that she wouldn't.

But something else was going on. He was too quiet. He looked exhausted. And the shadow of worry in his eyes seemed so deep, so very dark.

"What is it? What's happened?"

He closed his eyes. "Abby…"

She sat in the chair opposite him, leaned across the table and put her hand over his. He stiffened, and then he turned his hand, enclosing hers. At that moment, they were what they had once been: Cash and Abby. Comrades. Family.

"Tell me," she said, willing strength into his hand, drawing strength from him at the same time.

"It's Edna…."

"God." The single word was a prayer. She squeezed Cash's hand, and felt him squeeze back.

"Something's happened," he said. "They think a heart attack, but they're not sure yet."

"She's...?" Somehow Abby couldn't make herself say the word *dead*.

Cash hastened to reassure her. "She's alive. I swear to you. I called Zach just a few minutes ago, before I came in here, so I could tell you for certain. They say she's stabilized. But something's wrong. Only half of her heart is working."

"Where is she?"

"They took her to Buffalo first, and then put her in a helicopter and flew her to Billings."

"You flew your own plane here?"

"Yeah."

"You'll take me to her?"

"You know I will."

She pulled her hand from Cash's grip and pushed back her chair. "Let's go."

Mac muttered a few choice epithets when Abby said she had to go. But then he wished her Godspeed and called his wife, Millie, to come in and finish out Abby's shift.

Abby returned to her apartment just long enough to throw some things in a suitcase. She didn't have time to think about the recently sensitive state of her stomach until she was strapped into one of the seats in Cash's little plane. But she needn't have worried. She'd never been sick before in small planes, and she wasn't this time, either.

It was nearly dawn by the time they got to Billings.

Cash had a rental car waiting. He drove them straight to the hospital.

They found Zach in the little waiting room outside the intensive care unit. He stood when he saw them. Abby rushed to him, and he enfolded her in his arms.

"Good to see you, Pint-Size," he whispered in her ear.

She held on tight. "Same back to you."

Zach was actually younger than Cash by a couple of years. But to Abby, he always seemed older, so mature and settled down. He possessed a deep calm that never failed to soothe her.

She stepped away and mustered up a smile. "So. How is she doing?"

Briefly, he brought them up to date. The doctors had run more tests. Evidently, a certain enzyme always showed up in the blood when a heart attack had taken place. Edna's bloodstream had no trace of it. Still, half of her heart wasn't functioning. So they'd gone in through an artery in her thigh and inserted a device that would help her heart to beat regularly until they could figure out what the hell was going on.

"She has to lie completely still," Zach said, "so they've got her pretty doped up."

"Can I see her?"

"Come on." He led them through a pair of swinging doors and past a large central nurses' station. He waved at a nurse and she gave him a nod, so he moved on to one of the rooms.

In the room, Edna lay faceup on a metal-railed bed. Tubes seemed to be everywhere: they emerged from the back of one hand, the crook of an elbow and also from the sheet that covered her thin chest. Around her were way too many machines and monitors, each one ticking or bubbling or beeping or making strange breathing sounds.

Cash and Zach hung back as Abby walked around the far side of the bed. At the metal railing there, careful of all the tubes and machines, she stood looking down at her mother.

Edna's eyes were closed. Her eyelids looked paper-thin and bluish. And her face looked...so old. Her hair was all smashed down, too. Abby hated seeing her like that. Because she knew how her mother would hate looking like that. Edna always took care to keep herself neat and tidy. And she wore a little mascara and lipstick, too, as a rule—applied with a very light hand, of course.

The paper-thin eyelids fluttered open. "Abigail." There was such relief on that old-looking face. "You've come."

"Mom." She wanted to touch the thin hand, but she feared she might disturb all the tubes stuck in the back of it. "How are you doing?"

"I've been better."

Abby nodded in understanding.

"I must remain very still. But it's not hard, with whatever it is they've been giving me. So tired...." Her eyelids fluttered down again.

Abby didn't move. She watched her mother sleep, thinking of all the battles they'd fought with each other over the years. Sometimes Edna drove her crazy. But still, there was love between them. Right then, Abby felt that love as a physical force, deep, fierce and true. Death might have snatched away her father, but death could not have her mother. Not for years yet. Abby wouldn't let it.

Edna opened her eyes again. "You'll come home now?" she asked in a thin, plaintive voice.

It was blackmail, pure and simple. Emotional blackmail. And Abby knew it.

She thought of the baby growing inside her, but instead of feeling overwhelmed as she had for so many weeks now, she felt energized. It came to her: she wanted the baby, *really* wanted it, with no doubts and no ambivalence. She had never been a girl who'd played with dolls, who'd dreamed of a husband, babies and a home to keep. But now, at last, she truly understood that she would be a mother, like her own mother. And that she would give herself heart and soul to the task.

"Abigail?"

She thought of Cash, not ten feet away, watching. All she had to do was turn her head to see him. It had finally become real to her: he would have to know. Somehow, she would have to tell him.

And he would want to take over. He'd insist on marriage. At first.

But she would just have to be strong enough and sure enough of herself that she could tell him no and mean it. She wouldn't marry any man just because they had made a baby together; he'd have to accept that. They'd learn to work together to raise their child, with respect for each other as independent adults.

"Abigail." Edna's reedy voice was petulant now. "Will you come home?"

Abby smiled at her mother. "Hush. Settle down. You know I will."

Except to go to the bathroom and grab a few bites in the cafeteria, Abby refused to leave her mother's side through that entire day. Finally, around seven that night, after a lengthy consultation with a doctor who insisted that Edna would not expire if Abby took a break, Cash convinced her to check into a hotel.

But she would only stay there long enough to shower and change. And then she made him drive her back to the hospital.

"Now," she told Cash and Zach, "I want you both to get out of here. Get a good dinner and get some sleep."

They tried to argue, but she held firm. At last, they gave in and left. The ICU nurses, seeing how tired she looked, took pity on her and had a bed rolled into her mother's room. She fell into it gratefully and closed her eyes.

"Abigail?"

Her mother's voice sought her out through the darkness and the beeping and bubbling of all those lifesaving machines.

"Umm?"

"Thank you."

"What for?"

"You know."

Abby smiled to herself. "I'm here. I'm not going anywhere."

"Exactly."

"Good night, Mom."

Instead of saying good-night, Edna murmured dreamily, "Your father always promised me my own house, did you know that?"

Abby opened her eyes and stared into the darkness. She didn't speak.

Edna went on anyway. "But I never got my house.

We never had that kind of money. So I spent our life together taking care of the Bravo house. And I didn't mind it, really. Not most of the time. Those boys needed me. They're like my own...but not really my own.''

Edna fell silent. For a moment, Abby thought she had dropped off to sleep again.

But then she said, ''Abby? Are you still awake?''

''Yes, Mom.''

''I'm fortunate, I know. I've managed to save some. And we did have a little life insurance, because I insisted. So I won't be destitute when I can't work anymore.'' She made a low sound, perhaps a chuckle. ''Zach. Mr. Responsible. He's seen I have good health insurance, so this episode will all be taken care of.''

''Good.''

''But we both know Cash would take care of me anyway, even if there was no savings and no insurance at all.''

''Yes. He would.''

''And Nate would come all the way from L.A. if necessary, to help me.'' Edna made that sound again, that sound that might have been a chuckle. ''Your father. Like the wind. Who can tie down the wind?''

''No one.''

''I did love him. I don't think I knew...how much. Until he was gone.''

''Mom...''

''I loved him.'' She sounded almost defiant. ''And I love you.''

''I know you do, Mom.''

''So very much....''

''Go to sleep now.''

Edna sighed and said no more.

Abby lay in the darkness, listening to the machines for a while. Soon enough, exhaustion claimed her.

She awoke in the middle of the night when a nurse came in to check on Edna. And she felt her stomach rise and roll.

Stifling a groan, she slid from the bed. Luckily, the bathroom was only a few feet away. She pushed the door closed and got her head over the toilet basin before the scanty contents of her stomach came up. She tried to be as quiet as she could.

When the retching finally stopped, she turned on the light and held back another groan at the sight of herself in the medicine cabinet mirror.

"So attractive," she whispered to her own haggard image.

She cleaned up as best she could. Then she turned off the light and waited for her eyes to become accustomed to the gloom.

Slowly, quietly, she pulled open the door. The room beyond was quiet, except for the machines. The nurse had gone. She tiptoed to the bed and looked down at her mother.

Sound asleep.

Abby went back to her own bed and slid beneath the sheet. Within minutes, dreams embraced her.

It was a week before Edna left the hospital. Zach went back to the ranch the day after Abby arrived. The next day, Cash got a call from one of his business associates about a land deal they were working on. Abby told him to go handle it; she could look after her mother just fine on her own. She felt relief when he agreed to go, because sometimes, when he looked at her, she was sure he knew her secret—which she did intend to tell him about.

Soon. Very soon.

Before he left, Cash made sure she had a rental car so that she could get around.

The doctors ran more tests. Finally, they told Abby that Edna had experienced a coronary vasospasm, and not a real heart attack.

"A coronary vasospasm," the doctor said, "amounts to severe, extended cramping of the heart muscle. It is not a heart attack—there is no disease involved. It's like a big charley horse. But it's dangerous because it's happening to the heart."

They couldn't say why it had happened. But they did say that Edna's arteries were surprisingly clear, with very little plaque buildup. Thus, with time, she would probably recover completely. Of course, she'd have to take it nice and easy for a while. And for the rest of her life, she would require medication to keep the problem from recurring.

Cash returned on Sunday, a week after Edna became ill. By then, they had taken her off the device that helped her heart to pump and moved her from intensive care into a regular room.

He appeared in the afternoon, while Edna was napping and Abby sat in a chair in the corner playing Super MarioKart on a Game Boy that one of the nurses had lent her. She was so intent on trying to pass Yoshi without spinning off the track that she didn't know Cash had come in until he spoke.

"Are you winning?"

Her nimble thumbs went slack. Mario whirled off into oblivion. She looked up. "I was."

Those gorgeous blue eyes scanned her face.

"You look better. More rested."

Her foolish heart trip-hammered against her breast-bone. She prayed he couldn't hear it. "Not a lot to do around here *but* rest."

He went on looking at her. And she looked back.

Then he seemed to shake himself. "How is she?"

"I'm right here, Cash Bravo," Edna said. "Turn around and see for yourself."

He did turn. "Well, well," he said. "Beautiful. Downright beautiful."

Edna was blushing. Abby thought she really did look pretty, in a new bed jacket, with her hair neatly combed—and just a touch of blusher and lipstick.

"You look like you're ready to go home," Cash said, taking her hand.

"They said I could. Tomorrow."

For a moment, he just held Edna's hand.

Then she asked, "Are you staying the night here in Billings?"

"You bet."

"Then would you do a favor?"

"Name it."

"I want you to take Abigail out for dinner."

Panic lanced through Abby. Of course she needed to tell Cash her secret. But she wasn't quite ready yet. And until she *was* ready, she wanted to avoid spending time alone with him. She jumped to her feet. "No, really. I'd rather—"

Edna didn't let her finish. "Nonsense. All you do is sit here with me. And I'm getting along just fine now. A nice dinner out will be good for you."

"Mom..."

"Cash. Will you do that for me?"

* * *

They went to a steak house.

Abby's stomach had been behaving much better in the past few days, probably a result of the extra rest she was getting. Confident she could handle a nice, juicy porterhouse, she ordered one, along with a salad and a baked potato smothered in sour cream and chives.

"And hot tea." She smiled at the waitress.

As soon as the waitress had walked away, Cash demanded, "What's this tea you're always drinking lately?"

It occurred to her that he'd given her the perfect opening. She should tell him the truth right now. But she just wasn't ready yet. "I like tea. So what?"

He took a sip of the drink the waitress had brought him earlier, then shrugged. "I don't know. I just wondered."

She felt defensive—because she knew that she was going to sit across from him through the entire meal and not say a word about something that would change both their lives irrevocably. "If I want tea, I'll have tea."

"Abby, come on."

She glanced away, knowing herself to be petulant and cowardly—and not liking herself much at all. "I'm sorry." She met his eyes.

He looked back at her in a way that made her more uncomfortable than ever.

"I know you didn't want to come out to eat with me. And believe me, I understand your feelings."

No, you don't, she wanted to say. You don't understand at all. Because I can't seem to tell you. I can't *stand* to tell you....

"Abby, we're going to have learn to get along. We're going to have to get past what happened."

She swallowed. "I know."

The waitress came with their salads. For a few blessed minutes, Abby concentrated on forking up lettuce leaves and putting them in her mouth.

Cash sipped his drink again. "I'd like to just…let it go. Forget it ever happened. If you could do that. Could you?"

She almost dared to answer, Well, that might be kind of difficult, considering I'm pregnant. But she didn't dare. She didn't say a word, only looked at him.

He set down his drink. "Okay, stupid suggestion."

She put down her fork. "Look. Can we just eat, please? Can we just…not talk about it? I mean it, Cash. If every time I'm with you, we have to rehash it all again, I, well, I think I'll go plain crazy, you know?"

"Yeah. Fine. I get the message." He picked up a piece of bread and tore it in half.

They finished their salads and the waitress brought the main course. Abby cut off a bite of her porterhouse. It was delicious. But her appetite had fled. Across from her, Cash looked miserable.

She forced herself to speak in a bright tone. "Well, it seems like I'll be coming home for the summer after all."

He kept watching her, broodingly. "That's something, I guess." He raised his hand for the waitress.

She appeared from thin air, eager to serve him, as all waitresses were. "What can I get you?"

He pointed at his drink.

"Coming right up." She bounced happily away.

Abby tried again to talk about everyday matters, to get them back on some kind of even ground with each other. "I think as soon as we get Mom settled at home, I'll fly to Denver."

He lifted a bronze eyebrow. "Why?"

"Well, to get my things, to close up my apartment and to pick up my car." She had already called Mac and the manager of the coffee shop where she worked days and told them she wouldn't be returning.

"Forget that," Cash said.

For a moment, Abby thought he was talking to the waitress, who'd just reappeared with his fresh drink. But then he went on.

"I handled it."

Abby frowned. "You what?"

"I arranged to have your things sent home and told the manager at your apartment that you wouldn't need the place anymore. I also hired someone to drive your car home."

She stared at him.

He waved a hand. "Your mother needs you now. You can't be fooling around in Denver."

"That's not the point."

"It sure as hell is."

"They were *my* things, Cash. This is *my* life."

"You're making a big deal out of nothing."

"No, I'm not." She reached for her water glass and then set it down, hard enough that water sloshed on the tablecloth.

"Abby…"

"No." She leaned across the table and kept her voice to a whisper. "You can't take over my life, Cash. You can't fix everything for me. I'm twenty-one. It's time I fixed things for myself. Do you understand?"

He sat back and sighed. "You always used to let me

do whatever I thought was best for you. You'd just say thanks and let it be.''

He was right, so it took her a moment to compose a reply. When she spoke, she made her tone gentler than before. ''I know. You've been good to me. But I really do want to make my own decisions now. And I want you to let me.''

''You wouldn't be saying this if it wasn't for—''

She didn't let him finish. ''Look. I've told you more than once that I don't blame you for what happened. And I meant it. So just give up feeling guilty, why don't you?''

He looked sheepish—and so handsome it hurt.

''I'll try.''

They managed to get through the rest of the meal without incident. He took her back to the hospital for a while after that. And then he returned her to her hotel, where he had a room, too.

She thought that maybe she'd gotten through to him, at least about trying to run her life for her—until the next morning, when she went to check out of her room and learned he'd already paid the bill. She spoke to him about that briefly, before they went to drop off her rental car and pick up Edna for the drive home.

''Cash, you can't just pay all my bills.''

''Why not?''

She remained calm. ''Because they're *my* bills.''

''Are you coming back to work for me?''

''Cash...''

''You know it's the best thing. How do you expect me to keep track of my money, without you and all those damn spreadsheets of yours? And you won't find another job that pays as well—or that you can do at home, where you can keep an eye on Edna at the same time.''

She was shaking her head.

He put on that boyish look that knocked all the women dead. ''Come on. Work for me.''

And she heard herself giving in, saying yes.

He grinned and told her he'd take the cost of the hotel room out of her paycheck, over time, if she insisted. And the same went for her rental car.

Abby told herself they'd come to some sort of understanding, that even though she'd agreed to work for him, which was bound to cause some problems, at least he would stop trying to take over her life. But then, when they went home, he drove to Medicine Creek instead of out to the ranch. He pulled onto Meadowlark Lane, a street a few blocks from his.

Abby saw her battered Rabbit right away, parked in the driveway of a neat two-story brick house with a big, spreading cottonwood tree in the front yard. Cash turned in and parked beside the Rabbit.

''What's this?'' Edna asked, her eyes shining.

''I think it's about time you had your own house,'' Cash said.

Chapter Four

"Oh, Cash." Edna sounded young, full of life and joy. "I just...I can't believe it!"

Cash basked in her excitement. Over a year before, Ty had told him how much Edna longed for her own house.

That had been during the spring trail drive, which took place every April; Zach would get together whatever hands he had working for him, and a neighbor or two, and move a good half of the herd up to higher pastures for the warmer months. Cash had been helping out with the spring drive since the first year he'd come to live at the ranch. Some years, if they stopped at fenced land for the night, they'd go on home to sleep.

But last year, they'd taken a little different route and ended up spending one night on open land, in a camper trailer, watching over the herd. Early on, as the hands took a turn circling the herd, Cash and Ty sat out under the stars for a while, sharing a nip or two, talking about nothing in particular. Somewhere in the conversation, Ty had mentioned that he'd never bought Edna the house he'd always promised her.

"If there's anything I got regrets about, it's that," he'd said. Then he'd looked up at the shadows of the Big Horn Mountains, capped with their glittering mantle of snow, and lifted a thermos with whiskey-laced coffee in it. "Nothin' else. Nothin' else at all."

On the day Ty died, Cash had remembered what Ty had said that cold spring night under the stars. And he'd decided to see to it that Edna got her house.

What had happened after the funeral between him and Abby had nothing to do with his decision. Nothing at all.

He'd bought the house two weeks after Ty's death. It was just right. It had a master suite downstairs for Edna, and two spare rooms upstairs: one for Abby when she came home, and one, as it turned out, that Abby could use as an office. Escrow had closed without a hitch. But he'd wanted to fix it up nice before giving it to Edna, so he'd sort of back-burnered the project until he'd had a little spare time to finish it up right.

Edna's illness had motivated him. During her hospital stay, he'd overseen the delivery of two moving vans full of furniture in solid, conservative styles. Then he'd spent all day last Saturday moving the stuff into the rooms with the help of a couple of local kids. He'd even hired a woman to come in and put the new sheets on the beds, as well as to fill the kitchen cabinets with packaged goods.

"Oh, Cash." Edna hung on his arm as he gave her and Abby the tour. "How could you have known? It's exactly as I always dreamed it might be. Even the furniture...."

"I've seen you studying those JC Penney catalogs. I think, after all these years, I know what you like."

"I don't know what to say."

"Then don't say a thing." He glanced at Abby. Her face wore that closed, tight look it wore too much lately. He looked at Edna again, drank in her smile. "It's your retirement present—if you want to retire, I mean. You know you won't have to. Zach would be more than glad to have you back, when you're feeling better. But this house will always be here, waiting for you."

She gave his arm another squeeze. "I think I'll have to pinch myself. Is this really real?"

"You bet it is."

They walked slowly up the stairs, in consideration for Edna's weakened condition. He showed them the room that would be Abby's bedroom.

Abby pulled open the closet door. "Why, all my clothes are here," she sneered. "Already put away. Isn't that convenient?"

Cash just looked at her, feeling reproachful. He had only wanted to help.

"Abigail..." Edna murmured warningly.

Abby fell silent, but her eyes were mutinous.

And then, when she saw her computer and all her accounting software and books in the office room, she looked madder than a teased hornet.

"Thank you," she said in a tone that didn't sound grateful at all.

He just went ahead and smiled at her. "You're welcome. Renata will be expecting you over at the office tomorrow. You can pick up the books and things from her.''

''Fine.''

''I'll let you get them in order, and then I thought I'd drop by in a few days so we can go over everything.''

''Great.''

Edna patted his arm again. ''Cash, I am just completely overwhelmed.''

Abby muttered something too low to make out.

''What was that, Abigail?'' Edna asked sharply.

''Nothing.''

She stuck out her lip. Cash thought she looked just like the kid she constantly insisted she wasn't anymore.

Cash smiled at Edna. Her eyes sparkled with happiness. Still, she had to be careful not to wear herself out. The doctors had said she'd need a lot of rest, that she wasn't to do anything strenuous for at least the next month. ''You should get yourself to bed.''

''Yes. Of course. You're right.''

He took her back down the stairs and saw her settled in the big reclining chair he'd bought for her, in the nice little sitting area of her bedroom where she could look out on the box elder tree that grew in the backyard. Then he went outside to bring in the two small suitcases in the trunk.

Abby had beaten him to it. She was trudging up the stairs when he got to the front hall.

''Abby.''

She stopped at the top and looked down at him, her straw-colored hair falling in her eyes, her mouth set in a defiant line.

''I would have brought those in.''

''Oh, I know you would.''

He mounted the first step. "Abby..."

She just looked at him, daring him with those eyes of hers to take another step. She was breathing a little fast. He could see her breasts, beneath the white shirt she wore, rising and falling.

He knew what those breasts looked like naked, what they felt like in his hands....

"What?" she said.

"Nothing." He turned before she could look down and see that he hadn't put that one night behind him— not by a long shot.

"Cash." Now she sounded sorry.

He froze, looking away from her, a few steps from the front door, not daring to turn back on the chance that she might see his shame. "Yeah?"

"She wanted a house...so bad. How did you know?" Her voice was soft.

"Ty told me. A year ago."

She was quiet for a moment, then she sighed. "I'm mad at you."

"I know."

"You will not run my life."

"You've said that."

"But...thank you. For her."

"Welcome," he muttered. And then he got the hell out.

Cash returned on Thursday. He visited with Edna, and then he and Abby retreated to her office.

Abby thought that he seemed edgy at first, once they were alone. He took pains to stay well away from her, on the far side of her desk. But she had decided that she would really put some effort into getting along with him. After all, they did have to work together.

And he *was* the father of her baby—which she intended to tell him about. As soon as she could reestablish some semblance of the old easiness between them.

She'd set a goal for that day: to get their working relationship back on track. To that end, she stayed cheerful and professional and never once hinted that she sensed any tension in the air.

She showed him how she'd started to pull his books back together and promised to have everything pretty much under control within a week or so. She smiled and sat back in her chair and asked him about his latest land deal.

He seemed to relax as he talked about it. They discussed grain futures and the encouraging rise in uranium prices.

Before he left, she brought up the subject of Josh DeMarley. Josh, an old high school buddy of Cash's, always had some oil well that was supposed to make him rich. But he never got rich. Between loans and "investments," Cash had passed a significant sum Josh's way over the years—money Cash would never see again.

Abby tried to sound stern. "I want you to promise me that the next time he comes to you with some crazy wildcatting scheme, you'll tell him no."

Cash looked at Abby reproachfully. "You know I can't promise anything like that. Josh and I go way back. He's got a wife and a little girl. And he's had bad luck."

"He *is* bad luck," Abby said.

"It's only money. And you know me. I can always make more."

That much was true. Money seemed to seek him out. It had been like that since he was a very small child.

He had earned the name Cash at the age of seven when his parents, Johnny and Vivian, had taken him to Vegas. John-John, as Cash was known at the time, had begged to play the slots. Vivian had patiently explained that only grown-ups could gamble. But John-John had a few quarters tucked away in a pocket. And when his mother turned around, he stuck one in a machine and pulled the handle. He'd won ten thousand dollars—and Vivian had thought fast and pretended that the quarter had been hers.

Later, when she and his father got him alone, they chided John-John for what he'd done.

His father had announced, "But you know we'll put that money away for you, son. When we get home, we'll open you your own savings account."

This statement was considered humorous in itself, since Johnny Bravo had never saved a cent in his life. If he needed money, he made a deal or placed a bet, and somehow he always came out ahead.

Seven-year-old John-John was a chip off the old block. He looked at his father levelly. "Thanks, Dad. But I'd rather just have the cash."

The way Abby had heard it, no one had ever called him "John-John" again.

Cash got to his feet. "Next week all right? Say, Wednesday? We can go over everything then."

"Sounds fine."

He left, and Abby felt really good. Really positive that they would work through all their difficulties, eventually.

Things weren't going nearly so well with Edna. Already, after just a few days in the same house with her mother, Abby found herself longing to slam a few doors and say some rude things.

It was the same old problem. Edna had been born to make a home. She baked biscuits that dissolved on the tongue and put little plastic sleeves on the pages of her recipe books so no unruly grease spatters would dirty them up.

Abby couldn't fry an egg without breaking the yolk. And her idea of hell would be somewhere that they made you separate the whites from the colors when you did the laundry.

They had started to have their little nitpicky fights again. Edna wanted her new house kept up a certain way. But she wasn't supposed to keep house; she was supposed to take it easy. Keeping house was Abby's job.

Abby tried. She really did. But she could think of a thousand more interesting things to do with herself than dusting the tables or separating the wash. Such as the work Cash had hired her to do. Or reading the *Wall Street Journal* and *U.S. News and World Report,* keeping up on events in the world. Inevitably, when she'd start to do some housewifely chore, she'd end up picking up a book or a calculator. She'd sit down for just a minute or two, perhaps to read about poultry futures; she and Cash had been discussing how much he should have tied up in poultry futures.

The next sound she'd hear would be her mother's querulous voice. "Abigail. Abigail! What are you up to now?"

Her morning sickness, which had seemed to fade during Edna's stay in the hospital, got worse. Her stomach constantly seemed on the verge of rebelling.

Once it did rebel, right at the table, while she and her mother were eating and arguing. She'd had to run for the bathroom. Which had caused no end of questions from Edna when she returned.

"What is the matter with you, Abigail? Are you ill? Is it something you've eaten? I don't understand."

"There's nothing wrong with me."

"What were you doing in the bathroom?"

"Mother. I am fine. Let's just drop it now. Eat your dinner. Please."

"This chicken is bloody. That's probably your problem. E. coli. Or ptomaine."

"I'm fine, Mom. Just fine."

"It's food poisoning. I know it. We should call the clinic right away."

Finally, with continued soothing and groveling, she got Edna settled down. But then, two days later, it happened again; she and Edna argued at the dinner table, and Abby had to run for the bathroom. After that, Abby realized she had to come to grips with her hatred of housework.

She made an effort; she really did. And things started to smooth out a little. Edna found less to complain about. And Abby was scrupulous about not letting arguments get started.

Cash visited on both Saturday and Monday, after that Thursday when he and Abby had met in her office. But those were strictly social calls, for Edna's sake. He chatted with Abby's mother awhile and then left. It seemed to Abby that he avoided talking to her, which she didn't really mind, as she still hadn't worked up the nerve to say what she had to say to him.

She knew she had to stop putting it off. She was in her eleventh week of pregnancy, not showing yet because her stomach was too queasy most of the time for her to put on any weight. She knew very well that she should have seen a doctor a month ago, in Denver. But she'd been walking around in a daze there, working two exhausting jobs, just trying to get through each day as it came along.

She wasn't walking around in a daze anymore. But here at home, she knew everyone at the local clinic. She felt certain they would try to keep the news confidential, but she couldn't see herself showing up there for prenatal care without the word leaking out. And she couldn't bear that: to have Cash or her mother find out the truth from someone else.

They deserved to hear it from her. Cash first. And then Edna.

So, at last, Abby came to a decision. Wednesday, when Cash came to go over the books with her, she would tell him that she carried his child.

He arrived right after lunch and closeted himself with Edna for half an hour. Abby sat up in her office, trying not to bite her fingernails, wishing he would hurry up so they could get down to it.

Then, when she heard his boots on the stairs, she reminded herself of how she was going to handle this: to be cordial and professional while they discussed business, and to keep calm and levelheaded when it came time to break the news.

"Hi." He was standing in the doorway, looking as if he wasn't sure she would let him in.

"Hi." She smiled. He smiled back, cautiously. "Come on in." She had the hard copy of his expense ledger in front of her. "I've got everything ready."

She'd pulled the visitor's chair around to her side of the desk so they could look at the figures together. He frowned at the chair, as if it somehow displeased him. But then he came and dropped into it.

For a few minutes, everything seemed to be going along just fine. They went over the entries, Abby pointing out the places where his natural extravagance should be curbed, asking him why he'd bought certain things at all—making notes as she went so she could move some of the entries to other columns later.

She did find herself terribly distracted by his nearness, by the warmth his body generated, by the smell of his aftershave, which was very faint but nonetheless hard to ignore. Maybe it hadn't been such a good idea to sit next to him. But things had gone so well the week before that she'd become a little complacent about being around him.

She was just nervous enough that she pressed too hard with her pencil when she pointed to a line in the ''Travel and Entertainment'' column. ''What's this?'' The lead snapped.

The noise seemed magnified, like a pistol shot in the room. They looked up from the spreadsheet and into each other's eyes.

And it was that night in April all over again. Her whole body leaned toward him.

She knew she had to stop it. She rose from her chair. He stood, too.

She couldn't talk, couldn't say a word. She looked up at him, and he looked down at her. She saw in his eyes what she felt in her heart—and all through her body. A hunger. A yearning.

Memories flooded her. Memories of the two of them. Doing forbidden things.

The humid sweetness of hay was all around her. Zach's favorite mare, Ladybird, snorted nervously in a nearby stall. The wind outside whistled a little as it found its way through the cracks in the walls. And Cash wasn't standing there in front of her, staring into her eyes, but looming above her, his powerful shoulders cutting out the light from the fluorescent lamps overhead, casting the world into seductive shadow.

She had cried out when he covered her, shocked at the heavy, hard feel of him, bewildered at the way he hurt her at first. But the hurt had quickly melted, becoming something altogether different, something wondrous, something frightening, something that lifted her up and turned her inside out. Something that made them more to each other than they had been before— yet less at the same time....

Downstairs, a door slammed, yanking Abby rudely back to the present.

Neither of them moved. They stared at each other, waiting, not breathing.

No other sound came from below.

Cash seemed to shake himself. "I...gotta go." He reached around her, scooped up the papers from her desk. "I'll look these over." He backed away. "And we'll get together again. In a day or two."

She remembered her promise to herself, took a step toward him. "Cash, I want to talk to you. There's something I—"

"No." He held up the hand with the papers in it, warding her off. "Not now. Can't talk now."

"But, Cash, I—"

"Look. I mean it. Gotta go."

"Cash, please. Just listen. Just let me—"

He backed another step, reached behind him for the door. If she hadn't been so desperate, so in conflict within herself, she might have laughed. Cash Bravo was scared to turn his back on her!

"Cash. I'm not kidding. It's important—it really is."

"Not now. I can't talk now. I can't stay here. I have to get out." He yanked open the door, spun on his heel and disappeared.

She just stood there, listening to the heavy tread of his boots as they retreated down the stairs. She heard the front door open and close and then, within moments, his car starting up and driving off. She despised herself a little for not chasing after him. Because she knew he wouldn't visit again for a while—and that until he did, she would put off the grim job of telling him he was going to be a dad.

At his own house, Cash threw some clothes in a bag and left. He drove down to Cheyenne to meet with a few buddies of his. They went to good restaurants and they did a little business.

He returned to Medicine Creek on Monday morning, July 3. He wanted to go over and check on Edna, see if maybe she felt well enough to head over to Ucross for a while tomorrow evening. A tiny town about eighteen miles north of Buffalo, Ucross always put on a nice Independence Day celebration, complete with music and fireworks after dark. He was thinking he'd ask Abby to come, too. There shouldn't be any trouble between them out in the open with Edna along.

Trouble between them. That was how he thought of this…problem he had when it came to Abby. Trouble. Because he couldn't stop thinking about her, in ways that he had no right to think about her. It made no sense. It wasn't like him. He adored women. But he never let himself get crazy over one. Until now. Now he was stark raving out of his head. Over Abby. Of all the women he might have chosen to drive himself nuts over, it had to be her.

He just hoped that, over time, he'd get past it. Hell, he *had* to get past it. She was just an innocent kid and she had her whole life in front of her. And he was a dyed-in-the-wool bachelor, set in his ways. He wanted them to get back to the way they used to be with each other. And they would. Somehow.

He was just reaching for the phone to call Edna, when it rang. He snatched it up and barked into the mouthpiece. "Yeah?"

"Cash? Is that you, Cash?"

The voice was familiar. "Yeah, this is Cash."

"Cash, this is Tess. Tess DeMarley?"

Josh's wife. He smiled into the phone. "Tess. How's everything?"

"Cash, I..."

She hesitated, and all at once he knew she had bad news.

"Tess, what's happened? Is it Jobeth?" Jobeth was her six-year-old daughter.

"No, not Jobeth. She's fine." Tess spoke very carefully. A woman picking her way over a verbal minefield. "It's Josh."

Cash realized he was holding his breath, and let it out in a rush. "What about Josh?"

"He fell from the rig. This morning." She paused, as if composing herself. Then she said it: "Josh is dead."

For a moment, Cash's mind rejected the information. He thought of Ty out under the stars, lifting his thermos of fortified coffee. And Edna, still with them, thank

God—but it had been pretty damn scary there for a while. And now Josh? It wasn't possible.

"Cash, I thought you'd want to know." She sounded so calm. But Tess was like that. So young, but still a hell of a woman, one who always kept her head.

He ordered his mind to function. "You sit tight. I'll be there in a few hours."

"Oh, no. You shouldn't…"

He could hear her relief, even as she tried to protest.

"That same apartment? There in Laramie?"

"Cash, it's not your—"

"A few hours. Count on me."

"Where is Cash lately?" Edna asked. They were at the dinner table.

Abby tried to make her shrug offhand. "I don't know. He's probably away on business."

"It's been days since we heard from him."

"Mom, he has a life."

Edna frowned. "Did something happen between the two of you last Wednesday?"

"Why do you ask that?"

"Well, he left without saying goodbye. And I heard his boots on the stairs. He *ran* down the stairs."

Abby sipped a little tea.

Edna wouldn't be put off. "Well, *did* something happen?"

Abby set down her cup. "No," she lied without remorse. "Not a thing. We went over his expenses. And then he left. He took his ledger sheets with him."

Edna stared at Abby's barely touched plate. "What's happened to your appetite?"

"Mom—"

"No, I've noticed that you've hardly been eating at

all since you came back from Denver. And I know that
sometimes you don't hold your food down.''

''Mom.''

''Are you developing an eating disorder of some
kind?''

''If you don't stop, I'm getting up and leaving this
table.''

Edna shook her head. ''I don't understand. Cash dis-
appears. And you're not…right. Something's going on.
I just want to—''

Abby picked up her plate and started to rise.

''Sit down,'' Edna said.

After a beat, Abby dropped back into her chair. They
ate in silence for a moment.

Then Edna said plaintively, ''I just wish you felt you
could trust me, whatever it is.''

Abby put on a smile. ''I do trust you, Mom.''

Edna shook her head and turned her attention back
to her plate.

Tess wouldn't let Cash pay for the funeral, though
he knew she hardly had a dime to her name. And she
had no family left, either—none that could help her,
anyway. Tess's dad was dead. Her mom lived on Social
Security and barely had the funds to make it to Laramie
for Josh's funeral. Tess was young, not yet twenty-five,
if Cash remembered right. Too young to be widowed
and flat broke.

''I'll manage,'' Tess assured him, smiling that brave
smile he'd always admired.

He stayed in Laramie till Saturday morning, through
the funeral and the day after, at a hotel not too far from
the tiny apartment Tess and her daughter now shared
alone. He thought a lot about Josh, about the old days,

the good times they used to have. But even more, he worried about Tess and Jobeth. Before he left, he pressed a few bills into Tess's hand, a small enough amount that she could call it a loan and accept it.

She explained, "I've been picking up a few hours here and there down at the corner market. But they told me last week that they'd have to let me go." Her voice turned hopeful. "If you hear of a job in Medicine Creek, something for a woman who might not have a lot of skills but is willing to put in a good day's work...."

He nodded. "I'll see what I can do."

Her eyes hardened. "A job, Cash. Not charity."

And he had to reassure her that there'd be no charity involved.

He was back at his house in Medicine Creek by a little after one in the afternoon. He had a raft of messages on his machine. More than one of them was from Edna.

He dialed her number. She answered on the second ring.

"Hello, Heller residence."

He felt both relief and disappointment that it wasn't Abby who'd answered. "Hi there. How are you doing?"

"Oh, Cash..."

He didn't like the way she sounded. "Edna, are you okay?"

"Of course. I just...I've missed you."

"I'll come right over."

"Yes. Good."

He could have sworn she was crying. "What's the matter?"

She sniffled a little. "Nothing. Everything. Please. I would so like to see you."

He was there in five minutes. And when she opened the door, her red-rimmed eyes said it all. She led him into the living room.

He tried not to ask, but he couldn't help himself. "Where's Abby?"

"Grocery shopping. She'll be back soon." A box of tissues waited on a nearby table. Edna yanked one out and dabbed at her eyes. "So we don't have much time."

"Time for what?"

"To talk."

"Damn it, Edna. What the hell is going on?"

"Oh, I shouldn't say anything. I know it. But I have to talk to someone. And when you called, I was just going crazy, wondering what in the world I was going to do."

"About what?"

Edna dabbed her eyes some more. "I just don't know who else to turn to."

"About what, Edna?"

"It's Abby...."

His mind conjured a million disasters. If someone had hurt her, he'd do murder, he would. He tried to stay cool. "What? What about Abby?"

"She's... Oh, Cash. She will be so angry at me if she learns that I've turned to you about this. But I do count on you. And she won't talk to me."

"Tell me."

Edna smoothed out her tissue, then wadded it up again. "Well, she hasn't been eating much since she came back from Denver. Have you noticed that?"

What did Abby's lack of appetite have to do with disaster? "Yeah. All right. I've noticed."

"And sometimes she gets sick. She goes in the bathroom and she—"

"Fine. I get the point. What are you telling me?"

"I've been over and over it. At first, I thought she was trying to hide an illness. Or maybe an eating disorder. But the past day or two, I've finally admitted to myself what it has to be."

"What?"

"Oh, I'm so worried for her. But why else would she take off for Denver like that, with hardly a word of explanation? And why, once she got there, would she refuse to return our calls? Refuse to come home until her own mother was at death's door? Even now, she won't confide in me. Won't turn to me. She always thinks she has to handle everything herself, has to shoulder all the burden alone. Ever since she was a tiny thing, it was that way. She wouldn't—"

"Edna. What the hell is wrong with Abby?"

Edna gulped. "Oh, Cash."

"What? God. Tell me."

Edna closed her eyes. A shudder racked her slim shoulders. And then she hung her head. "She's pregnant. Isn't it obvious? She's pregnant. Some awful man has taken advantage of her and then left her to deal with the consequences all on her own."

Chapter Five

Abby saw Cash's Cadillac in front of the house when she turned onto Meadowlark Lane.

So, she thought grimly, wherever he's been, he's back.

This time, she decided, she would tell him the truth before he could get away—if she had to shout it at his back as he tried to run out the door. She pulled into the driveway and opened the garage door with the remote control. Then she slid the Rabbit in beside her mother's old station wagon.

Carrying a bag of groceries in each arm, she entered through the kitchen.

''Abigail!'' her mother called from the living room.

Abby slid the groceries onto the end of the counter. ''Coming!'' She smoothed her hands down her jeans, pulled her shoulders back and marched into the other room.

Cash stood from an easy chair as she entered. Their eyes met.

And she knew that he knew.

Two steps and he was beside her, taking her arm. "Let's go."

She stared at him, her mind gone suddenly to mush. "Go where?"

"My house. We have to talk. Alone."

Edna, in the other easy chair, started sputtering. "Cash, no. Really, I didn't mean for you to—"

"Edna, don't worry. I'll handle this." He started pulling Abby toward the front door. "Come on."

Abby dug in her heels. "What is going on?" she demanded, as if she didn't already know.

Edna stood, putting her hand to her heart. "Oh, Abigail. I was so worried about you. I *had* to talk to someone...."

Cash turned to Edna then, his concern for her health crowding out his determination to get Abby alone. "Now, settle down, Edna. I'm going to fix everything—you'll see. I just want you to trust me. I don't want you to get yourself too worked up about this."

Abby clenched her teeth so hard she wondered why they didn't crack. "Worked up about what?"

"Oh, Abigail," Edna cried in abject misery, "why is it you've never felt you could talk to me?"

Abby sucked in a deep breath and let it out slowly. Then she spoke with great patience. "Mother, go lie down."

"No, no. We have to *talk* about this."

"We will. When I get back."

"Back from where?"

"Cash's house."

"But that's not right. Cash has nothing to do with this."

"He really wants to be involved." She sent Cash a telling glance. "Don't you, Cash?"

His eyes bored through her. "That's right. I really do."

"Oh." Edna wrung her hands. "I feel so useless. I had to talk to someone. And then Cash called. And I—"

"Shh," Abby soothed. "You are not to worry. I promise. It will all work out."

"Oh, honey..."

Taking her mother by the hand, Abby headed for the downstairs bedroom. Once she got there, she led Edna straight to the bed. "Come on. Sit."

Obedient as a child, Edna dropped to the edge of the bed. Abby knelt, slipped off her mother's house shoes and helped her to stretch out. Then Abby stood. "We'll be at Cash's. And you will be fine. If you just rest."

"Abigail."

"What?"

"Are you going to have a baby?"

The time for denials had passed. "Yes, Mom."

A whimper escaped Edna. "Oh, dear..."

"Rest. Please. It will be okay."

"I should be more help."

"Just rest. That will help a lot—I promise you."

Edna sighed, a deep, weary sigh. "You'll be at Cash's?"

"Yes."

"Cash will help you. Cash always helps."

"Yes. He does. And he will. You'll see."

"All right, then." Edna closed her eyes. "We'll talk when you get back from Cash's."

Abby turned. Cash was standing in the doorway to the hall.

"Let's go," he said.

"Why the hell didn't you tell me?" he demanded, as soon as they were alone in his big living room, with its plush area rugs, soaring windows and vaulted ceiling.

"Cash, listen—"

He paced the floor. "You lied to me. I asked you directly in Denver. I said, 'Are you pregnant?' and you looked me straight in the eye and you told me no."

"I wasn't ready to talk about it then."

Cash stopped pacing and raked a hand back through his hair. "Hell. How could I not have figured it out? The way you eat. That tea you're always drinking. And the way you look so skinny and green." She was standing in front of the long, off-white sofa, opposite him. He frowned at her across the coffee table. "Are you all right?"

Abby sighed and dropped to the sofa. "I'm fine. And my mother should have come to me first."

Cash made a snorting sound. "You know she could never talk to you." He marched to a caramel-colored leather chair a few feet away and sat down. "She doesn't know I'm the father." He braced his elbows on his knees and hung his head in shame. "God help me, I didn't have the guts to tell her. It's going to break her heart. I've abused the trust she and Ty had in me." He studied his boots for a moment, then he glanced up and into her eyes. "Let alone the trust *you* had in me."

She held his gaze firmly. "It *is* your baby, Cash."

Now he looked injured. "How could you think I would doubt it?"

"I just wanted to say it. I've been meaning to say it. Trying to say it."

"Abby..." He didn't seem to know how to go on.

"It *is* your baby," she said again. "And I want it. I do."

His eyes darkened. "What does that mean? Did you think I would try to stop you from having it?"

"No, I never thought that." She leaned forward, to the edge of the sofa, willing him to understand, to see how it had been for her. "It's just that I've been trying to figure out a way to tell you for what seems like forever now."

"Well." He looked grim. "Now I know."

She felt defiant. "And I'm *glad* you know—even if my mother was the one who ended up telling you."

He stared at her for a long moment, then he turned and flipped open a little carved box that sat on a small table by his chair. He took out a cigarette and tapped it on the edge of the table. Then, the cigarette poised in mid-tap, he shot her a reproving glance. "You should have come to me." With a low oath, he tossed the cigarette back in the box. "But then, how the hell could you?" He snapped the lid of the box shut. "How could you turn to me ever again after I—"

She stood then. "Cash Bravo."

He scowled at her. "What?"

"You've got to stop beating yourself up about this. You have to remember how it was that night. I was...willing. More than willing. No matter how much you want all the blame, you can't have it."

He was shaking his head. "You're only a—"

She glared at him. "If you call me a kid, I will do serious bodily harm to you."

He glared back, but only for a moment. Then he was looking at his boots again. "I know you hate me."

"When will you hear me? I do not hate you."

"I'm too old for you, I know."

At first, she didn't realize what he was getting at. "What does how old you are have to do with anything?"

"Abby...." He looked so sad, a man on a first-name basis with regret. He got to his feet and walked over to the tall windows at the end of the room. Outside, the wind filled the air with feathery white fluff from the cottonwood trees. The sun shone down. In the distance, however, toward the Big Horns, dark-bellied clouds loomed. Cash looked out for a moment, at the distant clouds and the whirling white fluff. And then he turned. "I think it's best if we get married."

She swallowed. It was exactly what she'd expected he would say. Still, it had the power to surprise her. "What?"

"You heard me. We'll get married."

She drew herself up, tried to sound firm. "No. No, really. We can't do that."

"The hell we can't."

"Listen. I mean it. It would be a mistake—you know it would."

He shrugged, as if her words had meant nothing. "It's the right thing. And we'll do it."

She came out from behind the coffee table, into the middle of the room. "Cash, you're not listening to me."

"Yes, I am."

"Then hear what I'm telling you. I won't marry you. It never works when people get married for something like this."

He looked at her as if she'd said something incredibly foolish and juvenile. Then he replied quietly, "You'll marry me."

She shook her head. "No. It's not a good idea."

A weary half smile tugged on one corner of his mouth. "Why not?"

"I just...well, I don't think it's wise."

That half smile remained, making him look infinitely superior and worldly-wise. "You're twenty-one. You don't know a thing about wisdom." He strode to her and took her by the shoulders.

His touch felt so good. And she was so...confused. This wasn't working out. Instead of marshaling her very reasonable arguments against marrying him and laying them before him with calm self-assurance, she'd stammered and hesitated. She hadn't been convincing at all.

And he had just plain refused to listen to her.

She glanced away from him, toward the window. Out there, the air was heavy and moist—charged with the promise of a summer storm.

"Look at me."

She did, putting considerable effort into keeping her expression severe and composed.

"We'll get married," Cash said. "We'll make the best of it. It's better for the baby. Can't you see that?"

Abby shrugged free of his grip and moved around him, toward the window.

He spoke to her back. "The baby deserves whatever we can give him. And we can give him two parents who did their best to make a marriage between them, to make a family for him."

She looked out at the blowing cottonwood fluff and the slowly darkening sky.

"Abby, come on. You know it's the best thing—the *right* thing—to do."

She watched lightning fork down, and heard the thunder boom out far away somewhere.

"Abby…"

She spoke, but it was more to herself than to him. "I never wanted to be a wife. I wanted…to work with you. And to run my own life."

He came up behind her, but he didn't touch her. She could feel him standing there. "I know, Abby. And I do understand."

She smiled to herself. "I'll bet."

"What's that supposed to mean?"

Lightning flashed again. The dark clouds boiled in. "I just know you. I know how you are."

"How?"

She could hear the wind keening.

"How am I, Abby?"

She turned to him. "You're a bachelor to the core. You've never in your life wanted to get married, to anyone." She paused, halfway hoping that he would argue. But he didn't argue. So she went on, "Oh, you love the way all the women go gaga over you. And you treat them all so nice. But marriage has never been of much interest to you. You like your wheeling and your dealing. You like to get up and go when the mood strikes. You want to be free to follow a deal—or to ride out in your Cadillac to rescue some needy friend. You're everyone's knight in shining armor. But you're just not the marrying kind."

She could see by his expression that she had described him personally. And it made her sad, somehow. So very sad.

"Fine," he said. "We both like being single—but

now you're going to have a baby. A baby you say you want.''

She pushed the sadness away and replied with assurance, "I don't just *say* it. I *do* want it.''

"Then think of the baby. Do what's right. Marry me.''

"It will never work." Even as she said it, she was waiting for him to come back strong, to argue that it *would* work. That they would *make* it work.

He cleared his throat. "It might.''

She cast a put-upon glance toward the vaulted ceiling. "You sound *so* convincing.''

He grunted. "Well, all right. Maybe it won't work. In the long run. And if it doesn't work...''

"What?''

"Abby, people do get divorced.''

For some reason, that hurt. To have him already planning divorce when she hadn't even agreed to marry him. She stared up at him—and found herself thinking about how much she liked looking at him.

It made her feel good to look at him. As if all was right with the world. But she supposed that made sense. He'd always been there, in her world. The family story went that he'd held her in his arms shortly after she was born. All her life, she had counted on him. And confided in him. She had always known that she could tell him anything.

And it had been so hard these past grim weeks, feeling as if she didn't dare talk to him at all. But now, the long silence had been broken. They were saying things that had to be said. True, it didn't approach the old easiness they used to share. But it was something, at least.

And she had known that he'd demand marriage.

What she hadn't expected was to hear him speak so calmly of divorce.

She edged around him again, moving out into the middle of the room, where she turned and faced him squarely. "So you're not talking about a *real* marriage at all. Just a marriage on paper. You want to set it up so that when our baby asks about it later, it will look like we cared."

He frowned. "That is not what I said. I said we'd try."

"'Try.'" She braced her hands on her hips. "That's a puny little word if I ever heard one."

"Abby, you're fifteen years younger than I am. And you just said yourself that you never wanted to be a wife." He held out both arms to the sides. "And look here. See any strings? No, you don't. Because I like being single. It's just what you said. We're neither of us the marrying kind." He approached her again, cautiously. "Together we probably haven't got a snowflake's chance in hell of making a marriage last."

"Well, it's good to see you have such confidence in us." She started to turn.

He caught her arm. "Don't get cute."

She shook him off, but stood her ground. "I am not cute."

"Look, I know I did wrong by you."

"There you go again. Acting like I wasn't even there."

"But I want to do right by my child—as well as by the woman who is carrying my child."

"Cash, did you hear yourself? You just called me a *woman*. Are we making progress here?"

His eyes glinted dangerously. "You will marry me, Abby." He took her by the shoulders again. "Say you will.'' He pulled her marginally closer. She felt his strength, his determination to do what he thought was right. His breath across her face was warm, and a little uneven. ''Say yes.''

She knew at that moment that she *would* say yes. She even had enough self-awareness to realize that she *wanted* to say yes.

But some contrary devil inside her couldn't just give in and go along. She had to push it a little, to find out exactly how much he counted on the option of divorce. ''Did you mean that? About getting divorced if it doesn't work out?''

His eyes were like mirrors, giving only her own reflection back to her. ''Yeah, I meant it.''

''Then maybe we should just admit what we're doing. From the first.''

He blinked. ''You've lost me.''

''I mean, we could have an agreement between the two of us, right up front. The marriage would last until the baby comes. Or a little after. A year, say. We could be married for a year. And then, unless we change our minds and both decide we *are* the marrying kind, I'll go to Reno twelve months after our wedding day—and get a divorce. And after that, we will equally share custody of our child.''

He stared at her, his eyes wary. ''Is that what you want?''

It wasn't, not really. In spite of the way she'd scoffed when he'd said it, she would have preferred to leave things open-ended: to simply give the marriage an honest try. But what right did she have to tie Cash down permanently if he didn't want to be tied down? Wouldn't he be happier if he knew he could easily be free within a year? When she looked at it that way, her proposal didn't seem like such a bad idea. The local scandal would be minimized, because the marriage would serve as a public statement that both the mother and the father were committed to the child they'd made. And if it didn't last, well, people in Medicine Creek accepted divorce these days more readily than they accepted unwed mothers and illegitimate kids.

"It could work," Abby said.

"I asked you if it's what you want." His eyes challenged her.

Abby Heller had never been one to turn down a challenge. "Yes. It's what I want." Her voice sounded so sure, much more sure than she felt.

Idly, he brushed his thumbs along the sides of her neck. "It would have to be just between us, this agreement."

Down inside her something heated and pooled. She tried to ignore it, tried to keep her voice matter-of-fact. "That's what I said."

He went on stroking the sides of her neck—so lightly. "Fine. What 'between us' means to me is that no one else would know about it."

"Agreed." She tried to pull away.

He held on—so gently. "I'm not finished."

"Okay. What else?"

He caressed the tip of her chin. Resolute, she neither flinched nor sighed.

"We would also live together for the year. And for that time, it would be a real marriage." He put both hands solidly on her shoulders again, his expression grave. "We'd give it an honest try."

Something happened inside her, a little burst of joy. Because he did want to try. He wanted a real marriage, for as long as it lasted. She did her best to look sure of herself—and to stop thinking about his idle caresses, caresses that he probably didn't even realize aroused her. "Yes, all right. An honest try. But in a year, unless we both change our minds, it's over."

He frowned, dropped his hands from her shoulders and stepped back. "Would you want it in writing?"

She smiled, a businesslike smile. "I'll take your word—if you'll take mine."

He nodded. "Good enough." He held out his hand.

They shook to seal the bargain as outside lightning flashed, thunder boomed and the first drops of rain began to fall.

They made sure Edna was resting comfortably when they told her that Cash was the father of Abby's baby and that they were getting married right away.

But Edna surprised them both. After a few agonizing seconds where she stared in openmouthed disbelief from her daughter to Cash and then back to her daughter again, she smiled.

A slow smile. "Well." She went on smiling. "This isn't so bad after all—now, is it?"

Abby didn't like that smile at all. "What do you mean, it's not so bad?"

"Well, now, Abigail, we all know how you are."

"Oh. And how is that?"

"Headstrong, to put it mildly. Headstrong and rash."

"So?"

"So at least you were headstrong and rash with the right man."

Abby couldn't come up with a scathing enough reply for that one.

Edna went one better. "And you need a man strong enough to master you."

Abby groaned. "*Master* me?" She thought she heard Cash chuckle, but when she shot him a glance, his face was perfectly serious. She turned her attention to Edna again. "I do not believe you said that."

Edna huffed a little. "You did ask."

"And I regret asking, believe me."

"Also, Cash will take care of you."

"I can take care of myself."

Edna wasn't listening. "And we'll all be a family," she said. "At last. In the real, true sense. Cash's children will be my grandchildren. Nate and Zach will be their uncles."

She held out her hand—toward Cash, Abby realized. He stepped forward, still looking appropriately grave, and took that outstretched hand.

"Oh, Cash, I'm so happy. This is wonderful. I'm just…overwhelmed with joy."

Chapter Six

Two weeks later, on July 22, Cash and Abby were married in the neat little white-trimmed brick church where each of them had been baptized as children. Abby wore the dress in which Vivian Sellerby had wed Johnny Bravo thirty-eight years before, a stunning creation of silk and seed pearls, with a basque waist and lace sleeves that came to pearl-embroidered points on the tops of her hands. The dress was a pretty good fit, except for the waist, which had to be let out at the last minute to allow for the weight that Abby had finally started to put on.

The church was full. Of course the whole town had been talking; no one had ever thought there was *that* kind of relationship between Cash and Abby. In the days after the word got out, Abby had been congratulated frequently on her upcoming marriage. To her, some of those congratulations seemed a little forced, especially from the other single women in town. Though Cash had never come close to proposing to any of them, more than one had dared to dream that someday she would be his chosen bride.

They held the reception at Cash's house. Cash had hired a caterer from Sheridan, a small woman with a big ability to put a great party together in a hurry. She had the rugs rolled back in the living room and had hired a four-piece band. She'd put tubs of bright flowers everywhere, decorated the banisters with white silk roses that looked like the real thing and prepared a feast that included Rising Sun beef, lobster on ice and game birds stuffed with corn bread and chestnuts. The cake had four tiers and raspberry sauce between the layers.

Abby danced the first dance with Cash's father. Johnny Bravo had arrived the day before from some small South American country where he'd been enjoying retirement for the past few years. He looked like an older version of Cash: tan, fit and heartbreaker-handsome—and not a day over fifty, though his actual age was sixty-six. He'd brought along his new wife, his fourth. Her name was Allegra. Allegra spoke with a faint accent, one Abby couldn't place. She had platinum-blond hair and eyes the tropical green of a parrot's wing. She resembled the pop singer Madonna. A very young Madonna. If Allegra was over twenty-five, Abby would eat her wedding veil.

"You look beautiful," Johnny told Abby as she whirled in his arms. He seemed a little misty-eyed, and a little sad, too. Abby wondered if it bothered him that she had chosen to wear Vivian's wedding gown.

Everyone said that Vivian had been the great love of Johnny Bravo's life. She had died giving birth to their second child, a girl. The baby hadn't made it, either. People said Johnny had never gotten over the loss, and that his relationships with all the other women who came after were only pitiful attempts to get through the rest of his life without the woman he loved.

Abby wanted him to understand why she'd chosen the dress. "I always admired this dress, from the pictures of you and Vivian. And Mom remembered that it was up in the attic at the ranch. I guess it just seemed like a good idea to wear it today."

Johnny gave her a big smile. "There's no need to explain. Viv would have been honored that you chose that dress. And I am honored, too."

"Well, I'm glad, then."

When the dance ended, Cash came to claim her. Before he did, Johnny whispered in her ear, "My son's a lucky devil. You be happy, you hear?"

She whispered back, "I will."

Another tune started up. Cash took her in his arms. For a moment, they simply danced. Smiling, Abby closed her eyes and leaned her head on her husband's shoulder. She felt all shimmery. For the past two weeks, she'd been getting used to the idea that Cash would be her husband. It really hadn't been that difficult an adjustment after all.

"You seem happy," he said.

His voice was soft and teasing in her ear. She liked the sound of it. She also liked the feel of his arms, guiding her in the dance.

She cuddled a little closer to him. "It was a nice wedding. And this is a nice party."

"But are you happy? Right now, at this minute?"

"Yes. I am."

"Well, good. I want you to be happy."

They danced some more. Abby went on thinking

about how right it felt, to dance with Cash. But that shouldn't have surprised her. He had taught her to dance, after all, in the great room of the ranch house. He could dance to anything. From Glenn Miller to Billy Ray Cyrus, the fox trot to the achy-breaky. The first time he showed her how to waltz, she had stood on his feet as he glided her around the floor; she had felt as if she were floating on air.

"What?" he asked.

"What do you mean, what?"

"That dreamy look, that's what."

"Just thinking. Remembering."

"Remembering what?"

"Me standing on your feet, learning to dance."

He chuckled. "You learned fast."

"I'm a bright girl."

He pulled her close again and they finished out the dance. After that, he spoke to the boys in the band. They played a slow, stately number. Cash went to Edna and held out his hand. She rose and allowed her new son-in-law to squire her out onto the floor.

Abby danced with Zach and then with Nate, who had come all the way from Los Angeles for this event. As usual, Nate's black hair grew over his collar. Abby smoothed it a little, thinking how handsome and dangerous and semidisreputable he looked. Nate had always had a reputation as a bad boy. But Abby had grown up with him. She knew he wasn't nearly as bad as he liked everyone to think.

"If I'd known Cash would snap you up, I would have made a play myself," Nate said teasingly.

"Well, it's too late now."

"You let me know if he gives you any grief."

She faked a look of surprise. "Cash? Give me grief?"

He grunted. "He's a lucky son of a gun."

"His father said that, too. Apparently, I'm a real prize. I hate housekeeping and I can't cook. But there's something wonderful about me anyway."

Nate lifted an eyebrow at her and she realized from his expression that he'd guessed there was a child on the way. Well, what could she expect? After all, she *was* beginning to show. And she imagined a lot of people must have noticed—and remarked on it when they thought she wouldn't hear. And surely by the time she bore a full-term baby just six months after her wedding day anyone who could count would have figured it out.

She grinned defiantly up at Nate.

Nate tossed back his head and laughed out loud. But when he looked down at her again, his dark eyes had grown serious. "You mean the world to him. And I know that scares him. Don't let it scare you off."

Before Abby could think of what to say to that, they danced past Meggie May Kane, whose father owned a smaller ranch bordering Rising Sun land. Abby saw the swift, hot look that passed between Nate and Meggie.

Years ago, Nate and Meggie had been friends. But not anymore. Now they went out of their way to avoid each other whenever Nate came to town. Abby thought it was too bad. She had seen with her own eyes how strongly they were drawn to each other. That had been years ago, when they were both nineteen and Abby was just a little girl, crouching in the bushes, spying on her elders.

The dance ended. Barnaby Cotes, a local shop owner, was waiting for a dance with the bride. As he stepped in, Nate turned and walked away.

A little while later, the band took a break. Abby wandered over to the bar, where Tess DeMarley assisted the bartender by serving the punch and soft drinks.

Tess had come to town just last week, after Cash had called her and explained that Abby's mother needed a housemate. Tess would get food and board and a small salary for looking after Edna, taking care of the house and cooking the meals. And there was a gift shop in town that would hire her if she wanted more work as Edna's health improved.

Abby had never thought Edna would go for it. She couldn't see her mother letting any stranger—especially one with a child—move into her beloved house. But Tess DeMarley was gentle and soft-spoken, a great cook and a fine housekeeper. Edna had taken one look at her and known she'd found the daughter that Abby should have been. So Edna was as happy as a bee in clover. She even got along with Tess's quiet, self-possessed daughter, Jobeth.

Abby liked Tess, too. Who could help but like her? She had a sort of ingrained dignity and goodness about her. Yet she wasn't self-righteous in the least. She'd had a tough life, living with that reckless Josh DeMarley all those years. And now she was a widow, starting all over again.

"Punch?" Tess asked.

"I'd love some."

Tess dipped up some punch and handed Abby a cup.

Abby took a long, grateful drink. "I haven't seen you dance once."

Tess looked down modestly. "I've been busy helping out."

Just then, Zach wandered by. Abby reached out and grabbed him. "I want you to dance with Tess. Now."

Tess looked all flustered. "Oh, no. Really...."

"I'd be pleased to," Zach said, and held out his hand.

"Go on," Abby instructed. "It's my wedding. And I'll mind the punch bowl. Don't you worry about a thing." She watched, smiling fatuously, as tall, quiet Zach danced off with pretty, reserved Tess. She thought they made a nice couple. Who could say? Maybe she and Cash would start a trend, a rash of Bravo weddings. Zach would marry Tess. And Nate would finally get together with Meggie May Kane.

She told Cash about her matchmaking fantasies later, after midnight, when the guests had all gone and the little dynamo of a caterer had packed everything up and driven away. Cash grinned when she told him. But then he shook his head. "Nate's favorite song is 'Don't Fence Me In.' And you know Meggie May—she'll never leave the Double-K. It's got fences all around it. And as for Zach..." He let silence finish the sentence.

Abby took his meaning. Zach had married his high-school sweetheart, Leila Wickerston, a week after graduation. The marriage lasted three years. When Leila walked out, she took their only child with her. "It's been years since Leila left him. He *might* try again."

Cash only grunted. He went over to the bar, clear now of all the party paraphernalia, and poured himself two fingers of Jack Daniels. He sipped, leaning against the bar, regarding her over the rim of his glass.

She regarded him right back.

A long, slow moment went by before he seemed to shake himself. "It's late," he said. "I'll bet you're tired."

She shook her head. "No, I'm not tired. Not at all." She felt like the heroine of *My Fair Lady*—she wanted to dance all night.

Or make love.

She smiled to herself. It was true. She wanted to make love with Cash again. She'd had two weeks to deal with the idea. Like the idea of being his wife, it hadn't been that hard to get used to.

She was sitting on the couch, still in her wedding gown, though she'd long ago dispensed with the veil. She stood. "I don't know what's the matter with this dress."

He sipped some more. "There's not a damn thing wrong with that dress."

His voice sounded gruff. Deliciously so.

"For some reason, it seems a little tight."

"You're finally starting to put on some weight."

She approached him slowly. "I'll be as round as a water barrel before you know it."

He stayed where he was, but his big body seemed to tense. "You look good."

Now he sounded grim.

"Well. Thank you."

He saluted her with his glass, then drained the last of his drink.

She took the glass from his hand and set it on the bar. "You'll have to undo me."

He coughed. "Huh?"

She turned around and showed him the back of the dress. "Undo me."

For a moment, he did nothing. And then she felt his fingers on the topmost pearl button. It took several minutes; it was a long row of buttons. But finally, he'd undone each one.

Abby breathed deeply for the first time in hours. "Umm. That feels wonderful."

She turned to find him watching her. Intently. She smiled.

He didn't smile back. "Go on to bed."

She frowned—and then she understood. "Oh. I'm supposed to slip into something more comfortable, is that it? And then you'll join me in a few minutes?"

He said nothing. Not a good sign.

The pleasant, hazy feeling of sensual anticipation began to fade. "Okay. What is it? What's wrong?"

"Nothing."

She stared at him for a moment. Then she muttered, "Major lie."

He reached for the bottle of Jack Daniels again. "Just go to bed."

She watched him pour. "No."

He set the bottle down too hard. "Damn it, Abby." He drank, looked away, then back. "Why don't you just let it go?"

"Let it go? Are you crazy?"

He plunked down his glass. "This is ridiculous."

"No argument."

"Then go to bed."

"No way. I'm your wife. And this is our wedding night."

He gave her a long, hard stare. When that didn't work, he sighed. "Just go to bed."

"No. Forget it. I'm not putting up with this."

"Putting up with *what?*"

She put her hands on her hips—to show him her exasperation, as well as to keep her dress from falling off. "We agreed to a real marriage, Cash. For however long it lasts. It's our wedding night. And on their wedding night, people in a real marriage make love.''

"Abby, don't push me."

She closed her eyes and counted to ten. Then she mustered all her courage and dared to demand, "Are you saying you don't want to make love with me?"

"Abby, I—"

"Just answer the question. Do you or don't you?"

"Abby…"

"My name is not an answer."

"I just think…"

"What? You just think what?"

"That it's wrong for me to take advantage of you."

"Cash, get this—*I really want to be taken advantage of.*"

"You say that now."

"And I mean it. You're not going to prove anything by staying away from me." She paused long enough to slant him a sideways look. "Except maybe that you don't really want to give our marriage an honest chance."

His golden brows drew together. "You're twisting what I said. Of course I mean to give this marriage an honest chance. But you're just a—"

She put up a hand. "Do not say it. Please. Look at the facts. I'm legally an adult. Old enough to drink. Old enough to vote. Old enough to have your baby, Cash Bravo. Which is exactly what I'm going to be doing some time in the middle of January."

He shook his head wearily. She had no idea what was happening in his mind.

"What?" she demanded at last. "Say something."

"I want a cigarette."

She turned around, flounced over to the little carved

box by the caramel-colored leather chair and got him one. Then she flounced back, clutching her dress against her breasts with her free hand. "Here." She held it out.

He looked at it. "It's bad for me."

She granted him a look of infinite patience as she tossed it on the bar. Her dress slid off one shoulder. She yanked it up. "This thing is driving me nuts." She slanted another glance at Cash. "I'm taking it off."

"Abby…"

She stuck a finger under the neckline and gave a little tug. It dropped off of her shoulders. Unfortunately, the long, pearl-embroidered lace sleeves were too snug to slide easily down her arms. She looked down at herself. "Trapped. In my own wedding gown."

"I can see that."

Abby froze. She looked up into Cash's eyes. She saw equal parts humor and heat.

And she thought again of dancing. That she and Cash were dancing. He had almost walked off the floor. But she had held him there, somehow. And the music between them was beguiling him once more. The important thing right now was that she not stumble, not miss a step.

She wrinkled her nose, keeping the mood playful, keeping it light. "Give me a minute here." She took her sweet time, peeling the sleeves free of her arms. That accomplished, she let the dress fall to the floor. She stepped out of it slowly, then picked it up and carried it to a chair. There, she laid it out with great care. It was a lot more of a fuss than she ordinarily would have made over a dress. But this wasn't just any dress.

And besides, the process of laying it out, of smoothing the delicate silk, had become part of the dance she and Cash were sharing. When she straightened and looked at Cash again, he hadn't moved from where she'd left him.

"Pretty slip," he said.

She looked down at her floor-length ivory satin slip, then back up at him. "Thank you."

"Welcome."

She felt awkward, suddenly. She touched the shimmery fabric of the dress again, for reassurance, and spoke shyly, not looking at him. "Your dad said your mother would have liked it. That I wore her dress."

"Who knows what goes on with him?"

She looked up and saw him shrug, a shrug that dismissed her words—and discouraged further discussion on the topic of his father.

"You never would talk much about your dad," she said. In her heart, she thought he resented the way his dad had left him when Vivian died all those years ago. But they'd never really gone into it. Whenever Abby would bring up the subject of Johnny Bravo, Cash would always say it was useless to dwell on the past.

He said it now. "What's the point? It's history."

"He introduced me to Allegra," Abby said carefully. "She seemed nice. And I really think she's crazy about him."

Cash made a low sound in his throat. "Oh, come on. She could be his *granddaughter*."

"But she's not. She's his wife."

"For the moment."

"Cash, you're so cynical."

"Realistic is more like it."

"And you're too hung up on age differences."

He actually chuckled. "Have you been taking psychology courses at C.U. when I wasn't looking?"

"No. Strictly business administration." She put up a hand. "I do solemnly swear."

"Good. I don't need you analyzing me."

"But I do analyze you. Lately, anyway."

"What the hell for?"

"Because..." She wasn't sure how to explain.

"Yeah?"

"Oh, because I've always taken you for granted, I guess. Like my father or my mother. Like Zach and Nate. Only more so. You've always been there whenever I needed you. Like air. Or water. Like food. And then, for a while, you weren't there."

"Because you wouldn't let me be."

He sounded angry.

She longed for him to understand. "Because I *couldn't* let you be."

"You could have. You could have always come to me. And you should have."

"No, I couldn't."

"Yes, you could."

"Let's not argue. Please?"

He leaned on the bar and picked up the cigarette she'd dropped there. "Fine with me." .

She smiled, a smile she knew quivered a little at the corners. And she bravely announced, "I want my wedding night, Cash."

He tossed the cigarette down again.

"Well? Are you going to give it to me?"

He said nothing. Treading carefully, she closed the distance between them.

When she stood in front of him, she gazed up at him in honest appeal. "Say something. Please?"

He lifted a hand and touched the side of her face. Then, hesitantly, he asked, "You're sure that this is what you want?"

She shivered a little. His slightest touch seemed to burn her, to start off fires down below. "Yes."

He caressed her cheek, a long, slow stroke, over the rounded ridge of her cheekbone and down to the curve of her chin. "You won't go running off this time afterward?"

"No."

"Swear it."

"I swear."

"Whatever happens—now or in the future. You won't run away from me. Ever again."

She shook her head.

"Say it. Say you won't."

"I won't, Cash. I promise you. I won't run away from you ever again."

"All right, then."

She waited, holding her breath.

And then, at last, his hand strayed down, over her neck, out to her shoulder, where he slid his finger under the thin satin strap of her slip. He lifted the strap, lowered it back in place. "I think about that night all the time."

She let out the breath she was holding, but didn't dare to speak.

He lifted the strap again, guided it over the slope of her shoulder and let it fall down her arm. "That day in your office, I had to get out. I wanted to kiss you then. I wanted to do a lot more than kiss you."

She said nothing, only listened. And reveled in sensation. She loved the feel of the silky strap against her arm. And the weight of the slip, uneven now, since the top of one side had fallen down. She didn't look to see, but she could feel that the top swell of her left breast was exposed, as well as the tiny scrap of lace she wore for a bra.

Cash hooked up the other strap, guided it down her other arm. He pulled on that strap. She helped him, sliding her arms up and clear of both straps, then letting them fall to her sides once more. The slip slithered to her waist and stopped there, held up by the swell of her hips below.

"Pretty," he said. He touched her bare skin, at the top of her belly, between her bra and the slip. Her stomach tightened in response. He smiled, a lazy, knowing smile.

She felt as if she were melting, slowly, from the inside out. "Oh, Cash..."

"Shh." He brushed his fingers against her lips.

She obeyed his command, falling silent.

He touched the strap of her bra. "So pretty."

She ordered her suddenly wobbly legs to hold her upright as his finger slid down, tracing the skin along the edge of the bra strap, caressing the slope of her left breast. She shivered and sighed. He was still smiling, his sexiest smile. His eyes were like smoke.

Now *this* was dancing, she thought. Dancing in the truest sense. Right in tune, in perfect rhythm. Though neither of them had taken a step.

His finger moved on, to the center of her chest, and then up the rounded swell of her other breast.

She captured his hand, guided it to her mouth and pressed her lips into his palm.

His hand escaped her grasp, to slide around and cup her nape. He said her name on a breath.

And then he reeled her in.

Chapter Seven

Cash's fingers threaded up into her hair, beneath the tiny silk flowers woven there. He pulled her up into him. She went, lifting on tiptoe.

His mouth settled over hers, stealing her breath and then giving it back to her. She heard a moan—hers or his, she couldn't be sure.

He kissed her long and slow and deep, taking his time, tasting her, savoring her. And she let him do that, wanted him to do that. She hovered on tiptoe, her arms limp at her sides, and held her mouth up to him, sighing in delight as he took what she offered.

They kissed for the longest time, standing there in the middle of the living room. He undressed her as he kissed her, putting his big hands on the sides of her hips, sliding down the satin slip, making of the action one long, slow caress. They both sighed as the satin fell away to land around her ankles.

His lips played on hers, his tongue hungry and seeking, as he unhooked her bra and tossed it away. Her breasts, so heavy and hot, yearned for his touch. He gave her that touch, cupping them, seeming to ease the yearning for a moment, and then only managing to increase it.

His hands roamed over her flesh as his mouth plundered hers. It was heaven. Could this be real? After midnight on her wedding night. Standing here in Cash's living room, wearing nothing but her diamond ring, her panty hose and her satin shoes.

Kissing Cash.

Making love…

He lifted his mouth from hers.

"Let's go to bed." His voice caressed her, rough and tender. He lifted an eyebrow as if to say, Well?

She gulped and nodded, staring up at his mouth, which looked swollen from kissing her.

He scooped her up against his chest and carried her to the master bedroom, which was through a short hall off the living room. She kicked off her shoes as he bore her down the hall and heard them bump the wall when they fell.

In the room, he carried her straight to the bed, gently laid her down and turned a dial on the wall. The two lamps on either side of the bed came on very low. Swiftly, he got rid of his own clothes: the black silk tux, the stiff white shirt, the trousers, the black dress shoes. Everything. All of it.

He lay down with her, on his huge bed with its maple bedstead and its bold, red-and-blue-patterned comforter. He reached for her, wrapping his strong arms around her, then pulling back just enough to help her with her panty hose. By then, they were both too needful to go slowly; the panty hose tore. Neither of them cared.

When she was totally nude, he put his hand on her belly, felt its roundness. And on her breast again. "Fuller," he said.

She nuzzled him, claiming his mouth once more. He kissed her as she wanted to be kissed, slow and open and wet. And as he kissed her, his hand went roving, over her fuller breasts and her rounder belly and down, to the place where her thighs joined. His fingers delved in.

She gasped. He moaned into her mouth. She moved against him, urging him on, transported by the wondrous sensations of his hands and lips upon her burning skin.

He pulled his mouth from hers, looked down into her eyes. She saw bewilderment. And a need as strong and consuming as her own.

"Abby, I'm sorry. Can't wait. Don't make me wait." Her rose up above her, blocking the light, as he had that one other night they'd shared.

She pulled him down to her, taking him in, crying out in wonder as he filled her. She looked up at him, into his beautiful eyes. And she felt him pulsing into her. She smiled, feeling powerful, triumphant. And totally free.

He relaxed on top of her. And then he rolled to the side, taking her with him, so they lay facing each other. She felt him start to pull away.

"No. Don't go...." She wrapped her top leg over his hip, holding him inside.

He chuckled then, and pushed himself against her. Oh, she did like that, to feel his body joined with hers.

For a time, they just lay there. She put her hand

against his hard chest, felt his heart beating strongly, slowing a little as the minutes went by.

He touched her hair, smoothing it out of her eyes. "You looked so pretty, with all those little flowers in your hair."

"Umm...."

"Now all your little flowers are crushed."

She kissed his square chin. "Yes. So sad. My hair's a mess."

"I was too fast," he confessed ruefully, tucking her head beneath the chin she'd just kissed.

She snuggled up. "It's a wedding night. You can be fast if you want. And maybe slow later."

She could hear the smile in his voice when he asked, "Is that a hint?"

"I never give hints. I'm an up-front kind of girl."

"Oh, yeah?"

"Yeah."

"So tell me, how come you know so much about wedding nights?"

"I don't. I'm making it all up as I go along."

He pulled her closer. "You're doing a hell of a job."

"We've been over this. I'm a bright girl and I learn fast."

"Amen to that."

In one slow, lazy stroke, he ran his index finger down the side of her neck, into the curve where her collarbone started and then out over the rounded slope of her shoulder. She closed her eyes, enjoying the little sparks of sensation that his touch seemed to leave in its wake.

"Abby?"

"Umm?"

But he said no more. His hand continued on its teasing course, sliding over the outside of her arm. She kept her eyes closed. He touched each of her fingers, tracing them one by one. And then he pulled back from her a little. She sighed as she lost him. But her sigh turned to a gasp as she felt his hand there, at the secret heart of her, his fingers moving in the moistness and the heat.

"Cash?" Her breath came ragged. "Oh, Cash…"

And again, he said nothing. He let his caresses talk for him. Her body lifted; her thighs opened. Fulfillment washed over her in a warm, sweet wave.

Sometime later, as they lay side by side gazing up at the ceiling, she whispered, "Over the past couple of weeks, since I've known we would get married, I've started to wonder."

"About what?"

"About your bathroom."

Clearly puzzled, he repeated, "My bathroom."

"Your *private* bathroom."

"What about it?"

"Well, I've never seen it. All the times I've been in this house, I was never allowed in your private rooms."

"So?"

"So, I'll bet it has a big bathtub…."

He made a low sound in his throat.

She went on, "With whirlpool jets."

She felt him turn his head on the pillow. She turned her head, too, and their eyes met.

"Want to see it?" His straight white teeth flashed with his grin.

She nodded.

So he showed her his bathroom. They stayed there

for quite a while, in the deep tub, enjoying those whirl-pool jets.

Eventually, they went back to the bed, turned off the lights and snuggled beneath the covers.

Much later, Abby awoke to darkness and the warmth of her husband lying beside her. She reached out for Cash and felt him reaching for her. They made love again, in the dark, saying nothing, finding fulfillment at one and the same time.

Late the following afternoon, they drove to the Sheridan airport and took Cash's little Cessna to Mexico.

They stayed for a week, in an out-of-the-way place where the beaches sparkled like white sugar in the sun and the sky was the same clear blue as Cash's eyes. Cash had rented a small villa, with a red-tiled roof and pink walls and bougainvillea spilling over the fence that surrounded the pool and the back patio. They did nothing there but eat and sleep and swim and make love.

Next, Cash wanted to conduct a little business with some of his buddies in Cheyenne. So he took Abby along. She'd met most of them before, over the years. And she enjoyed seeing them again, from Chandler Parks, who lived in Phoenix and had recently married an Olympic volleyball star, to Redbone Deevers, who was an expert on the grain market.

Back in the eighties, when the FCC divided up the country for cellular phone franchises, Cash had bought the rights to a few remote areas. He was ready to un-load them now. And Redbone knew a guy who knew a guy who wanted to buy areas for an independent cellular phone company that was just starting up. Abby sat in on most of their meetings, her head bent over the financial calculator she always carried with her, and kept track of the figures they threw around.

Cash had to put up with a little teasing about robbing the cradle and marrying "the kid," as they'd always called Abby. But it was good-natured teasing, and Abby thought he took it pretty well.

Of course they stayed in a luxury hotel. The bathtub in their suite was as deep and inviting as the one at home. And it had whirlpool jets, too. So when Cash wasn't making deals, they spent their time in the bathtub. Or in the king-sized bed. Every once in a while, they ate at a nice restaurant. Or went dancing at a country-and-western club.

There in Cheyenne, they ran into one of Cash's ex-girlfriends. Abby recognized her immediately by how casual she tried to be when she said hello to him. She was a gorgeous woman. And she seemed nice. Abby could feel the effort she exerted to be cordial and to keep things light.

Cash, on the other hand, exerted no effort. He didn't need to. He smiled at the woman and asked how she was doing. He was friendly and charming. And when he walked away from her, she watched him go with hungry eyes—while he never looked back.

After meeting the ex-girlfriend, Abby couldn't help dwelling a little on the agreement she and Cash had made. A year of marriage, and that would be it. She could end up like the ex-girlfriend, staring after him every time she saw him, with longing in her heart. Unless both of them wanted it otherwise.

After their wedding night, after the week in Mexico, the agreement had come to seem unreal to her, something that had never actually taken place. But running into that old girlfriend brought the truth home to Abby:

they *had* made the agreement. And it would have to be dealt with.

Eventually.

She was stretched out on the bed in their suite, thinking about the old girlfriend and her own foolishness in having proposed the agreement in the first place, when Cash returned from one of his meetings with the cellular phone franchise buyer.

He came and stood over her. "Okay, what's up?"

She gave him a distant smile. "Hmm?"

"What are you moping about?"

She closed her eyes and evaded his question by teasing, "Moping? Me?"

He dropped to his knees on the side of the bed and brought his face down to hers, so they were nose to nose. "Yes. Moping. You."

She wrapped her hand around the back of his neck. "I am not moping." And she wasn't, not anymore. She smoothed the hair at his nape.

He brushed his lips back and forth against hers.

"Kiss me," she said.

"I am."

"Those are just little kisses."

"You don't like little kisses?"

"I love them. But I want more. I want a long, deep, slow kiss."

He gave her what she wanted. And as he kissed her, he unbuttoned the blouse she wore. When all the buttons were undone, his lips left hers to burn a path over her chin and down her neck. He pushed the shirt open, out of his way. And he put his mouth on the swell of her breast, above her bra.

Abby moaned and clutched his golden head, pushing her breasts up at him, wanting him to suck them. With his index finger, he guided one cup of her bra out of the way. And then he took her nipple in his mouth.

She cried out. It felt so good, so right, so exactly what her body needed. What *she* needed: Cash. Loving her.

He joined her on the bed, and they helped each other to undress. He guided her to ride him. She took him inside her slowly, the way they both liked it done. And by the time she was rising and falling above him, she had no thought at all of old girlfriends or foolish agreements.

She thoroughly enjoyed the rest of their stay in Cheyenne.

But the best time of their honeymoon came at the end. When they got home to Medicine Creek, Abby admitted how much she sometimes missed the ranch. So they went out to the Rising Sun to stay for a while.

For four days, they rode out every morning early. It was the best time to ride, when the sun was just starting to rise, turning the sky to flame in the east. They rode side by side, their horses' hooves making dark trails in the dewy grass, grass that was turning dusty golden now, as the summer sun baked it brown. Abby loved the feel of the wind in her face; she loved riding into the cold shadows of the coulees and draws and then up into bright daylight on the high, windy ridges. She felt right inside herself to watch the light spread across the land as the sun rose, all the way to the Big Horns, making the snow on Cloud Peak reflect back, clean and pure and blindingly white.

Sometimes, they'd scare up an antelope or a jack-rabbit. Their horses would shy, prancing sideways. And Cash and Abby would laugh together, as they had laughed together all the years of her life, and watch the spooked animal bound away, leaping with swift, sure economy through the golden grass.

Of course they'd make their rides useful, checking the ponds where the cattle gathered, seeing if any of the ponds had dried up too much. Cattle weren't terribly bright. They'd wade out into deep mud and get themselves stuck there, so Zach always tried to move them to a better water source before they got themselves in trouble in the mud.

After breakfast, sometimes Cash and Abby would head out with Zach and the hands, to cut hay or poison weeds or move the cows around. And sometimes they'd take off by themselves, to a secret place they'd always known of, on the banks of Crystal Creek, which ran in a lazy meander across much of the Rising Sun. There, in the shadows of the cottonwoods and willows, with the creek gurgling along nearby, they'd spread a blanket and share a picnic. Then later, since they couldn't keep their hands off each other, they'd make love with most of their clothes on, always ready to pull apart and button up if someone should chance to ride by.

They talked a lot about Ty, about the way he used to drive that old pickup of his up and down the ridges and draws of the Rising Sun as if there never had been such a thing as a road. They agreed that they missed him. That something had gone out of the world when he died. But they also agreed that it was almost possible to believe he'd never left them, when the sun shone on the Big Horns and when summer lightning forked across the sky.

It was a beautiful, perfect time. And Abby reveled in it. Her morning sickness had completely vanished. She felt fit and strong—and bonded to Cash in the most complete kind of way. She no longer yearned for the old days, when they had been mere comrades. Because now they were so much more to each other. She dared to hope that their marriage might turn out to be a lasting thing after all.

But then the notice about the University of Colorado's fall semester came in the mail, addressed to the ranch because that was the address Abby had given them the year before.

Abby tossed it in the trash basket in the front hall. And Cash retrieved it. He came out on the porch to find her, slamming the screen behind him.

"You need this stuff, don't you?" He waved the papers at her.

She'd been feeling nice and comfortable, sipping lemonade, her boots up on the railing. She dropped them to the porch boards. "What stuff?"

"This stuff from C.U. It's got the day you're supposed to call, a tentative schedule and your PIN number so you can reregister."

She frowned at him, wondering what all that mattered. "But I'm not going back—not this semester, anyway."

His jaw hardened. "The hell you're not."

"But Cash…"

"What?"

"Think. It makes no sense for me to go back right now. The school's in Boulder. And Boulder's in *Colorado*."

He made a snorting sound. "I know where Boulder is."

"Well, Cash. I'm pregnant."

"So?"

"So I'll be as big as a barn in a few months. I can't be off in Boulder—you know that."

"The baby isn't due till the end of January."

"January 20. That's the *middle* of January."

"Right. Fine. The semester ends before Christmas. And they always say first babies come late."

"*Who* says that?"

"Hell if I know. I heard it somewhere. Use your head, Abby. Your education matters. And you want to get as far along as you can. You could be within a semester of a four-year degree when the baby's born."

"Right. I could also end up having the baby in Boulder."

He frowned. Apparently, that idea gave him pause. But then he shook his head. "That's not going to happen."

"Have you told that to the baby?"

"Very funny."

"My doctor's here in Medicine Creek." She had started seeing Dr. Pruitt, at the Medicine Creek Clinic, the day after she and Cash had agreed to get married.

Cash waved that objection away. "So you'll have *two* doctors, one in Boulder and one here."

She stared at him, wondering what he could be thinking. Her education did mean a lot to her. But she would be *very* pregnant by the time finals came along; perhaps too pregnant to be going to school—let alone flying back and forth between Boulder and Medicine Creek.

And why was he suddenly so eager to send her away? Everything seemed to be going so well between them. Did he want to get rid of her?

Because she did not want to leave him. In fact, every day she spent with him, it became more clear to her that she actually *was* the marrying kind—as long as Cash was the husband in question.

The agreement came into her mind again. Why in the world had she ever suggested it?

She plunked her lemonade glass down on the railing. "Cash, come on. I could end up going into labor during finals."

"You won't."

"How do you know?"

He chuckled then. And he reached for her, wrapping an arm around her, drawing her close. She put her hands on his arms, resisting a little, refusing to meet his eyes.

"Come on, look at me," he coaxed. And he tipped up her chin with a finger. "Hey. Think of it another way. You just might get through the whole semester. And that would put you one semester further along than you would be if you didn't give it a try."

She searched his eyes. She could see no hints of hidden agendas in them. But still, she couldn't help reminding him, "I thought we agreed to spend the whole year together. How can we do that if I'm off in Boulder and you're Lord knows where?"

"Ah." He looked smug. "You'd be lonesome without me."

She pushed at his arms a little. "Don't bet on it."

He pulled her closer. "Come on. Admit it. You can't stand to be away from me."

It was true. Too true. But she had no intention of admitting it.

He tipped up her chin again. "Kiss me."

"Cash..." She squirmed some more. But she kept her mouth tipped up so he had no trouble claiming a long, sweet kiss.

That night, back in the house in Medicine Creek after they'd made love, he promised her, "We won't be apart that much. I'll fly to Boulder every chance I get. And you can come home a lot. I'll *bring* you home. You want to be 'together' with me—you will be. Wait and see. But the baby coming is not going to interfere with your education any more than it absolutely has to, and that's that." He pulled her close, into the crook of his arm.

She snuggled against him and dared to whisper what was really on her mind. "Are you trying to get rid of me?"

He pulled her closer still. "Never. I swear it. I only want what's best for you."

He kissed her some more and then he made love to her again. While he was loving her, she believed him.

The next day, though, her own mother told her she was a complete fool.

"Your place is with your husband now," Edna said when Abby explained her plans. "You're a fool to leave him—and in your condition, too. It's irresponsible, totally irresponsible."

Abby spoke with all the patience she could muster. "Mother, Cash is the one insisting that I go."

They were having lunch together, in Edna's kitchen. Edna set down the sandwich she'd been nibbling on and announced stiffly, "I've noticed that when you want something, Abigail, you're not above pretending that everyone else wants it, too."

"Mother—"

"Please don't interrupt."

Abby sighed. "All right. What?"

Edna pushed her plate away and folded her hands

on the table. "I'm going to be frank with you. Cash is a real catch. You're lucky you got him."

Abby held on to her temper by speaking with great care and precision. "I did not *get* him, Mother."

Edna waved a hand. "You know what I mean. He's a fine man, a man who could have had just about any woman. But he's always preferred the single life. Still, he did right by you, when another, lesser, man might not have. But he's only human. And if you leave him..."

"I'm not *leaving* him."

Edna sent darting glances around the bright kitchen, as if someone might be lurking nearby, listening in. Then she leaned forward and spoke low and intensely. "I'm just telling you that a woman has to look after her own interests. If she doesn't, take my word, there will be other women who won't hesitate to try to steal what's hers."

Abby made a conscious effort not to roll her eyes. "Mother, you just said it yourself—women have always been after Cash. And if one of them was going to *steal* him, don't you think she would have done it by now?"

Edna clucked her tongue and sagely shook her head. "I'm only warning you. You could lose him."

Just then Tess came in from the garage, where she'd been taking care of the laundry—separating the colors from whites, humming while she worked, Abby had no doubt.

Edna beamed at Tess. "Here's Tess. Let's talk about something more pleasant, why don't we?"

Abby was only too glad to oblige.

Cash and Abby flew to Boulder a few days after that. He wanted to get her all set up for the fall semester.

They stayed in a nice hotel and ate at the best restaurants and looked through the want ads for just the right place.

The year before, Abby had lived with three roommates on the Hill, a few miles from campus, where most of the students who didn't live in the dorms found housing. The Hill consisted of an eclectic assortment of older houses, many of them run-down. Most of the frat and sorority houses were on the Hill, where keg parties went on almost nightly and stereos played into the wee hours. But in spite of the distractions and the noise level, a lot of the students who lived there worked hard and earned good grades. Abby had.

However, now she wanted her new husband to come and see her often. And Cash had grown a little beyond keg parties and Red Hot Chili Peppers playing all night long. Also, as her pregnancy progressed, Abby figured she would probably appreciate less hectic surroundings. So they chose a nice two-bedroom apartment far enough from campus that not many students lived in the area. As soon as they'd signed the rental agreement, Cash insisted that they go and buy furniture, linens and kitchenware. Then, while Abby was putting all the new things away, he went out and came back with a red Blazer.

"Cash, it's too much," she told him, when he pulled her out to her carport space to admire it.

"That Rabbit's on its last legs. I want you to have a dependable vehicle, one that's safe in the snow and on the mountain roads."

"Cash—"

He picked her up and swung her around. "Don't argue, Abby. Let me do this, please?"

She wrapped her arms around his neck as he slowly let her slide to the ground. "You've got to stop buying me things," she chided, rather breathlessly.

He kissed her nose. "No, I don't. You're my wife."

You're my wife. The words sang through her, causing such a burst of happiness that she did what he wanted, and said nothing more except, "Thank you," for the car.

He pressed himself against her. She felt how he wanted her, and wanted him right back.

"Come on," he whispered. "Let's go inside. Did you get the bed made?"

She shook her head.

"Hell. Who cares?" He grabbed her hand and towed her back inside and straight to the bedroom, where they fell across the brand-new bed. The mattress plastic crackled in protest beneath them.

They didn't care at all.

Once the apartment was all ready to live in, they returned to Medicine Creek. Cash went off to Cheyenne alone for a couple of days, while Abby stayed at home, helping Renata update the files on the office computer and driving up to Billings to choose the furniture and linens for the baby's room.

When Cash returned, he said he felt lucky. He would be thirty-seven the next day and he wanted to celebrate. They flew the Cessna to Vegas. There, they took in the shows and Abby played the slots, smiling, one hand on her softly rounded belly, as she thought of the little boy who'd tossed a quarter in a slot over thirty years ago and won ten thousand dollars when his mother's back was turned. Cash played poker with some buddies of his, two all-night games—one of them on his birthday. By the time he was ready to leave, he was just a little richer than when they'd gotten there.

Once again, they flew back home and then from home, they flew to Boulder. Cash stayed at the apartment for several days, while Abby got into her routine of classes and studying. Then he left; he had deals to make.

She missed him. And as soon as he was gone, her mother's dire admonitions returned to haunt her. She tried to keep her mind on her studies, but she just couldn't help wondering if her husband felt relieved to have some degree of his old freedom again.

On Friday, after he'd been gone for two days, she found herself sitting at her computer in the spare bedroom, trying to study. But her mind kept wandering. She kept thinking about how big she was getting. And wondering if perhaps Cash didn't find her very attractive. If maybe he...

With a grunt of disgust, she stood. Two days ago, before Cash had left, he'd made love to her at length, with enthusiasm. If he no longer found her attractive, he was one heck of an actor.

She just had to stop dwelling on the negative.

She needed some physical activity. Instead of sitting around stewing, she should get up and *move*. She could straighten up the apartment. It was starting to look just a little bit messy. In Medicine Creek, where they had a cook-housekeeper who came in five days a week, things always looked so neat and tidy. Cash had wanted to hire someone here. But Abby had vetoed that. It was only a two-bedroom place. Surely she could keep it up on her own.

She looked around her. "Ha!" she said to the books

and clothes strewn everywhere. She should definitely do something about it.

But it was Friday night. She needed people, company—something to take her mind off her own silly doubts. She'd run into Melanie Ludlow, one of her roommates from last year, at the student union just yesterday. They'd spent a few minutes talking over old times. Melanie had congratulated Abby on her marriage and the coming baby, then she'd invited her to drop by the house anytime.

"Things are pretty much the same as last year," she'd said. "There's me, Sasha Thompkins, Libby Sands—and since we lost you, we got a friend of Libby's, Mandy Parks. Everybody would love to see you—and that rich cowboy of yours, too." Her roommates had all met Cash once or twice. "Well? What do you say?"

She'd promised Melanie that she'd call her. Real soon.

And now was as good a time as any. She picked up the phone and dialed the number of the house on the Hill where she'd lived the year before.

Melanie answered the phone on the first ring. Abby could hear music and voices in the background.

"How can you guys study with all that racket going on?" Abby asked.

"Abby. Hey. You coming on over?"

"Yeah. I think I will." Abby glanced at the clock on her desk as she hung up. A little after seven. She'd go over to the Hill for a couple of hours and enjoy the company. That should take the edge off of missing Cash so much. She'd be back home in bed by ten at the latest.

* * *

At seven-thirty, Cash pulled up in front of Abby's apartment building. He was grinning. She didn't expect him back until next week. But he'd missed her. And he had nothing to do that couldn't wait awhile. Tomorrow was Saturday. And Monday was Labor Day.

They could take off for the weekend—fly back home to Medicine Creek. Or maybe just drive over to Denver and stay someplace with decent room service and a big bathtub. He should have thought of it sooner.

Well, he had thought of it sooner. But they'd virtually been on one long honeymoon since the wedding. A holiday had seemed a little like overkill. And Abby had said she wanted to get some focus on her studies.

Hell, if she needed to work, that was all right with him. He could hang around, make sure she ate right, sleep next to her at night. He liked having her next to him when he slept, which bothered him a little. Made him feel dependent on her for his own peace of mind. He'd never in his life cared before if a woman spent the night or not.

But he supposed it was nothing to get his gut in knots over. They were married—for the time being, anyway. And married people slept together. No big deal.

He got out of the car, went around to the trunk and grabbed his suitcase. Then he jogged up the stretch of lawn and around the side walkway that led to the apartment's door. He reached for the handle and discovered it was locked at the same time as he really registered the fact that all the lights were off.

He got out his key and let himself in. "Abby?"

But he got no answer. The kitchen was right off the tiny entry hall. He reached in and flipped on the light, smiling indulgently as he saw that the remains of her last meal still sat on the table at the far end of the room. He glanced at the sink: full of dishes.

He picked up his suitcase and carried it to their bedroom. The bed wasn't made. He set down his suitcase with a sigh.

Chapter Eight

Melanie came running out when Abby pulled up in front of the slightly run-down two-story brick house with the broad, deep porch and the scraggly elm in the center of its patchy front lawn. "Nice wheels," she said.

"Thanks." Abby slid down from the driver's seat and walked around the front of the Blazer. As soon as she was out of the car, she could hear the music coming from the house.

"You are definitely looking ripe," Melanie declared. She was tiny, with big brown eyes and brown hair cut short.

"You mean fat, right?"

"No, I do not. You're not *that* big yet. Just kind of round and rosy. Your skin looks great and you sort of glow."

"I do?"

"You do." Melanie hooked her arm through Abby's. "Come on in. Party in progress."

By an hour after he'd arrived at the apartment, Cash had straightened the place up a little. And he was starting to wonder where the hell Abby could have gotten herself off to.

He found a can of cola in the refrigerator and took it into the living room. Dropping to the couch, he turned on the television. For a while, he just sat there, sipping his cola, switching from channel to channel. He watched a rerun of *Cops* for a while, hardly paying attention as two spousal abusers were towed off to jail and a major drug bust was accomplished with the aid of a battering ram.

By nine o'clock, he started getting worried. And not long after that, he started getting mad.

And then he saw himself for the moonstruck fool he was. Abby didn't know he was coming. She'd probably gone to spend the evening with one of her old girl-friends. She could be out until late—and there was no reason she shouldn't be.

He punched the "off" button and tossed the remote control on the couch. No sense sitting around here, waiting and wondering. He'd find himself a nice restaurant where he could get a strong drink and a thick steak. And maybe after that, he'd go cruising for a poker game.

Grabbing up his keys, he headed for the door.

"A woman never looks so beautiful as when she is with child!" the skinny guy in the black turtleneck shouted at Abby.

His name was Sven and he had backed her up

against a wall of the living room about five minutes before. She wanted to escape him, but she felt a little sorry for him. So she just stood there, trying to look interested as he yelled in her ear in an effort to compete with Boyz II Men, which someone had turned up loud on the stereo.

Sven hollered, "There's such a deep, inner calm about a pregnant woman! Such a feeling of being in touch with the earth forces! Don't you think?"

Gamely, Abby attempted a reply. "Well, Sven, I don't know if I—"

He cut in loudly before she could finish. "I do believe I remember you! You lived here last year, didn't you?"

Abby nodded.

"Some kind of boring business-admin major, right?"

"Right," Abby replied. "With an emphasis in accounting and finance."

"Of course!" Sven looked down at her left hand, which was wrapped around a can of Sprite. Her diamond winked at him. "And now you're married!"

"Yes."

"Married!" Sven indulged in a chuckle. "How quaint!"

Abby gave him the kind of smile he deserved for a remark like that, and then took a sip of her Sprite. Right then, somebody had the good grace to turn down the stereo.

"Is your husband here?" Sven asked—more quietly, thank God.

She swallowed. "No."

Sasha Thompkins, on her way to the kitchen, paused

long enough to lean in and inform Sven, "Give it up. She married a rich older guy. A total hunk."

"Ah," Sven said knowingly as Sasha moved on by.

Abby frowned. "Pardon me?"

Sven waved a skinny hand. "Nothing, nothing. It's just…predictable, that's all."

Abby wondered what had possessed her to feel sorry for him. "What's predictable?"

"Good-looking young women marrying older men with money. And having their babies. It's biology. What more is there to say?"

That did it. "How about, 'See you around, Sven'?" She ducked and tried to dodge beneath his arm.

He shifted his body slightly to keep her there. "I've offended you."

She leaned back against the wall and gave him a long, cool look. "Get out of my way."

Sven sighed. "How boring that you're angry." He leaned in close. "It is a simple fact that older, successful men look for young, healthy women of breeding age. Having made their mark on the world, they feel driven to propagate themselves. And there's no *blame* to it. The men can't help themselves, any more than young women can help being drawn to them, to the power and protection they represent."

"Goodbye." Abby moved faster that time, sliding beneath his arm, even shoving at him a little when he tried again to block her escape.

He called after her, "The truth hurts—I know it does!"

Abby set down her soda can on a scratched side table and kept walking. It was too smoky in the living room anyway, and now someone had put *Nirvana* on the stereo. She could do without Kurt Cobain. And she could use a little fresh air. She went through the hall to the kitchen, where Sasha was helping herself to a glass of white zinfandel from the wine box in the refrigerator.

"Abigail, Abigail." Sasha held up her full glass. "Where have you been?"

"Stuck in the living room with Sven."

Sasha burst out laughing. Then she blushed and covered her mouth with her hand. "Sorry, I'm a little plotzed. Love this white zin." She took a long drink, then looked straight at Abby, her expression suddenly severe. "But seriously. How have you been?"

"Great."

"You look..." Sasha waved her glass, seeking the right word.

Abby suggested, "Pregnant?"

Sasha gulped more wine. "Right on." She left the refrigerator and moved to Abby's side, where she lowered her voice to a conspiratorial level. "We've missed having you around." She drained her glass. "I know *I* have. You always minded your own business. And you never came up short when it was time to put in for the rent and the food." She brought a hand to her mouth again, this time to pat her lips, as if they'd grown numb. She frowned. "But then again, you *were* kind of a slob...." She lifted her glass to drink some more, then stopped and looked into it, puzzled. "Uh-oh. All gone." Giggling to herself, she moved back to the refrigerator, where she pulled open the door and stuck her glass beneath the spigot of the wine box once again.

"God, Sasha." Libby Sands had appeared in the arch from the living room. "You better slow down."

Sasha straightened and shut the refrigerator. "I pay

for my share." Defiantly, she raised her glass and drank long and deep.

With a sigh, Abby wandered on out the back door.

In the backyard, several guys from a fraternity house down the road had rolled out a keg. They sat around the lawn, drinking beer and talking about everything from obscure Danish philosophers to the Denver Broncos. Abby sat on the back step for a few minutes, listening to their banter, appreciating the cool September night.

Then Melanie came out and found her. "Come on. Up to my room. We've hardly had a chance to talk."

Abby glanced at her watch. It was 9:35. "I should be—"

"Forget it. The night hasn't even begun. And your guy's in Vegas or something, right?"

"Cheyenne, probably."

"So there's no one waiting for you at home. You can stay for an hour or two. C'mon. Please?"

So Abby went upstairs with her friend. They sat on Melanie's bed together, the way they used to do. Melanie complained about her roommates a little, then told Abby all about the guy she'd met that summer, who'd turned out to be married and had broken her heart. And then she wanted to know about Cash and what it was like to be married—and having a baby.

Melanie asked gently, "You were pregnant at the end of spring semester, weren't you?"

Abby nodded.

"I knew it. I knew something was bothering you, big time. Something on top of losing your dad."

"It was…rough going there for a while."

"But everything worked out all right after all."

Abby thought about the agreement.

"Well," Melanie said, "didn't it?"

"Yes, it did," Abby said, sounding more sure than she'd been feeling the past couple of days.

"I gotta say, I admire you." Melanie widened those big eyes even more. "Your due date can't be too long after the end of the semester."

"January 20."

"Wow. That's cutting it close."

Abby nodded and tried to look self-assured. "If I don't make it, I don't make it. I'll take the semester over. But I wanted to give it a try."

"Well, your guy's really understanding to let you put so much focus on your education at the beginning of your marriage, with a baby on the way."

"He was the one who insisted I come here."

Melanie frowned. "Maybe he's trying to get rid of you."

Abby must have looked worried, because Melanie trilled out a laugh and poked her in the ribs.

"Not."

Abby made herself laugh, too.

Finally, at a little after eleven, Abby said she had to go. Melanie walked her out to the Blazer and told her not to be a stranger. Abby said she wouldn't, but as she drove away, she realized that it had been a polite lie. So much had changed in her life. She just didn't have a lot in common with her friends on the Hill anymore.

She knew that Cash was home the minute she walked in the front door and saw how neat everything was.

"Cash!" She ran to the bedroom and flicked on the

light, sure she would find him lying right there on the bed, all rumpled and sleepy, waiting for her.

But the room was empty. She checked in the office room, just in case. No luck.

Back in the living area, she looked for a note. But he hadn't left one. She had no way to know if he would even come back that night.

She wandered back to her office, where she sank to the swivel chair at her desk and stared at her computer screen, feeling forlorn.

Cash returned at half past two the next morning. He parked in front of the building, then walked around back, to the carport. When he saw the red gleam of Abby's Blazer, right in her space where it belonged, he felt a sweet wash of relief.

An unpleasant, angry feeling swiftly followed. It was anger at himself, for skulking around back to look for her car instead of just heading straight for her door. And—unfairly, he knew—anger at her. Until this thing between him and Abby, Cash Bravo had never been a man who prowled around in the dark, checking to see if a woman's car was in its parking space or not.

A few moments later, Cash let himself in the dark apartment. Carefully, he shut the door behind him, putting his hand against it so that the latch wouldn't click too loud. He turned the dead bolt slowly so it wouldn't make a sound. Then he leaned against the wall and pulled off one of his boots.

He'd already decided to stretch out on the couch, instead of joining her in the bedroom. He told himself that he didn't want to disturb her.

But that wasn't the real reason. He wanted to feel casual about dropping in, not to make a big deal of it.

But he didn't feel casual. He was bugged because she'd been gone when he showed up earlier.

And he didn't want to be bugged.

He didn't want to hold on to her too tightly. He didn't want to feel jealousy—or this hungry need for her. He wanted to go easy with this whole thing between them. He knew that was the right way to go.

Or at least, he knew it in his mind. The rest of him, however, seemed to have other ideas.

Cash pulled off his second boot and quietly set it on the floor beside the first one. Then, with a heavy exhalation of breath, he straightened and leaned against the wall.

He probably never should have let her talk him into making love on their wedding night. That night had set a precedent for all the nights to come. If he'd kept his hands off her, everything would have remained in perspective. He could have kept his mind on the real goal he'd had for this "marriage" of theirs: to provide for and protect both her and their child—period.

As for anything more, they could have taken it more slowly. They *should* have taken it more slowly.

But she wouldn't allow that.

And somehow, with him, Abby always got her way.

Cash closed his eyes, remembering....

Abby at seven, a streak of red dirt on her face and her hair in her eyes. "Cash. I'm big enough. I want my own horse." It was always a big deal for a ranch kid to graduate from some safe old nag to a green-broke horse you got to work into shape yourself. "Daddy says next year. You tell him I'm ready now. And I know the horse I want. She's a pretty little chestnut mare and she has a blaze on her forehead. Daddy got her last week at the wild-horse adoption over at the county fairgrounds.''

"Listen, Pint-Size, if Ty says—''

She had grabbed his hand. Right now, more than fifteen years later, he could still feel that—her small, grubby paw in his.

"Come on, Cash. You tell him I should have that mare.''

So Cash had found himself talking to Ty. And Abby had gotten her first horse.

"I'm coming to work for you,'' she had announced the summer she was sixteen.

He had grinned at her, thinking she was growing up to be kind of cute, in a skinny-as-a-fence-post kind of way. "Abby, you should enjoy your summer. And if you really want to work, I'm sure Zach would let you—''

"I love the ranch, Cash. But I'm no rancher. I'm not like Zach. I'm like you, only with less of an instinct for bringing it in and more of a brain for the bottom line. That's why we're going to make a great team.''

He'd had to stifle a grin. She was always so damn sure of herself, even when she didn't know what the hell she was talking about. "Look, if you need money for something specific—''

"I don't want you to *give* me any money, Cash. Forget that. I want a job.''

"Well, you'll have to look somewhere other than my direction, Pint-Size.''

"Do not call me 'Pint-Size.' I'm five foot six now. It's a perfectly respectable height.''

"Sorry. But get real. I don't need anyone to work for me. I've got Renata in the office and she doesn't have enough to do as it is. She types a letter when I need it, and gets all the receipts together for the IRS boys when they insist on it. What are you going to do for me that I don't already get done?''

"I'll organize you. And you know I'm good with math. You know that computer you bought me? They have this program now, Lotus 1-2-3. You won't believe what it can do. You just have to know how to break it all down. Cash. I'm telling you. You need me. You need me bad....''

"Cash?''

He opened his eyes. She was standing in the tiny hall that led to the bedroom, a light on behind her. He saw her in silhouette, a shadow rimmed in gold. She wore one of those big T-shirts she liked to sleep in. It obscured the top of her. But he could see those long, smooth legs just fine.

"Cash!'' She came flying at him. "You're back!''

She landed against him, and his arms wrapped around her all by themselves. He buried his face in her sweet-smelling hair, felt her soft thighs, the roundness of her belly with his baby in it, the fullness of her breasts.

She pulled back enough to kiss him, little pecking kisses all over his face. And while she kissed him, she babbled.

"I'm sorry I wasn't here. I didn't know you were coming. Oh, I have missed you.'' She wrinkled her nose a little. "You smell like cigarettes.''

He wrapped his fingers in her hair, pulled her head back enough that their eyes could meet. "I had a few cigarettes, so what? I found me a friendly bar and got into a little game of five-card stud. A man can't play poker without a smoke or two.''

She scrunched up her nose at him. "I thought you quit."

He tried to look innocent. "I did. I am."

"Yeah, right."

"Hey. If anyone should be able to do it, it's me."

She gave a little snort. "After all, you've had so much practice."

"Exactly."

They looked at each other. He still had his fingers twined in her hair. Her mouth looked so soft. He wanted to take it. So he was putting off taking it, just to prove to himself that he could.

She grinned, a naughty-girl grin. "I can feel that you're glad to see me."

Still holding her head so he could see her eyes, he rubbed himself against her, slowly, teasing both of them.

Her eyes went dreamy. "Kiss me, Cash. Please?"

He wanted to ask her where she'd been, who she'd been with, what they'd done. But he refused to act like the jealous fool he knew he was.

"Cash?" A note of uneasiness had crept into her voice. "Is something wrong?"

"Not a damn thing."

"Then why won't you kiss me?"

"I'll kiss you."

"When?"

"Now." And he lowered his mouth to hers.

As he kissed her, he put his hands on her hips and slowly pulled up that T-shirt. She had nothing on under it. He cupped her bottom and pulled her closer, tighter into him.

"Oh." She sighed against his mouth. "Oh, yes, yes, yes...."

He scooped her up and carried her toward the light at the end of the hall.

The next morning, when they were sitting at the table, eating oatmeal, Cash told Abby that he was hiring a woman to come in three times a week.

"And do what?" she asked, irritated by the suggestion.

"You know what."

She felt defensive—and so she attacked. "That's ridiculous. We don't need a maid for a two-bedroom apartment."

"We *shouldn't* need a maid for a two-bedroom apartment."

She set down her spoon and took three deep breaths. "I'll do better."

He looked pained. "Abby, it doesn't mean a damn thing to me if you can keep a house or not. I just don't want to walk into a pigpen every time I show up here."

That hurt. Probably because her own idea of a real woman was someone who kept a nice house. She knew for certain that there were a lot of women out there just dying for their chance to pick up after Cash Bravo.

"Abby, are you listening?"

"Yes. And I understand."

"You say that, and then you leave your junk everywhere. I don't want to live like that."

"I know. It's a...problem I have. I understand why I do it, I swear."

His brows drew together. "Why?"

"Rebellion."

"Against who?"

"My mother. You know how she is. The perfect homemaker. And I'm not her. I don't want to be her."

"Fine. So you're all grown up now, right? You don't have to get even with Edna anymore. Get over it."

"I'm trying."

He looked doubtful. "Abby..."

"What?"

"Maybe you just don't give a hoot about picking up your junk. I don't like to pick up after myself, either. So I hire people to do it. *They* make money. And *I* get to live comfortably. Everybody wins."

He had a point, and she knew it. But still some frugal, self-sufficient part of her hated to admit that she was a hopeless slob who couldn't be bothered to put her own clothes away—let alone that she wouldn't do for Cash what a *real* woman would be eager to do. "I just want to try, Cash. Please. Let me try. It just seems wrong to need a maid for a place this size."

He sighed.

And she knew he would give her another chance. She smiled. "Thanks. I'll do better."

"Eat your damn oatmeal."

Obediently, she picked up her spoon and dipped it into her bowl.

And in the weeks that followed, Abby's housekeeping did improve slightly—enough to keep Cash from actually going out and hiring that maid.

Cash kept his promise and came to see her often. Sometimes he stayed at the apartment for days at a stretch. He was passionate and attentive. He went with her to the doctor and they signed up for a childbirth class, which took place on Wednesday nights in October and November. He promised to knock himself out to be there, and he did. In the six weeks of classes, he only missed two.

Twice, over weekends, they flew home to Medicine Creek. And two other weekends they drove in to Denver and spent Friday and Saturday night in one of the best hotels in town. The first weekend they spent in Denver, they dined at the Brown Palace and saw Dwight Yoakam live.

The second weekend, they ate at the Brown Palace again on Friday night. On Saturday, they tried a new Italian place.

"Right this way," the maître d' said. He led them to a nice corner table and promised that the wine steward would be right with them.

As the maître d' left them, Cash opened his menu and pretended to read it. But he was really watching Abby. He'd been having a ball with her the past several weeks, spending every available moment with her, giving in, really, to his craving to be near her. She seemed to want it that way. And besides, that had been part of their agreement when they'd decided to marry: to be together as much as they could.

She glanced up from her menu and their gazes locked. She grinned. He grinned back. She went back to deciding what to order. He went on looking at her.

He liked looking at her, studying the various parts of her. Right now, he was watching her hands as they held the menu. They were slender hands and she kept the nails trimmed short. Pretty hands, but useful-looking, too. And clean. He smiled to himself. Edna might have failed in her efforts to turn her only daughter into a happy little homemaker, but at least she'd won out when it came to personal hygiene. The grubby urchin of yesterday existed only in Cash's fond memories now.

"Abby? Is that you?"

Cash glanced up, frowning. A handsome, dark-haired kid hovered by Abby's chair.

Abby looked up from the tasseled menu and smiled. "Tony! Tony Ellerby. How are you?"

"Fine. I can't believe this."

Cash watched Tony Ellerby. The kid was trying not to stare at Abby's stomach. But he'd put two and two together, all right. Cash watched the kid, thinking that he was just about Abby's age, wondering how Abby knew him, what he might have been to her.

Tony asked, "Are you, uh, living here now? In Denver?"

"No, I'm still at C.U. We just came into town for the weekend." Abby looked at Cash, then back at Tony. "Tony, this is my husband, Cash."

Tony grinned. "Hey, how are you?"

Cash took Tony's outstretched hand, gave it a quick shake and then let it go.

Abby inquired, "What about you, Tony? I haven't seen you around campus."

Tony forked a hand through his thick black hair and explained that he was taking a break for a semester or two. Getting his "priorities" in order, trying to figure out what he really wanted from life. Abby laughed and said it was good to see him and she wished him luck, whatever he did.

"Old friend?" Cash asked casually, after Tony had said goodbye and walked away.

Abby nodded at him over the top of her menu. "We dated a couple of times last year."

Cash looked at his own menu. Then the wine steward appeared. Cash ordered wine for himself.

Abby waited for the wine steward to leave. Then she

said quietly, "It was nothing serious between me and Tony."

Cash continued to study his menu, scanning the pasta selections, considering the veal entrées. "You never mentioned him, that I remember."

"We just had dinner once, and went to a show another time. No big deal."

Cash believed her. He knew her that well. If it had been a big deal between her and Tony Ellerby, he would have heard about it.

What bothered him had nothing to do with how many dates Abby and Tony Ellerby had shared. It had to do with the way his gut had knotted at the sight of that kid bending over his wife. With the possessive streak he'd discovered in himself. Never in his life had Cash felt possessive about a woman. Until Abby.

And then there was the guilt. Guilt that he was the one sitting across from her now, her belly so big with the child he had put there. As much as he hated the thought of her with anyone else, he knew that she should be sitting across from someone like Tony Ellerby tonight. It was the time of her life for casual dates with guys her own age, guys who would take her home later to that shabby brick house she used to live in last year with a bunch of other college girls. Instead, she went home with a husband fifteen years older than she was. And very soon, she'd be dealing with motherhood.

"Cash..."

He felt her foot, under the table, rubbing his leg.

He looked at her over the top of the menu. "Put your shoe back on."

"Are you jealous?"

"Do you know what you want?"

She picked up her water glass and sipped from it.

Provocatively. "Oh, I do." Under the table, her toes trailed up and down his pant leg. "I know just what I want."

"Good. Because the waiter's coming."

She kept on stroking his leg with her toes all through the process of placing their order. By the time the waiter walked away, Cash's jealousy and guilt had taken a back seat to lust.

He didn't know how she did it. She was due to have the baby in just two months—and she was sexy as hell. Sometimes, he tried to control himself, worrying that all the lovemaking might hurt her or the baby. But she would remind him that the baby was fine, that the doctor said it was okay as long as she wanted to and he wanted to.

And they both did want to. All the time.

He shifted in his seat, coughing, trying to readjust for his arousal without being obvious.

Across from him, Abby grinned like a Cheshire cat. She knew exactly what she'd done to him. And she was proud of herself. He slid a hand down and captured her ankle.

"Oh!" she said.

He grinned right back at her. "Something wrong?"

She batted her eyelashes. "No. Not a thing, honestly."

"Good." He scooted his chair under the table a little farther—and then he put her foot on top of his thigh.

It took concentration; her big belly got in the way, but she managed to scoot closer, to put those naughty little toes right up against the part of him that was straining at the front of his pants. He tried not to gasp.

She went on grinning. He glanced around. People nibbled their antipasti and chewed their veal piccata and chatted casually between sips of wine. No one seemed to notice what the pretty pregnant lady was doing to her husband under the long white tablecloth.

Just then, the wine steward appeared with the bottle Cash had ordered. He uncorked it with a flourish, then poured a small amount for Cash to sample. Cash took a sip, then nodded. The wine steward filled his glass and left.

Cash raised his glass to Abby, as under the table she continued to drive him out of his mind. He knocked back a long sip, then set the glass down a little more firmly than necessary. "Are we going to eat?"

She looked rueful and adorable. "Well. I do keep thinking about that tub in our suite. It's so nice and big and deep."

"Fine." He pushed back his chair and threw a hand-ful of bills on the table. "We're gone."

Abby took a minute to slide on her shoe and push back her chair. And then they were heading for the door.

"Is there a problem?" the maître d' inquired as they fled past the reservation podium. He glanced at Abby's belly. "Signora, are you all right?"

"She just needs a little rest," Cash said.

"But—"

"I left enough to cover our meal on the table." Cash kept walking, pushing Abby slightly ahead of him.

The maître d' kept sputtering. "But, wait. Are you—?"

Abby gave him a smile over her shoulder as Cash pushed her out the door. "I'll be fine. Honestly. I just need a long, hot bath."

A couple of hours later, they lay together on the big bed in their suite, Abby on her side in a nest of pillows and Cash wrapped around her, spoon-fashion. He had his hand on her belly, feeling for kicks. He smiled. "A good one."

She gave a little mock groan. "I know—I felt it."

He nuzzled the back of her neck, breathed in the sweet scent of her. "I've been thinking."

She shifted a little, readjusting herself on the pillows, trying to get comfortable. It got harder and harder for her as the days went by.

"Abby? Did you hear me?"

"Umm-hmm. You've been thinking…"

"About next weekend.…"

She groaned again, took his hand, kissed it and put it back on her belly. "Forget it. We're going home."

The next weekend was Thanksgiving. Abby wanted to go home to the ranch, where she'd spent every Thanksgiving of her life. Edna was planning a huge feast, to be prepared by the capable hands of Tess DeMarley.

"Abby, I don't think it's such a great idea for you to be flying now."

She put a hand over her ear—the one that wasn't buried in the pillow. "I can't hear you."

"Abby…"

She jerked away from him then and dragged herself to a sitting position, Indian-style. "We've been over this." She smoothed her big T-shirt over the heavy curve of her stomach. "I'll see the doctor Wednesday. If he gives permission—which he will, because I feel fine—then we are taking the Cessna home and we are having Thanksgiving the way we've always had it."

"But—"

"No. Listen. My mother drives me nuts. But I do

love her. And she is expecting us. It will break her heart if we don't show up.''

"Edna will understand.''

"No. Edna will *say* that she understands. And inside, she'll be hurt. And anyway, you should have listened to me back in August when I told you I wasn't sure about getting in another semester.''

"I know. I was a damn idiot.''

"Well, fine. You were an idiot. But just because you talked me into coming here doesn't mean I'm giving up my Thanksgiving.''

"I just didn't realize...''

"What?''

"How *big* a pregnant woman gets.''

She sniffed and tried to act wounded. "Thank you very much.''

"I mean it, Abby. We'll have a great Thanksgiving, the two of us. In Boulder, or here in Denver if you want to get away a little.''

She dropped the wounded act and gave him that straight-on, will-to-will look she had perfected over two decades of unremitting practice. "We are going. And that's that.''

"No, Abby.'' He spoke firmly, to show her he could not be swayed on this. "We're not.''

Chapter Nine

They flew back to Wyoming on Wednesday evening and spent the night at the house in Medicine Creek. Then, early in the morning, they drove out to the ranch in the Jeep Cherokee that Cash kept next to his Cadillac in the garage.

It was a cold, clear morning. Abby looked out the window of the Jeep at the rolling prairie land. To the east, from the higher points in the road, the fields seemed to go on forever, overlapping ridges and draws, rising to distant hills somewhere at the ends of the earth. But to the west, rising starkly, black and tipped with blinding white, the Big Horns loomed high, rough and proud, wreathed in feathery gray clouds.

Abby felt good for a woman who was as big as a cow, and pleased to be headed for her favorite place in the world. All the grass in the pasturelands had gone dusty brown months before. Abby watched it bend before a strong wind, rippling away toward the mountains. White patches of snow from a recent storm dotted the land, giving back a glare in the bright sun that made Abby squint. A line of fence ran along the ridge above the road and Abby spotted a sage grouse, scared from cover by some unseen predator. Its plump body rose from the ground in a flutter of gray wings, then dropped back to earth, bomberlike, not far from where it had taken flight.

She glanced at Cash. Sensing her eyes on him, he turned his head. He smiled, and she knew he'd forgiven her for keeping at him relentlessly until he gave in and brought her home.

Her mother came out of the house when they pulled up beneath the big Russian olive tree that grew in the center of the yard. The wind that had bent the brown grass of the prairie now whipped the skirt of Edna's Sunday-best wool dress around her legs. Abby felt satisfaction at the sight of her. She looked better each time Abby saw her, both stronger and happier, too. She was healing—from her illness and from the loss of Ty. Abby grinned to herself. Clearly, living with Tess DeMarley suited Edna—far better than living with her own daughter ever had.

Cash shoved open his door and headed for the porch. But Abby hung back, in the warmth of the Jeep, looking at the house, loving everything about it, from the shingles on the side-gabled roof to the four double-hung windows on the full-width front porch. Ross Bravo had built the house more than forty years ago, after a string of good years when beef prices had run high and the snowpack had measured deep. Before then, he and his wife, Matty, had lived in what was now the foreman's cottage, across the yard. Ross's daddy, the first John Bravo, had built the foreman's cottage sixty-five years past. Until then, John, his wife, Belinda, and their son had lived in the small, dark homesteader's cabin. John's father, Matt, had built that cabin back when the Bravos had laid claim to the first acres that would become the Rising Sun. It still stood on the other side of the horse pasture, behind the barn.

On the porch, Cash and Edna waited for her. Abby got out of the Jeep and approached her mother with her arms out. Edna smiled and opened her own arms.

"Abigail," Edna said in her ear as they hugged—rather awkwardly, because of the size of Abby's stomach. "Oh, this is so good. To have you both home." Then she stood back. "My, my. You are getting…"

"Huge?" Abby supplied helpfully, and then shivered as a gust of frigid wind whipped around the corner of the porch and sliced right through her heavy sweater and pregnant-lady stirrup pants.

"Brrr," Edna said. "Let's get inside before we all freeze."

In the late afternoon, they sat down to the feast Tess had prepared. Zach had spent the morning out checking tubs—fifty-gallon barrels cut in half and filled with a molasses-based mineral mixture meant to supplement the cattle's diet of pasture grasses. He'd taken Tess's daughter, Jobeth, along with him. The six-year-old was pink cheeked and excited at having been included in the work of the ranch.

"Those tubs looked pretty good, don't you think, Zach?"

"Yep." He smiled at Jobeth. "Still pretty full."

She beamed down the table at him, worshipful, but restrained.

"This is wonderful, Tess," Edna said.

And it was. Abby looked up and down the long table in amazement. Even Edna, in her heyday, had never whipped up such a spread. The huge turkey was golden brown, and a steaming bowl of bread-and-chestnut stuffing sat beside it. The mashed potatoes looked as fluffy as clouds, the yams temptingly sweet under a drizzle of brown-sugar sauce. Tess had provided three kinds of green vegetables: steamed squash, peas and a broccoli casserole baked with cheese that set the mouth watering with its delicious scent. She had also set out two kinds of cranberry sauce, savory creamed onions, so many different pickled things that Abby couldn't count them all, a couple of yummy-looking gelatin molds and a tray of crudités, with the radishes cut to look like flowers and the carrots and celery all sliced at an attractive slant. Abby found it truly impressive, and regretted that in recent weeks the baby seemed to have pressed her stomach into a tiny corner beneath her ribs, leaving her appetite seriously impaired.

The two ranch hands, Tim Cally and Lolly Franzen, both murmured how good it all looked. It was Rising Sun tradition that the hands ate with the family on holidays if they didn't have somewhere else they wanted to go.

Cash took a bite of dressing. "Incredible," he said.

"I'm glad you like it," Tess replied.

Something in Tess's tone stopped Abby in the process of sampling the yams. Abby glanced at her mother's housemate. Tess was looking at Cash, a look that didn't last more than a split second. Cash himself hadn't seen it; his attention was on his plate.

But Abby saw it.

And knew what it meant.

It was the look Cash's old girlfriend had given him in Vegas. Yearning. Adoring. And hopeless.

Gentle Tess was in love with Cash. Abby set down her fork, what appetite she'd had a moment before suddenly fled. It was so obvious! How could she not have known before? Abby slanted another glance at Tess, who held out that wonderful broccoli casserole to Zach. Jealousy poked at Abby, a sharp, mean little jab. Tess was lovely, so slim and sweet—and so accomplished in all the womanly arts—arts in which Abby had absolutely no interest.

"I only wish Nate could have come, too," Edna said wistfully.

Cash laughed. "He'll be here for Christmas—just you watch."

"You think so?" Edna asked, brightening.

"Absolutely. Think back. He always makes it for either Thanksgiving or Christmas."

"Well, I wish he'd make it for both."

Cash shook his head. "If he showed up for both, we might get the idea he can't stay away."

Everybody laughed at that except Tess and her daughter, who hardly knew Nate.

Cash moved his thigh beneath the table so it brushed against Abby's. "Hey. You okay?" He indicated her untouched plate.

She gave him a smile. "You bet." And she picked up her fork and tackled the bread-and-chestnut stuffing.

Once they'd all sworn they couldn't eat another bite, Abby helped Tess clear the table and clean up the dishes. Then they played double-deck pinochle, Abby partnering up with Cash against Zach and Tess. Through the entire evening, Abby watched her husband closely.

By bedtime, she was positive he didn't have a clue about Tess's feelings for him. He treated Edna's housemate with the good-natured courtesy and warmth he'd always bestowed on the numberless women who had adored him over the years. And no one else seemed to notice what Abby had seen.

And really, as the evening had progressed, Abby began to suspect she might have only imagined that quick, worshipful glance of Tess's. Because after that single look, Abby caught no other hint that her mother's companion might be in love with Cash. Perhaps Abby was just being a paranoid pregnant lady and Tess DeMarley hadn't fallen for Cash at all—except in Abby's own jealous mind.

Besides, even if Tess *were* attracted to Abby's husband, she would never do anything about it. Because Tess DeMarley was every bit as exemplary a woman as everyone believed her to be.

And yet, lying in bed in one of the guest rooms later, listening to the wind whip and whistle around the eaves outside, Abby couldn't stop remembering the way Cash and Tess had laughed and talked together. And she couldn't help recalling her mother's warnings—and thinking of the agreement that still hung like a shadow over her relationship with Cash. If both of them didn't change their minds, in eight more months their marriage would end.

Every time she let herself think about that, she felt terrible.

Because she did not want her marriage to end.

Recently, she'd accepted the truth: she loved her husband—deeply and completely. As a woman loves a man.

She didn't know exactly how or when it had happened. Probably that night in the barn—maybe even before that. Lately, she'd begun to suspect that she'd been in love with Cash all her life.

But that night in the barn had marked the turning point. After that, she'd seen him as a man.

She'd run off to Boulder and then to Denver, trying to get away from what she felt. And then they'd decided to marry. And she'd starting letting herself get used to her love.

And now, finally, she could admit it to herself. She didn't want their marriage to end. She wanted him beside her in the night, across from her at the table, just plain nearby in general, for the rest of their lives.

"What is it?" Cash asked, out of the darkness beside her. "You keep wiggling around."

She felt a surge of her old independence, of irritation at him for having such power over her heart. "Sorry," she whispered sourly. "I'm just having a real adventure here, trying to sleep with this basketball in my stomach."

"Aw, poor baby."

He slid closer, fitting himself around her. The hair on his thighs scratched her a little; his hard hips cradled her soft ones. It felt good. So very good. With a finger, he guided a swatch of hair off her neck and put a kiss there.

"Feel better," he commanded.

She snuggled back against him, readjusting the pillow beneath her belly at the same time. "I do." It was true. Something happened when he cradled her at night. His body seemed to speak of peace to her body. And her body always listened. "Thanks."

"Any time." She felt his breath against her neck as he brushed one more gentle kiss there. "Go to sleep."

"I will."

And she did.

They stayed at the ranch through the weekend. It snowed on Saturday, wet snow, the white flakes whirling, making everything look hazy, turning to water the minute they touched down. Abby and Edna stood on the porch together and watched the clouds roll in overhead and the first wet flakes fall. Everyone else, including Jobeth, had gone out with Zach to help move some bred heifers to a pasture nearer the ranch buildings.

"They'll all be coming in wet," Edna said. She had on her coat, and she held her arms tight around her waist, shivering with each gust of icy wind that blew.

Abby pulled her heavy jacket closer, wrapping it snugly around the bulge of her belly. "They're having a ball."

"You wish you were with them."

"How did you guess?" Abby leaned from beneath the porch and caught a soggy snowflake on her tongue. It had melted almost before she felt its coldness. "But Cash wouldn't let me." She patted her stomach. "Too far along, he says." She leaned out once more, welcoming the wet flakes on her upturned face.

"He's right," Edna declared. "There will be time later for moving heifers on a snowy afternoon. And besides, I think it's lovely the way he cares for you, how much he loves you."

When she heard those words, Abby wanted to whirl on her mother and demand, He does love me? Are you sure? How do you know?

Somehow, she stopped herself. Questions like that would only get her more questions from her mother in return—worried questions, prying questions. Questions to which Abby had no answers anyway.

She needed to talk to Cash. To tell him she loved him. And to let him know that she, for one, wanted their marriage to last.

But right now at the ranch, with all the family around, didn't seem like the right time. She decided to wait. Until they could really be alone, back in Boulder. She didn't want to think that it might go badly. But just in case it did, they wouldn't have the family to deal with, too.

"Let's go in," Edna suggested. "I'll make us some tea."

The kettle had started to whistle when they heard the horses and Zach's pickup in the yard. Abby ran out to meet them.

Cash's horse, Reno's Pride, a big gray gelding and a fine cutting horse, pranced to the side when she grabbed the bridle.

"Whoa, easy…" Cash soothed the horse. Then he leaned down and gave Abby a kiss. "Miss me?" he asked.

His lips felt icy against her own. She could smell the melted snow in his clothes and his breath made plumes in the cold air.

"Desperately," she told him, with just enough drama that he could think she was only playing.

Sunday morning, before they went downstairs, Cash actually tried to talk Abby out of returning to Boulder.

"Hey," she teased. "Remember? You were the guy who insisted I had to get in one more semester."

"That was insane of me. You should have had me locked up. I'm serious. We got back here safely enough. But let's not tempt fate. It can't be smart for you to fly now."

"The doctor said—"

"I know what the doctor said. And I don't care." He turned to the window and for a moment stood looking out at the gray day and the patches of sludgy snow on the roof of the barn. Then he turned back to her. "You can take the semester over again. Next year."

She was putting on one of the giant-sized tunic sweaters she wore all the time now. She smoothed it down over her maternity leggings and marched over to him in stocking feet, thinking of how she'd busted her butt in her investment and portfolio management course. And if she had to take the seminar in financial accounting again, she might just lose her mind. "No. Honestly, Cash. I really think I can get through finals before the baby comes. I feel good, I swear. And I've worked so hard...."

He smoothed a hank of hair out of her eyes. "I know. But—"

"No, really. I mean it. I want to finish out the semester. I really do."

He ran the back of his hand along her cheek and in his eyes she saw such tender concern.

I love you, she thought. The words sounded so sweet and soft in the back of her mind. She opened her mouth, almost said them....

But he spoke first. "I don't think it's safe."

She blinked. And remembered what he was trying to get her to do. "We are going. Today. I am finishing the semester, and that is that."

He sucked in a breath, then blew out his cheeks in frustration. "Abby, if you insist on going back, I think we should drive."

"Four hundred miles? Excuse me. I *will* go into premature labor if you put me through that right now." She placed a hand on his shoulder. "Look. We'll fly this one last time. And then, before Christmas, when we come home for good, we'll drive. How's that?"

He looked at her steadily. "If we're going there, we stay there. Until the baby's born."

She smiled at him, a coaxing smile. No way she was staying in Boulder for Christmas. But they didn't have to go into that right then. "Let's not worry about that now."

"Abby..."

"Cash..."

They glared at each other. And then they both laughed. He put an arm around her and pulled her close, so her big stomach bumped against him. Then he kissed her nose. "All right. I don't like it, but all right."

She smoothed the hair at his temples, thinking how she loved the little grooves that appeared in his cheeks when he smiled. Masculine dimples, that's what they were. But he would not have appreciated her pointing them out. So she didn't.

"I could shoot myself," he said softly, "for pushing you to go back in the first place. I don't know what the hell I was using for brains at the time."

He looked so worried. And so sweet.

Again, she almost said it: I love you, Cash.

But then she heard footsteps, out in the upper hall, and remembered her plan to tell him when they were really alone, when she didn't have to worry about dealing with anyone else. Best to stick with the plan.

They went down to breakfast a few minutes later.

And a few hours after that, they were on their way to Sheridan to get the Cessna.

More than once during the flight, Abby started to tell Cash how she felt about him. But somehow, the words never found their way out her mouth. She told herself that she'd be foolish to tell him something so important while he was trying to fly a plane.

In Denver, it had snowed, too. And a lot of it had stayed on the ground. Abby looked out the window of the Blazer at the soft blanket of white and thought of Christmas, which would be coming up before they knew it.

At the apartment, Cash carried their suitcases in. Abby headed straight for the thermostat to heat the place up, and from there to the bathroom. It was a funny thing about being pregnant. You spent the first three months bending over the commode, and the last three sitting on it.

"Do you want to go out to eat?" Cash asked, when she emerged from the bathroom.

She felt tired from the trip. But still, she wanted to say yes. Abby loved to eat out. It always seemed festive to her—plus, when you ate out, you got fed without having to cook or clean. In Abby's perfect world, people would either eat out or eat at the houses of other people who actually *enjoyed* cooking and cleaning.

People like Tess—who might or might not be in love with Abby's husband, but, in any case, was exactly the kind of woman most men wanted for their wives.

"Abby?" Cash was frowning at her. "You in there?"

She shook herself. "Uh, yeah. And let's not go out. I'll just whip something up, why don't I?"

He stared at her. "Are you feeling all right?"

"What do you mean?"

"I could have sworn you just said you'd rather cook something yourself than eat out."

"That's exactly what I said." She turned for the kitchen. "Sit down and relax. I'll call you when it's ready."

She found linguine and a can of clam sauce in the cupboard. And there was lettuce and a lone tomato in the crisper. And frozen Pepperidge Farm garlic bread in the freezer. So they had pasta, salad and bread.

It wasn't that difficult. And when they sat down to eat, the linguine was only slightly beyond al dente.

"Are you turning domestic on me?" Cash teased.

Even with Tess's feminine perfection taunting her, Abby wasn't willing to go that far. "It's the nesting instinct. It'll pass."

Later, as they were going to bed, she decided that the time had come to tell him. "Cash?"

He pulled back the covers and slid in beside her. "Yeah?" He canted up on an elbow to look at her, since she was sitting against the headboard.

"Well, I…"

And before she could say another word, a memory rose up to taunt her; a memory of something that had happened years ago.

It had been at a dance. A Fourth of July dance, out in Medicine Creek Park.

Abby could picture the bandstand, with loops of red, white and blue bunting tacked to the sides—and the dance floor, its railings draped in red, white and blue, as well. Overhead, the summer stars gleamed like sequins on a midnight blue gown. The weather had been warm and humid, unusual for Wyoming. Folks had remarked on the heat. Their faces had glistened with sweat when they danced.

And Abby had been eight years old.

She could almost see herself now, in blue jeans and pigtails, standing on the sidelines, clapping along to a Bob Wills song, watching her mom and dad as they danced....

Chapter Ten

The child, Abby, stood by the bandstand, watching her mother and father as they whirled around the floor.

She felt good watching them, because they were smiling at each other, smiles with love in them. Sometimes Abby could feel a coldness between her mother and father. She felt a coldness inside herself when that happened. A fear that her world, her life, might go bad somehow. That everything could change and there would be no one to love her and take care of her.

But at times like this, when her mom and dad looked at each other and something warm and private happened between them, Abby knew that her world was safe. She could smile and feel good and not worry about anything.

The band started playing another song, a faster one. Abby clapped her hands and stomped her feet as the dancers moved faster, up and down the floor, laughing and breathing hard, their faces shiny with sweat.

Abby looked around. Where was Cash? Cash would dance with her and it would be such fun. A few moments ago, she'd seen him dancing with Marianne Bowers, but now Marianne was dancing with Bart Crowley and Cash was nowhere to be seen.

Abby turned from the bandstand and the circle of light that glowed from the lanterns strung overhead. She took the trail that led down to the bank of Medicine Creek, which ran along one side of town and after which the town had been named. Down by the creek it was cooler, but moisture still made the air seem thick, as if you could taste it while you were breathing it. Frogs croaked in the darkness and the cottonwoods and willows grew thick and shadowy, hanging over the burbling stream and the trail. It was kind of creepy, but Abby could handle it. She could hear the music from the bandstand behind her. And if she looked back, she could see the gleam of the lanterns lighting up the night. She wouldn't get lost or anything, no danger of that.

Up ahead, she heard voices. She froze on the trail for a moment, listening. A man and a woman, she felt pretty sure. When she started walking again, she walked more carefully, trying not to snap any branches, not to make any noise. She was sneaking, really. And she probably shouldn't. But she did it anyway.

The voices stopped suddenly, but Abby knew where they had been coming from: a little picnic area on a clear spot above the trail. Abby slid in behind a clump of willows to see who it was.

She saw Nate and Meggie May Kane. Nate had come home again for one of his visits a few days before. He had a bandage on his hand, where the bull he'd ridden in the rodeo that day had stomped him. Nate liked to tempt fate by riding in the Powder River Roundup every year. That was what Abby's mom said. Just this morning, she had told him, "You just have to tempt fate, don't you, Nathan Bravo? You'll break your fool neck one of these days."

Nate was leaning against the picnic table in the middle of the clear spot. He had his arms around Meggie May and she was pressed up real close to him, closer than dancing, that was for sure. Their mouths were all mooshed up together in a kiss. A very *private* kind of kiss. One that went on for a long, long time. The white bandage on Nate's hand seemed to gleam in the darkness, like the lanterns back at the dance, as he held Meggie May so tight against him.

Abby knew she shouldn't be watching. But she just stayed crouched there, behind the willows, watching anyway.

Finally, Meggie May pulled back. She looked up at Nate. "I mean it, Nate. I love you. And I will always love you."

Nate took Meggie May by the arms. He pushed her back from him and stared down at her. "Give me a break," he said.

Abby could see his face pretty well. He had on his mean look, the look he gave people when he wanted to be safe from them.

"Nate." Meggie May sounded like she might start crying. "Please…"

"Look." Nate held Meggie May farther away than before. "If you want a good time, fine. But you shouldn't have followed me out here for anything else.

Because you're never gonna get anything else from me.''

Meggie didn't say anything for a minute after that. Abby discovered she was holding her breath. Very carefully, she let it out and then started breathing, real quiet, again.

Meggie stepped back. And Nate dropped his hands.

Meggie said, her voice all tight sounding, "I guess I always thought that if I told you, it would make a difference.''

Nate made a disgusted noise in his throat. "Well, now you know. It doesn't make one damn bit of difference. Not to me, anyway.''

Meggie started backing up, toward the slope that led down to the trail. She went past Abby's hiding place and took a few more steps backward. Then she whirled around and started running, off down the trail toward the lights and the music.

Abby turned back to watch Nate again. She thought he looked sad. He took a cigarette from the pocket of his shirt and lighted it, the match flaring, blinding Abby a little, so she closed her eyes. When she opened them again, Nate was just leaning there, against the picnic table, smoking.

Abby heard a sound on the trail. And Cash came out into the clear spot. Abby's heart lifted up high in her chest, in that happy feeling she always got at the sight of him. She almost leaped from her hiding place and grabbed him to come dance with her.

But then she realized that if she did that, Nate and Cash would both know she'd been spying and sneaking. So she stayed crouched in the willows.

"You seen Abby?" Cash asked. "Edna wants her.''

Nate shook his head and blew out smoke.

Cash went over and hoisted himself onto the picnic table, a little ways from Nate, with his boots on the long bench. "Got a smoke?"

Nate gave him one and held up a match. This time Abby closed her eyes before it flared.

Cash blew out smoke. "Meggie May almost ran me down on the trail. She didn't look happy."

Nate grunted. "Am I gonna get a lecture here, Cousin?"

"She was crying."

"She's better off crying than if she'd stayed here with me. We both know that."

"Maybe you should give her a chance," Cash said.

Nate threw back his head and laughed a mean laugh. Then he turned so he was looking straight at Cash. "Don't give me advice, Cash. Not about getting serious over some woman, anyway. I'm never getting serious over a woman." Nate leaned closer to Cash. "And you understand that. Because even though you treat them so much nicer than I do, you're just like me. If some female wants to get rid of you, all she's gotta do is start sayin' how she loves you. And you will be gone."

Cash and Nate stared at each other, then Cash nodded. "You know, Cousin, you're brighter than you look."

Nate didn't say anything; he just went on smoking.

Cash got down from the table. He dropped his cigarette and crushed it with his boot. "Help me find the pint-size, will you, before Edna gets to worrying?"

"Sure." Nate ground out his cigarette, too. Then they went off down the trail together.

As soon as Abby was sure they were gone, she jumped up and ran the opposite way. She took the

higher path, and she was back among the lights and
the people a few minutes before the Bravo cousins got
there.

Her mother got mad. "Where have you been, Abigail? I've been worried sick."

Abby lied and said she'd just walked on the high
path for a ways. But in her mind, she was remembering
the lesson she'd learned.

She should never say "I love you" to Cash. Or he
would go away.

"Abby?"

Cash was grinning up at her, still leaning on his elbow in their bed.

"Hmm?" She brought herself back to the present
and put on a smile for him.

"What?" he asked.

She frowned.

He reached up and pulled on her hair, a teasing little
tug. "You were going to say something?"

She couldn't do it. Not right now. She just could not
do it. She shook her head. "No, it's nothing. Really.
Nothing at all."

He put his hand on the hard mound of her belly, a
possessive, tender gesture. She put her hand over his.

"Come on down here," he said. "Let's get some
sleep."

She scrunched down and turned to her side. He
helped her with her pillows and then he wrapped himself around her back.

"Are you all right?" he asked, after they'd lain there
silent in the dark for a while.

"Sure. Why?"

"I don't know. You seem…"

She reached behind her and patted his hip. "I'm fine. G'night."

He pulled her closer. A few minutes later, she could tell by his breathing that he had dropped off. It took her considerably longer to get to sleep.

After that, it became a kind of game Abby played with herself. She knew she should tell Cash about her feelings, about wanting to make their temporary marriage a lifetime thing. But somehow, every time she was just about to do it, she found an excuse to back out.

And there were plenty of excuses to be had. Cash was forever leaving and coming back. He had his deals to make, but he seemed to want to be near her as much as possible as the time that the baby would be born approached. So she never knew, when she left for classes in the morning, whether he would be there or not when she returned. How could she plan a serious talk with him when she couldn't even be sure if he'd be there to listen to what she had to say?

Also, her end-of-semester workload kept her hopping. Finals seemed to be coming at her like a speeding train. And she kept thinking about Tess, the perfect woman, who just might be in love with Cash. So she expended more effort than usual in taking care of the apartment and keeping the refrigerator stocked. Plus, she wanted to Christmas-shop. And she did. She bought several gifts for her mother and Zach and Nate and that little girl of Tess's. And, of course, for Cash. Somehow, she managed to get them all wrapped, as well.

But something had to give. She ended up missing one of her scheduled visits to Dr. McClary, her Boulder ob-gyn. When she called and he fit her in two days later, he said her blood pressure was somewhat elevated. He made her stay for hours, to check it again and to run urine and blood tests. Then she had to come back the next day so he could tell her that her tests had turned out fine.

"Everything looks pretty good," he said. "We found nothing to worry about in the blood work. And no traces of protein in the urine, which might point to PIH. Are you familiar with that term?"

She nodded. "I think they talked about it in our childbirth class. It's like toxemia, isn't it?"

"Pregnancy-induced hypertension. And yes, it is what we used to call toxemia or preeclampsia. Basically, it's late-pregnancy high blood pressure and it's nothing to fool around with. Right now, your blood pressure is within the safe range. But it's higher than it has been, and so it's something to watch. I think the best thing you could do at this point would be to reduce your salt intake as much as possible, get plenty of rest and carefully monitor your stress level. By that I mean, cut out anything that puts pressure on you."

She gave him a look of great patience. "I'll be even more careful than I have been about salt. But as far as the rest of it, well, my finals are in one week."

He shook his head. "You are having a baby, Mrs. Bravo, and very soon now. I understand that you are young and strong and that you imagine you can handle anything. But maybe you should consider taking those finals at some later date."

"In a pig's eye, Dr. McClary."

He chuckled at that and then grew serious once more. "Take it easy, please. I want that blood pressure back down nice and low again the next time I see you.''

"But this is my last visit," she reminded him. "Remember? I'll be going home in a week and a half. I already have my next appointment scheduled with my doctor in Medicine Creek."

Dr. McClary frowned. "Where is this Medicine Creek, now?"

"Northern Wyoming."

"That would be a very long trip for you at this point in your pregnancy."

"Dr. McClary, I am going home as soon as my finals are through, and that's that."

The doctor looked at her over the top of the half glasses he wore. "On your way out, check in with Annie at the reception desk to make an appointment for next week."

"But—"

"There's no harm in being too careful. When I see you then, we'll discuss your flight to Medicine Creek."

"But I'm not going to fly. My husband won't let me. We're driving. That should be safe, right?"

"Probably," he said grudgingly. "But I'd still like to see you before you go."

Abby restrained a sigh. Just what she needed—something else to do next week.

Dr. McClary was still talking. "Also, you have some swelling now, around your ankles especially. And that's normal. But you're to call me immediately if you get any swelling in the hands or face, blurred vision or headaches."

Abby promised that she would contact his office if any strange symptoms appeared. Then she went out and told the receptionist that she'd give her a call as soon as she had a chance to check her schedule for next week.

At home, Abby hit the books good and hard. Cash asked her how her visit to Dr. McClary had gone. She lifted her cheek for his kiss and muttered, "Fine," thinking that she had to remember to call and schedule that last appointment. Then she went back to her studying.

The next week, she took her finals. She felt she did well on them, though she wouldn't know for sure until she received her grades. By December 21, she was done with school. She went to the registrar's office and told them she wouldn't be back until next fall. They agreed to mail her a copy of her transcript as soon as the new grades were posted.

She and Cash were packing for the trip back home when Annie, Dr. McClary's receptionist, called. Abby remembered at that moment that she'd never made that last appointment. She apologized profusely and then asked Annie to reassure the doctor that she was fine and had an appointment scheduled with her Medicine Creek doctor on the twenty-sixth, just a few days away.

"I'll need to speak with the doctor before I let you go," Annie said. "Please hold."

Abby waited, then Dr. McClary came on the line. He asked her several questions and then, reasonably satisfied with the answers, instructed her to stop every hour on the trip home to rest and stretch her legs. Abby promised that she would.

She hung up and looked around at the apartment. There were boxes everywhere. When they left this time, they wouldn't be back. Cash had already made arrangements for the sale of the furniture. And the few things they wanted to keep that wouldn't fit in the

Blazer would be shipped back to the house in Medicine Creek.

Though Abby wanted to go home, she felt a little sad about leaving. She'd enjoyed the life that she and Cash had shared in the apartment. It felt more like her own home than the big house in Medicine Creek. To her, that house always felt like Cash's house alone. True, she liked the house. She liked the design and the decor; she and Cash had similar tastes. But it wasn't *her* house, not in any way. Cash had built it and chosen the furnishings years before. He had a cook and housekeeper who kept the place ready for him whenever he wanted it. To Abby, in some ways, that house didn't seem much different from the hotels they had stayed in together.

Here, it was another story. Here, she'd chosen most of the furniture herself. And she'd done good work here on her studies. She'd even learned to cook a few simple dishes in the tiny kitchen—thanks to the inspiration provided by her silly jealousy of Tess DeMarley. In this apartment, she and Cash had really *lived* as a married couple. Remembering their lives together here, Abby could almost tell herself that their marriage was a secure, permanent thing.

Abby lowered herself to the sofa, groaning a little at the effort it took her now to do something so simple as sitting down. Just as she got settled, Cash appeared from the bedroom, carrying a packing box. He lugged it over to the door and left it there to take out to the Blazer when the time came to load up. When he turned for the bedroom again, he smiled at Abby—a tender smile. Then he came over to her and dropped down next to her, stretching his arm along the back of the sofa behind her. With a sigh, she leaned her head into his shoulder.

"Tired?" He rested his head against hers.

"A little." She found herself thinking about the agreement. She never had managed to make herself talk to him about it. And she did want to deal with it, to tell him that she longed for nothing more than to put it behind them and stay his wife for the rest of their lives.

Her heart beat a little faster. Maybe now would be a good time. Today. Before they went home, while they were still here in this apartment where things had been so good between them.

He took her hand, turned it over and traced a heart in the center of her palm. "Who was that?"

"Hmm?"

"Just now, on the phone?"

"Dr. McClary's office."

He traced the heart again.

She knew he was waiting for her to tell him what the doctor had said. Reluctantly, she admitted, "Dr. McClary wanted to see me once more before we left. But it's all been so crazy I forgot to schedule an appointment."

"So when are you going in?"

"I'm not. There's no time."

"Abby…"

"No, listen. It's not a problem. He asked me a few questions, then said it was all right if I waited until Tuesday and saw Dr. Pruitt."

"Questions about what?"

She explained about her blood pressure. "But it's no big deal. He did a thousand tests on me last week and everything was fine."

"You're sure?"

"I'm sure."

He gave her shoulder a squeeze. "So you'll see Dr. Pruitt on Tuesday?"

She raised a hand, palm out. "I do solemnly swear."

"Okay."

He kissed the crown of her head. In a second, he would get up, go back to the bedroom, pack another box. Her opportunity, once again, would have passed her by.

"Cash?"

"Yeah?"

"Do you, um, ever think about the agreement we made before we got married?"

His body seemed to stiffen a little next to her. But maybe that was only her overactive imagination. He didn't pull away or take his arm from around her shoulders.

After a moment, he said, "The agreement we made?"

She had no idea how to read that. Had he forgotten about the agreement? Or was he simply stonewalling her?

She clarified. "You know, the agreement that we'd get divorced in a year unless—"

He cut her off. "I remember." He definitely did move back then, pulling his arm from around her and putting a few inches between them on the sofa. "What about it?"

"Well, how do you feel about it? Now, I mean? We've been married for a while. Do you still feel the same?"

His eyes gave nothing away. "If you want to talk

about the agreement, Abby, maybe you should start with how *you* feel.''

She stared at him, knowing he was right. And irritated at him, too. He just couldn't make this easy on her. Oh, no. He had to make her do it all.

Abby felt too antsy to remain seated. Grunting a little, she pushed herself to her feet. She went over to the glass door that looked out on a central courtyard. It was a gray day. Shrinking patches of snow sat on the tops of the hedges and on the grass, as well.

"Abby?"

She made herself face him. "I'd like to forget it, that's all."

"Forget it?"

What was the matter with him? He knew what they were talking about.

She spoke with exaggerated patience. "Yes. I'd like to forget the agreement. I'd like to go on from here as if we'd never made any bargain at all. I'd like to stay married come July."

He was sitting forward on the couch, watching her. But she couldn't read his look. She had no idea what he might be thinking.

"Well?" she demanded after about a half a century had elapsed without him saying a single word. "I told you what *I* think. What about what *you* think?"

He stood. "Abby…"

She wrapped her arms around her huge belly and hugged herself, feeling lost and ungainly. And faintly nauseated. Her stomach ached suddenly, a dull, inflamed kind of pain. Dr. McClary had been right. All the stress had started to catch up with her. She made herself breathe deeply and told herself she would not feel angry at Cash because he was behaving just as she'd feared he would behave if she dared to broach this subject with him.

He approached her cautiously. She watched him come through wary eyes. Gently, he reached for her. She let him pull her close, her anger draining off a little in the comfort of his embrace.

"I think we should wait to decide on this."

She leaned her head against his shoulder. "Wait for what?"

"Until after the baby's born and you're more yourself."

She pulled back and scoffed, "Oh, please. I may look like I swallowed a watermelon, but I'm still the same person I've always been. I'm not going to be any more *me* after the baby's born."

"I think you know what I mean. You're eight months pregnant."

"So? My brain still functions. I still know what I want."

"I'd just rather wait to make any permanent decisions, that's all. Until the baby's born and you're absolutely sure of how you feel."

"I *am* sure. I just told you that. If there's anyone who's not sure here, it isn't me." She stepped back then, out of the circle of his arms.

"Abby, don't get all worked up."

The baby chose that moment to kick against her ribs. "Ow!" She grabbed her side.

"Abby..." He reached for her again.

And she let him gather her close. "I'm fine." She leaned into his embrace. "I just got a little boot in the ribs from you know who, that's all." She turned so his arms encircled her from behind. Then she took his hand and put it where he could feel the movement.

He chuckled. "Whoa, there. The kid's got a wicked punch."

"Yeah. Tell him to stop it."

Cash said nothing, only tenderly rubbed the spot. Abby allowed her body to relax more fully against him. Her stomachache and the feeling of nausea faded.

After rocking her lazily for a moment, Cash kissed her neck. Then he whispered in her ear. "Why don't you sit down and put your feet up for a while? I'll get back to packing things up."

In spite of his tender tone, she knew what he was telling her: the conversation was over.

And nothing had changed.

Abby felt drained. She looked around at all the open packing boxes, most of them still waiting to be filled. There was so much to do. Lately, there was always so much to do.

She murmured wearily, "I should be helping."

"Just rest for a little while. Please."

She let him lead her back to the sofa, where he propped her up against the armrest, with two pillows at her back and her legs stretched out along the cushions. "Comfortable?" he asked.

She nodded.

He kissed her on the nose and returned to the bedroom. Abby settled back among the pillows, trying not to feel sad. And trying not to let herself think that her husband had no desire at all to make their marriage last.

Chapter Eleven

They left for home the next day, early in the morning.

To Abby, the drive seemed interminable. Her back ached a little and the baby kept moving, poking her from the inside every time she just about got comfortable. Cash was wonderful the whole way, saying nice things to her while she muttered complaints and squirmed against the pillow she'd used to cushion her lower back. He insisted they stop every hour on the hour so that she could go to the bathroom and move around a little.

She bore the stops with bad humor, though she knew they were good for her. She didn't want to stop. She just wanted to get there. For some reason, all of a sudden, her bladder had decided to give her a break. She had to go to the rest room only once during the entire trip.

They arrived in Medicine Creek late on Saturday afternoon. Mrs. Helm, the cook-housekeeper, had been warned of their arrival and had left homemade soup and bread for them to heat up. Abby had very little appetite. She ate a few spoonfuls of soup and then got ready for bed.

Cash called the ranch from the bedroom as soon as Abby was settled in among the pillows. After he'd talked briefly to Zach, he handed her the phone. Abby spoke with her mother, who had driven to the ranch with Tess and Jobeth the day before.

Edna sounded happy and excited at the prospect of the holiday. "Tess and Jobeth went out today to collect cedar boughs. We decorated every mantel and banister with them. They're so festive, and they really make the place feel like Christmas. And you should see the tree. It's beautiful, honey. Tess has done so much. She is amazing. She put up the tree yesterday, right after we got here. And you won't believe the menu for the dinner she's preparing Christmas Day."

"I can't wait," Abby said dryly.

"The Panklevys quit." Sandy and Bill Panklevy had hired on at the ranch not long after Edna became ill. Sandy had been filling Edna's shoes.

"What will Zach do?"

"He'll hire someone else, of course. And that Sandy wasn't worth yesterday's coffee grounds anyway. Did you see a sign of her at Thanksgiving? No, because she and Bill had to take a week's vacation, that's why. And she has not kept the place up, not at all. Tess has been cleaning and cleaning."

"Tell Zach he shouldn't take advantage of her."

"Don't worry. I did. Tess will be getting a nice little bonus in her Christmas stocking. And guess what? Nate arrived this afternoon."

Abby grinned. "Cash said that he would, remember?"

"Well, Cash was right. I just can't wait for you two to get here. Then we'll all be together." A silence followed, then she added softly, "Except for your father. Oh, I do wish he could be here with us."

"Me, too."

"But I'm finding that it's not as bad as I thought it would be, this first Christmas without him."

"I'm glad."

"How are *you* feeling?"

Not so great, Abby thought. "Fine," she said.

"You've been pushing too hard, haven't you? I can tell by your voice. Honestly, what in the world possessed you to even attempt going to college at a time like this in your life? I don't understand it. I will never understand it."

"Mom. It's finished now."

"And you'll stay home, where you belong."

"I will. I promise." At least until next fall, she added silently.

"Well," her mother said. "Thank the Lord for small favors. And now that you're home, I can see to it that you get your rest."

"I'm counting on you to do just that," Abby said with some irony.

The irony was lost on Edna. "Good. After all, we're only a few blocks away from each other. And I'm feeling so much better lately. I can be with you whenever you need me."

"Thanks, Mom."

"Oh, well. What is a mother for?"

They spoke for a few more minutes and then Abby said she had to go.

"See you tomorrow," Edna chirped happily, and hung up.

Abby reached over and put the phone back in its cradle on the nightstand. Then she kissed Cash and snuggled down for sleep.

She felt better in the morning, though Cash said her face looked puffy. She remembered Dr. McClary's warning and considered calling Dr. Pruitt, even though it was Sunday—and Christmas Eve, to boot. But she put it off until after breakfast, and it seemed to her that after she got up and moved around a little, her face looked just fine.

They reached the ranch at a little before eleven. Edna came out to greet them. At the sight of Abby, she frowned. "You look terrible."

"Gee, thanks, Mom."

"Your face seems swollen."

"I tried to tell her that," Cash said from the back of the Blazer, where he was hauling out their bags. "She says she feels fine."

"I do," Abby said.

"You've pushed yourself too hard," Edna insisted. "It's written all over you. Have you seen Dr. Pruitt?"

"We just got in yesterday."

"Well, you'll see him right away, won't you?"

"The day after tomorrow, I promise."

Edna put her arm around Abby. "You come inside this minute and lie down." She cast an accusatory glance at the gathering black clouds overhead. "It's freezing out here and it's going to snow."

"Mom, the weather isn't my fault."

"I know, I know. Come on. I don't want you out in this."

Abby went along willingly, glad to be home and rather enjoying having her mother fuss over her.

"We'll put you right to bed," Edna said once they got inside.

"No way."

"But—"

Cedar boughs decorated the long table in the front hall. Abby grinned in pleasure at the Christmasy scent of them. "I'll lie on the sofa."

"But I think you—"

"Mom," Abby said sternly.

Edna let out a huff of air. "Oh, all right. Have it your way."

"Thank you. I will." Nate appeared in the entrance to the formal living room, which they hardly ever used. Abby held out her arms. "Nathan, you're really here!"

He enfolded her in a big hug. "It's good to see you, Pint-Size. *All* of you." The baby chose that moment to kick. Nate jumped back and looked down at Abby's huge stomach. "What was that?"

Cash spoke from behind her, on his way toward the central stairway with their suitcases. "The next Muhammad Ali. How's it goin', Cousin?"

"Can't complain."

Edna pulled Abby into the great room and over to a long, fat flowered sofa beneath the windows on the north wall. "This makes into a bed. Isn't that convenient?"

"Forget it, Mom. I'll lie there, but it stays a sofa."

"You are so stubborn."

"I am not going to bed in the middle of the great room."

"All right, all right. Sit down, then. And put your feet up." Abby lowered herself to the sofa, then Edna knelt in front of her and slid off her shoes. "We'll just make you comfortable...."

The tall tree stood opposite the windows and the sofa. A thousand ornaments, some of them generations old, winked at Abby from the green branches. Brightly wrapped gifts were piled knee-high around the base. "Oh, Mom, you were right. The tree looks fabulous."

"These ankles are swollen."

"Don't nag, Mom. Please?"

"All right, all right." Edna was arranging Abby the way she wanted her, with her feet along the cushions, her legs covered with an afghan and her back against a nest of pillows, when Tess came in through the central hall from the kitchen and breakfast room.

"Abby, how are you?"

Abby looked up into Tess's beautiful dark eyes. "Just fine. But Mom won't stop fussing over me."

"Isn't that what moms are for?"

"Oh, I suppose so." Abby looked at her mother, so busy tucking in the afghan and plumping pillows, fixing everything just so. When she glanced up, she saw that Tess was watching Edna, too. In Tess's face, Abby saw humor and affection. Perhaps even love.

Tess looked up, and into Abby's eyes once more. Abby had the strangest feeling right then. A *sisterly* sort of feeling.

Tess grinned at her, a conspiratorial grin.

Abby couldn't help it. Even if the woman *was* perfect and possibly in love with Cash, Abby liked her. A lot.

"How about a cup of tea?" Tess suggested.

"You twisted my arm."

"Is it decaffeinated?" Edna asked anxiously. "She doesn't need any caffeine. Just look at her."

"Decaffeinated tea," Tess said. "Coming right up." She turned back toward the hall just as Cash came down the stairs. "Cash," she said. "It's good to see you."

Cash gave her a hug, then stepped back. "Merry Christmas."

"Yes, Merry Christmas."

"Where's Jobeth?"

"Where do you think? Out with Zach, probably pulling a calf out of a ditch or something equally exciting."

Cash laughed. "A born rancher, that kid."

"I do believe so."

Abby watched this innocuous exchange with eagle eyes—and couldn't drum up a shred of suspicion. Tess and Cash smiled at each other like old friends and nothing more. Cash turned for the front door to go and bring in the Christmas presents, while Tess continued on toward the kitchen.

Not too much later, Zach and Jobeth appeared, half-frozen and splattered with mud.

"We pulled a bull out of a ditch," Jobeth announced proudly.

Tess, who'd just come in with Abby's tea, couldn't resist a knowing laugh.

"What's so funny?"

"Nothing, nothing..."

"That bull didn't seem too grateful," Jobeth added. "He tried to kick Zach."

"He was just being a bull," Zach said.

"You. Bath. Now," Tess said to her daughter.

Jobeth scrunched up her nose, but headed for the stairs.

"I suppose you expect me to clean up, too," Zach said.

Tess looked him up and down. "It certainly wouldn't hurt."

"I'm going, I'm going," Zach said. He turned and followed Jobeth up the stairs.

Abby watched Zach go, remembering how Cash had brushed aside her suggestion that Zach and Tess might get together. Cash was just too cynical; Tess and Zach would make a perfect couple.

Outside, it had started to snow. Abby watched the flakes whirl and dance beyond the window, coming down harder as each moment passed. "It looks like a mean one out there."

"But we're in here, all safe and warm," Edna said contentedly from over by the old stereo, where she was thumbing through the records. "Ah. Bing Crosby. 'White Christmas.' Just what I was looking for." She put the record on the turntable and Christmas music filled the air.

The snow kept up all the rest of that day, so everyone stayed inside, drinking hot cider, playing board games and visiting. Tess laid out a lunch of chili and corn bread that Nate said was the best he'd ever tasted. For dinner, Tess served them a savory venison stew.

In spite of the wonderful food, Abby couldn't drum up much of an appetite. Edna chided her for not eating. Tess asked if maybe she'd like soup or something lighter.

"Will you two stop fussing over me?" Abby complained. She felt just a little agitated, uncomfortable in her own skin.

Edna clucked her tongue and tucked the afghan around Abby's legs again. Tess went off to get more tea.

Again, Abby went to bed early. She was sure that by tomorrow, with another good night's rest, she would feel just fine.

But instead, she awoke in the middle of the night with an aching belly and a pounding head.

Abby groaned and pushed the covers down. It was too hot in the bed. And her skin felt so strange, all itchy and prickly.

She turned to her other side, moaning a little in the process, hoping the change in position might soothe her headache and make her stomach stop hurting.

"Abby, what is it?" Cash asked out of the darkness beside her.

She knew at that moment that she would throw up. She shoved back the covers the rest of the way and windmilled her feet, groping her way out of the bed.

"Abby?"

Her feet found the soft bedside rug. With an agonized moan, she pushed herself to a standing position and headed for the bathroom, which was two doors away.

"Abby…"

She heard him jump from the bed, but she didn't dare turn to him or open her mouth to answer. Pressing her lips together, willing the nausea down, she shuffled along, one hand under her stomach for support. As soon as she made it into the hall, she used her other hand to drag the wall. That kept her from falling down—and helped her to find the way through the dark. The pain in her stomach doubled her over, though her distended belly didn't give her much room to bend.

At last, she came to the door of the bathroom. The

white porcelain of the commode glowed at her fuzzily through the dark. She shuffled toward it.

"Abby?"

She waved a hand behind her, the best she could do for him right then.

"Let me help you." And his strong arms were there, supporting her, guiding her down over the basin.

What little she'd eaten came up. Cash held her shoulders, kept her hair out of the way.

When it was over, she didn't feel much better.

Cash found a washcloth on the edge of the sink. He ran water on it, wrung it out and then stroked it gently over her face. It felt cool. "Abby, my God," he whispered as he rubbed the cool cloth on her too-hot skin. "What's going on? You're burning up."

She leaned back against the side of the bathtub, panting, her stomach still aching and her head pounding evilly. "Something's wrong. I…" She closed her eyes, moaned, clutched her aching belly.

"Abby?"

She forced her eyes open, wanting to see him, to look at his beloved face in the soft glow from the nightlight next to the sink counter. He knelt before her, holding that soothing washcloth. She could make out the shape of him. But he didn't look right. He looked…

Her belly cramped again. "Cash. I…my stomach. Hurts so bad."

"Are you in labor?"

"No. Not like that. It's really my stomach, not…the baby. And my head. My head aches like the devil. My whole body feels awful, all itchy and…bad…."

"All right. I'll call emergency. Get you some help." He started to stand.

She reached out and grabbed his arm, thinking of the

storm outside, wondering where that help would come from. "Cash. There's more."

"God, Abby. What?"

"Everything's blurry. I...can't see very well."

"Cash? Abby?"

It was Tess's voice, coming from the doorway that led out to the hall.

"What's happened?"

She must have flicked on the light, because all of a sudden, the room seemed to explode into brightness.

"Turn it off!" Abby cried in a torn whisper that echoed in her head like a shout. "It hurts! Turn it off now!"

The room plunged back into blessed darkness once more.

Cash said, "Tess. Help us. She's vomiting. Her vision's blurry."

"And my head. It hurts so much...."

"I'll call emergency," Tess said.

Abby heard the soft thuds of her slippered feet running down the hall. She held on to Cash. "What about the storm? We'll never get out."

"Shh." He rocked her, held her so close, against his heart. "You'll be all right. I swear to you. You will be fine."

She pushed at him. Even the comfort he offered caused her pain. "Oh, Cash. The baby. The poor baby...."

"Shh. Quiet. Breathe. Relax."

She tried to listen to him, but she was so terrified. "Dr. McClary said I had to watch my blood pressure. He talked about toxemia. About how I should be careful."

"Toxemia? You never said anything about that."

"I know, I know. There was so much going on. And my blood pressure wasn't that high. I was sure it was nothing. Oh, Cash, what if—"

"Shh. I mean it. Breathe slowly. And relax."

It seemed like an eternity before Tess came back. But at last, she appeared again, a fuzzy shape in the doorway.

"They said the storm's broken up enough that they can send out the helicopter. They said to make her comfortable until they can get here."

"How long?" Cash demanded.

"Within an hour, they said."

Abby closed her eyes, against her own blurry sight, against the pain inside her head, against her whole body, which seemed to imprison her, itching and aching and hot. To her, an hour sounded like forever. She pressed her hand against her belly, where her innocent baby slept.

"Hold on," she whispered fervently. "Just hold on. For an hour...."

Chapter Twelve

Cash and Tess brought Abby downstairs to the great room to wait for help. They made her as comfortable as possible on the big sofa, which they opened up to a bed.

Nate and Zach appeared just as Tess had finished putting on fresh sheets and Cash was helping Abby to lie down. As yet, Edna and Jobeth remained in their rooms. Cash hoped to keep it that way, though he knew that was probably impossible.

"What's going on?" Zach asked quietly.

Tess calmly explained what had happened.

They all tried to keep their voices down, not only in the hope that Edna and Jobeth wouldn't wake, but also because loud noises hurt Abby's ears.

"They're ringing," Abby fretted. "My ears are ringing...."

Only one lamp burned in the room, turned down

very low, since bright light caused her real pain. Tess tried to get her to drink a little warm broth, but Abby swore she would throw up again if she tried to get anything down.

A few minutes after they got her settled on the sofa bed, she had some kind of seizure. Her body flailed and twitched. It took all four of them to keep her from hurting herself. Finally, after what seemed a grim eternity to Cash, the seizure passed.

Soon after that, Abby got the dry heaves. When that was over, she slumped to the pillows, weak and feverish, hardly able to open her eyes.

Cash bathed her forehead with a cool cloth. Her lashes fluttered open. She forced a wan smile. "Cash?"

"I'm here."

"Kinda messed up, didn't I?"

"Shh. No, you didn't. You didn't mess up. Not one damn bit."

He was the one who'd messed up. From the first. He'd taken her innocence and put a baby inside her. And then he'd insisted that she go back to college. He'd seen himself as so damn noble, doing that. Making sure she got on with her education, in spite of what he'd done to her. Not even thinking that there was only so much one smart, scrappy woman could take. He'd ordered her to push herself. And so she had pushed herself.

And now, she would die for it. The way his mother had died all those years ago having his baby sister, who had died, as well.

"Cash?"

He looked down at her, hating himself, wishing only that there were some way he could switch places with her.

She whispered, "You're...good husband. Want you to know...love you...."

"God, Abby...."

"Just tell me...do you love me, too?"

It wasn't a big enough word for what he felt. Not by a long shot. Still, if she wanted to hear it, he would give it to her. "I do, Abby. I love you...." He couldn't be sure if she heard him. Her eyelids fluttered shut as he started to say it. She didn't open them again.

Tess put her hand on his shoulder. "You should get dressed. So you'll be ready when they come."

"Watch her."

"I will."

He flew up the stairs, yanked off the pajama bottoms he slept in and pulled on jeans, socks, boots and a sweater. Then he ran back down.

"Is she...?"

Tess put a finger to her lips. "She's resting."

He sat down on the edge of the mattress. Tess handed him the cloth she'd just dipped in cool water. He bathed his wife's hot forehead—and listened so hard for the sound of a helicopter outside that his ears hurt.

Twenty minutes later, they heard the beating of the blades as the copter set down out in the yard. Abby went into convulsions again just as Tess was letting the two EMTs in the front door.

Cash, Zach and the EMTs surrounded her. "Hold her gently, very gently," one of the EMTs said evenly as he pressed an oxygen mask over her face. "Just keep her from hurting herself. That's what we want to do now."

The other EMT expertly drew fluid from a vial into

a hypodermic syringe. "Hold her arm," he said to Zach. "Hold it absolutely still."

When the seizure finally passed, Abby lay unconscious. They took her blood pressure. If it had been high before, now it was dangerously low.

"We need to get her to the hospital in Billings right away," one of the EMTs said. "It's a tertiary care center. They have the facilities there to deal with this."

Cash stared at Abby, who lay there so frighteningly still. He turned to the man who'd just spoken. "I'm going with you."

"You're the husband?"

"Yeah. I'm the husband."

The man studied Cash, then shrugged. "Normally, we don't allow it. But you'd be hours getting there through all the snow. You can ride up front with the pilot."

"Fine. Thanks," Cash said, then couldn't help adding, "she's out cold. Is she…okay?"

The second EMT, who'd just come in with the stretcher, muttered something about a coma.

Cash turned on him, grabbed him by his down jacket. The rolled-up stretcher clattered to the floor. "What the hell did you say?"

The first man shouted, "Stop!"

Cash froze, then let go of the second man's jacket.

The first man said, "Look. Now's not the time for explanations. Or for you to be losing it. It's our job to get this woman and her baby to the help she needs. Do you understand?"

"Yeah," Cash said, breathing deep. "Sorry."

"We can't take you if you'll be a problem."

"I won't. I swear it."

Edna chose that moment to appear from upstairs.

"What is going on? Abby? Oh, no. Not my little girl...." She started for Abby.

Tess went right to her, embracing her—and, at the same time, keeping her from getting in the way. "It's all right. The helicopter's here. They're taking her to the hospital now."

"But what's happened?"

Tess led Edna to a chair. "Here. Sit down. I'll explain everything we know so far."

Cash realized he'd forgotten his wallet. Grateful that Tess was dealing with Edna, he ran up the stairs. He grabbed his wallet and a jacket. When he got back down to the main floor, they'd already taken Abby out to the helicopter.

"We'll get there as fast as we can," Nate promised.

"Fine," Cash said on his way out the door. "Look out for Edna."

"You know we will."

As it turned out, Cash found the helicopter flight the most bearable part of what followed. They were moving, at least, through the darkness, above the white, cold land. Moving fast toward the hospital where Abby could get help.

Things got unbearable pretty quickly once they got there. After filling out a ream of paperwork, Cash had to do what he hated doing: he waited. He drank machine coffee and sat. When he couldn't stand sitting, he paced. He realized later that the doctors had worked like demons and that he really hadn't waited that long at all—it only seemed like it.

Finally, a doctor came out and explained to him about Abby's condition: eclampsia, it was called.

"It's what we once called pregnancy-induced toxemia,'' the doctor said. "And nowadays, it's rare. Especially in a case like your wife's, where there's been adequate prenatal care, no indications of trouble during the pregnancy and no family history of high blood pressure. I will say that it occurs more often in young, first-time mothers, like your wife. And as has happened with your wife, it tends to strike very suddenly, in the last trimester.''

"How is she?"

"At this point, she remains unconscious, but stable.''

"The baby?"

"The baby seems fine."

"Seems?"

"We've conducted an ultrasound. And a stress test. We have no indications of fetal distress.''

"And?"

"I understand that the pregnancy is thirty-six weeks along.''

"That's right.''

"How confident are you of that figure?"

"Very confident."

"All right, then. At thirty-six weeks, the lungs are mature enough that the child should have no trouble surviving outside the womb. As you may have deduced, the only way to help your wife is to deliver the baby.''

"So deliver it. Deliver it now."

"We intend to. However, your wife's body shows no signs of labor. Dilation and effacement are minimal. And we feel that to induce labor with the mother unconscious is not advisable.''

Cash remembered a word from those classes he'd gone to with Abby. "A C-section?"

"Yes. It's the wisest course in this case. And cesarean procedures are quite safe nowadays. An incision will be made in the lower abdomen, through to the uterus."

Cash thought of them cutting into Abby and felt sick to his stomach. The doctor was still talking.

"The baby will be removed, and the incision closed up. Recovery takes a little longer than from a vaginal delivery, but for most women who have a cesarean, vaginal delivery of future babies is possible."

Cash didn't give a damn about future deliveries. As far as he was concerned, there wouldn't be any of those. "Fine. Do what you have to do."

"Good enough."

"When?"

"Immediately. We'll have some papers for you to sign and then we'll go ahead."

"Get the papers."

The doctor turned.

"Wait a minute."

The doctor stopped, turned back. "Yes?"

"She's in a...coma, isn't she?"

The doctor hesitated, then admitted, "Yes. I'm afraid so."

"You said she'd get better as soon as the baby's born. That means she'll wake up, right?"

"Yes. She should."

"She *should*?"

"In most cases—"

"Just tell me. Will she wake up?"

The doctor sighed. "The prognosis is good."

"That means yes."

"Yes. With reservations."

"What reservations?"

"Mr. Bravo, there are no guarantees in a situation like this one."

At first, they tried to tell him he couldn't be there for the operation. But he remembered what he'd learned in those childbirth classes. Fathers were often present during cesarean births.

"But the mother is not usually unconscious," the doctor argued.

"If she wakes up, she'll want me there."

"Mr. Bravo, she won't wake up. She'll be under a general anesthetic."

"A general anesthetic? But I thought—"

The doctor sighed. "We do often use spinal blocks when performing C-sections. But not in the case of eclampsia. Spinal blocks can lower blood pressure and your wife's blood pressure is too low already."

"Fine. Whatever. I want to be there. I *will* be there. I'll stay out of the way and I'll keep myself in hand."

In the end, they allowed it.

The surgery took place in a rectangular room, with the operating table in the center and bright lights above it. Cash saw a long table against one wall. And counters and sinks lining another wall. There was more, of course, much more: cabinets filled with equipment, machines and trays of instruments that Cash couldn't name.

Abby lay unmoving on the center table, draped in hospital green, hooked up to a number of machines that the surgery nurse explained would monitor her vital signs through the procedure. Several drapes hung from tracks on the ceiling, surrounding Abby's abdomen. There was a screen on wheels, which they placed at Abby's shoulder level. Cash stared at that screen, wondering what the hell it was for. And then he understood: as long as he didn't go around it, he wouldn't have to see what they were doing to her.

That was just fine with him. He'd stick with the top half of her. He'd promised to hold it together, and he would. But he could use all the help he could get.

He asked to be able to hold her hand. They said it would be okay. So he clutched her limp fingers in his rubber-gloved fist and prayed silently that she would be all right.

Once the anesthesiologist gave the go-ahead, the operation began. Cash stayed beside his wife, holding her hand, as the doctor on the other side of the screen described every move he made.

It didn't take that long. Cash heard a baby's cry.

"Look at those shoulders," the doctor said in satisfaction. "Mr. Bravo, you have a son."

Cash thought he'd sell his soul for a cigarette. "A son?" he repeated, as if the word were new to him.

"Yes," said the doctor. "A fine, healthy son."

Cash bent close to Abby and whispered through the mask they'd made him wear. "It's a boy. We have a little boy, and he's fine." He knew she couldn't hear him, but he didn't care.

Behind him, Cash could hear the baby crying. A nurse had carried him to the table against the side wall, where the process of examining, weighing and initial cleaning up took place. Through this, the baby cried louder than before. Cash clutched Abby's hand and told himself she would be okay as, on the other side of the screen, the doctor began the work of sewing her belly up again.

At last, after several minutes, the examining nurse

confirmed the doctor's diagnosis: the baby was whole and sound.

"Would you like to hold him, Mr. Bravo?"

Cash laid Abby's hand gently down and turned.

The nurse held out a tiny, squalling red thing, which she'd already wrapped up to keep it warm.

"Just for a moment," she said.

Even though a mask covered her mouth, he could see her smile in the crinkles around her eyes.

Cash backed up a step, and came up short when he hit the operating table on which Abby lay. He stared at the bundle in the nurse's arms.

And all at once he was fifteen again, and the tiny red thing was Abby. And Ty was there, grinning.

"Come on, hold this pint-size little thing. Don't you be shy, Cash. She won't break. She's gonna be a tough one—I can feel it in my bones. Tough, and beautiful, too. What more could a daddy ask for in his child?"

"Come on, Mr. Bravo," the nurse said. Cash could hear the warmth and humor in her voice. "Hold your baby. Here you go."

Cash opened his arms, hardly knowing now from then. And the nurse put the squalling bundle in them.

He looked into the wrinkled face. The crying stopped. And the blue eyes met his, so wise, so watchful.

"Tyler," Cash said, as the name came into his head. "For your grandpa on your mama's side. And Ross— for your great-grandpa on my side. Welcome to the world, Tyler Ross." Cash turned to Abby, grinning. "What do you think? Tyler Ross."

His grin quickly faded as he remembered that Abby couldn't hear him. She lay on that metal table, as still and quiet as the grave.

"A Christmas baby," the nurse murmured from behind him.

Cash looked up at the big institutional clock on the far wall. It was four in the morning. On Christmas Day.

He had a flash of the tree in the great room that Tess had decorated with such care. And all the presents under it. By the time he'd put the gifts he and Abby had brought under there, too, the presents had overflowed across the floor. Abby had bought so damn many, and insisted on wrapping every one herself.

"Christmas babies bring good luck," the nurse said.

Cash looked down at Abby once more. "I just hope to holy hell that you're right."

As soon as he left the operating room, Cash called the ranch. Zach answered. Cash gave his cousin the news and learned that Edna and Nate were on their way.

Eventually, when they had Abby settled into a room, they let him be with her. The room wasn't the same one that Edna had stayed in; it had a different number on the door. But it looked identical, with one tiny window, a white curtain that could be pulled around the bed and a single chair. The half bath, as in Edna's room, could be entered through a door about eight feet from the end of the bed.

Cash pulled up the chair so he could sit by the bed. He took his wife's slim hand and just looked at it. He thought about all the times he'd looked at it before, from when she was a baby and it had wrapped around his index finger, holding tight, through her childhood when it was always dirty and always grabbing for something she wasn't supposed to have.

More recently, he remembered that hand reaching

up, pulling him down for a kiss. And holding that menu, in that Italian place in Denver, just before that kid her own age had walked in, confronting him with his own scary jealousy—and reminding him once more of all he had stolen from her: her youth, and her freedom....

God help him, let it not be her life, as well.

He closed his eyes, rubbed them. The room seemed lighter, somehow. He turned toward the window. Out there, dawn was breaking. But inside him, it seemed there was nothing but endless night.

He laid his head down on the bed, beside her. Still holding her hand, he closed his eyes.

"Cash?"

He lifted his head. Edna was smiling down at him. He raked a hand through his hair, rubbed the back of his neck. "Sorry. Must have dropped off...."

She put her hand on his shoulder. "Nate and I are here now. We'll sit with her. You go get some food into your stomach."

"No. I don't want to leave her."

"Go on. You have to eat. And you can come right back."

"Did they tell you about the baby?"

"We've already seen him." In spite of the worry lines between her brows, there was real joy in her voice. "My grandson is a fine-looking boy."

"I named him. Tyler Ross Bravo."

Edna's eyes filled. She had to bite her lower lip to tame the tears. "Perfect," she said.

Cash turned to Abby, where she lay so pale against the pillows. "Do you think she'll like that name?"

"She will love it."

"She hasn't woken up yet. She's supposed to wake up. Soon. If she moves or makes a sound—anything—we have to call the nurse right away."

"Go get some food and coffee," Nate said from where he stood by the door. "We'll watch while you're gone."

Cash knew they were right. He should eat, walk around a little, maybe look in on Tyler Ross. "All right." He stood, then he glanced at his watch: after nine. "How was the drive up here?"

"Don't ask," Nate replied grimly. "There are two new feet of snow on the ground. We made it. That's what matters."

Edna sank into the chair Cash had vacated, and took up the hand that he had set down.

"If she moves—" he began.

"Go," Nate said. "We're here. We'll look out for her."

Cash went to the cafeteria, where he drank two cups of coffee and forced down some eggs and toast. Then he visited a rest room, where he splashed cold water on his face, rinsed his mouth and combed his hair. After that, he made a stop at the nursery, where they let him hold Tyler Ross. He was back in Abby's room within half an hour of the time that he'd left.

"Any change?" he asked hopefully.

Edna just shook her head.

Nate had talked the nurses into getting them two more chairs. They settled in for the vigil.

It was a vigil that lasted eight more hours, hours that seemed like years to Cash.

Then, at five-thirty in the afternoon, Cash felt Abby's hand move in his. He looked at her face.

And her eyes slowly opened. "Cash?"

He squeezed her hand. "I'm here, Abby. I'm right here."

Chapter Thirteen

"They do say mother's milk is best," Edna remarked in a tone of loving disapproval.

They were sitting in the living room at Edna's house. Abby looked up from her son, who was sucking happily at his bottle. "Well, now, Mom. Tyler seems to like this bottle just fine."

"He'll be colicky. *You* were colicky, even though I kept you on the breast for a full year, just the way all the books said."

"Tyler's six weeks old now. Not a sign of colic."

"Sometimes it comes on late. And allergies. Bottle-fed babies always develop more allergies."

Tyler drained the bottle and let go of the nipple with a rude little pop. Then he burped loudly and his mouth stretched wide in what his mama chose to think of as a great big smile. Abby bent down and kissed him, then looked up at her own mother again. "You know, Mom, there's really no point in talking about this. Your grandson's a bottle-fed baby. That is not going to change.''

"Well, for the next one..."

Abby let out a groan. "Mom. Let's not start planning the next one yet, okay? I'm just getting used to this one." She smoothed a diaper on her shoulder, lifted Tyler Ross and gently set him there. After a moment or two of gentle pats, he burped again. "There," Abby said. "That's better, isn't it?"

Edna watched adoringly. "You astonish me."

"Why?"

"You're so relaxed. You're going to be a good mother."

"I'm *already* a good mother. And you don't have to act so surprised about it."

"Well, but you know how you always were. More interested in horses and math books than in dolls. And you always swore that being a homebody wasn't for you."

"I'm still not a homebody."

"You know what I mean. You swore you'd never get married and have children. But now here you are, a wife and mother. And you're just a natural with that baby. I don't know how you do it. I remember with you I could hardly enjoy myself. I was always nervous, trying to do everything right."

"Well, you know me. No chance of doing everything right anyway, so I might as well relax."

Edna actually chuckled. And then she frowned once more. "But I do worry, about our Tyler not getting all the benefits of breast feeding."

"Edna, stop it." Tess had appeared from the kitchen, carrying a coffee tray. "Tyler's doing just great. Look at him." She stared, dreamy eyed, at the baby in Abby's arms.

Abby let out another groan. "Tess, you've got that silly look on your face again."

"I can't stop myself. He's so adorable." Tess carried her coffee tray into the room and set it on the low table in front of the sofa. "Let me hold him."

Abby held out her son. Tess gathered him close. "Oh, he feels so good." She cooed and rocked the baby a little, then she grinned at Abby. "I always wanted about a hundred of these."

"Better get to work."

"Abigail," Edna chided.

Tess and Abby shared a laugh, then Tess sat on the end of the sofa and cuddled with Tyler, as Edna poured the coffee and passed it around.

"When is your six-week checkup?" Edna asked.

"Tomorrow, 9 a.m. sharp," Abby said with a little flutter of anticipation. She hoped to get a clean bill of health at last, because she had plans. For herself and Cash. Very intimate plans.

She and Cash needed a little intimacy. Lately, it seemed to Abby that he'd become somewhat distant with her. He'd been absolutely incredible through her illness. But in the past few weeks, since she'd been feeling so much better, he was forever on his way somewhere. He would make a point to help with Tyler, getting up for night feedings and even changing a diaper or two. But he never seemed to have much time to spend with Abby alone—except when both of them were sleeping.

Abby understood, of course. He had his business deals to catch up on, and though Tyler was easygoing for a newborn, he'd still managed to change their lives in a thousand ways.

Abby felt that what she and Cash needed was a good shot of romance. The married kind, in their bed. And in their whirlpool bath. And in a number of other locations she could think of without a great deal of effort.

All the books said that they could have romance right now—just not actual intercourse. But with Cash so preoccupied, Abby hadn't found the way to approach him about those other kinds of lovemaking. She felt more confident that she could bridge the distance between them if she knew they could just do whatever came naturally.

So she wanted that okay from Dr. Pruitt. She wanted it a lot.

"You've recovered so quickly," her mother said. "It's a miracle, really."

"Dr. Pruitt says that in cases like mine, as soon as the baby's delivered, the mother usually improves right away—as long as she received help in time, I mean."

"Oh, you were so fortunate."

"I know. I had Cash. And Tess." Abby looked at the woman across the coffee table, who was cooing and gurgling just like the baby. Tess stopped cooing long enough to give Abby an affectionate smile.

"Well," Edna said, "even if you feel better now, it's nothing to fool with."

"I'm not fooling with it, Mom. I promise. I'm taking good care of myself." She sat up straight and drew her shoulders back proudly. "This morning, my blood pressure was 120 over 60."

"That's good," Edna admitted.

"It's better than good. It's terrific. Now, if I can just get my stomach back in shape."

Tess glanced up again from gumming Tyler's fingers. "One thing at a time," she said.

"I started doing stomach crunches a week ago."

"Are you crazy?" Edna asked.

"No, I am not crazy." She thought about Cash. She did want to look good for him. "Just determined."

"To hurt yourself."

"I'm not hurting myself. I'm careful. Honest. I take it slow and steady." She lowered her voice and leaned toward her mother. "And I'll be the happiest woman alive when that creepy numbness around my incision goes away."

Edna sighed. "You're just like your father. Every time he broke a bone—and he broke a lot of bones, if you recall—he would start exercising the minute the cast was off. I still remember him sitting in the kitchen of the foreman's cottage, lifting a weight on a leg that he'd broken, tears running down his face. I told him, 'Ty, the way you work that thing, you'll break it all over again.' 'No, Edna,' he says to me. 'What I'll do is make it strong.'"

"He was something," Abby said reverently.

"He was crazy," Edna declared.

Tess said, "I think we need a clean diaper here." They all looked at Tyler, who gurgled and cooed, content with the world and his place in it.

The next morning, Abby left Dr. Pruitt's office with a big smile on her face. The doctor had told her just what she wanted to hear. She was ready once more to be a wife in every way.

Abby longed to share the good news with Cash. But she would have to wait, for a little while, anyway. Cash had flown to Vegas early the day before—for a big card game, Abby suspected, though he hadn't been specific about details when he said goodbye. He was due back tomorrow afternoon. And then she'd give him the good news. She'd do it the best way: up close and personal.

At home, Abby counseled with Mrs. Helm, the cook-housekeeper, for forty-five minutes. She was taking no chances on her own cooking tomorrow night. Once they'd settled on a special menu, Mrs. Helm went out to shop for groceries. Abby took Tyler to her mother's and then drove all the way to Billings to do a little shopping of her own. She bought a sexy cocktail dress and some lingerie that was black and slinky and not meant for anyone but a husband to see. Abby thought she looked pretty good in both the dress and the lingerie—considering she'd had a baby and nearly died six weeks before.

It was after dark by the time she got home, and it had also started snowing.

"What can you be thinking of, out driving in that?" Edna complained.

Abby soothed her mother, collected her baby and went home to the big house that always seemed so empty when Cash wasn't there. But she didn't feel quite as lost and forlorn as she'd felt on the other nights recently when Cash had been gone. She had tomorrow to look forward to, after all.

She awoke in the morning all jittery and eager. When Mrs. Helm came in, Abby asked her if she could stay a little later than usual to serve the dinner.

"It shouldn't be much after eight, I promise," Abby said. "And as soon as it's on the table, you could go ahead and leave. And if you want a few hours off during the day today in exchange, that would be fine. Or

I'll pay you overtime. Whichever. It doesn't matter to me.''

"Now, now, slow down," the kindly Mrs. Helm replied. "I'll be glad to stay. It's no problem. And I think I understand what you want. A beautiful table with tempting food—and a little privacy as soon as dinner is served.''

Abby beamed. "Yes. That's it exactly. Mrs. Helm, you are an angel."

"I'll just take myself out the back way, as soon as you two are enjoying your meal."

"Oh, thank you. I can't tell you. I owe you. Big time."

Abby decided that as much as she adored her son, she didn't want him interrupting anything on this special night. So she called her mother next.

Edna was not so kindly as Mrs. Helm. "Abigail, what is going on? Yesterday, you drove to Billings in a snowstorm."

"It had just started to snow when I got home, Mother."

"And today, you want to drop your baby off with me again, this time for a whole night."

"Is that a 'no,' then? Are you telling me you won't take Tyler for the night?"

"Of course I'm not telling you that."

"Then what are you telling me?"

"I'm not telling. I'm asking. What is going on?"

Abby sighed. "Oh, all right. I want an evening alone with Cash."

After a silence, Edna murmured, "Well. Why didn't you say so?"

"Does that mean that you'll look after Tyler?"

"I'd be pleased to, honey."

Abby took Tyler to her mother's at three in the afternoon. Then she went home. At four, she sank into a scented bath from which she didn't emerge until five. Once she'd slathered lotion from head to toe and dabbed perfume at every pulse point, she dedicated an hour to fiddling with her hair and putting on her makeup. By the time she was all dressed in her sexy lingerie and new cocktail dress, it was after six—and Cash wasn't home yet.

Expecting him to walk in the door at any moment, Abby went out through the living room to the dining room, where she discovered that Mrs. Helm had outdone herself. The sight of the table made her sigh: a snowy lace tablecloth, gleaming silver and china, red roses in a cut-glass bowl and long cream-colored candles in crystal candle holders. Abby debated over whether to light the candles or not. She decided to wait until they sat down to eat.

She went to the kitchen. "Mrs. Helm, it's all just perfect." She sniffed the air, which carried the rich scent of Madeira-braised ham. "It smells like heaven in here."

Mrs. Helm turned to her. "And you look just beautiful. Mr. Bravo won't care about dinner at all once he sees you." Mrs. Helm held out a wooden spoon. "Here. Taste this."

Abby tasted. "Umm."

"More salt?"

"No. It's just right."

Abby wandered back into the dining room and then on into the living room. She put on a stack of romantic CDs and turned the lights down nice and low. Then she picked up a magazine and turned one of the lamps up a few notches so that she could read.

Half an hour later, she'd thumbed through the two *Western Horseman* magazines and the three *Architectural Digest*s on the coffee table. She got up and went to the kitchen again.

"Everything okay in here?"

Mrs. Helm smiled. "Just fine."

"Good. Terrific." She ducked out of there and went back to the living room, where yet another romantic CD was playing. She switched it off. All those strings were starting to get to her.

She went to the bedroom. The lights were low, the bedcovers turned invitingly back. Not a single article of her own clothing was strewn anywhere. All lay in readiness for the romance to come.

Only the husband was missing.

Fifteen minutes later, he called.

"Abby, I'm sorry. This is taking longer than I planned."

She could hear masculine laughter and glasses clinking in the background.

"I meant to call you earlier, but I couldn't break away."

"From what? A card game?"

"You guessed it." He sounded sheepish. "I'm on a roll. I can't quit now."

She wanted to scream at him, something shrill and hateful and totally unfair.

He asked carefully, "Abby, are you all right?"

She reminded herself that he hadn't known what she planned, that she shouldn't take her disappointment out on him. "I'm fine. When will you be home?"

"Tomorrow for certain."

Abby heard another man's voice, muffled, from his end of the line.

Then he said, "Listen, I have to go now."

She whispered, "Goodbye," but he was already gone.

She hung up very slowly. And then, for a few minutes, she just sat, her hands folded in her lap; she felt sad, disappointed and a little silly all at the same time. Finally, she dragged herself to her feet and went to the kitchen to tell Mrs. Helm that Mr. Bravo had been detained until tomorrow.

Mrs. Helm looked at her for a long moment. "Are you all right, then?"

She forced a smile. "I'm just fine."

"I'll clean things up, shall I?"

"Leave it all. Get it tomorrow."

"Let me just put the food away, then."

"Whatever you think." Abby turned to go, then stopped and turned back. "Thank you."

"You're very welcome, Mrs. Bravo."

"Just call me 'Abby.'"

Mrs. Helm promised that she would.

Abby leaned wearily on the door frame and slipped off her high-heeled shoes. Then, in stocking feet, she returned to the bedroom, where she took off her dress and her beautiful lingerie and put it all away. She washed her face and brushed her teeth.

As she climbed into the big bed alone, she couldn't help wishing that she had the nerve to go get Tyler from her mother's house. To hold his small, warm body would have been a great comfort right then. But that would only get Edna all stirred up, worrying that something was wrong.

And was it? Abby couldn't be sure. Cash was Cash, after all. He made his money gambling, whether it was poultry futures or five-card stud. She didn't expect him to show up at five-thirty every night. And she knew that, as his wife, there would be nights when she would sleep alone.

She didn't mind sleeping alone sometimes. As long as it didn't become a habit.

But her husband was a smart man. He'd read more than one book about childbirth and recovery. He'd gone through those childbirth classes with her. He knew what her six-week checkup meant. And he knew that it had taken place yesterday. She'd had it marked on the calendar since the day she got home from the hospital. And yet he'd chosen to be gone when she went in for it....

No, she had to stop thinking like this. Cash had no idea of her plans for a romantic evening. She had never told him. And she had no right to expect him to read her mind.

Still, she just couldn't shake the feeling that things weren't right between them. Things hadn't seemed right for a few weeks now.

She wanted to talk to him about it. But she didn't know quite how to broach the subject with him. And what would she say, anyway?

Are you avoiding me? Is something wrong? Are you tired of me? Are you just waiting for next July, when you can be free of me?

When she asked the questions to herself, they sounded weak and whiny. How would they sound like anything else to Cash?

And she couldn't stop thinking about the way he had reacted that other time, before they left Boulder, when she had tried to talk to him about their future as a couple. He'd made it painfully clear that he didn't want to discuss it.

Yet he had also promised that they could talk about it again after the baby came. So he had to be expecting to hear more on the subject.

Abby rolled over, punched her pillow, sighed aloud in the dark, lonely room. She just knew he wouldn't like it if she brought up the agreement again. She could feel it in her bones. Secretly, she feared that as soon as she brought it up again, she would lose him.

No. Actually, it was worse than that. In her deepest heart of hearts, she feared that she had already lost him.

At Christmas, before Tyler came, when she got so sick, she had told him that she loved him. So much else about that night was a scary blur to her now. But she remembered that moment, after the first set of convulsions had rattled through her body, when she had honestly feared she would die.

She had dared to whisper of her love. And then she had asked him if he loved her, too. He had hesitated, but then he had said it: "I do, Abby. I love you...."

She remembered his words exactly. It seemed they were engraved on her soul. Everything got fuzzy after that. She recalled no more until she woke up and learned that Tyler had been born.

But she *had* told Cash that she loved him.

And he had said that he loved her, too—which was true.

He had always loved her, *would* always love her.

But not the way she wanted to be loved. Not the way she loved him.

The past few weeks, she couldn't shake the growing conviction that the darkest fear of her childhood had come true.

She had told Cash she loved him.

And now he was going away.

Oh, he had stayed close during her illness. But now that she'd recovered, she would lose him. Because he just wasn't a marrying kind of man.

He'd given his son his name and he would see to it that his son's mother was well provided for. But other than that, he would want to be free.

And if she dared to try to talk to him about it, she would only lose him all the sooner.

Chapter Fourteen

Cash returned home the next day, as promised. But
he'd hardly walked in the door before he told Abby he
was heading out again—for San Francisco this time.
He wanted to talk to some old buddy of his about investing in a new computer chip that hadn't been put
on the market yet.

Carrying Tyler, Abby trailed after Cash into their
bedroom. She stood in the doorway, holding their son,
watching her husband as he emptied dirty clothes from
his bags.

"Cash, you just got home." She tried to sound reasonable, and thought she succeeded pretty well. "I was
hoping we could—"

"I'm sorry," he cut in without letting her finish.
"But this could be a big one. They say this chip is a
damn miracle. And if I miss out now, my chance won't
come around again."

She said nothing for a few minutes. Cash moved back and forth between the bureau and the bed, collecting clean underwear and socks. Then she tried a different approach. "I know. How about if Tyler and I go with you? You know it always helps to have me there to keep track of the numbers. And Tyler may as well get used to our traveling life-style."

Cash tossed a stack of underwear in his suitcase and turned to her. "Abby, it's not a good idea."

"Why not?"

"You've been very sick."

"But I'm fine now. I saw Dr. Pruitt day before yesterday. For my six-week checkup, remember?"

He turned for the closet and disappeared inside. When he came out, he was carrying a stack of shirts, folded and wrapped in plastic from the dry cleaner's.

Abby stroked her son's small, warm head. "Dr. Pruitt says I'm fine. Completely recovered. In every way."

"Well, that's good." Cash set the shirts in the suitcase. "But you have the baby to think of."

"I *am* thinking of him. He's coming, too, remember?"

"Abby, he's too young to be dragged all over the place." Cash headed for the closet again.

She waited for him to emerge. When he did, carrying two pairs of slacks and two jackets, she reminded him, "Your mom and dad dragged *you* all over the place, almost from the day you were born."

He marched back to the bed and tucked the slacks and jackets into a garment bag. "Tyler's not going to have that kind of life."

"Why not?"

"It's not a good life for a kid."

"You loved it. I know you loved it. You used to tell me how you loved it!"

He looked up from the garment bag, frowning. "Quiet down."

On her shoulder, Tyler was squirming. She realized her voice had become a little shrill. She patted Tyler's back and forced a low tone. "You were a happy little kid, Cash. You know you were. It was only later, when your mother died and your dad took off without you, that you—"

"All right." His tone sent a chill through her. "I was happy. And I'm going to San Francisco alone."

She rocked from side to side, rubbing Tyler's back. "We have to talk, Cash."

"Fine."

"When?"

"When I come back."

"When will that be?"

"I'm not sure. A few days. Maybe a week."

She looked at him for a long time, over the feathery newborn fuzz on their son's head. "All right, then," she said at last. "When you get back."

He returned in six days, flushed and happy, certain he'd made the deal of the century. He grabbed Abby around the waist and swung her in a circle—and her firm intention to sit down and talk with him just seemed to evaporate into the air.

Mrs. Helm served them a wonderful dinner, and afterward, they sat in the living room and talked. Tyler lay in Cash's lap, staring up at his father in what Abby would have sworn was pure adoration. Abby just couldn't bear to ruin such a lovely evening with a discussion of that awful agreement that she never, ever should have made.

Cash gave Tyler his bottle. Then, together, they put their son to bed.

After that, they went back to the living room for a while. They listened to some music and talked some more, about the computer chip deal, about how well Edna was doing. And about Tess's new job at a gift shop over on Main.

"She likes it," Abby said. "But I know she worries. She doesn't make enough to save anything. And she's bright. She wants more from life, for herself and for Jobeth, you know?"

"Yeah. I know."

"She told me she got good grades in high school."

"So?"

"If someone helped her out a little, she could go to college." Abby looked at her husband hopefully.

He shook his head. "Don't think I haven't tried. She won't take that kind of help. She considers living with Edna more charity than she should accept."

"But that's ridiculous. She's worked hard for Mom, and she understands Mom. And Mom's been so hungry for that, for another woman who puts value on what she values. It's just meant everything to her."

Cash was grinning. "Some daughters would be jealous."

Abby shrugged. "What for? Just because I admire Tess doesn't mean I want to be her. I like being me just fine."

"I can understand why."

Abby met his eyes. She saw warmth and affection. Admiration. And yes, love, too. And she was sure, at that moment, that everything would work out all right.

She stood and stretched, thinking about the diaphragm that Dr. Pruitt had prescribed for her. It waited in the cabinet in the bathroom of the master suite, along with the little tube of contraceptive jelly. Before she set about seducing her husband, she had better put the darn thing where it would do some good.

"Tired?" Cash asked.

She smiled. "Not at all. But I think I'll just go get ready for bed."

"I have a few calls to make."

Something in his voice gave her pause. An edge? A wariness?

Best not to dwell on it. "That's fine," she said tenderly. She crossed the few feet between his chair and her chair and bent to kiss him, a light but lingering kiss. "Don't be too long," she said softly when she pulled away.

"I won't."

In the bathroom, she set to work putting the diaphragm in place. After a couple of false starts, she accomplished the task. That done, she rushed back into the bedroom, yanked off all of her clothes, wadded them up and tossed them in the corner of the closet. Then she slipped on a little scrap of black satin that she'd bought on her shopping trip to Billings the week before. Over it she wrapped a matching robe.

She went out into the main part of the bedroom to wait. First, she sat in a chair. Then she stretched out on the bed.

When Cash didn't appear after about twenty minutes, she went looking for him.

She found him in the study, on the phone. His eyes widened a little when he saw what she wore. She smiled invitingly and arched a questioning brow at him.

"Just a minute," he said into the mouthpiece. He punched the "mute" button. "Abby, I'm sorry. This is going to take a while."

She felt the smile fade from her lips. "How long?"

"I can't say. Just go on to bed, all right?"

She had that same urge she'd had last week when he'd called and said he wouldn't be home—the urge to scream and throw things. She quelled it, reminding herself how great the evening had been up until now.

"Okay," she replied carefully.

"Good night," he said, with way too much finality.

Abby returned to the master suite, where she traded her sexy outfit for a big T-shirt. In the bathroom, she removed the diaphragm, washed her face and cleaned her teeth. Then she crawled between the covers and turned off the light.

She laced her fingers behind her head and stared up at the dark ceiling and wondered where she'd gone wrong.

Maybe she hadn't been direct enough. She thought of their wedding night, some of her misery fading at the memory of how beautiful it had been. That night, she'd come right out and demanded that he make love with her. And he had given in to her demand—with a good deal of enthusiasm, in the end.

But on their wedding night, he'd been committed to trying to make their marriage work. Now she kept getting the feeling that he'd done all the "trying" he intended to do. And if she pushed him, he'd simply head out the door. Fast.

Abby sat up, lay back down, turned over. And admitted to herself that lovemaking—or the lack of it—was only a symptom of the real issue here.

The real issue was their marriage—which Abby felt more and more certain would not last.

At this rate, she feared, they'd never make it until July.

The dilemma remained the same: they had to talk about their problems. But she knew in her heart that as soon as they did, he would tell her that he wanted to be free.

Fearing she'd lose him, she put off confronting him. For weeks, they lived like polite acquaintances in the big house on North Street.

Cash wasn't around that much. The computer chip deal went bad, and he flew to San Francisco to try to salvage the situation. But it turned out that the chip just didn't live up to its advance PR. Cash lost a lot of money.

He could afford it. But it didn't make him happy. He wheeled and dealed all the harder to make back what he'd lost.

Abby took all the papers from the chip deal and went over them in depth. Then she made the mistake of announcing that he'd never have made that deal if she'd been there to advise him.

"Don't ride me, Abby," was all he said in response.

She had that urge to shout at him again. But she didn't. She held it in, somehow. And she went on holding it in, though more and more often, she wanted to scream at him.

Sometimes she saw desire in his eyes when he looked at her. But he never made a move on her. And she hated him for that. Because his unwillingness to make love with her could mean only one thing: he really did intend to leave her. Cash Bravo, after all, was much too noble a man to make love with his wife when he planned to divorce her.

Abby's anger grew. He had trapped her—oh, yes, he had. She loved him and she wanted him. But as soon as she really started fighting for him, she would lose him. She knew it as she knew that the sun set over the Big Horns.

And so she held her anger in.

Until a gray day in March, when some old pal of his called from Provo with a sob story about needing the down payment on a pickup truck.

Abby peeked in the doorway of Cash's study to tell him that Mrs. Helm had dinner on the table.

He was talking on the phone. "Tell you what, Earl," he said. "You name the figure, and I'll write the check."

Abby pushed the door open and leaned against the door frame, waiting for him to look her way.

Cash listened for a minute, then chuckled. "But, Earl, I don't need to see the truck. If you want it, you buy it. I'll wire you the down, and you pay me back when you can."

Earl said something else.

Cash made a low, amused sound in his throat. "Earl, Earl. I trust your judgment. You want it, you get it. And I'm glad to help you out…. Earl. Listen." Cash let out a long breath. "All right, all right. I'll fly on down there tonight." He chuckled again. "Well, Earl. I'm not Superman, you know?" He grabbed a pencil, scribbled something on a tablet. "You're in Provo, Earl. I'll need a few hours to get there." He scribbled some more, then ripped the page off the tablet and stuck it in a pocket. "I know, I know. But I tell you what. If somebody else snaps it up, we'll find you another one. I promise we will.'' He got up from his big calfskin swivel chair. "All right. Yeah. As soon as I can.'' He put the phone down, looked up—and saw Abby. "What?''

"Dinner,'' she said with great care, a numb kind of fury rising inside her. He was leaving again. Because some guy named Earl couldn't buy a pickup truck by himself.

Cash forked a hand back through his hair. "Look. Something's come up. I have to—''

"Take the Cessna to Provo to look at a pickup truck. I heard.''

"Abby.'' His tone dripped reproach. "It's a favor. For an old friend.''

She pasted on a smile over gritted teeth. "We'll come with you, Tyler and I.''

"Don't be ridiculous. You can't drag the baby all the way to Provo just to look at a pickup truck.''

"Watch me.''

He tossed his pencil on the desk blotter. "All right. What's the problem?''

She glared at him. "I'm looking at it.''

He made a faint groaning sound. "Oh. That's funny. Really funny.''

"I don't think it's funny. Not at all.'' She stepped fully into the room and shut the door behind her, aware in every quivering nerve of her body that this was it. The big battle, the one she'd been avoiding by holding her temper. Well, her temper just wouldn't be held anymore. She could feel it straining at the leash of her good sense. It would break that leash. Very soon now.

He watched her close the door and then he sighed wearily. "Abby, let's not get into it. I have to go.''

"No, you don't. You don't have to go. You can send Earl a nice, big check and he can either buy that pickup or not, his choice."

He shook his head. "You don't understand. It's not just about money. Earl's been going through a rough time lately and he could use a friend right now."

"Well, I can certainly understand that."

"Right," he muttered.

"I can, I swear. I'm kind of like Earl, really. Only I could use a *husband* right now."

He came around the big desk. For a moment, she thought he would stride right up to her and confront her eye to eye. But he didn't. He wouldn't come that close. He kept several feet of gleaming hardwood floor between them.

"Abby, you know me. You've known me all your life. When a friend needs me, I help him. That's how I am."

She folded her arms under her breasts. "Great. Wonderful. Terrific. But what about your wife and son? What if we need you? Do we have to take a number and wait in line?"

He scowled at her, then he snorted. "You're being completely unreasonable. And I don't have time for it right now."

"You never have time. Not in weeks and weeks. And I am fed up."

He studied her. "You're fed up, huh?"

"Yes. I am."

"Well, all right, then. If you're fed up, you know what to do."

The words were cryptic. But she knew exactly what he meant by them. She dropped her arms, all the fight draining from her like water from a sieve.

"No, Cash," she said quietly. "I don't know what to do. That's the problem."

He looked away, then back. Like someone trapped. "Abby…"

"No. Please. Listen."

"Let's just not—"

"Please."

He fell silent, though he didn't look happy about it.

She dragged in a breath and forged on. "I…I want to reach out to you, but you won't let me. I want to get close to you again, but you're so far away. Help me, Cash. Tell me. What can I do to work things out with you?"

He looked at her for the longest time. And then he turned away. He stuck his hands in his pockets and stared at a couple of Remington prints on the far wall.

"Cash."

"Yeah?" He still didn't look at her.

She swallowed. "Cash, please.…" She took a step toward him.

He turned back to her then and put up a hand. "Look. Just don't, okay?"

"But it's all…falling apart. We hardly see each other. We never…make love.…"

He winced. "Stop."

But she wouldn't stop. "We had so much last summer and in Boulder. We got along so well. We were happy. At least, I know *I* was happy. Were you?"

"Abby—"

"Just tell me. Were you happy?"

He lifted one shoulder in sort of a half shrug. "Yeah. All right. I was happy."

"So what happened?"

He went on looking at her, but he didn't answer her question.

She felt as if they stood on opposite sides of the world. Somehow, she had to bridge the distance. Though his eyes warned her to keep back, she took a step toward him. And then another.

When she stood only inches from him, she whispered, "Cash. Please. You said we would talk about this, about *us,* after the baby came. Well, the baby's here. The baby's been here for months. And you just won't talk."

"I don't think…" His voice faded off.

"What? You don't think what?"

He closed his eyes, tipped his head toward the ceiling. "That there's much to say."

Her anger sparked again. "What do you mean, there's not much to say? You're my husband. I'm your wife. I want to spend the rest of my life with you."

He looked right at her, and didn't say a word. "Hell."

She threw up her hands. "What? What does that look mean? Talk to me, Cash. I've had enough of you sighing and shaking your head and turning away."

"You won't like it if I talk to you."

"Do it anyway."

"Fine." He sank to the edge of the desk, his big shoulders slumping. "Abby, I…this isn't working out. I'm not cut out for marriage. You knew it from the first. We gave it a good try, but—"

Though she'd demanded that he talk to her, now she couldn't bear to let him finish. She cut in, "No, we didn't. We didn't give it nearly enough of a try. If you'll only listen to me, you'll understand that we need to—"

"Abby, I'm through."

"No. That's not true. Don't say that. I won't accept that."

"You have to accept it."

"No—"

"Abby, it takes two to make a marriage. And I want out. You asked me, I'm telling you. I want that divorce. There's no point in waiting until July. You get yourself a decent lawyer. And we'll get it over with."

"But I don't want it over with. I just want *you*."

"Abby..."

"No. Wait." She couldn't stand it. She'd known this was coming. But now that it was here, she only wanted to stop, to go back to the moment before she'd pushed him to talk to her. "Listen. Let's just forget this. Let's just go on as if I hadn't said anything."

He looked at her with such sadness. And pity.

Shameless now, she couldn't stop begging. "Please. Listen. Cash, we can make it work. Just give it a chance. You know that we can!"

He stood from the edge of the desk. "Abby..."

She threw herself against him, grabbing his shirt in her fists. "Listen. Please. I want to make it work. We have to make it work." I love you, she thought. But she couldn't quite say it. It had always been too dangerous to say it. Only once had she dared, on the night when she thought she would die.

And a lot of good it had done her.

"Cash..."

"No."

"Don't tell me no!"

"Abby, it's over."

She wouldn't hear it. She *refused* to hear it. With a

low, desperate cry, she surged up—and captured his mouth before he could say any more.

He froze. And then he moaned.

She moaned back, in triumph and in hope. Because she could feel it—the shock of connection. The yearning. The hunger between them.

She pressed herself against him, her hands sliding up to wrap around his neck. And he responded, his mouth devouring hers, his arms like bands of steel around her, his hands roaming her back.

And then he stiffened. He tore his mouth away.

She clutched him tighter. "No, please. Please, Cash..."

But it didn't help. He took her arms and peeled them away. He looked down at her, his eyes like blue chips of ice.

"Stop. Just stop."

She stared at him for the longest time, into those cold, stranger's eyes. And then, very calmly, she commanded, "Let go of me."

He released her. She stepped back, turned away, tried to collect her shattered wits.

But all she could think of were the days and days she'd waited and hoped. And for nothing. To have it end like this. Over some old buddy of his and a pickup.

With him looking so distant and cold. And with her begging him.

Had all those other women begged him?

If they had, she was just like them now. And if they hadn't, she was less than them. Because she hadn't even managed to salvage her pride.

Now he was the one approaching her. He came up behind her, gently grasped her shoulders. She shrugged off his touch.

"Abby," he said.

His kindly tone set her teeth on edge.

"Once you get used to it, you'll see that it's for the best. You'll have your freedom and I'll have mine. And Tyler will get both of us, just the way we always planned it."

The way *you* planned it, she thought, though she didn't say it out loud.

He went on, "You'll always have whatever you want."

Except what I want most: you.

"I'll instruct my lawyer to give you anything you ask for."

It was too much. She whirled on him. "Forget it. If you won't be my husband, I don't need or want anything from you. I can take care of myself just fine."

"I'll always take care of you."

"No, you won't. Because I won't let you."

"Abby, you're acting like a child."

"Right. Call me a child. That's always your defense against me. I'm a child, and so you don't have to take me seriously. You don't have to listen to me. You don't have to love me like the woman you know I really am!"

"Abby, settle down."

She backed away from him, because if she didn't, she would have jumped on him—and not to kiss him this time. "Get this. I don't care about your money. I don't *want* your money."

"Come on, don't be like this."

"I won't take a damn penny from you, Cash Bravo. You won't ease your conscience about me by buying me off." She backed into the credenza against the wall by the door.

"Abby, stop it." He took a careful step toward her. "This is for the best. You'll see that I'm right as soon as you cool down a little and start to think rationally."

"Rationally? *Rationally?*" She felt behind her, and her fingers closed around the base of something heavy. She picked it up and brought it around so she could see it: a bronze figurine of a cowboy on a rearing horse.

"Abby, put that thing down."

Nothing in the world would have given her greater pleasure than to smash him in the face with it.

"Abby, come on...."

She settled for waving it at him, feeling like a fool, hating him almost as much as she loved him. "Out!" She felt the tears rising. She couldn't stand for him to see them. "Get out of this house."

"Abby—"

"Just get out. Pack a bag and go to Provo."

He closed his eyes. Drew in a deep breath. "All right. Fine." He strode to the door, pulled it open.

"Don't come back," she said.

He went out the door, closing it quietly behind him. She waited, holding her breath, until she was certain he was really gone. Then, carefully, she set down the bronze statue.

She gulped and swallowed, making ludicrous choking sounds, trying to hold the blasted tears back. But they wouldn't be held.

They spilled down her face. Gulping, sobbing, despising herself for giving in to such weakness, she went to the big desk and dropped into the calfskin swivel chair. She put her arms on the blotter and laid her head down and let the tears have their way.

Fifteen minutes later, she raised her head and slumped back in the chair. She shuddered. An animal

cry tried to get out. She forced it down. With the back
of her hand, she wiped her nose. She put both palms
flat on the blotter and pushed herself to her feet.

Not far away, on the side table by a leather love seat,
sat a box of tissues. Abby marched over there, grabbed
a handful and blew her nose repeatedly. Then she
squared her shoulders, smoothed her hair and went out
to sit down to dinner alone.

Chapter Fifteen

For the next two days, Abby didn't leave the house. She took care of her baby and ate when Mrs. Helm put the food on the table. She went through the motions of living. And she did not cry again.

The third day was Saturday, one of Mrs. Helm's two days off. There was no breakfast on the table. So after giving Tyler his early bottle, Abby went back to bed. She pulled the covers close around her, shut her eyes and dropped into a fitful, unsatisfying sleep.

The phone rang at nine. She groped on the night stand and found it. "What?"

"Well. Good morning to you, too."

"Mom."

"You sound so *happy* to hear from me."

"I was sleeping."

"Then it's time you got up. I'm coming by."

"No!"

A silence, then, "All right. What's wrong?"

She didn't want to think about it. She only wanted to go back to sleep.

"Abigail."

But could she afford to go back to sleep, really?

"Abigail, I don't like this."

No. She couldn't.

Fact: her husband had left her. The marriage that was supposed to have lasted at least a year had barely survived for nine months in the end.

She had told him she wouldn't take his money, yet here she lay in his bed, her stomach rumbling because his housekeeper hadn't come in today to feed her.

She needed a job, not more sleep.

"Abigail, I'm coming over there."

She shoved back the covers. "Don't bother. Tyler and I will be over at your place in half an hour. There's something we have talk about."

"I don't like the sound of this."

"You think you don't like it now, wait until I get there."

"Abigail, Abigail," Edna murmured sadly as she stood at the stove, poaching eggs. "Didn't I warn you that this would happen? You should have taken better care of that man."

Abby, at the table, shifted her son to her other arm. "I did take good care of Cash."

Edna took the lid from the pan, lifted the poaching tray out of the water and turned the two eggs into a cup. "I'm sure you believe you did."

Abby pulled in a deep breath and assumed a peace-making tone. "Let's not argue about it, Mom. I did the best I could. And I suppose you're right—it wasn't good enough.''

Edna carried the eggs to her daughter, along with a plate of golden brown toast. ''Here. Eat. Give me that beautiful boy.'' Abby handed Tyler to his grandmother and picked up her spoon. Holding Tyler on one arm, Edna got the coffeepot with her free hand and refilled the two cups on the table. Then she sat and watched her daughter eat.

Abby looked up from the meal. ''Thanks, Mom. These eggs are perfect.''

''You need your strength.''

''Amen.''

Gently, Edna rocked Tyler. ''He looks just like his daddy.''

''Do I need to hear that right now?''

Edna glanced up from the baby. ''It's not something you'll ever escape. Face it. You'll think of that man all your life. Every time you look at this boy.'' She leaned toward Abby a little and lowered her voice. ''You love him. And you have to find a way to get him back.''

Abby thought of his cold eyes, of the way she had begged him. ''I don't want him back.''

Edna retreated to her own chair. ''That's only pride talking.''

''So? What's wrong with a woman having a little pride?''

''It won't keep you warm in a blizzard.''

''It's better than nothing.''

''Not by much.'' She looked sideways at Abby. ''I don't know how you can let him go. He loves you so. I'll bet his heart is broken.''

''Mom. Try to get it straight. *He* left *me*.''

"What does that matter? I know he didn't *want* to leave you."

"Oh. And just how do you know that?"

"A million ways. The way he looks when you come in the room. The way he lights up when he hears your voice or when I talk about you. I know Cash. After all, I as good as raised him from the time he was ten years old. And I've been watching him since the two of you married. He loves you."

Abby sipped some coffee, then set the cup down firmly. "Sure he loves me. And he loves you. He loves Nate and Zach and Tess and Jobeth. And some guy named Earl in Provo."

"You know what I mean. He loves you as a man loves a woman. He loves you deeply. He loves you more than he's ever loved any other person on this earth."

"He has a strange way of showing it."

"You could get him back if you tried."

"Look. I don't want to talk about it anymore."

"Fine, fine. Ruin your life."

"Mom. I didn't come here to argue."

"No, you came here to listen to some good advice."

"I did not."

"Oh? Then what?"

"I need your help."

Edna frowned. "What kind of help?"

"I want to get a job."

"A job?" Edna rolled her eyes. "You don't need a job. Even if you've driven him away, Cash will always take care of you. That's the way he is."

Silently, Abby reminded herself that she wanted her mother's help—and if she started yelling at her, she probably wouldn't get it. With great patience, she explained for what seemed like the hundredth time, "I don't want him taking care of me. I want to take care of myself."

"Oh, I do not understand you. I will never understand you."

"Will you help me, Mom?"

Edna released a long, weary breath. "What kind of job?"

"I don't really know yet. But I have the better part of a business degree. So I think I can find something. But I need you to look after Tyler for me while I look. And then, when I do find something, I would want you to watch him while I'm working."

"This baby needs his mother."

"And this mother needs a job. Will you help me or not?"

Edna smoothed the blanket around Tyler's sleeping face. "What a little angel. A beautiful, perfect angel."

"Mother. Will you help me?"

"Just like his daddy."

"Mother. Yes or no?"

"Oh, do what you have to do. And I'll take care of this beautiful boy whenever you need me to."

"Thanks."

"But I won't stop hoping that you and Cash will work things out."

Abby pushed the remains of her toast away. "He's left me, Mother. And I don't want him back. Get used to it, because that's the way it is." She looked over and saw that Tess was standing in the arch that led to the living room. "Come on in. The coffee's hot."

"I don't believe what I just heard," Tess said. "Cash would never leave you."

"Believe it," Abby replied. "And can we please talk about something else?"

Just then the door to the garage flew open. Jobeth stood on the concrete steps beyond the threshold, soaking wet and shivering. "Mom!" she wailed.

"What happened?" Edna demanded as Tess hurried over and ushered her daughter into the warmth of the room.

Jobeth began babbling something about the boy down the street, a gate and a bucket of water rigged to a string in a cottonwood tree.

"You got doused," Tess said.

"I am never playing with that Nick Collerby again," Jobeth whined.

"Come on," Tess said. "Dry clothes. Now."

"Why would he do that to me, Mom?"

"I haven't the faintest idea. We'll get you dry, and you can go ask him."

"I will not ask him. I *can't* ask him. I'm not speaking to him. Ever again for as long as I live...."

Patiently, Tess herded her toward the stairs.

Edna grinned at Abby. "Children. Always up to something."

Abby stared at her mother, wishing she'd been one tenth that serene while Abby was growing up.

Moments later, Tess and Jobeth reappeared and Tess got to work making hot chocolate for Jobeth.

"Use the double boiler," Edna instructed. "It's down in that cabinet there."

Tess bent down and looked in the cabinet. "I don't see it, Edna."

Clucking her tongue, Edna handed Tyler to Abby and went to find the pans herself.

Abby cradled her son, enjoying the warmth of the

kitchen and the chatter of the others. She also felt relief that her mother had agreed to look after Tyler—and that the subject of herself and Cash seemed to be closed.

Tess appeared at Abby's door at eight that night.

Abby looked at the other woman with suspicion. "Is this about Cash?"

Tess shivered. "It's really cold out here, Abby."

"All right, all right." Abby stepped back and let Tess into the house.

In the living room, Tess perched on the edge of the sofa. "I just, well, I can't stop thinking about what I heard today. It makes no sense at all. You and Cash love each other. And you were meant to be together."

Abby sat in the caramel-colored leather chair and fiddled with the little carved box in which Cash kept the cigarettes he was always trying not to smoke.

"Abby. Talk to me."

Abby shut the lid of the box with a snap. "Look. He doesn't want to be married. He is not a marrying kind of man. He only married me because of Tyler, because we didn't...take precautions. And I got pregnant."

"It happens that way sometimes."

Something in Tess's voice tipped Abby off. The women shared a long glance. Finally, Abby asked, "You and Josh?"

Tess nodded. She looked down at her hands, which were folded in her lap. "I was seventeen." She raised her head, gave Abby a sad smile. "And he was so handsome. We had nothing in common. It was just one of those things that happen, between a foolish girl...and a reckless man.

"When I found out I was pregnant, he said he'd marry me. It seemed like the best choice at the time. But we were so different. He couldn't stay in one place—and all I wanted was to go home." She relaxed back onto the couch, her eyes far away now, lost somewhere in the past. "My parents had a ranch. In South Dakota. I always thought that in the end I'd go back there. But my mother lost it after my father died. And I can't ever go back."

"I'm so sorry...."

Tess shook her head. "Don't be. I do have Jobeth. She's a big consolation for...everything that might have been."

Abby thought of the baby sleeping in the other room. "I know exactly what you mean."

"No, you don't."

Abby blinked. "What?"

"You don't know what I mean. You can't know. You and Cash aren't anything like me and Josh. You and Cash are a good match."

"Tess..."

"You are. Better than good. You're exactly right for each other. I knew it the first time I saw you together."

Abby made a disbelieving sound. "Tell that to Cash."

"I would. If he was here."

"Well, he's not. Because he doesn't want me."

"Oh, come on."

"He doesn't."

"Of course he does. I was there, remember, the night Tyler was born? I saw with my own eyes how Cash feels about you. He loves you more than his life. You just have to find out why he thinks it's best for you if he leaves you. Because believe me, that's the only reason he would do what he's done."

Abby stared at Tess. "You think that Cash has walked out on me...for my own good?"

"I *know* that's what he's done."

Right then, looking at Tess's earnest face, Abby found herself wanting to believe—and thinking of how she had once imagined that Tess was in love with Cash. She had a crazy urge right then to ask her friend if there might be any truth to her suspicion. But to ask would be to cross some invisible boundary. And Abby didn't know if she could deal with what she'd find on the other side.

"When you love someone, *really* love someone," Tess said softly, "you want what's best for them, no matter what the cost to yourself."

A tight laugh escaped Abby. "But he won't talk to me. I've reasoned with him, I've yelled at him. I've tried everything. You just don't know...."

Tess smiled her gentle smile. "Have you actually told him that you love him?"

Abby looked away, then made herself meet her friend's eyes again. "Once."

"And?"

"It didn't do any good. If anything, I think it pushed him away. Like I said, he's not a marrying man. Talk of love makes him really nervous."

Tess stood. "So he needs to get adjusted to hearing it. You have to tell him again. You have to tell him a *lot*."

"But Tess, he won't *let* me tell him. Every time I try, he puts me off or walks away—or says he wants a divorce."

Tess moved around the coffee table and came to stand before Abby's chair. "Then you must be relentless."

"I've been relentless."

"Not relentless enough."

"I'm just..." Abby hung her head.

"What?"

Abby let out a long sigh. "So tired. Of having him reject me."

Tess dropped to her knees in front of Abby. "Of course you are. But tell the truth. Do you want to spend the rest of your life without him?"

"Oh, Tess..."

"Well?"

"No!" It was a cry of longing. "I want him back. I want him beside me."

"Then go after him."

"He won't give me the chance."

"Make the chance. And don't let your foolish pride get in the way this time."

Abby hardly slept all night. She tossed and turned, thinking of the things that Tess had said. By the time the first rays of the sun were turning the sky orange-yellow in the east, she had decided to give winning Cash Bravo one more try.

She talked to her son as she fed him and dressed him, explaining that he would have to stay with his grandma for a few days, but when she returned, she would bring his daddy back with her. "And from then on, Tyler, I swear to you. We will take you with us, wherever we go."

She prayed she wasn't lying. To her son. Or to herself.

Once she had Tyler ready, she searched Cash's office, checking for an address that might belong to Earl, in Provo, last name unknown. She came up with zero; she'd have to look elsewhere.

"I might be gone a few days, Mom," she said when she showed up at Edna's to drop off Tyler.

Edna let out a small cry of dismay. "You're looking for a job out of town?"

"I'm not looking for a job."

"Then what?"

"I just don't want to go into it now. Please understand."

And it seemed as if she actually did. At least she stopped asking questions.

She kissed Abby's cheek. "You call me. Let me know where you are."

Abby promised that she would.

And then she headed over to Main Street, and Cash's storefront office there. Abby let herself in with the key that Cash had given her years ago, during the first summer she came to work for him.

Inside, Renata's cluttered desk sat in the center of the rectangular room, with two chairs for visitors facing it. Renata wasn't in yet, of course. She rarely showed up before eleven and it was just past eight.

Abby headed straight for the desk. She booted up the computer and ran a search on the name "Earl" in the word processor address book she had taught Renata to use. No luck. Either Earl had never actually dealt with Cash Ventures, or Renata wasn't keeping up the file.

Abby tried the Rolodex, thumbing through every card since she didn't have a last name. Either she missed it, or Earl wasn't there.

With a sigh, she picked up the phone and called

Renata at home. Cash's secretary answered on the fourth ring.

"Huh?"

"Hi, Renata. It's me," Abby said cheerily. "I'm really sorry to wake you, but I've got a question for you."

"Uh. Yeah. Huh?"

"Do you recall a guy Cash knows named Earl, in Provo?"

"Uh. Earl. Sure."

"I can't remember his last name. Can you?"

"Uh." Renata yawned and sighed. "He just goes by Earl, I think."

"I was afraid of that. What's his address?"

"Uh."

There was a long pause. Abby feared Renata might have grown suspicious—or gone back to sleep. But she was only thinking.

"Oh, yeah," she said at last. "I remember. Cash called on Thursday. He gave me Earl's address and phone number just in case."

"Great. Where is it?"

"It's, um...the Rolodex?"

"I looked there. Didn't find it."

"Well, I *meant* to put it in the Rolodex...."

"Fine, Renata." Abby assumed her best fed-up employer voice. "But it's not there."

"Well, I don't...oh. Wait. Look under my coffee cup. There's a notepad."

Abby lifted Renata's coffee cup, which was shaped like a smiling cat with a tail for a handle. Underneath she found the notepad—and on it, Earl's address and phone number, only partly obscured by a dried coffee ring. "Here it is."

"Good."

"Go back to sleep."

"I will. Oh. Ab?"

"What?"

"Did you want Cash—is that it?"

Abby felt her stomach knot up. "Why?"

"Because he left Earl's on Friday."

Abby muttered something rude as she dropped into the chair behind the desk. All this silly sneaking around when she could have just come right out and asked.

"Did you try that cell phone of his?" Renata asked. Abby hadn't. She considered the phone a last resort. She wanted to track him down and confront him face to face.

"Where is he now?" Abby asked.

"The Nugget in Reno. I scribbled his room number somewhere…oh, yeah, I remember. The lower right-hand corner of the desk blotter. See it?"

"Well…" The blotter was a virtual explosion of scribbles and doodles.

"It's in purple ink, under a green smiley face, with a—"

"Right. I got it." She grabbed one of the hundred or so scraps of paper stuck under the edges of the blotter and wrote the number down. "What's he there for? A card game?"

"No, some meetings with Redbone Deevers and some investor group, about a time-share condo deal, I think." Renata paused to yawn again hugely. "He'll be there until Tuesday, he said."

Abby went back to the house to pack a small bag and line up a flight. Then she drove to Sheridan, to the small airport there.

She didn't touch down in Reno until late afternoon. She took a cab to the Nugget, which was actually in nearby Sparks. At the Nugget, she went straight up to the room whose number Renata had provided on the chance that Cash might be there, between meetings on the condo deal. She set her suitcase on the carpet, took three deep breaths and then knocked.

After what seemed like forever, she heard the lock turn on the other side. The door swung open. And Abby found herself face to face with a beautiful blonde in a slinky pink silk robe. "Yes?" the blonde asked politely.

Abby saw red. "All right. Where is he?"

"What? Excuse me?"

"Who is it, darling?" A man Abby had never seen before appeared in the door to the bedroom behind the blonde.

Abby gulped. "Er, I'm looking for my husband. Cash Bravo?"

The blonde and the strange man exchanged glances. "Sorry," the woman said. "No one by that name here." Swiftly and firmly, she shut the door in Abby's face.

Abby stared at the door for a moment, feeling foolish and lost. Then she picked up her suitcase and went down to the main desk.

The clerk punched some buttons on the keyboard of his reservations computer, then he shook his head. "I'm sorry. Mr. Bravo checked out this morning."

The desk clerk said he'd watch her suitcase, so she left it with him while she found a phone and called Renata. But Renata hadn't heard from Cash, not since he'd called to tell her he'd be staying at the Nugget. She gave in and tried Cash's cell phone: no answer.

She was just hanging up in despair, when a voice several feet away drawled, "I'll be damned. Is that you, kid?"

She turned to find Redbone Deevers lumbering toward her on his ebony cane. She ran to him and he enfolded her in a bear hug. Then he stepped back. She looked up into his broad face with its fringe of white hair. He sported a goatee and favored white three-piece suits. To Abby, he always seemed the image of the courtly Southern gentleman, though Cash claimed he'd been born in Detroit, son of a steel-mill worker and a grocery-store clerk.

"Investors like a little glamour and romance," Cash had told Abby. "So Redbone gives them what they want."

Now Redbone was looking appropriately concerned and solemn. "You come after that husband of yours?"

She nodded.

"Well, he's gone."

"I know. They told me at the desk."

"We finished our business. And profitably, too." His white eyebrows lifted. "You come to work things out with him?"

"Oh, Redbone..."

He patted her shoulder with his big, gentle hand. "Now, now. Come on over here. Sit yourself down." He led her to a pair of black leather chairs against a nearby wall.

Once they were both settled, she dared to demand, "All right, what did Cash tell you?"

"Not a thing." Redbone shrugged. "But you weren't with him. And he growled at me like a flea-bit hound when I asked him how you were doin'. I drew my own conclusions."

"I see."

He leaned a little closer. "You want to know where he's gone?"

Hope made her sit up a little straighter. "You know?"

Redbone chuckled. "He said he had a yen to get away from it all. Can you believe that? Cash Bravo with a yen to get away from it all?"

"It doesn't sound much like him."

"No, it does not. But I couldn't stand to see him looking so glum. So I offered him the use of my private cabin on the lake."

"Did he take it?"

"He did."

"Where is it?"

The old gentleman looked at her sideways. "Is he goin' to be unhappy with old Redbone when you show up lookin' for him?"

Right then, someone hit a jackpot on a slot machine not twenty yards away. Bells clanged and lights flashed. Abby glanced over to where the winner stood calmly, watching the river of coins as it poured into the tray.

"You ever heard the old story about how Cash got his name?"

She looked at Redbone. "I've heard it."

"One too many times, I'll bet."

Abby shrugged. She was more interested in finding her husband than in discussing what an amusing child he had been.

Redbone asked, with a gleam in his eye, "You goin' to answer my question?"

She confessed, "The truth is, he'll probably be mad at you if you tell me where he's gone."

Redbone laughed, a deep, belly-shaking sound. "Well, that's just fine. Let 'im steam. I can take it."

She leaned toward Redbone again. "Tell me, then."

"Fair enough. Got a pen?"

It was a sixty-mile trip from the Reno-Sparks area to Redbone's hideaway in the pines on the shore of Lake Tahoe. Abby took a cab. Darkness had fallen by the time the cab pulled into the clear space in front of the cabin.

Abby, in the back seat, looked out the side window at the tall, shadowy trees. In the distance, far across the black water, she could see snow-tipped mountains, as rough and craggy as the mountains of home. A sliver of moon hung over the highest peak, a bright star above it, so it seemed as if the moon swung from that star.

"This is it, lady," the cabdriver said. "And it looks to me like nobody's home."

Abby stared out the other window, toward the dark cabin, which appeared shut up tight. There was no sign of another vehicle anywhere, either.

"Could you wait here for a minute?"

"No problem."

Abby got out of the car and pulled her coat close around her against the night chill. She mounted the rustic steps and pounded on the heavy door. And then she waited.

No lights came on. And there was no sound from inside.

She went down the steps and around to the back, which turned out to be just as dark and deserted as the front of the place. With the key Redbone had given her, she let herself in the back door.

The cabin was as rustic inside as out, with unfinished

furniture and a set of deer antlers over the potbellied stove in the main room. It didn't take long to look through the whole place. And to find that there was no one there.

"Where to now, lady?" the cabbie asked wearily when Abby climbed into the back seat once more.

"Back to the Nugget," she said.

When she trudged into the Nugget again, Abby went straight to the front desk and asked for a room.

Once she'd checked in, she tried Cash's cell phone again and again and got no answer. Once she'd hung up, she considered calling her mother. But she felt too depressed to pick up the phone another time. And besides, she'd be talking to Edna soon enough. Because she would be on the first flight she could get tomorrow, headed for home.

It had been a crazy idea anyway to go chasing after Cash. Clearly, he didn't want to be found.

The trip home took forever. As on the flight to Reno, she had to go to Denver and then board a puddle jumper for Sheridan. The sun had long ago disappeared behind the Big Horns when she finally got off the highway in Medicine Creek.

She drove straight to her mother's. "Mom, I just want my baby," she said when Edna opened the door.

"Then go on home," Edna replied. "Your baby's there. With your husband, where he belongs."

Chapter Sixteen

Abby dropped her coat, purse and suitcase inside the front door and went looking for her husband and her son. She found them in the baby's room. Cash was sitting in the rocker, feeding Tyler his bottle.

He looked up and saw her standing in the doorway. He whispered roughly, "Where've you been?"

She felt so many emotions her body could hardly contain them all. Joy. Rage. Hurt. Relief. Hopeless, incurable love most of all, flooding through her, warming her flesh and weakening her knees. She swallowed and replied in a whisper as rough as his had been, "Looking for you."

He scanned her face. Then he glanced down at the child in his arms. "He's almost done."

She leaned in the doorway, waiting. Tyler finished his meal. Cash set the bottle aside and carefully lifted the small body to his broad shoulder. He rose from the rocker and came to stand before her. "Here." Gently, he held out their son.

She took his small, warm weight in her arms, brought him close to her heart. She snuggled his wobbly head beneath her chin and he burped against her neck.

Cash whispered, "He's ready to go down."

She looked into her husband's face—and felt anger rising. Without a word, she turned from him and went to sit in the rocker.

Cash stayed in the doorway. She could feel him there, watching her. But she didn't look at him. She closed her eyes and rocked her baby. And when she opened her eyes again, Cash had gone.

Tyler needed changing, so she performed the task. His sleepy eyes kept drooping as she cleaned him up. Once the job was done, she laid him in his bed and kissed the back of his warm little head. Already off in dreamland somewhere, he made no sound when she turned off the light.

She found Cash in their bedroom, sitting in one of the two big chairs beneath the window that faced the side yard. He looked at her when she appeared from the short hall off the living room, but he didn't say anything. Feeling nervous and wary—and more angry as each moment passed—Abby entered the room. She went straight to the bed, dropped to the end of it and kicked off her shoes.

She could feel Cash's eyes on her, though he remained silent. Leaning defiantly back on her hands, she looked at him. "Well?"

Still he said nothing, only shifted in the chair.

She waited, daring him to speak.

Finally, he did. "I'm scared to death."

She knew that—had known it all along, deep in her heart. And she had ached for him, that love frightened him so. But right then, she was dealing with her own pain—pain he had caused her. And she just couldn't drum up much sympathy for him.

"You're still mad at me, aren't you?"

She let several grim seconds go by before answering, "Furious."

He shifted in the chair again, but he still looked far from comfortable.

And that was just fine with her. She didn't want him comfortable.

"Abby, come on. Talk to me. Please."

She let out a low, rageful sound and sat up straight. "I begged you," she said, the words tight, brimming with her fury and love and pain. "*Begged* you."

"Abby..."

All at once, she couldn't just sit there. She jumped to her feet and turned on him, clenching her hands at her sides to keep them from reaching out and closing around his neck. "I am not someone who begs."

"I know."

Slowly and deliberately, she said the words: "I love you."

He had the grace not to wince or turn away. "I know."

She held her head high and she told him with pride, "I have always loved you."

"Abby, I—"

"No. Let me say it."

"But I—"

"I want you to just sit there and listen to me. *Really* listen. For once."

His blue gaze moved over her face, heartbreakingly intent. "All right."

She needed to move. So she paced the floor, back and forth from the bureau to the bed. Finally, she had her thoughts in order. She stopped, turned to face him.

"Since I was a little girl, I've loved you. Do you know that?"

He closed his eyes, breathed deeply—and nodded.

She went on, "But I knew so much about you, knew you were afraid of loving. So I tried, for years and years, to pretend that the love I felt for you was an innocent love. But it wasn't."

She paused, daring him to interrupt. He didn't, so she made herself continue. "Finally, the time came when I couldn't pretend anymore. I…" She swallowed convulsively. "I reached for you. As a woman, I reached for you…the night they buried my dad. And you reached for me. As a man."

Suddenly she couldn't look into those knowing blue eyes for one second longer. She turned, spoke to the far wall. "We…made Tyler. And we married. But still, you held back." She whirled to face him again, forced herself to confess, "Oh, I did, too, I know. I held back, too. I suggested that stupid agreement. I told you I wanted a temporary marriage, instead of admitting from the first that, as far as I was concerned, there was never anything temporary about you and me. I was afraid to say my love out loud. And I never did. For all those years I was growing up—and right into our married life together. I never, ever said my love out loud. Because I knew I would lose you if I did."

She looked toward the dark window behind his head. "And I was right. When I tried to get you to throw out the agreement, you wouldn't. You told me to wait. Until the baby came. Until I was—'' she paused, then sneered ''—*more myself.''* She grimaced at him. ''That was how you put it, wasn't it?''

His lips thinned; he coughed. Then he muttered, ''Yes.''

She went on, ''And then the baby did come. And it all happened just the way I always knew it would. The night Tyler was born, I did it. I said my love out loud. And from that night, you started to leave me.'' She stared right at him, hard and long. ''That is what happened, isn't it?''

He nodded.

''And in the end, when you said you were going, I threw out the one thing I had always kept for myself when it came to you—my pride. I *begged* you to stay. But you wouldn't.'' A chill shook her body. She wrapped her arms around her middle. ''And that was it, the final straw. I told myself I wouldn't take any more. That I was through with you.

''But then my mother started in on me. And Tess, too. Both of them telling me how you loved me. I could brush my mother off. But not Tess. She was so... convincing. She insisted that you would never leave me unless you thought it was best for me. And that, well, it kind of made sense.''

She shivered some more, hugged herself harder. ''So I chased you. All the way to Reno and Lake Tahoe, I chased you. But I couldn't find you.''

''Because I came home.''

She stared at him, loving him so, almost wishing she didn't.

He must have known he had some explaining to do.

Grimly, he admitted, ''Tess was right, up to a point.''

"How?"

"I told myself that I was doing the best thing for you."

"To leave me?"

"Yes. I told myself it was the right thing to do, to use that stupid agreement we'd made to set you free."

"The *right* thing?"

"Yeah. Because you're so young. You have so much ahead of you. And I...I took the choices away from you. I made love to you and got you pregnant. And I pushed you to go back to school. It was all too much for you. Because of the choices I made, you nearly died."

She felt totally exhausted, suddenly. She dropped to the edge of the bed once more. "Oh, Cash, when will you give me credit for being part of those choices, too?"

"I will. I do now. Just let me finish."

She cast him a glance, then looked down at the floor. "Okay. Fine. Finish."

"I know you were there, too. That *we* made those choices. But I wouldn't admit it to myself or to you. I was too busy being noble, the way you always said. Out saving the damn world. Saving you. From me. So I wouldn't have to deal with how scared I am...to love you."

Abby closed her eyes. He had said it. He had as good as said it. She asked in a voice that was torn at the edges, "And *do* you, then? Do you love me?"

"More than I've loved anything or anyone ever. I swear to you."

Those words meant so much. Abby felt her hurt and anger fading, melting away like snow in the path of a chinook.

They stood at the same time.

"You were right," he said. "I was happy when I was a little kid. And I've hated my father for turning away from me when he lost my mother. I didn't want to get hurt that way again. But when you almost died, I saw it happening to me. Just as it happened to me when I was a kid. Just like it happened to my father, losing the one who mattered most. And I thought...I could escape it. By turning away from you. But I didn't escape it. I only...lost you." He made a low, anguished sound. "You *hadn't* died, after all. And still I'd lost you...."

"Oh, Cash..."

"And I was setting myself up to lose Tyler, too. Doing the same thing my father did to me. Turning away, cutting him out. I don't want to be like that. Help me, Abby. Help me not to be like that...." He took a step toward her.

She took one toward him.

He held out his arms.

And then she was flying—straight to where she wanted to be. He crushed her close, his whole body trembling. She held on tight.

He let out a long, shuddering breath. And then he took her by the shoulders and looked into her eyes. "I love you, Abby. You can't know how much."

She wondered if it could be legal to feel happiness like this.

"Abby, we never should have made that crazy agreement."

"I know."

"I want to throw it out. I want you to be my wife. For real. Forever. Will you do that? Will you stay with me?"

She reached up, laid her hand on his cheek. "It seems I've waited my whole life for you to ask me that."

"Are you saying you will?"

She pulled his head down so his mouth hovered just above hers, on the brink of a kiss. "Oh, Cash. Yes. I will."

He whispered her name as his lips met hers.

Epilogue

Meggie May Kane stood at the edge of the dance floor that had been set up under the stars for the Fourth of July dance. It was just like old times, she thought, with the lanterns strung overhead, the bandstand, the dance floor—and the red, white and blue bunting looped everywhere. When Meggie was growing up, the Community Club used to put on a dance every Fourth. But lately, the custom had been lost. Then, this year, the Medicine Creek Merchant's Society had decided to revive the tradition. They'd done a beautiful job of it.

The band struck up a slow number. The lines of dancers broke, milled and re-formed into pairs. Embracing couples swayed and turned across the floor. Meggie watched Cash and Abby Bravo. They'd been married about a year now. And they looked so happy it almost hurt to watch them.

Once, Meggie had dreamed of happiness like that....

Swallowing down pointless tears, Meggie turned from the dance floor. There were a few rows of chairs set up in front of the bandstand. Meggie sank into one of them. As the music played, neighbors and family friends approached her.

"Meggie, I'm so sorry about your dad."

"How are you doin' there, Meggie?"

"Meggie, we're thinking of you. Our hearts go out…"

Meggie murmured her thanks for their kind words and tried not to show her pain and fury. Her father's funeral had taken place just the day before. She had loved him so much. And yet right now, she was so angry with him she couldn't even think of him without wanting to throw back her head and scream in rage.

But what good would that do? Jason Kane was far beyond anybody's wrath now.

"Meggie?"

She looked up—and smiled when she saw who it was. "Zach. How are you?"

"I think the question is, how are *you?*"

"Getting by."

"Meggie, if there's anything—" he began.

She didn't know what gave her the courage. But she heard herself saying, "There is."

Zach leaned closer. "Name it."

And she did. "I have to speak with Nate."

Zach blinked—and retreated from her a little in his chair.

She refused to drop her gaze as she asked carefully, "If I were to fly to L.A., would I find him in the phone book, do you think?"

Zach frowned. "Meggie…"

"You asked me if there was anything you could do.

And there is—you can answer my question. Can I find Nate's number in the L.A. phone book?''

Zach was still frowning, but he told her what she needed to know. ''Bravo Investigative Services. It's in the Yellow Pages.''

She nodded. ''Thank you.''

He shrugged, then held out a hand. ''Come on. Put your worries behind you for a while and let's have a dance.''

''Oh, Zach. You're kind. But I just don't feel much like dancing.''

He dropped his hand. ''I understand.'' He glanced away, off toward the dance floor—and then beyond it, to where Edna Heller and Tess DeMarley stood on the sidelines together.

Meggie saw the way his gaze lingered on Tess. She suggested lightly, ''I see Tess DeMarley over there. You might ask her.''

Zach looked at Meggie again and grinned. He had a charming grin—but then, all the Bravos did. ''I'm working up the nerve.''

Meggie stood to go. ''Good luck,'' she said softly.

He stared up at her for a long, slow time before he replied, ''Same to you.''

*   *   *   *   *

MARRIAGE BY
NECESSITY

For Susan Crosby,
the best kind of friend,
one who inspires, instructs
and makes me laugh.

Chapter One

In the pool area of the Hollywood Paradise Hotel, palm fronds swayed softly in a balmy summer breeze—a breeze only minimally tainted with smog. Tourists laughed and splashed in the pool. Gorgeous men and women lay on chaise lounges, dressed in skimpy swimwear and soaking up rays. Not far from the pool, at the Tropicana Poolside Bar, men in business suits enjoyed the shade and took their whiskey or vodka over ice. Meanwhile, at a table closer to the pool, a group of gray-haired ladies in bright-colored caftans drank strawberry daiquiris and argued over whether or not they had time to visit Universal Studios that day.

Four floors above the fun, a glass door stood open on a small balcony. In the room beyond the door, Megan May Kane lay on the bed and stared up at the ceiling fan that turned slowly overhead. Megan sighed.

She hardly heard the happy laughter from below. Her lips moved. She was praying silently for the phone to ring.

When it did, she sat straight up and cried out, "Oh!"

It rang again. Megan put a hand to her heart and made herself take three deep, slow breaths. She told herself that she would be calm. Still, her hand shook when she reached for the receiver.

"H-hello?"

"Meggie?" The deep voice came out of her past, out of her dreams, out of her future as she had once dared to imagine it might be.

Her foolish heart soared. He had found her message on that machine of his. And he had actually called back.

"Meggie, are you there?"

"Uh, yes." She gulped, paused, breathed slowly. In. And then out. "Yes, Nate. I'm here."

"What the hell are you doing in L.A.?"

"I'm..." How to explain this, how to even *begin?* A hot jolt of anger pulsed through her—fury at her dead father.

"Meggie, are you all right?"

She steeled herself, ordered the pointless rage away. "Yes. I'm all right. And I, um, I really need to see you. Right away."

There was a pause, a pure agony for Meggie. Then at last he asked warily, "See me about what?"

Meggie realized that her face was flaming. She laid her hand on her cheek in an attempt to cool the heat. It had been over a decade since that steamy Fourth of July night when she had thrown herself at him. She'd hardly spoken to him since. Still, she knew he must be wondering if she'd decided to try again—which, in a crazy way, was exactly the case.

"Look," she said, "I'd really prefer just to explain everything when I see you."

Another nerve-flaying silence occurred.

"Nate?" she asked faintly, fearing he might have hung up.

At last he spoke. "All right. One hour."

She felt breathless. She gulped in air. "Where?"

"The lobby."

"The lobby of what?"

"Your hotel."

Her hotel. That made sense. "All right, the lobby," she agreed. "Do you need the address?"

"I think I can find it," he said dryly.

"Well. All right." She confirmed the time. "In an hour then?" She got no reply. He'd already hung up.

Nate Bravo stood behind the ancient metal desk in his "office," which was really only a spare room in his apartment. His hand rested on the phone he'd just set down. He stared off toward the green bamboo blinds that covered the window. The blinds were rolled halfway up. Through the bottom half of the window, he could see the white stucco wall of the building next door. A hibiscus bush, blooming in lush explosions of coral pink, grew against that wall. A splash of sunlight made the green leaves shine and the white wall gleam. A pretty sight.

But Nate stared blindly, not really seeing the bright tropical flowers. His mind was filled with Meggie May Kane.

He could see her as if she stood before him, in Wranglers and a plaid shirt, her skeins of shining dark hair coming loose from under her hat, those big amber eyes staring at him with yearning—and a strange, defiant pride.

When he thought of Meggie May, he thought of contradictions. Of strength and innocence. Toughness and purity.

He was probably a damn fool to meet with her. What he wanted and what she wanted were worlds—universes—apart.

But then again, she'd sounded pretty upset. Just maybe she needed the kind of help he could provide: someone found. Or someone followed. He could do something like that for her. And he would. Willingly.

He found her sitting in a studded leather mission-style chair, wearing a sundress and sandals. Except for those strong, work-toughened hands gripping the chair arms, no one would have guessed that she was a woman who had pulled, cut and branded more than her share of calves. Her big eyes looked up at him, as pure and innocent as ever.

"Thank you. For coming." She stood and held out one of those calloused hands. He took it and they shook, awkward and formal. Then she cast a quick, uncomfortable glance around the lobby, with its Moorish arches, red-tiled floor and Persian rugs. A family sat in a group of leather chairs to their left, all dressed up for playing tourists, in shorts and sun visors, armed with cameras and binoculars. To their right, a man sat alone, reading the Sunday *Times*. And not far away, on a studded leather sofa, slouched four refugees from the punk scene, complete with safety pins in their ears and hair that went from Day-glo green to fluorescent purple. No one looked the least bit interested in the pretty woman in the sundress and the man who'd just shaken her hand.

Still, Meggie suggested, "Could we go on up to my room, do you think? Somewhere we could talk alone?"

Nate almost said no, since she had yet to tell him what the hell this was about. But then he scoffed at himself. What could Meggie May Kane do to him alone in her room that he couldn't handle?

They took the elevator up. In the enclosed space, Nate found himself overly conscious of her. Of her slightly woodsy perfume and those unwavering eyes, of the high roundness of her breasts beneath that pretty little dress. He had always found her physically attractive—which was why, from the time she started to fill out, he'd done his best to keep clear of her. A woman like Meggie, so rooted to the land, could never be anything but trouble to a man like him.

And really, by now, she should represent little to no threat to his peace of mind. All logic declared that physical attraction faded over time. Yet somehow, she still drew him. Now, in her early thirties, she seemed even more attractive than she had been in her teens. There was a lushness to her now, a ripeness she hadn't possessed before.

The elevator slid to a stop. The doors opened. She led the way down the hall to her room.

Once inside, she set her small purse on the round table in the corner, near a glass door that led out to a balcony. She gestured. "Have a seat." He walked past the end of the bed and dropped into the chair she'd offered. She indicated the small liquor cabinet not far away. "Can I get you something?"

"Why not? Jack Daniels. And ice."

He watched her as she got the key, unlocked the

cabinet and took out the miniature bottle. The ice bucket was empty. She held it up. "I'll be right back."

He let her get to the door before he stopped her. "Never mind. I'll take it straight."

"Are you sure? It won't take a minute to get the ice."

"Straight is fine."

She returned to the small mirrored bar area over the liquor cabinet and poured him the drink. He nodded his thanks when she handed it to him, then lifted the glass and sipped, watching her over the rim as he did.

She stood unmoving for a moment, managing somehow to look both nervous and thoroughly self-possessed. She eyed the other chair, but must have decided against sitting in it, because she backed up until her knees hit the edge of the bed. She scooped the back of her dress smooth, then sat.

They regarded each other. In the silence, he became more aware of the noises from outside, of people laughing and talking from the pool area below the balcony, of a helicopter in the distance somewhere and the far-off scream of a siren. Just another day in paradise, he thought with some irony.

He glanced over at the balcony door. "You shouldn't leave that open. This isn't Medicine Creek." Medicine Creek was the small Wyoming town where they'd both gone to high school. Meggie still lived on a ranch not far from there. "In L.A. the burglars tend to be fast and agile."

"I'll close it next time I leave the room."

"And at night."

She shrugged. "Whatever."

Exasperation rippled through him—at himself for giving a damn whether she left her balcony door open or not. And at her, for smelling so good and looking so good. For the power of the attraction that still existed, against all logic, between them.

He sipped again from his drink, then set it on the table and stared at the small amount of amber liquid in the bottom of the glass. "What do you want from me, Meggie?"

He heard her shift on the bed. "My father died. A week ago today. Did you know?"

Nate shook his head. He still had family in Medicine Creek. But it had been a month or two since he'd talked to any of them. "I hadn't heard."

Meggie's hands gripped the edge of the bed, on either side of her thighs. She stared down at her own knees. "It was cancer. But he would never let Doc Pruitt look at him. He just got thinner and thinner. And then, for a few weeks, he got really sick. And then he died."

Nate reached for the drink again. "I'm sorry." He offered the bland condolence, not knowing what the hell else to say. He drank. Then, with finality, he set the glass down. He looked at her, waiting.

She coughed, as if her throat had gone tight on her. "This is hard."

"I'm listening."

"Um, well, it was just assumed that he'd leave me the Double-K."

Alarm had him sitting up a little straighter. "You mean he didn't?"

"No, he did. Sort of. With a couple of conditions."

"What conditions?"

With a small sigh, she rose, went to the closet nook and took some papers from her suitcase, which stood open on the rack below the hangers. Looking solemn, she returned to him.

Reluctantly, he took the papers from her hand.

"That's my father's will." She moved over so she stood beside him. The woodsy smell of her taunted him as she pointed at the page on top. "Read from there."

He stared down at all the legal mumbo jumbo. "Look. Why don't you just explain it to me?"

He set the papers on the table by his empty glass.

She sighed again. "All right." She returned to the end of the bed, where she sat once more. For a moment, he felt some relief, because the scent of her faded a little with the distance. But the relief didn't last long.

"My father's been after me for years now to get married and give him some grandchildren. But I just never met the right guy." She paused. Her gaze slid away, then defiantly met his once more. "I mean, I didn't love any of the ones who asked. So I turned them down. And, well, it looks like my father decided to make sure I'd get a husband and some kids—from beyond the grave, if you know what I mean."

Nate did know what she meant—or at least he caught the general drift. And that made him long to bolt from the chair and head for the door.

But he hadn't heard her out yet. It seemed only right to give her that much. Somehow, he made himself sit still for the rest.

Meggie closed her eyes and rubbed her temples. Then she rested her hands on her knees. "This is the situation. According to my father's will, the ranch will be kept in trust, with me as the legal operator, for a period of two years. During that time, I am required to bear a child as a result of a lawful marriage."

His urge to get the hell out intensified. It was just as he'd feared. He asked, "And if you don't?"

"Then the Double-K will become public land."

"You'll get *nothing?*"

"Not exactly. My father set it up so that the herd will be sold at auction and all proceeds from that auction will be mine. I'll also get the money from the sale of the home place, which includes the main house, the old bunkhouse where my cousin and his family live now, the homesteader's cabin and the outbuildings, including the forty acres those buildings stand on. With that, and the profits from the sale of the stock, my father figured I'd have enough for a fresh start."

Nate found he could breathe a little easier. "So you won't be destitute."

"No. But I *will* lose the Double-K."

"What I mean is, you'll end up with a decent chunk of change, anyway."

Her generous mouth was a thin line. "Without the Double-K, who cares?"

He'd had enough of circling the point. He said flatly, "You called me here to ask me to marry you and try to get you pregnant."

She just stared at him with those big, soulful eyes.

"Have I got it right?" he demanded.

Very slowly, she nodded.

Nate stood. "No." He headed for the exit.

She jumped up, zipped around him and plastered herself against the door. "Nate. Just listen. Just give me—"

"Get away from the door."

But she refused to budge. "Nate. Please. You have to listen to me."

If she'd been anyone else, he would have shoved her

aside and gotten the hell out. But somehow, he couldn't bring himself to lay a hand on her.

"Nate." Her husky voice reached out, curled around him like smoke. "I told you how I felt about you once. And you sent me away. And I never meant to bother you again. I swear to you. But I had two dreams, Nate. My ranch. And you. How can you ask me to give up both?"

"I'm not asking a damn thing of you."

She let out a tight, frantic-sounding laugh. "I know. You never have. And you never will...."

"Find someone else."

She pressed herself harder against the door, her eyes burning with a purposeful fire. "That's exactly what I intend to do. If you turn me down."

That gave him pause; he refused to think why.

She talked fast. "Listen. This is my offer. I'm not asking for a lifetime from you. I don't want to fence you in and I'm not asking you to settle down. I want a ring on my finger. And a baby. And as soon as the baby's born, we can get a..." She hesitated over the next word, but she did get it out. "Divorce."

"This is insane."

"Not for me. For me, it would be the best of a bad deal. Because at least my baby's father would be the man I love."

That spooked him good. He fell back a step.

She must have seen the panic in his eyes. She put up a hand. "It's just a fact, Nate. I don't expect it to mean a thing to you. I swear. I love you, have loved you and will always love you. And if I'm going to have a baby, I want it to be yours. I won't tie you down. Just a ring and a baby, and then you're free."

He shook his head. What she asked was so much

like her: a total contradiction in terms. He spoke more kindly. "Meggie…"

"No. Listen. There's more."

"Meggie, this isn't going to—"

She ran right over him. "I have twenty thousand dollars that my grandmother Kane left to me. It's mine, free and clear. And I'll give it to you. As payment for…what I'm putting your through."

His gut tightened all over again. Essentially, she had just offered to pay him for fathering her child. The thought sickened him.

She wasn't finished. "I will go on my knees to you, Nathan Bravo. I will do anything. Anything at all."

"Stop."

She obeyed his command, waited there against the door, still begging with those big eyes.

He decided to try reason. "Look. Just slow down here. Let's just look logically at what you're asking."

"Yes," she agreed eagerly. "Fine. Let's look at it logically."

"Okay, then. What exactly are you thinking about here? Is this going to be some kind of test-tube thing?"

She stared. "What?"

"Are you talking about artificial insemination?"

Her face went crimson. She stammered, "Well, no. I mean, we would be married. And married people, um…"

"So you plan for us to have sex together?"

"Um. Well. Yeah."

"The more sex the better, right? To increase the odds that you'll actually conceive."

She frowned. "Yes. So?"

"Think. How are we going to do that, Meggie? I do have a life and a business to run—here, in L.A. I can't move to the Double-K for however long it takes you to get pregnant. And you can't run a ranch from my apartment.''

"We could work it out. I know we could. I've thought it through. You could stay at the Double-K as much as possible through the fall. Oh, I know you'd have to leave sometimes, when something just couldn't wait. But you're your own man, right? And we could it make a point to, um, get together at the most crucial times, when I'm...ovulating.''

Ovulating. Where the hell did they get words like that? "Meggie, listen—''

But she wouldn't listen. "No, really. It could work. It *will* work. And the money I'd pay you would help to make up for any business you might lose.''

Anger arrowed through him again at the mention of the money. "Forget the damn money.''

"No, really. I would want to pay you. I would want you to get something out of this for yourself.''

"I said, forget the damn money.'' It was a command.

She raised both hands, palms out. "All right. Whatever. But listen. We *could* work it out, so we could be together. You could stay with me as much as possible until the snows come. And then, when things get quiet at the ranch, Sonny and Farrah could handle things.''

"Sonny and Farrah?''

"My cousin and his wife. They work for me now, for the last three years or so.''

He thought he remembered hearing that somewhere. "Right.''

She rushed on. "Anyway, as soon as winter comes, I would come here and stay with you, until calving season. And with any luck, by then I'd be pregnant. You'd go back to your life and I'd go back to mine and when the baby comes, I'd send you the divorce papers in the mail. Okay?''

He only looked at her, shaking his head.

"Nate, please…''

He kept looking at her, showing her nothing—except his refusal. And then he said it aloud. "No, Meggie. I just can't help you with this. Now, get out of my way.''

"Nate…''

"I said, get out of my way.''

That did it. He watched the hope fade from her eyes. "That's your final decision?''

He nodded.

"Oh, Nate…''

"Move aside.''

She drew her shoulders back. "Fine. But I mean it. If you won't do it, I will find someone else.''

He looked her up and down. "That's supposed to change my mind? Give me a break.''

Give me a break….

Those were the words he had said to her all those years ago, when she had told him she loved him.

"I love you,'' she had sworn. "And I will always love you.''

He had looked down at her flushed face, at her full lips, which were soft and swollen from his kisses. And he had sneered, "Give me a break.''

She hadn't forgotten, any more than he had. He could see it in her eyes.

Now, foolishly, he felt remorse. For hurting her again. For dimming the brightness of those beautiful eyes. "Meggie…'' He reached out.

She ducked away, before he could touch her. And then she drew herself up once more. She turned and opened the door, stepping back, so the exit was clear. "Goodbye, Nate."

He had an idiot's urge to say more. But he quelled it.

With a final curt nod, he left her.

Chapter Two

Unfortunately, over the days that followed, Nate couldn't get Meggie out of his mind.

On Wednesday, three days after the meeting in her hotel room, he called his cousin Zach. Zach Bravo ran the family ranch, the Rising Sun Cattle Company, which shared more than one boundary with the Double-K. Zach and Meggie were good friends. When either came up shorthanded, the other would help out. The Kanes always put in an appearance during branding time at the Rising Sun. And there was usually a Bravo around if Meggie needed help in calving season.

Nate waited to call until nine at night, which was seven in Wyoming. By then, the day's work should be through and the dinner dishes cleared from the table.

Some strange woman answered the phone. "Yeah?"

Nate wondered if he'd dialed wrong. "Is this the Rising Sun?"

"Yeah."

"This is Nate. Nate Bravo?"

"Yeah, I heard of you."

"Let me talk to Zach."

"Hold on."

It took Zach forever to come on the line. Nate started to wonder if the strange woman had bothered to tell his cousin that he had a call. But finally, Nate heard the quiet, low voice.

"Hello, Nate."

"Hey, Zach."

"How are you doing?"

"Fine. Who the hell was that?"

Zach chuckled. "Mable LeDoux. She and her husband, Charlie, hired on about a month ago."

"She's keeping house and cooking?"

"You got it." Zach sounded grim. "And she's no Edna."

A year ago, Edna Heller, the ranch's longtime housekeeper, had become ill and been forced to retire. Edna had always taken care of the house—and the Bravos—as if they were her own. And the meals she used to put on the table, both in the main house and for the hands, kept everyone smiling. Zach was having a hell of a time trying to replace her. And it sounded as if Mable wouldn't last much longer than the others had.

Zach asked, "You coming home?"

"Not unless you need me."

"Nah, I'm dealing with things all right." Zach waited. He knew Nate. And Nate never called just to shoot the breeze.

Nate realized he probably should have thought this through a little better before picking up the phone.

"Nate? You okay?"

"Yeah. I'm fine. Listen. I heard that Meggie May's dad died."

Dead silence. Then Zach said, "Yeah. About a week and a half ago."

"How's she been?"

Another silence. Nate could almost hear Zach's mind working, as he carefully chose what to say. At last, he muttered grudgingly, "She's all right, I guess."

"You seen her much, since the funeral?"

More dead air. Then Zach said, "Meggie May's a good woman, Nate."

Damn. That was the thing about family. They always knew too much. "You don't have to worry about her and me," Nate said. "Nothing ever happened between us to speak of. And there's nothing going on now."

"Did she show up down there to see you?"

Nate muttered a word that would have made Edna Heller threaten to wash his mouth out with soap. "How did you know?"

"The Merchant's Society put on a dance, over at Medicine Creek Park, on the Fourth. I saw Meggie there. She asked about you."

"Asked what?"

"Asked if your name was in the L.A. phone book."

"What did you tell her?"

"I said, 'Bravo Investigative Services, in the Yellow Pages.' So. Did she come and see you?"

"Yeah, she came."

Another disapproving silence, then Zach asked, "Are you gonna tell me what this is all about?"

"No."

Zach grunted. "I don't think I like this."

"Don't worry, it's no big deal," Nate lied. Then he added, "I just need to know if she's all right."

"She's fine, last I heard. You remember that cousin of hers, Sonny? Used to come and stay over at the Double-K sometimes, in the summers?"

"Yeah."

"Well, Meggie and Sonny are running the Double-K together now."

"Yeah, I heard that."

"Sonny dropped by yesterday. Said they hired a new hand on Monday. Just temporary, Sonny says, until they get on top of things. I guess they fell behind some when Jason died."

A new hand. What did that mean? Did she plan to ask some no-account cowpuncher to father her child? "What do you know about him?"

"Who?"

"The new hand."

"Not a thing. Listen, Nate. That's all I can tell you. Because that's all I know. Last time I saw Meggie was on the Fourth. She seemed okay, for a woman whose dad had just died."

"Look…"

"What?"

He realized he didn't have anything worthwhile to say. So he muttered, "Hell. Nothing."

"Why don't you come on home for a while?" Zach suggested, more gently. "I'm not short of hands, but I can always use another pair. Lots of weeds to poison and ditches to burn. Not to mention hay to cut and fences to mend."

Nate felt the pull. He always did. If he closed his eyes, he could see the Big Horns, looming so high and proud over the endless, rolling prairie land. Overhead, there would be clean blue sky, with clouds like castles, white and high. And off to the east, a hawk soaring…

"Nate. What do you say?"

He remembered his freedom. He remembered his life. "Nah. Not right now."

"It *is* your place, too," Zach reminded him. Technically, the Rising Sun belonged equally to Nate and Zach and their third cousin, Cash. But Zach was the operator; he loved the ranching life and he made it pay.

"Some other time," Nate promised.

"I know, I know. Thanksgiving. Or Christmas. Don't let that L.A. smog fog your brain."

Nate promised he wouldn't and said goodbye.

He managed to hold off two more days before he got nuts enough to call Edna. Edna Heller was not only the former housekeeper of the Rising Sun, but also the mother-in-law of his other cousin, Cash. She could drive a man crazy, telling him what to eat and warning him to take care of himself, but Nate loved her anyway. She'd looked after him good, all those years ago, when his dad died and his mother turned him over to his grandpa Ross and took off for parts unknown. Edna had clucked over him and hugged him whether he liked it or not and generally treated him like a son, the way she'd done all three of the Bravo cousins. Widowed for two years now, Edna lived in a nice two-story house, which Cash had bought for her, in Medicine Creek.

And Edna always knew who was seeing whom.

"Why, it's funny you should ask about Megan May," Edna declared just a little too knowingly. "Because only this past Friday night Tillie Spitzenberger saw her at Arlington's Steak House with Barnaby Cotes. Kind of a surprise, everyone says, since we all thought she'd more or less told that boy she wasn't interested years ago...."

Edna chattered on, but Nate wasn't listening. Barnaby Cotes was the son of a Medicine Creek shop owner. And a smug, self-important piece of work if there ever was one. The thought of Cotes putting his slimy hands on Meggie made the blood pump too fast through Nate's veins. She deserved better than some fatheaded prig like that.

"Nathan, are you listening to me?"

"You know I am, Edna."

"Well then, what are you planning to do about Megan May?"

"Nothing."

"Then why did you ask about her?"

"Edna."

"Yes, Nathan?"

"Let's drop it."

"Always so prickly. When are you coming home? We miss you. And you should see that nephew of yours. He's getting bigger and better-looking every day. Just like his daddy." Cash's son, Tyler, had been born just the Christmas before. "Nathan?"

"I'm still here."

"Well? Are you coming home? We haven't seen you in months. It's too long. And I worry that you don't eat right, and it's bound to be dangerous, chasing after criminals and shady characters the way you do."

"I'm not planning to come home right now."

"When, then?"

"I can't say for sure."

She lectured him some more. And finally, about ten minutes later, he managed to say goodbye and get off the phone.

After that call, he swore to himself that he would make no more attempts to learn about Meggie May.

He told himself that her search for a husband to father her child was none of his damn business, and promised himself he'd put her completely from his mind.

But then, on Monday, a week and a day after meeting with Meggie at the Hollywood Franklin, Nate got a job offer to track an embezzler down into Mexico. The money was right and expenses were generous. And still, he heard himself turning it down.

The new hand, Lev Jarvis, jumped out to open the gate and Sonny drove the pickup through. Lev walked the gate closed and sprinted over to join Sonny and Meggie.

Meggie leaned out the passenger window of the cab as a pair of grasshoppers leaped out from under the wheels, their wings snapping and shining in the sun. Meggie looked up at the blue bowl of the sky. The few clouds in sight looked like little shreds of white cotton. It was hot. Not far off, barn swallows hovered, ready to swing away after any hopper that dared to jump too high.

Meggie smiled to herself. She was happy to be out, doing useful work. The days really weren't so bad. It was the nights that killed her lately. Thinking of her home. And what she must do if she hoped to keep it.

But when she trundled around checking the stock with Sonny, she could tip her face to the sun and keep her mind on work. She glanced out over the pasture. It had been a pretty good year, with respectable rainfall. The grass still had green in it. And here and there, even now in July, she could still pick out the tiny bright heads of purple flax and the sunny faces of black-eyed Susans.

Lev, who was shy and respectful and young enough

not to fear skin cancer, took off his shirt and tossed it in the back of the pickup. Meggie grinned at him and pointed. "There's a pond over that ridge there. I figure there should be fifteen heifers and their first calves hanging around it. We'll check the salt box and the mineral tubs." They'd also check the stock. They'd look for heifers with tight bags, which would mean a calf wasn't sucking. They'd search for any sick animals, which they'd take home to treat. They'd look over the calves for any sores. In the heat, a calf could be dead in a day or two from an untreated wound. And they'd hope to find only the Black Angus bulls they'd put in that pasture last month. Black Angus bulls produced a small, wiry calf that hit the ground running. They were the perfect bulls to put with heifers, both in their first and second years of calving out, because a smaller calf made for an easier birth.

"Hop in," Meggie said.

Lev joined his shirt in the back of the pickup. Sonny shifted into gear, but he didn't get ten feet before a horn honked, loud and long, behind them at the pasture gate. Sonny put on the brakes. Meggie leaned farther out her window and looked back.

It was one of the Bravo pickups. That big old GMC that Nate's grandfather Ross used to favor in the final years before he died. Meggie squinted, trying to see through the glare on the windshield to whoever was behind the wheel. But she couldn't make out the face.

She swung open her door. "I'll be right back." She sprinted toward the GMC. At the gate, she paused to slip the latch and slide through. As soon as she got past the glaring windshield and looked in the open window of the driver's door, she saw the man behind the wheel.

Her poor heart started thundering so loud she felt sure all of Johnson County could hear it.

She froze a few feet from the door and put her hand to her throat. "What?" she asked. The word sounded as numb and dazed as she felt.

Nate hung an elbow out the driver's door, looking perfectly casual, as if he drove out to her ranch in his granddaddy's old pickup every day of the week. "Your cousin's wife said I might find you here."

She gaped at him. She had absolutely no idea what to say. Stalling, trying to get her wits back about her, she took off her hat, fiddled with the brim for a moment, then put it back on.

Nate looked past her "Who's that?" He nodded at the pickup that still waited for her in the pasture beyond the gate.

She looked where he nodded. "Who?"

"That fool with his shirt off." He sounded angry.

"That's Lev. Lev Jarvis. He hired on to help out for a while."

"Doing what?" His tone was nasty.

Meggie saw no point at all in replying to that, so she didn't.

"Get in," he said.

"Why?"

"We have to talk."

She looked toward the other pickup again. "Now?"

"Now."

Meggie considered. It wasn't exactly the perfect time for a talk. Evening would have been better, after the day's work was through. But hope had lit a fire inside her again. Why else would he show up here, but to tell her that he had changed his mind about her request?

She'd go insane waiting till evening to hear what he had to say.

"Well?"

"Wait here." She turned and slid back through the gate.

"What's going on?" Sonny asked when she reached the driver's side of the cab.

"It's Nate Bravo." She knew she sounded breathless, but that was no big deal. After all, she had been running.

Sonny, who was tall, thin, sandy haired and pretty much like a brother to her, frowned at her through his open window. "Nate Bravo? What the hell's he doing here?"

Guilt poked at her. Meggie had yet to say a word to Sonny about the will. As far as he knew, he and Farrah and their two kids had a place to live and work for as long as they wanted it. She'd already lied to him outright about the situation once, when she'd told him she had to go down to Cheyenne to see about a certain Black Angus bull—when in reality, she'd booked a flight to L.A. She hated to lie, but she wanted to have some kind of solution to the problem before she told him about it.

And just maybe, today, Nate would give her a solution.

"Meggie, what's Nate Bravo doing here?" Sonny asked again.

She avoided the question. "I want to talk to him for a while. You and Lev go on over to the pond without me, okay?"

"You're going off with Nate Bravo?" Sonny sounded thoroughly disapproving. Nate had always had a bad reputation. Apparently even Sonny, who had only lived in the area for the past few years, had heard the rumors about him, about how wild he'd been while growing up, and how he'd always sworn he would never settle down.

"Like I said, I need to talk to him. And I'm not sure how long it's going to take. I'll just have to catch up with you."

Sonny was quiet for a moment, then he asked, "Is something going on that I should know about?"

Meggie forced a confident smile. "No. It's nothing." Guilt nudged her again. It was a lot more than nothing. But she certainly couldn't be expected to explain it all now.

Sonny studied her face for a long moment before he nodded. "We'll check the Deerling pasture after we're through here." He referred to the next pasture north. They called it the Deerling pasture because Meggie's father had bought it from the Deerlings when old man Deerling died and his family had to sell it to pay the inheritance taxes. The Deerlings had sold out altogether not long after that and moved to Oregon. But they still had a pasture in Wyoming named after them.

"Go on." Meggie slapped the door of the pickup. Sonny saluted her and shifted into gear again. She stood, watching, until the pickup crested the rise and disappeared on the other side.

Then she turned and ran back to where Nate waited for her.

Nate drove too fast. They bounced over the rutted dirt road as if one of the bad guys he chased for a living had turned the tables and come after him for a change. Meggie held on to the "chicken" handle over the door and didn't say a word. Finally, he jerked the

wheel to the side and pulled off into a patch of sage
and buffalo grass. He switched off the engine and
draped an arm over the top of the steering wheel.

He stared out the windshield at the rolling prairie
that went on forever up ahead. "Have you made your
offer to any other men?"

She looked straight ahead, too. "No."

Actually, she had tried to make herself ask Barnaby
Cotes. She'd run into him in town last week, and said
yes when he invited her to dinner. But an evening with
him had reminded her too thoroughly of all the ways
he wasn't Nate. And somehow, though she knew she
must find a husband, she just hadn't quite managed to
make herself propose to Barnaby.

"What about Barnaby Cotes?" Nate demanded.

She blinked and looked at him, wondering if he had
read her mind. "Who told you I went out with Barnaby?"

He still didn't look at her, but the side of his mouth
twisted with irony. "I'm a detective, remember?"

She figured it out. "You called Edna."

He grunted, still looking out the window. "Yeah. I
called Edna." He fisted his hand and tapped it on the
steering wheel. "So. Did you tell Cotes? About the
will? About what you need?"

"No, I did not."

She kept looking at his profile, at his hawklike nose
and his high cheekbones, at his straight black hair that
he always left just long enough to make him look disreputable. His mother, Sharilyn Tickberry Bravo, was
part Lakota Sioux. And the mark of his ancestors was
strong in Nate's face—on both sides. He had cheekbones like knife blades, a nose fit for a tribal chief and

the Bravo mouth, which was a little bit full for a man. A mouth that looked like it was made to kiss a woman.

"Who knows about this, Meggie?" Nate demanded.

She kept her head high. "You, me and G. Vernon Bannister."

"Who's G. Vernon Bannister?"

"The lawyer who handled my father's will."

"No one else?"

"Why does it matter?"

He continued to stare out the bug-spattered windshield. Then at last he said, "I guess it doesn't matter. I just wanted to know, that's all."

"Well, G. Vernon Bannister told me. And I told you. And that's as far as it's gone."

"Fine."

"And now it's my turn to ask a question."

"Ask."

"Why are you here?"

He turned to look at her then. His dark eyes were hard and fathoms deep. "I changed my mind. I'll marry you."

Chapter Three

Meggie found she couldn't speak.

But it didn't matter, because Nate had more to say. "If the offer's still open, I'll accept your proposition pretty much as you laid it out a week ago—with a couple of conditions."

She managed to croak, "Name them."

He did. "You agree from the first that if I do give you the child you need, I'll always be free to see him. He'll also be allowed to come stay with me whenever I can make decent arrangements for his care."

Meggie saw nothing wrong with that. "Agreed."

He added, "And I won't take any money from you, period."

She couldn't go along with that. It just didn't seem fair. Even though he'd never said the words, she knew in her heart that Nate cared for her in his own independent way. He understood how much the Double-K meant to her. And in the end, he was coming through to help her keep it. She wanted to pay him back for that, somehow.

"Nate, really. It's silly for you to be so stubborn about—"

"No money."

"But you should be getting *something* out of—"

He glared at her. "No money."

It was hot in the cab of that pickup. Meggie took off her hat and armed sweat from her forehead. "I'm not exactly in a position to argue with you." She tossed her hat on the seat between them. "So you just go right ahead and cheat yourself." Freed of the hat, her hair started falling down.

A hint of a grin came and went on Nate's mouth. "Thanks. I will."

Meggie twisted her hair tight again and anchored it more securely at the back of her head. She smoothed the last stray hairs into place.

She felt guilty, to be giving in on this issue. But the hard truth was, she needed that money. If everything went as she prayed it would, she'd have some hefty inheritance taxes to pay in two years. She didn't want to end up like the Deerlings, with someone else's pasture named after her. She wanted to keep her ranch. Now, with Nate's help, she just might manage that.

"Okay, then. That's settled," she said. "You get no money."

"Good enough." He was grinning again.

She couldn't help grinning right back. "So. Have I met all your terms?"

"You sure have."

They stared at each other, across the seat of the cab. Only her hat lay between them. She could have moved it. Or they could have leaned across it, to share the kiss that would seal this strange marriage bargain. But they didn't.

As Meggie gazed into those dark eyes, a memory came to her. Of the first time she ever saw him, the summer they were both fourteen—the summer Nate's grandfather had brought him to live at the Rising Sun.

Nate had been nothing but trouble to his grandpa that first year. And the day Meggie met him was no exception. He'd stolen a Rising Sun pickup that day, a pickup not much different from the one he and Meggie sat in now. And he'd gone joyriding on the rutted dirt roads that crisscrossed his grandpa's ranch.

Probably without even realizing it, he'd crossed over onto Double-K land. The muffler of the pickup must have been scraping the road ruts, setting off sparks. The sparks found dry grass.

Meggie had been lying just over a rise, next to Crystal Creek, naked, after a refreshing swim. Her favorite horse, a sorrel gelding she'd named Renegade, nipped the grass nearby. Renegade had lifted his head and sniffed the air. And then he'd let out a long, nervous whinny. Meggie looked up and saw the smoke—just a tiny trail of it. But on the prairie, a tiny wisp of smoke could become an inferno in no time at all.

She yanked on her underpants, her boots and her shirt, jumped into the saddle and took off. Over the rise, she rode up on a black-haired boy. He'd just managed to beat out the flames with an old blanket he must have found in the truck.

He looked up at her, his face smudged and his eyes wild—and then he burst out laughing. "You're damn near naked!" he crowed.

She called him a fool. An idiot. A jerk. And then she

started laughing, too. It was good, to laugh like that with someone. She and her father lived alone at the ranch, except for the hired hands that came and went. Jason Kane wasn't much of a talker, so Meggie sometimes found herself tongue-tied in company.

But she didn't feel tongue-tied with this boy. She sensed a kinship with him. She just knew that here was a friend. And she suspected that he knew it, too.

"Wait here," she told him when the laughter finally faded. "I'll go put my clothes on."

When she returned, he was still there. She gave him a hand up and he rode behind her, back to the creek again. He slid down from Renegade and knelt at the bank to wash the soot from his face and to drink long and deep. She dismounted, too, and joined him. They ended up splashing each other, laughing some more.

And then, for at least an hour, they sat there, on the bank, in the shade of the cottonwoods, with the cottonwood fluff like fairy dust blowing in the incessant wind.

He told her who he was. And that his dad had died a few months before—of blood poisoning from not bothering to get himself a tetanus shot after some tough character had bitten him in a bar fight. Once they put his dad in the ground, Nate's mom had dumped him on his grandfather. Nate said he hated his grandfather, who was always looking at him sideways and shaking his head. Nate just knew that Ross Bravo wondered why he'd let someone like Nate come and live at his precious ranch. Nate also hated Edna Heller, who had decided to civilize him. And he couldn't stand his cousin Cash, who was perfect. And he despised his cousin Zach, who did everything right.

Meggie listened and nodded. She'd seen in Nate's eyes that he didn't really hate the Bravos and Edna. In time, he would realize he was one of them, too. And then things would be all right for him at the Rising Sun.

When they parted, Nate promised to meet her for a swim the next day. But he didn't show up. Ross grounded him, for stealing the pickup. Meggie didn't see him for weeks. But it didn't matter. They were friends.

Their friendship lasted for two years. Until they both started to grow up. Nate's shoulders broadened and he put on muscle. Meggie began to fill out, too. And boys started looking at her the way men looked at women. But Meggie had no interest in just any boy. Her eyes turned to Nate, and she saw more than a friend. At the same time, Nate started dating the girls a guy only went out with for one reason—and avoiding Meggie whenever they met, as if he didn't even know her anymore.

Meggie always thought of that period as the first time he broke her heart. The second time occurred a few years later, on that Fourth of July night, when she'd finally worked up the courage to tell him of her love— and he had scorned her.

Now, in the sweltering cab of Ross Bravo's old pickup, Meggie couldn't help wondering if she had just set herself up for heartbreak number three.

Nate began laying out alternatives for the wedding. "We could fly to Reno right away, I guess. Or I suppose we could go into the clinic in town tomorrow, get the blood tests and then get married at the county courthouse as soon as the results come in."

All at once, another problem occurred to her. A very delicate problem. One she'd promised herself she would face when she came to it. "Nate?"

"Yeah?"

"Um, there's something more I think we really should consider."

"What?"

"What if one of us…can't have children?"

He let out a long breath, then he picked up her hat from between them on the seat. He smoothed dual creases in the crown. "I have a suggestion."

"I'm listening."

"There's only so much you can do here. And then you just have to let nature take its course." He held out her hat.

She took it, put it on her head. "You're right. I know. But…"

"But what?" He sounded grim.

"Well, I think we should be realistic here. I need a baby. And I want to be as sure as I *can* be, going into this, that it's going to work."

"Get to the point Meggie."

"The point is…"

He stared at her, one of those hard, dark, unreadable stares of his.

She made herself say it. "Um, would you be willing to take a few tests?"

For a moment, he went on staring at her. Then he swore crudely under his breath. "You don't ask much, do you, Meggie May?"

She turned her body toward him, hoisted a leg up on the seat and rested her hand on the ankle of her boot. "Let's be frank, okay?"

He squinted at her disbelievingly. Then, with a snort, he shoved open his door, braced it with a boot and muttered, "It's hotter than the south end of hell in here."

Wisely, she refrained from pointing out that he was the one who had chosen the cab of a truck in the middle of the prairie at midday in July to have this conversation. "Nate. Is there any possibility at all that you might want to...stay married to me, after this is all over and done?"

He was staring out the windshield again. Slowly, he faced her. "None."

She told herself that didn't hurt. "Okay. Then there's really no sense in putting ourselves through this if I'm infertile or you can't...father a child. Please. We're better off knowing where we stand."

He shook his head. "A few tests. You want me to take a few tests...."

Two days later, they drove to Billings together in Nate's rental car. Meggie had arranged appointments for them at a fertility clinic there. They sat in the waiting room for an hour, filling out forms.

Then they went in for an interview with the doctor.

Meggie explained their situation. They'd come to the clinic for a little assurance—in advance. They wanted to get married, but having children was a high priority for both of them. If there were any barriers to conception, Meggie hoped the doctor might discover them. "So we'll know where we stand on this right from the first," she said.

The doctor coughed into his hand. "Miss Kane. Most couples don't even contact a fertility specialist until they've been trying to conceive a child for at least a year."

"I understand that," Meggie replied carefully. "And I...respect that. I do. But Nate and I really want to know ahead of time if anything is going to keep us from being parents. It's just...terribly important to us."

The doctor frowned. "My dear young woman, even if I found no contraindications of fertility in either of you, there could still be a number of reasons conception might not occur. I am simply not in the business of providing guarantees.''

Meggie rushed to reassure him. "Doctor, really. We aren't asking for a guarantee. Not at all. We just want help in ruling out the obvious.''

"The obvious?''

"I mean, if either of us can absolutely *never* have children, we want to know.''

The doctor looked at Nate. "And just where do you stand in this, Mr. Bravo?''

Nate slid a glance at Meggie and saw her smile grow tight. He knew she didn't feel she could count on him to back her up. And that inspired a perverse desire to prove her wrong.

He reached out and took her hand. She stiffened at the contact, but only a little—not enough that the doctor would notice. Nate brought her fingers to his lips and looked over her knuckles into her slightly panicked eyes. "Meggie wants me to give her a baby,'' he said to the doctor, though he didn't break contact with those wide brown eyes. "And I want Meggie to have what she wants.''

"Do *you* want children yourself, Mr. Bravo?'' the doctor inquired.

He lowered Meggie's hand, but he didn't let go of it. Instead, he twined his fingers with hers. "Absolutely.'' He rested their clasped hands in his lap and gave the doctor a big smile. "I want a whole houseful of kids. It's my major dream in life, to tell you the truth.''

The doctor beamed back at him. "A real family man.''

"I'm afraid you've found me out.''

The doctor beamed some more. And then he coughed

again. "Well then. All right. I think we can perform a few basic tests, though of course you'll each have to sign a release stating your understanding of the issues we've just discussed."

"Thank you," Nate said. He squeezed Meggie's hand, and she immediately tried to tug free. He didn't let her go. Instead, he smiled at her adoringly. "Say thank-you to the doctor, darling."

He saw the confusion in her eyes. He had surprised her, by playing along so well. And she wasn't sure if she liked it. But she didn't let him throw her. "Yes, Doctor. Thank you," she said with great sincerity. "Really. I can't tell you how much this means to me."

They went to separate rooms for their physicals. Nate's was strictly routine. The doctor measured his blood pressure and heart rate. He thumped Nate's chest and back, checked his reflexes with a little steel hammer, poked at his stomach and prodded his privates. As soon as the doctor left the examining room, a nurse came in and drew blood.

And then the nurse led Nate to the rest room at the end of the hall. She handed him a plastic cup. "We'll need a semen sample."

"Gotcha."

"We have a selection of men's magazines, if you think they might help."

"No, thanks. I'll manage."

Nate took his cup and entered the rest room, where he conjured up a nice little fantasy—centering around Meggie, as a matter of fact. It worked out fine.

The doctor spoke to them once more before they left, informing them that the lab results should be back within forty-eight hours. They should make an appointment for another consultation.

The one hundred fifty–mile drive home didn't take that long, since Nate had the wheel and Montana had no speed limits. Meggie was silent for half of the ride. She stared out the window at the rolling land and the rows of drift fences positioned at a slant on the rises near the road, to catch the snow and control where it piled up.

Finally, she turned to him. "You were very convincing, with the doctor."

He shot her a single glance. "You're mad at me."

He saw her shrug in his side vision. "No," she said. "I admit you confused me. I don't think I've ever seen you so enthusiastic about anything, in all the years I've known you." She smiled out the windshield. "Actually, I kind of liked it."

Irritation rose in him. "It was only an act."

"I know that." She gave a soft little sigh and said no more.

He drove faster. They crossed into Wyoming. From the border, it didn't take long before he was pulling into the yard in front of the Double-K ranch house.

Meggie turned to him. "Monday, then? Early?"

"I'll be here to get you at eight. Is that early enough?"

"That's fine." She leaned on her door, climbed out and then paused before she shut it. "Nate?"

"Yeah?"

"Thanks. You were great. You really were."

A ridiculous flush of pleasure washed through him. He scowled at her. "You're welcome."

Still smiling that wide, gorgeous smile, she shut the door.

* * *

The next day was Friday. Nate spent it and the weekend that followed helping Zach out around the Rising Sun and avoiding his cousin's probing, suspicious glances. Zach knew something was up. But he'd never been a man who would pry. He'd wait for the right opening before he'd ask any questions. Nate made sure he got no openings.

Edna, however, never required openings. She considered the private lives of the Bravo cousins her own personal territory. And as soon as she learned that Nate had appeared at the Rising Sun, she insisted he and Zach must come to her place in town for Sunday dinner. Edna's housemate, Tess DeMarley, would cook.

The last time Nate had come home, over Christmas, Tess had cooked all the meals out at the ranch. Each one had been excellent. Nate looked forward to sampling her cooking again.

He did not, however, look forward to Edna's questions, which started the minute he and Zach walked in the door.

"Nathan." She hugged him and kissed him. "Come in. Sit down. And tell me. What's brought you home to us when it isn't even a holiday?"

"I just felt like a visit."

"Are you sure that's all? You were seen driving through town this past Thursday. With Megan May Kane."

"He was?" Zach glowered.

"Who saw me?" Nate demanded.

Edna patted his arm. "I'm sorry, Nathan. But I can't tell you that. Everyone knows about your temper. If someone was hurt because I opened my big mouth, well I simply could not live with myself."

"I'm not going to hurt anyone, Edna."

"I just don't think it's wise for me to say any more."

"Well, your source is mistaken," Nate lied—with authority, he hoped.

Edna smiled indulgently. "My source is not mistaken. And here's Tess with that wonderful cheese ball of hers. You boys help yourselves, now."

They sat down to eat half an hour later. With Zach glaring at him and Edna watching him like a hawk, Nate found it hard to give the great food the attention it deserved. Tess's little daughter, Jobeth, eased the situation somewhat. She'd been out to the ranch a number of times and fallen in love with the place. She had a thousand questions for Zach—everything from how all the barn cats were doing to whether he'd seen her favorite bull snake in the cake shack lately. At least Zach stopped giving Nate dirty looks long enough to answer Jobeth's questions.

But the ride home was grim and deathly silent.

Once they got in the house, Zach turned to him. "You got anything you want to say to me?"

Now, how the hell could a man answer that? Nate lifted a shoulder in a careless shrug. "Not a thing."

Zach looked at him, a long look full of pained disapproval. And then he turned for the stairs.

Nate watched his cousin go, still wondering what he should have told him. It would have been jumping the gun to say that he and Meggie were getting married. She wanted to know the results of those tests they'd taken before they told anyone. And besides, at its core, the marriage was hardly the kind of arrangement Zach would approve of. Nate realized that he and Meggie had to talk; they had to decide exactly how much everyone would know about this marriage of theirs.

* * *

As agreed, they drove to Billings early the next day. There they learned that Nate was perfectly capable of fathering a child and that all of Megan's equipment appeared to be in working order, as well.

On the ride home, Meggie told Nate that the next step should be explaining the situation to her cousin Sonny. "He doesn't understand why I keep taking off with you."

Nate grunted. "He's heard about how bad I am, right?"

She sighed. "Oh, Nate..."

"Hey. It's no big deal. I *am* bad. And you shouldn't be hanging around with me."

"You are not bad."

"Am so."

They shared a glance, then he turned his gaze toward the road again. She said, "Seriously. Lately, it seems that every time I look at Sonny, I see worry in his eyes. And he does have a right to know what's going on."

"Fine. So tell him."

She shifted in her seat a little, and he knew she was building up to laying something new on him.

"Go on, spit it out," he said.

For a moment, she didn't say anything. He shot her another glance and saw she was looking out the passenger window, in the direction of a flock of blackbirds perched in close-packed rows on a drift fence that ran along a rise above the highway. It was rare to see so many of them together, this time of year. Usually, they spread out in the spring and didn't gather again until time for the fall migration. And yet, there they were, in the middle of summer, a whole flock of them. Before the car passed them, the birds took flight, like a hundred tiny ink spots scattered on the wind.

"Meggie. Speak."

"I'm trying. I've just, well, I've been thinking, that's all."

"Sounds dangerous."

"Don't tease."

"Sorry. 'You've been thinking…'"

"Well, I think we should let Sonny—and everyone else, too—believe this is a real marriage, not one with a built-in divorce at the end of it. I think it'll be easier on everyone if we just play it out as if we plan for it to last forever."

"And when the time comes to call it quits?"

"We'll just say it didn't work out."

Nate thought of Edna and the disapproving stares she could lay on a man. And he thought of Zach, so moral and upright. And Cash, who until pretty recently had been a lot like Nate—determined never to let some woman get control of his heart. But now Cash and Abby were as good as joined at the hip, and Cash had suddenly developed a lot of respect for the state of matrimony.

Nate could read the writing on the bathroom wall, all right. He would get no peace from anyone in his entire family if they knew he was playing temporary husband and sperm donor to Meggie May Kane.

"Nate?" Meggie asked nervously. "What do you say?"

"That I've been thinking along the same lines myself."

"Really?" She sounded genuinely relieved. "Terrific." She laid her arm along the back of the seat. "What do you think about the will?"

"What do you mean, what do I think?"

"I mean, should I tell Sonny and Farrah about it?"

"What for?"

"Well, they have a right to know, don't they, that I may lose the Double-K? It is their livelihood, too, after all."

"Hell. I suppose so."

"Good, then." She leaned toward him a little, across the seat. He got a whiff of that scent of hers—and he knew another request was coming at him.

"What else?" he demanded bleakly.

"I think you should be there when I tell them. You know. As my fiancé, it's only logical that you would be there at my side, giving me the love and support I need at a time like this."

"Right."

"I think you should come for dinner. About six tonight. Oh, and I want to give them a percentage of the Double-K, too—in the end, I mean, if everything works out. I thought I'd tell them about that tonight, along with everything else."

"It's your ranch."

"So that means you'll be there?"

He glared at the road ahead.

"Nate? Will you be there?"

Grudgingly, he muttered, "All right."

That night, in the old-fashioned kitchen of the Double-K ranch house, after dinner had been served and cleared off, Lev Jarvis returned to his quarters in the homesteader's cabin out beyond the corrals and the horse pasture. Farrah took her little son and daughter back across the yard to the old bunkhouse, which Sonny had fixed up into a home for his family.

Twenty minutes later, Farrah returned alone. She took

the chair beside her husband, across the table from Meggie and Nate.

"Okay," Sonny said. "Suppose you tell us what is going on around here."

Meggie had the will ready. She stood and laid it before her cousin and his wife. "Read that section there."

Sonny and Farrah bent over the page. Then, after a few minutes, Sonny looked up. "This is some kind of condition that you have to fulfill to keep the Double-K, right?"

Meggie nodded. "I have to marry and have a baby within two years—or we lose the ranch."

Sonny and Farrah both frowned, then bent over the page again. At last, Sonny shoved the will away. "Are you sure?"

"Positive."

"Why the hell would he do a thing like that?"

Farrah put her hand over his. "Sonny…" she murmured soothingly.

"He's lucky he's dead," Sonny muttered. "If he wasn't, I'd kill him myself."

"Hush, now." Farrah squeezed his hand. "Don't speak ill of the dead."

"I'm sorry, Sonny," Meggie said. "I know I should have told you sooner. I just…I didn't know how to break it to you."

Sonny met her eyes. "What could have been in his mind? You meant everything to him. How could he do this to you?"

"He wanted me to get married. And have a family."

"Well, this is sure one crazy way to make that happen."

"I agree."

"We'll have to see a lawyer. We'll have to—"

Meggie was shaking her head. "I've checked into it. There's no breaking that will. Dad was sane. And he had a right to do whatever he wanted with what belonged to him. He had a lawyer draw that will up, and it's properly witnessed, too."

"So that means..."

"I fulfill the conditions—or we lose the ranch. Period."

Sonny groaned. "So what happens now?" And then his eyes shifted to Nate. The truth dawned. He looked at his cousin again. "Him?" he breathed in complete disbelief. "You're marrying *Nate Bravo?*"

Nate, who'd been pointedly ignoring the other man's dirty looks all evening, had to remind himself to keep cool. This was Meggie's show, after all. And he would let her run it however she saw fit. He would not lose his temper just because her uptight cousin considered him a bad marriage risk.

Hell, he *was* a bad marriage risk! So what was there to get offended about?

Meggie jumped right in to defend her choice. She reached for his hand and when she found it, she held on tight. "The truth is, I've always loved Nate."

Across the table, Sonny let out a snort of disbelief. He focused narrowed blue eyes on Nate. "You're some kind of detective in L.A., aren't you?"

"Yeah."

"So I don't get it. You live in L.A. Meggie lives here. How are you gonna get together to...uh..." His face turned as red as his hair.

Meggie swiftly explained that Nate would stay at the Double-K until fall. "And this winter, I'll have to ask you and Farrah to handle things here while I go to L.A."

Sonny looked totally unconvinced. "Right. And what

about after that? Are you trying to tell us that every year the two of you will disappear to L.A.? You're planning to be a part-time rancher—is that what you're trying to say? There's no such thing, and we all know it.''

Meggie's face turned red. ''No. Of course I don't mean that, Sonny.''

''Well, then, what do you mean?''

''I mean that...well, after this year, we'll have a better grip on everything. And we can...decide what to do next.''

Meggie's half-baked, stammered explanation didn't convince Sonny of anything—except exactly what they'd been trying to keep him from figuring out. ''I get it. You've made some deal with him. He'll marry you and try to give you...what you need. And after that, it won't matter who lives where, because you won't be together anyway.''

''Oh, Sonny, no. You don't understand.'' Meggie looked miserable.

''What are you paying him?'' Sonny demanded. ''Your twenty thousand from Granny Kane?''

Nate decided it was time he stepped in. He held Meggie's hand tighter. ''She's not paying me a damn thing.''

Sonny blinked. ''I'm not talking to you.''

''Fine. But *I'm* talking to *you*. And I'm telling you that this is a real marriage.'' He spoke with outraged conviction, managing to sound as if he meant every word. ''And Meggie and I plan for it to last the rest of our lives.''

Sonny gaped, but still tried to keep up the cynicism. ''Right. Sure.''

''Bet on it. Come next spring, Meggie and I will be moving back here to stay.'' Where were all these lies coming from? Nate wondered vaguely—and then lied some more. "The truth is, this winter, while Meggie and I are in L.A., I'll be closing up my business there for good." As if there were a damn thing to close up, besides a two-bedroom apartment and a few utility bills.

Sonny took the bait. "You will?"

"Yeah. And once that's done, we'll be back here. Forever. Got that?"

Sonny gulped. "Well, yeah."

Nate looked Meggie's cousin up and down, then challenged, "So what do you think?"

"Uh, it sounds…"

"Good." Farrah provided the word for her floundering husband. "It sounds real good. If Meggie loves you and you love her, then we're happy for you both."

"And there's more," Meggie piped up.

She must mean the percentage she wanted to promise them. Nate gave her the floor. "Right. Meggie, tell them what you have planned."

Meggie gave him a look of pure adoration. Then she smiled at her cousin and his wife. "As soon as the terms of the will are met, Nate and I want to go into a real partnership with you two."

"A partnership?" Sonny looked a little dazed.

"Yes," Meggie said. "If everything works out, and Nate and I have the baby we need to keep the Double-K, I intend for you two to have a twenty-five-percent share of the place."

"No, Meggie…" Now Sonny looked stunned.

"Don't argue. You've worked hard for the Double-K for three years now. And you'll have to run things yourselves this winter. You deserve to be working for something you can call your own. When all this trouble is through, this will be partly your ranch, too. We'll all be in this together, in the best and truest sense." She turned her wide smile briefly on Farrah, and then focused on her cousin again. "So, what do you say?"

"I...Meggie, are you sure?"

"I am. Now, please. Make your peace with Nate, because the two of you will be working together from now on."

Sonny nodded. "All right." He met Nate's eyes. "I guess maybe I...jumped the gun a little."

Nate shrugged. "Forget it."

"No. The truth is, I heard a few things about you. That you were a wild kid. And not the kind of man who would ever be settling down. And I judged you on rumor. I can see now that I was wrong."

Nate felt about two inches high. Simple, hardworking men were always too damn easy to deceive. Still, the agreement he and Meggie had made was just between the two of them. He would keep up the act. He held out his hand. "Let's start fresh from here."

They shook across the table.

"You take good care of her," Sonny warned.

"I will," Nate promised. That wasn't a total lie. He *would* take good care of Meggie. He would give her what she needed to keep what she loved. And then, as her cousin had guessed before Nate started conning him, they would go their separate ways.

Chapter Four

Nate and Meggie said their vows that Saturday, at the Johnson County Courthouse in Buffalo, with Sonny and Farrah as witnesses. They planned to drive back to Medicine Creek, stop for dinner at Arlington's Steak House and then head on home to the ranch. Meggie walked out of the courthouse on her new husband's arm, feeling happy and full of hope—almost as if she and Nate had just married for real and forever. The sun shone down from a cloudless sky.

They didn't get five steps along Main Street before Cash, the blond, blue-eyed charmer of the Bravo cousins, pulled up beside them in his Cadillac. He slid across the seat and shoved open the back door. "Get in."

"What the hell is this?" Nate demanded.

"A kidnapping, what do you think?" Cash met his

cousin's dark stare. "So just do what I tell you—for once. Or there will be hell to pay."

"Says who?"

"Edna."

Nate turned to Meggie, a sheepish grin on his face. "If Edna wants us, then I guess we'd better go."

Meggie laughed. "Fine by me."

Nate took her elbow to help her into the car. But then he stopped and looked around. "What happened to Sonny and Farrah and the kids?"

"They're already on their way where we're going," Cash said. "Now, get in. We were supposed to be there ten minutes ago."

Cash took them to Medicine Creek—but not to Arlington's Steak House. Instead, he delivered them to the big house he shared with Abby and their son on North Street.

"March up to the door and knock," he commanded.

They did as they were told. Edna Heller answered, all dressed for a party in a blue silk shirtwaist, looking so dainty and feminine it was hard to believe that she possessed a will of iron and the relentless determination of a drill sergeant.

"Oh, here you both are, at last." Edna kissed Meggie. "Oh, my dear. I am so thrilled about this." She held out her arms to Nate, who obediently moved in for a hug. "Congratulations, Nathan." She patted his broad back. "You are a very lucky man."

She stepped back, beaming, and turned to lead them into the high-ceilinged living room.

Friends and family were waiting there. In unison, everyone shouted, "Surprise!"

Abby stepped right up, her pretty face alight and her blond hair, as usual, falling in her eyes. She grabbed

Meggie and hugged her. "I said this would happen," she whispered in Meggie's ear.

"You did?"

"Yep. Last year. On my own wedding day."

Meggie had no time to respond to that, because Zach grabbed her, spun her off the floor and hugged her hard. She was passed from embrace to embrace. It felt wonderful.

After all the hugging was through, Meggie looked around in delight. Cash and Abby had spared no expense. They'd hired a caterer from Sheridan, the same one, Abby whispered, who'd put on their own wedding reception—in this very house, the year before. An array of tempting dishes waited on white-clothed tables and the bar had been fully stocked. The caterer had also brought along a four-piece band.

"Oh, you really shouldn't have." Meggie sighed.

"Oh, yes, we should," Abby shot back. "Now, get out on that floor and dance."

Meggie didn't hesitate. She danced with Zach and Cash and Sonny. She whirled from partner to partner, having the time of her life. Everyone seemed genuinely happy for her and for Nate. And she was happy, too.

The only grim moment occurred when she danced with Barnaby Cotes.

"I wish you the best, Meggie," he told her stiffly. "But I can't say I believe you'll be happy with a man like that."

"Take a hike, Cotes," Nate muttered, cutting in on them before she had the chance to tell Barnaby that she could do without his condescending remarks.

Barnaby faded away into the crowd and Meggie found herself whirling in her husband's arms. She closed her eyes and smiled and wished the dance would never end.

"What did that creep say to you?" Nate asked in her ear.

"Nothing important."

"I never could stand him. He's a smug, self-righteous little—"

She put a hand over his mouth—her left hand, on which her wedding band gleamed. "Shh. Just dance."

He pulled her closer and didn't say another word.

They drove back to the Double-K together, long after dark, in the rental car that Nate planned to turn in on Monday. From then until they left for L.A., he would use the old GMC pickup from the Rising Sun to get around.

The nearly full moon seemed to light their way home. Meggie leaned her head on Nate's shoulder and watched it through the windshield, a silver disk with one side missing, in a night of a thousand stars. The moonlight spilled down on the rolling grasses, so they looked like sheets of liquid silver, rippling before the wind.

At last, Nate pulled into the yard. The lights were on in the bunkhouse. Sonny and Farrah had left the party to take the kids home over an hour before. Sonny's old hound dog, Scrapper, barked twice from the bunkhouse steps. And then he must have decided things were all right, because he didn't bark again.

Nate swung the car around and pulled up in front of the main house. He turned off the engine and the lights. They sat there, for a moment, with the wind sighing outside and the moonlight pouring down, silvering the yard.

Then Meggie lifted her head from Nate's shoulder. They shared a long glance.

And Nate said softly, "It shouldn't be in a bedroom."

She knew just what he meant. "Let's get going, then."

Half an hour later, Meggie rode out beside her husband, toward the Big Horns, black and craggy, like an absence of light against the night sky to the west. She rode Patriot, a fast little mare sired by her dear old Renegade. Nate had chosen a big black gelding that Meggie had named Indigo, since his coat shone almost purplish in the sun. Nate carried a rifle in his saddle scabbard, just to be on the safe side. And both of them had bedrolls tied on in back, with jackets wrapped inside.

They rode clear of the home place and then, as one, they reigned their horses in. For a moment, they just sat there, looking out over the land. Meggie leaned on the saddle horn, smiling into the wind, smelling sage and just a hint of pine from the mountains not far off. Somewhere an owl hooted. And a coyote let out one long, lonely howl.

They clucked their tongues softly at their horses and started out again. They didn't need words. They knew where they were going: to that spot by Crystal Creek where they had sat and talked for hours so many afternoons those first two years when they were almost children—and the best of friends. They rode overland, in and out of gates that took them back and forth from Rising Sun pastures to ones that belonged to the Double-K. They came up quiet and easy on the cattle in those pastures. As they went by, the long heads would lift. Wide-set bulging eyes, gleaming in the moonlight, would stare at them curiously. Then, in dismissal, the eyelids would flicker down—and the long heads would turn away.

At last they came to the dirt road that Nate had used at fourteen, when he went for a joyride in his grandpa's pickup. Meggie dug in her heels and Patriot took off, headed for the rise and the creek beyond. With a low laugh, Nate followed.

They raced over the ridge and down to the creek, laughing, the cool, clean wind in their faces, the moon showing the way. Over the years, successive spring thaws had changed the channel slightly. The old spot they used to favor no longer existed. They had to slow down and ride along above the bank, peering into the shadows of the willows and cottonwoods, looking for a likely place.

"Here," Nate said to her at last.

They unsaddled and hobbled their horses several yards from creek side. Then they hauled the saddles and bedrolls down to the grass near the water, where the trees and the lowness of the land made a break from the incessant, keening wind. Nate spread his sleeping bag on the grass; they would use Meggie's to put over them.

Finally they sat side by side on their makeshift marriage bed and pulled off their boots and their socks. Shyness found Meggie just as she started unbuttoning her shirt, making her heart beat too fast and all her fingers turn to thumbs. She sat still, licking her lips that had become as dry as late-summer grass, staring at the dark water rushing past not far away, thinking that she was absolutely terrified.

"Need some help?" Nate knelt before her.

A break in the tree cover overhead showed him to her, silvered in moonlight. Unreality assailed her. Was this really happening?

It was. She knew it. He was her most precious, hopeless fantasy. And he was here with her tonight because she had sought him out and begged him to help her. And, in the end, he had come to her, unable to refuse her need. Her knight in shining armor, in spite of himself.

Wordless, she stared at him, at the shaggy jet hair, the chiseled face. His dark eyes, which so often watched the world in cold appraisal, were less cold now, maybe—but no less watchful.

To escape that gaze, she glanced down. He'd already taken off his shirt. She found herself staring at the hard muscles of his shoulders and arms, at the silky trail of black hair that curled out across his chest and then went down in a line over his hard belly, to disappear beneath the waistband of his worn jeans.

"Meggie?"

She made herself look into his eyes again. "I'm so scared all of a sudden...." The words came out sounding as weak as the cry of a sick calf, because her silly throat had clamped tight on her.

A rueful smile took one corner of that full Bravo mouth. "Meggie. You didn't go and *save* yourself, now, did you?"

Her face was flaming. She couldn't speak. She closed her eyes.

"Hell, Meggie," he whispered tenderly.

Not far away, one of the horses whickered softly. And the wind, beyond the shelter of the bank, whistled and moaned.

"Come on," he said. "Look at me."

She did, with great effort. And she tried to explain. "I just, well, I didn't see any point, with anyone else, you know?" She laughed then, a pained sound, at herself more than anything. She remembered the girls he used to date, the wild ones, when he was so busy breaking her heart for the first time. "How could I ask you that? Of course you don't know."

"Meggie…"

She closed her eyes again, willed the hurts of the past away. Nate had never made any promises to her. He had always been honest. Brutally so. She had known she would never lie down with him. Because she wanted forever—and he wanted to be free.

Yet by some crazy miracle, here they were. On their wedding night. One moment in time that would never come again.

"Meggie."

She looked at him and gave him a smile that quivered only slightly at the corners. "Yes. I could use a little help," she said. "Somehow all my fingers have stopped working." She took his big hands, so warm and so strong, and put them on the top button of her shirt. "Please?"

His fingers moved, from one button to the next. The cool night air kissed her skin. He pulled the shirt out of her jeans, then took her wrists, one at a time, and undid the buttons there. His hands moved to her shoulders. And the shirt was gone.

Her bra was white lace; she'd worn it beneath the knee-length white dress she'd married him in. It had a front clasp. His fingers worked briefly there, pressing at the exact center of her chest. And the clasp came apart. He slid the bra off her shoulders and away, gently, considerately, reminding her of the way a child will do a task, with serious and complete concentration on every move.

He put his hands on her hips. "Stand up."

He steadied her as she rose. When she stood above him, he looked up the length of her body and she looked down at him, between the mounds of her own breasts, into the darkness of his eyes, a darkness she had longed for, always, all of her life, it seemed to her. She put her hands on her own belly, undid the top button of her fly. Then pulled. The zipper came open.

He hooked his hands in her waistband and took her jeans down, along with the white lace panties that matched her bra. She had to rest a hand on his shoulder for balance when she stepped clear of everything.

Swiftly, before she had time to ponder her own nakedness, he rose before her, and stripped down his own jeans. They faced each other at last, each totally nude. The wind blew, crying low. She shivered a little, still somewhat fearful—and poignantly aware that he was very much ready to make a baby with her.

He reached out a hand, ran it over the goose bumps on her arm. "More than damn *near* naked now."

She smiled, remembering that first day, when she had ridden up on Renegade without her jeans to find him beating out a fire with blanket.

"Cold?" he asked.

She rubbed her arms. "Yeah."

"Come on, then."

He guided her down to their bed on the grass, and pulled the cover over them. The sudden, cozy warmth was sheer heaven. He held her close, his body against hers, and he stroked her back—long, slow strokes. She understood his intention: that she become accustomed to his touch.

Meggie breathed slow and deep and let the sensations wash over her. She took in the scent of him. To her, he had always smelled like home, like breathing in the wind on the prairie: sage and dust and a hint of pine.

His body felt hot, hotter than her own, really. And big. And so strong, all sleek bone and ready muscle. The hair on his thighs scratched her a little. But it felt good. It felt right.

A few minutes before, he might have looked at her with tender pity, thinking her foolish to have *saved* herself. But right now, this moment, wrapped up tight with him, naked, she didn't feel foolish. She felt glad, right down to the deepest part of herself, that she would have the one man she wanted. That she had never settled for less.

He continued to stroke her, his hands moving over her neck, her shoulders and then between their bodies. He touched her breasts, tenderly, knowingly, bringing the nipples to hard, hungry peaks. His mouth followed his hands. When he took her nipple in his mouth, she threw her head back, moaning, as the sensation trailed its way down to her woman's core, which suddenly felt like a hot, moist flower, blooming, opening.

His hands were all over her. She lost track of each individual touch. The caresses were all one. He touched the blooming center of her, and she opened all the more for him.

Then he was rising above her, blocking out the dark trees, the night sky and the moon. He braced himself on his elbows. She knew he gazed down at her, serious and intent; though, with the moon behind him, she could not actually see his eyes. She felt him, at her tender entrance, as he positioned himself.

He thrust in, hard and clean. She let out one sharp, wounded cry.

And he lay still inside her, letting her body know him, giving her time to accept his invasion. He bent his head and found her mouth. The kiss they shared went on forever.

Three times, she thought. Three times, she had kissed this man. Once fourteen years ago, on the Fourth of July. Once just hours ago, so briefly, a light brushing of his lips on hers, to seal their wedding vows. And now. A third kiss. As they lay mated on the grass by Crystal Creek, beneath a cottonwood tree....

Down where he pressed into her, there was pain. And a fullness. Slowly, as he kissed her, the pain was fading. Becoming pleasure. And a hunger, to move. To seek a rhythm that would bring fulfillment shattering through them both.

With a long sigh, she adjusted herself, wrapping her legs around his. He simply kept kissing her, pausing only long enough to make a growling sound and to smile against her mouth.

She lifted her hips, taking him even more fully into her. Then she relaxed back into their grassy bed. He made that growling sound again.

And then he was moving. And she was moving with him. And their eternal kiss continued as their bodies moved together in an endless, rolling wave—like the grasses of the prairie, rippling on and on forever before the incessant wind.

Something rose within her, reaching. And she followed it, up and over the edge of the universe. Into a darkness that exploded with light. She held on to Nate, crying out. And he held on to her.

He whispered her name at the very end, as if it was

the only name that mattered, whispered it in agony and joy, against her parted lips.

"Yes, Nate," she whispered back. "Yes." And "Yes," again.

Chapter Five

Meggie woke at dawn to the sound of a meadowlark trilling out its high, piercing song. She looked over at Nate. Surprisingly, he slept on. And very peacefully, too, his cheek resting on his arm. Though she didn't want to wake him yet, she couldn't keep herself from staring at him just for a moment or two, knowing she wore a fool's grin on her face, and not giving a darn. Or course, Nate Bravo could never look soft, but he came pretty close to it, now in sleep. She thought of last night and her foolish grin widened.

Carefully, Meggie slid from under the covers and pulled on her clothes, including the jacket she'd left flung over her saddle, ready to pull on against the morning chill. Patriot, not far away, saw her moving about and snorted at her in question. She shot the horse a look and the mare snorted once more, then bent her head to nip delicately at what was left of the grass around her hooves.

Nate stirred a little, as Meggie was pulling on her boots. She sat very still, watching him, but he didn't open his eyes. Quietly, Meggie rose and tiptoed away. Once she was far enough from Nate that she didn't think the sound of her boots brushing the grass would wake him, she picked up her pace. She walked briskly, up the rise they'd come down the night before. At the top, she sat facing the creek.

From her perch, she could see the horses, nibbling the stubs of grass they'd already chewed down during the night. She could also see Nate, under the blankets by the side of the creek. And if she raised her eyes, she could see the Big Horns. Very soon, the sun would break over the horizon behind her and flood the craggy peaks with morning light.

She reached in the pocket of her jacket and found the envelope she'd stuck in there the night before. It contained a letter from her father, which G. Vernon Bannister had given her on the same day he informed her of the contents of her father's will.

Meggie opened the letter carefully and smoothed it on her knee. She had read it before, of course. A hundred times, at least—during those first awful days after she'd learned what Jason Kane had done to her. She had read it in rage and hurt and a faint hope that someday, somehow, she would let herself forgive him.

She read it now as the sun hit the Big Horns and the day truly began:

My dearest Megan,
I know how you must be feeling right now. And I got to admit, I'm glad I don't have to face you.

But something had to be done. And I have done it. And that's that.

I've told you more than one time how I fear for you, fear that you've put all of your love into the land. And how I worry it's not healthy. That if you're not careful, you'll end up like me, with no one beside you in the darkest part of the night. In plain speaking, Meggie girl, you could end up worse than me, because at least your mother gave me you before she took off. But the way you're headed, you won't even have a child to give the land to when you go.

It pleases me that your cousin has brought his family to the Double-K. I hope they stay on. But a cousin is not a husband. And those two children of Sonny's are not your own. I want you to have children of your own.

And don't go thinking I don't know my own part in what's happened to you. Your mother was the only woman I ever loved. And if I couldn't have her, I didn't want anyone else. I waited and waited for her to come back to us, though she told me when she left that she was never coming back. Still, even after I got word of her death, some crazy part of me kept hoping to see her again. I'm still hoping, to tell you true. And I know I passed that narrow way of loving on to you.

You never talked about Nathan Bravo to me. But I know that he was the one. And I don't know whether you told him and he turned you down— or he just plain never asked. But he is gone from you now, living far away. And all you've allowed yourself is the Double-K. It's not enough.

Anyways, I guess you know I have been sick

for a while. And the closer my time came, the more it got clear to me just what I needed to do.

By now, Mr. Bannister has told you the terms of my will. And I know you're probably mad as a peeled rattler at your old man. But I sincerely hope, over time, that you will come to understand why I've done what I've done. To understand, and maybe even to forgive. Hell, if you find happiness because of this, you might even thank me one day. And in any case, if my plan doesn't work out, the sale of the herd and the home place should give you enough of a stake to start again.

Megan May, when I look back on my life, I see your eyes. It feels to me that *you* are why I lived at all. And what I want for you is a shot at a marriage. A damn long shot, I know. But a chance, anyway. And at least one child. Someone to be the reason why *you* lived, when you're old and used up and waiting for death to ease the pain that eats you from inside.

I do love you, Meggie. And I did this for you.

> Your father, Jason Levi Kane

Carefully, Meggie folded the letter and put it back in the envelope. She put the envelope in her pocket. Right then, from somewhere behind her, another meadowlark burst into song. She stared at the Big Horns, now bathed in sunlight. And she thought of her father.

Jason Kane *had* loved Mia Stephens Kane with all of his heart. He had met her on a trip to Denver, and brought her home to share his life. She stayed long enough to have their baby. And then she left. Meggie had no memories of her at all. Still, Meggie's child-hood had felt complete—because of Jason Kane.

The sun on the mountains shone so bright it made her squint. She drew up her legs, wrapped her arms around them and rested her cheek on her knees.

Her father might not have intended for her to go after troublesome Nate Bravo in order to fulfill the terms of his will. But she *had* gone after Nate. And for a time, she would have him. Thus, in a way, her father had forced her to go out and pursue her heart's desire.

Of course, it wouldn't last....

Meggie closed her eyes and smiled to herself. What ever really lasted anyway? God willing, she'd have a few shining, wonderful months with the man who owned her heart—and she'd have his baby. It was much more than she had ever dared to hope for in all the lonely years since he had turned her love away.

Keeping her eyes shut, Meggie lifted her head and tipped her face to the wind. Right then and there, she made a promise to herself. She vowed that she would not try to hold Nate when it ended. She'd take these few precious months to treasure and she would set him free with a smile when the time came. Moreover, while they were together, she would not cling to him, or pres-sure him with talk of love.

Just as the vow was made, she heard Nate's foot-steps, whispering through the grass. The footsteps stopped a few feet from her. She opened her eyes and looked at him.

"You okay?" he asked.

She nodded. He hadn't bothered to pull on his shirt and his muscular chest was pebbled with goose bumps in the cold morning air. Also, his hair stuck out at all angles and he had a red sleep mark on his cheek where he'd lain on his arm. She thought he was the most gorgeous sight she'd ever beheld.

He faked a mean frown. "What are you staring at?"

"You." Suddenly suspicious, she narrowed her eyes at him. "How long have you been awake?"

He grinned. "Since you slid out from under the covers. But you seemed like a woman on a mission, the way you pulled on your clothes so carefully and then crept away. I figured you wanted a little time alone."

She would have shown him the letter then if it hadn't included mention of him and how much she loved him. References to her undying love could be read as putting pressure on him, which she had just silently sworn not to do.

"Well?" he asked.

"Well what?"

He dropped down beside her. "*Did* you want a little time alone?"

She leaned his way, still clutching her drawn-up knees, so their bodies touched. "I did. Thanks."

He looked in her eyes and something lovely and intimate passed between them. "No problem."

She dared to wrap her arm around his shoulder. His skin felt wonderful under her hand, so smooth and tight, the muscles beneath as hard as stones, but more resilient. "Aren't you cold?"

He shrugged and looked out toward the sun-bright mountains. "It's not bad."

Behind them, the meadowlark sang some more. Along the crest of the rise, about fifty feet away, a jackrabbit rose up on its hind legs, sniffed the air and then turned to hop off, long ears twitching. Somebody's stomach growled, but they were sitting so close Meggie couldn't tell whose.

She chuckled. "We should get back to the house. Get some breakfast. And some oats for the poor horses."

He looked at her again. "No."

His curtness startled her a little. "What?"

He turned toward her slightly and slid his hand between the open sides of her down jacket. She sucked in a quick, surprised breath as he began unbuttoning her shirt.

"I've always wanted you," he said conversationally, "since we were kids." His fingers had made swift work of the buttons. Now she felt his hand sliding under the cup of her bra. His hand was cold. She shivered a little. He made a low, soothing sound as he cradled her breast.

He spoke in that casual tone again. "I wanted to do all kinds of things to your body. And you knew it." He toyed with her nipple. "You were furious at me, because I wouldn't give in and come after you. Weren't you?"

Meggie said nothing. She felt pretty much pole-axed—but in a delicious sort of way. The moment he touched her, her body came alive. Every sensation became acute. Arousal spread through her, pooling in her belly, making everything loose and ready. Even the slight soreness caused by the night before had a need to it, as if it hungered to be made sorer still.

"Weren't you mad at me, Meggie May?" He unclasped her bra.

She melted. Opened. Bloomed.

"Meggie. Answer."

She forced herself to reply. "Yes. I was mad at you."

He smoothed the sides of her bra out of his way. "But I didn't touch you, except that one kiss, on the Fourth of July. I knew the price of touching you—marriage. Turn toward me." She did as he commanded. He took her hips and pulled her to him, lifting her so she straddled his lap, there on that rise, with the wind and the dewy grass moving all around them.

She could feel him, through her jeans, as hard and ready as she was meltingly willing. He smiled, a slow, devastatingly sexy smile. "But now. Hell. I've paid the price. I've married you. And for the next few months, it's kind of my job. To want you. Right?"

She drew in a long, shaky breath. "Right."

He slid both hands inside her coat and tugged on her shirt, until it was out of her Wranglers. Then he gathered her close, his hands splayed on her bare back. "Before breakfast is always a good time," he whispered in her ear.

She quivered, and pressed herself closer to him, her breasts against his broad, hard chest.

He instructed, "Say, 'Yes, Nate.'"

Obediently, she parroted, "Yes, Nate."

"Wrap your legs around me. I'll take you back to the blankets."

She hooked her boots around his waist. He got his feet beneath him and rocked back on his heels. With a low grunt, he stood. And then he started down the rise to where the blankets waited.

In the golden days that followed, Nate worked right alongside Megan and Sonny. As it turned out, they needed the extra pair of hands, because Lev found a better-paying job and left them a few days after the wedding. The day Lev took off, Meggie told Nate that she would just go ahead and pay him Lev's wages.

Nate laughed. "Forget it, Meggie May. I'm not taking your money."

"But if you're going to work, it only seems fair that you—"

"Quiet. I don't want to hear it."

"But it's not right."

"Look at it this way. I'm working for something that will someday belong to my kid, right?"

"If everything goes the way we hope."

"So consider it child support."

"But—"

He only shook his head. "Say thank-you."

She did.

"And give me a kiss."

She did that, too.

Nate fit right in. He knew the work—better than Lev had, certainly. After all, Nate was Ross Bravo's grandson and had helped out at the Rising Sun from the age of fourteen on. He could string a fence with the best of them.

And he never shirked in the endless, backbreaking work of clearing the ditches so that precious water would find its way to the cattle and the alfalfa fields. Sometimes they dug the ditches out; sometimes they burned out the swamp grass that choked them. And sometimes, when they burned, the fires got away from them, creeping along underneath the thick grasses to pop up here and there, taunting them with how easily a prairie fire can get a hold.

When they cut hay that summer, Nate usually drove the swather. The swather was designed to both cut and windrow the hay, leaving it laid out in a neat row, ready for the baler, which they wouldn't bring round until the hay had a chance to cure in the hot summer sun.

Once, when they were cutting alfalfa, Meggie climbed onto the small platform near where Nate sat to drive. She held on tight while he went up and down the field, with the big blades turning, throwing the hay up into a pair of canvas rollers that spit it out in a long row behind. She laughed, over the noise of the engine, enjoying herself immensely, in spite of the bits of grass and dirt blown in her face by the wind. Life never got much better than this, to be here with Nate, essentially living out her dearest fantasy—of the two of them, married and working together every day.

Nate yelled, "Pay attention—hang on." She glanced back at the big sharp blades and took his advice to heart.

When the field was cut, that wonderful smell perfumed the air. There was nothing like the scent of cut alfalfa. Sweet and grassy, with a hint of spice from the little purple flowers it produced. Cut alfalfa was the smell of summer, pure and simple, to Meggie's mind.

Beyond haying and fencing and burning ditches, there were always weeds to poison. Especially sage and leafy spurge. Sage had been the bane of the prairie for generations. But spurge had been brought over from Europe more recently by some botanist who didn't know the kind of trouble he would end up causing.

Leafy spurge was a pretty green plant with tiny yellow flowers. Its roots went deep and it grew in dense clumps, forcing out the native grass wherever it took hold. And in the western United States, it seemed to be taking hold with a vengeance. Cattle wouldn't eat it; even most of the wildlife left it alone. And it was hard to kill, even with powerful herbicides. So, for local ranchers, poisoning spurge had become a summer-long activity. They treated it with Tordon, a chemical weed killer that came in both liquid and pellet form.

Most often that summer, when they poisoned leafy spurge on the Double-K, Nate drove the pickup, since he was so adept at getting a vehicle in and out of the kind of places Meggie wouldn't have even imagined it could go. As Nate drove, either Meggie or Sonny would work from the bed of the pickup, spraying like crazy or scattering pellets.

And of course, there was the constant work of checking the cattle, bringing in the ones with foot rot or cancer eye for treatment, keeping an eye on their watering holes to make sure they still had water and that no animal had gotten itself bogged down in the mud. And moving them, making choices about the culls—cattle they planned to sell off—so they would be ready for shipping day in the fall.

Then, at night, the big, old bed in the master bedroom was waiting for them. They worked hard there, as well, to make the baby that Meggie needed so much. Neither of them minded that particular job in the least.

Naturally, Nate insisted on bull riding in the August rodeo in Buffalo. Meggie's heart stopped beating for the entire seven seconds he stayed on. The bull he drew was a mean one, and he barely avoided getting stomped. When it was over, he told Meggie he was getting too damn old for such foolishness. She knew him well enough to disagree with him.

She said, "You love it and you know it. And you'll be riding bulls when you're sixty if you don't break your neck first."

He put his arm around her and bussed her on the cheek. "Hell. You got me nailed."

He smelled of manure. She looked up at his dirty face and wondered how it was possible for her heart to hold so much joy without bursting apart.

Once in August and once at the beginning of September, Nate returned to L.A.—the first time to testify in a trial and later to do a little sleuthing for some software firm that had sent a lot of business his way. But he never stayed away for more than a week. Meggie was happy, living in the now. She strictly honored her secret vow; not once did she speak of love or permanence. And Nate seemed as content as Meggie had ever seen him. She couldn't help priding herself on how well things were going between them.

But neither Meggie's happiness nor Nate's apparent contentment could stop the seasons from changing. Jealously, Meggie noted the signs of autumn's approach. The blackbirds gathered in the fields, getting ready for the long trip south. And the geese could be seen flying in their vee formations through the cloudy sky. The cottonwoods along Crystal Creek started to turn. And mornings brought frost that blackened the leaves of Farrah's pumpkin vines.

Meggie and Sonny discussed the different offers that had been made on the steers they were planning to sell. They were still holding out, at that point, for a better price.

One September morning, Meggie and Nate decided they'd take the GMC pickup out to what they called the Ridge Pasture, a couple of miles from the house. They had loaded the back of the pickup with half barrels full of a molasses-based vitamin-and-mineral supplement, which they fed to the cattle to round out their diet.

Meggie pointed to the black clouds rolling in over Cloud Peak. "Storm coming," she said. She was smiling. She loved a storm, loved the charged smell in the air as the storm clouds gathered.

"We can beat it," Nate said.

They took off at Nate's usual breakneck pace, along the dirt roads made by mining companies and oil speculators that crisscrossed the ranch. In the Ridge Pasture, the empty tubs were ranged along the crest of the high ridge after which the pasture had been named, away from any water source. To get to the sweet, sticky mixture, the cattle had to move around, rather than sticking by their favorite holes, eating the grass down to nothing in one spot. Nate shifted the pickup into low and it groaned its way up the dirt road to the crest.

At ridgetop, under a heavy, threatening sky, they jumped out and began switching the full barrels for the empty ones, which they tossed into the back of the pickup. Lightning forked down on a neighboring ridge just as the last empty barrel hit the pickup bed. The air smelled of ozone. Thunder reverberated across the dry, waiting land.

All at once, the wind grew fierce. The soot-black clouds piled overhead began to drop their rain. Meggie tipped up her face and opened her mouth. The wetness tasted wonderful. She giggled to herself.

She could almost hear her father's voice. "Meggie May, you're a durn fool. You want to make yourself a human lightning rod?"

So all right. She was a durn fool. And it felt terrific. Lightning flashed again and thunder struck out and rolled, booming, off toward the mountains. The rain came thick and fast, big, cold, sloppy drops, blown hard against her by the whipping wind.

Down by the creek in the lower part of the pasture, everything had become shrouded in mist.

The rain turned to hail just as Nate grabbed her hand. "Come on!"

She went with him, into the cab of the truck.

The hail pelted the roof, pinging and snapping. Unlike Meggie, who was having a ball, Nate had his mind on getting the hell back to the house before the roads turned to gumbo. He reached for the key he'd left stuck in the ignition.

And Meggie put her hand on his arm. She laughed.

God, he did love her laugh....

"Nate. Wait. Listen."

He looked at her. Water dripped off the brim of her hat and onto the seat between them. She was soaked through. And so was he.

"We should get the hell back to the house," he grumbled.

"It's all right. The lightning can't hurt us now that we're in the truck."

"What about the roads, Meggie?"

She wrinkled her nose, because she had no answer to that one. Finally, she simply shrugged. "Forget the roads."

"Meggie..."

"Shh."

"Meggie."

"You're not listening."

"Listening to what?"

She pointed at the roof of the cab, her head cocked, one eyebrow lifted. "Hear that?"

"Right. Hail. What a surprise."

"No. Imagine we're popcorn. Popping."

He glared at her for a moment more, and then couldn't keep it up. The hail beating down on the pickup did sound a little like corn exploding in a hot pan.

She slid across the seat and right up against him. "Nate." She took off his hat and dropped it on the dashboard. And then she did the same with her own. She nuzzled his neck.

"What are you up to?" he asked, though he had a pretty good idea. And so did his body. Already his jeans had become too snug.

"Nate," was all she said. She put her hand on his cheek and guided his mouth around. And then her lips touched his, cool at first, from the rain and the wind. But not cool for long...

With a groan, Nate gave himself to the kiss.

He loved the taste of her, so clean and sweet. And the smell of her, that woodsy scent with something flowery in it, just a little bit musky now, from tossing the mineral tubs around.

Outside, the hail had turned to rain again. The two in the cab didn't notice.

Nate pulled Meggie's thermal shirt out of her jeans and undid her bra. But he didn't take anything off, just in case someone happened to come along.

With a low laugh, she leaned back against the passenger door and stuck out a boot. "Pull."

Nate pulled—one wet boot and then the other. He helped her shimmy out of her jeans and her white cotton panties, too. Then he slid over to join her on the passenger side of the seat, so the steering wheel wouldn't interfere.

The windows had fogged over completely by the

time she unzipped him and got his own clothes out of the way enough that she could mount him. He slid into her heat and softness, groaning with the sweet agony of it.

"Nate, Nate, Nate..." She whispered his name against his lips as she rode him in slow, long, deep strokes. Now and then, she would pause, with him halfway out of her. He would stand it for as long as he could. And then, with a moan, he would take her hips and pull her down onto him again.

Outside, the hard rain slowed to a steady downpour. To Nate, the drumming sound of it against the roof and hood of the pickup was mesmerizing. Erotic.

Meggie moaned and kissed him. Her body moved on his. He didn't know what it was about her. Somehow, she made it all stronger, fiercer, more complete—and more plain fun—than any sex he'd ever had. She fit him just right, as maybe he'd always known that she would. She knew how to laugh. And how to play. When to tease. And when to give him what he wanted without any frills.

He let his head drop back as completion rolled over him, mowing him down like a waiting hay field under the blades of a relentless swather. He pushed himself high and hard into her. She whimpered—and pushed right back. He felt her going over with him, her body expanding and contracting around him. He reached out, blindly, and pulled her close against him, rucking up her shirt and bra so that he could feel her bare skin.

For several minutes, they just sat there, all wrapped up together in the steamy cab, as the rain droned on outside.

Finally, he muttered, "We're in for it now, trying to get out of here."

She had her hands under his shirt and was idly stroking him. "We'll manage."

He returned the favor, running his hands back and forth along the smooth length of her bare thighs. She sighed a little and nuzzled closer. Nate went on caressing her, thinking that he almost wished they would never make that baby, that they could just go on working at it indefinitely.

And boy, had they been working at it. Once or twice a night, since the wedding. And sometimes in the daytime, like now. Any time the slightest opportunity presented itself. If that doctor in Billings had been right about them, she should be pregnant already.

He frowned, his hand going still on her thigh as he realized that, to his knowledge, she hadn't had a period since he had started sleeping in her bed. But then he relaxed again, as he remembered those days he had been gone. The two trips had been just about a month apart.

With a long sigh, he rolled his head toward the driver's side of the cab. Through the fog on the window, he saw something move.

"Meggie," he whispered low.

"Um?"

He signaled with his head. She looked over.

Meggie gasped. "Oh, dear Lord..."

And then Nate reached out and brushed a hand over the foggy glass. As the glass cleared, they found themselves staring into the wide, solemn eyes of a Hereford steer.

Meggie leaned across the seat. "You are *steak*," she said to the long, white face on the other side of the window.

The steer turned his head and let out an extended, thoroughly insolent, "Mooo!"

Fall work began.

They gathered the cattle they planned to drive to the feedlots for sale. Gathering days were long ones, spent mostly in the saddle, herding and moving the culls into separate pastures from the breeding stock and the calves.

Soon after fall gathering came shipping day, when they drove the cattle to the feedlots, where the vet and the brand inspector checked them over and then Meggie collected her money from the buyers waiting there.

In the last weeks of October, they began weaning the calves. Weaning allowed the cows a little time to build up their nutritional stores, before the calves that were growing inside them started draining off their energy once again.

By then, the long Wyoming winter had begun to close in. Meggie, Nate and Sonny gathered and moved the calves with the wind in their faces and sleet stinging their cheeks. During weaning, they also took the time to put the calves in the chute and pour Spot-On over their backs, a topical medication for the control of grubs. They had the vet over to vaccinate the heifers against certain contagious diseases. In the end, weaning amounted to a lot of messy work in bad weather.

But they got through it. By the first week of November, that year's calves were on their own.

And Nate wanted to return to L.A.

Meggie knew it was time to go. But she didn't even want to think about leaving. She wanted to go on as they had been. She longed to enjoy with Nate the relatively quiet time that was coming up, to spend the holidays together with him here, at home.

She knew she had no right to want those things. She had vowed not to cling or try to hold him. And stalling about leaving brought her perilously close to breaking her vow.

But she didn't care. She cheated on her vow and stalled. Twice, when he reminded her that they had to make plans to leave, she pretended not to hear him. The third time he brought the subject up, they were in bed. Since she was lying right on top of him, kissing him, it was pretty difficult to fake inattention. So she suddenly found she had to go to the bathroom. She slid out of the bed.

"Meggie, what the hell—" Nate demanded.

"I'll be back in a flash."

"Meggie..."

She flew across the room and disappeared into the bathroom before he could say any more. She stayed in there for a very long time. And when she came out, he'd turned off the bedside lamp.

"Nate?" she asked nervously into the darkness.

"Come to bed, Meggie," he answered, sounding resigned. "Go to sleep."

But Meggie knew that Nate wasn't the kind of man a woman could stall for long. And she was right. After dinner on the second Saturday in November, she went up to the room they shared and found him packing. He zipped up the big duffel bag he used for a suitcase and carried it with finality over to the door where she stood watching him.

He dropped the bag at her feet. "I'm leaving in the morning."

She looked down at the bag and then up at him, her

love for him washing over her like a powerful wave, cutting off her air. She wanted to grab him. And hold him. And never let him go.

"Cash will fly me to Denver," he said. Cash had his own plane. "And from there, I've got a direct flight to LAX."

His hair had gotten hung up on the collar of his shirt. She reached out and freed it, then stroked it smooth.

He caught her hand. "Are you coming with me?"

She closed her eyes, swallowed and then made herself drag in a breath and speak. "I'll...be along."

He looked at her piercingly. And then he dropped her hand. "I know you don't want to leave. I know how you are, about this ranch. About your life here. But I have to go, Meggie. I have a damn life, too, you know."

"I know."

"I can't keep turning down jobs. Word gets out I'm unavailable. It cuts into the offers I get."

She thought of the money she'd wanted him to take. It would have helped to make up for the business he'd lost. But she wasn't going to bring up the money. He'd made himself more than clear on that issue. "I understand."

"We agreed—"

She reached out, put her fingers over his lips. "Shh. I know. I just...need a little time. Is that okay?"

"Hell." He grabbed her wrist. And then his lips were moving against her fingers, kissing them.

"Oh, Nate..."

He tugged. She went into his arms. His mouth came down on hers, hot and demanding, full of fire and need.

He kicked the door closed, scooped her up and carried her over to the bed.

* * *

Nate woke well before dawn. He turned his head and looked at Meggie. She slept on her side, facing him, a slight frown marring her brow. He wanted to reach out and stroke that frown away. But he knew if he woke her, she'd only try to keep him from going.

And not with words. Meggie May Kane was too honorable a woman to argue against something she'd already agreed to. No, she would work to hold him with looks. And with touches. With soft sighs. With the formidable power her sweet body had over his.

But Nate Bravo did not intend to be held—no matter how tempting the looks, the sighs and the caresses. He'd never lied to her about that. He was doing what he could for her. If she wanted to keep her ranch, she would just have to come to L.A. as she had agreed to do.

The frown lines faded as he watched her face. Her wide mouth turned up in a dreamy smile. She made a small, contented sound and snuggled lower into the nest of blankets.

All he wanted at that moment was to touch her. To put his hands and his mouth on her. To pull back the blankets and—

He had to get the hell out. Now.

Quietly, he turned toward his side of the bed and slid carefully out from under the covers. The room was icy. But he didn't mind the cold. It got his blood pumping faster, made him want to hurry. He pulled on his clothes—all but his boots—mindful not to make the slightest sound. Finally, he took an envelope from a side pocket of his bag. Just as he was propping it against the alarm clock on the nightstand, Meggie rolled toward him with a sigh. He froze.

But she didn't wake. She slept on. And he stood

there like the fool he'd somehow allowed himself to become for her, watching. Wanting…

Nate closed his eyes. He sucked in a slow breath. And then he turned, scooped up his bag and walked out the door.

Meggie opened her eyes at the sound of the front door closing downstairs. Instantly wide-awake, she looked over her shoulder to where Nate should be sleeping. He wasn't there.

With a small, frantic cry, she threw off the covers, scooped up her nightgown from the end of the bed and yanked it over her nakedness. She heard a car door creak open outside, so she flew to the window. Below, in the yard, melting patches of dirty white spotted the dark, bare ground, the remains of the first real snowfall a few days before. She watched Nate toss his bag into the pickup and then climb in after it.

Meggie shivered. The floor felt like a slab of ice under her bare feet; the fire she always left burning in the old black heat stove downstairs must have gone completely out. Rooted to the spot in spite of the cold, she wrapped her arms around herself and stared out the window as the reluctant engine of the pickup sputtered to life. She went on watching as Nate drove down the drive, past the bunkhouse and the barn, the corrals and the outbuildings, toward the gate that led to the road. She didn't move from the window until he turned onto the road and she could no longer see his taillights through the thick darkness of the cloudy, moonless night.

Her gaze fell on the envelope propped on the nightstand. She grabbed it and dropped to the edge of the bed, scooping up her heavy shawl from the bedpost and wrapping it around herself. As she tore into the envelope, her toes found their way into her warm sheepskin slippers, which she always kept waiting by the side of the bed.

Inside the envelope she found a business card and a key. She reached out and flipped on the lamp. The card read *Bravo Investigative Services* at the top, then on the second line: DOMESTIC * CIVIL * CRIMINAL. Below that, with asterisks between, was a list of the kinds of services he performed: Background Checks * Missing Persons * Child Custody * Skip Tracing * Premarital * Divorce * Process Serving. At the bottom was the phone number she'd found in the L.A. phone book four months before, and what appeared to be the number of his private investigator's license.

Meggie turned the card over. On the back Nate had scrawled an address, an apartment number and another phone number—presumably, his private phone. His message was clear: she had his address and the key to his apartment. The rest was up to her.

Up to her...

Meggie's stomach clenched. And then she felt everything in it start to rise.

Tossing the card and the key on the nightstand, she ran for the bathroom.

Chapter Six

The porcelain commode was so cold Meggie's hands ached when she touched it, but still she was grateful to have made it in time. When the heaving finally stopped, she sat in a heap for long minutes, bent over the bowl, waiting, just in case it wasn't over. Finally, when nothing more came up, she slumped against the tub beside her, breathing slowly and carefully, feeling weak, lost and lonely.

And more than a little bit guilty.

She had not had a period since before her wedding night. And she had been sure, for weeks now, that she was carrying Nate's baby.

Strange, she thought bleakly, as she clutched her shawl closer around her, how easy it had been to maintain the lie. At first, she had told herself that she couldn't be absolutely certain. What did a missed period or two mean, after all?

Since she was normally as regular as clockwork, a missed period meant a lot. But she'd just put that idea right out of her mind. And later, when she could no longer deny the truth to herself, she simply didn't allow herself to think about it.

Surprisingly, Nate had helped her. He had never once asked about those periods she didn't have. More than likely, he'd trusted her honesty, believed that she'd tell him if all of their lovemaking had produced its intended result. And nature had colluded with her as well; the rare times, like just now, when morning sickness had overwhelmed her, Nate hadn't been nearby.

Shame sent a flush up her neck, pushing back the cold a little. Nate had a living to make, after all. She had kept him from it needlessly—and even told herself it was his own fault if he lost money, since he'd turned down the sizable amount she'd offered him to make up for whatever business he lost.

Groaning a little, she dragged herself to her feet and turned on the bathroom light. Her face, in the mirror over the sink, looked pale and sunken eyed. She splashed freezing water on her cheeks and brushed her teeth.

Then she wandered back into the bedroom. It was after four. She might as well get dressed, get the fire going downstairs and get a head start on the day.

But instead of pulling on her clothes, she dropped to the edge of the bed again. She picked up the key Nate had left her and looked down at it in her open palm. She had to tell him. He should have been told weeks ago.

And he would be told. Immediately. She would give him time to make his way home, and then she would call him and say that their goal had been reached; she'd be sending him his divorce papers as soon as the baby was born.

Her fingers closed around the key.

Then again, to call him would be cowardly. The least she could do would be to tell him about the baby face-to-face....

Two days later, on Monday, Meggie got off a plane at LAX. A cabdriver in a black pin-striped suit with a pink turban wrapped around his head took her to Nate's apartment in West Hollywood. Meggie spent the long drive staring out the window of the cab at palm trees, a cloudless sky and streets clogged with cars. She felt a little dazed. When she had boarded the small commuter plane in Sheridan, it had been fifteen degrees outside, with snow in the forecast. She'd been bundled into her heaviest coat, grateful for its warmth. In Denver, where she'd caught a commercial flight, it had been cold and gray and well below freezing. Here, the sun shone down, the temperature had to be in the seventies—and her heavy coat was just something unnecessary to lug around.

Finally, the driver pulled up in front of a two-story Spanish-style building with rough white walls and a red tile roof. "Here we go, yes," he said in a pleasant, rather singsongy voice. White teeth flashed in his brown face. "Your place to which you are visiting." He pointed cheerfully at the meter and sang out the exorbitant cost of the ride.

Without so much as a gasp of dismay, Meggie paid him, adding on a generous tip. She smiled to herself, thinking that she was really getting cosmopolitan. This was her third cab ride—the other two having occurred during her brief visit last July. Already she could pay a cabbie without flinching.

Apparently pleased with her and the tip she'd given him, the cabbie jumped out, took her small suitcase from the trunk and opened the car door for her. He held out his hand. "Allow me, yes?"

She gave him her hand and he helped her to the sidewalk.

"You have a real good time, now, okay?" His turban bobbed up and down as he nodded.

She promised that she would, and then found herself standing there on the sidewalk, with her coat over her arm, waving as he got back in his cab and drove away. Once he disappeared around the corner, she shook herself, picked up her suitcase and squared her shoulders. Her head high and her step determined, she marched up the walk to Nate's building.

She walked up one side of the building, discovered she'd gone the wrong way and retraced her steps, trying the other side next. By the time she found Nate's apartment, in the back, upstairs, she'd seen the dimensions of the place. It was small, with six apartments, three up and three down, each with an outside entrance.

By the time she stood before Nate's door, Meggie's heart was beating way too fast and sweat had broken out on her upper lip. Determined to face him and get it over with, she set down her suitcase and lifted the iron knocker. She gave three good raps. And then she waited.

Nothing happened.

She knocked again. Still no answer.

At that point, Meggie's heart had stopped trying to beat its way out of her chest. It looked as if Nate had gone out—which meant a possible reprieve. Coward that she was, she suddenly felt much better about everything. If she could just go inside and sit down for a few moments, collect herself and relax a little, she felt certain she'd be much more ready to tell Nate about his upcoming fatherhood the minute he walked in the door.

Meggie dug the key out of her purse and unlocked the door. Just in case he might be there after all, she stuck her head in first and called, "Nate? Are you here?"

As expected, she got no answer. There was a mail slot in the door. And the floor beyond the threshold was strewn with envelopes.

Feeling like an intruder, Meggie stepped inside and set her suitcase and purse on the floor, draping her coat over them. Then she closed the door. Nate had three locks: one on the door handle, the dead bolt she'd unlocked to get in and a heavy chain. Remembering that this was L.A., Meggie engaged them all.

By then, she was tired of trying to step around Nate's mail. So she bent and scooped it up, after which she rose again and leaned against the door, getting her bearings.

She stood in a long hallway that extended to the left and right from the door. To the right, she could see that the hallway opened up to a living area.

She went left, where she found what she needed: a bathroom—and a very attractive one, too. It had built-in cabinets, a big, deep tub, plush wine-colored towels and black and white tile. She set the mail on the sink counter and made use of the toilet. Once she was through, she washed her hands and gathered up the mail again. She peeked into the other two rooms at that end of the hall. One contained a huge bed on a wrought-iron frame with a fabulous silk comforter of a deep-maroon color. There were black-lacquer bureaus and beautiful lamps with black wire-mesh bases and raw-silk shades in maroon and midnight blue. The other room contained a beat up old desk, a file cabinet, a computer, a phone, an answering machine and a fax machine.

Down the hall the other way, not far beyond the front door, Meggie discovered a small kitchen. The kitchen was tiled like the bathroom, in black and white. A sturdy oak table stood beneath a big window at the far end. On the table, sat a blue ceramic pitcher. Out of the pitcher bloomed a bouquet of yellow lilies.

An envelope waited, propped against the pitcher, bearing her name in Nate's bold hand. Meggie set Nate's mail on the table and reached for the envelope. She opened it slowly, not sure she wanted to know what was inside.

She found a note, two keys and three one hundred–dollar bills. The note read:

> I've taken a job and should return by Wednesday or Thursday, the thirteenth or fourteenth. I figure you'll need transportation. The keys are to the blue Volvo in the carport in back. It should get you wherever you need to go. The money's in case you're short of cash. For anything else you need to know, ask Dolores Garnica, who owns and manages the place. She's downstairs in the front apartment.

Still carrying the note, Meggie wandered into the living room and dropped into a big, jewel-green easy chair. She stared down at the note: Wednesday or

Thursday. That would be two or three days. She'd wanted a reprieve—but not that much of one.

Feeling slightly stunned, Meggie slumped back in the chair and looked around the high-ceilinged room. A few feet away, two sapphire-blue couches faced each other, a low glass table between them. The bare hardwood floor gleamed in the spill of light from the tall, six-over-six windows on two walls. There was even a leafy, healthy-looking palm in one corner. The teak bookcases held lots of books—as well as an extensive collection of crystals, geodes and shells. Meggie found the room spare and dramatic. And quite beautiful.

It surprised her. So did the rest of the apartment—except for Nate's office. That room, so Spartan and utilitarian, with its scarred desk and green roll-up blinds, seemed more like Nate's kind of place.

Meggie smiled to herself. It came to her that she'd always thought of Nate as living in a kind of exile. The way she saw it, Nate had been born to be hers. Born to work the Double-K beside her, just as they'd been doing for the past few perfect months. Meggie had learned to live with the fact that Nate refused to surrender to his fate with her. But she'd always been certain he must be living a mean and barren life. Instead, she found lots of windows and intense colors, hardwood floors and seashells. And yellow lilies in a pitcher on the kitchen table.

Tired from the long trip, reprieved for a while whether she liked it or not, Meggie leaned back in the big, soft chair and closed her eyes.

When she woke, the room was dark and someone was knocking on the door. Yawning, Meggie pulled herself from the chair, flicked on a lamp and went to answer. She looked through the peephole before opening the door. On the other side she saw a pleasant-faced older woman with gray wings in her black hair. She wore a flowered housedress over her plump, full-bosomed figure.

Meggie disengaged all the locks and pulled open the door.

"You are Megan Bravo." The woman smiled, a smile that made her pleasant face beautiful. "I hope."

"Yes. I'm Megan."

"And I am Dolores." She stuck out a hand, which Meggie shook. Her grip was warm and firm. "This building is mine," she said with great pride. "And so is the one next door. Mr. Bravo said to watch for you. It is something very special when Mr. Bravo asks a favor."

"Yes. I guess you're right."

"So I want to show him, since he is a good tenant, that I do not take this honor lightly. I have been gone all day, but Benny, my husband, who owns these buildings with me, said he saw you go by our door in the afternoon with your little suitcase." She cast a quick glance down at the suitcase in question, which still waited near the door with Meggie's coat and purse. "Hmm. That is a *very* small suitcase for a bride to bring to her new home."

"I'm, um, having everything else shipped." Meggie remembered her manners—and changed the subject at the same time. "Come on in." She stepped back and gestured toward the living room.

Dolores took her lower lip between her even teeth. "Oh, Mr. Bravo never lets anyone in." Her black eyes gleamed with bright interest. "But now, it is your apartment, too, *si?*"

"*Sí.* Now, come on." She took Dolores's arm and

pulled her into the hall, then closed the door behind her. She led the way to the living room. "Have a seat."

Dolores perched on the end of one of the sapphire sofas. Her dark gaze scanned the room. "Very nice," she said, sighing and smiling, as if the room gave her physical pleasure.

"Yes," said Meggie. "I think so, too."

"So." Dolores folded her plump hands in her ample lap. "You will come to dinner *a mi casa?*"

"Well, I…"

"We would be so pleased to have you."

Meggie grinned. "All right. I'd love it."

That night, Meggie met Dolores's sweet, quiet husband, Benny, as well as two of the Garnicas' grandchildren.

"This is Yolanda. We call her 'Yolie,'" Dolores said of a slim, serious girl with a trigonometry book under one arm and a pencil behind her ear. "She lives here, with Benito and me. She is fourteen and a genius."

"Oh, Grandma," Yolie protested, her face coloring prettily. "Don't."

"But it's only the truth. You are *muy lista,* one very smart girl." Dolores turned to a tall, leanly muscled young man with black curly hair, a devilish smile and eyes of a startling blue. "And this is my Mateo. He comes just for dinner. He is becoming a great movie star. Too bad that he thinks he must call himself 'Matt Shane.'"

"I'm an *actor,* Grandma, not a movie star," the young man corrected with somewhat strained affection. "'Matt' is short for Mateo. And Shane *is* my real name."

Dolores made a disgusted sound. "The name of that terrible man who broke your poor mama's heart. He does not deserve to have his name in the movies when you become a famous star."

"Grandma, give it up. It's *my* name. I don't even think of it as his." Dolores made more disapproving sounds as Mateo turned that gorgeous smile on Meggie. "Call me 'Matt.' And welcome to L.A."

Dolores slapped him on the arm. "She is a married woman. You watch yourself."

The next morning, Dolores showed Meggie the coin laundry in the building next door and explained that the tenants in both buildings used it. She also gave Meggie directions to the supermarket several blocks away, and walked her down to Pahlavi's, the corner store, where a loaf of bread or a quart of milk could be bought if she didn't feel like driving all the way to the supermarket.

In the afternoon, Meggie went shopping. As she pushed her cart up and down the aisles, she saw a lot of ordinary-looking people like herself, wearing ordinary clothes with hair of ordinary colors: blond, brown, auburn and black. She also saw a woman with silver rings in her lips and her nose and a man all in leather with tattoos covering his arms to his elbows. She saw a lot of young people wearing black, with spiky hair of green or purple.

L.A. was a place of great diversity, Meggie decided. People came in all colors here. They spoke with a variety of accents. It made getting the groceries into something of an event.

Later, Meggie met the Tyrells, an ebony-skinned couple in their fifties. Their apartment shared a landing with Nate's. The Tyrells came out of their door just as

Meggie was bringing her groceries in. She introduced herself.

"Lovely to meet you," said Mrs. Tyrell, who looked absolutely stunning in a white linen dress.

"Charmed," said her husband. He wore an immaculately tailored black three-piece suit, complete with a gold watch chain hanging from his vest pocket.

As they exchanged pleasantries, Meggie caught a glimpse inside their door, which had a tiny foyer that opened right onto the living room. She saw an oppressive abundance of heavy, dark, ornately carved furniture.

"If you should need anything…*anything,* please feel free to call us," Mrs. Tyrell insisted as Mr. Tyrell closed and locked the door.

Meggie promised that she would and then watched, bemused, as the regal pair turned and descended the stairs.

The next day, Wednesday, Meggie met Bob and Ted, a screenwriter and a caterer's assistant, who shared the apartment beneath Nate's. She also introduced herself to Peg Tolly, an exotic dancer with enormous breasts, who had a one-bedroom upstairs around the opposite side of the building. Below Peg lived Edie Benson, who had once been a nurse and now rolled an oxygen tank around with her wherever she went, due to her steadily worsening case of emphysema. Meggie met Edie on a quick trip down to the corner to buy some butter, which she'd forgotten to pick up at the supermarket the day before. The older woman had just toddled out to the sidewalk with her oxygen tank on its little rollers, when Meggie came dashing out herself.

After introductions had been accomplished, Edie confessed that she was headed to the corner market, too. "I'm just going down to pick up my special little sandwich," Edie panted. "Mr. Pahlavi always makes it for me." The store's owner ran a sandwich counter in back of the store, by the beverage cases.

Meggie offered to get the sandwich for her.

"No, no. Can't have that. I like to do for myself. That's how I am."

So they walked together, picking their way carefully over the cracks and humps in the sidewalk, stopping now and then for Edie to catch her breath, down to the bottom of the street and into the cramped, dim store run by Mr. Pahlavi.

That night, Meggie invited the Garnicas over and served them chicken with dumplings, the way her grandma Kane used to make it. Benny remarked that the dish could use a few jalapeños, but was otherwise delicious. Meggie enjoyed their company, though she felt a certain anxiety all evening. Nate was due back any time now. He would very likely return that night.

All through dinner, and later, as she got ready for bed, she kept thinking of the answering machine in Nate's office. She had heard the phone ring in there more than once over the past two days. She knew his machine was taking the calls. Nate had a small remote device that he used to pick up his messages from an outside phone. She kept picturing him calling from a phone booth or that cell phone of his, beeping for his messages, listening to them play. She had a burning desire to go in there, to sit in the chair behind his desk and snatch the phone from its cradle the minute it rang. Maybe she would catch him calling in. She could tell him she was here, waiting for him.

But then, if it wasn't him, she'd only be interfering with his message system. And he probably wouldn't think much of that. So somehow, she restrained herself from answering his business phone.

Nate didn't return that night. Meggie woke early the next morning to find herself alone in Nate's big bed.

After a quick trip to the bathroom, she returned to the bed, pulled the covers up around her and reached for the phone on the black-lacquer nightstand. She punched out Sonny's number. Farrah answered on the second ring. Meggie asked her how things were going. Farrah reported that the mercury had dipped below zero again last night and as soon as it warmed up a few degrees, Sonny would be heading out to check on the heifers in the South Pasture.

"We're watching the ground freeze around here, Meggie," Farrah said. "We can handle it without you, believe me."

"I know. I just…feel a little homesick, I guess. And I miss you all."

Farrah made a tender sound. "And we miss you, too. But it's only for a few months, right? And then you and Nate will be back here at home where you belong."

Meggie pulled the covers a little closer around her. She considered herself an honest person. Yet, in a day or two, she'd be flying home with some trumped-up story about how things hadn't worked out between her and Nate. Nate would look like the bad guy. And Farrah and Sonny would feel sorry for poor Meggie, pregnant and deserted by the man who, they believed, had promised to stand beside her until death.

"Meggie, are you all right?" Farrah asked after the silence went on too long.

"Fine. And yes, I'll be glad when we get home for good." That was the truth, more or less. Meggie slid her hand under the covers and laid it on her stomach, which was beginning to round out the tiniest bit. She would be part of a "we" when she went home, because Nate's baby would be with her.

"You need some kind of project," Farrah said briskly. "You know how you are."

Meggie smiled and relaxed a little. "No, how am I?"

"A *doer*. So don't let yourself sit around just because you're in the big city. Find something to keep yourself busy."

Meggie heard herself agreeing before she stopped to think that she didn't really have time for a project; in a day or so, she'd be out of there. Right then, from Farrah's end of the line, Meggie heard a loud, outraged wail.

"Oops," said Farrah. "Davey wants Mommy. Gotta go."

Meggie told Farrah to kiss the crying toddler for her, said goodbye and headed for the kitchen to rustle up some breakfast.

Meggie ate to the sounds of L.A.: horns honking, someone shouting out on the street, a siren in the distance, coming closer and then fading off again. She watched the sun come up over the carports, spilling its hot orange light in the kitchen window, over the yellow lilies and across the wall to the black and white tile. As she stared at the lilies, with the sun on their freckled petals, a wave of longing moved through her. She wanted Nate—and dreaded his return at the same time.

Somehow, she got through the endless day, reading a little, walking down to Pahlavi's with Edie around noon. In the afternoon, to keep busy, she baked cookies, *lots* of cookies. The smell of them baking soothed her; it was something she would have done at home, this time of year, with a blizzard blowing outside and a roaring fire in the stove.

Once the cookies were done, she took them around to the other tenants in the building. Everyone was sweetly appreciative. Even Peg, who said she couldn't eat them, seemed pleased at the effort Meggie had put in.

"Well, honey, this is real nice. But a fat exotic dancer is an unemployed exotic dancer, you hear what I'm saying?" She thought a minute, tapping a long crimson nail against her front teeth. "You know, though, a lot of men got a yen for a little home cookin'. So how about if I take these babies to work with me tonight and pass them around?"

"Good idea," Meggie agreed, trying her best not to gape at Peg's breasts, which besides being huge, were very high and rounded. They seemed to float out from her chest, hard, perfect spheres, totally defiant of gravity.

That night, Meggie hardly slept at all. Every slightest sound had her eyes popping open. Then she'd stare into the darkness, straining her ears to hear if it was Nate coming home.

But it wasn't. She woke before dawn, still alone, and decided she'd had enough of trying to sleep.

She ate a light breakfast and tried to think of something to do with herself to make the time pass. Since her meager wardrobe needed washing, she put on a pair of Nate's black sweats and an old L.A. Lakers T-shirt that she found in one of his drawers and carried her own clothes next door to the laundry room. The sky beyond the carports had just started to pinken when she got the wash cycle going.

Someone had left a tattered copy of *People* magazine
on one of the chairs, so Meggie settled in to read about
Julia Roberts. She was studying the photos that accom-
panied the article, trying to decide whether the actress
looked better with her hair short or long, when Meggie
heard strange noises coming through the wall behind
her—bumps and grunts and the sound of furniture top-
pling. Meggie tried not to listen, tried to concentrate
harder on the news about Julia and how she was over-
coming divorce and career difficulties.

A sharp, pained cry from the other side of the wall
mobilized her. Someone in there was getting beat up.
Bad.

Meggie dropped the magazine and jumped from her
chair, which she took in both hands and hurled against
the wall. Then she shouted, at the top of her lungs,
"Help! Police! Fire! Police!" She grabbed a second
chair and hurled it, too. "Fire! Police! Help!"

She waited. There was dead silence from the other
side of the wall. Meggie shouted again, "I know who
you are, and I've called the police!"

That did it. She heard a door slam, and footsteps
pounding away. She ran out in time to see a thin male
figure in jeans and a mesh shirt disappear around the
front of the building. A door stood open a few feet
away—the door to the apartment that shared a wall
with the laundry room.

Meggie peered inside, through a tiny hall. The living
room beyond the hall was chaos, a welter of overturned
furniture, broken lamps and ripped cushions. Meggie
heard a pitiful moan.

Her feet moved of their own accord, carrying her
over the threshold and down the short length of the
hall. A slender man, who might have been anywhere

from forty to sixty, lay on the floor in the corner. He seemed to be covered in blood.

"Please," he whimpered. "Take the money. Take the money and go...."

Meggie spotted the phone on the floor beneath a broken chair. She picked it up: still working. She dialed 911. When she'd completed the call, she knelt beside the bleeding man to see if there was anything she could do for him.

A cursory examination led her to suspect that all the blood had come from a couple of scalp wounds and a number of minor cuts, many of them on the poor man's face. But it didn't look as if any major artery had been sliced. She tried to make him comfortable, sliding a pillow under his head and a blanket over him, since he'd already started shaking with shock.

She was sponging his face with a moist cloth, trying to wipe off a little of the blood without disturbing any of the cuts, when the paramedics arrived. They drove the white ambulance van down the driveway between the buildings and into the parking lot by the carports.

All the commotion brought Dolores and Benny. Edie came, too, toddling along with her oxygen tank, and Peg, still in her bathrobe, as well as Bob, the screenwriter, and a few other people Meggie didn't know. Dolores let out a stream of frantic Spanish at the sight of one of her tenants so badly used. She clung to Benny.

"Ah, *Dios mio*, it is a bad world sometimes! Poor Señor Leverson. A quiet man, *muy amable*. Did he ever hurt a fly? No, never. But the bad ones, they come and do the bad things to him anyway...."

It was full daylight and the paramedics were loading the injured man into the ambulance when the police car turned into the driveway. The two patrolmen inside took one look at all the blood on the Lakers T-shirt Meggie wore and decided to take her statement first.

She explained who she was, what she had heard, what she had done and what she had seen. The ambulance drove away. The tall, blond patrolman who had questioned her began congratulating her on her cool head and quick response in a crisis.

Right then, a black sports car turned into the driveway and rolled toward them. It was Nate.

Chapter Seven

Nate swung the sports car into the space next to the blue Volvo. Then he jumped out and slammed the door.

Meggie's heart lifted as she watched him stride toward her. He looked so handsome, in rumpled khakis and a midnight-blue polo shirt. There were circles under his eyes, though. He'd probably been going without sleep—on a stakeout, or something.

Just as Nate reached Meggie's side, the older of the two patrolmen, Officer Rinkley, came out of Mr. Leverson's apartment. He strolled over and stood next to his young partner, folding his arms across his chest. "Hello, Bravo."

"Rinkley." Nate dipped his head in a brief, ironic nod.

It surprised Meggie that they knew each other. But

then she realized that in Nate's line of work, he probably crossed paths with a lot of policemen.

Nate turned to Meggie, his dark eyes running a quick, ruthless inventory of the sweats and T-shirt she'd borrowed from him—and the blood all over them. "What the hell's going on?"

The younger officer launched into a glowing account of Meggie's bravery in rescuing a helpless man from assault by a burglar. Nate cut him off in midsentence by turning to Meggie. "Are you hurt?"

"Oh, no. I'm fine. Really, I just—"

He grabbed her hand. His touch felt wonderful. But his scowl worried her a little. "So you're done with her, then?" he said to the officers.

Rinkley shrugged. "Sure. We know how to reach her if we need her for anything more."

"Good." He cast Meggie another dark look. "Let's go."

"But, Nate, I—"

"Meggie. Inside. Now."

"But I've got laundry. I need to—"

Nate turned to Dolores, who still stood with Benny and the others, not far away. "Dolores, will you take care of her damn laundry? Please."

Dolores drew herself up. "I would be honored to care for her laundry."

"Thank you."

"*De nada.*"

Nate yanked on Meggie's hand. She stumbled after him, feeling a little foolish and a lot bewildered, across the parking lot to the stairs that led up to Nate's door.

Terrified and furious, Nate dragged Meggie in the door, shoved it closed and turned the dead bolt. Then he backed her up against the wall, took her sweet face in his hands and demanded, "What the hell is wrong with you?"

Her brows drew together. "Nothing. Nate, I—"

"You've got blood on your chin." He scrubbed at it with his thumb, frantic, scared to death at what might have happened to her.

She shook her head, trying to escape his hold. "Nate—"

But he wasn't letting her go. "Meggie. This isn't Medicine Creek. You can't just jump into the middle of things here, understand? You could get yourself killed."

"That poor man needed help."

"Meggie—"

"I'm not going to apologize for what I did, Nate. I would do it again. In a heartbeat." She gave him one of those hard, level looks that seared right through him. "And so would you."

"I'm different."

"How?"

"I'm—"

"A man," she sneered.

"Meggie, listen to me—"

She put a hand on his chest, firmly, to hold his attention on what she was about to say. "No. You listen. I've been doing a man's work since I was a kid. I know how to handle myself. And I am not a fool. All I did was scare the guy off."

"Meggie—"

"I'm not done. When someone's in trouble, I help them if I can. Whether I'm in L.A. or Timbuktu."

He knew that look in her eye, knew she wouldn't budge on this. He drew in a long, steadying breath and

let it out slowly. Then he released her, stepped back
and slumped against the wall opposite her. They regarded each other across the width of the narrow hall.

"You were scared for me," she said after a moment.
"That's nice."

"It is not nice. Not nice at all."

"You look tired," she said softly.

"It was a grim job."

"Tell me all about it."

"Maybe later." He looked her up and down, wondering how it was possible to be so damn glad to see
someone. "You're a bloody mess."

She lifted her chin and grinned. "It's good to see
you, too."

"When did you get here?"

"Monday."

Four days. For four days she'd been here, waiting
for him. If he'd called on his private line, she probably
would have answered. The idea pleased him. Too
much.

He asked, "Other than having to prevent a murder,
how have you been getting along?"

"Just fine. Dolores is great. And everyone—all your
neighbors—have been sweet to me."

"Good." He reached out and took her hand again,
but this time gently. "Come on. You need a bath."

She went along, as docile as a lamb, into the bathroom with him. He ran the water and removed her
bloodstained clothes and guided her down into the big
tub. When all the blood was washed away, he bundled
her in a towel and carried her to his bed, where he laid
her down and peeled the towel from her.

He looked at her, lying on his own bed, where he
had never dared to dream he would have her. Her still-

damp hair was spread out across his pillows. He loved the full, womanly curves of her body, the deep breasts and the slightly rounded belly, the soft, thick triangle of curls between her long, strong legs.

She reached up her arms. "Nate. Come here to me."

He went on looking at her—as he quickly removed every stitch he was wearing. She sighed when at last he bent down to her. Her arms twined around his neck and he stretched out along the soft, waiting length of her.

"I wasn't sure you'd be here," he confessed against her lips.

"I'm here." She kissed him through the words.

"Yeah. I can feel it."

She shifted slightly, parting her thighs, lifting her body in clear invitation. He slid between them—and home.

She moaned into his mouth.

He took the sound, tasted it, found it satisfying in a way no other woman's moans had ever been. She wrapped her legs around him. They began the long, slow dance that he always wished might never end.

At the end, he pressed in deep and she held him. So close. So complete. So exactly as lovemaking always should be.

Afterward, they just lay there, talking, filling each other in on the past few days. He told her a little about the divorce case he'd been working on, a surveillance deal down in Baja, where he had to hide in the hibiscus bushes outside a bungalow love nest, taking pictures of a certain wealthy, famous woman and her cabana-boy lover. The whole thing had depressed him. He had to turn in the pictures and the report at the Bel Air mansion of the woman's husband that afternoon.

Meggie talked about Dolores and the other tenants in his building. He had to smile when he learned that she knew all of them already. He'd lived there for five years and had done no more than exchange perfunctory greetings with a few of them.

She fell silent, lying there so peacefully, with her head on his chest. She stroked his arm in an idle, affectionate way and he thought it wouldn't be half-bad to just lie there with her like that for about a century.

"Nate?"

"Um?"

"The paramedics said that Mr. Leverson will probably be all right."

"Leverson?"

"The man from the building next door, the one who got beat up."

"Right. Well, good."

"They were taking him to Cedars Sinai Hospital. They said it's not far from here. I think I'll…go visit him, tomorrow."

Something in her tone bothered him, a hesitation, as if she had another issue entirely on her mind, beyond the injured man and a visit to Cedars.

"Okay?" she asked, still hesitant.

Maybe she thought he might tell her no and they'd end up in another argument. Well, she didn't have to worry on that score. If he couldn't talk her out of playing hero, he certainly wouldn't waste his time trying to convince her not to visit some beat-up burglary victim.

"Nate? Is that okay with you?"

He shrugged. "Fine. If that's what you want to do."

"It is." She lifted her head enough to plant a kiss on his chest, then lay back down again. "And Nate, I've been thinking..."

He chuckled. "Oh, no."

She slid off his chest and scooted up onto the pillow, bracing her head on her hand so she could meet his eyes. "What does that mean, 'Oh, no'?"

"Forget I said it. Think all you want."

"Thank you very much." Her thick, dark hair, shot with strands of gold and red, tumbled around her face; her wide eyes gleamed with humor.

He kissed the nose she'd wrinkled up at him. "All right. What have you been thinking?"

"I read an article a few months ago—in *Newsweek* or *Time*, I think. I can't remember where for sure, really. Anyway, it was an article about neighbors in big cities banding together, organizing themselves to look out for each other."

He knew what she was talking about. "You mean Community Watch?"

"Right. That's it. They had an eight-hundred number you could call, to have someone come and explain how to go about it."

"Why am I picturing meetings in my living room?"

"Maybe because there are going to *be* meetings in your living room." She reached out, pulled him close against her soft breasts. He went without reluctance, sucker that he was for her. She held him in her arms and stroked his hair. "Nate, I'd like to call that number. I'd like to get everybody in this building and the one next door organized. I'd like to know they can look out for each other. Is that all right with you?"

He made a low sound of agreement.

She went on stroking his hair. "I'd like to help them be safe, before I leave here."

There it was again, that strange tone. He pulled back and met her eyes. "What's wrong?"

She bit her lip, shook her head. "Nothing. I just…I really like all the people here. I don't want to see them hurt."

He swore low. "Meggie. It's okay. If you want Community Watch, you can have Community Watch."

She grabbed him then and hugged him hard. He felt like a million bucks. When she let him go, he realized he was starving. "What's in the kitchen?"

She laughed. "A stove. A refrigerator. A sink. Counters."

"I mean in the way of food."

"Eggs. Milk. Bread. The usual."

He was already tossing back the covers, reaching for his slacks. He looked around at her. She hadn't budged from the bed. "Come on. Get dressed. I want some breakfast."

"I've had mine."

"Then come watch me eat."

"Nate?"

He zipped up his pants, then lifted an eyebrow at her.

"Could I borrow another pair of sweats, maybe, and a shirt?"

"Sure." He gestured at the bureau. "Help yourself." He pulled on his shirt. Then he watched as she jumped from the bed, found some sweats, put them on and tied the drawstring, her pretty breasts bouncing temptingly as she moved. Damn, she was beautiful. It seemed to him that she got softer and riper looking every time he looked at her. "Meggie?"

"Um?"

"Where are your own clothes?"

She looked up, blinked and pushed her hair away from her face. Then she turned to the bureau again and opened another drawer. "Dolores has all my things." She took out a T-shirt and pulled it over her head. "The laundry, remember?" She flipped her hair free at the neck.

"Everything you brought with you was dirty already?"

"Well. Yes. I didn't bring much. I…hate checking my suitcase at the airport. I'm afraid they'll lose it. And besides, I thought while I was here I might pick up a few things. I'll have to cart them back with me, but I could use some new clothes."

Her explanation made perfect sense. And he had no idea why he'd made such a big deal out of it, anyway. "Whatever. Now, are you ready? I'm starving."

She beamed at him. "Lead the way."

Meggie went to see Mr. Leverson the next day. He was conscious. The nurses told her before she went into his room that he would be released in a day or two.

He smiled at her through his bandages and asked her to call him by his first name, which was Hector. "Thank you, young lady. You saved my life."

Meggie took his thin, bruised hand.

"My home is destroyed, isn't it?" He sounded as if he might cry.

Meggie hastened to reassure him. "No. No, really. It's pretty messed up, but nothing a new sofa, some lamps and a little paint won't fix."

"I have no family," Hector confessed in a whisper. "My wife died ten years ago. And we were childless.

But I have good insurance—I've been careful about that. I wonder…" His voice trailed off.

"What? Come on. Tell me, please."

"It's too much to ask."

"No. It's not. Come on. Ask me."

"Well, I'd like to get my insurance company moving on this. But from the hospital, it's a little difficult."

"Would you like me to call them? Dolores and I could show them the damage to your apartment."

"Oh. Would you?"

Meggie smiled. "I'd be glad to."

Nate called her a pushover when she got home. But when Hector's insurance company gave her the runaround, Nate took the phone and bullied the insurance agent until the man agreed to send someone over that afternoon.

The agent showed up right at five. Dolores and Meggie worked on him together, leading him through the trashed apartment, bemoaning the pain poor Hector had suffered.

Before he left, the agent promised that all Hector needed to do was send him the receipts for the cost of the repairs. On Saturday, Meggie, Nate and Benny cleaned the place up and painted the living room and kitchen. The intruder had never entered the single bedroom or the bath, so they remained intact. By Saturday evening, the apartment looked fresh and new. The living room lacked furniture, but Hector could handle that problem himself, with the money from his insurance company.

Hector returned home on Monday morning. Dolores and Meggie took the blue Volvo to get him. When they helped him inside and he saw what his landlady and neighbors had done, he sat down on the one chair left at his table and cried. Dolores clucked over him and told him not to upset himself, that they had all been happy to help out.

He wanted to get out his checkbook right then. Dolores reassured him that they could settle up later.

"Money isn't enough anyway," Hector protested. "What else can I do to repay you?"

"Come to the Community Watch meeting tonight," Meggie replied. "At my apartment, next door."

Amos Abel, the volunteer counselor from Community Watch, came to speak to the tenants of Nate's building at seven that night. Everyone in the building showed up, as well as four people from the building where Hector lived. Hector came, too, his face still bandaged, his left leg so stiff that Benny had to help him up the stairs.

Meggie and Dolores provided coffee and cookies. Amos Abel passed around brochures that explained the steps to a safe neighborhood. He advised them to tell each other their schedules, to learn each other's routines and to try to have one person in each building keeping an eye out at all times.

"I know, I know," Mr. Abel said. "You have to sleep sometimes. But do your best. Be aware. There is no substitute for vigilance." He gestured around the room. "And this—all of you here together, getting to know each other—is the first and most important step. People who know each other look out for each other. They take action when something seems strange in a neighbor's apartment." He advised the tenants on the ground floor to consider barring their windows. "I realize some of you just don't want to live that way. But you must understand that an unbarred ground-floor window is virtually impossible to truly secure.''

Before he left, Amos gave them all Community Watch stickers to put on their doors and in their windows, explaining, "The idea is to let the bad guys know that this is a place where people look out for each other.'' He also gave Dolores signs to put up in front of the buildings. The tenants agreed to meet again on Thursday, to exchange schedules.

Meggie felt pretty good by the time they all returned to their own apartments. She dared to hope that maybe, working together, they could protect themselves against predators like the one who had attacked Hector.

"Proud of yourself, aren't you?'' Nate teased, after the meeting, when they lay together in bed.

With a small, abashed groan, she snuggled in closer to him.

"Oh, now you're going modest on me.'' He started to tickle her.

She laughed and squirmed and batted his hands away. And then he kissed her. She kept on squirming, but for an entirely different reason—and she stopped trying to push him away.

Later, while Nate slept, Meggie lay wide-awake. The inner glow she'd felt at helping Nate's neighbors had somehow turned to a guilty heat down deep inside her.

She had come here to L.A. for one reason: to tell Nate face-to-face about the baby.

But instead, she had only lied some more. And Nate, whose ebony eyes always saw through the cleverest deceptions, seemed totally oblivious to the lies she told—lies she would not stop telling for as long as he continued to believe them.

Meggie understood herself now. All her vows to the

contrary, she would go on lying until Nate finally couldn't help but see the truth; until her own thickening waistline at last betrayed her. She would steal every glorious moment with him, each last second that God was willing to give her.

Just a little while longer, she whispered silently to herself, *here, in this place of palm trees and odd, sweet people. A little while longer. With Nate. Is it too much to ask?*

Meggie knew it *was* too much to ask; her agreement with Nate called for her to let him go as soon as she got pregnant. But she just didn't care. She would continue her deception with evasions and half lies. Gentle lies, she told herself. Lies that hurt no one, really. Lies that only bought her a little more precious time with Nate.

Nate left again on Wednesday, after warning Meggie that he probably wouldn't return until the weekend. As soon as he was gone, she looked up an ob-gyn in the phone book. On Thursday morning, she went to see him. He told her she was well over three months pregnant and doing just fine. He asked for urine and blood samples, then said that the office would call her if there were any abnormalities in the tests.

Meggie knew a moment of panic. What if they called and Nate answered?

But then calm descended. If Nate answered, so be it. Her foolish deception couldn't go on forever anyway. And she owed it to their baby to get decent prenatal care.

After she left the doctor's office, Meggie went shopping, as she'd told Nate she would. She bought some underwear, T-shirts, two loose jumpers and three pairs of jeans with elastic waists, clothes that she would be able to wear through most of her pregnancy—clothes that would also help to disguise her condition for a while. As a pure indulgence, she also picked up a bottle of perfume that smelled of roses. She smiled to herself as she sniffed it on her wrist, picturing Nate kissing all her pulse points, whispering that she smelled like a rose.

She got back to the apartment at four-thirty, but all she did was drop her shopping bags inside the door. She needed to pay a quick visit to Dolores, so they could talk about the refreshments for the Community Watch meeting that night.

However, Dolores wasn't in the mood to discuss refreshments. She opened the door with eyes red from crying. "*Hola,* Meggie," she said miserably.

"Dolores. What's wrong?"

"Come in." She turned and left Meggie to follow after.

In the kitchen, Dolores dropped to a chair by the table in front of a tissue box and a pile of used tissues. A sob shook her plump shoulders. She ripped a tissue from the box and buried her face in it.

Meggie went straight to her and laid a comforting hand on her shoulder, which inspired Dolores to erupt from her chair and into Meggie's bewildered arms.

"Ah, sweet virgin, oh *Dios mio. Mi familia—¿dónde está?* Where is my family, Megan? *Todos mis niños,* where have they gone?"

Meggie soothed and clucked and looked around frantically for Benny. "It's okay. It's all right. Settle down, now. Where's Benny?"

Dolores moaned. "He goes. Whenever I get like this.

I give him the ache in *la cabeza,* the head, you know?'' Dolores wailed some more.

Meggie hugged her and patted her until she settled down. Then she sat her back in her chair and took the one next to her. ''All right, now. What is it?''

A long, rambling, Spanish-punctuated explanation ensued. Dolores had borne her Benny five beautiful children—two sons and three daughters—all of them citizens of this great land. Between them, all those children had given Dolores and Benny eleven handsome grandchildren. Yet, out of all those children and all those grandchildren, only one—Yolie—would be home for Thanksgiving. Even Mateo, who always came, was off on the road somewhere, playing a gang leader in *West Side Story.*

When the sad tale had been told, Meggie sympathized some more. And then it occurred to her that they could share Thanksgiving together: Dolores, Benny and Yolanda—and Meggie and Nate. She suggested the idea to Dolores, who actually started to smile through her tears.

Then Meggie had an even better suggestion. ''Wait. We could invite everyone. In the two buildings. That way no one would have to spend the holiday alone.''

Dolores declared it a brilliant idea. ''A fiesta. *Una celebración grande.* For all the lonely ones. For everyone. *¿Sí?* Yes. Wonderful!''

They had the menu half planned by the time Dolores promised to bring cookies to the meeting that night and Meggie took her leave.

Nate returned ahead of schedule, on Friday afternoon. After a lovely hour in bed, Meggie told him all the news. He groaned when he heard how several of his neighbors would be coming to his place for dinner next Thursday, but he didn't try to change her plans.

The days that followed were happy ones. Nate took Meggie out for a little sight-seeing. They walked down Hollywood Boulevard, hand in hand, reading the names of the stars on the sidewalk, looking in the windows of the rather rundown stores, all decorated for Christmas now, in shiny red garlands and twinkling party lights. They visited the Descanso Gardens, where there were roses blooming even now, in November. They took in a movie at Mann's Chinese. And Dolores had tickets to a Sunday matinee at the Mark Taper Forum, a new play starring one of her grandson's friends. She and Benny didn't feel like going, so Meggie and Nate went, instead.

On Monday, Nate spent a few hours in his office at his computer, then he went out to meet with a client. He came back with the news that he'd be leaving Tuesday.

Meggie's heart sank. "For how long?"

He grinned. "Don't want me to miss the big feast, huh?"

She sighed. "You're right. I really want you here."

"Settle down." He came and put his arms around her. "This thing will take a day and a half, max. I have to serve some papers to a guy in Crescent City, up near the Oregon border. I know right where to find him, and he's going nowhere from what my client told me, so I don't even have to go looking."

"What are you saying?"

"That I promise I'll be back Wednesday at the latest, Tuesday night if I'm lucky. I wouldn't miss your Thanksgiving—you know that."

* * *

The next morning, Nate tried to get Meggie to sleep in. But she wouldn't. She insisted on getting up with him at 4 a.m. to fix him some breakfast before he took off.

She had set the timer the night before, so the coffee was already made. Nate offered to help fix the food, but she wouldn't hear of it. So he sat at the table, letting her wait on him, sipping caffeine and watching her bustle around in his bathrobe, whipping up eggs and toast.

He loved to watch her. He thought that she could do just about anything. She was equally at home treating cattle and baking cookies for her Community Watch meetings. She could pull on her Wranglers and eat dust in the drag during a trail drive—or put on her party duds and dance until dawn.

Even the few pounds she'd been putting on lately looked good on her. She seemed softer, rounder, sexier than ever.

Right then, she stood on tiptoe, reaching inside the cabinet above the stove to bring down the little bowl she liked to use for serving jam. Her slightly rounded belly pressed against the counter rim.

Something shifted inside Nate at that precise moment. And he saw the truth he'd been managing not to see.

Meggie was pregnant.

Chapter Eight

Meggie found the little bowl, closed the cupboard and set the bowl on the small section of counter between the stove and the refrigerator. She spooned out the jam. Then she put the jam jar away and took the bowl to the table. She looked up and smiled at Nate as she set the bowl down. "More coffee?"

He returned her smile mechanically, shaking his head. "I'm fine."

With a tiny shrug of her shoulders, she went back to the stove to stir the eggs. The toast popped up. She buttered it, put it on a small plate and cut it into neat triangles.

Nate went on watching her, stunned. In the space of one brief second, everything had changed. She set the food before him and a smaller portion at her own place, then went about brewing herself some herbal tea.

Herbal tea. It came to him that he hadn't seen her

drink coffee in weeks—maybe months. But that made sense. Caffeine couldn't be that good for the baby.

When the tea was ready, she carried it to the table and sat down opposite him. She took a bite of egg and looked up. Before she could ask why he wasn't eating, he picked up his own fork and began putting eggs in his mouth. As he dutifully chewed the eggs and ate the toast, she talked about her Thanksgiving party, about who would be there and how she would seat them all.

Nate watched her mouth move, nodded at the right places and made interested noises when required.

He said nothing at all about what he'd just realized— no doubt for the same reason she hadn't: because as soon as they got it out in the open, there would be no more reason for them to go on sleeping together, go on *being* together.

He had a ridiculous urge to throw back his head and laugh out loud at his own ability to deceive himself. Talk about clues....

He recalled all those menstrual periods she never seemed to have. And all the times when he would glance up to find her watching him with a strange, guilty look on her face. He remembered the way she sometimes stayed awake nights—fretting, he knew, by the stiff, bottled-up way she lay beside him.

He might have asked her, "What's on your mind?"

But he hadn't.

Because he hadn't wanted to know.

Meggie happily chattered on. "There's a party rental place a few blocks down on Santa Monica. I can get long folding tables from them, and good, sturdy folding chairs with padded seats. Not to mention table linens. Mrs. Tyrell is letting us use her china, glassware and silver."

She paused, but only for a sip of tea. Then she continued, "The Tyrells have gorgeous stuff, Nate. You should see it. Plates with gold rims and cut-crystal goblets. Mrs. Tyrell seemed really pleased to contribute them to the party. The table will be beautiful—just you wait. I've ordered a turkey, a really big one. Fresh, not frozen. And I'm going to go ahead and spring for a spiral-cut ham, because I think people like a choice...."

Damn. This was bad. This was trouble. This was exactly the reason he had kept himself clear of her for all those years. Because she was a woman who could make wearing a ball and chain seem like a great idea.

And maybe it was. Just not for him.

Nate had spent most of his childhood living over the bar his mother owned in Cheyenne. Sharilyn Tickberry Bravo hadn't been the most attentive of mothers; she worked nights and slept days. She had the bar to run, after all, because Nate's father—Bad Clint, as everyone called him—was not the kind of man a woman could depend on.

But Nate hadn't minded. He'd *liked* things that way. He'd gone where he wanted and kept his own hours from about the age of five on.

At fourteen, he'd gone to live at the Rising Sun. Under protest. He'd gotten used to it after a year or two. He'd even ended up forging strong bonds with his grandfather and his cousins. And Edna and her family, too. But those bonds didn't hold him there, with the Bravos; no bonds could hold him. Even at the Rising Sun, he'd only been marking time—until he was eighteen and could be free.

He left the ranch not long after he graduated from high school. He'd lived in a lot of places since then and acquired a number of disparate skills. He'd even put himself through four years of college, though few people knew that.

But most of all, he'd kept himself free. Nate was a man who needed to live free. It was something bred in the bone, this hunger to stay free. His mother had it. And so had Bad Clint.

And nothing, not even big-eyed Meggie May Kane and that baby she just had to have, would make him start thinking about settling down.

"Is something wrong, Nate?" She'd stopped chattering and started watching him across the table, those incredible eyes just a little bit troubled.

Yeah, I just noticed you're pregnant, he thought. "No, nothing," he said. "Why?"

"You seem...quiet, all of a sudden."

"Just thinking." He pushed back his chair. "And it's time I got out of here."

"Oh, Nate..." She looked adorably sad at his leaving.

More reason to get out quick.

They had a few things to talk about. But not now. He had to go now. They could face the music when he returned.

Before or after the big Thanksgiving feast? a voice in his mind taunted.

Ignoring that voice, he carried his plate to the sink, ran some water in it and then kept on going, back to the bedroom, where he had his bag already packed. He pulled on his jacket, scooped up the bag and headed out.

She was waiting for him by the front door. "I'll miss you." Her soft, warm body leaned toward him.

And he couldn't stop from dropping his bag and reaching for her. He pulled her close and settled his mouth over hers. She twined her arms around his neck. She tasted of peppermint tea and jam. And she smelled like a rose.

It took everything he had in him to pull away. "Lock up after me."

"I will. I promise." She watched him pick up his bag once more. "Come back by Thanksgiving."

"Right. Gotta go." He drew back the chain, turned the dead bolt and opened the door. The brisk predawn air greeted him. He stepped onto the landing and then ran down the stairs.

He knew she stood there in the doorway, watching until he disappeared, though he never turned to look back.

Nate flew to San Francisco and rented a car to take him up the coast to Crescent City. There, he discovered that the guy who wasn't going anywhere had decided to spend Thanksgiving in Chicago. Nate got out his cell phone and called his client, who reiterated that cost was not a factor and he wanted those papers served yesterday. Nate called the airlines and managed to get a seat on a flight out of San Francisco. And then he hopped in his rental car and drove like hell to get back there in time. He made the call he dreaded as he sped down the coast highway.

As soon as she picked up the phone, he laid it on her. "It turns out I've got to fly to Chicago."

Meggie's disappointment came at him through the silence on the line, as palpable as any words would have been.

"Dammit, Meggie. I have to work."

He heard her sigh. "I know." Then she made her

voice pleasantly brisk. "Any chance you might make it back for Thanksgiving?"

"How the hell should I know?"

Another reproachful beat of silence, then she said, "Don't be mad at me, Nate."

"I'm not."

"You sound—"

"Meggie."

"What?"

"I'll try to get there for your party. That's the most I can do."

She sighed again. "Okay."

"I have to go now." He didn't, but talking to her only reminded him of all the things they needed to say.

"All right. Nate?"

"Yeah?"

"Just…" She seemed not to know what to say. "Be safe," she finished at last, rather listlessly.

"I will." He disconnected the call and tossed the phone on the empty seat beside him, wondering what in hell had ever possessed him to imagine that this whole crazy plot would work out. One way or another, it was a setup for heartbreak.

He understood Meggie. To the very soul of her. He knew that for almost twenty years she'd maintained an irrational attachment to him. And he'd always been scrupulously careful not to encourage her.

Until he'd managed to let himself get roped into her scheme to save the Double-K. They'd played house— and slowly she had let herself believe the game was real.

Hell, to be totally honest, so had he.

Now he could see it coming. She had the marriage license and the baby she needed. But it wasn't going to be enough for her. He'd agreed to be temporarily roped. She wanted him tied and branded, as well.

But a lifetime arrangement wasn't the deal.

He stepped on the gas and pushed the speedometer needle over the speed limit. He had a plane to catch.

And his own heart to outrun.

In Nate's bedroom, Meggie hung up the phone feeling wounded and weepy. She sat on the edge of the bed for several minutes, her shoulders slumped, staring at the far wall. Then, with a soft, pitiful sigh, she got up and plodded out to the living room. She dropped into the jewel-green chair. She stared at an amethyst-centered geode on one of Nate's bookcases and allowed a grieved litany to play through her mind:

He promised before he left that he would be here. And now he suddenly has to fly off to Chicago. It's not fair. I've planned such a beautiful party. He could make a little effort. It's a special, special time. And he should be here. He should keep his promise and get home in time. Because I want him here. And he said before he left that he would be here....

About the third time through, she started to get sick of herself.

By the fifth time through, she'd had enough.

"I am being disgusting," she said to the amethyst-centered geode, since there was no one else to hear. "I am acting exactly like the clingy, demanding wife I swore I would never be." She stood. "I just better buck up."

The next morning, early, she knocked on Dolores's door. "Come on," she said, when the landlady opened the door.

"Where?"

"To the store. We have a lot of shopping to do."

Dolores beamed. "You know I adore to shop. Let me get *mi bolsa.*" She disappeared down the hall and reappeared a moment later, clutching the big black patent-leather purse she carried with her whenever she went out. Then she called, "Benito, we are going shopping!"

From somewhere in the living room, Benny shouted, "Go! Have fun!"

"We will!"

They went to Dolores's favorite *carnicería* to pick up the turkey and the ham—and to Ralph's supermarket for most of the rest of the food. They visited a florist shop for fall leaves and autumn-colored flowers, with which Dolores planned to create twin centerpieces, one for each end of the two long pushed-together folding tables. They went to the party supply house, where they bought orange candles and adorable miniature turkeys and Indians and Pilgrims, which Dolores planned to include in her centerpieces.

They ate lunch out, at a little Mexican café Dolores liked. Of course the landlady insisted on treating. When they got home, in the late afternoon, they made pies. Mince and pecan and pumpkin and apple, rolling out the dough and filling the pie pans at Nate's, and using both their ovens for the baking.

Mrs. Tyrell came over for a few minutes while they were putting the pies together. They already had two in the oven.

"Oh, my, is that pecan pie I smell?" she asked.

"It is," Meggie answered. "Get yourself some coffee," Meggie said, "and have a seat."

Mrs. Tyrell helped herself and they talked for a few minutes of the party tomorrow. Mrs. Tyrell explained that she and her husband had been married only a few years. They had met as tenants of the same building, in the Valley. After their marriage, they had decided to move to West Hollywood when Mr. Tyrell found a part-time job with a recording company nearby.

"He likes to keep his hand in, you understand," Mrs. Tyrell said. "Once, he was a record producer. But that was years ago."

Dolores winked. "See? They are newlyweds, the same as you and Nate."

The sound of Nate's name sent a small surge of yearning through Meggie. She banished it with a nod and a grateful smile for Mrs. Tyrell. "I can't tell you how much we appreciate the loan of your beautiful things."

Mrs. Tyrell waved a perfectly manicured hand. "It will be lovely for me to see them put to use." She sighed, and for a moment she looked very sad. "Times change, don't they? But still, we cling to our mementos of the past."

Meggie wondered what Mrs. Tyrell meant by that exactly. But she didn't ask. It would have felt too much like prying. Each day, she learned a little more about Nate's neighbors. But friendship and trust weren't things a person could rush; they made their own timetables.

Her stay here was temporary. Meggie had to remember that. She might or might not remain long enough to learn of Mrs. Tyrell's past.

Strange, she thought later, lying in Nate's bed alone, she felt so comfortable here. How quickly these two little Spanish-style apartment buildings in West Hollywood had become almost like home.

* * *

The next morning, Meggie and Dolores were up and cooking before the sun. All morning, the neighbors wandered in and out, bringing contributions to the feast or just stopping by for a few minutes to see how the preparations were getting along.

At nine, Benny took the van he and Dolores owned and drove over to the party store, which was open until noon that day so that customers could pick up any rental equipment they'd reserved. By ten-thirty, the two long tables extended from the kitchen halfway into the living room and Dolores had begun the intricate process of setting and decorating.

Meggie had just checked the turkey when Dolores asked her where the bag from the party store had gone.

"You know, the one with my little Indians and Pilgrims?"

"It's in the bedroom. I'll get it." Meggie headed down the hall.

As she passed the office, she heard Nate's business phone ring. She froze, her heart lurching in her chest. It could very well be Nate, calling from Chicago to check his messages.

Well, all right. It probably wasn't.

But it could be. And if she answered, she could wish him a Happy Thanksgiving. She could be upbeat and cheerful, show him that she'd gotten over her attack of the sulks the other day.

The phone rang for the third time. On the next ring, the machine would take it.

She shouldn't...

But she couldn't help herself. She shoved open the door and raced to the desk.

"Yes. Hello?" She remembered she probably ought

to try to sound professional. "Um, this is Bravo Investigative Services, Megan speaking."

On the other end, there was nothing but silence. She wasn't sure how Nate's message-pickup device worked. Maybe it was all electronic, which would mean that if Nate were on the other end of the line, he would have no idea that she had answered instead of his machine.

"Hello?" she said, trying again.

She heard a cough, and then a throaty woman's voice asked hesitantly, "Is Nate Bravo there?"

It wasn't Nate. Disappointment made Meggie sigh.

And then she realized that she would have to take a message. She yanked open the center drawer of the desk in search of a pencil and paper.

"Are you there?" the woman asked.

Meggie found a pen and a yellow legal pad and shoved the drawer shut. "Yes, I'm here. But Mr. Bravo isn't."

A silence, then, "Oh. I see. Well. All right, then."

Meggie sensed that the woman meant to hang up. Nate would not be happy that she'd picked up his phone—and possibly cost him a job. She spoke briskly. "May I take a message?"

The woman let another silence elapse before admitting with reluctance, "It's…personal."

A girlfriend. Meggie just knew it. She wanted to scratch the woman's eyes out. She wanted to shout, "Stay away from my husband!" But then, she had no claim on Nate. Not really. And she had no right to try to frighten his girlfriends away.

And come to think of it, wouldn't a girlfriend call on the house line?

The woman said grimly, "I suppose, though, that I

might as well leave a message. Would you wish him a happy Thanksgiving?''

"I'd be glad to. From who?"

"From his mother, Sharilyn.''

Chapter Nine

"Hello? Are you still there?" asked Sharilyn.

Nate's mother. Meggie couldn't believe it. She'd never met the woman herself. People said Sharilyn had grown up in South Dakota somewhere. She and Bad Clint had met in Cheyenne and stayed there through the years of their marriage. Since Bad Clint and his father, Ross, never could stand each other, Clint refused to go near Medicine Creek or the Rising Sun.

But then, when Bad Clint died, Ross had convinced Sharilyn to let Nate live with him. And after that, Nate's mother had pretty much disappeared. To Meggie's recollection, Nate hadn't mentioned her since that first year he came to the Rising Sun—and then only to say how he hated her for making him live there.

"Hello?" Sharilyn asked again.

"Yes. Don't hang up. I'm still here. I'm just... surprised, that's all."

A wry laugh came over the line. "Didn't think Nate *had* a mother, did you?"

"Well, I—"

"It's all right. Just give him the message, okay? Goodbye."

"Wait."

A pause, then warily, "What?"

"I tried to make you think I was Nate's secretary. But I'm not really his secretary."

Sharilyn chuckled. "Yeah. I was onto you. I don't know a lot of secretaries who work on Thanksgiving."

"I'm...Nate's wife."

"Oh. I see."

Was she sad or happy to hear such news? Meggie hadn't a clue. "Everybody calls me 'Meggie.' I own a ranch not far from the Rising Sun, back in Wyoming."

"Well," Sharilyn said. And nothing else.

"Does Nate have a number where he can reach you?"

Sharilyn laughed, but there wasn't much humor in the sound. "He knows how to reach me. We...don't talk much. But we kind of keep tabs on each other."

"I understand," Meggie said. Though she didn't, not at all. Nate's Rolodex sat in the right-hand corner of the big, old desk. She pulled it close and flipped to the *B*s.

And there it was. First name only: Sharilyn. With a phone number. And a Los Angeles address.

"You live here," Meggie blurted out.

"What do you mean?"

"Here. You live here in L.A."

"So?"

"So...what are you doing this afternoon?"

"Excuse me?"

"It's Thanksgiving. Have you made plans for dinner?"

"Well, I—"

"Stop. I can tell by the way you said 'Well.' You're free."

A low sound escaped Sharilyn. "Free," she murmured, as if she didn't think much of the word.

"Well, are you? Are you free?"

"Yeah, all right. I'm free."

"Great. So that means you can come here, to Nate's. We're having a feast."

"A feast," Sharilyn repeated, sounding a little dazed.

"Yes. A big Thanksgiving Day feast. Most of the people in Nate's building will be coming. And some from next door."

"Oh, really, no. I couldn't."

"Yes, you could."

"Nate wouldn't—"

"Look. Don't worry about Nate. He'll be glad to see you, I'm sure." Meggie spoke with a good deal more confidence than she felt.

"But I—"

"And besides, to tell you the truth, I can't even be sure he'll be here for dinner. He had to fly to Chicago unexpectedly. He said he'd try to get back in time, but I don't know if he'll make it. So will you come?"

"I really—"

"Please, Sharilyn. Say you'll come."

Sharilyn said nothing.

Meggie added in a wheedling tone, "I would really like to meet you."

"You're...a very sweet girl."

"Great." Meggie spoke with finality. "You'll come."

Sharilyn let a lengthy silence elapse before conceding apprehensively, "All right. I will."

An hour later Meggie answered the door to find a tall, slim woman with black hair waiting on the other side.

Meggie smiled tentatively, thinking that the woman must once have been stunningly beautiful, though signs of a hard life showed in the lines that bracketed her mouth and fanned out from the corners of her dark, deep-set eyes. "Sharilyn?"

Sharilyn nodded. "And you're Meggie?"

"Yes."

The two women regarded each other. Meggie felt misty eyed. Here was Nate's mother, standing right in front of her. And for some crazy reason, she found herself thinking of her own mother, Mia, who had left her adoring husband and infant daughter behind to go in search of bright lights and good times.

Mia had found what she sought. She had died on a Manhattan street corner, run down by a reckless driver at dawn after a night spent club hopping and drinking fine champagne.

Always, in her most secret heart, Meggie had nurtured an impossible fantasy. That her mother hadn't really died. And that someday, Mia would come to see her. She would be beautiful, but a little sad, a little worn—a lot like Sharilyn, actually. She would have tears in her eyes. And she would say, "Whatever I did, wherever I went, I thought of you, Megan May. And I always, always loved you...."

Sharilyn arched a dark eyebrow. "Well?"

Meggie shook herself and stepped back. "Come on in." She led Sharilyn to the kitchen, where Dolores stood at the stove and Yolie worked at the sink, cleaning shrimp for the seafood cocktail that was Dolores's specialty.

"Welcome," Dolores said, beaming her wide, warm smile.

Sharilyn smiled back. "Thank you." She looked around anxiously.

"No está aquí," Dolores murmured gently.

Sharilyn frowned. "Excuse me?"

"Mr. Bravo. Your son. He is not here right now."

"Yes," Sharilyn replied in a mild voice. "I can see that."

Around one o'clock, the other guests began arriving. They would share an hour or two of cocktails, appetizers and good talk, then sit down for the huge meal.

After an initial nervous reserve, Sharilyn seemed to fit right in. And she and Peg knew each other.

"Sharilyn's the best damn waitress on Sunset Boulevard," Peg announced with great respect.

It turned out that Sharilyn worked as head waitress on the morning shift at a place called Dave's Café. Often, after a late night, Peg would drop in for breakfast before heading home. "Sharilyn takes care of her people," Peg said.

Sharilyn muttered a dry, "Thanks," and then swiftly changed the subject to the beauty of the table setting.

Meggie served appetizers, declined champagne with some regret and made sure everyone was comfortable. The talk ranged from football to Community Watch to the Christmas season and how it seemed to start earlier every year. Hector, who had most of his bandages off now, but still looked pretty gruesome at first glance, took an instant liking to Sharilyn. And she seemed friendly enough toward him. Meggie smiled at the two of them, sitting side by side on one of Nate's blue sofas, speaking in low, careful voices of the weather and their mutual love of musical theater. As she moved among her guests, Meggie tried not to let her mind stray to thoughts of Nate. She tried not to keep hoping that maybe, just maybe, he might still make it home before the end of the party....

After a miserable flight home, Nate picked up his car in the long-term parking lot at LAX. It was a quarter of two.

He had to have holes in his head. Nobody tried to get a last-minute flight out of O'Hare on Thanksgiving. It couldn't be done.

But Nate had done it—because he couldn't stop thinking about Meggie, and how hurt she'd sounded the last time he talked to her.

He felt like a jerk for copping out on her party— even if, once the party was over, he planned to get down to hard reality with her. He'd started thinking that if he could just make it in time for Thanksgiving dinner, then at least he could tell himself he hadn't stood her up for the big event.

His reasoning was stupid. Irrational. Nonsense. But he'd waited half the night anyway, for a chance at a flight. And then he'd lurched and bumped over the Rockies, listening to his flight mates toss their cookies as, from the cockpit, the pilot issued constant reassurances that this "minor turbulence" would pass.

Nate paid the excessive long-term parking fee and headed home. Once he got clear of the airport, the streets were relatively empty; most people would be in their houses, watching football and getting ready to pound down a little turkey and dressing.

He pulled into his carport space at two-thirty, got his bag from the trunk and headed for his front door. He was sticking his key in the lock, when the door swung back.

And there she was, her eyes shining, her dark hair with its gold and red lights curling softly around her flushed, happy face.

The warm air from inside came out and wrapped around him, scented of ham and roast bird, of cinnamon and cloves. He could hear laughter and voices from the other room.

"You made it," she said.

Something rose up inside him, something that ached and longed and scared the hell out of him. He dropped his bag inside the door and reached for her. She came into his arms, warm and soft, smelling of roses and Thanksgiving.

"Nate…" She breathed his name against his mouth.

He kissed her hard and long. Only a burst of laughter from the other room stopped him from swinging her up in his arms and carrying her down the hall to his bedroom.

She stepped back, her face pink, a tender smile on her lips. "Come on. We're just sitting down."

"Let me get rid of my bag."

"Sure."

She was still standing in the same place when he came back down the hall after dropping the duffel in the bedroom. And she looked a little flustered. "Nate, I…wanted to tell you…"

"What?"

"Well, we have an extra guest."

He had no idea what she was babbling about. "That's okay by me."

"Well. Good." Still, she looked undecided. And maybe a little bit guilty.

"What's going on?" he asked quietly.

"Happy Thanksgiving, Nate," said a familiar voice.

Nate looked over to see his mother standing in the doorway to the kitchen.

He was careful to treat the woman civilly. Meggie seated him next to her, a move he didn't appreciate at all. He passed the woman the gravy when she asked for it and tried not to look into her deep, sad eyes.

At the end of the meal, he turned to her. "I think you and I could use a few minutes. Alone."

Her eyes looked sadder than ever and her stiff shoulders seemed to droop. "All right."

As most of the others gravitated back toward the living room, Nate led Sharilyn down the hall and into his office.

"Have a seat." He gestured at the chair opposite his desk.

Sharilyn looked at the chair warily, then shook her head. "I think I might as well stand."

"Suit yourself." He shoved the door closed and moved into the room, leaving her standing uncomfortably by the door. When he got beyond his desk, he turned and looked at her, letting a beat or two elapse before he asked, "All right. What's going on?"

She put her hand against her heart. "I called. To wish you a Happy Thanksgiving. Meggie answered. She invited me to come over for dinner."

"And you came."

She lifted her chin and said nothing.

He demanded flatly, "Why?"

Her brows drew together in a pained expression. "Nate, I just want—"

"What? You want what?"

"Some kind of…understanding, between us."

"We understand each other. Perfectly."

"Oh, Nate, that's not true. You know it's not."

"Do you need money?"

"No. It's not money. You know that."

"Do I?"

"Please, Nate…"

He let out a long, bored breath of air. "You shouldn't have come here. And I think you know that."

"I only wanted—"

He waved a hand to cut off her pointless explanations. "If you're short of cash, I'll help you out. Otherwise, I've got nothing to say to you." With that, he turned away from her, toward the window. As usual, the green blind was halfway up. He looked across the next-door neighbors' driveway at the hibiscus bush—a little scraggly this time of year—that grew against the building there. The shadows were lengthening. It would be dark soon.

"Nate…" Sharilyn said, trying again.

He refused to turn or to say a word.

She murmured sadly, "All right, then."

He resolutely continued staring out the window, ignoring her. After a moment, he heard the sound of the door opening and her footsteps on the hardwood floor, moving out into the hall. He waited another few seconds, to be sure she had really gone. Then he turned and followed after her.

In the living room, Sharilyn headed straight for Meggie. Nate stood in the hall entry, watching her make her goodbyes.

"Thank you so much for a great meal. But I'm afraid I've got to get going now."

Meggie frowned. "But, Sharilyn, there's still dessert."

"No. I really have to go."

Meggie tried teasing. "Sharilyn. These are incredible pies. My grandma Kane's secret recipes. People have fought their way through blizzards for pies like these."

"Thanks. Really." Sharilyn was backing toward the door. "Nice to meet you all." She glanced around, a wooden smile stretching her mouth.

Meggie looked up then and right at Nate. Her eyes accused him. He stared back at her, meeting her glare with one of his own. When Sharilyn reached him and went on past, he followed her to the door, watched her go out and closed it behind her.

Then he joined the party, where everyone seemed to be having a great time. He poured himself a glass of champagne. And then, refusing to let himself be snared by Meggie's reproachful glances, he went and sat by the old guy from next door, Leverson, who still looked like a refugee from a horror movie, but claimed he was feeling better every day.

"Call me 'Hector,' why don't you?" Leverson suggested. Then he added rather dreamily, "Your mother is a lovely, charming woman. It's a shame she had to leave so soon."

Nate made a low noise in his throat that Hector could interpret any way he chose, and then got up to pour himself more champagne. He figured he was going to

need a river of the stuff before the evening finally came
to an end.

Three hours later, most of the guests had said goodbye, all smiling and laughing and swearing they'd had
a terrific time.

Mrs. Tyrell suggested, "We'll have to do it again
next year."

Meggie smiled and made a noncommittal noise in
response. Next year, she wouldn't be here. But now
was hardly the time to mention that fact. She glanced
over to find Nate watching her. She looked away. She
had a few things to say to him—later, when they were
alone.

The Garnicas lingered to help clean up. Dolores and
Yolie worked with Meggie washing dishes, while
Benny and Nate lugged the tables, chairs and linens
down to the Garnicas' van so they'd be ready to go
back to the rental shop the next morning.

As soon as all of the Tyrells' treasured china sparkled like new, they toted it across the landing, where
Mrs. Tyrell put it away. Then Meggie and Dolores
packed up two-thirds of the leftovers for the Garnicas
to enjoy.

Finally, at a little after nine o'clock, the Garnicas
departed. Meggie stood at the top of the landing and
watched them bustle down the stairs, laden with their
booty of pies, candied yams and turkey—and a generous portion of spiral-cut ham.

When she turned back to the apartment, Nate was
leaning in the doorway, watching her.

They shared a long, telling look. And then Meggie
tried to move past him.

He shifted in the doorway to block her path.

She made a low noise. "Come on, Nate."

He shook his head, the action slow and insolent. He'd been drinking champagne steadily since he'd thrown his mother out. It hadn't seemed to affect him during the party, but now the signs of one too many were starting to show. His eyes were heavy lidded and his full mouth looked just a little bit mean.

Meggie understood his desire to dull the pain that his own actions must have caused him. But she didn't approve—either of the way he'd treated Sharilyn, or of drinking too much as a solution to anything. She'd thought they would talk over what he'd done. But now that she realized his condition, she only wanted to get away from him until he'd had time to sober up.

"Nate. Move."

"Meggie May." He said her name with great solemnity.

"Just move. Please."

His bloodshot eyes bored through her. But then, with a lazy shrug of his big shoulders, he let her pass.

She went straight down the hall to the bathroom, where she intended to take a long, soothing bath. Unfortunately, Nate followed after her and slid in front of the door when she tried to swing it shut.

"Get out of the way, Nate."

He didn't move, only crossed his arms insolently over his broad chest and leaned his head back against the door. "What is your problem?" he asked the ceiling, in a tone of infinite weariness.

"You. You keep blocking my way. Move."

He lowered his head and looked at her. "No."

With some regret, she gave up the idea of that nice, tension-relieving bath. "Fine." She turned on her heel and started back down the hall.

She got about three steps before he grabbed her arm. Meggie froze in midstride. "Let go of me."

"We have to talk."

She turned on him then, her lip curling in a sneer. "I don't want to talk to you now. You're drunk."

He wiggled a finger at her. "No. Incorrect. I am not drunk. I am...slightly numb."

"Right."

"But not numb enough." He pronounced each word with great care, as if he feared his own tongue might trip him up.

"Just let go of me, Nate."

"Meggie—"

"Let go."

He closed his eyes. "Meggie..." The word held utter exhaustion.

Her heart turned over then and her anger at him melted away. He looked so tired, and so bewildered. Gently, she laid her hand over his and peeled the fingers away from her arm.

"Come on." She eased around him and started pulling him toward the bedroom. "Sleep it off. We can talk in the morning." Surprisingly, he followed after her, obedient as a child.

In the bedroom, she sat him down on the bed. Then, kneeling, she pulled off his boots. He stuck out one foot and then the other for her, murmuring "Meggie, Meggie, Meggie," making a weary litany of her name.

When she had the boots off, she rose and took his shoulders, guiding him onto his back. He stretched out with sigh, his eyes already closed. She took the spare quilt from the top shelf of the closet and settled it over him.

"Meggie..." he whispered, already asleep.

She kissed him on the forehead and then tiptoed to the door. She would have that long bath after all, and then she'd slide under the quilt beside him and get some rest herself.

Tomorrow, she'd let him sleep late. And then, after she poured a few cups of coffee down him, she'd tell him just what she thought of the way he'd behaved with Sharilyn.

But it didn't work out quite as Meggie planned.

She woke around three to a feeling of loneliness. She sat up in bed. "Nate?" No answer came. His side of the bed was empty.

Worried, and telling herself not to be, Meggie pushed back the blanket, pulled on the robe she'd borrowed from Nate and padded out to the hall.

Past the front door, a wedge of light spilled from the kitchen onto the hardwood floor. The smell of freshly brewed coffee scented the air. Meggie pulled Nate's robe closer around her and moved toward the light.

She found Nate sitting at the kitchen table, staring into a coffee mug. "Nate. Are you all right?"

He looked up. His eyes were still red, but piercingly alert. He picked up the mug and drained the contents. "I'm fine." He stood and carried the mug to the counter, where he refilled it. Then he held the pot toward her. "Coffee?"

She shook her head.

He lifted an eyebrow at her, smirking a little. "How surprising."

She frowned. "What does that mean?"

He waved a hand, dismissing both her question and his own remark. Then he shoved the pot back on the warmer and returned to the table, where he dropped into his chair again and gestured at the seat across from him.

"Come on," he said. "Sit down. Time to talk."

She did want to discuss the way he'd behaved with Sharilyn. But there had to be a better time to do it. "Nate, it's three in the morning. I really think we might as well let this wait until—"

He leveled a hard stare at her. "Look. I'm stone sober now. And it's time we hashed this out."

Reluctantly, she murmured, "Fine."

"Sit down, then."

She marched to the table and plunked herself into the chair across from him.

For a moment, once she was seated, he stared at her—a totally unreadable kind of look. Then he brought the full mug to his lips and took a careful sip.

She assumed he must be waiting for her to begin. So she plunged right in. "You were really rotten to your mother."

He winced at her accusation and must have burned his mouth. He swore and set the mug down, hard enough that coffee slopped over the rim. "I wouldn't have been rotten to her," he said silkily, "if she hadn't been here. But *somebody* invited her here. Who was that, do you think?"

"You know who."

"Say it."

"Me."

He faked a surprised look, one that scraped her nerves raw. "Oh, really? You? What a revelation."

She kept her head high. "And I'm glad that I did it."

"I can see that."

Meggie breathed deeply, trying to keep her anger

leashed. She felt that he was totally in the wrong about this—and making it worse by taunting her. "Nate. She called on your *business line*. Your business line. She doesn't even have your private number, does she?"

"No, she doesn't."

Meggie's disbelief wouldn't be contained. "She lives right here. In L.A. I didn't even know that. You never said a word."

He made a harsh sound. "So?"

"So, we could have had her over. We could have spent a little time with her. We could have—"

He raised himself halfway out of his chair, put both hands on the table and leaned across at her. "You refuse to get the picture here," he said in a furious whisper. "I don't want her over. I don't want anything to do with her."

Meggie met his attack with quiet dignity. "That's cruel."

He snorted. "Life's cruel."

"If you would only—"

He dropped back into his chair and slapped a hand on the table. "Stop. You don't know what you're talking about. You don't get this situation at all. So let it be."

"No, Nate. It isn't right. She's your mother. And I think she really loves you. All she wants is a chance to—"

"Listen to me, Meggie. *I* want you to leave this alone."

"No. It's not right. You won't even give her a chance. I know you feel she abandoned you, after your dad died. But everything worked out all right, didn't it? You had a much better life with your grandfather and your cousins than you ever would have had with Sharilyn.''

''You don't know a damn thing about the life I would have had with her if my grandfather hadn't butted in.''

''I think I do know. I think Sharilyn did what she thought was best for you. She was a woman alone, and you weren't exactly an easy kid to handle. And she knew that your grandfather would take you in hand and—''

''Stop.''

''No. Listen. She knew that your grandfather would be able to deal with you.''

''That's garbage, Meggie May. Sentimental garbage.''

''No, it's not. She wanted—''

''You don't know her. You don't know what the hell she wanted.'' His red-rimmed eyes gleamed brightly now, with anger. And something else. Something deep and old and ugly with hurt.

''Oh, Nate…'' Involuntarily, she reached across and touched his hand.

He jerked back as if she'd burned him. ''Don't.''

''Nate, please—''

''No. Back off.''

''If you'll only give her a chance.''

''Forget it. She'll get no chance from me.''

''But why not?''

''You don't need to know.''

''I do. Please. Tell me. Let me understand.''

He looked out the window, at the lights of L.A. beyond the carport, and then back at her. ''You just have to keep pushing.''

''I really want to understand.''

"Fine. All right. The damn woman *sold* me."

Meggie frowned. "Sold you?"

"When I was fourteen years old, she sold me to my grandfather."

"Sold you—for money?"

Nate looked at her squarely; now his eyes were flat black stones. "Yeah, for money."

"But how—"

"When my father died, my grandfather offered my mother fifteen thousand dollars if she would give me up."

"No…"

"Yeah." He looked out the window again, at the darkness and the tiny lights that went on and on, up onto the surrounding hills and all the way to the horizon line.

"But how do you know that?"

"I overheard him make her the offer."

"Overheard?"

"Right." Nate rubbed a hand down his face. "My mother thought I was out running wild when she had her little talk with him. But I came in through the back. And I listened in. I heard my grandfather say a lot of nasty things about my father—what a loser he was, what a disgrace to the Bravo name." Nate made a low, scoffing sound. "Everything he said was true, of course. But all the same, I hated him for saying it, for being so damn smug about it. He talked a lot about how he knew it was partly his fault, the way my father had turned out. That he'd been too tough at the wrong times—and not loving enough in general. He told my mother he wanted to make sure I had a chance to be the man my father wasn't. And that she'd be doing me a favor to take the money and disappear."

"What did she say to all that?"

"Not a damn thing. He did all the talking. Finally, when he'd said it all, he told her he'd come back the next day for her answer. Then he left."

"What did you do then?"

"I came out of my hiding place. I begged her not to do it. I said we could make it, together, that we could get by. Maybe we didn't have the kind of life other people thought was a good life. But it was *our* life. I thought it mattered. I thought we had each other and that that was the bottom line."

A small, sympathetic sound escaped Meggie.

Nate shot her a hard glance, then turned away again. "Don't look at me like that. It was years ago. And you're right. I did well enough at the ranch, in the end. But I'm not giving an inch when it comes to that woman. She took the money and sent me away. She *said* it was the best thing for me. But that was just an excuse she made so that she could get rid of me—so that she could be free."

Meggie watched him as he stared on at the lights beyond the window. She ached for the boy he'd been—and she understood at last why he'd grown so angry every time she tried to give him money in return for all he'd agreed to do for her. What she couldn't understand was why he wouldn't let go of his anger at Sharilyn. It had been so many years, after all. Certainly time enough to get beyond the hurt. And Sharilyn so clearly wanted to reach out to him. What ever kind of mother she had been years ago, anyone could see she was a kind, thoughtful person now. Why not make peace with her? What harm could that possibly do?

Nate looked down into his empty mug and then up into Meggie's eyes. "So that's that. She wanted to be free. And she *is* free. And I don't want a damn thing to do with her.''

"Oh, Nate, I still really believe that—"

"Look. It doesn't matter what you believe. She wanted freedom, and she's got it. And I understand her. Because I'm just like her."

"But you *don't* understand her. Not really. You're just getting even with her, that's all. You're just nursing a grudge—hurting her and yourself, too—because you felt abandoned when she gave you up. Have you ever thought that it's just possible she really did do it for your own good? It's just possible it hurt her to lose you as much as it hurt you to be sent away. You should—"

"Meggie." His voice was as hard as his eyes.

"What?"

"I don't need anyone telling me what I *should* do."

"But I—"

"This is my damn life. You've got no right to tell me how I ought to live it. Am I making myself clear here?"

Meggie stared into his cold, remote face. And it occurred to her that she'd got herself into a losing battle here, one that had only ended up making him angry at her.

"Am I making myself clear?"

She sighed. "Yes. All right."

"All right, what?"

She spoke with measured calm. "You've made yourself clear."

"Good." He lifted his mug from the table and set it away from him, in a gesture of finality. "And now that we've wrapped up the subject of Sharilyn, let's finish up the rest of this mess."

She frowned at him, not understanding. "Finish up?"

"Meggie, let's stop playing games."

"Games?"

He shook his head. "You've been keeping something from me, for a while now. Haven't you?"

Reality started to dawn. "Well, I—"

"A pretty important little piece of information."

Her heart thudded to a stop, then started thundering. "Nate, let's not—"

"We've been having such a great time, playing house."

She opened her mouth, but no words came out.

He prodded. "Haven't we?"

She closed her eyes.

"Haven't we?"

"Yes. All right."

"All right, what?"

She gave him the words he'd demanded to hear. "We've been having a great time."

"But there *was* a goal. Wasn't there?"

She only stared at him.

"Wasn't there?"

"Nate, please—"

"Just give me an answer."

"Yes. All right. Fine. A goal, yes."

"And what was the goal, Meggie?"

"Stop it."

"Meggie. What was the goal?"

She looked out the window. "For me to get pregnant."

"What was that? Speak up."

"You can be so cruel."

"The goal, Meggie. Name me the goal."

She faced him. "That's enough."

"Then just tell me. Have we reached the goal here?"

She sat very straight.

"Have we, Meggie?"

She made her tone as cold as his. "Yes, Nate. We have."

"Fine, then. You've got everything you needed from me. And it's time you went on home."

Chapter Ten

Nate started calling the airlines right then, at three-thirty in the morning. He wanted her out of his hair ASAP. But it was Thanksgiving weekend. After an hour of calling, he found nothing available—unless she wanted to try standby—until Monday morning. He reserved a seat on the Monday flight.

He looked at Meggie with grim expectation when he gave her the information. She knew he was waiting for her to volunteer to go and sit at the airport. She didn't volunteer. Monday was three days away. A lot could happen in three days.

She had no right to hope he might change his mind, and she knew it. Yet hope burned like an eternal flame within her. She had promised herself not to try to hold him. But now that the moment to let him go had come, she refused to rush toward it. She would take the flight on Monday. But until then, he could just put up with her.

Which was exactly what he did: he put up with her. He slept on the couch Friday night and he spoke to her only when necessary. He waited for her to get on that plane and get out of his life.

Saturday afternoon, while Nate was out doing heaven knew what, Dolores knocked on the door. One look at Meggie's face and Dolores demanded, "Okay, what did that man do to you?"

Meggie ushered her in and gave her coffee and pumpkin pie and told her everything.

After calling Nate several shocking names in Spanish, Dolores told Meggie, "Still, we must remember, that man is wild and crazy for you. He cannot keep his hands off of you. And sometimes, when he looks at you..." Dolores made a show of fanning herself. Then she winked at Meggie. "Maybe you will just have to drive him mad with desire, eh? So he cannot let you go."

Meggie shook her head. "Dolores, he slept on the couch last night. He's very careful not to give me a chance to drive him mad with desire."

Dolores muttered more imprecations in Spanish. Then she brightened a little. "Ah well, at least there will be a little one. A woman needs her babies. A baby is life. And who can say? You do have a little time, to tempt him, before you go. And that baby will always be there, something you both share for all eternity."

Meggie sighed, not particularly heartened. "I guess so."

That evening, Nate didn't come home. Meggie made turkey noodle soup and ate alone, hardly tasting the food, staring out the window, longing for him and calling herself a fool.

She went to bed at ten, then tossed and turned for hours. Finally, sometime after two, she drifted into a fitful sleep.

When she got up in the morning, she found Nate sleeping on the couch. They sat down to breakfast together. He read the *Times* as he ate. When he was finished, he rinsed his dishes and stuck them in the dishwasher.

"I've got to go away overnight," he said.

She looked up from her half-empty plate. "Liar."

He shrugged. "I'll be back tomorrow, in time to take you to LAX."

"Don't bother. I can take a taxi."

"I said I'd be here in time. I will."

She couldn't stop herself from giving it one more try. "Nate, if you'll only—"

"We had an agreement. You have what you needed. Now let it go."

At that moment, hope finally left her. It drained from her, leaving her empty. And sad. She looked out at the parking lot and the carports. "All right. See you tomorrow, then."

He went back to the bedroom—she supposed to pack an overnight bag. A few minutes later, she heard the front door close. She watched him, when he appeared at the carports, tossing his bag behind the seat, pulling his black car out. And driving away.

Mrs. Tyrell knocked on Meggie's door that afternoon. "I hear you're leaving us."

Meggie gave her neighbor a rueful smiled. "Dolores has been talking."

Mrs. Tyrell laughed, a low, velvety sound. "Everybody in both buildings knows. And we will miss you."

Meggie stepped back. "Will you come in? I could use a little company."

Mrs. Tyrell nodded.

Meggie asked, "Coffee?"

"How about tea, for a change?"

Meggie brewed a pot of herbal tea and they sat at the table, sipping.

"My mother always drank tea," Mrs. Tyrell said musingly. "She felt coffee was for barbarians."

Meggie asked, "Were you raised here, in L.A.?"

"Oh, no. I'm from Philadelphia. And I lied about Terence."

Meggie didn't know anyone by that name. "Terence?"

"My husband."

"Oh." Meggie stared across the table at her neighbor, recognizing the moment when an acquaintance becomes a friend. "I didn't know your husband's first name."

"Now you do. And I'm Lurline."

"It's pretty."

"My mama chose it. And I didn't meet Terence at the apartment in the Valley."

"You didn't?"

Lurline shook her head. "I found him again there, almost thirty years later. But I met him when I was eighteen years old."

"In Philadelphia?"

"Um-hm. I loved him the moment I saw him."

Meggie instantly thought of Nate. "Oh, I know how that is. What happened?"

"My mama didn't approve of him."

"Oh, no."

"Oh, yes. 'A wild boy in a cheap suit,' she called him. She forbade me to see him. And I always did what Mama said."

"You turned him away."

"I did. He went to New York. And then came here. Had his big, fancy career in the record industry. He married three times, before I came to get him."

"Three times?"

Lurline smiled. "He has five children. I adore them all."

"And what about you?"

"I never married," Lurline said. "Until I found my Terence again." She leaned closer to Meggie. "That was after Mama died, of course." Lurline laughed her velvety laugh.

"You went looking for him when your mother died?"

"Yes, I did. When Mama died, I sold her house and packed up most of her fine, old things and moved out West—all the way to the San Fernando Valley."

"You knew where to find him?"

Lurline nodded. "That was my one rebellion against Mama in all those years. I kept track of my Terence."

"You wrote to him?"

"Never." Lurline's full lips were pursed in disapproval. "He was a married man. Most of the time."

"But how—"

"I had ways."

"So. You found him and married him."

"That's right. So never say that love is over. It might

just be waiting. Sometimes it waits for years and years."

"I'll try to remember that."

"Yes. Do."

Meggie cast Lurline a hesitant look.

"Go ahead," Lurline said. "Ask."

"All right. Did all of your fine things once belong to your mother?"

"Yes." Lurline sighed. "Sometimes, quite frankly, I feel as if *they* own *me*. Especially all that mahogany furniture. The scale is so wrong for our apartment. What I wouldn't give for a little bleached oak here and there."

Meggie laughed. "So sell some of it."

"Oh, I couldn't. Terence wouldn't let me."

Meggie blinked in surprise. "Why not?"

Lurline's smile grew secretive. "Oh, I shouldn't say."

"You should. Come on."

"He gets such...pleasure from it all."

"From your mother's things?"

"Yes. He says every time he sits at her table, eats off her dishes—or sleeps in her bed, he has the satisfaction of knowing that the wild boy in the cheap suit got Mama's precious daughter after all." Now Lurline looked pensive. "But maybe someday the thrill will wear off. Don't you think?"

"Who can say?"

"Oh, Meggie, you are so right. Who can say? When it comes to a man, who can ever say?"

Meggie spent another night alone. Nate showed up as promised, early the next morning, in time to drive her to the airport.

The sun shone down bright and cheerful when they went out to get in the car.

The Garnicas, Hector Leverson, Edie and Peg all came out to tell her goodbye. Dolores grabbed Meggie and burst into tears. And Hector told her he would never forget her.

Edie said, "I will miss our little strolls, dear."

Peg added, "Don't stay away forever. Come back and see us sometime."

And Nate just stood there, waiting for his neighbors to go back to their apartments so he could take Meggie to the airport and be free of her.

Strange. Meggie had told herself during the whole of their brief time together that she knew it was destined to end. She had convinced herself that she believed it.

But she hadn't believed it, not really.

Deep in her heart, she'd been sure that Nate would see the light. That the happiness they'd shared would finally convince him he should spend his life at her side.

It hadn't worked out that way. Instead, he had given her exactly what she'd asked of him.

And no more.

Chapter Eleven

Meggie arrived at the small airport in Sheridan late that afternoon. Farrah was waiting to take her the rest of the way home. Both six-year-old Kate and little Davey had come, too.

Meggie was relieved to see the children. Because of them, she wouldn't have to answer any uncomfortable questions during the drive to the ranch. The questions would come later, of course. But Meggie told herself she'd be better able to deal with them then. And if both Farrah and Sonny were there when they talked, then Meggie would only have to tell the sad story once.

Meggie spent most of the drive staring silently out the window at the miles and miles of pastureland, now cloaked in a glaring mantle of stark white. The cotton-woods in the creek bottoms were stripped bare, sticking up their naked branches toward the steel-gray sky.

* * *

That night, Farrah and Sonny insisted that Meggie have dinner at the bunkhouse.

As soon as the kids were in bed, they sat her down and asked what was going on. Fed up with lies and half-truths, Meggie told them everything.

"So he never meant to stay with you," Sonny declared indignantly when she was through. "He planned all along to walk away as soon as he got you pregnant."

Meggie sighed. "Sonny. It was what I asked him to do. What I *needed* him to do. Or we would have lost the Double-K."

Sonny shook his head. "You're a good-looking woman, with a big heart and a working ranch. You've had offers—I know you have. You could have found yourself a real husband. Someone who would have stood by you."

"I didn't want just *someone*. I only wanted Nate. And for a little while, I had him." She put her hand on her stomach cherishingly. "And there *will* be a baby. Nate's baby. It's not everything I dreamed of. But it's a lot closer than I ever thought I was going to get."

Sonny and Farrah exchanged baffled glances.

Meggie smiled. "I know you don't understand. And that's okay. I just want you to know that I am fine. That we're going to keep the Double-K. That in the spring, you'll have a new niece or nephew. I hope that you'll help me to raise him—or her—right."

Of course they promised that they would.

A bit later, Meggie returned to her own house. In spite of her exhaustion after the long flight home, she stayed awake late. She missed Nate's warmth beside her. And the wind was up, beating around the eaves, making a haunted, crying, lonely sound.

The next morning, born rancher that she was, Meggie rose in the dark. She made a fire and drank her tea and watched the winter sun lift its face slowly to light the new day.

A week later, Meggie received her first letter from Dolores. It read: "Your husband is gone. Off on one of those jobs of his. And when he his here, I do not talk to him. I give him looks like dirt. Did you know that my own grandmother was a *bruja,* a woman of magic? Maybe I will do something ugly, with chickens. He will suffer. And then he will beg you to return to him...."

Meggie shot a letter back, commanding Dolores to do no such thing.

Dolores replied that she had only been joking. She was a modern Catholic woman, after all, and not superstitious in the least.

After that, the letters went back and forth. Meggie tried to write once a week and Dolores did the same. Meggie loved reading all the gossip, how Edie's son had tried to make her move to a rest home, but Edie had steadfastly refused.

Community Watch was still going strong. "We meet every two weeks," Dolores wrote. "I usually make the cookies. No one is attacking us, so I think we must be doing the job right. And I learned some hot gossip. Mr. Hector Leverson goes very often to a café on Sunset. You know the one I mean. It is called Dave's and we both know who is the head waitress there...."

Christmas came and went. Meggie, Sonny, Farrah and the kids spent it together. On the Sunday before

New Year's, Meggie saw Cash and Abby at church in town.

Abby took Meggie aside and spoke frankly, as Abby tended to do. "You're pregnant, aren't you?"

"Am I getting that big?"

"Well, it does show. But you look good— Oh, Meggie. I'm so sorry."

"Don't be. I want this baby."

"I don't mean about the baby. You know what I mean. Nate." Abby groaned. "He is hopeless. Worse than Cash was, I think. And Cash was pretty bad, let me tell you. He ran away from happiness as fast as he could. You don't want to know what I went through with him. I'll spare you the details, but it was bad. Very bad. And Nate's a lot like Cash, really. Oh, I know. Nate's got that bad-boy thing going. And Cash was always everyone's knight in shining armor. But I mean, Cash lost his mother when he was twelve. And Nate lost his father when he was fourteen. And both of them ended up pretty much orphans, since the parent they had left dumped them off at the ranch. So my theory is, they're both terrified to love." Abby laughed. "You're looking kind of cross-eyed, Meggie. I'm talking too much, huh?" She frowned. "But all kidding aside, Nate didn't even come home for Christmas this year. That's a bad sign. He always comes home for that, at least. To tell you the truth, we're all a little worried."

Meggie offered the reassurance Abby seemed to be seeking. "He's all right. I keep in touch with his landlady. She says he's working a lot, but he's fine."

"Well. Good. I guess. Oh, Meggie. I know he loves you. He's always loved you."

"He wants his freedom."

''He is a complete fool.''

Before they said goodbye, Meggie remembered to congratulate Abby on her recent graduation, with honors, from the University of Colorado.

Abby smiled her thanks and then told Meggie that Tess DeMarley's mother had died. Tess was housemate to Abby's mother, Edna. ''Poor Tess. She had to spend her Christmas in Rapid City, taking care of all the funeral arrangements.''

Meggie made a mental note to send Tess a condolence card.

''But the good news,'' Abby said, ''is that Zach finally asked Tess out.''

Meggie smiled at that. Everyone in town knew that Zach Bravo had had his eye on the pretty widow who looked after Abby's mother. They'd all been waiting for him to make his move. And now, at last, he had.

''They'll end up married—just you wait,'' Abby predicted.

Meggie saw no reason to disagree.

In the first weeks of the new year, Meggie spent her days getting feed to the stock and her nights trying not to give in to depression. She did pretty well, actually. The baby helped. When things seemed loneliest, she would put her hand on her growing stomach and think loving thoughts of the life she would share with her new little one. Soon enough, she would find herself smiling, feeling that things weren't so bad after all.

Dolores wrote faithfully, alternately praising her grandchildren and complaining about them, reporting all the news from her two apartment buildings. In every letter, she made some mention of Nate:

He is doing fine, that man of yours. As fine as he deserves to do, staying all alone and acting like he hates the world....

Yesterday, he came down to pay the rent. He tried to stick the money where the mail goes. But I am watching for him. I pull open the door and give him a big, mean smile. "Good morning, Mr. Bravo," I say to him. "And how are you doing lately?" He coughs and looks very scared. He should be scared. I am thinking bad thoughts about him. "I'm just fine, Dolores," he tells me. And then he sticks out the check. "Here. The rent." "Thank you, Mr. Bravo," I say, so polite. He turns to go and I say to his back, so sweet I know it makes shivers down his spine, "You take good care of yourself now."

Meggie, I can promise you. A little chicken blood and a few words of power and that man will come running to your side. Just kidding. Ha-ha....

January faded into February. Meggie was six months pregnant and serious winter feeding of the stock was well under way. Mostly, Meggie drove the vehicles, leaving the heavy lifting to Sonny as much as she could. Dr. Pruitt, who ran the clinic in town, warned Meggie to start thinking about the baby more.

"You're coming to the point where you'll just have to back off a little," he said.

"Come on, Doc. It's almost calving time."

"Hire an extra man or two. And talk to Farrah. Maybe you'll have to take over some of the work close to home and let her go out with Sonny to look after the herd."

That night, Meggie sat down with her cousin and his wife. She laid out the doctor's orders. Farrah declared that she'd do her best to fill Meggie's boots, even though she'd never be the rancher Meggie was. They decided that when calving time came, Meggie would handle the cooking for everyone and look after the kids. Farrah would take over Meggie's work as best she could and Sonny would work even harder than usual, to pick up the slack.

Meggie put out the word that she could use an extra hand, but it was the dead of winter and cowboying didn't pay much. She just hoped someone worth hiring would show up in the next month or two.

On the fifteenth of February, Edna Heller and Tess DeMarley threw Meggie a surprise baby shower at Edna's house in town. Abby came, too, of course, and so did Farrah, plus a couple of women Meggie had known since her school days. They played silly games and ate cake and punch.

Edna clucked over Meggie constantly through the party, asking her if she was feeling all right, fetching her pillows to support her back—and muttering complaints about Nate under her breath.

Meggie opened the brightly wrapped packages to find a full layette from Edna, a set of receiving blankets from Tess and a windup swing from Abby. Sonny had already made her a changing table, but still there was a gift from Farrah, too.

"You shouldn't have," Meggie told her cousin's wife.

"Oh, yes, I should."

Inside the box was a handmade quilt, mittens and a hat. "Oh, Farrah. They're beautiful."

Farrah smiled in pleasure at Meggie's obvious delight in her gift.

When she got home, Meggie took the new things up to the room next to her own, which she'd been fixing up for the baby over the last few weeks. Meggie put the tiny shirts and soft rompers away in the bureau, struck with wonder at the thought that in a few months, her baby would be wearing them.

The cold, dreary days went by. Meggie still went out with Sonny. But the time drew steadily nearer when she would have to switch places with Farrah and do a ranch wife's work—not an easy job, by any means. But at least Farrah's work didn't include things like pulling cows from frozen streams. Even driving the pickup was something Meggie would have to give up soon; her stomach was starting to get in the way of the wheel.

Meggie did worry that when calving time came, they'd have more work to do than hands to do it; yet still, a kind of peace had settled over her. A fullness. An acceptance. That she and her family would get by, one way or another. That her baby would be born and life would go on.

She looked for beauty where she could find it. And even on the dreariest days, beauty managed to find her.

One freezing evening at the very end of February, Meggie came in alone at dark. Sonny had knocked off early and taken Farrah and the kids into Buffalo for a visit with Farrah's mom, who ran a motel there.

As Meggie climbed from the pickup, seven hungry heifers bawled at her from the corral. They were close to their calving time, well ahead of the rest of the herd. Meggie and Sonny had put them in the corral so they could keep a close eye on them. Meggie grinned at the sound of them. She felt a real affinity with them lately;

like them, she was big and ungainly and getting close to her time.

Crusted snow crunched under her boots as she tossed the heifers hay and grain cake, a process that took her much longer than it used to. Her back ached a little and her growing stomach slowed her down. Plus, she tried to be careful not to hurt herself or the baby whenever she attempted heavy work.

When the heifers had their feed, Meggie leaned on the corral rail for a minute, watching, listening to them crunch on the cake, feeling the cold down to her bones, but feeling kind of peaceful, too. The sky overhead was studded with stars—stars that always looked so much brighter, somehow, in the winter.

The chinook, a warm southern wind, came up as Meggie leaned there watching the heifers. It blew in the way it always did, seemingly from nowhere, to warm the winter world. Meggie sighed and smiled. She closed her eyes and let the warmth whip at her, swirling around her, feeling the temperature rise and the winter cold retreat.

The melting snow had started dripping from the eaves and cutting tiny rivulets in the blanket of white on the ground by the time she went inside. Meggie ate and got ready for bed smiling, as the chinook blew around the house, rattling the windows and making the roof creak.

She dreamed of a night, years and years ago, when she'd stood in the yard and, like tonight, a chinook had blown in, wild and warm, to thaw the frozen world of winter. That night Meggie had seen the aurora borealis: the fabulous many-colored northern lights. The chinook had whipped around her, pulling at her jacket and playing with her hair, and the great pipes of shimmering

color had come alive in the north sky, long, leaping
tubes of light, jumping high and fading down, water-
falls of pure color, dancing against the darkness of the
night.

In her dream, Meggie lived it all again. And it
seemed as if the rising towers of colored light were
blown by the warm wind, pushed higher by the gusts
of the chinook.

In her dream, she tipped her head to the sky, smiling.
And she felt a hand slide into her own. She whispered,
"Nate," and heard him gently answer, "Meggie."

And she woke, suddenly, alone in the bed that had
been her father's.

Outside, the wind still blew. And the sound of Nate's
voice was in it, warm and tender and full of all the
promises she had longed for that he would never make
to her. She rested her hand on the pregnant swell of
her belly, turned her head and closed her eyes, hoping
to slip back into the same dream.

But Nate and the dream of the northern lights had
faded to memory. Only the roundness beneath her
hand, the promise of the life he'd given into her care,
remained.

By the next morning, the chinook had blown itself
out. The deep, hard snow of the night before had
melted down to patches on the wet, cold ground. A
blizzard moved in that night, turning the world into a
blur of flying white. By the time the blizzard moved
on, the snow lay thick and white on the land once more.

In the first weeks of March, the heifers started to
calve. Meggie had no choice by then but to stay close
to the house, cooking and watching the kids and hand-
feeding any calves too premature or ill to suck. The

heifers they'd worried about, the ones they'd kept in the corral, had dropped their calves and been let out to pasture by the second week of March.

By the third week of March, the older cows started to calve. A good portion of the Double-K became one huge maternity ward. Sonny and Farrah were out every morning before dawn, trying to keep track of births that ranged over several thousand acres, to get to any cows that were having trouble, to help any calves that had gotten separated from their mothers in the spring storms that blew across the prairie, full of cold, blinding fury, driving the cows before the wind.

If possible, they brought the problems home to Meggie in the bed of a pickup, or even slung over the front of a saddle. She helped the weak ones eat and treated the sick ones as best she could. But she felt useless, so big and ungainly now, leaving her cousin and his wife to do the rough work, pulling calves in open pastures, catching the little critters to put on the dehorning paste, finding the lost calves and the dead ones, grafting the orphans onto cows that had lost their own. It went on and on. And Meggie cooked and doctored, went in for supplies and watched the kids and wished her baby had been born months ago so she could get out and do her share in this season when the Double-K needed her the most.

Zach came by on horseback the last Saturday in March, which was the day before Easter. Meggie's heart seemed to expand in her chest at the sight of him. Maybe he would have news of Nate.

But he only said he'd been checking the cows in a pasture that bordered the Double-K and decided to stop in and see how she was getting along. His eyes widened when he looked at the size of her stomach, but he was too well mannered to say anything about how big she'd grown.

Meggie had a pot of minestrone soup warming on the back burner of the stove. She served him a bowl.

Since they'd been friends for so long, she felt comfortable ribbing him a little about Tess DeMarley. "I hear the two of you have been seen around town."

"Tess is a good woman," he said quietly.

"And a pretty one."

"Yes, that's so."

"And I hear she knows ranch life. And loves it."

"You heard right."

"Some other man will snap her up, Zach. Don't drag your heels."

He pretended to glare at her. "Meggie, don't crowd a man."

She laughed and let the subject drop. Zach had been hurt pretty bad once when it came to love. It made sense he wouldn't be rushed the second time around.

"Good soup," he said, and then smiled wryly. "Maybe you ought to sell this place. You can come on over and cook for me."

"Not a chance."

"Just hoping out loud."

Zach's never-ending quest to find someone to replace Edna Heller was getting to be something of a joke to everyone who knew him. Meggie asked, "So who's cooking over at the Rising Sun now?"

"Her name's Angie Iberlin. She's a widow, in her fifties. Her biscuits could sink a battleship, but she's not half-bad at keeping the place clean. And she's polite. That's a real plus in someone who answers your phone, believe me."

"So you're saying that she's working out?"

"I'm saying I haven't done better since Edna left. Just cross your fingers this one will last."

She almost teased him a little more about Tess. After all, if he married Tess, he'd have his housekeeping problem solved. Everyone said that Tess DeMarley was a model of womanly accomplishment. But Meggie thought she'd probably teased Zach enough for the time being. So she kept her peace. Instead of Tess DeMarley, they spoke of the eight bred heifers that had been rustled off the Rising Sun just a month before. Zach said they still hadn't a clue as to who had committed the theft. Meggie wished she could reassure her friend that the theives would be caught in the end. But it didn't look likely at that point, and she and Zach both knew it.

"You doing all right over here?" he asked just before he got up to go.

"I've got Farrah and Sonny. We're managing."

"Maybe you ought to take on an extra hand, just for the next few weeks, until calving season's past."

"I've put the word out, but so far, nobody's knocking down my door."

"I'll check around for you."

She thanked him and then walked him back out to his horse. As she watched him prepare to mount, her heart set up a clamor in her chest. Each beat seemed to echo a name: *Nate, Nate, Nate, Nate,* tempting her, *taunting* her to ask after the husband she hadn't seen in months. If she was going to ask, it must be now, before Zach rode away.

"Zach?"

"Yeah?"

"Do you...hear anything from Nate?"

He paused with one foot in the saddle, then hoisted

himself up. "Not a word," he said, once he'd found his seat.

She looked down at the worn boards of the porch.

"I'm real sorry, Meggie."

She looked up and gave her friend a smile. "Hey. It's not your fault. You take care, now."

He saluted her and turned his horse for the gate.

Meggie stayed on the porch to watch him go, thinking that lately no one seemed to know much about Nate. Even Dolores hardly mentioned him anymore— other than to say he was gone most of the time.

Meggie had begun to feel as if he were fading from the world she knew. As if someday soon, Dolores would write and say he'd given up his apartment.

He would disappear completely, find an entirely different life for himself. And Meggie would never see— or hear—of him again.

Nate's private line was ringing when he let himself in the apartment after flying home from a five-day surveillance gig in Boca Raton. He had a cracked rib and a black eye, both caused by a run-in with the object of his surveillance—a hotheaded type who hadn't appreciated having his picture taken. Nate had managed to escape with the information he needed, but he'd lost a very expensive camera. Also, his side hurt like the devil and his head felt as if some fiend was in there with a hammer and an ice pick, pounding away.

He got the door open and bolted to the phone, catching it just before the answering machine switched on. "Yeah, hello?"

"Happy Easter—a day early." It was Zach.

Nate pressed his sore side, wincing, silently calling himself a damn fool for not letting the answering machine do its job. Lately, he found himself driven to break speed records whenever the phone rang. He never intended to get near Meggie again. But a phone call might bring news of her, news that something had gone wrong, that there was a problem with the baby, that Meggie needed him....

"You there, Nate?"

"Yeah. What's up?"

Zach didn't hedge. "I stopped by your wife's place today."

Nate blinked, dropped into the green chair and then groaned as his cracked rib protested. "So?"

"It's calving time around here."

Nate pressed his side some more. "Get to the point."

"Meggie's big, Nate. Really big with that baby you gave her. Before you dumped her."

Nate closed his eyes and said nothing. He was used to being the bad guy. His cousin's hard words didn't bother him much. But having to listen to him say Meggie's name did.

Zach went on, "I know you, Nate. I know there's more going on here than I understand. More than you or Meggie will ever explain to me. But an eight-months-pregnant woman running a ranch at calving time without enough hands to do the work—it's not good."

"She didn't hire anybody?"

"Is that a question?"

"Yeah."

"She says she put the word out, but got no takers. I did a little calling around, and I can't come up with anyone, either. I suppose I can send one of my own men over. It's not like I have them to spare. But for Meggie—''

''All right.''

''Pardon me?''

''You heard what I said.''

''Good. Cash says he'll fly the Cessna down to Denver to meet you. So let us know when you're coming in.''

No way, Nate thought. Cash would bring Abby and Abby was just too damn much like the sister he'd never had. Nate would get lectured on what a low-down rat he'd been to Meggie all the way from Denver to Sheridan. ''I'll manage on my own. Thanks.''

''Nate—''

''I said, I'll manage on my own.''

''I'll tell Meggie you're—''

''Tell Meggie nothing. I'll get there when I get there. Understand?''

Zach sighed. ''Sure. As long as you're coming, and soon.''

''I'll get the next flight out. Is that good enough?''

''I guess it'll have to be.''

Sunday, though they couldn't afford to do it, Sonny, Farrah and Meggie took a half day off. They hid eggs in the yard for the kids to find. And they drove into town to go to church. Then they went back to work.

On Monday, Sonny and Farrah rode out early, as usual. Meggie saw Katie off to the school bus and then took Davey around with her as she did her chores. The day passed uneventfully. Katie came home at three and took Davey back to the bunkhouse with her.

About three-thirty, Sonny and Farrah appeared, leading a prolapsed cow.

"We decided to let you handle this," Sonny said, his eyes gleaming with humor.

"Thanks." Meggie didn't bother to inject any gratitude into the word.

Farrah went on in to check on the kids. Sonny took the cow into the shed off the main corral and coaxed her into the chute. When he had her in, he winked at Meggie. "She's all yours."

Meggie considered using a plastic sleeve, but that gleam in Sonny's eyes made her sure he would razz her that she didn't need a sleeve for a little job like this. Just looking at that smirk of his got her rancher's pride up—as he knew it would.

Meggie stripped off her down jacket and the sweater she wore underneath it. Then she rolled up the sleeve of her maternity smock and moved behind the cow.

The prolapsed umbilical cord was swelled as round as a cantaloupe, and flame red. Meggie tried to lift it gently, to see if the cow could get a little relief, since she probably hadn't emptied her bladder in a while.

But nothing happened. Very carefully, Meggie began the delicate process of trying to ease the prolapse back where it had come from. It was important to be gentle, to take it very slowly.

After what seemed like a lifetime, Meggie finally managed to accomplish the goal. The umbilical cord slid back inside the cow where it belonged.

By then, the cow had voided both her bladder and her bowels. Repeatedly. Meggie had a good amount of the stuff—and quite a bit of blood, as well—splashed on her jeans and shirt. Also, her hand had gone right into the cow with the retracting prolapse.

The cow seemed a lot happier, though. She took cake from the trough in front of her and crunched away on it as if she'd never had a care in the world. Meggie waited, to be sure the cow was really settled down before she pulled out.

Right then, out in the dirt drive that turned around between the bunkhouse and her own house, Meggie heard the sound of a vehicle barreling in, tires spraying gravel as it braked. Sonny's hound barked out a warning.

Meggie felt the cow tighten up a little at the noise. "Go see who that is," she commanded. "And make that dog quiet down."

Sonny marched off to do her bidding. A moment later, she heard him order the dog to be silent. The barking stopped. A vehicle door opened and closed.

Meggie held still, listening to the cow munch on the cake, waiting for the interior muscles to relax a little more.

"Meggie…" Her cousin's voice came from behind her, full of something Meggie didn't like—wariness or worry, she wasn't sure which.

She turned her head. Between the wide-open doors of the shed, right beside Sonny, stood Nate.

Chapter Twelve

Meggie could only gape. She must be seeing things.

But no, he was real. His black hair gleamed in the thin spring sunlight. He had a livid black eye and a frown on his full lips.

He took in Meggie's situation at a glance, and moved swiftly to the other end of the cow. Quietly, he spoke to her, petting her forehead, saying soft, tender things.

Meggie felt the muscles inside the cow relax. Slowly, she eased out and stepped back. What was splattered on her pregnancy-paneled jeans and smock was also thick and pungent all the way up her arm.

Sonny, his face all pinched up in disapproval of Nate, handed her some medication. She poked it inside where her hand had been. She asked, "Any string around here?" Sonny came up with some packaging string. Meggie used it to stitch up the cow, and then, as a final preventive measure, she administered a shot of penicillin.

"You can have her back now," she said to her cousin.

"Terrific," Sonny replied, with a minimum of enthusiasm.

Meggie, her foolish heart racing in joy, turned to Nate. Masking her elation at the sight of him, she gave him a long, assessing stare. "What happened to your eye?"

"A minor disagreement with an object of surveillance."

"You favor your right side."

He shrugged. "A cracked rib, I think. It'll heal."

She went on looking at him. He looked right back. His eyes gave nothing away—beyond a kind of grim determination.

Whatever he'd come for, it wasn't a reunion. She would bet her favorite cutting horse on that. Her silly heart settled into a more reasonable rhythm.

"I want to clean up," she said. "And then we can talk."

Meggie took a long shower. Then she put on a clean pair of pants and a tunic-length sweater, dried her hair and went downstairs.

Nate was waiting at the kitchen table. As she walked toward him, she tried not to shuffle. She couldn't help feeling like the cow she'd just treated, and hating the way he watched her, so distant and measuring.

She pulled out the chair opposite him and sat down as gracefully as she could—which wasn't very graceful at all.

"When's the baby due?" he asked.

"The first of May."

"A month."

"Yes."

A silence descended and hung as heavy as a lead weight between the two of them. She knew he was counting. "So that means you were—what? About four months pregnant before I figured it out?"

She refused to shrink from the accusation in his eyes. "Just about."

"You knew you were pregnant. And you didn't tell me."

"Yep. I wanted to stay with you. Pretty stupid, huh?"

He gave no answer, only went on looking at her with that remote, brooding stare.

The baby kicked. Meggie put her hand on her belly and rubbed, looking down at the spot, letting a small, soothing noise escape her.

When she glanced up, he was still watching her. At that moment, she dared to think she saw tenderness in his eyes, but not for long. He announced flatly, "I'm staying, until the baby comes."

Her foolish heart leaped. But her mind knew better. "Why?"

"To help out."

Meggie rested a hand on the table and studied her short, ragged fingernails.

"I'm staying, Meggie," he said, as if her silence implied argument.

And it did. She didn't want him around if he was going to brood and sulk and watch her with eyes as hard as a banker's heart. "It's not necessary for you to stay. We're doing all right."

"Who's working the herd with Sonny?"

"Farrah."

He grunted, a very self-vindicated sound.

"Farrah's doing just fine," she said defensively. "She works hard, and Sonny takes up the slack. And I...do what I can."

A cold smile played at the corners of his mouth. "I saw. You looked damned uncomfortable standing there with your hand inside that cow and your belly out to here."

"I did fine by that cow."

"Whatever. You need help around here. There's no shame in admitting what you need."

She met his eyes square on. "I'm fine, Nate. Go back to L.A."

"No. That's my baby you've got inside you. Maybe I'll never be much of a father to it. But I can ride a horse and pull a calf—things you can't do right now. You're going to have to let me take care of this damn ranch of yours so you can ease up and take care of yourself for a while."

"I *am* taking care of myself."

"Fine. And now you'll take *better* care of yourself."

The baby kicked again, right in the spot where Meggie's hand already rested. She rubbed it some more.

"Meggie. You know I'm right."

She did, of course. It *was* his baby, too. And if he wanted to take some of the burden off her now, she owed it to him and their child to let him.

With some effort, she pushed herself to her feet. Her back ached, and she rubbed it, sighing a little, making no pretense now that her burden didn't tire her. "Bring your things in. You can take the front bedroom upstairs."

He looked up at her. "Are you really all right?"

She saw the concern in his eyes, all mixed up with the coldness and the determination to remain indifferent to her. She forced a smile. "Doc Pruitt says there's nothing wrong with me that a few more weeks and several hours of labor won't cure."

"The baby's healthy?"

"As far as anyone can tell."

"What about your cousin?"

"What about him?"

"I could tell by the look he gave me that I'm not his favorite person."

"I told him the truth."

"What truth?"

"That you helped me out to keep the Double-K, and now you want your freedom back—as we agreed from the first."

"Hell, Meggie," he said grimly.

"I just got sick of all the lies, Nate. And I couldn't see any reason to keep telling them anymore, anyway."

He let out a long, weary breath. "Fine. The question is, will he work with me?"

"I'm sure he will."

"I'm glad *you're* sure."

"We'll talk to him tonight."

"Terrific," he muttered as he rose. "I'll get my bag."

Sonny and his family and Meggie and Nate all ate together that night in Meggie's kitchen. It was an ordeal of hard looks between Sonny and Nate, worried glances between the women—and acting up from Davey, who had the radar of most children and seemed to sense that things weren't right with the grown-ups. Meggie hardly ate a bite, which worried Farrah all the more. "Are you all right?" she asked. "Are you sick?"

"What are you talking about?" Nate demanded. "She told me today that she's fine."

"She *was* fine." Farrah shot him a glare. "Until *recently,* anyway."

"Are you going to throw up, Aunt Meggie?" Kate asked, her eyes wide. "I could get you a bowl if you are. Mommy always gets me a bowl."

"No, Katie," Meggie said gently. "I am not going to throw up. I am not sick. I just don't have a big appetite tonight, that's all."

"Yucky, yucky. Hate cawots," chanted Davey. He picked up a handful of boiled carrots and dropped them over the edge of his high chair onto the floor.

"That's enough, young man," Sonny said sternly.

Davey beat on his chair tray and chanted, "No, no, no, no...."

"That does it," Farrah murmured. She stood, scooped Davey into her arms and started for the door. He wailed and cried and flailed his fists, but his mother just kept going. His outraged wails continued as she carried him down the short hall, through the living room, out the front door and across the yard to her own house.

The rest of them ate in silence for a while.

Finally, Kate said, "Daddy, I'm all done. Mommy bought some Tootsie Pops. Can I go home and have one?"

"You go right on, baby."

Kate rose, as well behaved as her brother was wild, and carried her plate to the sink, where she rinsed it and stacked it on the counter, ready to wash. Then she went to Meggie's side. "I think I'll kiss you good-night now, Meggie."

"Good night, honey." Meggie put an arm around Kate and kissed her on the cheek, a favor that Kate then returned.

"Should I kiss you, too, Daddy? Just in case I go to bed and you're not home yet."

"Good idea."

More kisses were exchanged.

Then Kate looked at Nate, a frown creasing her smooth brow. "Who hit you in the eye?"

"Katie..." Sonny warned.

Nate actually grinned. "It's all right. An angry man hit me."

"Did you hit him back?"

"Well..."

"That's enough, Katie," Sonny said. "Go on back to the house."

Kate started to leave, then turned back to Nate. "Good night," she said sweetly.

Nate nodded. "Good night, Katie."

Once Kate left, the three adults ate in silence for a few minutes—minutes that seemed to Meggie to crawl by like centuries. Then Sonny rose to carry his plate to the sink.

Meggie knew that in a minute he would be leaving for his own house. She cleared her throat. "Sonny?"

He set his plate down and turned. "Yeah?"

Meggie shot a glance at Nate. No help there. His face was impassive, his eyes fathomless.

She forged on. "Sonny, I suppose you're wondering what Nate's doing here."

Sonny tipped his head to the side. "Well, yeah. I suppose I am."

"Nate's come back to help out for a while, until calving time's through."

Sonny leaned on the drainboard, his wary expression turning to one of frank disapproval. "You mean he'll be leaving you again, right?"

Meggie dragged in a breath and answered carefully, "Sonny, he hasn't come back here for me. He's come for the baby's sake, to help out, since we're short-handed right now."

Sonny looked down at his boots. "Well. That's real big of him."

Meggie glanced at Nate again. His face betrayed nothing beyond a watchful, bleak patience. "Sonny," she said. "You're wrong to blame Nate for…what's happened. I told you before that he only did what I begged him to do. He helped out a…friend. And he got nothing for it. In fact, it's cost him. To be here through summer and fall, he lost—"

"Stop it, Meggie," Nate said.

She shook her head. "No, I want to say this. I don't think Sonny understands that you missed months of work to be here when I needed—"

Meggie stopped in midsentence as Nate stood. "There's no point in going into this." He winced and pressed his hand against his injured rib. He turned to Sonny. "Look. I'm here to help out for reasons that should be pretty damn obvious to everyone. You're going to have to work with me. Can you handle that?"

Sonny looked at Nate for a long, hard time. Then he shrugged. "I can do what I have to do, sure."

"All right, then," Nate said.

Sonny echoed, "All right." He looked at Meggie. "Thanks for the fine dinner. I'll be going home now."

Meggie murmured good-night and Sonny went out

the same way Farrah had, through the house to the front door.

"Don't make excuses for me," Nate said into the silence Sonny left behind. "I don't need them or want them."

"I was only trying to make him see—"

"People see what they want to see."

"But Sonny is a reasonable man. I think if he really understood all you've done for me, he would—"

"Drop it."

Meggie mentally counted to ten. "Fine." She pushed herself to her feet and went about the task of cleaning up after the meal.

"Where's the dish towel?" Nate asked belligerently a few moments later.

She snared the towel from the towel rack and tossed it to him. He set to work drying the pots and pans while she finished wiping up the counters. When the pots were all put away and the counters gleamed, Meggie went into the living room to watch a little television before she turned in.

Nate went straight upstairs to the front bedroom without even bothering to say good-night.

Chapter Thirteen

In the days that followed, Nate discovered that Sonny Kane was a man of his word. He'd agreed to work with Nate, and he put his personal disapproval aside to do what had to be done. Before long, Nate even started to wonder if Sonny and his wife had decided that maybe he wasn't so bad after all.

It was Meggie who drove Nate crazy. Even with her huge belly leading the way everywhere she went, she drew him just as she always had. And the attraction went far deeper than physical desire. She seemed so peaceful within herself, so content with the burden she carried around. He'd always admired her. And now he admired her more than ever. He not only wanted her—he wanted some of that peace she had.

Sometimes, when he looked at Meggie now, a question would come sneaking into his mind. He would wonder why the hell he was doing this: to her and to himself. Why did he continue to refuse her? Why did he continue to push her away?

He would look at her and think, *She is my wife.* And there seemed to be such rightness, such completeness, in that thought.

He would remember all the years he had stayed away from her. And he would see his future, remote from her and their child. And his solitary life would start to look more like a sentence than a choice; the emptiness inside him would seem all at once aching and vast.

But then, at night, when sleep finally found him, he would dream old dreams, of a dark place. Of the smell of musty wool. Of a vow he had made to himself long, long ago.

Someday I will be free....

He'd wake in the morning certain once again that all he wanted was to get through calving time and be on his way.

At first, Meggie hesitantly attempted to bridge the gap between them. At breakfast, she would ask him things like how he'd slept and did he need anything from town. He answered her questions curtly—"I slept fine and I don't need a damn thing from town"—trying not to be drawn in by her. There were, after all, a thousand and one ways she could get to him—from a bright smile to a gentle word, to a tender look across a room. He tried to keep his heart armed against her.

And she caught on quickly, as she always had. Within forty-eight hours of his arrival, she began beating him at his own game, looking away before he did. Asking no questions that didn't absolutely require answers. Staying clear of him whenever possible. Marking time. Until calving time passed. And he would be gone.

And, though he knew it was unfair, he resented her for giving him just what he'd been asking for. He wanted to grab her and shake her. He wanted to break through that wall she'd put up around herself as armor against his own indifference.

He wanted her to reach for him. So that, at least for a little while, he could allow himself to be touched.

But she didn't reach for him.

The tension between them seemed to grow by the hour. Sometimes, he felt as if he might explode. Yet, through a pure effort of will, he reined in his temper most of the time—except when she took stupid chances with her health. Then, he felt justified in letting his temper get loose.

After all, he'd come to help out so that she could take it easy. But she refused to take it easy. She would not stop working. Even though Farrah stayed home more now and offered to take on Meggie's work with the animals, Meggie wouldn't hear of that. She insisted on treating the sick and weak stock herself.

She would spend hours with a calf that wouldn't suck. About a week after Nate's return, Sonny brought in a spindly black Angus calf that must have been premature; it simply refused to eat. The mother cow came with it, her bags swollen with unsucked milk; she wore that bewildered look a cow gets when something's not right with her calf.

Since the cow was tractable, Meggie started out each feeding session trying to coax the calf to feed from the source. She'd get herself into a backbreaking, half-bent-over stance, her own belly an obstacle to be both protected and worked around. Holding the calf's head steady, pressing her own cheek up against the side of the cow, she'd stick the fingers of one hand in the calf's mouth while she tried to pump milk into it with the other hand.

Finally, when her arms were running with milk to the elbow, she'd give up on the direct approach. She'd milk the cow into a bucket, stick a rubber teat in the calf's mouth and force milk into it that way. Through the whole procedure she'd whisper soothing, gentle things. And then four or five hours later, she'd do it all again.

One night, when she came in from the shed with milk drying on her arms and down the front of her shirt, Nate told her he wanted her to let Farrah do the feeding from now on. "Or let me," he added, "if Farrah's got something else to do."

"I don't mind."

"You should mind. It's too much for you right now."

"I know what's too much for me. I can handle feeding a few calves."

"I mean it, Meggie. You're through feeding calves. As of tonight."

She gave him one of those looks of hers. A look no woman that big eyed and pretty ought to be able to manage. "I know what I can handle, Nate. Don't you try to tell me I don't."

He reminded her about Abby, who had insisted on finishing a semester at the University of Colorado last year when she'd been pregnant with Tyler Ross. Abby had pushed herself to the brink, and ended up with something called eclampsia that had put her in a coma and almost caused her death.

"Eclampsia is extremely rare, Nate, and there's no proof that it's caused by stress," Meggie told him.

"Oh, so you're an expert on the subject, huh?"

"I know what it is. And I'm not going to get it."

"You're pushing yourself."

"I am not. And I'm through discussing this."

"The hell you are."

"Please don't swear at me."

He started shouting then. "Dammit, you have to take care of yourself!"

She remained maddeningly calm. "I am taking care of myself."

"You're taking chances...but not anymore."

"What do you mean by that?"

"I mean, *no more feeding calves.*"

She looked him up and down, a slow, dismissing kind of look. "Don't try to make my decisions for me. You won't succeed." Then she turned around and headed for the stairs.

"Meggie, get back here!"

She didn't stop; she didn't even glance back. She just left him there in the kitchen, wanting to chase after her, wanting to shout at her some more, wanting to do a lot of things to her that he didn't dare even think about.

That happened about a week after he came back. And every day after that, he found something she needed to be lectured about.

One morning in the barn, when he'd brought in a half-frozen calf for her to warm up with one of the propane heaters, he warned her that she'd better stop driving the pickup.

"I know you drove Katie out to the bus stop today," he accused, as she was making the calf comfortable on a bed of straw.

"It was freezing. And it's a half mile out to the stop."

"If Katie needs driving, Farrah will have to do it."

"Farrah went out with you and Sonny at the crack of dawn."

"Meggie. Hear me. *Do not drive the pickup.* If you need to go somewhere, I'll drive you. Or Farrah or Sonny will. Understand?"

Meggie rose, with some effort, from her kneeling position in the straw. Panting, she glared at him. "Fine. Whatever you say." Then she turned around and lumbered out the barn door.

Nate shrugged. She could stomp off all she wanted. She wouldn't drive that pickup again if she knew what was good for her.

He looked down at the calf, a little black-baldy. It was a miracle, really, how fast heat could work on them. When he'd found the little critter, he'd looked half dead. And yet now, already, he was lurching around trying to get up.

Farrah came in and stood by Nate. "How's the little feller doing?"

"Take a look. Meggie went to get some milk for him—I think."

"You *think?*"

"She's mad because I told her not to drive herself around anymore."

Farrah made a noise in her throat. "Don't see why she's mad. Doc Pruitt already warned her about driving, now she's so big."

"He did?"

Farrah met Nate's eyes and then shook her head. "Now, why do I want to go and get myself between the two of you? Forget I said that."

But he didn't forget.

That night, Farrah made dinner for everybody. During the meal, Meggie asked Farrah to drive her to her appointment with Doc Pruitt. "It's tomorrow. At ten-thirty. Do you think you can take me?"

"I'll take you," Nate said. He wanted to have a few words with Pruitt, find out if there was anything else Meggie shouldn't be doing that she hadn't bothered to mention to him.

Meggie blinked. Clearly, she'd only intended to rub it in to him that she wouldn't be driving herself. The last thing she'd expected was for Nate to volunteer to do the job. She knew how he tried to avoid being alone with her, even in a vehicle. "Farrah can take me."

"I said, I'll take you."

"Farrah—"

Farrah exchanged a quick, grim glance with Sonny. "Leave me out of it. Please."

The next day, Nate made sure to be there waiting, with the GMC running and all warmed up, when Meggie came out to leave for town. She gave him a sour look through the driver's side window, but she didn't say a word, just waddled on over and lugged her weight up into the passenger seat.

They rode the whole way to town in silence.

At the clinic, Meggie signed herself in. The receptionist gave her a little cup and asked her for a urine sample.

When Meggie returned from the bathroom and took a seat in the waiting room, she didn't even glance his way. She buried her nose in a tattered magazine with a picture of Cher on the cover. Nate looked around for something he could read. But women's magazines and kids' books were all he could find.

After about a century, Trudy Peltier stuck her head out the inner door. Trudy was Pruitt's assistant, and an old classmate of both Meggie's and Nate's. "Meggie, come on in," Trudy said.

Meggie put down her magazine and got to her feet. Nate rose and followed right along behind her. When she realized he planned to go in with her, Meggie turned around and gave him another of her sullen looks. But she had sense enough not to try to tell him to keep out.

"Well, Nate Bravo," Trudy said in that too-sweet way of hers, "isn't it nice to see you here with Meggie for a change?"

"Think so, huh?" He gave her a long, cold look.

She pursed up her lips. "Now, now. No need to get snippy."

Nate just went on looking at her. The black eye he'd brought back from Boca Raton had faded almost to nothing by then. But still, he was sure Trudy could see it and that she was making judgments about him because of it. She had never been a big fan of his. She flashed him a wide, fake smile and then asked Meggie to step on the scale. "My, my," she clucked. "You're gaining nicely."

"Too nicely," Meggie murmured when Trudy finally stopped nudging the counterweight down the bar.

"This way." Trudy led them to an examining room. "The doctor will be with you in a few minutes."

When Trudy closed the door and left them in the small space, Meggie wiggled up onto the examining table and Nate took the visitor's chair in the corner. They sat and waited, both trying, as they usually did lately, not to make extended eye contact.

But the room was too small. Nate had to look somewhere. Once he had studied the color poster of the human heart and read the nutrition chart with its cartoon renderings of happy fruits and vegetables, his gaze just naturally turned Meggie's way.

She had more fortitude; she steadfastly refused to look at him. She sat awkwardly on the end of the examining table, her hands resting in what was left of her lap, her gaze cast down.

Nate studied her bent head, and couldn't help noting the way her shoulders drooped and the sad curve of her mouth. She looked tired and a little dejected. He often saw her rub at the base of her spine, as if it troubled her. He wondered if it ached now.

He stood. "You want this chair? Until Pruitt comes?"

She looked up and blinked. His tone had been gentle, for once. It must have surprised her. "Oh. No. I'm fine." She put her hand at her back and sat up straighter for a minute, stretching her spine a little.

"Sure?"

"Positive."

He stood there for a moment, then dropped into the chair again, feeling like a fool. She took to watching her knees once more. And he looked at her. He studied the soft curve of her cheek and wondered at the thickness of her dark hair, remembering in spite of himself just what the silky strands felt like when he ran his hands through them or pressed them against his mouth.

Finally, Pruitt came in. He greeted Meggie, then nodded at Nate. "Good to see you."

"Same to you, Doc."

Over the years, Nate had been in to see Doc Pruitt more than once—for everything from a persistent case of strep throat to a bone or two he'd broken riding bulls in the local rodeos.

Nate watched the doctor take Meggie's blood pressure and perform a thorough examination. As he tapped and poked and prodded, the old guy murmured things like, "Um, yes. I see. Fine."

When Pruitt stepped back and told Meggie she could button up, Nate saw his chance. "Doc?"

"Hm, yes?"

"Are there any...special precautions Meggie should be taking right now, for the baby's sake?"

Doc Pruitt frowned. "Did she stop driving her pickup on those rutted roads out at the Double-K?"

Meggie shot Nate an indignant glance and jumped to her own defense. "I did. I stopped."

"Well, then, I'd have to say that what we have here is a very healthy, very pregnant woman who appears to be taking dandy care of herself. Just take it easy, Meggie and—"

Nate leaned forward in his chair. "That's it, Doc. That's my point. She won't take it easy. She's got to hand-feed every damned orphaned calf herself."

Meggie glowered at him. "That's not true. I'm careful. I do take care of myself. And the baby."

"Tell her, Doc. Tell her she's got to ease up."

Doc Pruitt looked at Nate, then at Meggie, then back at Nate again. "Hmm. I think the last thing I want to do right now is to get in the middle of a private discussion between a man and his wife."

Nate snorted. "What the hell are you saying? This is a medical question. A question of Meggie's health. And the baby's, too."

The doc patted Meggie's hand. "It's real sweet that he's so concerned. Tell him to get more rest and to eat right. He'll need his strength for when the baby comes."

Meggie grinned. "Right, Doc."

Nate wanted to throttle them both. "I fail to see the damn humor here."

"You take care of yourself, Nate," Doc Pruitt said. "And, Meggie, from here on in, you come see me once a week."

"I'll make an appointment before I go."

"Hmm, yes. Sounds good."

"Hey, wait…" Nate began, but the doctor had already opened the door and stepped out into the hall.

Before she went home, Meggie wanted to buy groceries. Nate went into the market with her and then wheeled the cart out to the parking lot and loaded the shopping bags into the big lockbox in the back of the pickup for her, so she wouldn't strain herself.

"Oh, and I want to stop off at Cotes's," she said just before they headed for home. "I ordered a few things for the baby and I want to see if they came in yet."

Cotes's Clothing and Gifts took up half of a huge old brick building on Main. Nate dropped her off in front of the store and then told her he'd keep the motor running for her, since all the spaces along the street were taken. But then, just after she disappeared inside, a Bronco pulled out of a space right in front of the store. Nate turned the GMC into the empty spot.

A few minutes passed. Nate began drumming his hands on the steering wheel, wishing to hell she'd hurry up.

Then he started wondering if Barnaby Cotes could be in there with her. Since his father had died a few years before, Cotes had take over the store. And he'd always been after Meggie. Nate could just see the little weasel now, leaning across the counter at Meggie, smiling that slimy smile of his, stalling on telling her the status of her order just so he could keep her there a few more minutes and drool over her. It wouldn't mean a damn thing to Cotes that Meggie was married and eight months pregnant. Nate had seen the way Cotes looked at Meggie. The smarmy little twit would take Meggie May any damn way he could get her.

Nate had just begun to contemplate the idea of marching in there and dragging Meggie out, when she emerged on her own. She had a shopping bag in her hand and a sweet, happy smile on her face.

He knew for sure then: Cotes had been buttering her up.

She spotted the GMC and shuffled over to it, then pulled open the passenger door and dragged herself up into the seat. She shut the door and turned her smile on him—not on purpose, just because he happened to be sitting there. "Thanks for waiting for me."

He glared at her. Her smile faded to nothing. He shoved the old pickup into reverse, making it lurch when he let off the clutch. Beside him, Meggie buckled her seat belt and looked straight ahead.

She didn't speak the whole way home—and neither did he. When they got to the house, he carried her groceries in without saying a word, then changed into work clothes, tacked up the bay mare he'd been using and set out to join Sonny in the South Pasture.

For the next week, Nate avoided even minimal conversation with Meggie. He knew if he ever said more than a few words to her, he would say too much—about Cotes, as well as about the way she refused to take care of herself. Avoidance seemed to work pretty well. They shared a few testy exchanges, but somehow he managed to keep from losing it so bad they had a full-blown fight.

Then on Wednesday, the sixteenth, a spring blizzard blew in. It came in fast, rolling down from the Big Horns, turning the world blind white in a matter of hours. All Nate, Sonny and Farrah could do was find their way back to the buildings and wait inside for it to blow over.

For the whole of that afternoon, they were stuck in the houses. Since Meggie had been handling most of the cooking lately, they gathered at her house until after dinner, playing checkers and double-deck pinochle, while the wind screamed outside and, beyond the windows, it looked like midnight in the middle of the day.

The power went off around four, but it wasn't a big problem. Sonny fought his way around the side of the house through the driving snow and got the generator going. Both houses and the outbuildings had electricity again by four-thirty. And there was plenty of wood in the lean-tos built against Meggie's house and the bunkhouse. They could last indefinitely, cozy and warm inside, no matter how brutal the weather outside.

But the calves were another story. A calf didn't take the cold well. It's short coat would quickly soak through. Unless it could huddle against its mother or find a sheltered spot out of the wind, a calf out on the range could freeze to death quickly in a bad spring storm.

And Meggie was worried about how many of them this storm would take from her. She tried not to show it, since she was a practical woman and didn't go around moaning when moaning would do no good anyway. But Nate felt her worry as if it were his own. He watched her, the way she would glance toward the windows when she thought no one was looking, as if she might at last see something beyond them but a wall of whirling white.

She could usually wipe up the table with her opponents at pinochle—which was why Nate liked to partner up with her. But that day, she forgot which cards had been played and she got caught reneging twice.

By the time evening rolled around and Sonny and his family had struggled across the yard to their own house, Nate was starting to think that he would go nuts watching her try to pretend she wasn't half-crazed with anxiety. He found the whiskey bottle she kept in the pantry and poured himself a couple of fingers, just to settle his nerves a little.

But then, when he went out to the living room and sat down to enjoy his drink, she was standing at the window, looking out at the darkness, and at the snow driving against the panes. His nerves started singing all over again, just looking at her.

"You won't make it stop by staring at it," he said, maybe a little too harshly.

She turned, saw his drink and frowned.

He dropped to the sofa and took himself a warming sip. Then he shrugged. "What?"

She sighed. "I just don't think you should start drinking now, that's all."

"It's one drink, Meggie. That's all it is. One drink is not *starting drinking*."

She pressed her lips together and sighed again. "Fine. Whatever." She turned and headed for the stairs.

He raised his glass to her. "Right. Run off."

She stopped, smoothed her hand down her belly. She looked so frustrated and sweet and ripe he wanted to strangle her—or kiss her. Or both. "Let's not get into it, Nate."

He leaned forward and set his glass on the coffee table in front of him. "Get into what?" he asked, as if he didn't know.

She shook her head. "There's no point in talking to you." She took another step toward the stairs.

"Wait."

She glared at him—but she did stop. "I mean it, Nate. I don't want to fight with you."

He rose. She looked so vulnerable, even with that angry frown on her face. He wanted to touch her. He wanted to—

Her eyes widened. "Nate, don't."

He'd moved to within a few feet of her. And out of nowhere, he heard himself asking the question that had been eating at him for days. "Last Friday, in town. Was Cotes there when you went in his store?"

She shook her head and sighed. "Oh, Nate..."

"Was he there? Just tell me."

She studied him for a moment, then admitted, "Yes."

"I knew it."

"Why are you looking at me that way? There's nothing between Barnaby and me."

"Tell that to Barnaby."

"This is ridiculous."

"The hell it is. He'll be after you, you know that, once I'm out of the picture. He's going to think he's got a chance with you, that you're going to need a husband to help you raise our kid."

"Nate, stop it."

"I'm just telling you."

"Fine. I heard you. Now, let's drop it."

"Will you say yes to him?"

She made a low, incredulous sound in her throat. "I can't believe you're asking that. You have no right in the world to ask that."

She was right; he knew it. He'd let himself get completely out of hand here. The storm, her fear for the calves, all the damn tension caused by having to be near her and not being able to touch her, was finally pushing him over the edge.

He made himself lift his shoulders in a lazy shrug. "Consider the question retracted."

She studied him for a long, bleak moment. Then she nodded. "Can I go to bed now?"

"Go."

She turned and left him there, with his half-empty drink and the howling, lonely sound of the wind.

By the next morning, the storm had blown on by. They woke to a white and silent world. The power had come on again, so Nate went out and turned off the generator. Then Meggie served him breakfast.

Nate, Sonny and Farrah rode out with the sun, which shone harshly on the new snow, blinding them with its reflected glare. They found calves weak, sick and dying in the pastures, stretched out and stiff the way they got when the cold took them.

Right away, they got three warming huts set up— sheds with propane heaters in them—in the pastures farthest from the home place. All day they loaded calves into the GMC and Meggie's pickup and carried them to where they could get them warm.

In the barn and the corral shed closest to the house, they had heaters going steadily. Meggie worked as hard as the others, tending the calves they brought in to her.

By the end of the day, they were all about to drop from exhaustion. But the situation with the calves didn't look as bad as they had thought at first. Most of the them were at least a week or two old, ready and able to suck again as soon as they got warmed up. In general, it turned out that if a calf was still breathing when they got to it, it survived. After they warmed it up, it could be turned right back to its mother—given that its mother could be found, which wasn't always the case.

Orphaned calves meant more hand feeding, at least until they found a cow that would take on the motherless one. And though the season had started to wind down, there were still a few day- and two-day-old calves. Even after they'd been next to a propane heater for a while, some of them wouldn't suck.

Which meant that at nine-thirty that night, Meggie was still out in the shed. She had her fingers down the throat of a big newborn Charolais-cross, trying to get him to take a little nourishment.

Nate worked right beside her, feeding another of the calves, one that seemed to be doing pretty well. Once the calf Nate was tending had finished eating, he took a minute to make it comfortable in the straw under one of the heat lamps.

Then he went to stand above Meggie. "It's time to turn in."

She looked up at him, her eyes flat with exhaustion. "You go on."

"Meggie—"

"I won't be but a few minutes. Really."

He didn't believe her. She'd stay out here all damn night, more than likely. But he was too tired himself to argue with her.

"Come in soon. Or I'll come out and get you."

"I told you. A few minutes, that's all."

He decided to take her word for it and left her there, with that half-dead calf. It seemed as if it took every ounce of energy he had left to drag himself into the house and trudge upstairs, where he stripped and stood under the shower for a while.

When he came out, all he wanted to do was fall across a bed and not get up for a year or two.

But he knew that woman too well. He hadn't heard her come in. Because she *hadn't* come in.

Muttering crude things to himself, he pulled on his boots and yanked on his jacket and went out across the frozen yard to drag her bodily back to the house, where she belonged.

He found her sitting in the straw, the calf's limp head on her knees.

She looked up at him. "He died," she said. "He just gave a big, tired breath and that was it. His eyes rolled back." She looked down at the sprawled body, then put her hand against the neck, as if some flutter of pulse might still beat there. "Such a waste." She shook her head, stroking the smooth hide. "A waste of a fine animal."

Nate understood. It wasn't the death so much. A rancher lived with death, day in, day out. In the end, a rancher fought for the lives of his animals—in order to take those lives.

But Meggie had a good touch and a powerful will. She had put her mind and heart and hands into saving this animal. For nothing.

He dropped to his haunches beside her in the straw. "You're beat. It seems worse than it is, you're so tired."

She just went on slowly stroking the calf's neck.

"Meggie."

Still, she kept up that stroking, dried milk gleaming like snail tracks along her arm. Raising her other hand, she waved absently at the air. "Leave me alone. I'm okay. I'll be in soon."

"Meggie…"

"I mean it. Go."

"No. You're coming in."

Her hand stopped its stroking for a fraction of a second. And then she shrugged. The stroking began again, a total dismissal of him and his demand.

His anger, always right beneath the surface lately, rose up. His blood felt hot in his veins. He controlled the heat, channeling it into determination.

Damn her, she would do his will in this.

Slowly, deliberately, he reached out and put his hand on the back of her neck, below where she'd anchored her hair out of the way.

She stiffened. He held on.

The smoothness and warmth of her skin stunned him. The little hairs at her nape felt like the softest strands of purest silk.

God. How long had he kept himself from touching her?

Too damn long.

She batted at his hand. "Don't."

He kept his hand right where it was. His blood pounded in his veins, a primitive, possessive rhythm. "Come inside. Now."

She looked up at him then, her eyes widening, the flat, defeated exhaustion turning to something else. Something that burned him even as it surrendered to him.

"Nate…"

"Now."

"I don't want—"

"Now."

He felt her shudder—and then give in completely, the stiffness leaving her as she relaxed under his hand. Carefully, tenderly, she eased the calf's head from her knees and onto the bed of straw beneath them. The cow she'd milked to do the feeding shifted nervously nearby. She gave it a look. "Easy," she whispered. "It's okay, now."

"Meggie." He rubbed his thumb on her nape.

She turned her big eyes on him. "What?"

"At some point, you've got to let it go."

"I know."

He gave a tug, to pull her close. She sighed and drooped against him, her head fitting into his shoulder, her arm finding its way around his waist.

"So tired," she murmured.

He stroked her hair. "It's all right. All right.…" He kissed her forehead. "Come on, now. Let's go in."

He helped her to stand. Once on her feet, she leaned heavily on him and glanced blankly around her at the heat lamps suspended from the roof of the shed, at the three other calves still recovering from the effects of the blizzard the night before—all orphans, as far as they knew now.

"Everything's fine," Nate told her.

She looked down at the sprawled, lifeless body of the Charolais calf. "We should—"

"I'll see that it's taken care of. In the morning."

"I just wish—"

"Shh. Let's go."

She acquiesced to be led by him, out into the icy spring night, across the yard and into her house.

Chapter Fourteen

Inside, he helped her out of her jacket and hung it by the door, shrugging out of his own and hooking it there, too. He sat her down and took her dirty boots from her. Then he led her up to the room they had shared in the summer.

In the bathroom there, he removed the rest of her clothes, peeling them off swiftly, letting them fall to the tiles at her feet. Her eyes had gone blank on him again. She looked down at her big belly and her swollen breasts and then up at him, as if she wondered how she'd gotten there, in the bathroom with him, naked.

He turned to the tub and worked the faucets, getting the water running and hot, then pulling the lever that would engage the shower nozzle. He tested the temperature and stepped back. "Get in."

She turned obediently to do as he'd told her.

"Wait."

She stopped. He pulled her close to him and worked at the big tortoiseshell clip that held up her hair. The clip opened. The heavy, red-shot brown waves dropped to her shoulders. He couldn't stop himself. He buried his face in the strands. They smelled of hay and milk, of dust and sweat. Of Meggie in her most elemental form.

She made a small, questioning sound. He raised his head from the silky mass and smoothed it on her shoulders. "Go on. Get in. Wash your hair, too. Wash everything. You'll feel better once you do."

She got in under the shower spray, pulling the curtain closed behind her. He leaned against the wall, watching her blurred shape through the semiopaque curtain. She took a long time. The room filled up with fragrant steam, warm and wet and soothing. He was there, holding her towel, when she pushed back the curtain and stepped, dripping wet, from the tub.

He handed her the towel. As she dried herself, he got her heavy winter robe from the back of the door and held it up for her. She handed him the towel and slipped her arms into the sleeves of the robe. He moved behind her and began drying her hair.

"Hungry?" he asked.

She shook her head. "Just tired."

He dropped the towel atop the pile of discarded clothes. "Come on."

But she resisted.

"What?" he asked.

"My hair's too wet. If I go to bed with it this way..." Her voice trailed off, as if she'd forgotten in midsentence what she'd set out to say.

"All right." He got her blow-dryer from the little cabinet under the sink, feeling a strange kind of elation that he knew where it was, that he had been a true husband, at least for a while. One who knew the things a husband knows: where she kept her hair brush and her aspirin, her blow-dryer and the lipstick she so seldom wore.

He plugged in the dryer and handed it to her.

A few minutes later, he took it from her and put it away. Then he led her into the bedroom, where he switched on the lamp beside the bed.

He pulled back the covers, smoothing them down. Once all was in readiness, he turned to her, untied the robe and took it away from her.

Totally unconcerned about her own ungainly, pregnant nakedness—and so incredibly beautiful to him—she took a pillow from the pile at the head of the bed. He watched as she climbed in and curled up on her side, tucking the pillow under the heavy bulge of her stomach—for support, he realized.

"Comfortable?" he asked.

She made a low noise in the affirmative.

He settled the covers around her. And that was it. The moment when he should leave her.

But he couldn't leave her.

He backed up and dropped into the small armchair a few feet away. By the light of the lamp between them, he looked at her soft face. Her eyes seemed bruised, she was so tired. And her clean hair shone against the white pillowcase.

Those bruised eyes held a deep sadness. "I don't want to go on like this," she whispered. "It hurts, Nate. And it makes me so tired."

He knew exactly what she meant. It hurt him, too. This forced closeness they lived in, the armed camp each inhabited in the same house, the hostility that grew between them, filling the echoing, lonely space left by the intimacy they had once shared.

"I just want...to lie down with you." The low words came out of him all by themselves. "Let me, Meggie. Let me do that. Tonight." Some tiny part of him that still had scruples felt shame to ask such a thing of her.

But not enough shame to keep him from asking.

She sighed.

"Meggie."

She closed her eyes—and then opened them again.

He chose to take that as consent and rose quickly. He yanked off his clothes and his boots, tossing the clothes across the chair, shoving the boots against the wall. She watched him, her eyes sorrowful and knowing and full of hopeless yearning.

When he lifted the layers of blankets to slide in beside her, he half expected her to tell him no. But she said nothing, only scooted back enough to give him room.

And then at last, he was there with her, where he'd dreamed of being for months now, wrapped up warm and close, the fresh-showered scent of her taking all his senses. With a groan, he pulled her against him. She came—sighing, soft, willing, sad.

She kissed him, a long, slow, hungry kiss. Her belly pressed against him, and her heavy, ripe breasts, too. She reached down and touched him, a loving touch that turned to stroking.

"No, Meggie..." he groaned.

"Shh..."

He lost it, like some kid who'd never known the feel of a woman's hand.

Shattered, shamed, he threw an arm across his eyes and looked away from her.

She only pushed back the covers and went to the bathroom for a towel.

A little later, she lay beside him again, in the warm cove the blankets made. He reached for her. And he began to touch her. He could no more stop himself from touching her right then than he could make himself quit breathing. He had to feel every inch of her, to know her again as he had known her before, when they were man and wife, when he had allowed himself to forget for a while that freedom was what he wanted most.

This time, instead of facing him, she lay tucked right into him, spoon-fashion. That gave him free reign to caress her, and also put his body in the best, most complete contact with hers.

He found her somehow softer to the touch than before. Her skin felt hotter, too. And if most of her seemed softer, that didn't include her belly. The hard tautness of it astounded him. He rubbed the stretched skin gently, felt a movement. She sighed and put her hand over his.

"Does it hurt when he kicks?"

"Not too much. Not most of the time."

His hand strayed up to cup her full breast. And then down again. All the way down.

"Is it all right?"

"Yes. Carefully. Oh, Nate. Yes."

He touched her, his fingers parting her, delving in. She moved against him, eager, hungry, totally his. Within moments, she cried out.

As her ragged breathing slowed, he pulled her even closer than before, his body absorbing the heat of hers.

"Sleep now," he whispered.

"Oh, Nate..."

"Just sleep."

* * *

In the morning, before dawn, Meggie woke and slid out from under the blankets. Not allowing herself to glance back at the warm bed and the man sleeping there, she pulled on her robe. Then she tiptoed around the room, taking clean clothes from the bureau and closet, pulling them on quickly, staying as quiet as she could.

Downstairs, she built up the fire, put on the coffee and whipped up batter for pancakes. Nate came down just as she was pouring the first batch on the griddle and cracking eggs into a pan.

"Sit down," she said.

He came and stood by the table, looking sheepish and vulnerable. "Meggie, I..."

"Sit down," she said again.

He dropped to the chair. She moved around the room, pouring him coffee, turning the pancakes, then sliding them onto a warm plate along with three eggs. She set the food in front of him. "Eat."

He spread butter, poured on syrup, then picked up his fork.

A few minutes later, she joined him. They ate in silence, until the food was gone.

Meggie pushed her plate aside and sat back in her chair.

Nate looked at her broodingly from his end of the table. "All right. What? I shouldn't have last night. I know."

"I love you," she said.

He turned away, toward the still-dark windows that looked out on the yard behind the house.

She folded her hands on the table, stared down at

them, then up at him. "Last night was...beautiful for me."

He looked down, up, toward the window again. Everywhere but at her.

"Nate? Did you hear me?"

"I heard." He spoke harshly—and then added in a ragged whisper, "And it was...the same for me."

She waited for him to look at her. But he didn't. So she asked, "Where are we going together, Nate?"

He shrugged, still looking toward the dark windows.

"Are you my husband?"

He said nothing.

"Nate. I think you're going to have to decide."

He made himself look at her then. "I just...I came to help out."

She closed her eyes, breathed deeply, and leveled her gaze on him again. "For calving time."

"Right."

"Calving time is almost done."

"Not quite done."

"Enough so that we can manage now without you."

His expression darkened. "What are you talking about? We drove ourselves to the brink yesterday. You need me. If I hadn't been here—"

"It was the last big storm. You know it. And most of the cows have calved." She thought for a moment. "But come to think of it..."

"What?"

"You're right."

He looked at her sideways. "About what?"

"About how I need you."

He made a scoffing sound. "I meant you need my help, here, now, to run this damn ranch of yours."

"And you're right. I do need your help. I always will."

"What are you getting at?"

"Well, branding time comes next. And then the spring drive. And after that, it'll be summer, which means haying, mending fences, trying to keep the weeds down. It goes on and on. You know it does. So you're right, I do need you. The Double-K needs you. Your baby needs you. And not just for now. Forever."

She watched his defensiveness turn angry. He didn't like words like "forever." "You won't get any forever from me, Meggie. You knew it all along."

"Yes. I did."

His lip curled in a snarl. "But still you came after me."

"Because I love you. I told you from the first—if I needed a child to keep my home, I wanted that child to be yours."

He made a low, derisive sound. "Hell, Meggie. What is it with you?"

"What do you mean?"

"You know what I mean. You live in some crazy romance inside your own head. You have...no damn judgment at all."

She opened her mouth to speak, but he ran right over her.

"After all," he sneered, "you went and chose me as the object of your undying love. That's pretty damn deluded, if you think about it—first that you chose *me*. A losing proposition if there ever was one. But even if it had been someone else, someone not quite so...impossible as I am, it's still nothing more than some big, pointless fantasy, telling yourself for all these years that there's only one man in the world for you. It's not normal. No one carries a torch for that long.''

Meggie refused to be shamed by his cruel words. She faced him proudly. ''Maybe you're right. Nobody does. Nobody in the world—except me.''

''Oh, so you're something rare, are you?'' Her rose, his chair scraping the floorboards as he stood. ''Something special, in your delusion?''

''Stop it.'' She pushed herself to her feet so she could meet him eye-to-eye, grunting a little with the weight of the baby. ''Just stop that mean talk. It won't work on me anymore. I'm not some poor nineteen-year-old girl now, someone you can reduce to tears with a few cruel words. I've lived with you, and I know you in the deepest ways. And sometimes, in the best of our days together, I've dared to dream that it would work out all right between us.''

He just looked at her, so hard and guarded. ''Stop dreaming. It'll get you nowhere.''

She gave his own hardness right back to him. ''Fine. Then it's time for you to go. For good and all. It's time I stopped dreaming of what will never be. And it's time you stopped hanging around here, angry all the time because you want me, but then not letting yourself have me. If you want to see someone who's deluded, you just take a good, long look at yourself.''

That reached him, for some reason. His hard mask of angry defensiveness slipped. He allowed her to see the pain underneath. ''Meggie, I...''

''What?'' She looked straight at him.

He gazed back at her hopelessly.

''Say it,'' she prodded. ''I can take it. I've taken so much. You've got no idea how strong I am.''

''I just...can't be what you want me to be.''

She shook her head. "That's not true."

"Hell, Meggie..."

"No. Listen." She leaned toward him across the table, as much as she could with her stomach in the way. "You *are* what I want you to be. I've never asked you to change."

"You want me to come here." He gestured with a sweep of his arm. "To live here. To spend my life working the Double-K. With you."

"That's so."

He grunted, a vindicated sound.

She added, "But it's not the only option, not as far as I'm concerned."

He frowned and dropped his arm to his side. "What are you saying?"

"I'm saying that I learned something in November when I lived with you in L.A. I learned that...I could make my home anywhere. If there was love enough. If there was you. I'm saying that I would go with you. Me and our baby. If you would take us. Wherever you wanted to go."

He gaped at her. "You really mean that. You'd leave the Double-K."

"I would. For you. To be with you." She smiled at him then, a sad, resigned smile. "But you won't take us, will you?"

"I..."

"Will you?"

Slowly, he sank back to his chair.

With a sigh, she sat down, too, and waited for him to answer her. He said nothing. And that was all the answer she required.

She rested a hand on the swell of her belly. "Oh, Nate. I swore to myself, on the morning after our wedding night, that I would take the time we had together and find joy in it—and not ask for more. I've tried to do that. I truly have. Maybe I didn't always succeed. Maybe I...hoped more than I had a right to. Maybe I held on longer than I should have. But when you finally said it was truly over, I accepted your will. I came home and set my mind to leaving you behind.

"But then, you wouldn't stay away. You had to come back, temporarily, for calving time. And maybe you're right. Maybe we wouldn't have made it through without you. But it's no good, the way you treat me now. It's as if you have to hurt me. You've been riding me all the time, picking fights with me over every little thing. And then, finally, when neither of us could bear it anymore—you fell into bed with me. For what? To relieve the tension a little? So you can start the meanness all over again?"

"Meggie, I didn't—"

"Don't lie to me. Lie to yourself if you have to, but not to me. You want me, but you won't stay with me. You can't keep your hands off me, but you won't be my husband. I'm not going to take it anymore. It isn't any good for me, or for our baby."

Outside, the sky was beginning to lighten. Meggie pushed herself upright again and picked up her plate, as well as his. She carried both plates to the sink and set them down carefully.

Then she turned to Nate once more. "You're going to have to make up your mind, Nate. For good and all. Do you stay and make a real marriage with me—or do you go?"

He looked toward the window and the coming dawn. Out in the yard, one of Farrah's roosters crowed.

Sonny's hound took up the cry, letting out one long, doggy wail to the new day.

"Nate. Make up your mind."

He turned to her then. She knew his answer before he spoke. She could see it there, in the loneliness of his eyes.

"All right," he said at last. "I'll go."

Chapter Fifteen

Not long after breakfast, Nate rode out with Sonny. But before he left, he kept his word about the Charolais calf. Meggie never knew where he took it, but when she went out to the shed to feed the other calves, it was gone.

Nate stayed for two more days, until all the calves weakened by the blizzard were back on their feet again. Through that time, he and Meggie were unfailingly kind to each other. Kind, and as polite as strangers.

On Sunday, after breakfast, Nate rose from the table and went back upstairs.

Ten minutes later, he came down. Meggie was in the living room, feeding wood into the heat stove. She shoved in a log and shut the small iron door in the side of the stove.

"Meggie."

She rose and faced him. He carried that big duffel he used as a suitcase.

She rubbed her hands down the sides of the jumper she wore. Inside her, the yearning rose up, to reach out, to whisper, *Don't go....* She pushed the yearning back down, into the deepest part of her, where it made a dull, never-ending ache.

"Well," she said in the false, bright voice she'd been using with him for the past two days now. "You're all ready."

"Yeah." His tone was gruff. "All packed and ready."

"All right, then."

He seemed to struggle with what to say next. "If you need me..." he began.

She shook her head. "I'll let you know. When the baby comes."

"Thanks."

"And I'll send the papers, as soon as I get out of the hospital."

"Papers?"

"For the divorce."

His jaw tightened, and then relaxed. "Good enough."

They stared at each other.

He shrugged. "Well. Goodbye, then."

"Goodbye, Nate. And...thank you."

He actually grinned. "What for? Making you miserable for weeks on end?"

"You know what for. If there's ever anything I can—"

He put up his free hand. "Don't."

She closed her eyes, bit her lip and nodded.

"Goodbye, Meggie."

She nodded again, because her throat had tightened up and she didn't think she could push any words through it. And she kept her eyes closed, so she wouldn't have to watch him go. She heard his boots moving toward the door.

And then they stopped. "Meggie?"

She made herself open her eyes.

"The other night, when I asked you about Cotes...that was wrong of me. You said it then—I had no right to ask a thing like that."

She still didn't speak. She couldn't.

"Meggie, what I'm trying to say is, if you find someone you think you could make a life with—even if it's that smug little twit Cotes—I want you to go for it. All right?"

She swallowed and managed to whisper, "All right."

It was a lie, of course. There would be no other men for Megan Bravo. She was like her father. A person who gave her love only once. She felt in her heart that Nate knew she lied.

But he didn't let on. He only gave her one last too-brief smile. And went out the door.

How did she live through that parting? It was worse than it had been when he sent her away after Thanksgiving, as if a big piece of her heart had been torn out.

Yet Meggie was a strong woman. And she had her land and a baby to live for. She knew that as calving time passed and the first wildflowers begin to appear in the snow-patched meadows, she would find peace inside herself once more.

* * *

Nate had no such expectations. Peace was a word in a language not his own.

In the days immediately following his departure from the Double-K, he slept little. Every time he did, he dreamed the dream of darkness. Of musty wool. Of his vow to get free.

Or else he dreamed of Meggie. Calling him. He saw her eyes, looking into his, just the way she had looked at him when he went out her door that last time: a look of undying love—and pure determination to get on with her life.

Without him.

He knew that he could not go back to her. Ever. That he had to leave her alone to put her life back together again.

And he *would* leave her alone.

He swore to himself that he would.

Maybe he would move. His neighbors all seemed poisoned against him. They had adored Meggie. And they blamed him for her departure.

Rightly so.

For five years, he'd lived just fine with their indifference. But their simmering resentment set his teeth on edge. That damn Dolores looked at him as if he'd just done murder and buried the evidence.

On Tuesday, two days after he returned to L.A., Nate took a job tracking down a runaway, a kid of fifteen who'd stolen his father's Mercedes and gone south. Nate found the kid on Wednesday night, in a seedy bar just over the Mexican border.

It was a disaster. The kid had taken up with some teenaged gangster types. The gangsters had guns. Nate ended up in a shoot-out, and took a bullet in the left arm, midway between the shoulder and the elbow. The gangsters got nervous. They ran out, guns blazing, and jumped into the Mercedes. They took off, peeling rubber—and leaving the runaway in tears in a back room.

The barmaid, a kindhearted type, poured tequila over the bullet hole in Nate's arm and then wrapped it in a bar towel. The kid, by that time, was more than willing to go home.

They started back around three on Thursday morning. The trip was pure hell. Nate's arm burned as though someone had stuck a hot poker in it, and the kid cried the whole way, swearing that his parents didn't care about him, that all he wanted was his freedom.

Near Blythe, just before dawn, Nate pulled over to the side of the road. "Get out."

The kid sniffed and gaped. "Huh?"

"You want your damn freedom, you got it. Get out."

The kid blinked, then looked frantically out the windows. The highway was deserted in both directions. A lone Joshua tree stood a few feet from the passenger door. "It's the middle of the desert. I can't get out here."

Nate scowled across the distance between them. "You want your freedom or not?"

The kid whimpered. "I just want them to care about me."

Nate carefully pressed his arm and wished with all his heart for some heavy-duty painkillers.

"Don't kick me out, mister."

Nate let out a growl. "Then don't tell me one more

damn time about how you want freedom. I've had it up to here with freedom. Understand?"

The kid gulped and nodded. "Yeah. Okay. I got it. Sure."

"You hungry?"

"You bet."

They stopped at a McDonald's for Egg McMuffins and reached the Malibu beach house where the kid lived at a little before noon. The kid's mother made a big fuss over him. The father, however, seemed more concerned about the loss of his Mercedes than anything else.

"Do you have any idea what a machine like that costs?" the man demanded, when he and Nate were alone to settle up.

Nate mumbled something unintelligible—he always tried to be unintelligible when he wanted to say something he knew wouldn't be wise.

"And you'd better have someone look at that arm," the man suggested with distaste.

"I'll do that." Nate found himself thinking *to hell with wisdom,* and added, "You know, if you cared half as much about your kid as you do about your car, he probably wouldn't be risking his life hanging around with gangsters."

The man gaped. "I beg your pardon."

"You heard me."

The man's ears turned red. "I want you out of my house. This instant."

Nate couldn't help grinning. "I guess I'll get no referrals from you, huh?"

"Out."

Nate left, heading over to Cedars, where he had the bullet dug out. Then, at around four in the afternoon, armed with a vial of codeine tablets, he went back to his apartment.

The codeine worked great. At five, after an unsatisfying shower where he tried not to get his arm wet, he fell across his bed and slept for a drugged, blessedly dreamless twelve hours.

He woke at five in the morning. His arm was throbbing again. Somehow, he managed to pull on his jeans, though his arm screamed in pain as he did it. Then, unwilling to go through the agony that putting on a shirt and shoes would have cost him, he dragged himself into the bathroom and washed down another codeine with water straight from the tap.

It occurred to him then that he hadn't eaten since the Egg McMuffin yesterday morning. So he wandered down the hall toward the kitchen, stopping on the way to gather up two days' worth of mail; it had gotten scattered around the floor a little when he came in the evening before. In the kitchen, he flipped on the light. And groaned at the sudden brightness. He switched the light off. It was that time of half-light, just as the sky began to brighten. He could see well enough to make coffee and toast. And the mail could wait a little longer for his attention. He threw the pile of envelopes and circulars on the table and went to brew the coffee and make toast.

When the food was ready, he sat at the table to eat, wishing the codeine would kick in and stop the throbbing in his arm.

He saw the movement in the parking lot out of the corner of his eye. He turned to look, glad he'd left the light off or he never would have noticed.

Two skinny guys were sneaking around down there.

One carried what appeared to be a crowbar. And the other had some kind of handgun.

Not good news for whoever they were planning to visit.

Community Watch to the rescue, Nate thought grimly as he picked up the phone and dialed 911. He reported two armed prowlers and gave his address. Then he got his own Beretta 9 mm, shoved in a loaded clip and headed for the door.

Nate crept down the stairs, wishing the Tyrells had left their porch light off, keeping to the side wall, his bare feet making no sound on the smooth concrete steps. At the bottom of the stairs, he waited, listening, pressed against the wall inside the enclosure provided by the stairwell. He heard nothing.

Slowly, he made his way around the side of the building, moving silently, even breathing with care. When he peeked around into the parking lot, he saw no one.

Beyond the lot loomed the carports, each one a dark cavern with the end of a vehicle sticking out of it. Terrific places for bad guys to hide.

Nate waited some more, listening for a giveaway noise, alert for any movement. He saw and heard nothing. He was just trying to decide whether he wanted to chance cutting across the open parking lot to get to the carports, when he heard splintering noises, then a window being shoved up.

The sounds came from somewhere on the other side of the building next door. Nate sprinted across the driveway that ran between the buildings, then raced around the laundry room. He saw a figure disappear through a pried-open window on the ground floor. Nate knew whose window it was: Hector Leverson's. On the other side would be Hector's living room. Since Nate saw no one else, he assumed the other prowler had gone inside first.

A number of choices presented themselves, none of them particularly appealing. He could wait for a response to his 911 call. Maybe they'd show up in time to handle the situation.

He could try Meggie's technique and set up a racket. That might possibly make the prowlers—who had just attained the status of burglars—break and run. It also might freak them out enough that they'd shoot Leverson, if the poor guy was home.

Nate's third option was to crawl in the window after them. They had thoughtfully left it open for him, after all.

Nate just couldn't resist that open window. He approached it with caution and crouched below it for a full sixty seconds, listening for sounds from inside, thinking that the good thing about a little excitement like this was that it got his adrenaline up and he could hardly feel his throbbing arm at all now. But then, of course, that could just be the codeine starting to work.

A light went on, in a window several feet down the wall—in what he judged would be Hector's bedroom. He heard a cry, slightly muffled, a cry that seemed to come from the room where the light had just come on.

More than likely both scumbags had stalked their prey there. Which meant the living room would be deserted—he hoped.

Muttering a short prayer to the patron saint of fools and PIs, Nate slid over the sill and into the dark living room. His bare feet hit the floor soundlessly and he stayed crouched low when he landed, weapon ready.

Luck was with him. There was no one there. But from the bedroom, he could hear voices speaking in low, intense tones.

He rose to his feet and moved silently across the floor, to the short hall that branched two ways—straight on toward the front door and to the left toward the bedroom and bath. He turned left and then plastered himself against the wall, moving as close as he could to the open bedroom door.

He listened.

"Please—" that was Leverson's voice "—there's money there. On the bureau. Take it and go."

"You got more stashed around here somewhere," one of the scumbags insisted. "I know you do. I got a sense about this stuff. You've got yourself a hidey-hole. I would have found it last time if we hadn't been…interrupted."

"No," Leverson said. "I keep my money in the bank. I swear to you. What's there on the bureau is all we have on hand."

We, Nate thought. Leverson wasn't alone? That would make four people in that room.

He listened, to place them.

He heard footsteps. And rustling sounds. "There's only about fifty bucks here." It was the same scumbag who had spoken a moment before.

"That's all you'll find in this apartment." Leverson's voice again.

"You come up with more." Bingo, Nate thought. Scumbag number two. "Or the woman gets it."

"I will, I will. I'll…go to my bank, withdraw all I have," Leverson said. "Just, please. Don't hurt her."

"Don't beg them, Hector." Nate's heart stopped. He

knew that voice. ''They're low-life trash. You don't beg low-life trash.''

The second scumbag muttered something foul. Nate heard the thudding impact of what might have been a fist or a pistol grip against flesh. Then he heard his mother's groan.

''Now,'' said the first man. ''The bitch is quiet. And we want more money, or—''

''Or what?'' Nate stepped into the doorway and aimed his Beretta at the man who'd spoken last.

For a moment, everyone froze. Nate found himself noting the fact that his mother and Hector Leverson were wearing matching pajamas.

Then the first scumbag swore. And the second scumbag turned the .38 special in his hand away from Sharilyn toward Nate.

''No!'' Sharilyn cried.

Nate opened his mouth to warn her not to move. But he was too late. She launched herself across the bed and threw herself in front of him.

The scumbag fired his .38.

And pandemonium broke out.

When it was over, Nate had the guy with the crowbar in a chokehold and Hector had beaten the one with the .38 unconsciousness, using a bronze statuette he'd grabbed off of the bureau.

Sharilyn lay on the floor, as still as death, with a .38 slug in her back.

As it turned out, it was a busy morning for the LAPD and prowler calls had gotten low priority. They had to call 911 again to get a patrol car and an ambulance.

Help came right away, however, for a call that included breaking and entering and possible murder. All the tenants came out to see what was happening. Dolores wailed on her husband's shoulder, outraged at all the evil in the world.

Within an hour of the incident, the patrolmen had taken the bad guys away and Sharilyn had been wheeled into an operating room at Cedars for emergency surgery.

Nate stayed with Hector.

They sat in a waiting room and drank bad coffee.

And Hector talked. "The one with the gun," he said for about the tenth time. "That was the same guy who attacked me last November. It's amazing. He actually came back to try again."

"It was his last try," Nate promised, as he'd done more than once already. "Don't worry about him, Hector. They'll lock him up for good now."

Hector lowered his head. "Do you think she'll be all right?"

Nate had to swallow hard before he could speak. "Yeah. Sure. She'll be fine."

"We were married yesterday," he said to Nate, as he'd said already to the tenants and the patrolmen. "It was the happiest day of my life."

Nate was still having trouble dealing with that news. He knew his mother. She had wanted only to be free. And yet, she'd chosen to marry again.

Hector sighed. "She's a wonderful woman. I'm the luckiest man alive."

"Right."

Hector's hands were clenched. "I don't believe in violence."

"Gotcha."

"But I can't help it. I wish I had killed the one who shot her."

Nate grunted. "You did him serious damage, I promise you. His head will never be quite the same."

"Good," Hector whispered. He looked hard at Nate. "She would like to make peace with you, more than anything in the world."

Nate closed his eyes and looked away.

But Hector wouldn't take a hint. "I know, I know. She told me. About the money she took from your grandfather, about how she sent you away. But she really did believe things would be better for you at the Rising Sun than they would have been with her. She never could control you, and she felt that you were headed for trouble. She thought that your grandfather would take you in hand."

"Look—"

"And about the other, when you were a small child. She always felt you were deeply...damaged by that. She feels she should have known earlier. I told her that she has to forgive herself, that she had been so busy trying to support the family all on her own. And at least when she did find out she took action. And it never happened again, did it?"

Nate said nothing. He felt strange. Nauseated, suddenly. And a little light-headed. He thought of the dreams. The dreams of the darkness...

"Are you all right?" Hector was asking.

"Yeah. I'm fine."

Hector's kind eyes widened as understanding dawned. "You don't remember, do you?"

Nate only looked at him.

Hector swallowed. "Oh, God."

Nate's palms were sweating. "What...are you talking about?" As he said the words, he wanted only to call them back.

Hector drew in a long breath and faced Nate. "It's not my place. I was wrong to say anything. I'm sorry. Please. I'm so worried. About her. I'm just not thinking straight."

Nate stared at Hector; he was still talking. But his voice seemed far away. And his face blurred before Nate's eyes, became his father's face, scowling at him, scaring him...

"A man needs some damn freedom in his life," Bad Clint muttered as he pushed Nate into the closet.

Then he closed the door.

And Nate was alone, in the darkness, with the smell of musty wool from the coats and rubber from the rain boots stored back against the wall.

The darkness was all around him, pressing on him, making it hard for him to breathe.

But then, just when he though he would start screaming, he looked down.

And saw the thin line of light that came in beneath the door. As long as there was that thin line, he told himself, he could stand it.

Nate heard the lock turn. And then he got down on the floor where the light was, put his thumb in his mouth. And waited.

He didn't know where his father went. He didn't know what his father did. But he did know that his father would let him out before his mother got home.

"Nate. Oh, please..."

He heard Hector's voice from far away. He waved a hand at the voice absently. He was wondering...

Had there been a time when he protested, when he cried and screamed and fought what his father did to him? He didn't know. Right now, all his memory would show him was acquiescence. And a terrible patience.

A promise to himself that he would wait. To get out. That he would grow up, be a man, eventually. And then, like his father, he would have his freedom. No one would box him in ever, ever, again.

"Please..."

He felt Hector's hand on his arm. He shook it off.

He must have been about five before his mother discovered what his father did with him when she went to work. That was after she somehow scraped enough together to buy the bar and they were living over it. She came up in the middle of her shift one time. And Bad Clint was gone. She called for Nate.

But he stayed quiet, waiting, the way his father always warned him to do.

"If you know what's good for you, you'll keep your yap shut," Bad Clint always said.

Nate heard his mother moving through the apartment, looking in the closets and calling his name.

At last, she opened the door. The light came in, all over him. Banishing the darkness. Making everything all right.

"Oh baby, my baby," she cried as she scooped him close to her body. She was warm and smelled of cigarettes from the smoky bar downstairs. He cuddled against her and didn't say a word.

"Nate..."

Nate shook his head, blinked. And Hector's insistent voice faded into nothing again.

Later, when Bad Clint showed up, Sharilyn was waiting for him. She screamed at him. She told him she'd have him arrested if he ever tried a trick like that again.

"How long?" she demanded, "How long have you been locking him up in the dark like that?"

"A man needs a little damn freedom," was all his father would say.

"I mean it," she told his father. "I will see you in prison if this *ever* happens again."

How Nate loved her then. Fiercely. Totally, for saving him from the darkness, for telling his father he'd better not ever put him in the darkness again.

Nate swore to himself that he would do anything for her. Anything at all.

He ran free after that, until his father died.

And then his mother sold him to his grandfather.

And he learned that she was just like his father: she would do terrible things, just to be free.

He had hated her then, a thousand times more than he ever hated his father. He had hated her more because she had made him love her before she sent him away as if he was nothing to her.

And then this morning, she had taken a bullet in the back to protect him.

It was just possible he would have to reevaluate his judgment of her.

"Nate. Dear God. Nate..."

Nate blinked. And Hector was looking at him, his gentle eyes full of fear and concern.

"Are you all right, Nate?"

Nate armed sweat from his brow, feeling numb and strange and not all there.

Was that it, then? Was a dark closet the place where the hunger for freedom had been born?

Over the years, he'd managed to forget the horror of the darkness. Only the hunger to be free had remained.

Had that hunger served him in any way?

The answer came instantly: yes. It had given him the patience, the will to stay sane, a child locked in a dark place for what must have seemed like forever.

But did it serve him now?

Was it worth the price now—of love? Of connection? Of knowing his child? Of holding Meggie in his arms every night, for as long as both of them lived?

"Nate. Please. I never meant to—"

Nate made himself smile at Hector. "No. It's all right. It's been…a hell of a morning, that's all."

An hour later, the surgeon came out to talk to them. "She's going to be all right," he said.

Hector and Nate went in to see her. She looked pale and she was still unconscious, with tubes taped to her nose and her mouth, and an IV drip hooked up to the back of one hand. She had a huge, dark bruise on her chin, where one of the scumbags had clipped her. Hector pulled up a chair and took the hand that had no needles stuck in it. Nate stood across the bed from him, waiting.

It was a few hours before she woke up. Nate was there when she opened her eyes.

She looked at his face and she knew instantly. She whispered in a papery voice, "I guess things will be all right now between you and me."

"Yeah," Nate said. "If you want it that way."

"I want it."

"Okay, then." He smiled at her. "But next time, if there are guns involved, keep your mouth shut and don't move."

She didn't even bother to reply to that, only whispered, "I heard Meggie left."

"Yeah."

"And that she's going to have a baby."

"Yeah."

Her brows drew together. "I bet you don't want to miss that. Seeing your baby born. It's going to be soon, from what I've heard."

"Yeah. Real soon."

"Then what are you doing here?"

"Well, my mother's in the hospital."

Sharilyn cast a loving glance at Hector. "Don't you worry about me. I have someone special to care for me. You go on home now, Nathan, to Meggie and your baby, where you belong."

Chapter Sixteen

The last Saturday in April, Meggie woke in the morning to a rippling contraction that moved over her stomach and down into the deepest part of her. Smiling, she put her hands over the place where her baby lay.

Over the past several days, her belly had lost its high roundness. Now her baby lay low inside her, ready to be born.

"Um, yes. All right. Very good," Dr. Pruitt had said when she'd gone to see him on Thursday. "Effacement is progressing nicely. And you're even a couple of centimeters dilated. That baby should be showing up here very soon."

Dr. Pruitt had been right, of course.

Very right. Meggie lay in her bed thinking that before the next day dawned, she would hold her baby in her arms.

She rose from the bed and went down to make the

fire. Farrah called from her house just as Meggie got a good blaze going.

"Come on over. Biscuits and gravy."

"I'll be right there." Meggie damped the fire a bit, grabbed her jacket from its hook by the door and went out across the cold, dark yard to the bunkhouse.

Another contraction took her in the middle of the yard. Meggie stopped, put her hands on her stomach again and looked up at the stars overhead.

Not a cloud in sight. Her baby would be born on a sunny day.

Farrah knew what was happening the moment she saw Meggie's face. "How far apart are they?"

"Ten minutes at least, and they're not very regular. It could be quite a while yet."

"Did you call Doc Pruitt?"

"Not yet."

"By nine, though, all right? If the contractions keep up."

"Sure. By nine."

When Meggie called at nine, the contractions were still several minutes apart. Doc Pruitt told her to call again in two hours.

At eleven, he still advised her to wait awhile before heading to the hospital in Buffalo. Meggie cleaned her house and made sure she had everything she'd need for her short stay in the hospital. She checked the baby's room, opening all the bureau drawers to see the little shirts and hand-knitted sweaters, running her hand over the stack of diapers that waited on the shelf above the changing table.

"It won't be long now," she whispered to the yellow teddy bear propped up in the side of the crib.

Lunchtime came and went. Meggie felt too excited

to eat. But Farrah talked her into sipping a little soup and chewing a few crackers.

Finally, around three in the afternoon, Meggie reported to Doc Pruitt that her contractions were coming about every five minutes. They were longer, and stronger than before, too.

"Get Farrah to bring you on in, then," the doctor said. "I'll meet you there."

Meggie put her suitcase in the back of Farrah's little hatchback 4x4. Then she returned to the house to check one last time that all was in order.

Farrah was waiting with the motor running and her kids in the back seat when Meggie came out of the house again. Smiling, she walked across the sunny yard toward the waiting car. She had just reached the passenger door, when a contraction came on. She leaned on the roof of the car, waiting for it to pass.

Farrah rolled down her window. "Okay?"

Meggie groaned. And then she smiled. "Yeah. They're getting stronger."

"Come on, then." Farrah pushed the door open from inside.

Meggie started to lower herself to the seat.

And right at that moment, an old GMC pickup came barreling into the yard.

"Nate," both Meggie and Farrah said at the same time.

Spraying gravel, Nate spun to a stop a few yards from the hatchback. Sonny's hound started barking.

Meggie called out, "Scrapper! You stop that now!"

The dog gave one last "Whuff," then slunk off the side of the bunkhouse porch.

Nate shoved open his door and slid down from the seat.

Appalled by the tenacity of her own unwavering heart, Meggie hungrily drank in the sight of him. He looked wrung out, rakish—and disreputable as always. He was the handsomest man she'd ever seen.

She asked, "What happened to your arm?"

He shrugged. "It's nothing. A scratch."

"That's no answer."

He gave a cursory glance toward Farrah and the kids and the waiting hatchback. "Where are you headed?"

"To Buffalo."

"What for?"

Instead of telling him, Meggie turned and spoke to Farrah through the side window of the hatchback. "Go ahead and take the kids back inside. I'll give you a call. Soon."

Farrah frowned. "Meggie, it's a ways into Buffalo."

"There's time."

"But—"

"Please. Go on in. I'll talk to Nate. And I'll call you soon enough."

Farrah shot a disapproving look past Meggie's shoulder at the man who waited behind her. "If he gives you any trouble, you send him to me. I'll show him the sharp side of my tongue."

Meggie forced a grin, trying to telegraph a confidence she didn't feel. "Will do."

Farrah wasn't buying. "Look, Meggie…"

Meggie pushed back from the door. "Go on. I'll be fine."

Reluctantly, Farrah drove the car the short distance to her own front door, got out and began removing Davey from his carseat.

Meggie and Nate were left standing alone in the middle of the yard, looking at each other. Neither of them seemed to have a clue what to say.

Meggie was the one who broke the silence. "What do you want?"

His mouth opened, and then he closed it. His brows drew together in a pained frown.

She demanded again, "What do you want, Nate?"

His jaw tightened beneath a couple of days' worth of beard. He coughed, and then he asked quietly, "Will you please invite me in?"

She thought of all the times he had left her, of all the times he had sent her away—of how each of those times, he had broken her heart. She didn't want her heart broken anymore. She'd had all the heartbreak she could take. Behind her, the screen door to the bunkhouse squeaked shut as Farrah took her children inside.

"Please, Meggie…"

"You told me you would leave. For good. I believed you, Nate."

"Please."

With a grim sigh, she turned and led him up the steps and in the front door of her house. In the living room, she gestured at a chair. "Sit. And whatever you have to say, it had better be good."

But he didn't sit. He stood in the middle of the room, looking at her with the most intense and burning expression she'd ever seen on his face in all the years she'd known him.

"What?" she demanded. *"What?"*

And he said, "Meggie, I love you."

Meggie blinked. "What?"

He said it again. "I love you."

She gave a small, bewildered cry.

He added, "And there's more."

She gulped. "There is?"

"Yeah. I have always loved you, since the first minute I saw you, minus your Wranglers, on the back of that big sorrel gelding you used to ride. I know I don't deserve you. I know I've hurt you bad every time I walked away from you. You shouldn't take me back. But if you will take me back, I will never walk away from you again. I swear it."

A contraction took Meggie, right then, as Nate was saying all the words she'd made herself stop dreaming she would ever hear from him. She dropped into an old rocker that had been her granny Kane's and, moaning, she let the pain have its way with her.

Nate covered the distance between them and knelt at her side. He felt for her hand. She gave it and squeezed hard, bearing down the way the pain bore down on her.

At last, it passed off and away. She panted and leaned her head back. "Whew."

Nate let out a groan of his own. "My God. You're in labor."

She rolled her head to look at him. "Yeah."

"Buffalo," he muttered in dawning understanding. "The hospital. That's where you were going."

"Right."

He jumped to his feet. "What's the matter with you? Why didn't you tell me?"

"I'm fine, really. I have plenty of time."

"We're going. Now."

She didn't move. "Soon. I promise. Soon."

He dropped down beside her again. "Look. I really think we should get out of here."

"We will. In a minute. But first, there's so much…to decide."

"Not now. Later. Right now, we should be—"

"Listen. I have a ranch to run. You live in L.A. How are we going to work that out?"

"Meggie—"

"Answer me. How will we work out this problem?"

He stood once more and raked his fingers back through his hair. "I can't think about this now."

She wasn't accepting that as any excuse. "If I can, you can. Now, tell me how we'll handle this, or I'm not getting out of this chair."

"All right. Fine." He paced back and forth in front of her. Then he stopped and shrugged. "I don't see it as a problem. I've got nothing against ranching. I'll move back here."

Meggie gaped. This was so crazy. Her wildest, most impossible fantasy come true. "You will? You're serious? You're not just saying it because—"

He knelt once more. "Hell, no. I'll come back. I know how you feel about this place. I expected, if you'd have me, that I'd move back home and work the Double-K with you."

"You did?"

"Yeah."

"Oh, Nate…" She reached out, put her hand against his stubbled cheek, partly in pure love—and partly to reassure herself that this wasn't some crazy, labor-induced dream. He grabbed her hand, kissed her palm. She smiled at him adoringly. And then she frowned. "But all you ever wanted was to get away from here." She pulled her hand away.

"No."

"Yes. You always said—"

He stood again. It seemed he couldn't stay in one place. "Meggie, look. A lot has happened in the past couple of days. I've figured out a lot of things I never really understood before. I'm going to fill you in on all of it. Soon. While we're driving to the hospital, and after we get there. So let's get on the way. All right?''

''What things?''

''Meggie...''

''Just tell me a little. Come on.''

''My mother got married.''

''To Hector?''

''Right.''

''I knew it.'' Her face lit up. ''Wait a minute. I know. You made up with your mother.''

''More or less.''

''Oh, Nate...''

''I was really off base about her.''

Meggie couldn't help it. She felt wonderfully smug. ''I told you so. She really does love you. But people are people. They make mistakes. And I honestly believe she did the best thing for you when she turned you over to your grandfather. Don't you?''

''I do, Meggie.''

''Good.''

He bent down and took both her hands. ''Can we go to the damn hospital now? Please?''

''In a minute. Let me think what else we have to deal with...I know. I would want to go back to L.A. sometimes, to visit Dolores and our other friends there—and your mother and Hector, too. Could we do that?''

''Whatever you want, Meggie. Anything you want, I swear.'' He still had her hands, so he pulled her from the chair. ''Let's go.'' He pushed her ahead of him, toward the door. ''Do you have a suitcase or something?''

"It's in Farrah's car."

"Fine."

She turned and faced him before they went out. "Nate, I'm just so proud of you. I can't believe it. You made up with your mother...."

He groaned and rolled his eyes. "Meggie. Out the door. Now."

"I'm going. But listen—"

"No more. We are leaving now." He reached around her, groping for the door handle.

She kept talking. "I just want to say this. I may get clingy sometimes. Especially in the next several hours. And clingy was something I swore I'd never be with you."

Nate looked down into her flushed, earnest face and understood that he couldn't go another minute without holding her. Instead of pulling the door open, he pulled her close.

Sighing, she cuddled against him. He groaned—in pain, this time.

"Oh!" she said. "Your arm..."

"It's okay. It's fine. Don't pull away." He cradled her tenderly, moved beyond imagining by the feel of her huge belly pressing against him and her soft arms sliding up to encircle his neck.

"I really didn't want to be clingy, Nate," she murmured ruefully into his ear.

"Cling to me, Meggie," he whispered against her silky hair. "Never, ever let me go...."

From the *Medicine Creek Clarion* week of
April 31 through May 7:
HELLO, WORLD...
Born: April 26, to Megan May Kane Bravo and

Nathan Justice Bravo,
a son, Jason James, 7 lbs. 6 oz. Mother and child
are doing just fine.

*   *   *   *   *

PRACTICALLY
MARRIED

Chapter One

It was one-thirty in the afternoon on the last Sunday in April when Zach Bravo turned to Tess DeMarley and asked, "Will you go for a drive with me, Tess?"

Tess met his steady gray-blue eyes and knew immediately what would happen on that drive.

Ignoring the sudden acceleration of her heartbeat, she sat a little straighter and gave him a bright, direct smile. "Yes. I would enjoy a ride, Zach."

Edna Heller, with whom Tess lived, sat on the sofa a few feet away. Tess turned to the older woman. "Edna, would you mind if we left you on your own for a while?"

"Not at all. You two go on."

Tess thought of her daughter, Jobeth. After lunch, Jobeth had gone out to play with some neighbor kids. "Jobeth is off down the street at the Collerbys'. Do you think you could look after her while I'm gone?"

"Of course I will. Don't you worry about Jobeth. You two have yourselves a nice little ride."

Zach and Tess stopped in the small entry hall at the foot of the stairs to put on their coats. Then they went out together into the cold and windy afternoon.

When Zach opened the pickup door for her, Tess couldn't help noticing that he'd brought the best one, the newest one of the three he used out at the Rising Sun Ranch. It was a Chevy, a deep blue in color. And there wasn't a speck of mud or manure on it, inside or out. He must have washed it before he came to call.

That touched her, made silly tears push at the back of her throat. She swallowed them. She was not a woman who indulged in tears.

And there was no reason for tears anyway. Tess and Zach had spent a long, careful time with each other, slowly getting acquainted, each learning the other's ways and wants. And now Zach would make her an offer. It was nothing to cry over. It was a good and logical thing for all concerned.

As the pickup sped down the road, the wind whistled outside, blowing hard enough to make the cab shake. Tess stared through the windshield at the rolling prairie, the wide pale sky and the Big Horn Mountains in the distance, so tall and proud, silvery snow still thick on the tops of them and white clouds snagged on the crests. She had lived in Northeastern Wyoming for almost two years now. It was grand, harsh country; rich and green in early summer, cold and unforgiving in winter. More and more, she had begun to allow herself to think of it as home.

As they rode, Tess and Zach talked a little, about the newest addition to the Bravo family, Jason James, who'd been born just yesterday to Zach's cousin Nate and Nate's wife, Meggie. Zach had driven in to Buf-falo, to the hospital there, to see the baby early that morning.

"Nate looked so proud," Zach said. "And I've never seen Meggie so happy. I think things between them have worked out, after all."

There had been some trouble between Nate and his wife. Tess was glad to hear the trouble was over. "That's good."

Zach chuckled. "Already that baby's got a set of lungs on him. You should hear him holler."

"I can't wait to get my hands on him." Tess thought of when Jobeth was a baby, of her tiny, perfect hands, her fat pink cheeks. Of the smell of her, that lovely, milky, baby-powder scent.

Zach took his gaze from the road long enough to turn his smile her way. He had a wonderful smile. All the Bravo men did.

A funny, weak feeling swept through Tess. Right then, for the first time, it became real to her that she might have more babies. With this man. It seemed an awfully intimate subject to consider—for a woman who would soon be made a strictly sensible offer.

Zach was looking at the road again. If Tess's face had turned red, he hadn't noticed—or else his natural tactfulness made him pretend that he hadn't.

A moment later, Zach slowed the pickup and turned onto a smaller road. A few minutes more, and the pave-ment wore out; the road turned to dirt. They bumped along, skirting ruts for a while.

Then Zach pulled to the shoulder next to a barbwire fence that stretched on in both directions as far as the eye could see.

Zach turned off the engine. In the quiet, the wind

outside seemed to rise up louder and bump itself even harder against the truck. Zach gestured toward the snow-patched sweep of land beyond the fence. "This is Rising Sun land, as far as you can see."

The Rising Sun Cattle Company belonged to the Bravos, to Zach and Nate and their third cousin, Cash.

Cash. Tess thought the name, registered the inevitable ache it caused, and pushed it from her mind.

She smiled at the man behind the wheel. Of the three Bravo cousins who owned the Rising Sun, Zach was the one who lived there and worked the place full-time. A born rancher, everyone said of him. And from what Tess had seen in the past two years, everyone was right.

Zach pointed toward a stand of cottonwoods several hundred yards away. "Would you walk out there with me?"

Tess nodded, feeling formal and stiff—and a little bit scared. "Yes. Certainly."

They got out of the pickup. The wind, sharp and chill after the warmth of the cab, tore at Tess's jacket and tried to whip her hair out from under her wool hat. She hunched down into her jacket and stuck her gloved hands into her pockets.

Zach held the wires apart, so she could slide through the fence. She gave him a warm nod in thanks and eased through the space he'd made for her, taking care not to snag her clothes on the sharp barbs. Then, together but not touching, they slogged out to the bare cottonwoods, which clustered around a swiftly running stream—Crystal Creek, the stream was called, if Tess remembered right. It twisted and tumbled its way across a good portion of the Rising Sun Ranch.

"It's a pretty spot in summer," Zach said when they reached creekside. He sounded a little bewildered.

She hastened to let him know she found no fault with the place he had chosen. "It's just fine, Zach." But in truth, it looked barren and drab, the ground half-frozen and muddy. The trees, still leafless this time of year, reminded her of weather-bleached bones.

Zach's strong shoulders lifted in a shrug. "It'll have to do."

She could hear the nervousness in his tone and knew just how he felt. Even though this was a practical matter, it was still a big step. She assured him once more, "It'll do just fine."

They shared a smile. The wind blew strands of her hair across her mouth. She caught them and eased them back under the edge of her hat.

He seemed to shake himself. "Here." Between them crouched a big, round boulder. He bent and brushed it off. "Sit down."

"Thank you." She perched on the boulder. It was an extremely cold seat; it made her bottom ache. But she didn't get up. It had been so thoughtful of him to offer it to her and to brush it off and all. Tess believed that thoughtfulness should always be appreciated.

Zach coughed. "Tess, I..." His courage seemed to fail him.

She sat up straighter, willing him to be able to go on. "Yes?"

He coughed again, into his gloved fist. Then, at last, he made the words come. "I suppose you have a pretty good idea what this is about. It's a practical offer from a practical man. I need someone to keep the house and to keep me and the hands fed. Someone who knows the loneliness and plain day-to-day drudgery of life on

a ranch.'' A ghost of a grin came and went on his face.
''And someone just crazy enough to want that kind of
life for herself.''

She stared at him, thinking of the South Dakota
ranch that had been her childhood home. Zach was
right. It hadn't been an easy life. But it had been a life
she'd loved, a life she'd only left to follow her husband. She had believed at the time that she could always go back.

Oh, what a foolish girl she had been.

Zach hitched a booted foot up on the side of the
boulder where she sat, looked down at the frozen
ground by his other boot—and then up into her eyes.
''Do you know what I'm getting at here, Tess?''

Her heart had set up a terrible clatter. It sounded like
thunder in her ears. She'd never imagined that she
would be such a bundle of nerves about this. ''I...I
think so.''

He took his boot off the boulder, slid his hat off his
head and rolled the brim nervously in his two hands.
''Tess, I'm asking you to marry me.''

In spite of the gentle way he said those words, they
came at her stronger and sharper than the Wyoming
wind. She found she couldn't sit still, so she shot to
her feet, walked in a circle, and then sat back down.
''I see.''

He frowned, fiddled with his hat brim a little more,
then stuck the hat back on his head. ''I thought you
knew. I thought marriage was where we were headed.''

''Well, yes. I...I did know. And we've talked of
marriage, of what we both wanted from marriage,
haven't we? Often.''

''But you seem surprised.''

She gulped. ''No, really. I'm not.''

"Tess. You should see your face."

She blinked, shook her head. "No, I'm not surprised. I mean, I *am* surprised, but not about you proposing. I mean... Oh, I don't know...." She made herself stop babbling, took a moment to breathe deeply, to try to find some shred of composure somewhere in her agitated mind and heart.

Silently, as she breathed carefully in and out, she reminded herself of what mattered: that Zach Bravo offered her the life she longed for. That she liked Zach. And that the two of them sought the same things. They were both honorable people who would work hard to build a good future together. Zach Bravo would make a fine husband. He was a man who would always take care of his own, a man she would be able to count on.

And to a widowed single mother with minimal wage-earning skills, a man she could count on sounded pretty darn good.

Still...

"Tess?"

She closed her eyes. "Just...give me a minute, okay?"

"All right."

She rose again from the freezing rock, and turned away from Zach, to look westward toward the rugged peaks of the mountains. Somewhere behind her, from the other side of the creek, faintly, she heard a mournful cry, as of a dove, a sad, cooing sound.

And she couldn't stop herself; she saw Cash's face. She saw him grinning that warm, teasing grin of his.

Her heart seemed to get small and tight inside her chest. He was so splendid: golden-haired, blue-eyed Cash. Zach's cousin. And the one who had always come through for her and Jobeth when all hope was gone.

Cash had been her dead husband's buddy since high school. And Cash Bravo never deserted a friend.

Tess could almost feel the touch of his hand now, pressing money she hated to take but couldn't afford to refuse into her palm. Over and over, though he must have known he was only throwing good money after bad, he had bankrolled her husband's crazy wildcatting schemes. All it ever took was a phone call—and Cash would come.

When Josh died, Cash was there to help her through the funeral. And to offer her and Jobeth a new start, in Medicine Creek, living with Edna, who had been ill at the time and needed someone to care for her.

Cash was her friend and her hero. And she loved him with all of her heart.

Tess held her face up to the biting wind and closed her eyes again, tightly, as she ticked off the hard facts.

Cash Bravo was happily married and deeply in love with his wife, Abby—who was Edna's daughter, and who considered Tess her friend. Cash had no idea of Tess's feelings for him—and he never would. It was her guilty secret, a secret she would carry to her grave.

A secret that would never hurt Zach. Because Zach wasn't asking for her heart. He'd made that clear from the first. Zach wanted a loyal wife and a life's partner, a suitable mother for any children they might have. Tess could be those things for him. There was no reason he would ever have to know of the hidden, pointless yearnings of her stubborn heart.

From somewhere within the wind that blew around her, Tess could almost hear a sad voice chiding, *If he's to be your husband, he deserves the truth.*

Tess ignored the voice. She would tell no one of her love for Cash. No one. Ever.

"Tess?"

She turned back to Zach and gave him a wobbly smile.

He asked, "Are you worried about Jobeth?"

Her smile grew brighter. The answer to that question was easy. "I'm not worried in the least. Jobeth is crazy about you."

Strangely Jobeth was enough like Zach that she could have been his natural daughter. She had light brown hair like his, and eyes of a similar shade. But more than looks, she had a temperament like Zach's: even and serious, cautious in a touching and tender way. Jobeth had always looked at her own father with wariness. She'd shied away from Josh's loud voice and pulled into herself when he grabbed her for a hug. Yet she reached out to Zach, she followed him around. She lived for visits to the ranch, where she loved nothing more than to go out with Zach in the morning and come home at noon, grinning and covered with mud, to announce proudly that she'd helped pull a calf from a ditch or been chased by a bad-tempered bull.

"She's a fine girl," Zach said. "Marry me, and I will treat her as my own—if she'll let me."

Tess wrinkled her nose at him. "She'll let you. And you know she will." An extra hard gust of wind hit her, cutting right through her heavy jacket like an icy knife. Tess wrapped her arms around herself and shivered.

Zach watched her shiver and felt like a fool for dragging her out here. It had seemed the right thing, the fitting thing to do: to bring her out on the land to make his proposal. But now they were here, he could see that a warm living room with a cheery fire blazing in the grate would have been a wiser choice.

She cupped her gloved hands over her red nose and blew on them, warming her face a bit with her own breath. The harsh wind pulled wisps of her curly dark hair from under her hat and blew them wildly around her face.

Zach wanted to reach out and put his arms around her, to protect her from the cold. But he restrained the urge to shield her with his body. That was something a lover would do.

And love was not the issue here. They both knew that. They'd discussed what they each wanted from a life's partner often and at length.

Both of them had married once for what they had thought was love; and both were determined they wouldn't make that mistake the second time around.

This time, Zach had chosen a woman purely for compatibility. Tess had been born to ranching people and she loved the ranching life. He'd learned the hard way that a woman's love of his chosen life mattered a lot more than any passion she might feel toward him.

There was one more subject to tackle before he asked for her answer. "We should probably talk about Starr, too."

Tess nodded and dropped her hands away from her face. "Oh, yes. Your daughter. She's...?"

"Sixteen," he supplied flatly, wanting to get the information out, to get this talk of his lost, messed-up child behind them. "She lives in San Diego, with her mother. She used to come and stay with me in the summertime. But the past few years..." He didn't know how to finish, so he just shook his head.

Sympathy and understanding made Tess's fine dark eyes look even softer than usual. "I'm sorry."

Zach took off his hat again, hit it against his thigh and then eased it back on once more. "It's how it goes sometimes. Over the years, with the distance between us and the...hostility between her mother and me, well, somehow I lost Starr. She's like a stranger to me now. But I just wanted to be sure you understood that she's still my responsibility. I send her mother regular support checks. And it's always possible she could turn up one of these days. If that happened..."

Tess finished his sentence for him, with much more assurance than he could have mustered. "...we would welcome her, for a visit, or to live with us, whichever it turned out to be. And I sincerely hope to meet her soon."

Zach quelled the urge to mutter, Not damn likely and you'd be sorry if you did. Instead he asked the big question, directly this time. "Will you have me as your husband, Tess?"

After a long and agonizing silence, she gave him the words he sought.

"Yes, Zach. I will."

Chapter Two

During the drive back to Medicine Creek Tess asked, "What about Angie?"

Zach shot her a quick look. "Didn't I tell you? She's leaving a week from Monday. Going to live with a daughter in Denver."

Angie Iberlin was Zach's current cook and housekeeper, the latest in a long line of them in the past couple of years. For over two decades, Edna had handled the job. But her illness had forced her to quit and she'd decided not to return. Zach hadn't had much luck in trying to replace her.

Tess hid a smile. Now she understood what had finally pushed Zach into popping the question. He would rather take a chance on marriage again than to try to find another housekeeper. That was okay with Tess. She didn't care what had inspired him to take the big step. He had done it; that was good enough.

When they got to the house, they found Edna waiting for them.

"Did you have a nice ride? *Brr.* It's so cold out today. Come in, come in." She took their coats and hats and gloves and hung them on the rack by the door, then she herded them into the kitchen. "Coffee?"

Tess took the older woman by the shoulders and aimed her at the table. "Sit down. I'll get it."

"It's made. Fresh. I knew that when you came home, you'd probably want—"

Zach laughed. "Edna, sit down."

Edna dropped to the chair and looked from Zach to Tess and back again. "I...I had the strangest feeling, while you were gone. I thought that maybe..." Her voice trailed off on an expectant note.

Tess got the cups from the cupboard and the little cream pitcher, too. "You thought that maybe *what?*"

"Oh, you know. I know you know."

Zach laughed. "You know we know *what?*"

Edna pursed her mouth. "Zacharius Bravo, don't tease me. You know I hate to be teased."

Zach gave in. "All right. The truth is, I proposed."

Edna let out a glad cry. "I knew it. I knew it." She turned to look at Tess. "And?"

Tess filled the cream pitcher. "I accepted."

Edna put her hand to her heart. "Oh. I can hardly believe it. When? When will it be?"

With Angie leaving, Tess knew Zach would want the wedding soon. She shot him a questioning look.

"This coming Saturday?" he suggested. "At the county courthouse?"

"Sounds fine with me."

"And we'll have a party after," Edna announced. "Out at the ranch. Oh, there's so much to do...."

Jobeth came in a few minutes later. At the sight of Zach, her face lit up. "You're still here. Are we going out to the ranch?"

Tess answered for Zach. "Not today." She watched the excitement fade from Jobeth's eyes. "But sit down. We want to talk to you."

As soon as she heard the news, Jobeth was beaming again. "We'll live at the ranch, won't we? Forever and ever. When can we move in, Zach? When can we go?"

"Right after the wedding. How's that?"

With shining eyes, Jobeth declared that right after the wedding would be just fine with her.

Tess worked full-time at a gift shop, Amestoy's Treasure Trove, over on Main Street. First thing Monday, Tess told her employer, Carmen Amestoy, that she was marrying Zach Bravo and that Friday would be her last day.

Carmen threw up her plump hands and exclaimed, "Oh, no! How will I get along without you?" And then she went on, in that way she had of never waiting for the answer to a question. "Well, it's not exactly tourist season yet. And things have been slow as molasses in January flowing uphill. So I guess I'll manage somehow. And it's about time Zach Bravo proposed. I want you to be happy. You will be, won't you? And please don't be a stranger. All the customers will miss you. Am I invited to the wedding? Well, of course, I am."

"Carmen, we're only going to the courthouse, over in Buffalo."

"The party after, then. I'll come to that. It'll be at Cash and Abby's, am I right?"

Tess shook her head. "Well, no. It'll be—"

"If not at Cash and Abby's, then out at the Rising Sun."

"Yes. At the ranch. But it's only going to be a small—"

"Whatever. I'll come."

"Of course, if you'd like to."

"I suppose you'll want to shorten your hours a little, for the rest of the week, in order to get everything ready."

"As a matter of fact—"

"All right, all right. Consider yourself part-time."

"Thanks."

"Now, where are you going for your honeymoon? I think, this time of year, someplace tropical would be—"

"We're not."

"*What?* That's insane. Zach Bravo's got plenty of money. He can certainly afford to leave his precious cows for a week or two and take his new bride someplace she'll always remember."

"Carmen, we can't spare the time to go on any honeymoon."

Carmen looked crestfallen. "But...you're newlyweds."

"We have a ranch to run."

The older woman muttered something about ranchers and the total lack of romance in their souls. Then she spoke briskly, "All right, all right. If you don't want a honeymoon, that's your business. Who am I to tell you how to run your life? Who am I to point out that a man and a woman should have a little time, just for the two of them, when they first start out? I'm only Carmen. Your boss, part-time, until Friday...."

"Oh, Carmen..."

"No, no. It's all right. It *is* your life, after all. What will you wear to be married in? I know. You'll wear the dress you love. Come right this way."

Carmen kept a small clothing section in the rear of the shop. She led Tess there and made her try on the lavender silk dress with the peplum waist that Tess had been coveting from the day it came in.

"I know you love it," Carmen said. "And I know you couldn't afford it. But now you don't have to. Because I'm giving it to you. As a wedding present."

"Oh, no, Carmen, I couldn't—"

"Don't argue with me. I'm your boss. Until Friday, anyway. That dress was made for you. No one else will have it. And you will not pay a cent for it. Now here, try it on...."

Tess tried to keep saying no, but Carmen was determined and Tess did want the dress. In the end, she accepted the gift—and spent money she shouldn't have spent on a satiny nightgown and lacy negligee in almost the same shade as the dress.

"Just be happy," Carmen sniffed. "That's all I ask. Now, don't stand around. Check that shipment of hurricane lamps. See that none of them are broken. Can you do that? Of course you can. You're a gem and I don't know how I'll get along without you...."

Tess spent Monday and Tuesday nights packing up for the move. She and Jobeth didn't have a lot, but still, getting everything ready to go took time.

On Wednesday, Jobeth turned eight. They had talked the week before about inviting a few of her school friends over for cake and party games. But with all the excitement about the wedding, Tess had dropped the ball. The party just wasn't going to happen.

"I'm so sorry, honey," she told Jobeth that morning.

Jobeth looked puzzled. "Why be sorry? Zach's coming tonight, with a stock trailer to move our stuff, isn't he?"

"Yes. And instead of celebrating your special day, we'll be moving our things."

"But, Mom, we'll go out to the ranch! I'll see Tick and Tack. And Bozo." Tick and Tack were her favorite barn cats. And Bozo was a bum calf, orphaned during a big blizzard a few weeks before, a calf that Jobeth already thought of as her own. "*That's* the way to spend a birthday, if you ask me."

"Well," Tess said indulgently. "I'm glad you're not *too* disappointed."

"Mom. How could I be disappointed? We're going to the *ranch.*" And with that, she slung her pack onto her shoulder and headed out for school.

Zach arrived with the stock trailer, as promised, at a little after four. They had everything loaded within an hour. Naturally Jobeth begged to ride with Zach. So Tess followed behind them in her ancient 4X4 Tercel. She had a gift for Jobeth on the seat beside her. She planned to present it to her daughter during dinner—which she had prepared herself and put in plastic containers, all ready to heat and serve. Angie Iberlin, Zach's soon-to-be-ex-housekeeper, was a neat and polite person. She kept things tidy. But her cooking left a lot to be desired. With Tess bringing the meal, she could be sure they would eat well. Earlier that afternoon, she'd called Angie and told her not to worry about fixing dinner for them.

When they pulled into the yard at the ranch, Tess looked out the windshield at the two-story ranch house and just couldn't help feeling a little proprietary. The wood siding on the house had been painted a soft dove gray. Tess liked the color, but had noticed during other visits that the paint had started to fade and peel in a few places. She would have to do something about that—after the weather warmed, of course, after she got her garden going and whipped the interior of the house into reasonable shape.

Zach pulled the trailer around back. Tess followed where he led.

They found the house empty, as expected. By now, Angie would have gone on over to the foreman's cottage across the yard, where she stayed when she wasn't engaged in her housekeeping duties. The three cowhands who worked alongside Zach lived in individual house trailers not far from Angie's cottage. Angie would serve them their meals in the trailers.

By six, the stock trailer was empty. Tess's things waited in the big master bedroom. And Jobeth had carried hers to the room Zach had chosen for her. Zach began lugging the rest—a few pieces of furniture and some kitchen equipment—down to the big basement, where Tess could deal with it later.

In the master suite, Tess discovered that Zach had cleared out one side of the walk-in closet. Half of the huge double bureau was likewise empty, ready for Tess's clothes. As she hung her new nightgown and negligee in the closet, Tess couldn't help thinking that in just a few days, she and Zach would be sharing more than a closet and a bureau in that room. She blushed at the thought, and felt grateful that no one was there to see.

It would be awkward, she was certain, to make love when they didn't have that kind of feeling for each other. But she wanted more children so very much. She had always wanted more little ones to raise, though she'd taken great care never to get pregnant again during her marriage to Josh. They'd had too much trouble getting by as it was.

But now, with Zach, things would be different. Zach knew how she felt about children and he had agreed that having more would be fine with him. So after they married on Saturday, they would sleep together, in the big four-poster bed with its pineapple finials. And if God was kind, soon enough there would be a new Bravo baby for Tess to love.

Tess hung her few good dresses on hangers and filled three of the bureau drawers. The rest of her wardrobe she left in boxes, which she pushed into the closet on the side Zach had cleared for her. She would put it all away properly after the wedding.

She had just gathered up the empty boxes to carry downstairs when she thought she heard a car pull up out in the yard. The big windows of the master bedroom faced the front of the house, so she drew back the curtain and looked out. Down below, Cash's Cadillac gleamed in the gathering twilight.

Tess's heart leapt in guilty joy at the thought of seeing him—of sharing a few friendly words, of watching him smile. Dropping the empty boxes to worry about later, she flew to the mirror over the bureau and smoothed her hair. Then she hurried from the room.

She found Edna waiting at the foot of the stairs, holding a layer cake on a silver plate. Tess could make out the words, Much Happiness—Tess and Zach written in blue icing on top.

"Surprise!" Edna exclaimed. Then she grinned. "We're here to make a party. An engagement and birthday party. We've brought food. And two cakes.

One for the birthday girl. And this one—'' she lifted the cake she held higher ''— for you and Zach.''

"But...I brought our dinner," Tess explained idiotically.

Cash, who stood a few feet behind Edna, laughed his deep laugh and held out the second cake. "The more food the better, especially if you cooked it, Tess."

Thrilled at the sight of him, warmed by the sound of his voice, Tess beamed at him in pure adoration—but only for an instant. She quickly caught herself. She blinked and looked away—and right into Zach's eyes as he came up the basement stairs across from where she stood.

Tess's stomach lurched. For a second that seemed to stretch on into forever, time stopped.

Tess thought, He knows. He saw. It's all over now.

Then Zach asked in a perfectly normal tone of voice, "What's going on?"

"A party," Tess said faintly. She forced a light laugh. "They're giving us a party."

Just then, they heard voices in the front hall.

"That will be Nate and Meggie," Edna said.

"And the baby?" Tess asked, always excited at the prospect of a little one to hold—and right then eager to focus on anything else but what Zach might or might not have seen. "Are they bringing the baby?"

Edna nodded. "Let's go have a look at him. And then we must help Abigail. She's bringing in the rest of the food."

Ten minutes later, Edna had commandeered the formal dining room and bidden Angie to come back across the yard and help her with the table. The men and Jobeth had wandered out to the barn to have a look at a Black Angus bull that Zach had just bought. The younger women, Meggie, Abby and Tess, had moved into the great room with the new baby and Abby's toddler, Tyler Ross.

Meggie and Abby sat on the big sofa. Tess sat across from the Bravo wives in an easy chair, with tiny Jason James cradled in her arms. Tyler Ross, standing on his own two pudgy legs, clutched the side of her chair and gazed up at her through eyes as blue as his father's.

"Bay-bee," Tyler Ross said with great care.

"Yes," Tess replied dreamily, reveling in the sweet, warm weight of the bundle in her arms. "Baby. A big, handsome, incredible baby boy."

Over on the couch, Abby chuckled.

Tess looked up and caught the other two women sharing a glance. "What?" she demanded.

Abby brushed a hank of blond hair out of her eyes and spoke with affection. "It's just you. You're such a...*woman.* Put a baby in your arms and give you a menu to plan and you're in hog heaven."

Tess pursed her mouth. "And this is bad?"

Meggie, who had circles under her eyes as a testament to her new motherhood—and a soft smile on her face as proof that things really were going well with Nate—spoke up. "No, it's not bad. It's terrific. *You're* terrific. And we're so relieved Zach has finally snapped you up."

"I'll second that." Abby laughed. "Though of course, I knew from the first that you and Zach were meant for each other."

Tess tried not to think of blond hair and sky blue eyes. "You did?"

Abby nodded, looking smug. "On my wedding night, after all the guests went home and Cash and I were finally alone, I predicted that Nate would marry Meggie. And that Zach would get hitched up with you. Cash said I was nuts, that Zach would never marry again and Nate would never marry at all. But who'll have the last laugh here?''

Tess smiled and gently rocked the baby in her arms. ''You, Abby. Definitely you.''

Abby pushed her hair out of her eyes again. ''You bet I will.''

Tess went on smiling. She cared deeply for Abby. And she knew that Abby cared for her. Over the past two years, since Tess had come to Medicine Creek, they'd been through some scary times together. And when Abby and Cash had hit a rocky patch in their marriage, Tess had gone right to Abby and urged her to work things out. For Tess, there had been no thought of doing otherwise. She had known from the first time she saw them together that Abby and Cash were born to be man and wife.

Abby leaned forward on the couch. ''What is going through that mind of yours?''

Tess only kept smiling and rocking the baby. ''Nothing. Nothing at all.''

Right then, Edna appeared in the door to the hall that led to the kitchen. ''Tess, there is simply too much food. I'm going to have to put what you brought in the refrigerator. Angie can heat it up for tomorrow. Is that all right?''

''That's fine.''

Edna looked at her daughter. ''Angie and I could use a little help around here.''

Tess shifted the precious bundle in her arms. ''Let me—''

''No,'' Edna said firmly. ''You will sit there in that

chair and relax for once. You're always waiting on us. Tonight, it's our turn.''

Abby laughed. "As much as I hate to agree with my mother, she's right. Stay there. I think I can manage to put the food into serving bowls and carry the bowls to the table.''

"Just as long as you don't actually have to *cook* anything,'' Tess teased. Abby had little skill in the kitchen—and was darn proud of it.

"Don't worry,'' Abby promised. "If she tries to make me do anything resembling actual food preparation, I'll run out the back door—for everybody's sake.''

"Come on, Abigail, don't dawdle,'' said Edna, turning back toward the kitchen and the food waiting there.

Alone with the little ones, Meggie and Tess talked mostly of mundane things, of the weather, which should be warming to true spring very soon, and of Tess's various plans for getting the house in order.

At one point, Tess couldn't resist remarking softly, "It's good to see you and Nate looking so happy.''

Meggie colored a little. "He's the only one I've ever loved. And he's finally realized he loves me, too.'' She reached for her nephew, Tyler Ross, who had toddled over to drool on her leg. He went into her arms and she pulled him up to perch on her lap.

"You'll be working the Double-K together, I take it?'' Tess asked. The Double-K was Meggie's ranch.

"Yes,'' Meggie said. Tyler Ross had started squirming. She set him on the floor and handed him a rubber ring to chew on. "We'll be working together.'' She looked up and met Tess's eyes. "From now on.'' Her tired face seemed to glow with pure happiness.

Tess felt glad for her. And just a little bit jealous,

too. Meggie and Nate were like Abby and Cash: a man and a woman perfectly suited to each other, who also happened to be deeply and passionately in love.

Tess knew that she and Zach were well suited. But as for the rest...

Well suited is fine, she told herself firmly. Well suited is a lot more than you ever dared to hope you would get.

She was no longer some dreamy-eyed teenager. She knew now that the world could be a cruel, unforgiving place, that a person had to work hard—and grab her chance when it came.

She also knew that passionate love was a luxury, one that rarely came in the same package with a good and dependable man. A fortunate few, like Abby and Meggie, might find everything rolled into one. But for people like Tess, a productive life and a solid partnership would just have to do.

Right then, Abby appeared from the central hall. "Somebody go get the men and Jobeth. They have to wash up. My mother, the drill sergeant, says we're sitting down to dinner in ten minutes."

"I'll go." Tess rose from the chair and gave the baby to Meggie.

Outside, it was a clear night with only a mild wind. Tess left the house through the rear door off the enclosed back porch, and started across the backyard to the barn and sheds. But the night beguiled her. For a moment, she paused and looked up at the pale stars that would grow brighter as the night deepened. The air smelled sweet, of new grass with just a hint of cedar blown down from the distant mountains. Oh, yes, it was spring, all right.

She heard a sound, and turned to find that little black-baldy calf, Bozo, ambling toward her. He came right up to her and nuzzled her fingers.

"Sorry, boy. No milk here," she told him.

The little bum figured it out himself after a few seconds, and trotted off on his spindly legs. She smiled, watching him, thinking that she'd have to insist he stayed fenced once she got going on her garden. He was a bandit already; she could tell by the way he'd tried to suck from her fingers, a survivor who would steal milk from any cow who stood still long enough. Tess respected survivors; she considered herself one. But Bozo wouldn't get a chance to devour the tender leaves of her bedding plants if she had anything to say about it.

She started toward the outbuildings again, but she didn't get more than a step or two before the men appeared around the side of one of the sheds. They saw her standing there and they stopped for a moment, three tall, proud figures against the night.

They moved toward her with their long strides again. As they approached, Zach asked, "What is it, Tess?"

Through the darkness, Tess tried to read the secrets behind his eyes. *What did you see?* she wondered silently. *And what did it mean to you?* But his eyes gave nothing away.

Over the months they'd been seeing each other, she had thought that she'd grown to know him. Yet right then she felt as if she didn't know him at all. He was the stranger who would soon be her husband.

"Tess?" He was frowning at her.

She realized she hadn't answered his question. "Dinnertime. Where's Jobeth?"

He turned and called for her daughter. Jobeth appeared immediately, sliding out from between the big doors of the barn. "I'm here, Zach."

"You let Bozo out," he told her in that kind, careful voice of his. "Better get him back behind a fence."

"I will, Zach. Right away."

"And then come in and wash up. It's time for dinner."

"Okay." The child hurried after the calf.

Tess sighed when she looked at what Edna had wrought, at the ivory lace tablecloth, the gleaming china and silver, the snowy linen napkins, all set off so perfectly by the soft glow of candlelight. "Oh, Edna, it's beautiful."

Edna went to one end of the table and pulled out the chair there. With great formality, she instructed, "You will sit here." She gestured at the other end. "And Zacharius will sit there."

Tess remained standing. Edna always took the hostess's seat at any formal meal. Tess knew how much that seat meant to her. "Oh, Edna. No…"

Edna pulled the chair out farther. "I mean it. You sit down. You sit down right here."

Tess obeyed, sliding into the seat of honor. She felt Edna's slim hand touch her shoulder lightly and she reached back long enough to give that hand a quick squeeze. Then she busied herself with sliding the silver filigree ring from her napkin and smoothing the napkin across her lap.

When she looked up, she found Zach watching her from down the table. She thought of that moment on the stairs and her heart kind of froze for an instant, then commenced beating too fast. He smiled. She smiled back, praying that she looked more composed than she felt, wondering if his smile was a *real* smile, thinking that his eyes looked a little bit cold.

She picked up her water glass and drank from it. As she set the glass down, she told herself to quit worrying. It must be okay, with Zach. If he had seen anything in that look she'd given Cash, he wouldn't be smiling at her.

Would he?

Abby appeared then, bearing a huge rack of lamb. Everyone *oohed* and *ahhed* over it.

"Don't worry," she assured them all, laughing. "I didn't cook it. It'll taste just as good as it looks."

It turned out that Abby's housekeeper, Mrs. Helm, had prepared the feast. Everyone agreed that it was *almost* as good as something Tess might have done.

Cash had provided several bottles of excellent wine. The toasting went on long after most of the food had been eaten. Through the meal, Tess took great care never to look too long in Cash's direction. And when she thought Zach didn't notice, she watched him a lot. By the time dessert was served, she had succeeded in convincing herself that Zach had noticed nothing. Everything was just as it had always been. Her secret remained hers alone.

As Edna carried Jobeth's cake to the table, Cash produced a pile of presents to go with the one Tess had brought. Tess felt the usual flush of adoring thankfulness toward him. He was so generous, so thoughtful, so kind.

But this time, she kept her guard up. Her expression remained composed and her smile was no more than appropriately grateful.

Jobeth made a wish and blew out her candles. Then she opened her gifts.

Next came the engagement cake. And more toasts. It was near nine before Meggie and Nate insisted they just had to go. Everyone trooped outside to say goodbye. Then Edna kept Cash and Abby there an extra half hour, getting the plates scraped and stacked so that Angie wouldn't have too big a job the next morning.

Finally Tess and Zach stood together on the porch, waving, as Cash and his family piled into the Cadillac.

As soon as the big car drove away, Tess turned to Zach. "It's almost ten. We should get going, too."

He said nothing.

She pulled her sweater closer around her and folded her arms across her waist. "Zach?" Her pulse picked up, as the guilt and worry she'd managed to push to the deeper recesses of her mind came popping to the surface once again. "Is something wrong?" The dangerous question escaped her of its own accord.

Zach's brows drew together. Hardly daring to breathe, cursing herself for a thousand kinds of fool for asking a question to which an answer would most likely bring disaster, Tess waited for him to speak.

But he didn't speak. Instead, very gently, he put out a hand.

Wary, not knowing what he meant to do, she almost jerked back.

But then she stopped herself. He would be her husband. She shouldn't shy away from his touch.

His hand slid under her hair, to wrap around her nape. His skin felt rough—and warm. She gasped a little, in surprise. It was crazy, but now she thought about it, she couldn't remember ever having felt his touch before.

Was that possible? They would marry in three

days—yet this was the first time he had laid a hand on her. How could that be so?

Really, he must have taken her arm now and then, grasped her hand in greeting or in aid.

Yet she could not remember any of those casual contacts. Surely they had occurred. So why couldn't she recall a one of them?

Somewhere out in the night, an owl asked, "Who? Who?"

Tess started to turn her head toward the sound.

"No. Don't," Zach whispered softly.

She blinked and met his unreadable eyes, trying to appear calm and relaxed, praying that he couldn't hear the rapid pounding of her heart.

His rough thumb moved. It caressed the pulse point at the side of her throat.

And she realized that whether he heard it or not, he did know. Oh, yes. He knew how fast her heart raced. He could feel it, right under his hand.

Gently, relentlessly, he pulled her closer. She didn't fully believe that he would kiss her until his lips met hers.

Chapter Three

At first, Tess kept her arms wrapped protectively around herself, so that her body hardly touched Zach's.

But the distance she maintained didn't seem to bother him. He kissed her sweetly. Slowly. Tenderly. He didn't try to pull her closer.

Tess closed her eyes. She found she liked the scent of him, a healthy scent of soap and clean skin and leather. He tasted faintly of coffee, which Edna had served with dessert. After a moment, she stopped clutching her middle and dared to reach up, to put her hands on his shoulders. They were lean and hard under her fingers, the shoulders of a man who used his body in his work.

He let go of her nape and slid both hands to her waist, grasping firmly, stepping a fraction closer, brushing himself against her, but just barely. It felt nice. It felt as if his body was kind of whispering to hers.

She heard herself sigh.

And then he lifted his head and put her carefully away from him.

She let her eyelids flutter open. The night seemed so still. In the light of the porch lamp, she could see him quite clearly. She stared up at his craggy, serious face—and couldn't think of a thing to say.

She felt stunned. As tender as the kiss had been, there was no mistaking its intent. It was a kiss a man gives a woman. The kind of kiss Tess had only shared with one other man in her life—her husband, Josh.

Hardly knowing she would do it, she reached up and touched her lips. It seemed she could still feel the kiss there, so warm and sweet. So full of the promise of what was to come.

He smiled, just a little.

And she smiled back. She was glad he had kissed her, glad to learn that she could enjoy kissing him. Maybe when they got to the big bed with the pineapple finials, it wouldn't be so terribly difficult, after all.

"Come on," he said, taking her hand.

They went back inside to find Jobeth snoozing on the sofa in the great room.

Tess perched beside her and tenderly stroked the brown hair back from her forehead. "Honey, wake up. Time to go home."

Mumbling and groaning, Jobeth sat up and stretched. "Oh. Do we *have* to?"

Tess nodded. "Yes, we do. And right now."

A few minutes later, Zach stood in the back drive-way watching the taillights of Tess's battered little car as it disappeared around the front, headed for the gate and the highway beyond. He heard the car's tired engine revving as Tess turned onto the road. Moments later, the sound had faded to nothing.

He was alone with the night.

He started for the house, but then a nighthawk called from somewhere nearby. Turning that way, he saw the shadowy outline of the bird as it dived through the dark after some luckless insect.

Zach changed his mind about going in. Right then he would feel trapped in the house. He turned and headed for the horse pasture instead.

At the split-rail fence, he whistled. Ladybird, his favorite mare, came trotting over.

He stroked the blaze on her forehead and blew in her nostrils. "Sorry, sweetheart," he whispered, when she nuzzled his palm. "No carrots tonight."

She gave him a little snort and allowed a few more strokes before she turned and took off. Leaning on the fence, he watched her go, then ended up staring off blindly across the dark pasture toward the mountains and the quarter moon that hung low in the sky.

He kept thinking of Tess. Picturing her face, remembering her expression just after he'd kissed her. She'd looked so sweet and pretty and surprised, putting her hand to her mouth, as if his kiss still lingered there.

She had liked that kiss. And her expression had told him as clearly as any words that she hadn't expected to like it.

Probably, he shouldn't have kissed her. Not tonight, anyway.

Maybe not ever...

Zach turned and braced the heel of a boot on the bottom rail of the fence. He stared at the house his grandfather had built and tried to get used to what he'd probably suspected all along, but knew for certain as of tonight.

He had seen the look she'd given Cash. And now he had to face the truth: Like nearly every other female for miles around, his wife-to-be was totally gone on his big-spending, blue-eyed cousin.

Zach tipped his head back toward the sky and looked at the stars as thick and shiny as glitter-glue overhead. He knew damn well that, whatever Tess felt, nothing would come of it. Cash belonged to Abby, heart and soul. And, anyway, Zach had learned a lot about Tess in the months it had taken him to ask her to be his wife. He knew, with no doubt whatsoever, that she wasn't the kind who would let herself get too close to another woman's man, no matter what she felt for that man.

Ladybird wandered back over. She let out a playful snort and nudged Zach in the shoulder. He turned around and petted her some more, whispering to her softly, thinking that, from a practical standpoint, Tess DeMarley was exactly the wife he wanted. He'd look the rest of his life before he found another who suited his needs so well. And Jobeth. That kid was something. He wanted the chance to raise her to be the rancher she was meant to be.

Zach gave his horse a final pat and turned for the house.

He just had to *stay* practical about this, that was all. He didn't have to go and make a big deal out of some *feeling* that Tess was never going to act on, anyway. Maybe, in time, what she felt for Cash would fade by itself. Meanwhile, she could keep her little secret, and they could still have a good life.

They just had to take time. Take it slow.

Yes, she did appeal to him as a woman.

But he wasn't some breeding bull driven by urges he couldn't control. He'd been a virgin when he married his ex-wife, Leila, and except for that tough time right after she walked out on him, when he was looking for any way to dull the pain she'd left behind, he'd kept his equipment inside his pants. Unlike Cash, who'd been a real ladies' man, and Nate, who'd been just plain wild, Zach's sexual experience was pretty limited. He supposed he was old-fashioned. He felt that there were some things a man only ought to do with his wife. And that those things should not be taken lightly.

Zach's dog, Reggie, was waiting by the back door for him. Zach bent long enough to give him a scratch behind the ear and then went ahead and let him in to sleep on the back porch.

By the time he headed up the stairs, he knew what he would do. He would marry Tess on Saturday, just as they'd planned. And then he would give them both a little time to discover how close they really wanted their marriage to be.

"Great food, good music and fine company," Carmen Amestoy told Tess that Saturday evening, three hours after Tess and Zach had exchanged their wedding vows. The older woman talked with her usual animation as she balanced an overflowing plate on her plump knees. "Did you change your mind and decide to go on a honeymoon after all? Never mind, forget it. I can see by your face that you didn't." She popped an olive into her mouth and gave Tess's sleeve a pat. "You look lovely, honey. A beautiful bride—for the second time around. The dress is just right. Are you happy? I know you are. My loss is Zach's gain...."

Angie Iberlin appeared at Tess's shoulder. "Mrs. Bravo, your husband wants you. In the office."

It took Tess a moment to realize that "Mrs. Bravo" was herself. "Oh. Certainly." She smiled at the housekeeper. "Thank you, Angie." She turned to Carmen, who was already hard at work on that full plate. "Excuse me."

Carmen waved a plump hand and dug into her thick slice of Rising Sun prime rib.

Zach's office was on the first floor, off the dining room. Tess hurried there, slipping inside to find him at the big cherrywood desk, talking on the phone. He signaled her over, then put the mouthpiece under his chin.

"My folks," he whispered.

Tess herself had no family left to speak of. Her dad had died four years ago, and her mom had passed on just the previous December. But Zach's parents, Elaine and Austin, were still alive and well and living in New York City. They hadn't been able to get away on such short notice.

"It's nice of them to call," she said.

He held out the phone, his palm over the mouthpiece. "Tell them how much you wish they were here."

She took the phone and spoke with Zach's mother and then with his father. Each said how much they regretted not being there and how they wanted to meet her and would try to get out for a visit sometime soon.

"Thank you," Tess replied. "We'd love to see you—anytime." She said goodbye and hung up.

The phone started ringing again the second the handset hit the cradle.

It was one of Zach's two sisters, the one who lived in Philadelphia. She said the same things his parents had said, to Tess first and then to Zach.

When they hung up, he turned to her. "Let's dance."

She put her hand in his and he led her out through the dining room to the great room, where the big rug had been rolled back and the furniture pushed close to the walls. The three-piece band the caterer had brought was playing "It's Just a Matter of Time." Zach took her in his arms and they moved out on the floor.

A half an hour later, Zach's other sister called. Zach and Tess trooped back into the office to be congratulated some more. The second sister lived in some place called SoHo. Tess made polite noises and listened to the very East Coast sounding voice and wondered how in the world a cattleman like Zach could have come out of such a family.

Edna had told Tess months ago, "Zach's daddy, Austin, only wanted one thing from life—to get out of Wyoming and find someplace *civilized*. Zach was born in New York City. But then Austin made the mistake of letting him come to the ranch for a visit when he was ten. And Zacharius knew the minute he set foot on the Rising Sun that ranching would be his life. He convinced his father and mother to let him come to us three years later and he has pretty much been a fixture at the ranch ever since—except for that stint at Texas A&M after Leila left him. He was an AG major, of course. Even when his grandfather and his parents made him go to college, all he wanted to do was learn about how to raise better beef."

"She says she might come out for a visit real soon,"

Tess said when Zach hung up the phone from talking to Melinda, the sister from the place called SoHo.

Zach made a snorting noise. "When pigs fly. Melinda considers Wyoming the north end of nowhere. None of our restaurants are interesting enough, shopping opportunities are limited—and she might break a nail. Forget it." He pulled Tess back toward the great room, where he put his arms around her and led her out onto the floor again.

Tess closed her eyes and let herself enjoy dancing with him. She was a little scared about the night to come, but felt sure she would be able to get through it all right. He was a considerate man, after all. They would manage it, and in the morning they would be husband and wife in every way.

It was midnight when the last guest drove off. And another hour had passed before the caterer from Sheridan headed for the highway in her panel truck. Zach had settled up with the woman a while before. Still, out of politeness, Tess stood in the dark yard to watch the woman leave. Then she turned for the house.

Inside, she called quietly for Zach. When he didn't answer, she assumed he was either back in the office for some reason—or already upstairs in their bedroom.

Their bedroom. Her cheeks grew warm at the thought and a thousand fluttery things got loose inside her stomach.

She drew in a deep breath and headed for the stairs.

In the upper hall, she decided to peek in on Jobeth. Pausing outside her daughter's room, she slipped off her shoes and set them on the hall floor. Then, oh-so-quietly, she pushed open the door.

Across the room in the single bed, beneath the window that looked out on the side yard, Jobeth slept. She lay curled in a ball, her lips curved in a contented smile—despite the fact that she'd kicked the covers away and had to be just a little bit chilly. Careful not to disturb her slumber, Tess pulled up the blankets and tucked Jobeth in.

Jobeth snuggled down and muttered something that was almost a word, "Mmnph…" But she didn't open her eyes.

Very lightly, Tess smoothed the feathery bangs from Jobeth's forehead and brushed a kiss there. Then, for a few precious moments more, she stood staring down at her daughter, enjoying that wonderful feeling of lightness that sometimes came over her when she looked at Jobeth. She found herself thinking, Ah, yes. So many mistakes. But this one thing, my daughter. This one thing, I'm doing right…

Finally, when Tess knew she could no longer postpone the short walk down the hall to the master bedroom, she turned and tiptoed out the way she had come. Pausing only to scoop up her shoes from the floor, she went to join her new husband.

He wasn't there.

She felt a moment of sheer relief. His absence meant she could put off what would happen just a little while longer. But then she started wondering where he might be. And then she understood.

He was being thoughtful, giving her a few minutes alone, to prepare herself, before he joined her. With those pesky fluttery things kicking up a ruckus in her stomach again, she began unbuttoning her buttons and slipping out of her beautiful lavender dress.

A few moments later, feeling totally naked though she still wore her slip and all her underwear, she padded to the closet to hang up the dress and collect her waiting nightwear. She was already reaching for a hanger before her mind actually registered what her eyes had seen. Zach's side was bare.

Chapter Four

Moving automatically, Tess hung up her dress. Then,
still in her slip, she left the big closet and strode to the
double bureau. Slowly, one at a time, she pulled open
each drawer on Zach's side.

Every one of them was empty.

Tess stood staring down at all that emptiness and
wondered what in the world was going on.

With a small cry of dismay, she shoved a drawer
shut. Then, quickly, in succession, she closed the other
ones.

It didn't help. She could still see all that emptiness
in her mind.

Numbly she turned and walked to the bed. Once
there, she clutched one of the posts for a minute, and
then she dropped to a sitting position on the quilted
maroon counterpane.

Several moments passed, during which she sat

hunched over, rubbing her bare arms, confused...and afraid.

Zach did not plan to sleep in the same room with her. Some time after Wednesday night—when he might or might not have seen a thoughtless look she had turned Cash's way—he had decided, without bothering to mention it to her, that he would move to another room.

He must be very angry with her.

But he hadn't seemed angry. He'd been kind and attentive all afternoon and evening. He'd danced with her several times. And they had laughed together often. She remembered clearly how easily he had joked with her, about his family, about his sister from SoHo, who wouldn't come to visit because she might break a nail.

Could he have only pretended to be kind and to joke? Could this be some cruel revenge? Had he seen the look she'd given Cash, correctly read its meaning—and decided to show her exactly what he thought of a woman who could love one man and still agree to wed another?

She shook her head. She couldn't believe that of Zach. He wasn't a vengeful man. If he'd seen by her face that she loved Cash, he'd have confronted her. Or simply called off the marriage.

But whatever he might have done, he wouldn't do something so cruel as this, removing his things from the room they were supposed to have shared—and letting her find out she'd sleep alone when she went to don her wedding negligee.

Yet he *had* done it.

Tess lifted her head and straightened her shoulders. She had to face him, to find out what he meant by this. He might imagine that she wouldn't dare confront him, because of her shame and guilt at the secrets in her heart.

And to a degree, he would be right. She did feel great shame. And crushing guilt. She didn't *want* to love Abby's husband. Every day she prayed that the love she felt would fade away. But still, she did love Cash.

And she clung tightly to her belief that no one else knew.

Yet she *had* to confront Zach. If she didn't confront him, they had no marriage. She might as well put everything back in boxes and head for Edna's—not that Edna would take her in, once she learned why it hadn't worked out between her and Zach.

Determined, Tess rose to her feet. She returned to the closet and found her old blue plaid robe in one of the boxes she'd yet to unpack. She pulled it on over her slip and belted it firmly at the waist. Next, she went to the big, battered suitcase that waited by the door to the hall. It contained the rest of the clothes she'd brought from Edna's just today. She found her house slippers and slid them on. Finally she turned to the mirror over the bureau and met her own eyes.

She didn't like what she saw there: worry, misery and guilt. Too much of her life had been wasted, living those emotions over and over again.

For nearly all of the rough years of her marriage to Josh, worry had dogged her. She worried that the landlord would catch her on the stairs and demand the rent today—or else. She worried that Josh would drink away his paycheck before he brought it home. Worried that he would quit his job before he ever got a paycheck. And once he'd quit, she worried that he'd never work again. Josh's dreams had always been so much bigger than anything he ever actually managed to accomplish. And it depressed him, to have to go to work every day at some dead-end job when he wanted to be out drilling the oil well that would make him a millionaire.

He had been a good-hearted man. But still, whenever Tess thought of him, she remembered the constant, nagging worry she had known during most of her life with him.

She had done what she could to combat the worry. She had worked, whenever she could find something. But with Jobeth so young, it could never be more than part-time. And it was always for minimum wage. And she never had a chance to get anywhere on any job she found, because they inevitably packed up and moved on to someplace that Josh swore would be better.

Wherever they moved, the worry went with them.

The worry had caused the misery, the hopelessness, the growing certainty that they would never get out of the financial hole they had dug for themselves. The only bright spots had been the wonder of having a daughter like Jobeth—and the light of hope that Cash inspired, with his generosity to them.

Three or four years ago, Tess had realized that she didn't love her husband—and she did love Cash.

That had brought the guilt.

Finally, Josh had died. Roughnecking on an oil rig was dangerous work and an accident had killed him. The guilt had gone on, after Josh's death. Because her feelings for Cash hadn't faded.

Still, in the good life she and Jobeth had lived with Edna, much of the worry and all of the misery had slowly melted away.

Until tonight—when she had walked into that half-empty closet and looked in those accusing, vacant bureau drawers. Tonight, the misery and the worry had come crowding back on her, joining her guilt to make the whole world seem bleak and without hope.

She would not live that way. In spite of the mistakes she'd made the first time around, Tess *believed* in marriage. She believed that a man and a woman could and should form a lasting commitment, raise children, help each other through the tough times and share the joys as well.

But she *could* build a life on her own, just herself and Jobeth, if she had to. She was determined that this marriage would be different, *better* than the other. Or she would end it now.

Tess turned away from the face in the mirror and headed for the door.

The minute he saw her, standing in the arch that led to the stairway, wearing a threadbare plaid robe and a look of grim determination, Zach knew he'd handled the situation all wrong.

She said his name, softly, hopelessly. "Zach."

They stared at each other for what seemed like a bleak eternity.

"You moved your things," she said at last, her voice breaking a little. She dragged in a breath and finished, "from the bedroom."

He went to the liquor cabinet, which stood against the wall opposite the windows and the sofa. There, he got out a little false courage, pausing, once he had the bottle in his hand, to hold it up toward her.

"No, thank you," she said.

He shrugged, poured himself a shot and knocked it

back. It burned a fortifying trail of liquid heat into his belly. He set the glass down.

She stuck her hands into her pockets and spoke with great effort. "You never said anything about us not sharing a room. When I brought my things on Wednesday, your clothes were there. But now, the closet and the bureau, it's all half empty and I just don't—"

He put up a hand and she fell silent. "Look," he said. "Sit down."

She hovered there in the arch to the central hall, biting her lip, looking at him through wounded eyes.

He felt like some kind of heartless wife abuser. "Please, Tess. Come here and sit down."

She hesitated a moment more and then, at last, she padded across the giant rag rug his grandmother had braided herself forty years before. She went to the sofa, where she perched on the edge like some terrified little bird ready to take flight at the slightest hint of a threat.

She folded her hands on her knees and then she looked at him good and long. "You changed your clothes," she said at last. "That's where you were, when I came in from outside a while ago."

"Right." He gave a quick glance down at his Wranglers and flannel shirt, shrugging as he had when she refused the drink he'd offered. "The party's over. I wanted to get comfortable. So what?"

"You know what. You came back down here after I went up. Since everyone left, you've been purposely avoiding me, purposely going wherever I'm not."

He closed his eyes, ran a hand down his face. "I didn't avoid you, Tess. Not really. I didn't think on it much. I was restless, that's all."

"You didn't think on it much?" She looked even more wounded, if that was possible, than before.

"Tess. Listen."

"I am. I'm listening. You tell me. Whatever it is, you just tell me. Okay?"

"Okay."

"Good."

"Okay."

She waited.

He made himself try to explain. "I, well, I've been alone for a number of years now. As a man, I mean. A single man."

She pressed her lips together, nodded, gave a little cough. "Okay."

He stumbled on. "I, well, I can see I should have thought about you, about how you would take it, when you saw I moved my things. But I didn't. And I do apologize."

She looked down, smoothed her robe over her knees. Then she looked at him again, in rising hope that made her eyes look misty and her skin all sweetly pink. "You apologize?"

"I do. And I hope you'll forgive a man for not knowing how to behave."

She looked away, uncertain, embarrassed.

Damn. She was pretty. A pretty woman. He liked the soft way she could smile and the exotic way her brown eyes tilted up at the corners. He recalled, for some crazy reason, the day that Cash married Abby. Tess had been there, newly widowed, hiding behind the punch bowl, waiting on the guests, trying, it had seemed to him, to make herself invisible.

Abby hadn't allowed that. She'd grabbed him and grabbed Tess and ordered them to dance with each other. He'd done it willingly, smiling at the way the widow DeMarley blushed and got all flustered, thinking that she looked like the type of woman who would make a man the perfect wife—*if* a man was willing to take another chance on marriage.

Which he hadn't been. Not right then, anyway.

But then, in the months that followed, he'd seen her in action. Tasted the food she cooked. Watched the way, whenever she came to the ranch with Edna for a visit, everything suddenly ran smoothly. Mouthwatering meals appeared right on time. There was cleanliness where there had been a layer of grime, order in place of chaos.

She was frowning again. He realized she wanted a little extra reassurance.

"Tess. I am sorry. Please won't you accept my apology?"

Her brow smoothed out. She lifted a hand and put her fingers to her lips, the way she had done the night he'd kissed her. But this time it wasn't because of a kiss. It was a way to gather courage. To ask a question whose answer she probably didn't really want to hear.

She got the question out on a shaky breath. "Why? Why did you change your mind, about…the room? The bed…" She winced and then swallowed. "You know what I mean."

He considered his answer, pondered going straight for the throat, hitting her with something like, I saw that look you gave Cash the other night. And I believe I'll take a pass on making love with a woman who just might be pretending that I'm someone else.

But he couldn't bring himself to do that. She was a good woman, a fine mother—and she had been a loyal wife to that damn dreaming fool, Josh DeMarley. Looking into her sweet, scared face, Zach understood exactly how her love for Cash must shame her. It went against all she held true and right. He didn't doubt that her only consolation in the matter was the belief that no one else knew her guilty secret.

He just couldn't tell her that *he* did know. He couldn't do that to her.

Or to himself.

He was a man, after all. And a man had a right to a little damn pride. He didn't need to hear how his new bride loved his cousin. Not now. Probably not ever.

Time. That was what they needed. Time to work side by side. Time to forge a real bond. Time to let what she felt for Cash fade by itself.

What makes you think it's going to fade? a cynical voice in his mind demanded.

"Zach?"

He realized he'd made her wait way too long for his answer.

"Zach, please." She stood and dared to approach him, her slippers making no sound as she tiptoed across his grandmother's rug. "You have to tell me why." She stopped three feet from him, close enough that he imagined he could smell that light, flowery perfume she wore, close enough that the soft luster of her skin taunted him, close enough that he couldn't help thinking, Why the hell not just take her to bed? She *is* my wife. As of today, the state of Wyoming says we are joined....

Grimly he kept to his original intention. "I think we need time, Tess."

She stared at him. Then she asked doubtfully, "Is that all? Just...time?"

He nodded. "I got to thinking how we really don't know each other all that well. That we could take our time about this. There's no law that says we have to jump into bed together." As he spoke, he watched her face. She wanted to believe him. Desperately. If time was the only issue, that would mean her secret was safe.

And then she frowned again.

"What?" he demanded.

Haltingly she argued, "But Zach, we *are* married. And it really does seem like married people ought to, um, be intimate. That they should—"

To cut off that dangerous line of reasoning, he invaded her space a little, stepping forward, eliminating what was left of the distance between them. "They should what?"

She stared up at him, her eyes widening. "I..."

"What?"

"I just..."

He'd accomplished his goal: to make her lose her train of thought—but at a certain cost to his own self-control. This close, the scent of her was all around him. He breathed it in, looking at her mouth, thinking of what he *wasn't* going to do. Very slowly, because he wanted to and he had the right and he wasn't going to do anything more, he lifted a lock of her hair and rubbed it between his thumb and forefinger.

She struggled to continue her debate. "I, um, told you I wanted children. I thought...you agreed about that."

"I have a child." The strands of hair felt like silk. Warm silk. "And so do you."

Her breasts rose as she sucked in a big breath. "Well, I know. But I mean, um..."

He knew exactly what she meant. "Children we made together?"

"Yes."

He let go of the silky strands and made himself step back. "If it works out that way, sure."

"Well, but..."

"What?"

"Well, Zach, as I just said, I *do* want more children. I know I told you that more than once. But maybe you didn't really understand. I've always wanted at least three or four."

He had understood. Perfectly. Again, he suggested, "Give it time."

She stared at him. "Time," she repeated. Her eyes seemed to ask How much time? But she didn't get the question out, which was fine with him. He had no answer to it, anyway.

He decided he could use one more drink. He turned back to the liquor cabinet.

Tess watched him pour the second drink.

She was trying to tell herself that maybe what he suggested wasn't such a terrible idea. They could play it by ear, day to day. She could earn his trust. And a place at his side. And the children she longed for, as well.

And maybe, with time, it wouldn't feel quite so... awkward to imagine the two of them together, in the bed upstairs. Maybe he had grasped the situation better than she had. Maybe he was right. And in the meantime, as they grew to know each other better, she would work hard as mistress of the Rising Sun. She would take care of him and the hands, just as she'd promised. She would have her garden and paint the house. She would be his wife in every way but one.

It wasn't so terrible. She could handle it, she was sure.

And clearly, this had nothing to do with Cash. Nothing at all. Her fears on that score had been groundless.

Zach knocked back the second shot and set down the glass. "Well?"

What else was there to say? Except, "All right, Zach. We'll give it time."

Chapter Five

The next morning, Tess was up well before anyone else. She set right to work whipping up a big breakfast, pausing only to murmur, "Good morning" to Zach when he went out into the predawn chill to tend the animals in the barn and sheds. Angie appeared from the foreman's cottage soon after Zach went out. Tess greeted her and told her to go on back to bed. "I've got things under control, don't you worry."

Angie yawned. "Do I look worried? I'll be out of here tomorrow, in case Mr. Bravo didn't tell you."

Tess paused in her work to smile at the housekeeper. "He did tell me. And we'll miss you."

Angie made a scoffing sound, as a wide grin broke out on her usually serious face. "Right. You cook circles around me, you're neat as a pin and I've never seen a better organizer. I'm not needed here anymore, and we both know it."

Tess tactfully moved the subject along. "Zach did give you a reference, didn't he?"

Angie shrugged. "He did. And a nice one, too. Not that I'll need it. I'm through taking care of other people's houses. Going to spend the rest of my days with my daughter and her family. And if you meant what you said, I believe I will steal another few winks."

"I meant it. You go on."

Moments later, Jobeth came bouncing down the stairs. "Where's Zach? Did he go out already?"

Tess pointed with a spatula toward the barn. Jobeth bounced on out the door. She and Zach came back inside fifteen minutes later, just as Tess was taking the second sheet of biscuits from the oven.

"Jobeth, go ring that bell for the hands," Tess instructed. "And then get washed up. Quick time."

Jobeth flew out to the front porch. The dinner bell clanged long and loud. A few minutes later, everyone but Angie was seated at the big pine table in the kitchen, passing mounds of biscuits and a huge bowl of gravy, helping themselves to orange juice and breakfast sausage.

Tess looked around the table and felt pretty good. Both Zach and Jobeth were packing it away. And the three hands had droopy eyes, hair still wet from a morning wake-up dunking—and full mouths.

"This is great, Mrs. Bravo," said Beau Tisdale, the youngest of the three. He sandwiched the praise between one huge bite and the next.

Zach had told Tess about Beau and his family. Not that long ago, the Tisdales had run their own ranch in the shadow of the Big Horns. But in the end, low beef prices and high bank loans had done them in. Much of the Tisdale land belonged to the Bravos now. And their youngest son worked for Zach.

It wasn't the first time Tess had heard a story like that. In fact, she had pretty much lived that story herself. When her father died, her own family's ranch had been badly in debt. Her mother had asked Tess and Josh to come home and help her out. Josh had been in the middle of one of his big schemes, one that he swore would come in a gusher. He said they just couldn't afford to go back then—and anyway, he wasn't about to waste another minute of his life knee-deep in cow manure.

Tess's mother hadn't been equipped to run the place herself. Soon enough, she had been forced to sell everything to pay off the debts.

So Tess felt a certain compassion for Beau. She gave him a smile. "I'm pleased you enjoy the food."

He grinned back at her. "I surely do."

"I want to head out to the North Pasture," Zach said flatly. "So eat up."

Beau turned his attention back to his plate. Confused, Tess looked down the table at Zach. "You won't be going to church with me and Jobeth?"

For months now, Zach had shown up at Edna's door every Sunday, smelling of soap and aftershave, wearing his best boots, ready to squire her off to the little white-trimmed brick building over on Antelope Street where the Reverend Applegate presided. Until just now, Tess had assumed that today would be the same. However, after last night, she supposed she'd better not assume anything when it came to her new husband.

"I'll be back by nine and ready to go by nine-thirty."

His tone was a little cold and his expression stern.

Still, he *would* go. A smile broke across her face. "Oh, good."

And something happened. His stern look melted. He smiled at her. And she smiled back. For one lovely moment, there was only the two of them, a warm feeling passing back and forth, each to the other.

And then Lolly Franzen, one of the other two hands, who sat to Beau's right, let out a small noise that just might have been a snicker. Tess blinked and looked at the man, who obviously thought he'd just witnessed some romantic interchange between smitten newlyweds.

. Zach was looking stern again. "Got a problem, Loll?"

"No, boss. No problem. Nosirree, no way."

"Good. Finish up. Work's waiting."

Lolly dug into the rest of his meal as if his life depended on how fast he could get it down.

The men were gone in ten minutes. Jobeth sulked a little at not being allowed to go with them, but once they'd cleaned up the table, Tess sent her out to hand-feed Bozo and that perked her up. When she came back in, a full hour and a half later, Tess ordered her upstairs to wash and put on one of her two nice dresses.

The phone rang as Tess was bustling around the bedroom, getting herself ready to go. It was Edna.

"Well," the older woman said cheerfully. "And how is Mrs. Bravo this morning?" The simple question had a thousand shades of meaning, most of them concerning the wedding night just past.

Tess had no intention of letting Edna know she'd spent her wedding night alone. She infused her voice with warmth and happiness. "Mrs. Bravo is just fine."

"I am so glad."

"And how are you?"

Edna sighed. "Well. Maybe just a *little* lonely. I'm used to having you to talk to—and Jobeth running in and out."

Tess caught sight of herself in the bureau mirror and smiled at her own reflection. She had figured this would probably happen. "You could come and stay here—for a while, or even indefinitely. You know that."

"Oh, no. Absolutely not. You have a right to your own life and I—"

"Edna. You are a part of my life. A big part. And Zach and Jobeth feel the same way." She thought, suddenly, of exactly what it would mean if Edna came to stay. She would surely find out that the new Mr. and Mrs. Bravo slept in separate beds.

Edna sighed again. "No. I couldn't. I'll be fine. I have my dream, don't I? This beautiful house that Cash bought me." Cash had given Edna the house during her illness, two years ago. "It's just that I'm a little down, getting used to the quiet around here without you and Jobeth. And I just called Abigail. She and Cash are taking off again—and my grandson, too, of course."

Cash made money in a variety of investments, from oil to real estate to computer software. If he heard of a good thing, he put money in it. And Abby, with her degree in finance from CU, was his business manager. They were forever packing up and heading for Reno or Cheyenne, to meet with Cash's wheeler-dealer friends. "Oh, well." More sighing. "I suppose I'll just be going over to church all on my own."

Tess took the hint. "We'll be there to pick you up."

She could actually *hear* Edna's grateful smile. "You're a dear."

"Be ready to go at ten-fifteen."

"You know I will."

At church, before and after the service, both Tess and Zach received endless congratulations and wishes for their long-lasting happiness. Tess smiled and said "Thank you" so many times, it began to seem to her as if the two words were nonsense sounds, without any real meaning at all. More than once, as she was saying those two words, she cast a quick glance at her husband. He was smiling and saying "Thank you," too. He seemed to be taking it all in stride. Really, no one in the world would have imagined anything at all wrong between him and his new bride.

Tess caught her thoughts up short. There *was* nothing wrong. They had agreed to take it slow, that was all. In their situation—not a love match but a practical pairing—taking it slow made perfect sense.

Or so she kept telling herself.

After church, Edna insisted they all come over to her place for lunch. She flitted around them, serving them, clearly excited over their newlywed state.

At last, Zach told her, "Settle down, Edna. All your fussing and fluttering will put me off my feed."

Edna put a hand to her throat. "Oh, I know. I'm terrible. But I can't help it. Seeing you two together. Seeing how *perfect* you are for each other, well, it does my heart good, that's all."

Tess felt a silly blush starting, moving up her neck toward her cheeks. She didn't realize she was staring at Zach until he turned and looked at her.

"We're very happy," he said, and he smiled.

Tess wondered how in the world he could hide his feelings so completely. In her mind's eye, she saw all those people at church, shaking her hand, hugging her, wishing her well. She felt like a complete phony. *Taking it slow* was just an excuse, and she knew it. Her husband didn't want her and her practical marriage was a total sham. She blinked and looked down at her plate.

"Mom?" Jobeth, always sensitive, asked in concern. "Are you crying?"

She wasn't, of course. She never cried. Not in years. She looked up and smiled. "I'm just fine."

Edna turned to Jobeth. "She's a bride, honey. It's a beautiful, magical, *emotional* time."

They got back to the ranch at a little after two. Zach took one of the pickups and drove out to the North Pasture again, this time letting Jobeth accompany him. They returned two hours later.

"We're branding tomorrow," Jobeth explained proudly as she set the table for dinner. "Way out in the North Pasture. Nate and Sonny will be there. Nate will handle the irons and Sonny will help in the crowding pen." Sonny Kane was Meggie's cousin. He and his wife and children lived and worked at the Double-K with Nate and Meggie. "Since this will be my first branding," Jobeth continued, "I'm gonna do the tallying. Zach says we have to be out by four in the morning, so—"

Tess knew a snow job when she heard one. "Jobeth. Stop."

Jobeth glanced up from her task, her eyes wide and innocent. "What?"

"Did Zach tell you that you could help with the branding tomorrow?"

Jobeth took a napkin, folded it with great care into a triangle and tucked it beside a plate. "Zach said that for a person's first time, she usually does the tallying."

"That was not my question, and you know it."

Jobeth looked down, up, sideways—anywhere but at her mother.

Tess said gently, "Tomorrow is a school day."

Jobeth groaned. "Mom!" She stretched out the word so it sounded as if it had several syllables in it. "We are ranchers now. Sometimes, when you're a rancher, you have to miss a little school."

Tess hid her smile. Jobeth had a point. As she grew older and acquired the thousand and one skills a true rancher needed, she would make herself invaluable. And she would be allowed to miss some school—all this assuming that Tess and Zach stayed married, of course, and that Jobeth got her chance to grow up here.

Jobeth was frowning. "Mom? What's the matter?"

"What? Nothing."

"We were talking. I was explaining to you how I have to miss school tomorrow and you just…stopped listening."

Tess pushed the nagging worry about her relationship with Zach out of her mind. "I apologize for woolgathering."

Jobeth pulled a face. *"Woolgathering?"*

"That's another word for not listening, for letting your mind wander."

"Oh."

"But whether I was woolgathering or not, you are not missing school. Not this time."

Jobeth moaned—and then fastened on the part of her mother's statement that she liked. "But later. When I know more. When Zach and the other guys can't get along without me. I just might have to miss some school then, right?"

Tess ran a finger down the center of her daughter's forehead, tracing the natural line where her bangs tended to part. "Yes. I imagine so."

Jobeth heaved a sigh. "It's better than nothing, I guess."

Zach went out again after dinner, and didn't return until after nine. Tess, in the great room with her gardening book open on her lap, heard the pickup drive in. He must have hung around the barn and sheds for a while, because it was a half an hour later when she heard him come through the back door.

Tess closed her book, marking her place with the scrap of paper on which she'd been scribbling possible garden layouts. From the sofa where she sat, she could see the central hall and the foot of the stairs. She waited, watching.

Sure enough, Zach appeared in his stocking feet, headed for the stairs.

"Zach?" She stood.

He stopped with one heavy wool sock on the first step, and looked at her through the arch that separated the two rooms. She moved toward him, carrying her book, and stopped inside the hall arch, about five feet from where he waited to see what she wanted.

She tried a smile. "Muddy boots, huh?"

He shrugged. "I left them by the back door."

"Best place for them."

"Yeah. I guess so." He waited, his hand on the banister, ready to get out of there as soon as she told him why she'd stopped him.

The stranger I married, she thought with more self-pity than she should have allowed herself.

But then he actually smiled and gestured at the book she held. "Planning your garden, huh?"

She returned his smile. "I should have done this in January or February. The planning, I mean. Well, I *did* plan in January. But for the garden at Edna's. And that was different. Smaller, for one thing. And then, the windbreak, with the fence and the surrounding houses and all, was so much more effective than I'm going to get here at the ranch...." She realized she was babbling and cut herself short. "Anyway, I'll work it out."

"I know you will." He looked at her for a long moment. It seemed a warm look. But how could she know for sure? Then he shook himself and glanced down at the mud that spattered his jeans and shirt. "I'm a mess. Gotta go." He started to move.

"Wait."

He stopped.

She rushed on, before he could leave her. "Tomorrow will be a branding day. Is that right?"

"You bet."

"In the North Pasture?"

"Right."

"I'm not sure where that is exactly. I wonder... could you draw me a map?"

He frowned. "A map."

"Could I get my Tercel out there, do you think? It's got four-wheel drive."

"Sure, you could. But I don't—"

"Then after I make certain Jobeth catches the bus, I thought I'd load up some food and come join you."

He said nothing for a moment. Then he told her gently, "You don't have to do that. If you'll just pack us up something we can take along, that would be more than—''

''Zach.''

''What?''

''I *want* to do it.''

He stared at her, looking wary and maybe a little hopeful, too.

For the first time since that brief, shared glance at the breakfast table that morning, she felt warmly toward him. ''Zach. You never know. I might even pitch in. I've been in on my share of brandings, in case I didn't mention it.''

He seemed bemused. ''Well.''

''Well, what?''

''All right. We can always use an extra hand.''

Since Sonny's wife, Farrah, had come along to do the tally of the calves they branded and to handle the vaccine gun, they let Tess work the crowding pen with Sonny and Lolly. It was the dirtiest, toughest job of the branding process, during which they not only branded the calves, but also vaccinated them and castrated the males. Between them, Tess and the others chased and shoved and wrestled the penned calves into the calf table, a special working chute that could be rotated sideways, laying the calf in position to take the brand.

Tess proved herself proficient at the job—and then, when they switched positions for a while, she got to take Beau Tisdale's place and hold a few hind legs. Hind leg holding could be quite challenging. You had to hold tight, or the one doing the castrating could get cut or kicked. And with all the stress the calves endured under the iron and the knife, they tended to be incontinent. So the hind leg holder got to hold tight—*and* dodge flying streams of manure at the same time.

Still, branding was its own kind of fun, with everybody working hard as a team to get the job done.

They took a beer break at nine. To them, after all, it was the middle of the day. And they stopped for lunch at eleven, with only about fifteen calves to go. Tess realized they were stopping for her sake, since she'd brought the food out there. They could have just finished up and ridden on home to eat.

But whether lunch out in the pasture was necessary or not, it was fun. Everyone said it made scrabbling around in the dust, manhandling cattle almost worth it, for a hot meal like this one.

"Where's Meggie?" Zach asked, between bites. "I can't believe she'd let a branding go by without at least showing up to see that we're doing things right."

"She's home," Nate said, somewhat grimly. "She was up half the night with Jace. I told her she was spending her day catching up on her rest."

Farrah laughed. "You know how she is. She kept insisting I should stay with Jace and Davy." Davy was Farrah's three-year-old. "Meggie swore she'd take it easy, if Nate would just let her come, that she'd handle the tally and the vaccine guns."

Nate added, "I said she'd take it easy, all right. In bed. Period."

Farrah chuckled some more. "Nate practically had to tie her up to get her to change her mind."

"Tell her we missed her," Zach said.

Nate snorted. "As if that'll make her feel better. You know how she is. She's not going to be happy until she's back on that bay mare of hers, running the rest of us ragged."

Zach was grinning. "Well, we've got several more days of this, between your place and the Rising Sun. You think you'll keep her home through all of it?"

"I'll keep her home," Nate said darkly. "If I have to lock her in the bedroom."

Zach kept on grinning. "She'll climb out the window."

Nate was not amused. "Don't say it. Don't even think it."

Tess watched the interplay between the cousins, thinking how handsome Zach really was—in a rugged, no-frills sort of way, with his sun-toughened skin, strong cheekbones and hawklike nose.

But then again, maybe he did have a frill or two. If you looked close. He'd taken off his hat and his thick brown hair shone golden in the sun. And there was a dimple in his chin—a cleft, Tess mentally corrected herself. Men didn't have dimples, they had clefts. And then he had such a nice mouth, as all the Bravos did. Kind of full for a man. A mouth that made a woman think about kissing it.

Strange. All those months they'd been seeing each other, she'd never thought much about Zach's mouth, let alone about *kissing* Zach's mouth. Truth to tell, because of her feelings for Cash, she'd tried *not* to think about kissing Zach. It had just been something she knew would happen someday, if things kept on between them. She supposed she had looked at it as kind of a necessity. He would kiss her. They would make love. And maybe they'd have children—which she saw as the real goal.

But now, the goal was…postponed, to say the least. And here she was, watching him razz his cousin out in the North Pasture, and thinking about kissing him just for kissing's sake alone.

As if he could feel her watching, Zach started to turn. Tess saw his head move and managed to look out across the pasture before he actually caught her looking. And then she felt foolish, for turning away. She might have simply smiled at him.

And he might have smiled in return.

Tess decided to head back to the house before the others. She had some washing to do, and she wanted to get the dinner under way. And then, once Jobeth got home, they would drive into town to the garden shop, where Tess would buy the equipment she needed, along with a few flats of seedlings to get things going.

The others were already back at the corral when she got in the car to go, but Zach broke away and came running over. He skimmed off his hat and leaned in her window. "Hey. That was good. Thanks."

She couldn't help teasing, "The food, you mean—or the great hand I've got with a hind leg?"

"Both." He gripped the ledge of her open window and looked down at the Tercel. "How did you manage to get out here in this thing?"

"It was iffy going, now and then. But I made it, as you can see."

His brows drew together. "How long have you had this car?"

She laughed. "Too long."

He stepped back. "Well. The rest of us should be home soon."

"Fine. After Jobeth gets back from school, I'm going to town to the garden shop. So if you get in later than you expect, and I'm not there—"

"I understand. You'll need money."

She hadn't even thought of that. She had a little money of her own and had expected to spend some of it. "No, really, I—"

"In my room. There's a money clip. Top dresser drawer, in back. You'll find several hundred in cash there, for emergencies. Hell. I didn't even think about this. You have any credit cards?"

She shook her head, the old shame rising. She'd been Josh DeMarley's wife, after all. They'd lived hand-to-mouth, paycheck to paycheck. Once, during the first years of their marriage, they'd had a few credit cards. Josh had run them past their limits and then, about five years ago, he'd ended up declaring bankruptcy. After that, no credit card company in the world would have been crazy enough to extend credit to them.

Zach went on, "I'll see about getting you a card on my Visa account, at least. And in the next week or two, we'll have to go in to the bank and put you on my checking account."

"I have a checking account."

He smiled. "Don't get prickly. We never discussed this money thing, and we should have. You need to get on my account. So you have access to my money, when you need it."

"I do not need access to your money."

"Tess." He said her name gently, carefully. "You're my wife."

She almost said it: No, I'm not. Not really. Not completely your wife. But somehow she held it back. She slid her hands up to twelve and then back out to ten and two on the steering wheel. "I want to get going. And you're needed at the corral."

He glanced over his shoulder. "Right." He backed

away from the door. "Well, see you at the house, then."

"Yes. All right."

He stuck his hat back on his head and then stood there, watching, as she shifted into gear and drove off.

Once he was behind her, she caught sight of him in her rearview mirror. He was still standing there, staring after her. Finally he seemed to shake himself. He turned to join the others.

Tess focused front again, and came up to the gate. She stopped to open it, her mind stuck, for some silly reason, on the image of him standing there, staring after her.

He had seemed a little lost, a little unsure.

As if he didn't quite know how to deal with her.

And he probably didn't, she thought, as she got back in the car, drove through the gate, and then stopped again to close it behind her. Really, for all their caution with each other, they had kind of jumped into the marriage when it finally came down to it. Between the proposal and the wedding there had been exactly six days. They'd never even taken the time to talk about things like money. Or sex.

Or secrets.

She slid behind the wheel again and shifted into gear. The car started down the rutted dirt road.

Secrets. Well, Zach was never going to know her secrets. And that would make it all the harder for them to become close.

Theirs was simply not your average marriage— which had to be just as confusing for him as it was for her.

Too often, he did seem like a stranger. Still, for all the distance he kept between them, he was a good man who treated her with courtesy and kindness. With the exception of his body, he seemed willing to share all he had with her.

And yet, in spite of his courtesy and kindness, she had felt bitterness toward him. She'd felt it more than once in the brief time since their wedding night. Bitterness was a danger. Bitterness could kill any chance of closeness before it could even be born. She knew *that* from hard experience.

Tess bumped over a particularly bad rut. The car bottomed out, the pan scratching along the ridge of the rut, the transmission letting out an ugly groaning sound as she shifted down from second to first. She willed the old car to keep going, to please just get her home.

And she vowed, no more bitterness. No more bad attitudes. No more self-pity. She would be Zach's wife on his terms, and have some faith that they'd truly find their way to each other in the end.

Chapter Six

Three days later, in the afternoon, Zach took Tess into town. They visited the bank and his insurance agent. Before they went home, Tess and Zach had a joint checking account, Tess had signed on for a Visa card and she and Jobeth had full health coverage.

Then, when Saturday rolled around, Tess found herself in the cab of the blue Chevy pickup on the way to Sheridan with her daughter and her husband. When they came back that evening, Zach and Jobeth were still in the pickup—but Tess was driving a brand-new Suburban, a roomy 4X4 station wagon on a pickup chassis.

"Oh, Zach, it's too much," Tess had protested when she saw the Suburban for the first time, so big and shiny and new on display in the car lot. "You can't—"

He cut her off in his firmest voice. "I can. And you need it. That Tercel was a great little car—at one time.

But for your purposes now it's too old, too small and way too close to the ground.''

When it came time to deal with all the paperwork, Zach wrote an enormous check, paying half in cash—to cut down on the interest, he said. After that, he signed loan forms for the balance. Then he handed the pen to Tess.

She stared at him, not understanding.

He pointed at the next form. ''So the registration will be in your name.''

She thought again of how much the car cost. ''Oh, that's not necessary. Truly, I—''

Zach took her hand and wrapped it around the pen. ''Sign. Right there on that line.''

His touch, so warm and rough and sure, shocked her to her toes. Since he touched her so seldom, each slightest physical contact had started to take on great importance.

''Sign, Tess.''

Rather numbly, she did.

After that, they went out to dinner. Then Tess drove her new Suburban back to the Rising Sun, loving the steady purr of the engine, smelling that incredible new-car smell, and swearing to herself that she would work her fingers to the bone to do what she could in return for all that Zach had given her.

That night, after she put Jobeth to bed, Tess sat in the great room sewing patches onto the knees of a pair of Jobeth's jeans. Soon enough, she heard Zach come in through the back door from his final rounds of the barn and sheds. She knew his routine, and went on with her mending, hardly listening for the sound of his foot-falls. He might pause in the kitchen, to drink a glass of water at the sink. But after that, he would go straight for the stairs and head up to his room. He always did.

Or at least, in the week since their wedding, he always had.

But this time, he didn't turn for the stairs. Tess almost poked her finger with her needle when she realized he was headed her way. He stopped just outside the room where she sat. She kept her head bent over the mending, but still, she could feel him there, in the arch to the hall.

"Always busy."

She realized she'd been holding her breath and let it out slowly, so he wouldn't know. Then she looked up and met his eyes. They shared a smile. She held up her mending. "Jobeth. She swears she doesn't walk around on her knees, but you couldn't prove it by me."

He laughed, a warm, friendly sound. Her heart felt featherlight.

"Listen, I…" His sentence died without ever really getting started.

She wanted to urge him to fully enter the room, to sit down, to *talk* to her. But she didn't want to push, either. If he wanted to come in, he would.

He moved forward. One step. And then another, until he stood over her. "I wanted to talk to you a little about Jobeth."

She nodded, very casually, and kind of tipped her head toward the sofa, in an invitation that he could accept or reject without saying a word. He did neither. That is, he didn't sit. But he didn't leave, either.

He strode to the woodstove over by the interior wall, knelt, opened the side door and stirred the coals with the poker. Then he added a couple of logs from the wood box nearby. She watched him, admiring the strong breadth of his back and the way it tapered down to his narrow, hard waist.

When he had finished with the fire, he rose and turned to face her.

"What about Jobeth?" she asked, wondering all of a sudden if he had some kind of problem with her daughter's behavior.

He must have read her expression. "Relax. It's nothing wrong."

"Good. Then what?"

"Well…" He frowned, as if choosing his words with great care. "The truth is, she's been after me."

Tess stuck the needle in the cloth and set her mending in her lap. "After you? For what? To let her quit school and take up cowpunching full-time?"

He grinned. "Not quite."

"But almost."

"No, truly. It's something else."

"What?"

He put his hands into his back pockets, then immediately took them out and folded his arms over his chest.

"*What?*"

He finally got it out. "She wants her own horse."

Tess sat back in her chair, thinking that she should have known.

Zach raised a bronze eyebrow. "What do you think?"

Tess was thinking of the Suburban and what he had spent on it. And now this. He wanted to give her daughter a horse.

"Tess?"

She hedged, "Don't you think Jobeth's a little young?"

Zach came down firmly in Jobeth's behalf. "She's eight. Abby had her own horse at eight—or maybe even at seven, now I think about it."

"But Abby was born here at the ranch. Jobeth hasn't been riding that long."

"Tess, she's a fast learner. You know she is."

Tess had seen her daughter ride. And Zach was right. Jobeth was a natural horsewoman. Still, Tess felt that she and her daughter had taken way too much from him already. She felt a little guilty to consider taking even more. She wanted to draw the line somewhere—for a while, at least. Until she and Zach knew better where they stood with each other.

"Zach, you just can't keep *giving* us things."

"Sure, I can."

"But we can't possibly pay you back."

He frowned a little. "Wait a minute. You're my wife. Jobeth is my stepdaughter. What I have is yours."

She stared at him. The basic problem between them seemed to hang in the air, unsaid—the little problem of the separate beds they slept in, of the way they were always so formal with each other, of the way he avoided her most of the time. Of whether their marriage was really a marriage at all.

She considered the wisdom of going for broke. Of laying it all out there. Of saying again that she didn't feel they were truly married, since they were so careful and polite with each other, since they didn't even share a bed.

Of course, if she went for broke, she'd be taking the chance they'd end up talking about Cash.

She cringed at the thought of that.

No. They'd only been married a week, today. She'd

agreed to give it time. And she would. Whether that amounted to cowardice or wisdom, she had no idea.

Zach spoke again. "You work damn hard, Tess. Harder, even, than I expected you would. You're never idle. You're either cleaning or cooking or working in your garden. And at night, you sit in here, mending and planning what other projects to tackle, working some more."

His words pleased her, reinforced her decision to remain silent for now on the deeper issues. She admitted, smiling, "I like to work."

"And people get paid to work. Do you want a salary?"

"No. Of course not, I'm—"

He finished for her. "—my wife. And my wife gets the benefit of what I have. She gets decent insurance and a decent vehicle—to help her do her work more efficiently. Just like my stepdaughter gets a horse, when she's ready for one. I'm not a fool, Tess. I see the potential Jobeth has. She takes to life on the Rising Sun like a duck to a pond. She's a responsible girl. And she's ready for the responsibility of training her own horse."

Tess stared at him, so touched by what he'd just said that she couldn't come up with more arguments.

"Come on, Tess," Zach said when the silence stretched out too long.

She let out a breath, puffing her cheeks as she did it. "I suppose you've already picked out the horse?"

"Yeah. A nice chestnut gelding. Four years old, part Arabian. Green broke, but that's about all. Jobeth really would have to train him. I'd help her some, of course. And Tim said he'd keep an eye on her progress, as well." Tim Cally was the Rising Sun's third hand.

He'd been a Bravo employee for over three decades. An old man now, he could still spend a day in the saddle when the ranch needed him. But he took it a little easier than Beau and Lolly as a general rule, helping out around the barn and sheds, mending tack, repairing machinery and handling any animal doctoring that didn't require a real vet.

Tess still just wasn't sure. "How about if we wait another year? Until then, she can still ride that sweet, old mare you picked out for her."

Zach smoothed his hair back with his hand—and kept to the goal. "Tess. I believe she is ready. And the gelding's a good animal. Smart and quick, but no meanness. Horse-ornery, now and then. But you want them to have a little damn spirit."

Tess opened her mouth to voice more objections. But he looked so hopeful—hopeful for the sake of Jobeth.

His eyes coaxed. His words cajoled. "Come on, Tess. Give the kid a break."

Tess made a noise in her throat and picked up her mending again. She knew exactly what was going on here. If she said no now, then Jobeth would come after her next. And probably Tim, as well. She wouldn't have a moment's peace until she gave in.

And she did trust Zach's judgment when it came to Jobeth. He was watchful and protective of the child. He wouldn't let her come to harm.

He'd just...done so much already, for the two of them. In spite of his generous words about how hard she worked, Tess felt it would be impossible for her contribution to the marriage to ever equal his. And what if it just didn't work out between them in the end? Then Jobeth would have to give up the horse. How much worse would it be to give it up than never to have had it in the first place?

"That garden of yours is looking good," Zach said, pulling out all the stops.

She looked up at him, saw his coaxing smile—and couldn't resist playing along with his game to butter her up. "Tim put up the wire fence for me. And it took me forever to turn and till that ground. Lots of clay in it. Maybe I could open a little pottery shop in my spare time. Throw a few bowls and such."

He chuckled right on cue.

She bent her head and took a stitch, and then another, drawing the needle through the cloth with precision and care. Then she shot him a look from under her lashes. "I've put in corn as a windbreak. That should help some, and a hedgerow, too. And you know the beds had to be raised good and high. That was more work. But there's no other choice, with the gully-washers we get sometimes."

"You're right," he said. "No other choice."

"But it's coming along."

"I can't wait to taste the results."

She looked up, a more direct look than before. "I know what you're doing."

If he'd had his hat in his hand, he would have been twisting the brim. "She's ready, Tess."

At that moment, Tess felt almost tenderly toward him. She wished they were intimate, just to have the right to touch him. To rise from her chair and put her hand on his arm.

When she spoke, her voice came out a little husky. "You're good to her. So good. Her own father..." She looked down, took a stitch, wondered if she'd said too much.

"What?"

She met his eyes again.

He commanded, softly, "Say it."

She chose her words with great care. "They didn't…understand each other. He wanted to lasso the moon for her. But Jobeth, well, you just can't *dazzle* Jobeth. She didn't want the moon. More than once, he brought her home fancy dolls, dolls with beautiful painted faces, all dressed up in gorgeous clothes, dolls that cost a lot more than we could afford. She would say thank-you and she would really try to mean it. But all she wanted was for him to get us an apartment that allowed pets. So she could have a kitten, you know?"

He nodded. Then he asked, even more softly than before, "And what about you?"

She looked down at her mending, and then up at him. "Me?"

"Can you be…dazzled?"

She stared at him, her pulse all at once rocketing into high gear. What did he mean by *dazzled?* Did he mean something about Cash? If any man could be called a dazzler of women, that man would be Cash Bravo.

But then she breathed easier. Her heartbeat slowed. Zach had gone to school in Medicine Creek, after all. And so had Josh. Of course, Zach had to mean Josh.

Tess was aware of a deep sadness then. She thought of Josh that first time she'd seen him, the day he came to work at her father's ranch. She'd never seen a man so handsome, with those green eyes of his and that devilish smile. He'd had an aura about him. Something that seemed to make the air shimmer around him. An aura of risk. Of wildness. Of things of which her parents were not going to approve. She'd been just seventeen. And he had been almost thirty.

Zach prodded, "Well?"

She kept her head high and answered honestly. "Yes. I have been dazzled. Foolishly. Dazzled. But Jobeth isn't so easily fooled. All she wanted was a cat. And now she's got a whole barn full of cats. There's a furry critter everywhere she turns. And you..."

"I what?"

"You never come up on her fast. You take your time. You let her come to you. And you never tried to give her a doll. Oh, no. If you give her something, it's exactly what she wants."

He was silent. Then he said with a slight smile, "Like a horse."

She made a little humphing sound. "So. We're back to the point."

"Is that a yes?"

She tried to look her most severe. "Do I have a prayer of saying no and making it stick?"

"Well now, you're her mother and you're the one who—"

"Just answer the question, Zach."

He looked abashed. "No, ma'am. Probably not."

She knew she was beaten. Still, she said, "Give me a little time. To think it over."

"Well, sure." He frowned. "How much time would that be?"

"A few days?"

"All right, then. Three days."

For the next three days, Tess could feel the weight of her daughter's yearning. Nothing was said. Jobeth knew better. She had let Zach fight this battle for her, and she wouldn't step in herself unless it appeared that the prize was truly lost.

But Jobeth couldn't keep the hope from her eyes. Over and over, Tess would look up from the sink or the stove to find her daughter's gray-blue gaze on her.

Say yes, say yes, those eyes seemed to chant. Tess would smile and go on as if she noticed nothing. In the end, she knew she couldn't deny such desire. And in her heart, Tess did agreed with Zach: Jobeth was ready for her own horse.

Still, Tess wanted the time to change her mind. And she felt it only fitting that her daughter should wait and wonder a while. A big dream like this shouldn't come true too easily.

On the third night, the night when Tess was to give him the answer on the matter of Jobeth's first horse, Zach brought an armload of wood with him when he came in for the last time. He went straight through the kitchen and central hall to the great room, where he knew Tess would be sitting. He strode right to the wood box and dropped in the logs. Then he picked up the poker, opened the stove door and prodded the coals a bit. After that, he shoved in a log and shut the stove door.

He stood, turning to face Tess. Their eyes met.

He thought she looked really good, sitting there so quietly with her knitting. The light from the lamp at her side gave her hair a curried shine. She had an inner peace to her, a calmness inside herself that he'd always admired. So different than a lot of women.

Sometimes, lately, looking at Tess, Zach would find himself thinking of Leila, his first wife. Remembering. Comparing a little, maybe. Leila was a woman who never could sit still. You wouldn't have found her sitting in the great room knitting happily away in total silence, not in a thousand years.

He had loved Leila. The kind of love he'd thought would never die. It had seemed to him that she had cut his heart out and taken it with her when she left.

But that had been so long ago. And now, looking at Tess, he could hear his heart. Beating a little too fast right inside his own chest. Leila didn't have it, after all.

And the point was not to go losing it again.

Tess looked over those flying knitting needles and smiled. Zach gestured toward the blue wad of yarn that was gradually taking the shape of a tiny foot. "What's that?"

"Booties. For Jace. I'm going to make a little hat, as well. And a sweater. I made the same set for Tyler Ross and Meggie admired it, so I thought I'd make one for her baby, too." She set the knitting aside and folded her hands in her lap.

Zach was pretty sure he'd get the answer he wanted tonight, but he felt a little nervous anyway. If Tess did say no, he would have to back her up. He would have to face the disappointment in Jobeth's eyes. He didn't look forward to that. Probably he had too damn much pride when it came to Jobeth. Pride that he had never let her down. Pride that she had taken to him so completely, that she ran to do the tasks he set her, that she looked up to him as if he had all the answers to all the questions ever asked.

Once he had let himself imagine that Starr would be like Jobeth. But instead, she was down in San Diego, cutting school all the time, hanging out with troublemakers and generally driving her mother crazy.

Tess coughed politely into her hand.

Zach realized he was stalling and bestirred himself. "It's been three days. Since we talked about that horse."

"Yes. It has."

"Have you come to a decision?"

"I have." She looked so serious. For a moment, he feared the wrong answer was coming. But then he saw the smile that kept trying to pull on the corners of her mouth. "All right," she said at last. "Jobeth can have the horse."

It took him a moment to register her words—and his own relief.

She filled that moment with instructions. "She's to take it slow. And have supervision. Either you or Tim should be there when she starts to put him through his paces, because she'll need training herself."

"I promise," he said. "I'll be there."

She looked all soft. Her eyes had a happy shine to them. "I know you will. Thank you."

He felt about ten feet tall. At that moment, the whole world belonged to him and him alone. It was almost as good as when he'd taken her to get the Suburban.

His body stirred as he imagined himself moving forward, closing the distance between them, putting out his hand. She would lay hers in it. He would pull her up, out of the chair and into his arms, her soft, slim body molding all along his. He would lower his mouth to hers.

And when she returned his kiss, he would not know for sure whose face she saw when she closed her eyes...

He looked down at his boots. And then over at the big windows above the sofa. Night had fallen not too long ago; the windows showed only a dark reflection of the room. "You're welcome," he said, and turned for the stairs.

"Zach." Her voice stopped him just before he cleared the arch to the hall.

"Yeah?"

"Good night."

"Good night, Tess." He went on up the stairs to his solitary room.

Jobeth got her horse the next day after school. When Zach took her out to the pasture to catch him, her eyes were shining so bright, it almost hurt to look at her.

For the next three days, as far as Jobeth was concerned, nothing existed but that horse. She named him Callabash, just because she liked the sound of it. She got up in the morning before her mother or her stepfather to give him oats and carrots and she groomed him until Tim Cally swore she was going to wear the hide right off of him.

Bozo, newly branded and now formally a steer, stood in the small pasture on the other side of the barn, mooing forlornly in longing for the attention Jobeth no longer had time to lavish on him.

In the afternoon, with either Tim or Zach looking on, Jobeth worked with Callabash, leading him around the corral on a tether, later tacking him up slowly and carefully, requiring a little help to get the saddle on and all the straps cinched up good—and finally mounting him and riding him in a circle, getting him used to the feel of her on his back.

On Friday, Tess stood at the sink peeling potatoes and stealing glances out the window, where Jobeth rode Callabash at a smart trot around the corral. Both Zach and Tim hung on the fence, watching and calling out occasional instructions.

Grinning in satisfaction at the sight, Tess looked down at her work once more. When she looked up, a sheriff's office 4X4 came rolling into sight from around front. Zach jumped down from the fence. He waved at Jobeth, calling out something that caused the child to smile and wave back. Then Zach got into the 4X4 on the passenger side and the vehicle drove away.

Frowning, Tess wiped her hands on her apron and went out the back door. She crossed the yard to the corral where Callabash still trotted in a circle with Jobeth on his back.

Tim obligingly dropped off the fence when he saw the boss's wife coming toward him.

"What happened?" Tess asked the old man. "I saw the sheriff's car. Is something wrong?"

Tim swiped his hat off and shuffled his feet. "Well, ma'am. I reckon Zach saw somethin' that shouldn't have been there. Out near the Crazyman Draw, it was. He didn't like it, so he got someone from the sheriff's office out here to have a look, that's all."

"I don't understand. What did he see?"

"Tire tracks, ma'am. Looked like a pickup and a stock trailer. And dog tracks, too."

Tess didn't like the sound of that at all. "More rustling, is that it?"

Back at the end of February, eight bred heifers had been stolen from a pasture not far from the ranch buildings. The heifers would have started calving two weeks after the theft, so in effect, that was sixteen head of cattle gone, amounting to several thousand dollars on the hoof. The story had made the front page of the *Medicine Creek Clarion.* Folks in town had speculated about it for weeks afterward. But then the sheriff had found no leads on the culprits. The talk had died down. Zach hadn't mentioned anything about the theft in a while.

Tim said, "Well, we don't know that it's rustlers, ma'am. Zach just wants that detective to have a look."

Tess thanked the old man just as Jobeth called, "Mom, Mom, look!" She reined in the gelding. He stopped smooth and easy.

Tess waved. "Real good, honey. He's coming along just fine." She thanked the old man and went back inside.

Tess watched for Zach's return. He was gone about two hours. She managed to catch him alone for a moment just before dinnertime. "I saw you leave in the sheriff's car. Tim said there was some problem out by the Crazyman Draw."

Zach shook his head. "It's just tire tracks. And a bad feeling. Don't worry about it. The detective says he'll write a report—and dig up the pictures of the tracks from the incident in February for comparison."

"Did the tracks look the same?"

"I thought so."

"Oh, Zach…"

"It's probably nothing." The words didn't match the disquiet in his eyes.

The next day was Saturday. At breakfast, Zach said he thought both Jobeth and her new horse were ready for a little ride around the horse pasture. It was near noon when the big event occurred, so Tess came out to watch, thinking she'd call them in for lunch once Jobeth and Callabash had trotted around a while.

Jobeth rode out smiling, her head high. Callabash

looked pretty proud of himself, prancing a little, but not too much. And Jobeth seemed to have him under control.

But then, about halfway to the far fence, something spooked the gelding. He rose up, letting out a neigh of fright and pawed the air. Tess's heart seemed to freeze in her chest. But Jobeth kept her seat as the horse's hooves hit the ground.

Tess almost allowed herself to breathe. Then the horse reared once more, tossing his head. Jobeth slid backward, twisting as she fell. The horse raced away, leaving the child in a small heap on the hard ground.

Chapter Seven

Zach was already halfway there when Tess jumped the fence and started running, too. Tim followed close behind. Tess could hear the old man's heavy footfalls, though all her mind and heart were focused on the little lump that lay so still and defenseless on the ground.

And then the little lump moved. Tess heard a groan. Jobeth sat up. She blinked and looked around.

Zach reached her. He knelt beside her.

When Tess got to them, Jobeth was cradling her left arm, her dirt-streaked face way too pale. Her eyes locked with her mother's—and she immediately began defending her horse. "It's not Callabash's fault, Mom. There was a snake. I swear, there was a snake." She turned her wide, anxious eyes on Zach, who was already searching the rough pasture ground.

Zach rose, took a few steps, then knelt again. "Here it is." He held up a brown-spotted snake with six neat little rattle buttons at the end of its tail. The head had been crushed, no doubt by Callabash's heavy hooves.

A prairie rattler, Tess though. Not as deadly as a diamondback, or as the sidewinders that basked in the Arizona and New Mexico deserts—but deadly enough to make a child very sick at the least. Tess dropped to her haunches beside her daughter. "Honey, did it bite you?"

Jobeth gazed back at her mother in stark fear—but not for herself. "It didn't get me, I swear. But we've got to check Callabash, see if he—"

Tim Cally spoke from behind Tess. "I'll see to the horse." He started off across the pasture to the far corner, where the gelding had backed himself up near the fence and now regarded them all with a look of edgy disdain.

Zach dropped the snake and knelt beside Tess. Tess glanced over at him, all at once aware of him, of the steady grace of his lean body, of the inner calm that seemed to radiate from him. At that moment, she felt like glass, like something that shouldn't move too fast, or she might shatter into a thousand pointed, ugly shards. Gently she smoothed her daughter's hair. "What's the matter with your arm, honey?"

Jobeth held the arm closer, wincing as she did it. "Nothing. It's nothing." The pain in her eyes gave the lie to her brave words.

Zach stood. "We'll have to take her in. Might as well go right to Buffalo. They've got an X-ray machine at the hospital there."

Jobeth whimpered. "No. It's not broke. It *can't* be broke."

Zach looked down at her, a knowing smile tugging

at the corners of his mouth. "You're gonna live, Jo. And you'll be riding again, as soon as that arm heals."

She stared up at him in open yearning, *willing* his words to be true. "You promise me?"

He looked at Tess, deferring to a mother's authority. Tess realized they both feared she'd change her mind about Callabash. Some part of her longed to do just that, to make sure that she'd never again have to live through a moment like the one when Callabash had reared up for the second time and she'd seen her only child go bouncing off toward the ground.

But she *would* live through such moments again, especially with a daughter like Jobeth, who would take a lot of physical risks in the process of making herself into a bona fide cowhand.

"Of course you'll ride again," Tess said.

Jobeth wanted more reassurance than that. "But soon," she cried. "Will I ride again soon?"

Tess felt a flare of irritation. Jobeth needed a doctor. It was no time to negotiate the question of when she would be allowed to get back on a horse. "I'll tell you this. You won't ride *ever* if you don't get that arm taken care of."

Jobeth let go of her injury and grabbed her mother by the shoulder. "Say you won't take Callabash away from me."

Tess met her daughter's eyes, amazed at the fierceness she saw there. Jobeth had always been such an easygoing child, a child who took things as they came. Tess had thought that her daughter's composure was simply Jobeth's nature. But maybe more than nature, it had been resignation. Jobeth had known she'd never have the things she really wanted, so what was there to get all fired up about?

Now, she was fired up but good. "Mom. Please. Just say it. Just promise you me you won't take Callabash away."

Tess realized she'd get nowhere fighting her daughter's new fire. She tried a more soothing tone. "All right. I understand that this accident wasn't your fault, or the fault of your horse. You can ride him again, as soon as your arm is okay—as long as you take care of him, and as long as you can handle him." And as long as Zach and I stay married, she couldn't help thinking. Shoving the ugly thought away, she smiled at Jobeth. "I promise you."

Jobeth let out a long, relieved breath. And then she gave in and allowed herself to consider her injury. Her brows drew together in a grimace of pain. "I guess it kind of does hurt. A lot." But then she thought of Callabash again. She turned, looking for Tim. "Tim!" she yelled, when she spotted him, with the gelding, over by the fence. "Is he—?"

Tim made a high sign. "He's okay! Don't you worry none!"

"Come on," Zach said. "Let's get that arm immobilized."

Zach improvised a splint with a piece of board, some newspaper and some strips of cloth, then Tess made a sling using a dish towel. They piled into the Suburban and started off, Zach driving, Tess cradling Jobeth against her side in the seat behind. Long before they reached the hospital, the shock of the accident had completely worn off and poor Jobeth was in considerable pain. But she tried to be brave, huddling against Tess, doing her best not to cry.

At the hospital, the X ray revealed a closed fracture

of Jobeth's left arm, midway between her elbow and her wrist. The doctor set the bone, put on a lightweight plastic cast, gave Tess a prescription for pain medication and said Jobeth could go home.

Even woozy from the anesthetic she'd been given when her arm was set, Jobeth had her eyes on the prize. "When will I be better?" she demanded of the doctor. "I mean, better enough to ride a horse?"

The doctor, a gray-haired woman whom Tess had never met before, looked at Jobeth over the tops of the half-glasses she wore. "Barring complications, the cast should come off in about six weeks. Please stay off all four-legged creatures until that time."

Jobeth threw her head back and let out a frustrated moan. "Six weeks! That's forever...."

The doctor chuckled. "Come back in four. I'll take a look at it, and we'll see, though I'm not promising anything."

Jobeth remained far from pleased. "Four weeks is like a *month*."

"Yes, it is," the doctor agreed. "Four weeks is very much like a month."

"I can't stay off Callabash for a month."

"Jo." Zach, watching from the corner, spoke quietly. Jobeth looked at him. He shook his head. She said no more.

Seney's Rexall was open till five-thirty on Saturdays. They made it just in time to fill Jobeth's prescription. On the way home, Jobeth stretched out in back. Tess took the wheel and Zach sat in the front seat with her.

Halfway there, Zach whispered, "She's asleep."

Tess glanced over her shoulder to see her daughter

slumped in the seat, dead to the world. Zach caught her eye as she turned to face the road again.

"She's a helluva kid."

"Yeah. She is."

"Aren't you glad we took care of the insurance?"

She nodded. Having health insurance did ease her mind. During her marriage to Josh, she'd lived in a kind of numb dread of some major illness or injury.

But those days were over now, she told herself firmly.

Outside, the sun still hovered above the mountains, though the shadows had begun to claim the coulees and draws. Here and there in the rolling sea of grass and sage, Tess could pick out the shyly drooping heads of yellow bells and the white, starlike blossoms of sand lilies. Oh, yes. Spring had truly arrived at last.

And Tess felt really good. Jobeth would be fine in a matter of weeks. And Zach had been so wonderful, right there with them through the whole ordeal. Tess had always known he would be a man she could count on. But never had she seen that so clearly as today.

In the great room that night after Jobeth had been tucked into bed, Tess sat reading her favorite book on high-yield gardening techniques. She heard Zach come in and listened to his footsteps moving toward the stairs—and then turning her way. He entered the great room, carrying a load of wood, the way he'd done the night he asked for Tess's answer on the matter of the horse.

Zach tossed the wood into the wood box, put some in the fire and then rose and came to stand over her shoulder.

"Today, it was a real spring day." He spoke in a

warm tone that had her smiling blindly down at her open book. "Did you notice?"

She kept her gaze on her book, though if anyone had asked, she couldn't for the life of her have said what she was looking at. "Yes. I noticed. I saw wildflowers in the pastures while we were driving home."

"But tonight..." He let his words trail off.

Tess sent a quick, questioning glance back at him.

And he finished his thought. "Tonight, we're getting another last taste of winter."

As if to punctuate his statement, the wind outside rose up and rattled the windowpanes. Tess spared a moment's concern for her garden, hoping it wouldn't get too cold, and wondering if the precautions she'd taken would be enough to protect the tender plants from the biting force of the wind.

"Hmm," Zach said. "Pixie. Early Girl. Beefsteak. Rushmore. Whoever would have guessed there were so many different names for a tomato?"

She realized he was reading over her shoulder and shut the book, shooting him another quick look as she did it. "How about a beer?" The suggestion came to her lips so naturally, she was glad she had made it— even though the minute the words were out, she felt certain he'd decline.

But a miracle happened. He shrugged. "Sounds good."

She almost blurted out, "Honestly?" in frank surprise, but managed to compose herself in time to keep her mouth shut. She stood. "I'll just get it, then."

Instead of waiting for her, he followed after.

They ended up sitting at the kitchen table, a couple of longnecks in front of them, talking at first about Jobeth and what a little trouper she was, and then later about the mysterious tire tracks Zach had seen on Rising Sun land.

He said, "The sheriff's office left a message on the answering machine while we were gone."

"What did they say?"

"The tire tracks from the Crazyman Draw match the ones from February."

"Oh, no."

"Yeah." He fiddled with the label on his bottle of beer. "I've seen tire tracks before, more than once, in the past few months."

"Did you report them?"

"No. Each time I would tell myself it was nothing." He'd peeled the label loose at the corner. Now he smoothed it back in place over the sweating bottle. "We've got a few mining companies who have legal access. And other local ranchers are always free to come and go across Rising Sun land. I told myself it was something like that. I guess I wanted to believe that what happened in February was an isolated incident. But I've been suspicious for a while now."

"Because cattle have turned up missing?"

He looked up from fiddling with the bottle and met her eyes. "You have to know how it is. With twelve hundred head of cattle, there's no way I can remember them all. But they do get familiar. I close my eyes, I can see them. Individual animals. For example, I remember a big red cow, mostly Hereford, with one white foreleg and a speckled udder. And a certain black-baldy with a bad attitude and a half sliced-off ear. I haven't seen either of them in months now." He let out a weary breath. "And I remember which pasture we put them in. And I know they aren't in those pastures anymore. But that's about all I'll ever know, unless they turn up in another pasture—or we find a car-cass somewhere. This is not like those heifers we lost back in February, a clearly identifiable group of animals, in a certain place for a certain reason. Most times, when they disappear, it's like a murder with no corpse. Just a few pitiful little clues. Like where did that black-baldy with the cut-off ear go and what are those pickup and trailer tracks doing out in the Crazyman Draw?''

She asked, ''Has the sheriff found out anything at all about those heifers?''

He shook his head. ''Come on, Tess. Those heifers have been on somebody's table by now. And the calves are born and branded, part of some other man's herd. It's not like the old days, when a rustler had to try to doctor a brand right out on the open range. Not like when a brand had to pass muster in a local stockyard—a place where the brand inspector knew all the brands. Now, sometimes they butcher them right out in the pasture, and load up that beef in the trunk of a car.''

Tess had heard such stories. Still, the thought appalled her. ''You think that's what's happening on the Rising Sun?''

He waved a hand. ''This is smoother. This is modern-day rustling at its smartest. It's somebody who knows the routines around here. Knows where we'll be and when we'll be there. Somebody with a good pickup and a stock trailer—and a stock dog to get the cattle loaded up with a minimum of effort. They're taking under ten head at a clip. And except for those heifers back in February, which they probably just couldn't resist, they're taking stock out of the biggest pastures, where we're keeping lots of animals. Once they get on the road, they're riding the freeways out of state. And unless we catch them red-handed, we'll never know for sure who the hell they are or how they're getting away with it.''

She repeated his words. '''Somebody who knows the routines around here…'''

Zach nodded. ''More than likely, it's one of our own.''

Tess thought of Beau and Lolly and Tim. Of Angie, who'd seemed so dependable. Could it really be one of them? ''But wouldn't you know, if it was one of the hands? I mean, they'd have to have an opportunity, wouldn't they? They'd have to be gone for a while, to do the job.''

He shook his head. ''You know how it is. We're not always all at the same place at the same time. And anyway, whoever it is, he's probably only on the look-out. He makes a phone call, that's all. And someone else actually does the job.''

''Back in February, the sheriff came out and talked to all the hands, didn't he?''

''Yeah. They interviewed everyone here at the Rising Sun—and everyone working the nearby ranches. They came up with zip.''

''But maybe now that you've found tracks to match the ones from February, the sheriff will send someone out to do some more interviewing. Maybe this time they'll find out something that slipped by them back in February.''

''Tess. This time, I've got no real proof of anything. It's tire tracks and a bad feeling and that's about all.''

''Well, why else would those tracks be there, except that more cattle were stolen?''

''Good question. But I still wouldn't expect a lot of action from the sheriff's office. They need more to go on, and that's a plain fact.'' He sounded tired and discouraged. Tess wanted to reach out and put her hand over his, in a gesture of support and reassurance. But she stopped herself. It seemed a big step, a touch like · that.

And they were doing so well. Why court rejection?

She kept her hands to herself and reasoned, "Still, the brands would have to be inspected before the cattle could be sold, wouldn't they?"

He took a pull off the beer. "Sure, though it's a real good possibility they're taking them somewhere and butchering them right off. But say they did sell them on the hoof. It's a damn sight easier to get away with an altered brand if you took the cow in Wyoming and you're selling her off in Chicago." He set the beer down and looked at it as if he couldn't figure out how the label had gotten peeled halfway off. "I heard somewhere that there are over 57,000 brands registered today—in the state of Montana alone, I think it was. Multiply that by all the beef-producing states. They keep track of them by computer. They do what they can, but it's just not enough."

"It's a crime."

He let out a dry laugh. "Exactly."

Outside, the wind cried. Tess got up and put another log in the wood-burning side of the big kitchen stove. The Rising Sun had all the conveniences, including central propane heat. Still, they salvaged a lot of wood—from out in the pastures, from the edges of the juniper forests that grew up the mountains and from old, falling-down buildings. They used that wood for heat, sometimes hardly needing the propane at all.

Tess stared down for a moment, into the flames that burned in the belly of the stove. Behind her, Zach was silent and outside, the wind moaned. Tess watched the flames as they embraced the log she'd just fed them. The heat rose up, warming her face.

She heard Zach shift in his chair, and smiled. He was probably wondering what she found so interesting down inside the stove. She put the iron cover back in place and turned to find him watching her.

He said, "You did great today, when Jo fell off that horse. You didn't get nuts, the way some mothers would have."

"I felt pretty nuts."

"It's what you *did,* Tess. That's what counts. You're always a plus in a crisis."

She loved when he praised her. It made her feel so good inside. She dared to tease, "Always? How would you know?"

"I've watched. Remember the Christmas before last? When Abby got so sick?"

Just before Tyler Ross was born, Abby had fallen victim to eclampsia—extreme pregnancy-induced high blood pressure that had put her in a coma and almost killed her. They'd all been at the ranch, snowed in by a Christmas blizzard, when the condition became acute.

Zach made a musing sound in his throat. "We were all useless as udders on a bull—me, Nate, and especially Edna." He didn't mention Cash, who had been absolutely terrified for his wife, and had stuck right by her side, *willing* her to pull through. "But *you,*" Zach said. "You called for the helicopter, and saw to making Abby as comfortable as possible. You dealt with Edna's near-hysterics. You kept your mind on what needed to be done, and you did it." He chuckled, shaking his head. "You were something that night."

Outside, the wind had died down for a moment.

Tess, positively basking in such praise, whispered, "I was?"

Zach whispered back, "Yeah."

And they looked at each other, a long look, a look that drew on Tess somehow, pulling down into the center of her, making a warmth, a pooling sort of feeling. A feeling of...

Desire.

The word bloomed in her mind, as the warmth bloomed down inside her. Zach went on watching her, his eyes so steady, his whole lean body absolutely motionless, waiting...for what?

She wished he would move. She wished he would stand up and walk around the table and—

She cut off the thought. It seemed a wrong thought. But why?

The answer came: because she loved Cash. She did. She had planned, as Zach's wife, to make love with Zach. To be true to Zach in the ways that Zach demanded—in all ways, really, except deep in her most secret heart.

But to *want* Zach? To yearn for the feel of his hands on her skin, for the touch of his lips against her hair...

That hadn't been part of her plan at all.

Which was crazy. He was her husband. For her to want him should be very right.

Except that it called into question her love for Cash, made it seem a transitory thing. Made her affection seem cheap, that its focus could so easily shift.

Zach picked up his beer and drained the last of it, watching her the whole time.

In her belly, in spite of her shame, the hungry heat grew, rising up like the fire in the stove behind her, as if she'd somehow just given it fuel.

Zach set down the empty bottle, then gestured at hers. "You haven't finished your beer."

She couldn't stop staring into his eyes. "I'm not much of a beer drinker."

He made no polite reply to that, only continued to stare right back at her in that arousing, fathomless way.

The shocking heat inside her burned hotter still. At the same time, his remark had her feeling obligated to drink the beer she'd opened. She stepped forward, picked up the bottle and took a sip, using the action to break the seductive hold of his gaze. When she lowered the bottle, a tiny bit of foam got away from her and dribbled over the edge of her lower lip.

She lifted her hand, to wipe it away—and her gaze locked with his again. She brushed at her chin, feeling mesmerized, lost somewhere in that level gaze of his.

All at once, her imagination got away from her. She pictured herself leaning across the table, stretching toward him, yearning, seeking—until her mouth met his and she sighed in both triumph and surrender.

In her imagination, he didn't turn away. In her imagination, he tasted a little of beer and a lot of the wind outside, with a slight tang of sage and cedar. In her imagination, he kissed her with longing. He kissed her with heat—slow, radiant heat, as from a well-tended fire that burned so hot beneath a layer of protecting ash. A fire that would last the whole night.

More than the night, a hundred nights.

A lifetime of nights...

Chapter Eight

In the stove behind her, a log must have shifted. Tess heard a dropping, settling sound. Zach went on watching her.

And she knew that if she didn't do something to break this strange erotic spell that had suddenly got hold of her, she would do something else. Something like what she had just imagined.

She would reach for him. And not just because they were married. Not just for the sake of another sweet child to hold in her arms.

But for him. For the feel of him. For the things they might do alone in the dark. For the sake of the act itself.

With him.

Tess dragged in a breath and made herself speak. "I'll get you another beer." She tore her gaze from his—that was what it felt like: tearing. And she turned to the refrigerator.

"No."

Startled at the flat, harsh sound of his voice, she whirled back to him. Their gazes locked again. Something—an energy, a current?—went zipping back and forth between them.

"One's enough," he said, and he stood.

She watched him, watched his tall, lean body unfold from behind the table. And she told herself he couldn't know what she'd just been thinking. Her mind was her own. No man could see into it.

All he could know was what had actually happened. They'd talked, and not one word of that talk had concerned the question of intimacy between them. He'd finished his beer. He didn't want another. Now he would leave her for the night.

He would go to his room and she would go to hers, just as they'd been doing every night since their wedding night.

"I guess I..." Her voice came out all ragged, revealing more than she wanted him to know.

"You guess you *what?*" It sounded like some kind of challenge.

She wasn't taking any challenge. No way. He was the one who'd said they were taking it slow, and if he wanted to take it faster, he'd just have to say so. Directly.

She ordered some starch into her tone. "Nothing. I guess *nothing.*"

He gave her a distant, completely unreadable smile. "Well, all right. Good night, then."

She nodded. "Good night."

He left her. A few minutes later, she poured the rest

of her beer down the drain and then climbed the stairs herself. She put on her nightgown and cleaned her face and her teeth and she got into bed.

Outside, the wind blew. It did sound like crying. It truly did.

She wished those moments hadn't happened—those moments when he'd looked at her and she'd imagined kissing him. Kissing him, and a whole lot more. Those moments had confused her, made her wonder if she really understood herself at all. And whether he'd guessed her thoughts or not, Zach had withdrawn from her afterward.

He was such a careful, wary man. She felt certain a lot of lonely nights would go by before he sought her out again.

But it didn't work out that way. The next night, he surprised her by coming to find her again, after all his work was done. He came, as the night before, bearing more wood. He stoked the fire, then asked, "How about a beer?"

She grinned in pure happiness. He *hadn't* stayed away from her, after all. She jumped from her chair. "I'll get you one."

"And one for you, too."

She made a face. "No, thanks. Maybe a cup of tea."

"Suit yourself."

They adjourned to the kitchen, choosing seats at the table just like the night before.

They talked of everyday things, which was just fine with Tess. They discussed which sections of fence needed mending and shook their heads over a prize bull that had got his hoof infected so bad, they had to have the town vet out to see him.

Then Zach said, "I want you to have something."

She waited, wondering what in the world he might mean, as he got up and left the room. He returned a few minutes later with a small pistol in a hip holster and a box of shells.

He slid the gun from the holster. "This is a .380 Colt. Simple and effective. A revolver with six shots." He flipped out the empty cylinder, spun it, then flipped it back in. "You know how to load and shoot?"

She nodded. "My father taught me. I wasn't much older than Jobeth. He took me out where I couldn't hit anything that mattered and set cans on logs for me. Believe it or not, I wasn't bad."

He reholstered the pistol and handed it to her, along with the box of shells. "Any time you go riding alone, load it and take it with you. It's useful against varmints—on four legs or otherwise."

She thought of the rustlers, who might or might not be making regular runs at the stock. If they really were out there, she wouldn't want to come up on them without a means of defending herself.

"Thank you, Zach." She set the weapon and the shells carefully on the end of the counter to take upstairs with her when she went to bed. "I suppose I couldn't talk you into having one more beer."

He grinned. "Sure you could. Just this once."

Tess poured more boiling water on her tea bag and Zach got a second longneck. They sat at the table again. Tess mentioned the paint job she thought the house needed. "I want to do both the inside and the outside. Inside, everything's looking a little gray. And outside, it's starting to peel."

Zach said, "Yeah. I suppose you're right. It has been a few years."

Tess wanted to do the work herself, inside at least.

But Zach said no. "We always use the Bartley brothers." Tess had heard of Brad and Chip Bartley. They'd been painting the buildings of local residents for the past thirty years. "They do a fine job and they don't fool around. Give them a call. They'll show up with all their samples and give great advice on colors and brands. Then they'll buy the paint, and do the job fast and right. All you'll have to do is work around them for a few days."

"But it would be cheaper if—"

Zach tipped his beer toward her. "I don't want cheap. I want it done right."

"I can do it right."

He shook his head, his expression bemused. "Oh, Tess. I know you can."

"So then, let me—"

"You've got plenty to do. You know it and I know it. Let the Bartleys paint the damn house. Please."

She looked down at her teacup. "Fine. Waste your money."

"Our money. And it won't be wasted."

She felt pleasure, a warm sensation all through her, that he would make a point of calling his money hers. She didn't agree with him. To her mind, she'd have no real share in what Zach owned for some time now. Not until she'd earned it with the labor of her hands. And not until she and Zach were truly man and wife.

Still, it meant a lot, that one little word: *ours*. The sound of it on his lips was like a gift.

"Tess. Say you'll call the Bartleys."

She looked across the table into his eyes. "I'll call the Bartleys."

"Good."

She went on outlining her plans. "I thought I'd get going on the inside of the house right away. And wait a while, till the end of June at least, when the weather should be more dependable, to try the outside."

"Sounds good. Call the Bartleys tomorrow, then."

"I will."

They talked a little more, and then he left her for the night. As she washed her teacup, she was smiling, thinking how well things seemed to be going between them lately.

Last night, it had been a little scary—when she'd turned from the fire and found the heat still burned inside her.

But tonight, it had been only good talk. And sharing.

Still smiling, she put her teacup in the cupboard and picked up the Colt and shells to put them safely away. Another few nights like this, and she would actually start thinking they were making progress toward true closeness to each other.

The next day, Tess called the Bartley brothers. And by the end of the week, they were painting the upstairs bedrooms. By the start of the following week, they'd progressed to the downstairs rooms, beginning with the formal living room and the dining room. The end of that week, the last week in May, was the toughest. The Bartleys took over the kitchen and the great room. Tess served meals in the foreman's cottage for two days— and didn't mind the inconvenience at all.

Cheerfully she stepped over drop cloths and skirted paint cans. With the Bartleys' help, she'd chosen colors that seemed to lighten and brighten the rooms—pale blues and butter yellows, warm mauves and cloud grays. It gave her a great feeling of contentment, to see that summery freshness taking over the rooms that to her had always seemed just a little too musty and dim.

And things between her and Zach were going so well. He came to sit with her every night now before bed. They talked over the day just passed, they laughed together. They spoke of Jobeth and how bravely she seemed to be bearing up under the deprivation of not being able to ride.

"Still, she's counting the days until we visit that doctor in Buffalo again," Tess said.

Zach chuckled. "Counting the hours, is more like it."

"Counting the minutes..."

"The seconds. And one thing's for sure. Callabash is the best groomed horse in Johnson County." Since Jobeth couldn't ride the horse, she spent what seemed like half of every afternoon brushing his hide until it shone like glass.

More suspicious tire tracks appeared in a pasture that shared a boundary with the Double-K. Beau and Lolly spotted them while out mending fences. Zach called the sheriff's office and the range detective came out, took pictures and asked questions. The next day the detective called back. He said the tire tracks matched the ones from the previous incidents, including the known thievery back in February. Then he went out and interviewed everyone over at the Double-K. Nate said they'd seen no evidence of rustling there, but they'd keep an eye out.

Zach and Tess discussed the grim situation a little more that night, at the kitchen table, over a pair of grape sodas.

"These guys are bound to get caught sooner or later," Tess predicted. "Someone will see them on Rising Sun land, or you or one of the hands will actually catch them in the act.''

Zach shook his head. ''We're talking roughly a hundred square miles of pastureland, Tess. And rustlers who know where and when to make a run at the stock. I just don't know. As long as they're careful and they don't get too greedy, this could go on for years.''

''Oh, I hate to think that's possible.''

''Sometimes the truth is not a pleasant thing.'' He drank from his soda and when he set the can down, he looked at her in that steady way he had—a level, measuring look that seemed to arouse her with its very directness. But then, after no more than a second or two, he glanced away.

Tess dropped her own gaze, feeling totally off balance, half-relieved and half-disappointed, wondering if he would ever make love to her, afraid that if he did, she might like it more than she ought to for a woman whose secret heart belonged to someone else.

When he looked back at her, he was smiling—a friendly, teasing smile. He asked how she was holding up with the Bartleys underfoot all the time.

She said, ''They're doing a great job. And I'm holding up just fine.''

In the first week of June, after the Bartleys had packed up their paintbrushes and cleared out until the end of the month when they'd be back to do the exterior of the house, Edna called with a hesitant but heartfelt request.

''I am just plain lonely, Tess. Isn't that silly?''

''No,'' Tess said firmly, knowing what was coming, wishing she could feel happier about it than she did. ''It's not silly at all.''

"I always thought I would love living alone. But I don't. I want family around me. Of course, Abigail and Cash have offered me a place with them. But they're gone so much. And I love my daughter dearly, but you know how we are with each other. I'd have her climbing the walls in a week. And she'd get me so crazy, I'd end up having to move out again."

Tess made an understanding sound in her throat. She'd seen Abby and Edna together a lot, seen the strength of their love and regard for each other—and also witnessed the way each always managed to say exactly the thing that would set the other on edge.

Edna went on, "However, for some reason, you and I always seem to rub along just fine together. You're patient with my tendency to tell everyone what to do. You're patient with *me*. And I miss you. I miss Jobeth."

Tess listened with half an ear, her mind on the separate beds she and Zach slept in, the separate beds that Jobeth, at eight, didn't see as particularly odd. The separate beds that no one else knew about.

But if Edna moved in, then Edna would figure it out. And Tess didn't want her to know. She didn't want Edna looking at her with worry in her eyes. And she most certainly did not want to answer any of the questions that Edna would eventually work up the courage to ask.

"Well, anyway," Edna said briskly, "I've been thinking about the foreman's cottage. It's empty now, isn't it?"

The foreman's cottage. Across the yard. Tess breathed a little easier. If Edna wanted to live *there,* then Tess and Zach's privacy on the matter of their current sleeping arrangements just might be maintained.

Edna sighed. "Oh, no. I shouldn't have asked, should I? I can tell by your silence that it simply isn't a good idea."

Tess smiled into the phone. "Oh, really? I haven't said a word, and already you're sure I'm saying no?"

Edna made a small sound of distress. "Don't tease me. You know I hate to be teased."

"All right," Tess replied more gently. "I won't tease you. When will you move in?"

There was silence, then some sputtering. "Oh, really. Let's slow down a little here. You'll have to talk with Zach."

"Edna, you are always welcome here. We both know that."

"All the same, I would insist that you talk with Zach. Maybe he doesn't want an old lady around, getting in the way all time."

"Edna. Stop it. The Rising Sun is your home anytime you want to return to it. We all know it. Zach will only ask what I'm asking, which is when do you want to move in?"

"Soon." Edna's voice sounded so small, suddenly. "Right away."

"Then we'll move you. Right away."

"Talk to Zach. And call me back."

"Edna, it's not necessary."

"You will talk to him first. And then you will call me." Now the older woman's tone would have done Queen Victoria proud.

"All right. I'll talk to him tonight. And call you first thing in the morning."

* * *

The night was mild. Tess sat out on the long gallery at the front of the house, a light sweater across her shoulders and Zach's sweet old mutt, Reggie, on the step beside her. Maybe she was testing Zach a little, seeing if he'd come all the way out to the porch to find her.

When she heard the door open behind her, she smiled. He had come. He had made the extra effort to seek her out in a different place. It was a small thing. But small things added up.

He came and stood over her. "What are you up to?"

She leaned her head back a little. "Watching the clouds float by that sliver of moon."

He made a small clicking noise with his tongue. With a heavy sigh, old Reggie dragged himself off the step and stretched out on the ground below.

Zach sat in the dog's place. For a moment, they were silent, staring out at the night together. A coyote howled, off near the mountains.

Then Tess spoke softly. "It's a nice night. Almost warm."

"It is at that."

She turned and looked at him. He was watching her. It was one of those moments, when his eyes said things his lips never did. In those eyes she saw promises. Pleasures. Fulfillment.

A shiver went through her. She gathered her sweater a little tighter, wondering, If I scooted over close to him, pressed myself shamelessly against him, would he put his arm around me?

"Cold?"

She should say yes, she should sidle on over like a cat seeking strokes. But her nerve failed her. "No, no. I'm fine."

He looked out toward the night again and the moment passed, leaving her a little let down, a little edgy. A little bit hungry for what might have been.

She remembered her conversation with Edna. "Zach?"

He looked at her again, cocking an eyebrow.

"Edna called today."

He went on looking at her for a long moment, then he said, "She wants to move back out here, to the ranch."

She stared at him. "How did you know?"

He shrugged. "Edna's more a mother to me than Elaine Bravo ever was. I know her. She was in heaven, in town, when you and Jo were there with her. But she's got to be lonely, all by herself. She needs people she cares for close by, to coddle. And to boss around." He reached out, tugged on the edge of her sweater. "You knew she'd be coming eventually. Didn't you?"

Tess felt breathless and lovely. That little tug on her sweater had almost been a caress.

"Tess. Didn't you know?"

"Yes. Yes, I did."

"Does she want her old room back?" Edna's old room was the room he slept in now; a nice, large, west-facing room with its own private bath. What would he have done, if Edna did want it back? Move to the one room that was left, and share a bath with Jobeth?

Oh, she didn't understand him. He seemed totally unconcerned about what Edna might discover if she lived in the house with them.

"Tess." He was looking at her sideways. "Did you hear my question?"

"Oh. Sorry. No, not her old room. She asked about the foreman's cottage."

He seemed to consider that, then nodded. "That's a good idea. She'd be close to us, but she'd have her privacy."

And so would we, Tess thought but didn't say. "Yes. It is. A good idea."

"When's she coming?"

"I take it that means you have no problem with her moving here."

His brows drew together in a puzzled frown. "How could I have a problem? She's Edna. She's always got a place here."

"That's exactly what I told her, but she kept insisting that I had to ask you first, before we agreed on the move."

He grunted, a sound of bafflement. "She's funny."

"She doesn't want to intrude."

"Intrude on what?" He was looking at her again, steadily. Probingly.

She just looked right back at him, saying nothing.

"Intrude on what, Tess?"

She felt angry with him, suddenly. For the way he could affect her lately, for this new and bewildering power he seemed to wield over her senses. And for his ability to hide whatever was going on inside him—if there actually *was* anything going on inside him.

She squared her shoulders and replied tartly, "She doesn't want to intrude on us, on our lives together as...man and wife."

He regarded her, taking his time as he always did, before he spoke again. Then he said, "She won't intrude, not as far as I'm concerned. What about you?"

She wanted to throw back her head and howl at that sliver of moon up above. Howl in frustration. In confusion. In pure aggravation. But she didn't. Oh, no. She could be every bit as calm and collected as he could, yessiree.

"No, Zach," she said, with excruciating sweetness. "It's not a problem for me. Not at all. Not one bit. I mean, why should it be? What's there to *intrude* on, anyway?"

Did he tense up, just a little? Had she gotten to him, just a tiny bit? She hoped so. It was small and petty and mean of her, but she did hope so. She hoped that he—

Her vindictive thoughts flew right out of her head as he reached for her. His hand—so warm, so rough, so exactly what she craved—slid around to cup her nape.

He pulled her to him, slowly. And when their lips were inches apart, he whispered, "What's your problem?"

His hand moved, at her nape, his fingers threading themselves into her hair. It felt good, so right, to have him touch her....

"Tess." He said her name in a whisper. "What is your problem?"

She made herself whisper right back at him, calmly, with assurance, "I don't know what you mean," as if he wasn't so close. Or as if he got that close all the time. "I don't have any problem."

He lowered his gaze to watch her mouth move, and then he met her eyes again. Almost tenderly, he murmured, "Good, then. Tell her to move in. Right away."

She whispered back, all sweetness, "That's exactly what I'll tell her."

And he said, "Fine."

And she said, "It's settled then."

"Yeah," he muttered. "Settled."

And then he moved forward, just a fraction, until his

lips brushed hers—so lightly, hardly more than a touch. Enough to make her yearn for more.

Almost instantly, he released her and stood.

She looked up at him, not trusting herself to speak.

He was already turning away, for the front door. "Good night." He tossed the words back at her, over a shoulder, then opened the door and went inside.

Once he was gone, she sat for a long time, watching the night, listening to a lone dove somewhere over near the foreman's cottage as it cooed forlornly in the dark.

Tyler Ross, retired to the foreman's cottage.

Chapter Nine

Edna moved into the foreman's cottage that Saturday.
Cash wanted to hire a regular moving company, but
Edna wouldn't hear of such an expense. So they rented
a moving truck to transport the furniture. Zach and
Cash provided the muscle.

By evening, they had it all moved in. Then Cash,
Abby and Tyler Ross stayed for dinner. Tess served
pork tenderloins and green beans and mashed potatoes
with pork gravy. The food was great, as usual. Zach
looked at his wife down the table. She glanced up and
smiled at him. As he smiled in return, he realized how
good it made him feel to see her there. Real good.
Maybe too good.

Cash made some offhand remark. Everyone laughed.
Zach watched his wife as she laughed, too, a thoroughly appropriate laugh, neither too warm nor too

long. She hid her feelings well. No one would guess how she felt about Cash.

No one but her husband, who just happened to have caught her at an unguarded moment, when her heart showed in her eyes.

After the meal, the women, along with Jobeth and Tyler Ross, retreated to the foreman's cottage.

Zach turned to Cash. "Come on. Let's have a look at the books."

Cash immediately tried to get out of it. "Zach. Give it a rest. I've been lugging Edna's damn furniture around all afternoon. I'd like another drink. And I'd really like a smoke."

"You quit."

"Don't remind me. Let's just go in the other room and get the bottle of Black Jack from the cabinet and—"

"Get the bottle. And bring it in my office."

Cash tried a stubborn glare. "Zach."

"You and Nate have to know what goes on around here."

"We do know. You're the operator and a damn fine one and when I'm curious about the bottom line, I'll let you know."

"Go get the bottle. And a couple of glasses. And come on."

Cash moaned and groaned some more, but he finally got the whiskey and glasses and followed Zach into the office.

They sat together at the computer and Zach scrolled through the spreadsheets, showing his cousin exactly how the ranch was doing in terms of dollars and cents.

"The count seems a little low," Cash said, referring to the number of cattle they'd counted during branding time just passed. "It's not all that bad, but it's just not quite up to what we thought it would be."

"No, it's not." With a frustration that made a burning in his gut, Zach thought of the mysterious tire tracks that kept appearing in his pastures. Cash knew all about the tracks. Zach kept both him and Nate posted on the situation.

"Come on," Cash said. "Don't look so damn grim. These numbers tell me we're absorbing the loss with no problem—if there really is a loss."

"There's a loss, bet on it. The tracks we found in February match the ones we've found since then. We're getting hit. And regularly. And if—*when*—I catch those bastards, there will be hell to pay."

Cash chuckled. "You're starting to get mad, cousin."

"That I am."

"But you *never* get mad."

"Never say never."

Cash looked at Zach for a long moment, then slowly shook his head. "I pity those poor S.O.B.'s—" he smiled that smile that drove the women wild "—*when* you find them." He frowned, then grinned again. "Hey. I almost forgot."

"What?"

"Wait right there." Cash got up and went out through the dining room.

Zach exited the spreadsheet program, switched off his computer and waited. His cousin returned a few minutes later, carrying a box.

"What now?" Zach asked grimly.

Cash was beaming. He pulled a cell phone from the box, a big one, about the size of an appointment book. "Your very own cellular phone. A bag phone, in this case. Three watts of pure power. That's enough to get pretty good reception anywhere on the Rising Sun. And don't give me that what-a-waste-of-money look. These things are damn convenient. You break your leg—or run into our phantom rustlers—out in the North Pasture, you'll be glad you can just phone home.'' He grunted. "'Course, cell phones have a drawback or two. Sometimes the reception's not so great on them—especially around these parts, even with a bag phone. Also if you don't recharge them, they go dead.''

"And a call on one costs a fortune.''

"Don't be a skinflint. You need to keep up with the times. This baby's all set up and ready to go. Let me show you how it works.''

"You mean the Rising Sun will be getting a bill any day now.''

"Come on, come on. You're gonna love this....''

A few minutes later, Zach set down his new cell phone. "Thanks.''

"You're welcome. Before you know it, you'll be wanting them for Tess and Edna, too.''

"We'll see.'' Zach shot Cash a sideways look. "Got a smoke?''

Cash raked a hand back through his gold hair. "You just said it an hour ago. I quit.''

Zach grunted. "Yeah. But have you got a cigarette?''

Cash studied Zach as if he were some strange new species of man. "How long's it been, since you had a smoke?''

Zach drained the last of his whiskey. "Six months, a year. I couldn't say for sure.''

"Haven't you heard? Smoking's addictive.''

"I can take it or leave it.''

"Right. Rub it in."

Zach set down his empty glass. "You didn't answer my original question."

Cash sent a furtive glance toward the door to the dining room, as if he expected Abby to come strolling through it the minute he lit up. Then he lowered his voice. "We could go out back, by the barn."

Zach grinned. "Yeah, that's a long way from the foreman's cottage, where your wife is right now."

Cash said, "Don't even give me that smirky-assed look. Abby worries about me, that's all. She cares about my health."

"Abby's right," Zach said, feeling bad all of a sudden, wondering where the hell his own good judgment had gone. Though Nate had quit years ago and Zach rarely smoked, Cash struggled constantly with a nicotine addiction that he never seemed to lick. Zach had no business suggesting that the two of them light up. "Forget I asked about it."

Cash laughed. "It's too late to forget now."

"No, it's not."

"It just so happens I've got a pack stashed in the moving truck."

"Look. I said let it go."

Cash peered at Zach more closely. "Something bothering you, cousin?"

Zach kept his face expressionless, though Tess's image flashed through his mind. "No. Why?"

"You seem edgy tonight. And you're always the upright one. It's not like you to even mention a cigarette around a nicotine fiend like me."

Zach figured extended denials would only make his cousin more suspicious. "Maybe I am a little on edge. It's the missing stock, I guess."

"Well," Cash said. "If you've changed your mind about that smoke, good for you. I haven't."

Zach turned for the door. "Fine. Go get the damn things. I'll meet you out back."

They hung on the fence to the horse pasture, the smoke from their cigarettes trailing up toward the stars. Callabash and Ladybird trotted over, accepted a little coddling, and then wandered away.

"So how's married life treatin' you?" Cash asked after they'd puffed away for a few minutes in silence.

Zach shot his cousin a look. But Cash just went on smoking, totally oblivious to Zach's problems—or to his own perfectly innocent part in them.

Cash turned and squinted through the cloud of smoke. "Well?"

"Good," Zach said. "Real good."

"Tess is a fine woman."

"Yeah. She is."

"She deserved a real chance for once."

"She sure did."

"And because of you, she got it."

Zach looked away, out toward the center of the pasture, where Ladybird was nipping at the grass.

Cash added, "And the house looks great. The new paint really lightens things up."

Zach sucked in more acrid smoke and wondered what the hell had possessed him to ask for a cigarette, anyway. "Yeah. Tess chose all the colors. She has an eye for stuff like that."

Cash fell silent, then asked, "Are you sure you're all right?"

"I'm good, Cash. Real good." Other than the fact that some rustling bastard is stealing us blind and my wife's in love with you. "And we probably ought to be heading on back inside."

Cash made a noise of agreement as he crushed the butt under his heel.

Zach put out his own cigarette and started to turn for the house.

Cash said, "Hey."

Zach turned back. "Yeah?"

"Maybe we should hire some men. To patrol the place. What do you think?"

Zach considered, and then shook his head. "Let's give it a while. See if it keeps up."

"You think they'll stop?"

"No."

Cash was looking at him real hard. "You don't want them to stop."

"I did at first. But now..."

"You just want to catch them in the act."

"You got it."

"Be careful."

Zach let out a humorless laugh. "You know me, cousin. Careful is my middle name."

That night, after Cash and his family left for town and Jobeth had gone to bed, Tess sat out on the front porch step with Reggie. Across the yard, the lights were on in the foreman's cottage. Edna would be settling in for her first night in her new home.

Tess drew up her knees, smoothing the skirt she wore down over them. Reggie gave a little whine, so she scratched him behind one of his droopy ears.

Actually, the foreman's cottage wasn't new to Edna. It had been her home for years before she moved to the main house. That had been back when Ross Bravo,

Zach's grandfather, had run the Rising Sun. Edna had lived in the cottage with her husband Ty, the Rising Sun's top hand. Tess had never met Ty. He had died just a few months before she and Jobeth had come to Medicine Creek.

Abby had been born in the foreman's cottage—during a blizzard when there'd been no way to get to the hospital in Buffalo. Cash, who was fifteen years old at the time, had been there when it happened. He had held Abby as a tiny baby, less than an hour after she first entered the world.

Tess smiled at the idea of a man holding his wife on the day of her birth. And then she frowned.

For some reason, right then, she found she was thinking of her father, dead now for several years. Roger Inman had been a tall, serious man—hardworking and kind. Even when he'd learned that his unmarried teenage daughter was pregnant, he hadn't raised a hand to her.

He'd only said, "It's time for truth, daughter. All of it, I think."

She had cried and told him about Josh. And he had listened, his eyes so sad and disappointed in her. But still kind. Still full of love.

He'd taken her out to the room off the barn where Josh slept. And Josh had looked so white and scared at first, but then he'd said he did love her. And would marry her.

So she had bound her life to him. That had been at the start of her senior year of high school. She'd been a straight-A student and she'd managed, just barely, to finish her required classes and graduate a semester early, before she got too big with Jobeth. At the time it hadn't occurred to her or her father—or Josh, either, for that matter—that there might have been some other choice besides marriage. She was seventeen and pregnant and needed a husband. Period.

Over in the foreman's cottage, the living room went dark. A few seconds later, the front bedroom light came on. Edna would be getting ready for bed.

Time for truth, daughter, her father used to say. Time for truth.

Tess pulled her sweater a little closer around her shoulders and thought of Cash, of the moment this afternoon when he'd driven up in the moving truck with Abby and Tyler. Zach had followed behind them in the blue pickup, with Edna on the passenger side.

Tess had been over in the foreman's cottage, freshening things up a bit for Edna's arrival. She'd heard the vehicles and run out to the porch. She'd seen the moving truck—and realized that Zach wasn't in it.

So she'd looked toward the pickup, seeking the shadow of Zach's hat in the window. And when she'd seen it, seen his profile and his strong hands on the wheel, she'd felt that rising, joyful feeling that she used to get at the sight of Cash.

Tess closed her eyes, drew in a long breath of the cool night air and laid her cheek down on her drawn-up knees. She felt so bewildered. And lost. So out of sorts with the world and her knowledge of herself.

She wanted Zach. She yearned for his touch, for a kind word, for a smile across the table during dinner. For a kiss on the porch after dark...

Oh, it felt like love. Exactly like love.

And it made her feel foolish and shallow, a woman whose affections changed with each shift in the winds. It made her wonder if she'd ever understood love at all—and if she was capable of loving a good man the way such a man deserved to be loved, with steadiness and loyalty, for as long as they both should live.

Behind her, she heard the front door open. Zach. It would be Zach. She hadn't thought he would come to talk with her tonight. He hadn't sought her out for the past two nights. Not since Wednesday night, when he'd kissed her and then gone inside so swiftly, leaving her to wonder if he regretted that sweet brushing of his lips against hers.

She heard his step, behind her. And then he made the small clicking noise with his tongue that signaled Reggie. The dog got up and moved out of the way.

Zach dropped down beside her.

The warmth of his body reached out to her. She kept her gaze on the foreman's cottage. She watched the light in the bedroom go out, but she watched without really seeing. Her mind was filled with the man sitting beside her, her senses humming with gladness and anxiety at his nearness. She felt shy, suddenly, and feared turning to face him. So she didn't. She just sat there, staring into the night.

And as Tess looked at the night, Zach looked at her, his gaze tracing her soft profile, wondering what she was thinking—but not sure that he'd like what he heard if she told him.

On one level, this practical marriage had turned out to be exactly what he'd hoped it might. The hands went to work smiling, their bellies full of good food. The house his grandfather had built was a place of order and comfort. Tess filled the rooms with warmth and light.

Beyond the good she did in his home, she had brought him Jobeth, who would make one hell of a rancher someday. Every day Zach felt more and more certain that there would be someone to take the reins from him when the time came to pass them on.

Things had worked out just as he'd hoped.

Except for the wanting. The wanting was the problem.

He wanted Tess too much. And he wanted her more and more all the time. He probably shouldn't have come out here tonight. But she drew him. He'd known she was out here. And he just couldn't stay away.

The thought came all the time now, that she was his wife and he had a right to her body. That she would accept him willingly in her bed, because she did want children, after all. That she was only waiting for him to reach out his hand.

It was damn scary. He felt so vulnerable to her. And he didn't want to be vulnerable. He just plain didn't need any woman having that kind of power over him— especially not Tess. Not Tess, his wife, who was absolutely perfect in every single way—except for the little problem that she loved another man.

She moved, turning her head slowly, seeking his eyes through the night. "I think it should work out just fine, with Edna in the foreman's cottage."

He looked at her, at her pretty, cat-slanted dark eyes and her smooth brow and that mouth with its neat little bow at the top. Her mouth drove him crazy, it was so soft and sweet.

She frowned. "Zach. Don't you think so?"

"What?"

"That Edna's going to be fine, living in the—"

"Oh. Edna. Yeah. Edna's fine."

"Are you...all right?"

"I'm fine."

She let out a little sigh and hugged her knees up

close to her chest so she could rest her chin on them. He thought of leaning over, putting his mouth against her neck, sucking a little, making a mark there. Then kissing that mark. Of pulling her to him, opening her shirt, seeing her breasts, in the moonlight, touching them, kissing them. Then taking her hand, leading her in the house and up the stairs…

She laid her head sideways on her knees, so she could look at him. "What is it?"

"Nothing."

"You seem so…"

"What?"

"I don't know…" She waited, probably for him to supply some explanation of his mood. He supplied nothing, so she sighed again and lifted her head to look out at the yard. He watched her lips curve as she smiled. "Jobeth was so sweet tonight, keeping Tyler Ross out of trouble while Abby and I helped Edna unpack." She closed her eyes, tipped her head up, as if she were offering her pretty face to the night. "One more week, and she can go back to the doctor. Maybe, if she's lucky, that cast can come off."

"Yeah."

She looked at him again. God, he could smell her, smell the special scent of her body, so warm and sweet and tempting.

Somewhere around the time he'd imagined sucking a red mark onto her neck, he'd become hard. A damn humiliation if there ever was one. If he stood and she looked at the front of his Wranglers, she would know.

He was out of control. Completely out of control.

She looked away again, and smiled out at the night. "Tyler Ross is so cute. And it's funny, even though he's hardly more than a baby, he's got that Bravo look stamped on him so strong.''

He watched her mouth. Watched that dreamy smile. And he knew she had to be thinking about Cash.

"What do you mean, that Bravo look?" It came out harsh, full of challenge, angry-sounding.

She snapped her head around. "What is wrong?"

He ached, that was what. For her. For her soft body. All around him. For the release that sinking into her tender flesh would bring. "Nothing. I just asked what you meant. What *Bravo* look?"

Her gaze scanned his face, lighting briefly on his mouth. "Well, the mouth."

"The mouth?"

"Kind of full, for a man. And the nose. A very strong nose. And the eyes…I don't know. It's just…the way you all look."

She kept smiling, and he knew, though it was dark, that her skin was flushed. He would feel the heat, if he touched her.

God. He wanted to touch her. To reach out and—

"Look," he said gruffly.

"What?"

"I'm going in." He stood, quickly, and turned away before she could see the proof of the power she had over him.

"But, Zach—"

"Good night." He headed for the door.

He heard her jump to her feet and start coming for him. "Wait. What's the matter?"

"Nothing's the matter."

"That's not true. What did I do?"

He reached for the door. "Nothing."

She caught up with him. He could feel her, at his

back. And then she made the mistake of putting her hand on his shoulder. "Zach—"

It was too much, that soft touch, that pleading tone. He spun on her and reached out, grabbed her by the hips and yanked her tight against him.

"Oh!" Those cat eyes went wide as she felt it, felt what she did to him.

"You happy?" he snarled, pulling her tighter still, feeling the heat of her, starving for more.

"I didn't... Oh, Zach..." No more words came.

And that was fine with him. He didn't want any words anyway. He could put that mouth of hers to use just fine doing other things than talking.

He lowered his head and took that mouth. It gave beneath his, parting, sighing, welcoming him. He ground his hips against hers, holding her tight, almost hoping she would refuse him, push him away.

But she didn't. She surged up with a small cry, and twined her slim arms around his neck. He felt her, the whole slender, sighing length of her. Her breasts pressed against his chest, so soft and round and full. And her hips—her hips pushed right back at him, answering, beckoning, welcoming him.

He bit her lower lip, not too hard, just enough to let her know that he might hurt her, might be rough with her, the need was so strong in him right then. She whimpered, a sound of surrender, a sound that said he could do what he wanted with her. He twined his hands in her silky hair, pulling a little, tipping her head back. And his mouth slid down, over the curve of her chin, to her neck. He licked the smooth, warm flesh and then he sucked, as he had imagined doing, putting his teeth against the skin, bringing a welt that would leave a slight bruise by morning. She clasped his head, holding him to her, as if she craved that mark.

He wanted to see her. All of her. To take her clothes away from her and have the whole of her body, all of her. For himself.

He froze.

And in spite of the roaring of his blood, the hunger in his body, he remembered.

He would not have her. Not *all* of her.

She tipped her hips against him, tried to tempt him to take her mouth again, to make him forget that what she offered wasn't everything. Wasn't complete.

"Oh, Zach…"

"No."

"Don't pull away. Please—"

He took her shoulders and very deliberately held her away from him. His body throbbed at the loss of a heaven not quite attained.

"Zach—"

"No, I said. No." He took his right hand from her shoulder and put it across those soft, tempting lips. "Listen."

She looked at him, waiting, her eyes begging with him over the mask of his hand. He dragged in a breath. "You'll listen?"

She nodded.

He said in a ragged whisper, "I loved my first wife. She cut out my heart and used it for buzzard bait. I don't need that again."

She pushed his hand away from her mouth. "I would never—"

He squeezed her shoulder. "Let me finish."

She swallowed. "All right."

He released her, stepping back. She swayed on her

feet a little when he let go. But then she collected herself, drew in a breath and stood tall.

He chose his words with great care. "This is a good marriage we have. A practical one. One that's working out fine for both of us. I say we don't mess it up."

She made a small, frustrated noise. "But how could we mess it up by doing...what married people do?"

He stared at her for a long, deep moment, knowing that she wouldn't like hearing the truth any more than he wanted to say it.

"Zach. Please. Tell me, talk to me..."

So he did.

"I know who's in your heart, Tess. And it's not me."

Chapter Ten

Tess gave a cry and put her hand against her mouth. Her eyes went wide and wounded. She couldn't have looked more shocked if he had slapped her hard across the face.

For a long, gruesome moment, they stared at each other. Then she dropped her hand. She whispered raggedly, "How did you know?"

Zach had a sinking, weary feeling, then. Until that moment, somewhere deep inside him, he had hoped that just maybe he'd been mistaken about this.

Her lower lip trembled. "It was that night, wasn't it? The night we moved our things out here. The night of the engagement party. You came up the basement stairs and you..." She seemed unable to finish.

So he finished for her. "I saw the look you gave Cash."

She wrapped her arms around herself and murmured

numbly, "I thought so. But I didn't want to believe it. And then, when you didn't say anything…" She closed her eyes, drew in a breath and then looked at him once more. "So. That means, on our wedding night, it wasn't just time you were talking about. It was…what you knew. You didn't want me, because of what you knew." She started shaking her head, her face pale as death through the shadows on the porch.

He took a step toward her. "Tess—"

She backed up, still shaking her head. "You don't understand. Nobody knows. Nobody was ever going to know.…"

"Well. *I* know."

"Oh, dear Lord." She turned away, went to the porch rail, looked out across the yard again, into darkness, into someplace he couldn't see.

He said, "I guess I've made a mistake, to come looking for you in the evenings, to think we could make more of this marriage than it is."

She said nothing. Her slim back was very straight.

He spoke again. "Look. I meant what I said. We have a good thing. A practical arrangement. I think we should just keep it that way."

Still, she didn't speak, only wrapped an arm around the pillar next to her and leaned her cheek against it. He felt alarm, then. Concern for her.

"Tess. Are you all right?"

She waved the hand that wasn't wrapped around the pillar. "Fine. Just…it's hard to think that all this time, you've known. But I'll be okay. Really."

He pushed his concern for her aside. After all, she said she would be okay.

And he wanted to get a few things settled. His desire had died with her admission that she loved his cousin.

He wanted it to stay dead. He wanted things back on an even keel. He wanted an understanding between them. And he wanted distance.

"Are you agreed, then? We'll keep things as they are. We won't go...stirring things up." He waited for her reply. When none came, he prompted, "Well?"

She seemed to shake herself. "Yes. Of course. Whatever you say."

"Good." As he said the word, he found he hated it. It wasn't good. Not good at all. But they would manage. It would be...bearable. She would take care of him and the hands and the house. And he would provide for her and Jobeth.

They'd treat each other with respect and civility. And they'd keep clear of each other in any personal sense.

She seemed awfully quiet. He said, "Are you sure you're all right?"

She didn't answer for a moment. He almost asked again. But then she let out a deep sigh. "I'm fine, Zach. And I'd like to be alone now, please."

She looked so lonely, standing there, staring into nothingness. Just about as lonely as he felt. He lifted his hand, to touch her, to reassure her.

But then he dropped it. Distance. That was what they'd agreed on. And she'd just asked him to leave her alone.

He said, "Good night, then."

And she replied, "Yes. Good night."

Once Zach left, Tess waited long enough for him to get all the way to his room. Then, moving very carefully because her silly legs felt so wobbly, she turned and went inside. She had to keep a firm grip on the bannister all the way up to the second floor.

And when she lay down between the cool sheets, she didn't close her eyes. She stared into the darkness, hearing Zach's awful words in her mind, over and over and over again.

I know who's in your heart, Tess.

She had always taken such comfort from the belief that not a soul had guessed her feelings for Cash. But Zach knew. He had known since before he married her.

The shame...it was burning all through her. So much worse, to think that Zach knew.

He knew. And he had married her anyway.

Because he thought they could make a good life together, whatever she felt in her foolish heart.

He had married her anyway.

Because, as he'd made so clear from the first, he didn't need or want her love.

With a small moan, she turned on her left side, then tossed to her right. But sleep didn't come for her.

She kept reliving that moment when he had told her that he knew.

And she wondered why she hadn't answered, Yes, Zach. It's true. I did think I loved Cash. For years, I thought I loved him. But now, Lord help me, I think that I love you....

Tess sat up in bed. And then she flopped back down.

Of course, she hadn't said such a thing. And she was glad that she hadn't. Because he never would have believed it. Hearing it in her mind, *she* didn't even believe it. It sounded so silly and impossible. It sounded like a desperate and pitiful lie, the kind of thing some low woman with no dignity would say to try to get a man to trust her.

Tess rolled to her stomach. She closed her eyes and wondered how she would face him, how she would live with him, day to day, knowing that he knew.

Should she leave? Just pack up Jobeth and their few things and go? She had about a thousand dollars in her old checking account, money she had earned working for Carmen Amestoy. She could manage on that, somehow, until she found a job—as long as she found a job fast.

She thought of Jobeth, of how she had changed since they'd moved here. Jobeth had pride now, in her new life and in her place within it. Jobeth adored Zach. If she took Jobeth away from here, it would break her heart.

Oh, Lord. She didn't want to do that to Jobeth. Not if she could help it.

Time, Zach had said on their wedding night, when he had already known her secret, but hadn't told her so. *Give it time.*

Yes. That was good advice, now as well as then. She was too full of shame and confusion to make any big decisions now, anyway. For a week or two at least, she wouldn't do anything at all. Except get by. Go through the motions. Do what needed to be done, day by day.

Zach had made it clear he still wanted her to care for his house, to put the meals on the table for the hands. And she loved it here. She did. She loved this life just as much as her daughter did.

Yes. She would give it time. She would face Zach in the morning with a smile. And she would get through the days, one hour at a time.

Tess turned on her back again. She stared at the ceiling.

She longed for morning, when she could rise and work hard and try to forget what had happened tonight.

In the morning, when she washed her face, Tess saw the red mark on her neck where Zach had kissed her. She blushed all over, remembering. And the blush deepened as she realized that everyone would see it and guess how she'd acquired it.

Under the circumstances, she could almost laugh. That little red love bite lied. Oh, how it lied.

She put makeup on the mark and buttoned her collar all the way to the top. But the mark would still be visible to anyone who looked hard enough.

At breakfast, Zach treated her kindly. He complimented her biscuits and took seconds on bacon. Once or twice, she caught him looking at her neck.

Well, fine. Let him look. He had put that love bite there himself, after all.

He finished his meal a little faster than usual and then he went out with Tim to check the mineral tubs in a pasture not far from the house, reminding her before he left to be ready for church on time.

Edna stared after him, beaming from ear to ear. "I am just so glad you and Zach found each other." She picked up her plate and began helping Tess load the dishwasher.

Tess rinsed glassware at the sink and tried to look glad, too.

"You were just...meant for each other."

Tess set the glasses in the top rack of the dishwasher. "Yes. We have the same interests."

"Oh, it's much more than that. Any fool can see, by the way he looks at you, that he loves you deeply. And of course, I know you feel the same way for him."

"Yes. I do. I...love him very much." Strange. When she said it, it sounded right. It sounded true.

"It's amazing, I never believed he'd find happiness again." Edna lowered her voice to a conspiratorial whisper. "After Leila, you know."

"Yes. Yes, I know."

"But it's worked out perfectly, between you, hasn't it?"

"Yes, Edna. Perfectly."

Zach came in right on time, cleaned up and took them to church. He sat beside Tess in the pew, a model husband, sharing a hymnal with her, his deep voice steady and sure when they sang. Once or twice, his arm brushed hers, when they rose and when they sat down again. He was so close. And yet he might as well have been a thousand miles away.

Tess noticed, as one day faded into the next, that Zach found a lot of work to do far away from the house. He avoided coming in for the substantial midday meal she always served. She saw him at breakfast and dinner, when he treated her gently, if somewhat distantly.

He never came near her when his day's work was through.

For the first couple of nights, that was just fine with her. At first, every time she looked at him, all she thought of was her secret. Her secret that he knew. But as the days passed, and she got used to the idea that he knew, she found that she missed him. Missed their evenings together, missed the sound of his voice as he talked about his day, missed his wry smiles and his occasional, unpracticed laughter. Heaven help her, she even missed the agony of wondering if, maybe, *this* was the night he would truly make her his.

She began to understand the real reason she hadn't packed up her belongings and taken her daughter away. She began to see that she wasn't through with Zach Bravo yet. Not by a long shot. And, whether he was willing to admit it or not, he wasn't through with her.

He could say that all he wanted was a housekeeper and a cook. But he'd signed on for a wife. And by golly, in the end, she would do all in her power to see that he got one.

She began watching him, covertly, every chance she got. And she saw the way he looked at her when he thought she didn't see, saw it much more clearly than she had before, when she'd been confused about her own feelings, and so jealously guarding her secret.

He did want her.

If she had any doubt about that, all she had to do was think of the way he had kissed her the other night, the way he had pulled her so hard against him—so she would know exactly how he felt. The mark on her neck had faded quickly, but not the memory of the way he had put it there.

As a claim. A brand.

There was a lot of passion behind Zach Bravo's impassive facade—if a woman just had the patience and stamina to pry him open and let it loose.

Shamelessly she pumped Edna for information. In the late mornings, after the breakfast things were cleared and she'd put in an hour on the house and an hour or two in her garden, she'd just wander on over to the foreman's cottage, where she knew Edna would have the coffee on.

They'd share a cup. And Tess would ask Edna things about Zach, about what he'd been like as a boy.

"A lot like he is now," Edna said. "Serious. Cautious. Honest. Upright. He used to drive Cash and Nate crazy. They both had the devil in them. And he was such a good boy. Yet they both wanted his respect. When either one of them would act up, all Zach would have to do was look at them with that direct, uncompromising stare of his. You know what I mean.''

"Oh, I do. I do.''

"Zach would give them a look. And they'd straighten up—or at least they'd feel good and guilty about whatever trouble they were up to. And that would mean that, soon enough, they'd stop.''

Tess asked about Leila. "Tell me. What was she *like?*''

Edna frowned, thinking about Zach's first wife, and then she sighed. "Leila Wickerston had black hair and big blue eyes.'' Edna laughed. "What am I saying? I'm sure Leila still has black hair and blue eyes. It isn't as if she's passed on or anything. She's down there in San Diego with that rich second husband of hers and that little hellion, Starr.''

"But what was she like, Edna? When she and Zach were together?''

"Beautiful. Spoiled, I suppose. All the boys were after her. But she only wanted Zach. And Zach, well, you know how he is.''

"Of course, but tell me anyway.''

"He tried to fight it at first. Even as a boy, he gave his heart…carefully. Does that make sense?''

"Yes. Yes, it does.''

"We all used to laugh, about the way Leila was always finding ways to put herself where he was. He was active in 4-H. And all of a sudden, Leila was raising chickens. The Wickerstons lived in town, so they had no room for big animals. But Leila got those chickens. Skinniest birds you ever saw. She didn't pay much attention to them, you see. They were only a means to an end.''

''The end being Zach.''

''Precisely. Of course, Zach saw how she treated those birds and he said he wouldn't have anything to do with her. She'd never make a ranch wife. But Leila had other tricks.''

''Like what?''

''Well, you know how Zach is. Church every Sunday. Not like Cash and Nate, both of whom I used to have to drag there. Zach's not terribly religious, but he believes in showing respect to the Lord on a regular basis. The Wickerstons were strictly Christmas and Easter churchgoers. But once Leila decided she wanted Zach, all of a sudden, that girl got religion. She always showed up in the same pew we sat in, waving and smiling and looking so sweet. She joined the Methodist Youth Fellowship and she bullied Zach until he joined, too. And then, naturally, he had to stop by her house to pick her up for the meetings. It took her about a year of constantly being everywhere Zach was.''

''And then?''

''Well, and then he surrendered.''

Tess wrinkled her nose at that. ''He *surrendered?*''

''I don't know what else to call it. He just…gave in and decided to love her. And when he did, he was so…devoted. It was lovely, really. And on her behalf, I'd have to admit that she seemed to be equally devoted to him—at first. They married right out of high school. And the trouble didn't start until then, until she came out here to the ranch to live.''

''She hated it.''

''That's too mild a word. After the first…romantic

flush wore off between her and Zach, all she wanted was out of here. She sulked and whined. And she had no pride or sense of privacy. She would start in on him right in the great room, where everyone could hear, or at the dinner table. She would get tears in those big blue eyes and beg him to get her away from here. He would sit there while she complained and pleaded, his face blank, looking like a turtle pulled into its shell, never fighting back more than to cautiously remind her that she had said she wanted what he wanted from life. And, really, it didn't matter what he said. She'd just keep crying and saying she wanted out and she wanted him to go with her.''

"But he wouldn't go."

"That's right. And when he wouldn't, she got mean. She threw tantrums. She sulked more than ever. And when she wasn't screaming or sulking or whining, she was criticizing anything and everything. Poor Zach. He didn't know what to do. He still loved her, but she was killing him. His grandfather Ross took him aside and advised that maybe a baby would settle her down. So when she got pregnant, we all had hopes that might make a difference with her. But it didn't. She just got meaner. And in the end, she left and took their baby with her."

Tess got up and refilled their cups.

Edna said, "I honestly thought, for years, that Zach would never take a chance on love again. But then you came along." She reached across the table and patted Tess's hand.

Tess said, "I want to make him happy."

"Oh, you do. I know you do."

As each day went by, Tess felt she understood Zach

a little better. Still the emotional chasm between them lay as deep and dangerous as the Grand Canyon.

Tess made no attempt to bridge it. She didn't really know how, though she sensed that complete honesty would be a start.

Complete honesty. Which meant she would have to tell him of those scary feelings she had for him—feelings that each day she became more and more certain added up to love.

And when she told him, how in the world could she expect him to actually believe her? Worse than that, how could she even expect him to care? He'd made it so painfully clear how he felt about love. He wanted nothing to do with it.

Still, he might let her get a little closer to him, if she could convince him that the specter of Cash no longer stood between them.

Or he might not.

Really, she had no way to know how he would react. And she just wasn't ready to take a chance on finding out.

Not yet, anyway.

On June 16, four weeks and three days after Jobeth broke her arm, the doctor in Buffalo took off the cast.

"I can ride, now. Right?" Jobeth demanded.

"You'll have to be cautious," the doctor warned. "That arm will be weak for a while."

"But can I *ride?*"

"Yes. You may ride."

Jobeth turned to Tess, her eyes as bright as stars. "Mom, I can ride."

"Yes. I heard."

"Let's get home. Right now."

But Edna had ridden with them and both she and Tess had shopping to do. Jobeth managed to contain her impatience until the groceries had been bought.

They arrived back at the ranch at a little before three—and found a dusty but very expensive-looking sports car parked in the turnaround in front of the main house.

"Whose car is that?" Tess asked, thinking Edna might know.

Edna only shrugged. "I haven't the faintest idea. But it appears they've gone on inside, whoever they are. Tim's around here somewhere. He must have let them in."

Tess pulled up in front of the foreman's cottage first. Jobeth leapt from the back seat and headed for the barn almost before Tess got the Suburban to a full stop. Tess considered calling her back and demanding a little help with the groceries, but then she decided to let her go. After all, Jobeth had waited weeks for this moment.

Tess did call out her window, "Don't get on that horse unless Zach or Tim is there to supervise!"

Jobeth turned, grinning widely, running backward in her eagerness. "I won't! I promise!"

"That child," Edna murmured fondly. "Such a dear..."

Tess smiled across the seat at her friend. "Come on. Let's take your things in, then we'll see who our company is."

Tess had gone around to the back of the Suburban and scooped Edna's two shopping bags into her arms when the front door of the main house opened.

A young girl came out—a girl with short, raggedly cut raven black hair. The girl wore a very tight black scrap of a skirt and a black T-shirt cut low enough to show a lot of cleavage and tight enough to reveal every curve of her fully mature torso. She wore no bra under the T-shirt. Stunned at the sight of the girl's lush, unbound breasts beneath the thin layer of cloth, Tess looked down to keep from gawking. The girl wore boots as black as the rest of her outfit—clunky, lace-up boots, with thick soles and round, heavy heels.

Tess straightened, holding a bag in each arm. The girl, looking bored to death, sauntered down the steps and across the yard toward the Suburban. When she got closer, Tess saw that she'd pierced her nose. A diamond caught the sun, winking from the side of her left nostril.

Tess just couldn't help herself. She stared. Even with the bad attitude and the crudely provocative clothes, the girl was drop-dead beautiful. A real traffic-stopper. She had eyes like Elizabeth Taylor's—so blue they appeared violet. Each feature of her face was perfection. And beneath a heavy layer of pale makeup, her skin looked flawless.

The girl came within three feet of Tess before she stopped and braced a hand on her hip. The violet eyes gave Tess a long, thorough once-over.

"You must be the new wife," the girl said. "I'm Starr. And I'm here to see my dad."

Chapter Eleven

Tess and Edna exchanged dazed glances. And then Zach rolled into the yard in one of the pickups, with Lolly in the passenger seat and Beau squatting in the truckbed behind the cab. Zach pulled in behind the Suburban.

Hips swaying, Starr strolled to the pickup. As she approached, Beau rose slowly to his feet. He took off his hat and laid it over his heart.

Zach leaned out the window. "Get your tongue back in your mouth, Tisdale."

"Yessir." Beau stuck his hat back on his head and jumped from the pickup bed. "Hi," he said softly to Starr.

Her violet gaze flicked over him dismissingly. Her eyes were only for Zach. She stopped right by his door. Cautiously he opened it and climbed down.

Starr smiled at Zach, a smile that taunted—and yet

seemed, at the same time, to beg for approval. The diamond in her nose caught the sunlight, glaring. "Hi, Daddy," she said. "I've had it with Mom. I've decided to come and live with you."

Zach went straight into the house, washed up quickly in the back porch sink and then headed for his office, where he called Leila.

"God, we've been frantic. Frantic." Leila spoke breathlessly. "When did she get there? Is she all right?"

"She just arrived. And she's fine."

"Oh. Of course. *She's* fine. It's the rest of us who are going out of our minds. You would not believe the things she said to me. And to Derek." Derek, Leila's second husband, was rich as Croesus and well into his sixties.

"You had a fight with her?"

"To put it mildly."

"What was the fight about?"

"Everything. You've seen her. The way she dresses. That thing in her nose. How she stays out all night with God knows who and then never bothers to show up at school. And her report card..."

"Bad?"

"Three *D*'s and two *F*'s."

"Damn."

Leila sniffed delicately. "Zach, I don't think I can take it anymore."

Knowing she couldn't see his face, Zach allowed himself an ironic smile. I don't think I can take it anymore had been one of Leila's favorite lines, way back when, during the hell that had been their marriage to each other.

Leila had more to say. "I simply cannot handle her anymore. She's totally out of control, *ruining* our lives. She's going to have to repeat her sophomore year. Derek feels we have to draw the line somewhere, and I'm afraid I'm to the point where I agree with him."

"Draw the line. What does that mean, exactly?"

"You don't have to become hostile with me."

"I'm not hostile, Leila."

"Oh, yes you are. I know how you are. Always so calm and logical, while inside, you're just...a seething mass of unresolved anger."

There had been a time when Leila's tongue could really cut into him. But not anymore. Now it just made him feel tired. He said, gently, "Let's talk about Starr, all right? And forget all the old garbage between you and me."

"That was precisely my intention until you started in on me."

"Leila. What do you want to do about our daughter?"

"Well." Leila let out a long breath of air. "You'll just have to keep her, that's all. She'll just have to stay with you for a while."

Zach felt relief then. Even though he knew his daughter would bring trouble, and he had his doubts about his ability to deal with her effectively, he wanted a chance with her. Apparently Leila was willing to let him have that chance. But he had to tread carefully. Leila could be damn vindictive. She had used Starr for years, keeping his daughter away from him as much as possible, just to get back at him. He wouldn't put it past her to change her mind now—if she thought he really *wanted* Starr to stay.

"Zach. Have you hung up?"

"No. I'm still here. And I'm willing to have her stay."

Dead silence, then Leila murmured in an injured tone, "I must say, I'm glad you've decided to be reasonable about this for once."

He refrained from pointing out how often he'd suggested that Starr come and live with him. Leila tended to rewrite the past to suit whatever ax she was grinding at the moment.

"I suppose you'll want me to send some of her things," Leila said.

"Not if they're all skin-tight skirts and combat boots."

"What does that mean?"

"It means I'll make sure she gets the clothes she needs here."

Leila made a small, harsh sound in her throat. "So superior. Always so damn superior."

Zach waited. No way he was going to buy into that one.

Leila said, "I guess, to be fair, I should send back half of this month's support check."

"That's up to you."

"All right. I'll send it back."

"Fine."

"You'll call me. If there's…anything I should know."

"Yeah."

"Well, then. I guess that's all, isn't it?"

He agreed that it was and they said goodbye. When he looked up, he saw Starr lurking in the doorway to the dining room, pulling on a hank of that chopped-off hair. "Well?"

He wanted to order her to wash her face and take

that thing out of her nose, but he didn't. He figured demands for changes in her appearance could wait a while. "You can stay."

She dragged in a huge breath and let it out dramatically. "Good. I couldn't go back there, Daddy. I just can't take it with her anymore."

He stared at her, trying to understand why such a good-looking girl would want to wear lipstick the color of dried blood. Watching her, he found himself wondering who the hell she was, anyway. Flesh of his flesh. A total and complete stranger to him. He could see how lost she was. And not damn likely to be found anytime soon. He thought, How could I have ever let her get this bad off?

"Daddy?" Her smooth black brows drew together over her perfect nose. Even with the punk outfit and all that goo on her face, she was so beautiful, it broke his heart.

"What, Starr?"

"You mad?"

"No."

"You seem mad."

"I'm not." He heard the back door close. It would be Tess, bringing in the groceries he'd seen in the back of the Suburban. A wave of relief swept through him as he thought of his wife and her calm, steady ways. Tess could be counted on. She would help him figure out how to deal with this messed-up almost-woman who also happened to be his child.

"Look," he said. "Tess is bringing in the groceries. Why don't you go on and give her a hand?"

Starr stiffened. "Ex-cuse me? Oh right, I'm going to be treated as a servant or something, is that it?"

Zach stared at her levelly, refusing to be baited. "Go on, Starr. Help Tess."

For a long moment, Starr glared right back at him. Then she shrugged. "Sure, fine. Whatever you say." She turned and left, hips swaying, ridiculous boots clomping.

Zach gave it a good five minutes before he followed his daughter to the kitchen. He found Tess alone, unloading grocery bags. He stood for a moment at the end of the counter, watching her, thinking how soothing just the sight of her could be to a man's troubled mind.

He shouldn't stare at her, and he knew it. The relationship they'd settled on didn't include self-indulgences like staring. But right now, after dealing with Leila and Starr, the sight of Tess was just too comforting to resist.

Tess emptied the bags first, setting their contents on the counter. After that, she folded the bags and set them aside. Then she put what she'd bought in the pantry and the refrigerator, stacking it all neatly, each item in the place she had reserved for it, never wasting movements or space.

"I sent Starr out to help you," he said after he'd watched her so long he could sense her discomfort with his silence. "Did she even come in here?"

Tess picked up a large bag of rice and a few cans of stewed tomatoes. "She was here—and she carried in some bags, too." She turned and disappeared into the pantry, reemerging seconds later, empty-handed. "She said she was going to be staying with us."

"That's right." He realized he probably should have discussed it with Tess before he'd made the final decision. "Is that okay with you?"

"Of course. I sent her out to get her bag from the car."

"Well. That's good."

"She said she didn't bring much."

"Yeah. I just talked to her mother. There wasn't a lot of planning involved in this trip."

Tess lowered her voice. "You mean she got mad at her mother and just took off?"

"Looks that way." He glanced toward the central hall, to make sure his daughter wasn't standing there, listening. "I warned you someday we might have to deal with this."

Tess gave him a calm, direct look. "And I said she would be welcome."

He felt some relief, that she wasn't angry, that she accepted Starr's arrival and all the upheaval it would probably bring. "All right then. I...thank you."

"There's nothing to thank me for. She's your daughter. And she has a place here." Tess leaned back against the rim of the sink and crossed her arms under her breasts. "There's just the one room left upstairs. I already told her to take her things up there."

"Sounds good." He thought of Jobeth then, remembering why Tess had taken her to Buffalo. "Did Jo get her cast off?"

"Yes." Tess tipped her head toward the window over the sink. "She went straight for the barn the minute we got home. She's probably lured that horse with the oat bucket by now. She'll have him tacked up in no time."

"Tim will help her."

"He'd better. I told her not to ride without supervision. She has to watch that arm for a while."

"You know she will. She's a great kid."

"Why is it I have the feeling you're not talking about me?" The voice came from the arch to the central hall. Zach glanced over his shoulder. Sure enough. Starr was there.

Tess explained, "I have a daughter. Her name's Jobeth. She's eight."

"Eight." Starr sneered. "How sweet."

Zach started to tell Starr to watch her mouth. But Tess caught his eye first. She gave a tiny shake of her head. He held his tongue.

Tess said, "Do you ride, Starr?"

Starr stuck out a hip and braced her hand on it. "Yeah. I can ride."

Zach reminded her, "It's been four years since I saw you on a horse."

"They have horses in California, Daddy."

"So you've been riding regularly, is that what you're saying?"

"No, I'm just saying that I have ridden since the last time I was here. I can still ride. If I want to ride."

Tess asked quietly, "*Do* you want to ride?"

Starr looked from Zach to Tess and back to Zach again, as if calculating ahead of time the adult response to her reply. Finally, she answered with a wary question. "Now?"

Tess raised an eyebrow at Zach. "What do you say?"

He shrugged, following Tess's lead, keeping the whole transaction offhand. "Sure. I'll ride with you. We can take Jo, too."

Starr looked pained. "The kid, you mean?"

"She's just learning," Tess warned. "You'd have to take it a little easy with her along."

The violet gaze darted back and forth between the

adults, measuring, gauging. Finally Starr forked a black-nailed hand through her spiky hair. "Oh, all right. She can come, I suppose. We'll look out for her."

Tess said, "You'll have to change. Do you have some jeans?"

"Oh, right. Like I'd come to Wyoming without jeans."

Tess smiled. "Then you'd better go put them on."

A half an hour later, Tess watched from the kitchen window as Zach rode past on Ladybird, flanked by Jobeth on Callabash and Starr on a handsome six-year-old mare called Sandygirl.

Edna, who had come over from her own house just a few minutes before to lend a hand with the evening meal, stood beside Tess.

"That girl is so beautiful," Edna said. "I find myself staring at her, marveling at the perfection nature can create. Too bad she has to dress like the bad guy's girlfriend in some awful science fiction movie."

Tess felt the urge to defend Starr. "She did put on jeans, to ride."

"So?"

"Well, the jeans were an improvement on that skirt, don't you think?"

"Not by much. There's still that horrible hair. And all that stuff on her face. And if God had meant for us to poke holes in our noses—"

Tess held up the potato she was peeling as a signal for silence. "Don't say it. You have pierced ears yourself."

"That's different."

Tess just looked at her friend. "Is it?"

Fondly Edna bumped her shoulder against Tess's. "All right. You just may have a point." She lifted an eyebrow at Tess. "But you will try to get her to wear a brassiere, won't you please?"

Tess remembered the dazed, flushed look on Beau Tisdale's face when Starr had strutted down the driveway in his direction. "Definitely. And soon." Tess handed her potato to Edna, who began slicing it thin for au gratin.

"What is it?" Edna asked gently.

Tess realized she'd been staring out the window at nothing. The riders were long gone. She picked up another potato and started in on it with the peeler. "I just think Starr is so sad, that's all. She needs love and attention so much. You can see it in those eyes of hers."

"But she'll reject anyone who tries to offer it," Edna predicted.

"I know."

"You must get together with Zach on this. Really talk this through. Decide what the rules will be for Starr—and then present a united front when she tries to get by you."

"Good advice," Tess said, and wondered, given the careful distance she and Zach maintained with each other, how in the world they would "get together" over the issue of poor, lost Starr.

"I think we should talk. About Starr."

Tess, on the porch step, stared up through the darkness into the shadowed eyes of her husband. "I was thinking the same thing."

His mouth twisted in a wry grin. "I just checked on her. She's up in her room, hooked up by her headphones to that boom box she brought with her. But I've noticed she can be sneaky. I look up and there she is, watching me from a doorway."

"I've noticed that, too."

"Got any carrots in that garden of yours yet?"

She chuckled, feeling so happy that he had sought her out again at last—that he had thought to consult her in this situation with Starr. "My carrots need another good month in the ground. Why?"

"We could wander out to the horse pasture, give them a treat."

"—And, at the same time, be sure no one will hear what we say."

"Exactly."

"How about apples? I bought a bag of them in town today, for pies."

"Get 'em. I'll meet you at the back door."

The horses saw them coming and trotted over, just Ladybird and Callabash at first. But as soon as the others saw the treat, they wandered over, too. Within five minutes, the apple bag was empty.

The horses snorted and nuzzled for more. But when they got nothing but empty hands, they turned one by one and ambled away. Tess folded the empty apple bag and tucked it into a back pocket to put away once she returned to the house.

Zach hoisted himself up to sit on the top rail of the fence. He looked back toward the house for a moment, then down at Tess. "The last time Starr came here, I told her she had to live by my rules if she wanted to stay with me. That drove her away completely, I think."

Tess could hear the regret in his voice and hastened to point out, "Still, a child does need rules."

"I think so, too. And she remembers, I know she does. She knows that in choosing to come here, she's chosen to do as she's told—at least, to a certain extent. So my bet is that she's going to be on her best behavior for a while."

Tess thought his reasoning made sense. So far, aside from a few snide remarks and sulky looks, Zach's daughter had done everything she'd been told to do. She'd carried in groceries, lugged her bags up to her room and put the sheets on her bed. She'd grudgingly agreed to let "the kid" go riding with her and Zach. She'd even set the table at dinner and helped clear off afterward.

Tess leaned against the fence post. "What do you mean, she'll be on her best behavior *for a while?*"

"I mean, sooner or later she'll be testing us out, trying to push the boundaries."

Tess thought of Starr's sullen looks and snide remarks. "I'm afraid you're probably right."

"So we need clear rules, for when she does start pushing."

"Agreed. Such as?"

"I was thinking a ten o'clock curfew, when she starts chomping at the bit to go out nights. And then only one or two nights a week. She's got to show us we can trust her. And then we'll see about letting her stay out later." He stared back toward the house again. Even in the soft, dim light from the half-moon, Tess could see the worry in his eyes. "I don't know," he said.

"What?"

"Starr. I don't know her at all. Her mother said she's

cut a lot of school. Stayed out all night, a lot of nights, with a bad crowd. Her grades were so bad, she'll have to do her sophomore year again. And who knows what else? Drugs?'' He met Tess's eyes. She knew he was wondering about the boys Starr might have been staying out all night with—and what exactly she might have been doing with them.

She started to reach out, to put her hand on his knee in a gesture of reassurance. But she stopped herself before she did it. They might be having their first real conversation in days, but that didn't mean he would welcome her touch. She folded her arms over her middle and looked down at the ground, then back up at him. ''Let's not borrow trouble, all right? We'll show her she can count on us. Trust us. And we'll show her we expect to be able to trust her. Over time, God willing, she'll open up to us a little.''

He made a low noise of agreement. ''That's the best we can do, I suppose.''

''We'll give her a choice, when it comes to chores. Housework or ranchwork. How's that?''

He groaned. ''I hope she chooses the house.''

She gave him a look. ''Thanks. But she should get a choice.''

''All right. And about that thing in her nose...''

''Don't even mention it.''

''What?''

''It hurts no one. Not really. And you know it. I'm sure it drove her mother crazy, when she did it. And if it drives us crazy, that's probably enough reason to punch a hole in some other part of her body. Let it be, I'm telling you.''

He shook his head. ''I hate it, but you're probably

right." His gaze sought hers again. "What about her clothes?"

"She didn't bring much with her. I'll take her shopping."

"I was hoping you'd say that."

"And since this is a ranch, she won't be running around in thigh-high tight skirts too much. I'll try to get her to work with me on choosing appropriate things to wear." Including underwear, she added silently.

He gave a low, humorless laugh. "Somehow, *appropriate* isn't the word that comes to mind when I think about things that Starr might want to wear."

"You'll have to trust me on this," she insisted, with a lot more confidence than she felt.

He was grinning. "Glad to. And good luck."

"Thanks. I'll need it."

They smiled at each other—for just a second too long.

Tess felt the yearning start.

And so did Zach.

His imagination, reined up tight of late, broke free.

He saw himself sliding down from the fence, reaching for her, pulling her close, lowering his mouth to hers the way he had done that night over a week ago on the porch. He remembered the way her body had felt, so soft and pliant, against his. He remembered the sweet, womanly scent of her, the velvet moistness of her mouth when it opened under his.

His own body responded to his thoughts.

He gritted his teeth and reminded himself of how she felt about Cash. For over a week now, all he had to do was focus on that, and any unruly spark of desire would immediately wink out and turn cold.

He ticked off all the things he couldn't afford when

it came to her. He couldn't afford to take her to bed. He couldn't afford to let her get too close, or to care about her too much. He couldn't afford to take any emotional risks with her at all, because he'd only end up the loser in the deal. The woman was in love with someone else.

But going over all the things he couldn't afford to do with her didn't help. And the knowledge that she loved his cousin just didn't seem to be working tonight. Tonight, his body didn't give a damn who the hell she loved or how it might hurt in the end if he started loving *her*. He simply wanted her. Wanted to touch and caress. To lose himself in her.

To take away all of her clothes and see her body naked. To kiss all the parts of her that only a husband should kiss. To bury himself in her. To find sweet release.

And then to start all over again...

He had to get the hell away from her, and he had to do it now.

He jumped down from the fence.

She sidestepped neatly, blocking his escape. And she looked at him so tenderly, so hopefully. "Zach..."

He shook his head. "Tess. Let it go."

"Zach, if we could just talk. If I could just explain how I—"

"There's nothing to explain. Just leave it. Please."

"I can't leave it."

"You can. You will."

"This isn't going to work, Zach. Not forever. We can't avoid each other all the time. We can't...feel like this when we finally get a few minutes together and not ever do anything about it. You do...want me, Zach. I can see in your eyes that you do."

"No…"

"Lying won't make the wanting stop."

"I don't—"

"Zach, we are husband and wife. And we have to find our way to each other. Somehow."

"We've been doing fine." He knew as he said the words how stupid and hollow they sounded.

And she knew, too. She looked at him with such sadness in those dark eyes. "Oh, Zach. I understand, at least a little bit, about how bad it must have been, with Leila. I know you're not a man to give your heart easily. And I can see how, the way she hurt you, it's really hard for you to trust a woman again. But I would never hurt you. I swear to you. I'll be true to you until death. I… Oh, Zach. I want you to know something. I have to tell you—"

He put both hands up, as if she held a gun on him, because, dammit, he *felt* as if she did. "Tess. Don't."

"I have to. I have to say it."

"No."

"Yes. I love you, Zach. I do."

Chapter Twelve

Tess stared up at him, hoping, praying, *willing* him to believe her.

But he didn't.

She could see it in his eyes.

He shook his head. "Hell, Tess."

She wanted to grab him, shake him, *make* him believe. "It's true, Zach. I swear it."

He dragged in a long breath and let it out hard. "Look. I think it's time to call it a night."

She wanted to throw herself against him, pound her fists on his chest, *demand* that he give credit to her words. But then she thought of Leila. Leila had made a lot of demands. Zach would only shake his head some more if she acted like Leila.

She drew herself up. "I'm sorry you don't believe me. I can understand why you don't. But I'm glad it's out in the open, anyway. And I sincerely hope that, over time, you will give me a chance to prove the truth of my love for you.''

He looked at her, a sad smile curving his mouth. ''You're a good woman and a good wife. You have nothing to prove to me, Tess. Not a damn thing.''

And with that, he turned and walked away, across the moon-silvered yard to the house. She watched him go, thinking how lonely he looked, longing to run after him—take his hand, walk beside him.

But knowing he would only pull away from her if she tried.

In the days that followed, Tess did her best to keep a positive attitude. She told herself she had done the right thing, that Zach needed to know of her love. And that someday—someday soon—he would come to her and reach out his hand. He would want to know more. He would want her to explain the how and why of her love for him.

And she *would* explain. Everything.

And after that, they would grow closer. Someday—someday soon—they would be husband and wife in every way.

In the meantime, she just had to wait, that was all. Now that her confused feelings for Cash no longer got in the way, she saw all the time how much Zach wanted her, that the looks he gave her when he thought she didn't see would set green wood aflame. He just needed time and space to come to her on his own.

But it was hard not to become discouraged. She wanted to stay positive, but a person had to deal with reality, too.

And reality kept whispering that she'd *been* giving

him time and space pretty much since their wedding day. And that it hadn't done a bit of good so far.

Starr decided she'd rather make beds and scrub pots than work cattle and help with haying. Zach hid a smile of relief when she made her decision. Tess knew he thought that no one noticed. But Tess saw it. She wished they were close. If they had been close, she would have teased him later, when they were alone, about getting off easy in terms of supervising his sulky child.

And Starr *was* sulky. Even in the first few days of her stay at the ranch, she never did anything voluntarily. Direct orders were needed. But at least she did obey orders—reluctantly, wearing a petulant frown.

When Starr had been with them for three days, Tess took her up to Sheridan to buy her some clothes. It turned out to be a relatively painless procedure. Tess chose items she thought appropriate, careful not to suggest anything too frilly or flowery, and Starr said, "Yeah, sure. That's fine. Whatever."

Tess saved the toughest part for last, when she led Starr to the lingerie department. She went straight to the bra racks. "Let's see, Starr. What size are you?"

Starr's lips pulled back from her teeth. "Oh, God. No."

Tess looked up from the rack and into the violet eyes. They stared each other down.

Then Starr said, "I hate them. They bind me up."

"Your breasts are full." Tess kept her tone strictly matter-of-fact. "You need them. At least for riding."

Starr sighed and tossed her head. Her diamond glittered. Then she grunted. "All right. But nothing with wires in it. Please."

The saleslady showed them some brand-new sports bras that gave excellent support without binding. Starr actually smiled when she tried them on. "Hey. These are okay."

After that, Tess didn't have to worry so much about what the hands might be thinking when Starr walked across the yard.

Four days after the shopping trip, Tess went into the barn through the tack room. She was after some straw to lay between the beds in her garden as a guard against the sun's heat and the moisture loss it caused. She'd just reached the inner door that led to the main part of the barn, when she heard voices.

Jobeth spoke first. "His name is Tick. He's a sweetie, don't you think?"

Then Starr's voice: "Pretty clean, for a barn cat."

"I brush him and Tim gives me stuff to put on his cuts. From the fights he gets in, you know. He's a tom."

Starr laughed. "I know about toms."

"And this is Tack, she's Tick's sister. She's also his wife, I think. Pretty weird, huh?"

Starr agreed, "Yeah. Pretty damn weird."

Jobeth explained, "She'll have kittens, in a few weeks."

A silence.

Tess knew she shouldn't, but she crept sideways, into the shadows, among the bits and bridles strung along the wall. From that angle, she could see the brown head and the black one, bent close together. Each of the girls was busy petting a cat. The cats reveled in the attention, arching their backs, rolling over, nudging and nuzzling at the girls' hands.

The door to the small pasture behind the barn stood

open. Bozo stuck his head in. *"Moo-oo-ooo!"* he said hopefully.

"Come on," said Jobeth.

The little steer came in and the girls petted him, too.

Jobeth looked at Starr. "It's hard. Not to care too much about him, you know?"

Starr nodded. She knew as well as Jobeth did that steers were raised to be sold and slaughtered. "Don't let it get you down," Starr said. She reached out and ruffled Jobeth's hair as the steer wandered back out into the sun. "Life's a bust. Then you die. For everybody."

Jobeth grinned. "Life's okay." She looked around the barn. "Especially since we moved here, you know?"

"Yeah, I know. You were like, *born to ranch.* It's all over you."

Jobeth looked at the older girl in frank adoration. "Starr?"

"Yeah?"

"We're sort of sisters, aren't we?"

"Yeah. I suppose."

"Would you mind a lot...if your dad adopted me?"

Starr leaned back against a hay bale and laced her hands behind her head. "Why? Is he?"

"I hope he will."

"Did you ask him?"

"Yeah."

"So what did he say?"

"He said he would talk about it with my mom— when the time's right." Jobeth frowned. "What does that mean, *when the time's right?* Is that one of those things grown-ups say when they're not going to do anything, really?"

Starr appeared to be playing some kind of ladder game with her fingers.

Jobeth leaned closer. "Whatcha got?"

"Ladybug."

"Cool."

Starr let her hands fall to her lap. They both watched what must have been the ladybug, flying off.

"Fly away home," Jobeth said.

"Yeah, get your ass back to that burnin' house, baby...."

Jobeth let out a guffaw that was part shock and part delight. "Starr!"

"Sorry." Starr leaned against the bale again, sighing—and picked up the conversation about adoption as if it had never been dropped. "No, if my dad says something, he means it. So, he will do it. He'll adopt you. I mean, after he finally gets around to talking to your mom. And *if* your mom says yes."

Jobeth picked up a piece of straw and began smoothing it over her knee. "So would that be okay, with you?"

Starr leaned her head back, closed her eyes.

"Starr. Would it?"

Starr lifted her head again and looked at Jobeth. "Yeah. I wouldn't mind, since it's you. I wouldn't mind at all."

Jobeth said, "Good." For a moment neither girl spoke, then Jobeth declared, "When I get bigger, I'll get a diamond. Just like yours."

"It's only a rhinestone, kid."

"It shines like a diamond. Like you. Like a star."

That night, when Zach came in from his last rounds, Tess was waiting for him in the kitchen.

"What?" he said warily, when he saw her.

She put on a smile that was friendly and no more. "I thought we should touch base a little."

"About what?"

She glanced toward the central hall, to be sure they were alone, and then she lowered her voice. "About Starr."

He frowned. "Did something happen? What did she do?"

Tess stood. "Relax. She didn't do anything. I just want to talk a little, that's all. Let me get you a beer." She waited a fraction of a second, and when he didn't refuse the beer, she went to the refrigerator, pulled out a longneck and screwed off the top. "Here."

He took it, muttering suspiciously, "Thanks."

"How about the front porch?"

"Fine."

He followed her through the house and out the door. She sat in her usual place on the step. He leaned against the porch post opposite her, clearly unwilling to get too close.

He lifted the beer. "All right. What?" He drank.

She said, "The shopping trip went fine."

He watched her broodingly. "Yeah, I noticed the jeans and T-shirts. She looks better. Much better."

Tess knew he also must have noticed that Starr was wearing bras now, but he didn't say anything. He probably thought his troubled daughter's underwear was too intimate a subject to discuss with her. Maybe he thought it would inflame her senses or something, make her grab him and kiss him and say terrible things, like I love you, Zach. And I wish you would give me a chance. I wish you would let me get close, let me tell you everything that's in my foolish heart....

"Anything else?" he said, already pushing away from the porch post.

No way she was letting him go yet. "As a matter of fact, yes."

"I'm listening."

"I saw her today, in the barn."

He was instantly on guard. "With who? Beau?"

"No. With Jobeth."

He relaxed against the post again.

"What made you think she might be with Beau?"

He drank from his beer. "I don't know. The way he looks at her. And yesterday, I saw them out by the sheds together."

"Doing what?"

He shrugged. "Just talking. It looked like no more than a Hi-how-are-you kind of thing. But it makes me nervous. She's sixteen, with problems. And he's a lonely cowhand. You know what I mean."

She thought of Josh and his green eyes and killer smile, all those years ago. And of her younger self, looking for excitement, for someone to sweep her off her feet. Oh, she did know. She knew exactly what Zach meant.

And yet Starr was so much more sophisticated than Tess had been. What real appeal could some penniless cowpuncher hold for her?

She said, "I've seen the way Beau looks at her. But she didn't seem interested in him in the least. I got the feeling she wouldn't give him the time of day."

"Who can say what goes on with her?"

Tess allowed herself a smug smile. "I can. A little, anyway."

He looked at her sideways. "What does that mean?"

She leaned toward him a little. "I have a theory."

Her enthusiasm must have been contagious. He actually cracked a smile. "A theory, huh?"

"Yes."

"Tell me."

"I believe she really is trying. That she sincerely wants to fit in here, to make things work, with us."

He grunted. "Right. By sulking all the time, making smart-mouth remarks and wearing a ring through her nose."

"It's not a ring. It's a rhinestone."

"Whatever. You know what I mean."

"Zach, aside from you, years ago, I don't think anybody's invested any effort in her at all. I don't think anybody's really cared what she did with herself or her time—until she became an embarrassment, I mean. You should have seen her, when we bought the clothes. Trying to act like she didn't care. But she did care. That someone would take the time to get her outfitted. I swear, I believe her mother probably just threw money at her and told her to get her own clothes."

"But not you," he said softly. "*You* took the time with her."

She looked away. The kind words moved her. Especially coming from him. But she had to be careful not to make too much of them, not to scare him off.

She spoke briskly. "Okay, she doesn't exactly knock herself out to be helpful. But she does what she's told to do. She's keeping the bargain you laid out for her four years ago that if she lives here, she lives by our rules.

"And today, Zach. Today, I went into the barn and saw her with Jobeth. They didn't see me. I probably shouldn't have spied on them, but I did. I hid in the shadows and watched them. And Zach, they are *friends.* I mean, I already noticed that Jobeth thinks Starr is about the most wonderful thing to hit this ranch since Callabash. But Starr cares for her, too. She hides it, when we're around, but you should have seen her, like a real big sister, petting the barn cats and dishing out advice about how tough life can be. And then...grabbing Jobeth, ruffling her hair. Jobeth said that they were like sisters, weren't they? And Starr nodded and said she supposed that they were.''

Tess glanced away for a moment, remembering the other subject the girls had discussed—the subject of Zach adopting Jobeth. Tess had stewed about that all afternoon. And then she'd accepted the fact that for Jobeth to be Zach's child legally could only be for the best, no matter what happened in the end between herself and Zach.

If Jobeth were legally Zach's daughter, then she would never lose her place with him, or on this ranch. It would break Tess's heart in two, to have to let her daughter go, should it come to that. But she would do it. If that was Jobeth's choice, and if Zach wanted it, too.

Still, Tess had no intention of mentioning the adoption issue herself. It was Zach's subject to broach.

Zach tapped his empty beer bottle against his thigh. ''Well. What you've told me sounds...interesting.''

''Come on,'' she scoffed. ''You know it's much more than *interesting*. It's progress, that's what it is.'' She considered telling him a bit more—such as how Jobeth admired Starr so much, she planned to get her nose pierced. But then she decided that probably wouldn't go over real big.

''What else?'' he demanded.

''Nothing.''

"I can see by that smile that there's something else."

"No," she said, playing innocent. "Not a thing. That was it."

He leaned his head back against the post and let out a breath. "Well. I guess you're right. It does sound like maybe Starr is working to get along, like maybe she *wants* to be here. And that's good."

"Yes. Very good."

A silence fell. The night sounds, imperceptible a moment ago, seemed much louder. Tess heard the soft whicker of one of the horses out in the back pasture, carried to them on the wind. And some bird she couldn't identify trilled out a long, sweet cry somewhere off to the east. And far off, as always, the coyotes howled.

Zach said, "Well..." He pushed himself away from the post and started for the door. He was leaving her, as he always left her, sitting in the darkness, alone.

"Zach."

He turned, his hand on the doorknob. "Yeah?"

"I've been wondering."

His eyes narrowed. "What?"

She cast about for something—anything—to keep him there a few moments longer.

"What is it, Tess?" Impatient. Eager to get away.

A subject finally occurred to her. "Well...about the rustling problem."

"What about it?"

"You haven't mentioned anything lately, about signs of trouble out in the pastures."

"Nobody's seen anything—not since Beau and Tim found those tire tracks back at the end of May."

"Almost a month ago," she said. "That's good, isn't it?"

He shrugged. "Could be. Who can say?"

"Maybe they've stopped."

"It's possible."

"But you don't think so."

"No, I don't. I think they've been smart and lucky. And that we've never been at the right place at the right time.

"And I think anytime you ride out by yourself, you should be sure and take that little Colt I gave you."

Chapter Thirteen

"It's hot," Jobeth whined.

"It's unbearable," Starr agreed. She was sitting next to Jobeth, on the top step of the front porch. She leaned her head against the porch post and groaned aloud. "What we need is a swim."

Tess and Edna, who sat back in the shadows of the porch, hemming twin panels of a set of curtains Tess had made for Starr's room, shared a smile at the girls' complaining.

Edna rubbed sweat from the bridge of her nose, sliding thumb and forefinger under the glasses she wore for close work. "Oh, yes. It feels like August and it's hardly the end of June."

"Mom," Jobeth said.

"Um?"

"When are Zach and the others coming back?"

They had headed out after the big noon meal, to fix a length of fence near the highway into town.

"I don't know," Tess said. "Anytime now, I'd guess."

"We could ride out to meet them." Jobeth looked at her stepsister with hopeful eyes.

Starr made a grotesque face, sticking out her tongue and rolling her lips back away from her teeth. "*Ugh.* Just what I need on a scorcher like this. To get on the back of some sweaty, fly-bitten nag and ride along a dusty road to meet up with my dad and two cowboys."

"Sandygirl's no nag."

"She's a horse. Horses sweat. They draw flies. I am not getting on a horse unless I'm riding it someplace I can swim. Get it?"

"Yeah. I get it." Jobeth gave Starr a nudge with the toe of her tennis shoe. "Meany."

Starr nudged back, playfully, with a bare foot.

"Hey!" Jobeth gave Starr a shove.

"Watch it...." Starr shoved back.

Seconds later, they were rolling around together on the little patch of scrubby grass at the foot of the steps, squealing and giggling. Tess and Edna shared another look and went on with their sewing.

Right then, Zach and the men drove into the yard. With a sigh, Tess stood from her comfortable swing chair. She gave a long whistle. The girls froze and looked up at her.

She pointed at the pickup. The girls pulled apart and jumped to their feet. Zach drove past them, no doubt on the way to park in the tractor barn on the far side of the sheds out in back. He waved as he went by— and so did Beau, who rode in the truckbed with the tools, the barbwire, and the leftover posts.

Tess glanced immediately at Starr, to see how she reacted to the sight of Beau. The girl appeared more interested in yanking her cutoffs back into place after her wrestling match with Jobeth than in making eyes at the ranch hand. Starr looked up and caught Tess's glance. "Listen, Tess. Crystal Creek runs along on the other side of the horse pasture, behind that old cabin where Great-grandpa John used to live. We can ride above the bank until we find a decent place to swim. Let me take Jo and go. We'll be back by five, I swear."

Tess had been wary of letting either of the girls head out for isolated spots. If those cattle thieves were still doing their dirty work on the Rising Sun, she didn't want Jobeth or Starr meeting up with them.

"Tess. Please. We are suffering here."

Tess chewed on her lower lip a little, thinking she wouldn't mind a swim herself, but she did need to get started on dinner soon.

Edna said, "You take them. I'll get the dinner going."

Tess grinned. "Mind reader. I owe you one."

"Good. Scrabble. This evening at my house. You'll let me win and pretend you didn't."

"We can go?" Starr asked, looking hopeful and younger than her years for once.

"Yes," Tess said. "Let's get our suits on and saddle up."

They'd caught the horses and were cinching up saddles when Zach came out of the barn and strode their way. Tess looked up and saw him coming. Patches of sweat darkened his old blue shirt, down the front and under the arms. Lines of sweaty dust had collected in the creases of his neck. His jeans were gray with dirt.

Tess thought she'd never in her life seen a better-looking man.

He asked, "What's up?"

Tess told her silly heart to settle down and answered with a calm she wished she could feel in his presence, "We're going hunting. For a swimming hole."

His glance flicked to the Colt at her hip. "You'll be careful."

"You know we will."

The little gray mare she'd chosen whickered softly. Tess patted her forehead. "Easy. It's okay."

The girls were already mounted and ready to go. Reggie, who'd appeared from the barn when they started tacking up, sat to the side, waiting patiently, looking expectant. Tess swung into the saddle. As she fiddled with the reins, Zach stepped up and took the headstall. She looked down at him. He smiled. She felt weakness all through herself. Longing that could hardly be borne. Yet she would bear it.

He gave her a crooked smile. "I'll get a shovel and follow along. If you don't find a good hole, we can make one."

She watched his mouth, wishing she could just bend down and plant a kiss on it.

He asked, "So what do you say?"

"Sounds good."

He started giving instructions. "Okay then, pick up the creek down behind the old cabin. Follow it about two or three miles, toward the mountains. You'll be on public land that nobody's been using this season. You should find some good places there." Tess took his meaning. Cattle tended to break down the banks of streams and flatten out the streambeds. On unused land, the creek would be more likely to keep a deeper channel. "I'll be along, in a few minutes." He let go of the bridle and backed away.

The girls started off and Tess followed after them, Reggie taking up the rear.

A half an hour later, they found a good spot, a wide bend in the creek that slowed down the water. It wasn't that deep. But it was clear and inviting. Cottonwoods and willows grew close to the bank, providing tempting, welcome shade.

Reggie flopped down in the shade as the girls quickly dismounted and stripped off their clothes, revealing the bathing suits they'd put on underneath. They ran for the bank, hooting like wild animals, yowling in glee when they hit the water, going under for several seconds and then shooting up in the air, shivering and screaming.

"It's cold!"

"It's *freezing!*"

"It's great!"

Tess spread an old blanket in the shade of a cottonwood and removed her own jeans, shirt and boots at a more sedate pace. She felt nervous, knowing Zach would come. She hoped she looked all right in her three-year-old suit. In the bright sun, the tropical print seemed just a little faded, she thought. Still, the colors were pretty and complemented her skin tone. And the cut was modest, so she didn't feel *too* naked.

"Tess, come on! Hurry up!"

"Yeah, Mom! Get in!"

She adjusted the straps of her suit, then turned toward the clear water and the waving, shouting girls. "Look out! I'm coming!" She took off at a run, pausing a split second at the edge to jump and gather her

legs up to her chest. Shrieking, she sailed out across
the creek, hitting the surface in a beauty of a cannon-
ball, sending water flying everywhere.

Zach heard all the screeching and shouting a quarter
of a mile away. He slowed Ladybird and listened. The
sounds told him that Tess and the girls had found a
perfectly fine place to swim and wouldn't need him or
his shovel after all. He might as well turn back.

But he didn't turn back. He just kept on moving
toward the laughter and happy voices. Finally he came
up a small rise and there they were below him, not
thirty feet away. He reined in. Leaning on the saddle
horn, he watched one doozy of a water fight—a battle
in which Starr showed herself willing to play dirty, but
Tess definitely had the best hand for serious water
spraying. Jobeth, outsized and outclassed, mostly cow-
ered between the other two, squealing and howling.

Tess, as pretty as a mermaid in a suit with big, bright
flowers all over it, spotted him first. She stopped and
tried to wave, which gave Starr a chance to mount a
serious attack.

"Come on, Jo!" Starr commanded, fanning water
hard and fast at a disadvantaged Tess. "Get her! Help
me get her!"

Jobeth turned on her mother with glee. The two girls
sprayed and splashed until Tess dived beneath the surface. The girls looked around. Tess came up near the
bank and started right for the edge.

"No fair! Chicken!"

Tess waved a hand at them, hardly glancing back,
leaving them to turn on each other—which they immediately did.

"Zach. You came." Her slanted eyes were on him,

only on him, as his eyes were only for her. Right then, their splashing, giggling daughters might not have existed.

She emerged from the creek, her long, slim legs revealed to him for what must have been the first time. She looked so good, the water running off of her—she looked *womanly,* everything sleek and strong and yet soft at the same time.

When she got up on the bank, she kept coming toward him. He watched her come, knowing she felt his gaze on her, though his eyes were shadowed by the brim of his hat. At a blanket spread beneath a cottonwood, near where Reggie lay asleep, she stopped to scoop up a towel, then came the rest of the way, drying herself as she walked.

I love you, she had told him the other night.

He didn't believe it. He knew it couldn't be true.

But damn. It had sounded good.

And now, looking into her welcoming eyes as she came on, he didn't know if he even cared anymore who she loved or how she might hurt him if he let himself get too attached to her.

He was already attached to her.

He couldn't imagine his life without her.

He might as well go ahead and surrender all the way to her.

Because she was going to have him in the end.

As he would have her.

Sitting there on his horse as his wife approached him on that hot June day, Zach Bravo at last came to understand that it was only a matter of time. He would keep her at bay as long as he could bear to—keep his pride and his distance till he just plain couldn't stand not having her. But sooner or later, he would fall.

She stopped a few feet from him and rubbed her hair with the towel. He watched the tender flesh of her inner arm, the hollow where her arm met her body, the slight rounding of her breast before it disappeared under the suit. She went on rubbing, drying her hair. His gaze trailed up, over the sweet curve of her shoulder and the singing line of her neck. He met her eyes and saw a woman's knowledge.

She knew exactly what she was doing, drying her hair that way, looking at him so steadily, a half smile on that mouth of hers.

Maybe he didn't have her love. But he had her desire. She wanted him now—as she had not on their wedding night. Now, when he took her, he would be able to tell himself it was his own face she saw when she closed her eyes.

That was something.

Not enough for him, but better than nothing at all.

"Come swimming," she said, hooking the towel around her neck.

"Naw." He reached back to put his hand on the shovel he'd tied behind his saddle. "I just came in case you needed help."

She gestured over her shoulder. "We found the perfect spot. And the water's great."

Starr yelled and waved from the bank across the stream. "Daddy! Come on!"

Jobeth, standing beside Starr, chimed in. "Yeah, Zach, come swim!"

He shook his head and waved. "Some other time!"

The two girls groaned in unison, then jumped back in the water and started splashing each other again. Watching them, Zach thought that Starr really did seem to be coming out of her sulky shell more and more every day. He also remembered the promise he'd made to Jobeth a while back. He would have to talk to Tess about it soon.

He saw no reason that she would say no. His adopting Jobeth would only give his stepdaughter a firmer claim on the land she loved so much. Still, he hesitated to bring the subject up with Tess. Somewhere inside himself, he couldn't help fearing that she would turn his offer down. Maybe it was all the years of dealing with Leila. It had ruined him for thinking a woman would ever do the right thing when it came to her own child.

"Thanks for coming to help." Tess stepped forward and took Ladybird's bridle the way he had done with her gray mare back at the horse pasture. "—Even if we didn't need you in the end." She patted the horse's neck and smiled up at him.

Something softened deep inside him. She was not like Leila. Not in any way. She would be kind in her power over him.

And she *was* fair.

He said quietly, "Jobeth would like me to adopt her."

She went on smiling, though the smile changed, grew tender and a little bit sad. "I know."

"Will you allow that?"

"Yes, Zach. I will."

Zach and Tess drove to Buffalo the next day to consult with the family lawyer, Philo T. O'Hare. O'Hare said that since Jobeth's natural father was deceased and Tess was the girl's sole guardian, the adoption should be no problem at all. He had them fill out a petition for adoption and assured them that the finalizing court date would occur within a month or so.

Tess seemed lost in her own thoughts on the way back. Zach didn't disturb her. He felt good, to know that within weeks, he could claim Jobeth as a true daughter. He also felt grateful to his wife, for granting him that claim.

At home, the girls and Edna were waiting for them, hungry for news of how it had gone.

"You'll be a Bravo within a month or two," Zach told Jobeth.

She let out a yelp of glee and launched herself at him, hugging him hard. From him, she jumped on Starr, then she grabbed Edna and squeezed her a good one.

Last of all, she went into her mother's waiting arms.

"Oh, thanks, Mom," she said. "Thank you so much."

"There's nothing to thank me for," Tess replied. "It's the best thing. The right thing."

"Oh, Mom. It is. I know it is."

They rang the bell for the hands and then went in to the midday meal that Edna had prepared.

After they ate, Zach decided to take Jobeth out to poison weeds. He invited Starr. She grunted. "No, thanks. I think I'll stick around here."

"You still have vacuuming to do, young lady," Edna reminded her.

"I know, I know. It's just a thrill a minute around this place." The words were sarcastic, but then she grinned.

Zach congratulated himself again on how much progress they were making with her.

* * *

An hour later, in her swinging chair on the front porch, Tess tied off the last stitch on the last hem of the last panel of Starr's new midnight blue curtains. By then, Zach and Jobeth were long gone, and Edna had wandered back across the yard to her own house for a brief nap. Starr was inside—presumably dusting, but probably sprawled across her bed with her headphones on, thumbing through one of her rock and roll magazines.

Humming happily to herself, Tess rose and carried the final two panels she'd been working on inside. The other four panels were folded and waiting in the master bedroom. Tess had set up her sewing machine in there, as well as the iron, all hot and ready for a final pressing. Tess ran the iron over the curtains.

Then she carried her handiwork across the hall to Starr's room. At the door, she gave a light knock. "Starr?"

No answer. The girl probably had her headphones cranked up loud. Tess peeked around the door. No Starr. Tess shrugged. Who could ever say where that girl might get off to? She was probably out in the barn, leaning against a hay bale, woolgathering.

Tess went on into the room, set the curtains on the midnight blue quilted spread she'd made a few days before and returned to her own room for the stepladder she kept in the closet there. Back in Starr's room, Tess set up the ladder, grabbed a curtain rod and began feeding a panel onto the end. Once she had the curtains strung on the rods, she moved to the window to hook the rods in place.

She'd just raised her foot to the first step of the footstool when she looked down on the backyard—and caught sight of Beau Tisdale as he pulled a very willing-looking Starr through the open door of the barn.

Chapter Fourteen

For an endless moment, Tess just stood there with one foot on the stepladder, staring blindly out the window at the door of the barn, wishing with all of her heart that she hadn't seen what she'd just seen.

Already, the cowhand and Zach's daughter had disappeared into the shadows beyond the door. Nothing marked their passing. If Tess had looked down a few seconds later, she wouldn't even have seen them.

And some part of her truly wished that she hadn't. Because some part of her—a very large part of her—did not want to deal with this at all.

Carefully Tess carried the curtains and rods back to the bed and set the whole apparatus down. Then, for several minutes, she just stood there, looking at her own handiwork, trying to decide what action she should take here.

Starr was sixteen. And probably not a complete innocent.

Beau had to be at least in his twenties. At this point in their lives, he was too old for Starr. Wasn't he? The law would certainly say so.

Tess put her hands to her mouth, shook her head.

And thought of Josh.

And the act she had done with him that had changed her life so irrevocably. The act that had created Jobeth, who was more precious to Tess than her own life.

No, Tess would never choose *not* to have had Jobeth, no matter what the price.

But, Jobeth aside—oh, to go back! To simply not make that choice to lie down in the barn with her father's hired man. To have been valedictorian of her high school class, as she would have been. To have gone off on an AG scholarship to college. To have been there when her father died, and to have done all she could to keep her place, her home, her heritage.

All those possibilities wiped out.

Because of a handsome man and an urge to wildness inside herself.

If, somehow, her parents had found out before it was too late—if they had talked to her—would it have changed anything?

Tess couldn't be sure. She just wasn't that girl anymore, that girl who flung herself at life without a care for the cost. That girl who was a lot like Starr—not so tough or so worldly-wise, maybe. But bright and passionate and hungry to see what the world had to offer.

Tess found she was turning for the stairs.

Maybe it would do no good. Maybe she had no right to intervene. Maybe she should wait for Zach to come home and discuss the situation with him, call him on that cellular phone he carried in the pickup with him now and tell him to hurry home.

But he couldn't get home fast enough to keep whatever was going on out in the barn from proceeding right through to its natural conclusion.

Which might be totally innocent.

Or might not...

No, she couldn't let it go. Not even for the time it would take Zach to come home and deal with it. She had to do what she could right now.

Tess went down the stairs, through the kitchen and out the back door, closing it rather loudly behind her, making no secret of her whereabouts. She marched straight for the barn and went right inside.

At first glance, it appeared deserted. And then she heard the rustling behind a stack of hay bales in the corner.

"Starr."

More rustling.

"Come on out. Now."

Slowly, her faced flushed and hay in her hair, Starr emerged from behind the bales. Tess stared at her, not sure what to do next. Starr stared right back, defiant.

Finally Tess managed to speak in a dry whisper. "You buttoned your shirt crooked."

Starr's lower lip quivered as she swiftly corrected the problem.

"Beau," Tess said more strongly. "Are you just going to hide back there and let Starr face the music alone?"

Beau appeared behind Starr, looking grim. All of his clothes seemed buttoned up right. Tess dared to hope that was because he'd never *un*buttoned anything. He had his hat in his hand and he beat it a few times against his thigh, watching Tess warily as he did it.

"You'd better go on back to your trailer for now," Tess told him.

His jaw twitched. For a moment, Tess thought he might argue with her. But then he turned without a word and started toward the door, brushing bits of hay from his shirt and hair as he went.

Starr watched him go, a look of injured disbelief on her beautiful face. She let him get all the way to the door, before she called out, "Beau! Wait! You don't have to do what *she* says. You don't have to..." She let the sentence die unfinished when Beau only shook his head and kept on walking.

Fuming now, Starr turned back to Tess. "Nice going. Thanks."

Tess stared at her stepdaughter. "The attitude won't work on me, Starr."

"What the hell are you talking about?"

"Attacking me isn't going to make this situation disappear—or keep me from telling your father about it."

Starr let out a disgusted breath, braced a hand on her hip and looked Tess up and down. "And I thought you were all right."

Tess only sighed. "I can see we're not going to get anywhere right now. Just go on up to your room. I'll send your father up after he gets home."

Starr was chewing on her lower lip. For a moment, Tess thought she might break down, say something honest, open the door for a real talk.

But in the end, she only drew back her shoulders and lifted her perfect chin. "Fine." Her rhinestone glinted; her eyes flashed in pure scorn. "And anyway,

I know what's up with you. I know why you're making such a big deal out of this."

Dread formed, a hard ball, in Tess's stomach. "Starr, look—"

"I *am* sixteen. I've got a brain. And eyes. I know you and my dad aren't married in any *normal* way. Because I know where my dad sleeps. And it's not with you."

Tess felt as if the girl had kneed her in the stomach. But somehow, she stayed upright and continued looking Starr right in the eye. "My relationship with your father has nothing to do with this. And I think you know that."

Another stare-down ensued. In the end, Starr's bravado cracked. She let out a tiny cry, whirled on her heel and ran from the barn.

Tess watched her through the wide-open door, made sure she ran toward the house and then listened for the slam of the back door. When she heard it, she found a hay bale and carefully lowered herself onto it. She sat there for a long time, staring at the rough floor, feeling numb and awful. She had thought that everything was going so well lately.

So much for what she had thought.

Zach and Jobeth stood out in a pasture near Saunderman Road, staring down at the tire tracks and the dragged spot the stock trailer ramp would have made.

"Is it them, Zach? Were the rustlers here?"

"Looks like it. Get me the phone from the pickup, will you?"

Jobeth took off. She was back with the phone in a flash. "Here you go."

Zach punched up the auto-dial number for the sheriff's office in Buffalo, got the dispatcher and explained what he'd seen, where he was and how to get there. Then he handed the phone back to Jobeth, who trotted to the pickup, put it away and ran back to him once more.

"What do we do now, Zach?"

"We wait for someone to come out and write a report."

Zach and Jobeth arrived home at five-thirty, both covered in mud. They left their boots by the back door and came trooping in in stocking feet.

Tess knew from the look on Zach's face that the afternoon had been no better for him than for her. "What happened?"

"We found tire tracks," Jobeth said eagerly. "Ones the rustlers must have left. So we called the range detective and he came out to make a report." From over at the stove, Edna made a sound of distress. Jobeth continued, "We got all this mud on us later, from pushing the pickup out of a mudhole."

Tess looked at Zach. "Do you know how many cattle are missing?"

"No way to be sure," he said flatly, "as usual." His tone grew brisk. "We need to clean up. Come on, Jo." The two headed upstairs to their respective showers.

Tess trailed after them to the foot of the stairs, dismayed at the news about the tire tracks, and worried about Starr, all alone in her room, probably fretting and fuming, wondering when her father would come. The girl had been up there for almost three hours now. It was long enough for her to suffer and wonder. And really, Tess thought, someone ought to go out and talk to Beau, too. Probably Zach. But Zach couldn't talk to anybody if he didn't know what was going on. And Tess didn't see how she would get Zach alone to share a word with him for hours yet. Sighing, she wandered back into the kitchen, wiping her hands on her apron, trying to remember what had to be done next to get the dinner on the table and everyone fed.

Edna, still at the stove stirring the beans, tapped the spoon impatiently against the rim of the pot. "Tess, you are nervous as a sinner in church. Something isn't right—beyond the news about those thieves. And where is Starr, anyway? We could use a little help with the table."

Tess hadn't planned to mention anything to Edna about the incident in the barn, at least not until she'd spoken with Zach—but then she turned and met her friend's eyes.

Edna set the spoon on the spoon rest. "All right. What's happened with Starr?"

Tess shot a glance around to be sure that they were alone. Then she swiftly explained the events of the afternoon—minus only Starr's comment about where she and Zach slept at night.

Edna said, "You must talk to your husband immediately."

"I know. But there's no time now."

"Of course there is. You just run on upstairs and catch him before he comes down from his shower."

Tess gaped at her friend. "Run upstairs? Now?"

"Yes."

Tess knew Edna's suggestion made perfect sense. She should have just followed Zach upstairs to his room in the first place and caught him alone. And yet she hadn't. Because she *never* entered his private space—except to gather his laundry when she washed his clothes. He made his own bed and tidied up after himself. With the kind of relationship they had, she wouldn't dare go near him when he was in his room. And never *ever* when he was doing something so private as taking a shower.

"Tess. What is the matter with you?"

"Nothing. Really. It's just that I'm so worried. About Starr."

"Well, then. Go talk it over with Zach. Now."

"But the dinner—"

"Oh, come on. I've been getting dinners on the table in this house for more years than I care to count. I think I can manage it this evening. I'll feed the hands and Jobeth and myself. You worry about Zach and Starr."

"Yes. You're right. I know you are."

"So get going."

"Yes. I am. Right now."

Tess stood in the upstairs hall, her ear pressed against Zach's door. The shower stopped. She would give it a slow count of two hundred, and then she'd knock.

"Mom?"

Tess let out a cry and turned. Jobeth stood at the top of the stairs, her hair slicked back and her skin still rosy from her own shower.

"Mom, what are you doing?"

"Jobeth, you scared me."

"Sorry. But what are you—?"

"Honey, I need to talk to Zach."

"Oh."

"Go on down and help Edna with the dinner."

"Okay. Where's Starr?"

"In her room."

"Can I get her?"

"Uh, no. We'll bring her. When we come."

"But—"

"Jobeth, would you please just do what I asked you to do?"

Frowning, Jobeth studied her mother. "Something's strange. What's wrong with you?"

"Nothing's wrong with me." That wasn't a lie, not exactly. "I promise you. I am fine. Now please go on down and give Edna a hand."

Reluctantly Jobeth descended the stairs. Tess moved to the top of the stairwell and watched her go, willing her not to change her mind and decide to come back up.

Finally Jobeth reached the bottom step and disappeared in the direction of the kitchen. Tess heard Edna's voice, faintly. "There you are. Come and set the table, please."

Good, Tess thought. Edna would keep Jobeth out of the way now. Tess turned for Zach's door once more.

It was open. Zach stood in the doorway, wearing clean Wranglers—and nothing else.

Tess blinked and stammered. "Oh. I didn't—"

"What the hell's going on?"

"I…" She gulped and stared and felt like a complete fool. "I have to talk with you."

"Right now?"

"Yes. And in private. Please."

He gave her one of those long looks of his, a look that measured and doubted and made her feel so confused. Then he stepped back. "All right. Come on."

She moved past him into the room, far too aware of his strong, bare chest, of the steam in the air, left over from his shower, of the clean scent of soap that came from his skin. He closed the door behind her, closed them in together...

She headed for the chair in the corner—as far away from him as she could get, thinking, Come on, get a grip here. This is about Starr, not about all the things you wish your husband would do to you that he *won't* do to you. She sat, drew her shoulders back, sucked in a good, long breath.

Zach remained by the door, watching. "Talk."

Suddenly she couldn't bear to sit. She stood. She went to the window and looked out at the barn, at the door through which Beau had pulled Starr only a few hours before.

The way to explain it all finally came to her. She would just start with herself at the window in the room next door and go right on through till the end.

So she did. She told it all, everything, right up to when Edna had sent her upstairs to talk to him. Everything *except* Starr's remarks about their sleeping arrangements. Somehow, she just couldn't admit that part. And really, it wasn't the issue anyway.

By the time she'd finished, Zach was already turning to the bureau, pulling out a white T-shirt and clean socks. She added, "I honestly thought it was going so well with her. I just...I had no idea about this thing with Beau."

Zach tugged the shirt over his head. "I told you I was suspicious. But we couldn't be sure anything was going on until now. Did you talk to her at all? Did you get any sense of how far the two of them have carried this?"

"No. She was so hostile. I just...didn't know how to reach her."

"It's all right," he said. "You did what you could. " He sat briefly and put on the socks. Then he went to the closet and got some boots. He sat a second time, just long enough to yank them on. Finally he stood.

Tess met his eyes. "I thought it might be good, to let her think things over for a while. But maybe I took it too far. She's been in there for hours, waiting. I believe I heard her go into the bathroom once, but that's all. I kept thinking you and Jobeth would show up, so I just left her in there. I probably should have—"

He waved a hand. "You did fine. I'll go talk to her now."

"And to Beau."

"He'll be next. Starr first."

"Yes. Good."

He turned and went out. Tess sank back to the chair, unwilling to go downstairs until he came out of Starr's room, just in case—well, she wasn't sure what. She only knew she wanted to be there waiting when Zach came out. So she stayed.

Zach tapped on Starr's door.

A moment, later, she pulled it open partway and peered out at him. "What?" Her eyes were hard and cold.

"Let me in."

Starr flung back the door and faced him. Behind her, he could see her bed, littered with magazines, her discarded headphones tossed on top of the heap. Over in the corner, wadded up in a pile, lay what looked like the dark blue curtains Tess had been making for her. The stepladder stood a few feet from the wad of blue cloth.

Starr saw the direction of his gaze. She made a low,

guilty sound in her throat. "Look. Those stupid curtains were in my way. All right?"

He crossed the threshold and closed the door behind him. For a moment, the two of them stared at each other. Zach had a feeling of total unreality. He didn't know what to do. Or how to begin.

Starr threw up her hands. "Okay. Say it. I have to go, right? You don't want me around anymore because I'm just...too trampy to live here. Right? Because I have to live by your rules and I blew your rules, going back behind the hay bales with Beau."

He focused on what he was sure of. "Starr. I don't want you to leave."

She dropped to the edge of her bed, to the one spot not littered with magazines. "You don't?" Her eyes seemed to ask, So what's the catch?

Zach despised himself then. How in the hell had he let her get so far away from him that she didn't believe she could get back? "You live here. With us."

The pile of magazines started to slide in her direction. She shoved at it with her elbow. "*She* hates me now."

"Tess does not hate you. She's worried about you."

"She'll tell Jo to keep away from me."

"No, she won't."

Starr looked down at all the magazines, then out toward the window.

"Starr. Look at me."

Her head snapped around and she glared at him, her mouth set in a mutinous line. "I'm not a tramp. I'm not."

"No one called you a tramp."

"*They* did. Derek and Mother. They called me worse than that. But I'm not. I don't do drugs. And I don't do anything with guys. I know how guys are. I learned early. When it comes to guys, it's simple. If you don't get humped, you don't get dumped.''

Zach cleared his throat. ''That's an…interesting way of putting it.''

''It's the truth, that's all.'' She sniffed and wiped her nose with the back of her hand. ''But Beau, he's different than other guys.'' Personally Zach thought Beau was a weasel and a snake in the grass. But he kept his opinion to himself.

Starr must have seen something in Zach's expression that betrayed his opinion of Beau. She cried, ''I can tell you blame him!''

''Starr. What he did was wrong.''

''But he *cares* for me. He does.''

''Then why didn't he come knocking on the front door and ask for you?''

She glared. ''And what would you have said if he did?''

''I would have said no.''

''Exactly. So I had to sneak out to see him. I'm not proud of it, but what else could we do?''

Zach thought, Stayed away from each other. But he didn't say it. It would have done no good.

Starr had more to say. ''Oh, Daddy, Beau *is* different than other guys. He understands what it's like to have everyone making judgments on you, deciding you're a certain way. Because of how you dress. Or because of what your family is like. He hasn't had an easy life, you know. He lost everything. And his father's always drunk now, since they lost their ranch. And his brothers get in trouble all the time. That's not easy for a man to live with, you know?''

''It seems like you've learned a lot about him.''

Starr studied her thumbnail, which was coated with a thick layer of purple polish.

"Starr, you said you'd been sneaking out to see him."

She began chewing on her cuticle. "He cares about me. He really does."

"Starr."

She pressed her lips together, recrossed her legs, shoved at the magazine pile again.

Zach tried to think of a way to reach her. He imagined what Tess might do. It came to him that Tess would get closer to her.

He moved toward Starr. She stopped chewing on her cuticle and watched him suspiciously. When he stood right before her, he dropped to a crouch, so he was the one looking up. "Starr. How many times have you sneaked out at night to…talk with Beau?"

She just stared at him. He waited. Finally she admitted in a small, lost voice, "I don't know. Six or seven."

He swallowed and sucked in a breath. "Look. I'm not judging you. I don't have the right. I haven't been…around enough to go judging you. But I have to know, if the two of you have…" He coughed. He was a reserved man. A *conservative* man. "I hate asking this."

The tears were there, now, in those beautiful blue eyes. "We haven't, Daddy. I swear. I…do care for him. And I probably *would* have. Soon. But not yet. Honest." She looked at him long and hard, as though *willing* him to believe her. Then, with a sad little hitch of her breath, she hung her head and swiped her nose with the back of her hand again.

He dared to reach out, to smooth her spiky hair. "It's okay. It'll be okay."

She only shook her head and kept looking down toward her bare toes that were painted the same intense purple as her fingernails. Outside, someone started banging on the dinner bell. Zach rose.

Starr looked up at him then, desperation in her eyes. "Don't fire him. I'll keep away from him. He needs this job, Daddy."

"What he's done is wrong. He's a grown man. And you're under eighteen. I can't trust a man like that. You have to see that."

"No. Please. You said you wouldn't judge me. Well, don't judge him, either. Give him a chance. Talk to him. You'll see. He does care for me."

"That's not the point."

"Just talk to him first. Please."

He studied her face, not knowing what to say to her. *"Please?"*

He couldn't completely refuse her. "All right. I'll talk to him first. But I really can't see how anything he could say would make me willing to keep him on."

"Just give him a chance."

"Starr—"

"All right, all right. As long as you listen to what he tells you. As long as you do that much."

"I said that I would. Now, why don't you go on down to dinner?"

"No. I'll just stay here. I couldn't eat. Not tonight."

He didn't argue with her. "We'll talk more later."

"Yeah. Okay."

Tess heard Zach come out of Starr's room. He went on down the stairs. She rose from the chair in the corner and almost followed him. But to what purpose? If he wanted to talk to her, Edna would tell him she was still upstairs. And if he just aimed to deal with Beau and get it over with, she didn't want to slow him down.

She sank back to the chair. She knew she probably ought to go ahead and join the others at the table. But she just wasn't quite up to that prospect right then. No, she'd just sit here for a bit, in the quiet room that had so much of Zach in it. She'd take some deep breaths and say a little prayer or two. And in a few minutes, she'd be ready to face the world again.

She was on the third deep breath and the first prayer when she heard Starr come out of her room.

Chapter Fifteen

Zach found Beau sitting at the kitchen table in the trailer he'd been assigned when he'd first hired on at the Rising Sun. His duffel was packed and waiting beside him. The trailer itself looked spotless—ready for the next man Zach hired to move right in.

"I guess I'd like my pay, sir," Beau said. "And then I'll be on my way."

Zach stared at the younger man, torn by opposing urges. He wanted to break every bone in his body for what he'd tried to do with Starr. And yet he felt sorry for him. Starr had been right. Beau hadn't had it easy. Once, his people had been proud folk. And now he was reduced to working another man's cattle to get by.

Zach remembered what he'd promised his daughter. "Starr asked me to hear what you have to say."

Beau looked right at Zach. "There's nothing. Just give me my pay and I'll go."

Zach gave it one more try. "Look. You'd better get a little honest with me here. You'd better tell me what the hell you thought you were doing with my daughter in the barn today."

Beau's jaw twitched. He looked away. "I kissed her. And unbuttoned her shirt. That's all that happened. All that ever happened."

Zach spoke with slow precision. "My daughter is sixteen."

"Yeah. I know."

"And you're what?"

"Old enough. Twenty-one."

"Then what the hell were you up to?"

Beau stared off into the middle distance. "Sometimes a guy gets hungry for more than he's ever gonna get. And then he sees something real pretty, something he knows it's wrong to take. But he's hungry. So he goes and acts like a fool. That's me. A guy who got hungry. A guy who isn't real bright."

Beau let out a long breath and turned his gaze toward Zach once more. "So, you want to beat me around a little or something?"

"Yeah," Zach said softly. "I suppose I do."

Beau got to his feet. The floor space in the trailer wasn't much, so when Beau stepped out from behind the table, he stood right in front of Zach.

"Okay," Beau said. "Do it."

Zach punched him square in the jaw, good and hard. Beau grunted and fell back against the table. Zach waited. The younger man gained his feet again and braced himself for another blow.

Zach considered, then shook his head. "That's all."

"You sure?" Beau rubbed his jaw.

Zach wasn't sure, not at all. Still, all he said was,

"Meet me by the back door of the house in ten minutes. I'll have your money in cash for you. Then you can get the hell off the Rising Sun."

Tess caught up with Starr just before she began to descend the stairs. "Starr."

The girl froze and whirled on Tess. "What?"

"Where are you going?"

"What's it to you?"

Tess looked down at Starr's feet. "Where are your shoes?"

"In my room."

"Go back and put them on. Then wash your hands and we'll go down to dinner together."

"I don't want dinner."

"Then where are you going?"

"Just mind your own business."

"You are my business."

"No, I'm not. You're no one to me." With a toss of her head, the girl started down.

Tess stood on the landing for a moment. Then, with a weary sigh, she followed Starr down.

At the foot of the stairs, Starr turned and gave Tess a fierce glare. But she didn't say anything—probably to avoid attracting the attention of everyone in the kitchen. She hurried on tiptoe out to the great room and through the entrance hall beyond. Tess followed close on her heels, closing the door behind them when they reached the front porch.

Starr whirled on Tess then, and hissed, "Stop following me!"

Tess looked at the girl levelly. "No."

Across the yard, the door to Beau's trailer opened. Zach emerged. He started down the driveway, heading for the back of the house. But when he saw them on the porch, he changed direction and strode to the foot of the front steps. "What's the matter?"

Starr leaned on the porch rail. "Daddy, what happened? Did you talk to him? Did he tell you—"

"Starr." Zach looked so weary and sad. "I thought you said you'd stay in your room."

"I couldn't. I had to know. Did he tell you how we have something special between us? Do you understand now that he never meant anything wrong to happen, that he—"

"Starr. Beau is leaving. I'm going to go get his pay and then he'll be gone."

Starr gaped at her father. "What? No. You can't do that. That's not right, not fair..." She started down the steps.

Zach blocked her path. "Go back upstairs."

"I have to talk to him."

"No, you don't. Just let the damn fool go."

"He is not a fool! He...he cares for me, that's all. He just wanted to be with me, like I want to be with him."

"Starr. Go upstairs."

She dodged to slide around Zach. He anticipated the move and stepped in her path once more, grabbing her by both arms as she ran square into his chest.

She cried, "No!" shouting now, a child denied some longed-for treasure, not caring in the least who might hear. "Let me go! Let me talk to him!"

"Starr, listen." Zach tried to hold her gently, though she kicked and squirmed and beat on his chest. "Starr. Settle down."

"No! I won't! I won't! Let me go!"

Right then, across the yard, the trailer door opened again. Beau stepped out.

Tess said, "He's coming."

Zach swore. Starr froze and glanced beyond Zach's shoulder. "Beau! Beau, he won't let me talk to you!" She tried again to break free, catching Zach off guard and almost succeeding that time. But somehow, Zach managed to catch one arm as she flew by. He hauled her back, against his chest, grabbing the other arm, too.

Beau came toward them, his stride long and swift. He stopped a few feet from where Starr stood, with her father holding her arms right behind her. Tess saw the bruise on Beau's chin—a big bruise, fresh and livid.

Starr noticed it, too. She gasped. "Beau. He *hit* you!" She shot an outraged glare over her shoulder at Zach.

Beau said, "Forget it. It's nothing."

Starr's gaze swung on Beau again. "No. He had no right to hit you! You didn't do anything. He can't—"

"Starr. He had a right."

She went still. "No!" It was a cry of pure distress. Though Tess stood on the porch, behind them all, she knew that Starr would be watching Beau's face, willing him to call her sudden, ugly doubts unfounded.

But Beau only smiled, a knowing smile. And then he actually chuckled.

"Tisdale," Zach warned in a growl.

"Zach," Tess said. "Let him tell her."

Zach turned his head and gave Tess a long, probing look. Then he released his daughter and stepped back.

Freed, Starr staggered a little, then righted herself. "Beau, please—"

Beau cut her off, his tone like a caress, "You thought you'd heard every line, didn't you, big-city girl? Heard 'em all and never fell for a one. But the lonesome cowboy routine got you goin', didn't it?''

''Wh-what are you saying?''

He made a low, smug sound. ''You know damn well what I'm saying.''

''No...''

'''Fraid so.'' Beau lowered his voice, as if sharing a secret. ''Come on, you know how guys are.''

Starr shook her head frantically. ''No! You wouldn't. You *couldn't*. All those things you said—''

He shrugged. ''They didn't mean squat. I was after one thing. And we both know what that was.''

''No.'' The word was barely a whisper.

Beau went on smiling. ''Yeah.''

Zach cut in then. ''Okay, enough. Go on, Tisdale. Around back. I'll get your money.''

Beau turned and walked away. Starr watched him go, her face as blank as a bleached sheet.

Zach's gaze sought out Tess again, in the shadows of the porch. ''Would you take her upstairs?''

Tess nodded and moved forward. Starr came to her numbly. Tess put an arm around the girl's stiff shoulders and led her toward the front door.

Inside, Edna and the others were still at the table. Tess caught sight of her friend as she passed by the arch from the central hall to the kitchen. Edna frowned. Tess shook her head.

Jobeth must have started to rise from the table, because Edna said, ''Sit back down, young lady. Finish your meal.''

Slowly, like very old people clinging to each other for support as they went, Tess and Starr proceeded up the stairs.

In Starr's room, Tess left the girl at the door and went to the bed. She gathered up the magazines and stacked them back on Starr's bookcase where they belonged. She set the headphones on the nightstand. Then she returned to Starr.

"Come on," Tess said, pushing the door closed and pulling Starr toward the bed. "Sit down."

The girl dropped to the edge of the bed. Tess sat beside her. They both stared toward the uncurtained windows for a time. Outside, it was still daylight, though to Tess it felt like it ought to be the middle of the night.

Starr murmured, "I'm sorry. About the curtains."

"They can be ironed again."

"I think I might have broken the curtain rod."

"It can be replaced."

"I said rotten things to you."

"Yes, you did."

"Do you hate me?"

"No. Never. That would be like...hating myself."

They'd both been sitting up as straight as soldiers. But then Starr let her head drop to Tess's shoulder. "I don't get it. You're not like me."

"Oh, yes I am. I'm a lot like you. Or I was. At one time."

They were silent again. Tess put her arm around Starr and smoothed her hair.

Starr said, "That stuff about where you and my dad sleep. That was none of my business."

"You're right. It wasn't."

"I just wanted to hurt you."

"I know. And you did. But I survived."

"I hit my dad. And kicked him."

"You behaved very badly. But it doesn't have to be the end of the world."

Starr sighed, a lonely, lost sound. "It feels like it is."

"I know. But it's not."

"I...*believed* him, believed *in* him."

"You mean Beau?" Tess felt Starr's nod against her shoulder. She stroked the black hair some more.

"I think I loved him." Starr let out another broken sigh. "I want to hate him now. But I don't. I'm just...numb."

Outside, they heard an engine start up. They both knew it would be Beau. Leaving.

After the vehicle drove off, when the sound of the engine had completely faded away, Tess asked, "Do you want to eat?"

"No. Not tonight. I'm just...so tired."

"Bed, then?"

"Yeah," Starr said. "Bed."

"Come on." Tess stood, pulled Starr to her feet and helped her get into her pajamas.

"I want to brush my teeth," Starr said, once she was all ready.

While Starr went to the hall bath she shared with Jobeth, Tess managed to hook the bent rod in place so the wrinkled curtains shut out the light.

"I really messed those up," Starr, back from the bathroom, spoke from over by the door.

Tess got down from the stool. "I'll fix them like new tomorrow." She noticed that Starr's face was scrubbed clean. "Feel better?"

"Yeah. A little."

Tess held back the covers. Starr climbed in. Tess tucked the blankets around her.

The girl sighed. "I'll say I'm sorry to my dad. Tomorrow."

"Good idea."

"Maybe it's kind of hard to believe, after today, but I really have been trying."

"We know you have."

"You'll give me another chance?"

"Absolutely."

"I'll do better."

"I believe you will."

Downstairs, Tess found Zach at the table, eating alone. Edna and Jobeth worked around him, cleaning up after the meal.

Jobeth whirled at the sound of Tess's footsteps, almost dropping the saucepan she'd been drying. "Mom. Where's Starr? Is Starr all right?"

Tess felt that all eyes were on her, waiting for her answer. "Starr is fine. A little tired."

"Will she eat?" asked Edna anxiously.

"No. She's not very hungry. She decided just to go to bed."

"Can I go up, Mom? And say good-night?"

Tess hesitated, unsure.

Zach glanced up from his dinner. "Let her go."

Tess met Zach's eyes, then turned to her daughter. "All right. Go."

Jobeth dropped the pan and the dish towel on the counter and headed for the stairs.

"Just say good-night," Tess warned. "Don't hang around."

Jobeth turned and held up a hand. "Just good-night. I promise." And she took off like a shot.

Edna turned to Tess. "Sit. I'll get you some food."

"Not much. I'm not too hungry, either."

"Some beans, a little salad. How's that?"

"That would be nice."

Jobeth kept her promise. She was back a few minutes later. She picked up the dish towel and started in where she'd left off.

Zach vanished into his office right after dinner, and later Tess heard him go outside.

Around eight, Tess walked Edna across the yard and stayed with her for a last cup of coffee. Quietly, as they sat at the table together, Tess related what had happened with Beau.

Edna shook her head. "The poor child. She acts so tough. But inside…"

"She's like all the rest of us. Looking for love."

"Maybe, after today, she'll know that love is right here. With us."

"I think she's starting to get the picture, Edna. I really do."

Tess returned to the main house at nine. She found no one downstairs, so she went up and knocked on Jobeth's door.

"Come in."

Tess pushed open the door.

Jobeth sat on her bed, wearing her pajamas, holding a black-haired doll that she'd named the Spanish Lady. The doll, dressed in red satin and black lace, was one Josh had given her not long before he died. Jobeth held up the doll. "Do you think she looks like Starr?"

Tess went and sat beside her. She smelled of toothpaste and soap. Her bangs had split in the middle, the way they always did. Tess traced the space with her forefinger.

"Mom. I asked you a question."

"Um?"

"Do you think the Spanish Lady looks like Starr?"

Tess turned her attention to the doll. "Hmm. A little, maybe. But Starr is more beautiful."

"Yes. That's true. I love Starr."

"Yes, I know you do."

"Do you love Starr?"

"I do."

"That's good. I think she'll be fine in the morning, don't you?"

"Yes, she'll be much better. In the morning. After a good night's sleep."

Jobeth slid off the bed and put the Spanish Lady back in her stand, next to four other dolls, on the bureau. "I never liked dolls that much. My real father always gave them to me. Remember?"

"Yes."

"It's hard to remember him sometimes." She straightened the skirt of a doll dressed like Scarlett O'Hara, all ready for the Wilkeses' picnic, in *Gone With The Wind*. "So it's funny, because now I'm glad to have these dolls. They help me remember him. Things like the way he would smile sometimes. And laugh."

"Yes, he had a great laugh. And a warm smile."

"Mom?"

"Yes?"

"I want to call Zach Dad. He feels like my dad. And now, after he's finished adopting me, he'll be my second dad, forever and for true, won't he?"

Tess nodded.

"Would it be all right, then? If I did?"

"It's all right with me. Maybe you ought to ask him."

"I did. I asked him first."

Tess hid her smile, thinking, Of course, she asked him first. She finds it so easy to talk to him. Easier than I find it, certainly. Easier than *she* finds it to talk to me. "What did he say?"

"He said it was fine with him, but to ask you, too."

Tess let her smile show then. "Well, all right. You've asked him and me. And we've both said yes. So what are you going to do?"

Jobeth grinned. "Call him Dad."

An hour later, Tess sat in her bed with the light on, trying to read a novel that had seemed really good last night, but tonight just didn't seem to hold her attention at all.

Someone knocked at the door. She thought it would be Jobeth. Or possibly Starr.

She looked up. "Come in."

The handle turned and the door swung open. It was Zach.

Chapter Sixteen

Tess lowered her book and put her hand to her throat. Though she had on a plain pair of summer pajamas and the covers were pulled up to her waist, she felt totally naked.

"Is it all right if I...come in?"

Since her throat felt too tight to let words out, she nodded.

He crossed the threshold and shut the door. And then he just stood there, a tall man in a clean chambray shirt, new Wranglers and tan moccasins. For a long time, they regarded each other. His hair looked wet, as if he'd taken another shower since the one before dinner.

Her heart beat with sweet fury, to think what that might mean.

Finally he said. "I went to Starr's room. She didn't answer my knock. So I looked in. She's asleep." He smiled a little. "She looks so sweet, when she sleeps."

Her throat still felt tight, so instead of speaking, Tess nodded again.

His smile turned rueful. "Do you want me to go?"

She shook her head, vehemently.

"Then maybe you could help me out a little here."

She forced out some words. "All right."

"There. Was that so hard?"

She tugged on the covers and smoothed the sheet. "I'm nervous, I guess."

His eyes said he understood. "That's okay."

She remembered what he'd been talking about. "Starr told me she'd apologize to you in the morning."

He looked beyond her, to the windows, over which the curtains were drawn. "Do you think it's going to be okay with her?"

"Yes."

"You really mean that?"

"I do. I don't mean I think it'll be easy. But I think it's going to work out. She wants to stay with us and she's willing to change."

"What do you think about Beau?"

Tess considered, then answered, "I think life's been hard on him. And that he does care for her."

Zach made a low sound of agreement. "I think you're right."

Tess closed her book and set it on the nightstand. "I also think he's good at heart—and that he gave Starr a great gift today."

"And that was?"

"He set her free of him."

Zach pondered her words, then asked, "Did you tell her all this?"

Tess shook her head. "If she realized that he said those cruel things for her own sake, she might chase after him. She's only sixteen, Zach. Whatever else you want to say about him and her and what's happened between them, she's just plain too young for him now.''

"I thought maybe she'd feel better, if she knew.''

"She's a proud and determined girl. And I think he's the first guy who's ever meant anything to her.''

"He is,'' Zach said. "She told me.''

"Do you think it would be the right thing, if she went running off after him?''

"Hell, no.''

"Then maybe we ought to just let it be.''

They shared another long look.

Zach said, "I always liked your eyes. Cat eyes, the way they tip up at the corners, the way they shine...''

Tess's heart beat even faster, to hear such words from him. Inside her chest there was a rising feeling. She tried to think of some appropriate reply to his compliment, but none came.

And apparently, he didn't expect a reply, because he turned away then and wandered over to her sewing area, against the wall near the big double bureau. He put his hand on her old Singer and asked without looking at her, "How long have you had this thing?''

"My parents gave it to me, as a high school graduation present.''

"That was only—what? Eight years ago?''

"That's right.''

"This machine looks a lot more than eight years old.''

"My mom bought it used. *Reconditioned,* I think they call it.''

He met her eyes at last. "Buy a new one.''

She smiled. "No. That one works just fine.''

"*I'll* buy you a new one."

"It's the same thing, and we both know it. And the answer is no. You've bought me too much already. Besides, I really love that old machine. And I'm used to it."

"I have not bought you too much."

She held his gaze. It felt so wonderful. Just to look at him, and have him look back. To dare to hope that his being here might mean a turning point in what they shared.

"Let's not argue about a sewing machine," she suggested in a voice that had somehow gone husky. "Or about how generous you are."

He grinned and her heart went weightless. "Then what should we argue about?"

"Nothing," she said. "Let's not argue at all."

"All right. I can deal with that."

He came closer. There was a small armchair, upholstered in maroon velvet, a few feet from the side of the bed where she lay. He dropped into it—sprawled, really, stretching his legs out and laying his arms on the armrests. For a moment, he let his head fall back and stared at the ceiling.

Then he straightened enough to look at her. She saw the heat in his eyes, as well as something else. Something that looked like resignation.

He said, in a low tone that affected all her senses, "Come here."

The breath fled her body and her mouth went as dry as a drought-stricken field.

He waited. He knew she would come. And slowly, the way a person moves in dreams, she pushed the covers away and swung her feet toward the floor.

He watched her, and the way he watched made her insides turn liquid, shimmery. Hot.

Her toes touched the small rag rug by the bedside. She could feel the pattern of the braiding all along the soles of her feet. All at once, everything, *everything* had gone so thick, so heavy—so unbearably sweet.

She stood, smiling a little, aware that the legs of her pajamas, pushed up by the covers, had dropped along her shins to their full length. She spared a moment of regret that on this night of all nights, she wore nothing more exciting than plain pink pajamas made of ordinary cotton.

She remembered the satiny nightgown and lacy negligee she had bought to wear for him. She wished she had them on right now.

But she didn't.

Some other night, she thought. And at the idea that there might be other nights, a delicious shiver went through her.

He was still waiting. She came on. His legs were open, so she stepped between them. He rested his head back again, looked at her through eyes that burned her in the most delightful way. And then he reached out. He clasped her waist. She felt the heat of his hand through the cool pink cotton.

He sat up straight and looked at her earnestly. "We got through today somehow, didn't we?"

"Yes."

"Together."

She closed her eyes for a minute, loving the sound of that word. Then she opened them. "Yes, Zach. Together."

"It's starting to seem a false thing to me, to sleep separate from you."

Her throat closed on her again when he said that, just clamped shut in pure joy. She dared to lift her hand and touch his hair. It *was* damp. And thick and silky. She felt a bright glow all through her, to think that she might begin to touch him whenever the mood struck. That they would share the closeness of two people who were truly and fully wed. She touched his jaw, found it smooth and fresh-shaven. He smelled so clean and good.

He said, "I want to stay here—in this room, in that bed—with you, tonight. Will you have me?"

She thought of the cold spring day he'd proposed to her, at that spot that she'd known must have been special to him. She remembered his bewildered look when he saw how bare it was, the way he'd remarked that it was pretty, in summer. He had asked, Will you have me as your husband, Tess?

She had answered, Yes, Zach. I will.

And then, more recently, when he said he wanted to adopt Jobeth, he'd asked, Will you allow that?

She had given him the same answer. Yes, Zach. I will.

Tonight was no different than the times before. She told him softly, "Yes, Zach. I will."

His hands moved to the bottom button of her pajama top. Trembling a little, she helped him, her own hands starting from above and moving down.

Their hands met in the middle, and she laid hers over his. Together, they parted the top, slid it off her shoulders and away. She felt his gaze on her breasts. She looked down at herself, saw the pale globes, the hard nipples. Then she looked at him again.

He whispered, "Beautiful..."

She smiled at him, still holding his hands. Gently

she pressed them against her belly. They were large hands, chapped and hard-used. They covered so much of her. His fingers wrapped around the base of her rib cage. His touch felt dizzyingly rough—and so wonderfully hot. She moaned a little as the encompassing touch slid upward. For one brief, exquisite moment, he cradled her breasts.

Then his hands glided down. He took the rest of her pajamas away, guiding them over the curve of her hips and off to the floor. She stepped back, out of them— and as she did, he rose.

Now, those burning eyes looked down at her. His broad chest confronted her. She put her hands there, against his chest, pressing a little, all at once intensely aware of the strength of him. The obdurate power.

He took her shoulders, pulled her so close. She felt her nakedness acutely, as the fabric of his shirt and jeans rubbed her tender skin. His arms went around her. She felt them, enveloping her, stealing her breath. His hands splayed at her back and her breasts pressed into his chest.

"Open your eyes."

She hadn't realized she'd closed them. But she had. She obeyed his command, raising her head fully toward his.

His mouth hovered inches from hers. She hungered for it. Longed for his kiss. And down below, she could feel him, could feel what he wanted.

The same thing she wanted: the two of them. Joined.

"Who do you see?"

She frowned, not following.

"Who? Who do you see?" He held her tighter, more urgently.

She understood then. He still thought she loved

Cash. He feared she imagined doing these intimate things with another.

She caught his lip between her teeth, worried it lightly. He moaned and she knew she had his full attention. "You, Zach," she said intently, releasing the tender flesh. "Only you."

With a low, male sound, he captured her mouth. He kissed her hard and hungrily. She melted into the kiss, totally his.

His hands roamed. He found the secret place between her thighs. She gasped, melting all the more as he caressed her there. She moved toward him, closer still, her mouth eagerly returning the demanding kiss, her body moving in welcome, encouraging his touch.

He lifted his mouth from hers, just enough to whisper raggedly, "I believe that—believe you want me." His hand continued its tormenting play below. "I believe your body is mine."

She couldn't think, couldn't answer. He lowered his head and took her breast, sucking strongly. She cried out in stunned delight as the thread of desire seemed to meet in the middle of her, stroked by both his hand and his mouth at the same time. Sensation overwhelmed her. Everything was shimmering, pulsing and contracting, then flowing outward and down in a shower of light.

Her knees buckled at the last. He scooped her up against his chest and carried her the few steps to the bed, where he laid her down.

She stared at him, as he removed his own clothes. She thought him so fine, so lean and strong. She wanted to cry and laugh at the same time.

He lay down beside her. She reached out and put her hand on his belly. It was hard and flat, with a tangle of brown hair below from which his manhood stood up proud and ready. She encircled him.

He gasped, and put his hand on her wrist, stilling any movement. "Don't. I'll lose it. I need you. Now."

He surged toward her. She fell back and he rose above her. A quick thrust, and he was inside.

He didn't move. "Stay still," he muttered between clenched teeth. A low oath escaped him.

She waited, for an eternity it seemed. Then, so carefully, she wrapped her legs around him, watching his face, seeing the intense pleasure there, and seeing pain, too, as he struggled to hold himself back.

He rested on his forearms, brought his mouth so close to hers. "I wanted this." She felt his words against her lips.

"Me, too. So much."

"And I lied."

"No."

"Yeah. To myself, mostly. About what I wanted from you. I wanted...everything."

"Oh, Zach. You have it. I—"

He cut off her words with a kiss, then lifted his mouth enough to mutter, "No more lies."

"They aren't—"

"No. Nothing. Nothing more. Just this. Just let it be."

She pressed her lips together. Nodded. And then moaned as he opened his mouth over hers. His tongue traced the line where her lips met. Slowly she opened for him, allowing him in, kissing him fully, letting him taste her, tasting him back.

Then, as he kissed her, he began to move.

She gasped and then sighed. They shared the same breath, in the kiss that went on and on, as he moved inside her, slowly, deliberately, making her feel every stroke. She thought she would pass out, from the sheer glory of it. Her whole being rose toward him, moved away, beckoned him back once more. She felt that she surrounded him, and yet was within him at the same time.

The rhythm grew wilder, rougher, harder. She clutched him tight, pushed herself up toward him.

And in the end, they found the peak together. She felt him stiffen, heard his guttural cry just as her body bloomed into a completion of its own.

She must have slept for a time. When she woke, the room was dark. She could feel the warmth of him, smell the scent of him. He was here at last, beside her in this bed, where she'd almost stopped dreaming he would ever come to claim her.

She thought he was sleeping. But then he touched her, his hand curving on her breast, trailing down over her belly, unerring, relentless. He found the female heart of her. She was ready for him, her legs falling open, her whole body so eager she gave not even token resistance.

He stroked her, slowly, touching everything, missing nothing. She moaned and moved at the command of his caresses. She cried his name. And tried to say her love.

But he wouldn't allow that. His hand stopped its play to move up and close over her mouth. She smelled her own desire, felt its wetness on his fingers.

"No," he said.

She nodded, like a captive sworn to silence on pain of torture or death. And shameless, she lifted herself toward him. He gave her what she sought, resuming the loveplay, finally entering her again when both of them were crazy with the scent and feel of each other.

It was frantic, needful. It went on and on.

Later, she woke again. Felt the slight soreness from the times before. Still, she couldn't stop herself. She reached for him once more.

Chapter Seventeen

When Zach woke beside his wife the next morning, the room lay in darkness. Slowly Zach turned his head to look at her.

She lay on her back. He studied her profile. She was smiling. Her arm was thrown back on the pillow by her head, the pale skin giving off a pearly glow in the darkness, her fingers loose and slightly open. He couldn't repress a smile. She looked relaxed. Content. She took up a good portion of the bed, too. Under the covers, her legs were wide apart. That amused him. She was such a tidy woman, and yet she slept in an abandoned sprawl.

He thought of the night before.

And wanted to reach for her, wanted to hear her welcoming sigh, feel her move toward him, twining her legs with his, eager and hungry for his touch.

But he didn't.

He belonged to her now. He understood that. That was just the way he was. He'd held out as long as he could. But when he gave his body, he gave his heart.

A glance at the clock on the nightstand told him that it was near six. Beyond the heavy drawn curtains, dawn would be breaking. They should have been up and around an hour ago, but neither of them had given much thought to setting the alarm the night before.

He considered the morning chores he always took care of before breakfast and decided that Tim could do them.

Zach needed some time. He needed a long ride on Ladybird, out somewhere he wouldn't see another soul. He needed time to accept what he understood now, to make his peace with it, and to clear his mind. Then he would feel up to handling the rest of the day. Up to dealing with Starr. Up to deciding whether to take Cash's suggestion and put together a little range patrol of his own.

Up to facing his wife and telling her honestly that he loved her with all of his heart and he would do his best to get past the fact that she didn't love him.

He thought of that place he'd taken her, in the spring, when he'd asked her to marry him. Now, the cottonwoods would have their leaves and the grass would be green. It was as good a destination as any—and fitting, in a way.

He slid from the bed with great care, sure he was going to wake her. But she only sighed and flung her other arm out, commandeering what was left of the bed.

Quiet as a thief, he crept around to where he'd dropped his clothes. Swiftly he scooped them up and pulled them on. Finally he tiptoed out, closing the door so carefully behind him that he managed to keep the latch from clicking when it caught.

He stopped in his room to put on a pair of socks. Then he went downstairs, where he found Jobeth at the table drinking hot chocolate and Edna bustling around the kitchen.

"We wondered if you would *ever* get up," Jobeth groused.

Edna asked anxiously, "Is Tess all right? She never sleeps this late."

He made his tone offhand. "She's fine. A little tired. We forgot to set the alarm. I thought I'd let her catch a few extra winks."

"Good idea." Edna attacked a big bowl of pancake batter with a wooden spoon. "I'll have this breakfast on in two shakes, just you watch."

"Great." He almost turned for the door where he'd left his muddy boots the afternoon before. They'd be dry now, and fine for a ride in any case. But then he decided he'd better say something to Edna about where he was headed. He'd get her all stirred up if he just rode off without a word. "Listen. I'm going out riding. For an hour or two."

Jobeth jumped up. "I'll come."

He gave her a smile. "No, I need your help here."

Her face fell when he said no, but brightened at the news that she could help him. "Anything. Sure."

"I haven't done my chores yet. I wonder if—"

"Yeah. I can do them. I can handle that."

"You get Tim. He'll help."

"Sure. All right. I will. I'll get going right now— Dad." Her face turned the cutest shade of pink.

He couldn't hold back a grin. "Thanks." She was

734   *PRACTICALLY MARRIED*

out the door almost before he got the single word out of his mouth. He heard her whistle for Reggie when she got to the back step, and a glance out the kitchen window showed the child and the dog racing for the barn.

He could feel Edna's gaze on him. He faced her. "When Tess wakes up, tell her not to worry. I'll be a few hours, no more."

"Where are you going?"

"Northwest. A little place I know along the creek, out near the Farley breaks."

"Are you…all right, truly, Zach? You seem—"

"I'm fine. And I'll be back soon."

"You *will* catch those cattle thieves. And Starr *will* be okay."

"I know you're right—at least about Starr. And don't worry." He grinned at her. "Get those pancakes on. Lolly and Tim are probably starving."

"Go on. Let me do my work." She made a shooing motion, then turned back to the counter and her breakfast preparations.

Zach stepped out to the back porch, shucked off his moccasins, pulled on his boots and went out the way Jobeth had gone. Within ten minutes, as dawn began to bleed the night from the sky, he was mounted on Ladybird and headed toward the Big Horns that towered so jagged and uncompromising on the western horizon.

Tess woke smiling—until she opened her eyes and found herself alone.

She sat up. "Zach?"

And then she looked at the clock. She blinked. Looked again. "Six-thirty!" she exclaimed aloud, imagining everyone down in the kitchen, seated around an empty table, wondering if breakfast would ever be served. She threw back the covers and jumped from the bed.

She'd just emerged from a two-minute shower, yanked on some clothes and raked a comb through her hair when someone knocked at the bedroom door.

She blushed crimson and grinned like a fool as an image of Zach flashed through her mind—Zach carrying a breakfast tray, all loaded up with two eggs, bacon, toast, a steaming cup of coffee—and maybe even a bud vase containing a single red rose.

Where he'd get the rose was a mystery, of course, since she hadn't got around to planting any yet. But maybe a wild rose. She'd seen a few, out near the creek. Now that would be something. Breakfast served to her on a tray, and a wild rose in a bud vase, brought to her by her husband, who ordered her back to bed where he would sit next to her adoringly as she ate.

Oh, she had to stop this foolishness. Any ranch wife who expected breakfast in bed either had a broken leg or an unclear understanding of her own responsibilities.

There was a second knock. Tess smoothed her hair and went to the door.

It was Starr, dressed in jeans and a clean T-shirt, her face scrubbed free of makeup, though the rhinestone still glittered in her nose. For some reason, Tess found the sight of the sparkly stone reassuring.

Starr said, "Edna told me not to bother you, but I thought I heard the shower going and I—"

Tess took her arm. "Come in." She pulled the girl into the room and shut the door. "How are you?"

"Okay. I was looking for Dad, but Edna said he was gone."

Tess waved a hand, dismissing that idea. "He's probably out in the barn. I...think he might have gotten a late start on his morning chores."

"Edna said he was having Jobeth and Tim handle his chores."

Tess frowned. "Why?"

"Edna said he went riding, about twenty minutes ago. That he'd be back in a few hours."

Tess made a low sound of disbelief. "A three-hour ride. By himself. That will take up half the morning." In summer, mornings were prime working hours. A lot could be accomplished before the heat of the day made tough jobs all the harder.

Starr said, "Edna told me he just wanted a little time to himself." She moved a few steps away, then turned back. "But I know what that means. It means he's trying to decide what to do with me, after what happened yesterday."

"Starr." Tess put on a stern expression. "Stop this."

Starr threw up her hands. "I feel like such a... nothing. All dirty and awful inside, you know?"

Tess reached out, put her arm around the girl. "Listen. Yes, your dad *is* worried about you. But there's more going on. Yesterday, he and Jobeth found more tire tracks."

"The rustlers?"

"I'm afraid so. He's worried about that—and a few other things, I suppose."

"What things?"

"Not-your-problem things."

Starr let out a groan, then grew earnest. "So then, what you're saying is, if he's really bugged, it's not only about me?"

"Exactly."

"And he didn't talk to you about anything like, um, sending me away?"

"Starr. Listen. No one is sending you away. No one wants you to leave. Unless you go back with your mother—"

"Never. Please. Don't make me go back there."

"We won't. Not if you don't want to."

"You promise?"

"I promise. Will you believe me?"

"All right."

"So. If your mother's not an option—"

"She's not."

"—then you belong here with us. We will insist that you stay at least until you're out of high school. And after that, you'll always have a place here, though by then the choice to stay or not will be your own."

Starr gnawed on her lower lip. "You mean that, don't you?"

"I do."

The girl let out a long breath. "Well. Okay."

Tess gave Starr's shoulder one last squeeze. "Now. I suppose Edna is getting the breakfast?"

"Yeah."

Just then, the bell started clanging outside.

Tess said, "Come on, then. Let's go down."

"I told that girl to let you sleep," Edna said when Tess and Starr got to the kitchen.

Starr jumped to her own defense. "She was up already, I swear."

"Well, all right then. It's just as well, I suppose. The food's on the table and ready to eat. Starr, pour the milk for you and Jobeth. And how about coffee, for the rest of us?"

"Sure." Starr went to work.

Tess hovered in the arch from the hall, thinking about Zach, feeling a growing unease. "Edna, where did Zach say he was going?"

"Some place along the creek, Northwest, out by the Farley breaks."

Tess knew the geography of the Rising Sun well enough now to be reasonably certain that was the place he'd taken her the day he proposed.

She recalled the night before, a pleasant weakness washing through her at the sweet memory. And she thought of his words to her.

I lied, he had whispered, To myself, mostly. About what I wanted from you. I wanted....everything.

She had tried to tell him that he *had* everything. Twice, she had tried to tell him—three times, if she included that night out by the horse pasture when they'd talked about Starr. But he wouldn't hear her.

He wanted her love. And he had her love.

But he wouldn't let her say it.

Because he thought it was a lie.

Now he'd gone and run off to sit by the creek and feel sorry for himself. Worrying everyone. Because he wouldn't see the truth when it bit him on the nose.

Lolly, Tim and Jobeth came trooping in.

"Sit down, sit down," said Edna. "And you, too, Tess. Come on now, the food will get cold."

Tess took her seat. The business of serving and passing dishes began. She helped herself to the food and passed the platters as they came by her.

But her mind remained on Zach.

Okay, she could understand why he didn't believe her. Her love was no real prize, to be fair. She had thought she loved Josh once, as a foolish girl of seventeen. And then she'd been so sure she would love Cash forever.

And now, those other loves were as nothing. Like lightning bugs in a long-ago night—next to her love for Zach, which shone as bright as the sun.

Oh, she shouldn't have let her body rule her last night. She should have pushed him away, ordered him to sit there in that maroon velvet chair, until she told him that he was the only one for her. Over and over, she should have told him. Until he finally got so sick of hearing it that he gave in and believed her.

But she hadn't. She had wanted him too much. She'd been afraid that if she tried to force him to hear her out, he might turn and leave her, as he had done so many nights before.

So she had kept quiet. And he had stayed. They'd shared a beautiful night.

And now, come morning, he was out there by the creek somewhere.

Feeling sorry for himself.

It had to stop, that was all. It had to stop now. Today.

"Tess, you haven't touched a bite."

She stood. "Edna, can you handle things here?"

"What now?"

"I'm going for a ride."

Halfway to his destination, Zach let himself through the gate into a pasture where he and his men had put several Hereford cows and their calves, along with a few registered Black Angus bulls. He closed the gate and then remounted, clicking his tongue at Ladybird, who started up a rise a hundred yards from the gate. Zach let the horse have her head as she carried him up to the crest. His eyes were on the clean morning sky,

on the mountains and on the striated ridges of the
breaks that became clearer up ahead as he topped the
rise.

His mind was on Tess. Which was why he let himself get in plain sight of the sweep of land below him
before he really registered what he saw there: a pickup
and stock trailer, two men and a dog.

Chapter Eighteen

The men below had a set of portable panels in place and it looked like the dog had already bullied a couple of cows and their calves up the ramp.

Where the hell was that cell phone when he needed it?

Swearing under his breath, Zach sawed on the reins and turned back—hoping to hell that he hadn't been spotted.

Once over the rise again, he slid off of Ladybird, pulling his rifle from its saddle scabbard, scanning the landscape for cover that would take him closer to the men below.

But he was too late. Just as his boots hit the ground, Beau Tisdale stood from behind a boulder ten feet to his left, a little below the crest of the rise. He held a .30-30 just like Zach's own.

Unfortunately Zach's rifle was pointing at the ground. Beau had his pointed straight at Zach.

"Throw it down," Beau said.

Carefully, Zach knelt and set his rifle on the ground.

Keeping Zach firmly in his sights, Beau commanded, "Move back, away from the weapon."

Zach did as he was told.

"Now go on." Beau gestured with the rifle barrel. "That way, back over the rise."

By then, Zach had got a good look at Beau. The younger man was a hell of a sight. His left eye was an ugly purple and swollen nearly shut. He had welts along his jaw, a mean-looking goose egg standing out from his right cheekbone and a lot more bruises than the one Zach had put on his chin. "What happened to you?"

"I ran into a door. Now, move."

Cautiously Zach backed up the rise. Still pointing the rifle at him, Beau slid between him, Ladybird and the .30-30 he'd thrown down. Zach reached the crest. His hands in the air, he stood silhouetted against the sky. The men below must have seen him then. He heard them shout.

"Turn around," Beau said. "And head on down."

Zach was putting it together. It all seemed so clear now. "Your brothers are down there, right? And you've been the spy for them, relaying which stock is where—and which pastures to keep clear of because we'd be working them."

Beau said nothing. He just kept that rifle trained on Zach's chest and his finger on the trigger. A gun went off, down below. The shot went nowhere, but Zach ducked beneath the crest again anyway.

Beau swore under his breath. Keeping his rifle

trained on Zach, he stalked up the rise. At the top, he shouted down, "I've got him! Stop shooting, dammit!" He spoke to Zach. "Come on. Move."

Zach held his ground and spoke gently. "They beat holy hell out of you, because you messed up their gravy train, didn't they? Getting mixed up with my Starr like that, getting stupid. Getting caught." Zach looked right in Beau's eyes over the barrel of that .30-30. "I bet there are Montana plates on that pickup. And your brothers got themselves a deal with some sleazeball in a packing plant over the state line."

"Move."

"This is bad business, Beau. You know it. That's why you didn't stop me before I hit the top of that rise and saw what was going on down below. You didn't stop me until I got off my horse. If I'd just ridden away, you would have let me go."

"I told you to move."

"Come on, Beau. You know it's over now." He took a step toward the younger man.

"Stop. Freeze."

"Give me the gun, Beau."

"Just don't, Mr. Bravo. Don't come closer. I'll shoot."

In the distance, over the rise, Zach could hear the other men yelling. They'd have started clawing their way up now, unable to drive the pickup and half-loaded stock trailer at such an angle, and having no horses to ride.

He had a minute or two, max. To talk Beau around to his side. Or to take him. Or to get himself shot.

Zach took another step. And another.

Beau said, "Damn your eyes." And pulled the trigger.

The shot exploded into the morning stillness. When the sound faded off, Zach was still standing. "Missed me. On purpose, I'd say."

Beau ejected the spent shell and chambered another. "Stop."

And Zach pounced. Beau grunted at the impact. The rifle exploded a second time, the sound so loud, it might have been the end of the world. Zach felt the bullet sizzle along his side.

Ignoring the stinging pain over his ribs, he concentrated on dealing with Beau, on getting both hands on the weapon and trying to wrestle it free. They rolled several yards with the rifle between them, off the crest and down the side Zach had come up. They'd both lost their hats by then. They rolled right over one of them.

When they stopped, Beau was on top. He pulled back and yanked the rifle away. Zach held on. Beau let go of one end and tried to land a punch. Zach blocked it with the stock of the weapon. Beau yelped with pain as his fist connected with wood. They rolled some more.

As they struggled, Zach could hear a dog barking, coming closer. And not far away, Ladybird snorted and pranced, not liking this one bit more than Zach did.

And then, at last, things started to go Zach's way. He got a firm hold on both the pistol grip and the barrel. He had himself on top. He rocked back onto his knees, then gained his feet in a crouch.

The rifle tore free of Beau's grip. Beau grunted and stared at Zach, stunned. For a split second, Zach thought he had things under control.

Then Beau's eyes shifted, widening, looking beyond Zach's shoulder. Zach didn't even have time to turn before something exploded against the side of his head.

The world went blindingly bright—and then narrowed down to a point.

And then faded away to nothing at all.

Sometime later, Zach came swimming up to a semblance of consciousness. He didn't feel so great. His head throbbed and his stomach roiled. His side still burned.

"You tie him up good, boy?" That would probably be J.T., the oldest of the three Tisdale boys.

"I did." Beau's voice. "Good and tight. He's goin' nowhere till we figure out where we want to take him."

Zach kept his head down and his body loose. He must have made no sound as he came to, because they talked as if he were still out cold.

"Okay, let's finish up here." J.T. again. "He's dead to the world and goin' nowhere. You get back up on lookout, Beau."

Zach heard footsteps turning, loping away.

"Don't you let us down again!" A third man's voice—had to be Lyle Tisdale—commanded.

No answer from Beau.

"You hear me, boy?" Lyle shouted again.

After a moment, Beau called back, "I heard!"

"Let's go," J.T. said.

Zach heard other boots moving away. A whistle. Cattle lowing, a dog barking. Hoofs pounding a ramp. Somewhere not too far away, a horse snorted and shifted. That would be Ladybird.

Zach identified the object at his back. A tire and wheel. It felt like Beau had tied him to the pickup wheel.

Carefully, making a supreme effort not to show

movement, he tested the ropes that held him. He felt a little bit of play.

Maybe Beau was thinking about changing sides in this game.

Damn, his head felt like a split-open watermelon. A wave of dizziness came washing over him....

Riding the gray mare, Tess topped the rise from which the Farley breaks started to show up pretty clear.

She saw what was going on down there—including Ladybird, tied to the front bumper of the pickup, and what had to be Zach, bound to the rear wheel.

She reached for her Colt.

"Hands up, Mrs. Bravo," said a voice from behind and slightly to her right.

She turned enough to see the owner of the voice— and the rifle he had aimed at her.

She shook her head. "Oh, Beau. What are you up to now?"

"Throw down that pistol, Mrs. Bravo. Real careful-like. And then slide off that mare, slow and easy."

He must have passed out again, briefly, because Zach found all of a sudden that he was awake again. He heard more shuffling of hoofs, and an endgate being lowered and hooked. He stayed limp, head hanging, though his hands were already working at the knots that bound him.

A man whistled and the cab door of the pickup opened, several feet to his right, on the opposite side. He knew then that he'd been tied to the rear wheel, on the driver's side.

"Get on in there, Queenie," J.T. said. The pickup

rocked a little as the dog jumped in the cab. The door was slammed shut.

From a few feet away, Lyle let out a shout. "Whooee! Look who Beau's caught now."

"Aw hell," J.T. said. "Just what we need. The little woman."

Tess staggered down the pasture side of the rise. Beau followed behind her, leading her mare, carrying his rifle over his shoulder and using her own Colt to keep her in line. The closer she got to the pickup and the man tied against the rear wheel, the less she liked what she saw.

She walked faster, wanting to get to him, wanting to prove to herself that he was all right. He had to be all right....

As the ground leveled out a little, she broke into a run, her hat blowing off her head and bouncing against her shoulder blades. Nobody did anything to stop her— probably because she was headed right where they wanted her.

One of the two men by the truck made a few rude, whooping sounds. Tess ignored him. She ran straight for the limp figure tied against the wheel.

"Zach, oh Zach..." She dropped down beside him, wrapped her arms around him. "What did they do to you? Oh, Zach. You wake up, now. *Please,* open your eyes. I mean it, Zach Bravo. Open your eyes right this instant!"

She felt so warm. Her neck was moist with sweat. She held him so tight, smashing his nose against the leather thong that held her hat on. It was so fierce and hungry, the way her arms clutched him. Her voice trembled in fear at the same time as she commanded, "Open your eyes right this instant!"

She sounded so frantic. She sounded like she might just go crazy if she lost him. She sounded like...

A woman in love.

Like a light going on inside his head, brighter than the sun, brighter than a thousand suns, the truth came to him: Tess loved him.

Dammit.

She loved him.

He had what he wanted from her. He had everything. He had it all.

But not for long, if he didn't get them out of this.

She stroked his head, letting out a small cry of dismay when she felt the hard lump where he'd been hit, pulling his face so close into the crook of her neck that he dared to whisper, "Be ready."

She stiffened, just a little. But she was a crackerjack in a crisis. He would swear the Tisdale boys didn't have a clue what she'd heard.

She started in on those Tisdales. "What is the matter with you? He needs a doctor, can't you see that? You untie him this instant. You get us straight into town."

J.T. started laughing. "A doctor? You think we'll take him to a doctor? That's a hundred-dollar hoot."

Lyle started cackling away, too. Only Beau was silent.

Then J.T. got serious. "All right. Listen up. We gotta get the hell out of here. What do we do with them?"

"Er, shoot 'em?" Lyle suggested helpfully.

Zach worked at the rope. It wouldn't be long now....

Tess held Zach's head lightly. She had heard and understood his message. She tried to look like nothing more than a distraught wife, while she used her body to shield his movements as he worked at his bonds.

"Do murder?" Even with his face all battered, Tess could see Beau grow pale. "Not that. Come on, J.T. Not that."

J.T. scratched his bearded chin with the pistol he carried. "Well, now. We can't just let 'em go. They've seen us."

"We got no choice, the way I see it," said the third man. "We gotta get rid of them for good and all."

"Lyle, no," said Beau. "Not murder. Murder's no good."

"Don't talk back to your elders," Lyle snarled.

Tess felt the slightest brush of Zach's hand against her back. He had done it! Somehow, he had worked his hands free. The moment to act would be coming up fast.

Hope and fear making her heart beat so loud it seemed as if she could hear nothing else, Tess glanced at their captors, one by one, assessing the possibilities for overpowering them. Beau had both her Colt and the rifle he'd drawn on her, one in either hand. At the moment, both of those weapons were pointed at the ground. J.T. had that pistol. The third man, Lyle, wasn't armed.

Tess knew that Zach always carried a rifle when he rode out alone, one similar to Beau's. But she didn't see it anywhere close.

"I know," J.T. said. "There's that old homesteader's cabin, out near the breaks. We'll take the two of them there, tie them up inside, and set fire to the place."

"Good idea," said Lyle.

"We'll start a damn grass fire," Beau argued.

J.T. shrugged. "A big fire wouldn't be half-bad. Wipe out any evidence good and proper."

"What about the horses?" Beau sounded desperate.

J.T. looked at him as if he had no brains at all. "We'll turn 'em loose. They'll wander home. So what?"

"Someone will find our tracks here. And with two people dead, they'll put a lot more effort into figuring out what the hell's happened than they have been so far."

"We'll be long gone, boy. Over the state line. The cattle will be hanging in a meat locker. And we'll take the pickup and trailer apart for junk." J.T. gestured with his pistol. "So come on." He gave the gray mare a slap on the flank that sent her galloping off. "Give Lyle all the hardware and tie up the woman. We gotta get gone."

Beau didn't move.

J.T.'s lips drew back from his yellowed teeth. "*Now,* boy. Like I said."

Beau stayed unmoving for a split second more. Then he said one word, "Tess," and tossed her the Colt.

Everything went crazy. From beside her, Zach erupted into action, pouncing on Lyle. J.T. fired his pistol, catching Beau in the thigh. Beau cried out, but not before he fired the rifle. J.T. went down, and fired again, hitting Beau in the shoulder. Somehow, Beau stayed on his feet. He aimed slow and steady at J.T.

J.T. tossed his pistol away and shouted, "Don't shoot, you little bastard! Can't you see I'm hit?"

Through the exchange of gunfire, Zach, his legs still tied, rolled around on the ground with Lyle.

Tess rose slowly. She pointed the Colt at her husband and the other man and commanded, "Zach, get me a clear shot."

Obediently he rolled beneath his adversary. She stepped up and put the Colt to the back of Lyle's head.

"Don't move," she said gently. "Don't even breathe."

Chapter Nineteen

As soon as Zach was on his feet, Beau handed him the rifle. Zach gave it to Tess to hold, along with J.T.'s pistol, which she stuck in her hip holster. She felt like a regular human arsenal.

Next, Zach ordered the Tisdales into the back of the pickup. They had some trouble getting the two injured men in there, but Beau and Zach managed it, with Tess keeping her Colt trained on the whole operation. After that, Zach tied up Lyle and J.T., though J.T. moaned and complained the whole time about how hurt he was.

"We have to take you in, too," Zach said, when he came to Beau.

"I know it."

"You need to be tied?"

"No, I do not."

"You're dead, boy, when I get my hands on you," Lyle muttered to Beau.

Zach said, "Shut up."

Lyle started to say something else, but Zach clipped him a good one on the jaw. Lyle was quiet after that.

Zach turned to Tess. "Keep watch on them. I'll get the cattle out of the trailer."

"Fine."

Tess stood guard as Zach bullied the cows and their calves out into the sunlight. Next, he unhitched the trailer and hobbled the horses. Then Zach jumped in the back of the pickup with the Tisdales.

"You drive. To the sheriff's office in Buffalo," he said to Tess.

She handed him Beau's rifle. Then, when she opened the driver's door, she saw Zach's rifle in the gun rack.

"Zach. They put your rifle right up here."

"Trade me," he said.

She took his rifle down and gave it to him, then put Beau's rifle in the gun rack. The whole time, the stock dog watched her from the passenger side of the seat, friendly and panting, as if he hadn't a clue they'd just tied up his masters.

Finally she drove them all to the sheriff's office in Buffalo, with the dog sitting happy as you please on the seat beside her.

Later, after Lyle had been booked and Beau and J.T. had been taken to the hospital under armed guard, Zach and Tess gave their statements and turned the dog and the Tisdales' weapons over to a deputy. They both made a point to speak kindly of Beau, to explain how he had come over to their side in the end. The arresting officer said Beau's change of heart would be considered, but there was probably no way he'd avoid doing time.

It was near noon before they were done answering

all the questions. They used the phone at the station to call the Rising Sun. Edna answered, and Tess told her an abbreviated version of the morning's events.

"Oh, my sweet Lord. Are you both all right?"

Tess looked at her husband, who stood right beside her. "Zach's got a bullet graze, along his ribs. And one heck of knot on the back of his head. But he's still standing. And still ornery. The doctor patched him up, but I can't get him to stay in the hospital."

"That man," said Edna. Tess knew she was shaking her head. "Well, then. You come on home now."

"Can't. Not yet. A deputy's driving us back to the pasture where it happened."

"Whatever for?"

"He wants to look over the scene. Plus, we left the horses there. And Zach lost his hat. He wants to look for it."

"And *then* you'll come home?"

Zach took the phone from Tess. "Look, Edna. Could you handle things there for a little more. Please." She must have said she would, because Zach grinned at the phone. "We'll be home for dinner. That's a promise."

Tess grabbed the phone again. "Give the girls our love."

"Well, certainly. I'll do that. I think I'll make Swiss Steak. How does that sound?"

"Delicious. Put those little bits of green pepper in it, like you always do. And not too heavy on the onions."

"Yes, I did go a little overboard on onions last time. I'll go lighter with them today."

Zach took the receiver for the last time. "Edna. We really have to go now."

Tess could hear her, giving one last bit of unheeded advice, as Zach hung up the phone.

The horses were there, nibbling the grass, pretty much where they'd left them. And they found Zach's hat, smashed flat, right where he'd lost it, on the far side of the rise. Zach beat it against his thigh to loosen it, then reshaped the creases as best he could.

"Good as new," he declared.

Tess refrained from comment.

The deputy looked around and took pictures of the scene before he left. As soon as he'd driven off, Tess took two aspirin from the first-aid kit in her saddlebag and passed them to Zach, along with her canteen.

He looked down at the little white pills in his hand, then up at her. "Always ready with whatever I need." He tossed the pills into his mouth and washed them down with a long drink from the canteen.

She watched him. "I really don't like the look of that goose egg you've got."

"Let it be," he muttered gruffly, settling his battered hat more firmly on his head.

"And I'll bet your side hurts like the devil. I think I should—"

"Stop fussing." He capped her canteen and handed it back. She hooked it in place.

They mounted the horses. And then, as one, they turned for that spot under the cottonwoods where Zach had asked her to marry him back at the end of April.

With the trees in full leaf, the spot was shaded now. Cottonwood fluff blew around in the air. The boulder that Tess had found so cold to sit on was warm and dappled with sun. She perched on it again, folding her hands in her lap, feeling almost as nervous as she had on that cold spring day two months before.

Zach cleared his throat. "Tess, I..."

She looked up at him, thinking of all the things she herself had to say, not knowing how to begin.

He said, "I guess I love you."

The words didn't surprise her, but they did fill her with joy. She looked down at her hands, swallowed and looked up at him once more. "And *I* guess I know that now. Since last night. Since...the way it was. And what you said, about wanting it all."

He had more to say. "I think I might have loved you almost the first time I saw you, hiding behind the punch bowl, the day Cash married Abby."

Her heart skipped a beat, and then started pounding faster than before. "You loved me since *then?*"

He nodded. He had to cough again. "But I didn't let myself admit it. I saw what a good wife you'd make. And I focused on that. I think I knew all along about your feelings for Cash."

"You did?"

"Yeah. But I didn't let myself see it. Not until after I'd asked you to be my wife. By then, I could tell myself it was too late to back out. That you were too perfect for my needs. That since it would be a practical arrangement, it didn't matter what you felt in your heart."

She dared to whisper, huskily, "But it did matter."

He looked off, toward the mountains. "Yeah. It did. I guess that, in the end, what goes on between a man and a woman can never be entirely...convenient."

"No, Zach. I suppose that it can't." She looked down at her folded hands, torn between joy that he truly did love her—and fear that he would never believe she loved him as well.

He confessed, "I rode off by myself today to…get myself straight with all of this. When I came back, I was going to tell you that I would try to live with loving you, even though you didn't love me. Because you and me together, well, it works so damn well. Don't you think?"

"Yes, Zach. It does."

He scooped off his hat and dropped it in the grass. "A hard day seems half the effort it used to be, since you became my wife. You finish what I start, you know what to do before I even have to tell you. And to have you in my house, filling it with your smiles and your laughter, with your caring ways—that's everything to me. But a man's heart is a headstrong thing, Tess. And I was having trouble. I couldn't help wanting you to feel for me what I feel for you."

Tears pooled in her eyes. She didn't know where they came from. She really was a woman who had been done with tears long ago. Dashing the moisture away, she nodded. "I do understand, Zach. And I'd…I'd like to say a few things myself now, please. If you'll hear me."

He looked at her for a long moment, then replied, "All right. Say your piece."

She gulped, brushed at her eyes again and began. She told him of the wild-hearted seventeen-year-old she had been. How what she'd thought was love for Josh DeMarley had quickly faded to grim duty. And she told him what he already knew—of the hundred ways Cash had come to her rescue, through all the tough times.

She said, "I honestly believed I loved your cousin.

For years. Lately it's occurred to me that believing I loved Cash was a way to keep love alive in me. A way to keep hoping, when there wasn't much left to hope for. A way to keep something shining and fresh inside me, when what I really felt was just plain used up and helpless—barely in my twenties, with a hopeless wandering dreamer for a husband, a little girl to raise, and no chance to advance myself on any job I did manage to get.''

She rose from the boulder, took off her own hat and tossed it in the grass beside his. Then she looked up intently into his beloved, craggy face. ''Oh, but, Zach, now, with you, I've learned what real love is. Because I've found it at last. And it's so much deeper and finer a thing than I ever knew. It's…having so much in common, wanting the same things. And yet still feeling that little catch of excitement, feeling my heart beat faster from a look or a smile. It's…it's you, Zach. You are my love.''

She thought for a moment that she saw tears in his eyes, too. And then he turned away.

She looked down at her boots, at their hats so close together, at the shiny green grass. ''I knew you wouldn't believe me. Why *should* you believe me? I haven't been honest, ever, I know it. I don't think I ever really loved Josh. And the love I felt for Cash was nothing more than gratitude, in the end. Why should you think I even know how to love?''

''Tess.''

She forced herself to meet his eyes again. And she gasped. His sun-lined face looked so young, suddenly. And full of joy. He took both her hands. ''I do believe you.''

She stared at him. ''You do? But how can you?''

"I felt it in the way you held me. I heard it. In your voice."

"But I don't understand. You mean last night, that you knew last night?"

"No, for some reason, I couldn't see it then. It wasn't till a few hours ago, when you found me tied to that pickup wheel, when you jumped on me and grabbed me and ordered me to open my eyes."

"A few hours ago?"

"Yeah."

She felt more than a little bit irritated with him. "You knew, you *believed,* when we got here, to the creek? You knew I loved you *then?*"

He released her hands and backed up a step. "Now, Tess. Don't go getting yourself worked up."

"But, Zach. You didn't tell me. You let me say...all those embarrassing things...."

"You asked to talk before I was finished." That mouth she loved curled in a sheepish smile. "And besides..."

She looked at him sideways. "Besides, what?"

"I guess I wanted to hear what you said. It was beautiful, what you said. And the part about me, about how I'm so special to you, how we think alike and want the same things. How you get excited when you see me. That was real...edifying."

"You liked it."

"Yeah. I did."

"It was...edifying?"

"Yeah, I believe that would be the right word."

They stared at each other. And then they were smiling at each other. They started to laugh—and then, all at once, Tess found she was crying.

He reached for her, pulled her close. "Hey. It's all right. It's good. You know it is."

She buried her face in his shirt. "I...I've been so ashamed."

He stroked her back. It felt like heaven, to have him hold her this way, to have him show her such tender care. "You've been on your own," he murmured, "struggling to make a life with some dignity in it. You've done your best."

"I've lied in my heart."

"Tess Bravo, you don't have to lie anymore."

She looked up at him, swiping at the darn tears. "That's good. I'm glad of that."

His gaze strayed to her mouth. "Kiss me, Tess."

And she did, there in the shadows of the cottonwood trees, with the creek rushing past a few feet away and the warm summer wind sighing all around them.

Not too much later they mounted up for the ride back. Zach gave her a smile. "Ready?"

She nodded, her heart so full, thinking how beautiful and impossible life could be. Eight years ago, she had foolishly left the ranch she loved. She hadn't known then that she would never return.

And yet, in her heart now, she felt just as if she had found her way back.

With her true love at her side, Tess Bravo turned her horse for home.

* * * * *

*Silhouette presents an exciting
new continuity series:*

**When a royal family rolls out the red carpet
for love, power and deception, will their
lives change forever?**

The saga begins in April 2002 with:

The Princess Is Pregnant!

by Laurie Paige (SE #1459)

**May: THE PRINCESS AND THE DUKE by Allison Leigh
(SE #1465)**

**June: ROYAL PROTOCOL by Christine Flynn
(SE #1471)**

Be sure to catch all nine Crown and Glory stories: the first three appear in
Silhouette Special Edition, the next three continue in Silhouette Romance
and the saga concludes with three books in Silhouette Desire.

———————————————

And be sure not to miss more royal stories,
from Silhouette Intimate Moments'

Romancing
the Crown,

running January through December.

Where love comes alive™

*Available at
your favorite
retail outlet.*

Visit Silhouette at www.eHarlequin.com   SSECAG

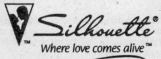

MONTANA
Bred

From the bestselling series

MONTANA MAVERICKS

Wed in Whitehorn

Two more tales that capture living and loving
beneath the Big Sky.

JUST PRETENDING by Myrna Mackenzie

FBI Agent David Hannon's plans for a quiet vacation
were overturned by a murder investigation—and by
officer Gretchen Neal!

STORMING WHITEHORN by Christine Scott

Native American Storm Hunter's return to Whitehorn
sent tremors through the town—and shock waves of
desire through Jasmine Kincaid Monroe....

Silhouette®
Where love comes alive™

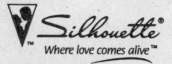

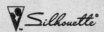

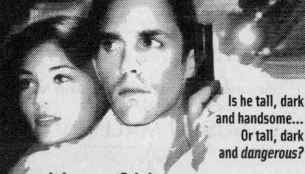